SERGIO LEONE

Christopher Frayling is Rector of the Royal College of Art in London, where he is also Professor of Cultural History. An historian, critic and award-winning broadcaster, he is well known for his writing and presenting of major television series such as *The Art of Persuasion, The Face of Tutankhamun, Strange Landscape: The Illumination of the Middle Ages* and *Nightmare: The Birth of Horror,* all of which were accompanied by best-selling books.

His other books include *Spaghetti Westerns, The Royal College of Art: 150 Years of Art and Design, Vampyres: Lord Byron to Count Dracula, The Art Pack* (with Helen Frayling), *Clint Eastwood* and a BFI monograph on the film *Things to Come.*

# SERGIO LEONE
## Something To Do With Death
### CHRISTOPHER FRAYLING

*faber and faber*

LONDON  NEW YORK

First published in 2000
by Faber and Faber Limited
3 Queen Square London WC1N 3AU

Published in the United States by Faber and Faber Inc.
a division of Farrar, Straus and Giroux Inc., New York

Photoset by RefineCatch Limited, Bungay, Suffolk
Printed in England by Clays Ltd, St Ives plc

A CIP record for this book
is available from the British Library

ISBN 0-571-16438-2

2 4 6 8 10 9 7 5 3 1

For Helen and the Wild Bunch,
twenty-one years on.

# Contents

# List of Illustrations

All photographs are from the Leone family archive, unless otherwise credited.

# Preface

*Brr. Brr. Brr.* The phone in the outer office of the Department of Cultural History at the Royal College of Art would not stop ringing. In the room next door, I was trying to run a seminar on Umberto Eco, *The Name of the Rose* and 'looking for a logic of culture'. It was February 1982.

*Brr. Brr. Brr.* There was supposed to be someone looking after phone calls in the outer office. She must have gone out to lunch. The seminar was overrunning.

*Brr. Brr. Brr.* Asking one of the postgraduate students to take over for a while, I went out to answer the call. Testily.

'Hello?'

'Is that Professor Frayling? I have Sergio Leone on the line, calling from the Cumberland Hotel.'

The voice was American: Leone's assistant and interpreter Brian Freilino, as it turned out. 'Sergio wants to talk to you about his father, Vincenzo. Your book *Spaghetti Westerns* had some material about him he didn't know about before.'

I had left a copy for Leone, at the offices of his production company Rafran, just before Christmas 1981. I did so somewhat apprehensively, knowing his strong views about the title. Had he read the book then? Apparently yet another long-suffering assistant had read the entire tome aloud to Leone, translating from English into Italian as he went along.

'Would you like to speak?'

'Sure.'

'*Salve Professore! Perché non ci incontriamo mentre a Londra?*'

It couldn't be that afternoon. He was going to look in on George Lucas, who was editing *The Return of the Jedi* at Elstree.

My meeting with Sergio Leone that evening at the Cumberland – I now realize – starting me thinking about this book. It began life as a study of his films, which, after fifteen years of lobbying by his aficionados, were beginning to attract the sort of critical attention they deserved.

xiii

Then, following Leone's death on 30 April 1989, the book began to turn into the first-ever biography; for some reason, no one in Italy had ever attempted one. And at the same time, it became a history of Italian popular cinema since the 1920s, the sort of cinema that is rarely mentioned in the standard works; and if so, rarely with more than a patronizing glance.

Sergio Leone once said 'I was born in a cinema, almost. Both my parents worked there. My life, my reading, everything about me revolves around the cinema. So for me, cinema is life, and vice-versa.' He first wandered onto a sound stage at Cinecittà in 1941, at the age of twelve, to watch his father shooting a film. And he died watching a film on television, in Rome, at the age of sixty. As we will see, for Leone, the passionate experience of movie-going, the ideas and sensations it unleashed in him, informed all of his work in cinema. Leone was the first modern cineaste to make really popular films: films which nevertheless remained personal to him. In the words of philosopher Jean Baudrillard, he was 'the first postmodernist director'.

Along the way, I have had conversations with many of Sergio Leone's professional colleagues, his contemporaries and his family, as well as with the man himself. I would like to thank them all: Ken Adam, Alessandro Alessandroni, Luis Beltran, Bernardo Bertolucci, Peter Bogdanovich, Dino De Laurentiis, Tonino Delli Colli, Sergio Donati, Clint Eastwood, Umberto Eco, Jean-Pierre Gorin, Charlton Heston, John Landis, Joaquín Romero Marchent, Elizabeth McGovern, John Milius, Fulvio and Luca Morsella, Franco Nero, Gillo Pontecorvo, Martin Scorsese, Carlo Simi, Tonino Valerii, Luciano Vincenzoni, Wim Wenders and Fred Zinnemann; Carla, Francesca and Raffaella Leone; and the late Sergio Leone. Dario Argento, Andrea Leone and Ennio Morricone were interviewed for my television programme *Viva Leone!*, broadcast on BBC2 in December 1989: many thanks to David Thompson and Nick Freand Jones for all their help, and for providing the transcriptions. The conversations with Mickey Knox and Luciano Vincenzoni were recorded by Cenk Kiral, to whom I am grateful for allowing me to use the results. Rod Steiger was specially interviewed for this book by Barbra Paskin, who generously gave her time and expertise. A supplementary conversation with Sergio Leone was recorded for a Channel 4 *Visions* documentary on Italian cinema in May 1984, on which I was consultant: thanks to Rod Stoneman for giving me the complete version.

Many others have helped unearth research materials for me. Raw materials: soundtrack specialist Lionel Woodman, film collectors Grant Kelly and the late Robert James Leake, René Hogguer of Ciné-City in Hilversum, Holland, and the man on that market stall in Whitechapel High Street. Personal materials: the Leone family has been welcoming and always supportive through thick and thin, even though they had no idea what I would be writing about Sergio. Euro Westerns: Lorenzo Codelli and Carlo Gaberscek at the Udine Film Festival; Ed Buscombe, ex-BFI; and Hubert Corbin at Montpellier. Spaghetti materials: Tom Betts and Tim Ferrante, the editors of *Westerns all'Italiana*, a journal published since 1983 in Anaheim, California. Leone's funeral: Barry Edson. Louise Swan and Adrian Turner helped to arrange interviews with Hollywood people, Françoise Jollant and Francesca Boesch sent printed materials, Jasper Hawker and Julius Cotter scouted locations in Spain.

But my greatest debt is to five individuals who, in their very different ways, have played a key role in the gestation of *Sergio Leone*. Luca Morsella, whom I first met in 1981, provided an entrée into Leone's circle in Rome, and has been a mine of useful information ever since, as well as a friend. Cenk Kiral, a Leone enthusiast and computer buff from Istanbul, has bombarded me with electronic information (good, bad and ugly), and kept me in touch with developments in the cyber-world. John Exshaw, a film scholar and filmographer who knows more about Italian popular cinema than anyone else could possibly hope to know, selflessly provided me with detailed advice and moral support at a time when I was flagging. Matthew Evans, my editor at Faber, said to me many years ago, 'Frayling on Leone – I'd certainly read that!' He had to be very patient indeed. Richard Kelly helped me to edit the final draft from the half a million words I originally submitted. I owe them all.

Various people assisted with translations: Barbara Bingola, Caterina Fadda, Sara Fanelli, Anna Negri, Lisa Ronconni, Ilaria Snowdon and Silvia Tonini (who helped with Italian materials); Britta Teckentrup (German) and Gabriela Salgado (Spanish). The librarians of the BFI, New York Public Library and the Bibliothèque Nationale were helpful, if sometimes baffled. Gill Plummer and Juliet Thorp processed and re-processed the text, in particularly frenzied circumstances, with good humour and efficiency.

And my wife Helen has put up with this project, for almost as long as

I have known her. We visited Cinecittà and Rafran on our honeymoon: since then, there have been countless late night viewings of Leone films in several languages. Now that is what I call devotion.

Don Quixote and Sancho went to the puppet-show, which was now set up and uncovered; and they found it looked splendid, being lit all round by a multitude of wax tapers. On their arrival Master Peter the puppet-showman got inside, as it was he who had to work the puppets in the play. But seeing the cavalcade of Moors on the puppet stage and hearing such an alarm, Don Quixote thought it only right to help the fugitives. So, rising to his feet, he cried aloud: 'Never while I live shall I permit an outrage to be done in my presence on so famous a knight and so bold a lover as Sir Gaiferos! Stop, low-born rabble! Neither follow or molest them or you will do battle with me.'

Matching his actions to his words, he unsheathed his sword, and at a single bound planted himself in front of the puppet-show. Then with swift and unparalleled fury he began to rain blows upon the puppet-heathenry, knocking down some, beheading others, maiming one, and destroying another; and, among other thrusts, he delivered one down-stroke that would have sliced off Master Peter's head as easily as if it had been made of marzipan, had he not ducked and crouched and made himself small. 'Stop, your worship!' he kept shouting. 'Reflect, Don Quixote, that these are not real Moors you're upsetting, demolishing and murdering, but only little pasteboard figures! Look out . . . you're ruining my whole livelihood!'

Miguel de Cervantes, *Don Quixote* (1614)

'Is the place really as big as that?' asked Karl.

'It's the biggest theatre in the world,' Fanny said. 'I haven't seen it yet myself, I admit, but some of the other girls here, who have been in Oklahoma already, say there are almost no limits to it.'

'But there aren't many people here,' said Karl, pointing down at the boys and the little family.

'That's true,' said Fanny. 'But consider that we pick up people in all the towns, that our recruiting outfit here is always on the road, and that there are ever so many of these outfits.'

'Why, has the theatre not opened yet?' asked Karl.

'Oh yes,' said Fanny, 'it's an old theatre, but it is always being enlarged.'

'I'm surprised', said Karl, 'that more people don't flock to join it.'

'Yes,' said Fanny. 'It is extraordinary.'

Franz Kafka, *Amerika* (1927)

# I

# Once Upon a Time in Rome

The American cinema as it was then was composed of a gallery of actors' faces unparalleled either before or after (at least as I see it), and the plots were simple devices (amorous, character-based, generic) for bringing these faces together in ever changing combinations. Around these conventional stories there was very little flavour of a particular society or period, but that was precisely why what flavour there was struck home without my being able to define what it consisted in . . . And just as a psychologist is equally interested when his patient lies as when he tells the truth, since either way he reveals something about himself, so I, as a film-goer belonging to another system of mystifications, could learn something both from the very little truth and the great deal of mystification the products of Hollywood offered me. With the result that I bear no rancour towards that fake and fabricated image of life; and although I wouldn't have been able to explain at the time, it seems to me now that I never took it as truth, but just as one of the many artificial images possible.
    Italo Calvino, *A Cinema-Goer's Autobiography* (*mid-1960s*)

Action! Once upon a time in Rome – and a very good time it later seemed to be – the nineteen-year-old Sergio Leone wrote his first screenplay, which, like most first attempts at writing for the cinema, was autobiographical: a rite of passage movie, which was also a calling card. The screenplay was called *Viale Glorioso*, and it told of the adventures of a gang of middle-class youths on the streets of Rome shortly before the outbreak of the Second World War. For this firmly all-male gang, their 'universe was the street and the cinema'. Meanwhile, in the adult world, the Fascist regime was deciding whether to gear up for Italian involvement in Germany's war. (Mussolini's decision, announced in June 1940, was 'to declare war, but not to make war' – whatever that meant.)

'I first went to the cinema round about 1939, when I was nine or ten,' Leone was to recall half a century later. 'I went with my little comrades. We formed a gang, and we were all like street urchins. When we were at home, we resembled good Dr Jekyll, with all the benefits of a refined education. The moment we got outside, though, we became proper Mr Hydes. Louts, really. And yet we were sons of good families. We lived in the Trastevere district of the city. Within this quarter, there was a distinct area. From the Via Dandelo up to the Gianicolo is one of the steepest hills of Rome, topped by the statue of Garibaldi. We're talking about a good address, where the Jewish bourgeoisie, members of the Papal court and senior professional people lived. Two hundred metres further on, though, was the more downmarket area. The kingdom of the real louts. And we had pitched battles with them. These scuffles happened on the steps of the public staircase, which led to the Viale Glorioso.'[1]

The gang's stamping ground was bordered at one end by the Viale Di Trastevere, just north of the Porta Portese, and at the other by the Gianicolo Park, atop the Gianiculum Hill. Just below the meeting of the Via Dandelo and the Viale Glorioso were 126 steep steps, flanked by cast-iron street lamps set into balustrades. The gang used to gather on these steps and play water games in the granite basin of the nearby fountain of Santa Paola (built for Pope Paul V when he renovated the old aqueduct down the road, and brought water to Trastevere). Above them, in the park, was the equestrian statue of Garibaldi and an avenue of sculptures of the Garibaldini. Below them were the cobbled streets, small shops and artisanal dwellings of Trastevere, a district that enjoyed a 'left-bank' atmosphere and reputation. (This was a legacy of the mid-to-late nineteenth century, when intellectuals, Mazzinians, and radical artisans rubbed shoulders with one another, and when the district laid claim to represent the 'traditional' independent Roman character.) Beyond the steps of the Viale Glorioso were large imposing villas and institutional buildings; at their base, a rabbit warren of smaller houses, workshops and garages.

Despite the highly charged political atmosphere of 1939, the children from the upmarket side of the steps were preoccupied by street fights, secret societies, friendships, plots against rival gangs, troubles at school, chasing girls and reading American comics. Above all they liked to take up an entire row of twenty seats in the front stalls of a *cinema della periferia*, a suburban cinema. Thus installed, they would yell cat-calls and generally make nuisances of themselves; especially during the interval between the first and second reels which was (and is) a distinctive feature of Italian cinema-going. It was particularly good fun to arrive late and to try to puzzle out the storyline together, while others in the audience were trying to concentrate.

As an only child, born fourteen years into his parents' marriage when his father was fifty years old, young Sergio found such companionship particularly nourishing. He was to regret the huge age difference, which made it difficult for him to have a close relationship with his father. By the time he got to know Vincenzo Leone, Vincenzo was a disillusioned senior citizen. The father never lived to see the success of the son, which was, Sergio was to tell *his* son Andrea, 'one of the greatest regrets of my life'. Sergio Leone recalled himself as a solitary, timid, dreamy sort of child. It was for this reason, he later decided, that in adult life he developed 'a fascination with the theme of friendship'. In the meantime, his solitary nature encouraged him to present a confident, bluff exterior, masking a much less confident personality within. He also developed a tendency to impress his circle of friends with tall stories.

In *Viale Glorioso*, the gang's anarchic life on the streets contrasted favourably with the pomposity of life during school hours and the restrictions of life at home. It showed, Leone was to say, 'how this quarter was in fact less than glorious. And it was about a Rome which has gone completely.' Above all, it was about a love affair with cinema, hinging on the difference between the richness and coherence of the world on screen, and the confusion and incoherence of the world outside the picture palace. As Leone recalled, 'We in the gang modelled ourselves on the heroes of the American films we'd seen. We were madly in love with American cinema. We always imitated Errol Flynn and Gary Cooper . . . We always went to see the films that came from Hollywood. Never the Italian *telefoni bianci*, the white telephone comedies. *That* form of cinema I was to discover after the war.'[2]

This identification with American heroes was experienced equally powerfully, and at precisely the same time, by the young Italo Calvino, a close contemporary of Leone's though he grew up in the seaside town of San Remo rather than in Trastevere. Calvino was skilfully to analyse the 'Hollywood firmament' of stars as 'a system entire unto itself, with its own contrasts and its own variables, a human typology. The actors represented models of character and behaviour; there was a hero available for every temperament; for those who aimed to tackle life through action, Clark Gable represented a sort of brutality leavened with boastful swagger; Gary Cooper was cold blood filtered through irony; for those who counted on overcoming obstacles with a mixture of humour and savoir faire, there was the aplomb of William Powell and the discretion of Franchot Tone; for the introvert who masters his shyness there was James Stewart, while Spencer Tracy was the model of the just, open-minded man who knows how to do things with his hands.'[3]

For Calvino, as for Leone, cinema at this time meant American cinema (albeit dubbed into Italian, as was the law). In the late 1930s, the Alfieri Law had attempted to reduce the importation and distribution of American films, and throughout the decade there had been several efforts to institute a protectionist 'quota' system (one Italian film for every ten foreign films shown; mandatory Italian newsreels) as a boost to home-grown productions. As a result, many more films, publicly or privately financed, were being made in Italy. Production had increased sevenfold since 1923, the year after Mussolini's March on Rome. The technical quality of these films was continually improving, and some of them were making use of the newly opened Cinecittà Studio on the Via Tuscolana, which boasted 144 acres of facilities, including twelve sound stages.

Quotas notwithstanding, Hollywood films – even the silent ones which remained in circulation – still tended to dominate Italian popular culture, and not just for middle-class youths on the streets around the Via Dandelo. Federico Fellini's novel and film *Amarcord* (slang for 'I remember') illustrates the extent of that domination from a vantage of fifty years later. Sergio Leone reckoned it was full of 'exact memories' of life in a provincial town north of Rome in the mid-1930s. Fellini depicts the parades of the young *Avanguardisti* and the *Ballila*, marching with the local militiamen and veteran blackshirts, but it is clear that the major cultural event to be celebrated in the town of Amarcord is the arrival of the latest Gary Cooper Western at the Fulgar cinema. References to the Hollywood dream factory abound. The mountainous woman in the tobacconist's shop has 'come-to-bed eyes like Kay Francis'; overexcited children discuss Comanche Indians over the family supper; a new *'Thin Man'*-style raincoat is much admired; and the children masturbate together in a stationary car to ecstatic cries of 'Jean Harlow!', 'Mae West!' and 'The tobacco lady's tits!' In the wedding scene which concludes both book and film, a young woman finally finds 'her Gary Cooper' in the unlikely form of a little *carabiniere* from southern Italy ('Gary is a cowboy and Matteo is a policeman, but love is always love'). The prevailing impression is that, where Italian collective fantasies were concerned, 'we are the sons and daughters of Americans'.[4]

The same fantasies were available to the 'Viale Glorioso gang', as

Leone was to recall. In 1938 Errol Flynn and Gary Cooper were still all the rage, at least in those films that had been passed by the censorship office of the Ministry of Press and Propaganda. But from 1939 onwards they became decidedly less accessible as the Fascist government insisted that the importing of all foreign films be controlled by the state monopoly, and the major American companies gradually withdrew from the Italian sphere of operation in protest. This was a deprivation that made young movie enthusiasts like Leone feel as if the Fascist regime was striking directly at them. RKO continued to distribute, so Leone was able to see John Ford's *Stagecoach* at the local *cinema della periferia* (much cheaper than the first-run houses in the centre of town, and with more audience participation). And thankfully, some of the films Leone remembers enjoying most, such as James Cagney in *Angels with Dirty Faces* and Charlie Chaplin's *Modern Times*, made it into the theatre without the intervention of the censor's office. Luigi Freddi, director of the film division of the Ministry of Popular Culture, had somehow come to the conclusion that *Modern Times* was 'a ferocious satire on socialism and communism'.

But the regime was by no means wholly opposed to the products of Hollywood. In pondering what sort of Italian cinema his ministry should be promoting, Signor Freddi had expressed no small admiration for the cultural values (not to mention the production values) of the mainstream Hollywood films of the time. 'The American film industry', Freddi wrote in the mid-1930s, 'produces films that are youthful, serene, honest, optimistic, enjoyable, generally of high moral value and most often of a noble meaning.' (Frank Capra was a particular favourite, whom Freddi duly invited to Italy to conduct a seminar at the new Centro Sperimentale di Cinematografia.) Freddi shrewdly reckoned that it would be much better to invest in positive-thinking films, such as Capra's, than to engage in overt propaganda, which would probably be both expensive and counter-productive. His views on this matter were shared by Vittorio Mussolini (editor of the magazine *Cinema*, as well as occasional producer and scriptwriter) and Vittorio's father Benito, whose preferred genres were light comedy and musicals. Benito Mussolini especially liked 'Stanlio e Olio'.[5]

So, while Leone may have thumbed his nose at the 'the Italian *telefoni bianca*', they were not always so divorced from the Hollywood product he revered. A comedy, released in 1938, called *Il Signor Max*, is a good example. It tells the story of Gianni (Vittorio de Sica), a humble Roman newspaper vendor who learns all about 'the American way of life' from the illustrated magazines (*Esquire, Time*) he sells at his roadside kiosk. Eventually, he is tempted to lead a double life, as the affluent and sybaritic 'Signor Max'. He picks up a few choice phrases in English ('How d'you do?', 'Cheerio'), learns to distinguish between superior and inferior brands of whisky, and ostentatiously smokes Samos Export cigarettes in a Roman cocktail bar where the international set hang out. But finally, after various farcical complications, Max decides that he prefers to settle down with a nice nursemaid, and to mix with the little people: people like him and his jolly bus conductor father, who are good-hearted and much better company.

*Il Signor Max* was directed by Mario Camerini, who throughout the 1930s specialized in Capraesque romantic comedies of this kind, wherein timid lower-middle-class characters (usually played by De Sica) gently rocked the boat, before accepting at the fade-out that stability was safest. From the mid-1940s on, Camerini was categorized by his increasingly neo-realist critics as the head of the 'calligraphic' school of film-making, one which emphasized *bello scrivere* (beautiful or over-decorated handwriting) at the expense of hard content, and which tended to insulate cinema from everyday political realities. Though Leone claimed that he avoided this sort of stuff until after the war, the claim is highly unlikely, for Mario Camerini was his godfather and a close friend of the family.

It is more likely that in 1939 the Viale Glorioso gang rejected any films that made overt political points and therefore stood out in bolder contrast to the dubbed American films they loved. They would have had little time for Flavio Calzavara's *Piccolo naufraghi*, a rare example of a propaganda film pitched at children, dedicated in fact to 'the fighting youth of Italy'. Calzavara's film was reminiscent of William Golding's *Lord of the Flies* turned on its head, for the edification of Fascist youth organizations. Between that and James Cagney, or *The Adventures of Tom Sawyer*, or Judy Garland and Mickey Rooney, there was no contest in the eyes of the Viale Glorioso gang: 'We went to see the films that came from Hollywood.'

Some of them (especially the serials, and series such as Charlie Chan, which Leone 'adored') bore a distinct family resemblance to the monochrome comics that Leone's friends looked at over and over again until they fell to pieces.[6] They couldn't read English, but the graphics were much more interesting in any case. The key titles were *Flash Gordon*,

*Jungle Jim, Mandrake the Magician* and *The Shadow*. The 'official' comics *Il Balilla* and *Jumbo*, with their inspiring tales of ancient Rome, and heavy-handed satire on little black sambos, seemed much less interesting. The one Sergio Leone liked best was Lyman Young's *Cino and Franco*, which featured his favourite theme, friendship, between two young people in a jungle setting. A little later, at the height of the Second World War, American comics, in common with books and graphic art, were much harder to come by, as the regime discouraged them. True, there were Italian-produced copies by then, but they were, according to Leone, invariably 'abominable'. At a glance he could tell that everything from the print quality to the way the message was expressed was just wrong. 'Luckily, there was a thriving black market, where you could buy all that was forbidden. American novels and comics were sold under the counter, or from suitcases. But we didn't read much. By then, we were too busy waiting for the arrival of the *real* Americans: the soldiers.'[7]

Sergio Leone was eleven when the war started, and fourteen by the time the Sicily landings took place. Rome in the war years was characterized by its chaotic food distribution system and resultant food shortages, by its black market and unrestricted luxury restaurants, and by its increasingly shrill and hollow propaganda, epitomized by the 'oceanic assemblies' in the square outside the Palazzo Venezia, and the newsagents' stands crammed with copies of Il Duce's speeches and news of Il Duce's orders. Latterly, Rome was racked by Nazi occupation and Allied aerial bombardments of the 'holy city'. For Leone, life in wartime must have made the world represented by American popular culture seem very like a dream of freedom and modernity, and an escape from the straitjacket of reality.

In Leone's *Viale Glorioso*, afternoon visits to the cinema lulled the gang of youths into a sort of daze, which didn't help their homework much but certainly fuelled their daydreams. Meanwhile, bootleg comics were full of images for an Italian adolescent to fantasize about: images of plenty, of a world of promise, of the wide open prairies of America. Umberto Eco reckons that the fascination of a group of Italian intellectuals with American 'mass culture' in the 1950s and 1960s had a great deal to do with their experience of comics and popular music during the latter part of the Fascist period, and of the backlog of Hollywood cinema unleashed shortly afterwards. These cultural products represented forbidden fruit, the 'other world'; and this made the ideology they represented seem doubly attractive. They were a rejection of official culture, which seemed to have had all the life squeezed out of it. The young Sergio Leone's love affair with Hollywood films and American comics happened within this atmosphere: the projection on to another world of all that was positive about modernity.

In the prewar years there was a further form of year-round entertainment on offer to children, albeit in the open air of the Gianicolo Park, near the Piazzale Garibaldi.[8] On occasional weekends Sergio Leone was taken there by his parents to see the glove puppets known as the *burattini*, often operated by Neapolitan families of puppeteers. Their name was said to derive from *buratto*, the coarse cloth used by Southern peasants both for sifting flour and to make the hard-wearing sleeve of the puppets' gloves. This brand of puppet theatre pre-dated the *commedia dell'arte*, but the stories usually enacted were in a line of descent from those of the *commedia*: the misfortunes of Pulcinella or Arlecchino or Gerolamo at the hands of the wily Brighella, as enacted by hand-waving puppets in masks. To the young Leone, they were magic. Often his parents had to drag him away from repeated viewings of the same performance, or prevent him from slipping off to yet another glove-puppet theatre.

'I remember late one afternoon', Sergio Leone said in 1976, 'as I was returning home to Trastevere, I walked past one of the puppet theatres which was just closing . . . Behind the lowered curtain of the theatre, I could hear raised voices, and the sound of things being thrown about. Looking behind the theatre, I could see the puppeteer and his wife having a scrap. It was a friendly fight, and very Neapolitan. But just after the puppets had been hitting one another with wooden sticks on the stage, here was this couple hitting one another with the wood and cloth puppets, whose "gloves" by now had become all too visible. As I watched this bizarre event, I understood – in my childlike way – that there were things as they appeared, and things that went on *behind* the things as they appeared. Fiction and reality. The fables of the theatre, and the human theatre which was more serious, tougher, more shabby, and pitiful even. I had just grasped my first lesson in the meaning of the word "spectacle". And it happened before I went to the cinema for the first time.'[9]

The *burattini* were just one form of traditional puppet theatre on offer in Rome's public spaces. Since Sergio's father Vincenzo hailed from Naples and could speak the Neapolitan dialect, he had a particularly soft spot for them. But there were also occasional visits from the *pupi Siciliani* of the South. These were rod-puppets, of up to five feet in height, rather than small glove puppets. They were used to perform Sicilian variations on stories of heroism and bloodshed, originally dating back to the era of Charlemagne: the same stories that were collected in the Old French epic *The Song of Roland* (written shortly after the First Crusade and describing an actual military disaster of AD 778). But these had been updated and made even larger than life in the Renaissance by the Italian poet Ludovico Ariosto, as *Orlando Furioso*.

Sergio Leone liked to say that *Orlando* was an excellent example of the ability of Italian culture to absorb outside influences, and turn them into a distinctive form of entertainment. Performances by the *pupi Siciliani* consisted of one from a repertoire of about 500 plays drawn from incidents in *Orlando*. Roland (or Orlando) would do battle against the Saracens, with help from his magic sword and his cousin Renaud (Rinaldo). But Rinaldo had mistakenly drunk from the fountain of hate, and declared that he, like Orlando, was in love with the fair Angelica. Consequently, there would be a great deal of gore, much clattering, shouting and decapitation, long interludes of courtly love, a complex language of puppet gestures, and (perhaps the most distinctive feature) the stiff-legged 'Orlando walk' which younger members of the audience became adept at imitating. This was the result of the two puppeteers moving two iron rods (one to the head, one to the right hand) to make a rigid five-foot puppet in metal armour traverse the stage. The action took place in front of brightly coloured fairground backdrops, over which the busy puppeteers would lean, yelling, improvising, and stamping their feet to create sound effects. Depending on the audience, performances could also consist of noisy, down-to-earth humour, and crude pastiches of 'high culture' from further north, as well as contemporary twists on the age-old stories. If the *pupi Siciliani* were on form, the audience wouldn't know whether to laugh or cry. Such was the magnificent confusion they evoked in *Don Quixote*.

When the thirty-five-year-old Sergio Leone was preparing *Fistful of Dollars*, he cast his mind back to the performances of the *pupi Siciliani* he saw as an adolescent in Rome's Pincio Park, south of the Borghese Gardens, where the puppet theatre was surrounded by merry-go-rounds, and statues of the great authors of Italian literature. He recalled: 'When I started my first Western, I had to find a psychological reason in myself – not being a person who ever lived in that environment! And a thought came to me spontaneously: it was like being a puppeteer for the *pupi Siciliani* . . . They perform shows which we can call legendary and historical. However, the skill of the puppeteers consists of one thing: to give each of the characters an extra dimension, which will interest the particular village the *pupi* are visiting; to adapt the legend to the particular locality. That is, Rolando takes on the faults – and the virtues – of the village mayor. He's the good guy in the legend. His enemy, the bad guy, becomes – say – the local chemist . . . The puppeteers take a legend or fable, and mix it with the local reality. The relationship with everyday life is a symbiotic one. You get the parallels? As a film-maker, my job was to make a fable for adults, a fairy-tale for grown-ups, and in relation to the cinema I felt like a puppeteer with his puppets.'[10] (By then, Leone was also aware of the parallels between the *pupi Siciliani* and the *bunraku* tradition in Japan, where the puppeteers 'shadow' their puppets on the stage, and the vocalists sit in a line beside it; as well as the cut-out shadow puppets of Java, which perform against a white screen. All three traditions would have an influence on his work.)

Like his father before him (and, incidentally, like Mussolini until he was expelled), Leone was schooled by the Salesian Fathers, a religious order specializing in education. Leone later remembered them as 'more open than the Jesuits, and some of the teachers were lay people'. In the classroom and playground of the Institute of Saint Juan Baptiste de la Salle, Sergio Leone had his first experience of Fascist youth and education policies. His father secured for him exemption from the so-called *Sabato fascista*, which was laid on by the regime as part of the youth programme, a mixture of athletics and pre-military training, with uniforms, banners and drums, marches and anthems. Instead Leone was registered on a fencing course, as a school 'extra' on Saturday mornings. 'By learning how to handle a sword,' he recalled, 'I at least avoided *that* form of Fascist cretinism.' But his favourite classroom subject, history, did not so easily escape the imprint of the regime. The textbooks had bundles of rods or *fasci*, the Fascist symbol, printed on their covers: 'Of course, under Fascism, the history textbooks were biased and abridged. So all had become fake. We knew it. During the period of the dictatorship, the lie had become an institution. Even the newspapers, transparently, never told the truth. When we read them, it was almost a kind of game to point out there was no longer an ounce of reality in the published articles.' And, as Leone recalled many years later, albeit with the benefit of hindsight, 'a game I particularly enjoyed playing was putting my history teacher into embarrassing situations – by asking him things he could not possibly explain truthfully'.[11]

In the late 1930s the curriculum placed great emphasis upon 'the four Romes': those of the Emperors, of the Popes, of Unification and of Il Duce. Similarly, it stressed 'the four great epochs' of Italian power and influence: the Roman Empire, the Renaissance, the *Risorgimento* and the present day. Each of these epochs had been the subject of a big-budget, partly state-funded Italian film, of the type that children were expected to view on school outings. Carmine Gallone's *Scipione L'Africano* (1937) starkly opposed the rural, idealistic, family-minded Romans with mercenary, loose-living Carthaginians, during the second Punic War of 207 BC. Luis Trenker's *I Condottieri* (1937) celebrated its superhuman Florentine hero Giovanni de' Medici. Alessandro Blasetti's *1860* (1934) recounted Garibaldi's liberation of Sicily from the Bourbons; and Blasetti's *Vecchia Guardia* (*The Old Guard*, 1935) was a tale of the Fascist *Squadristi*, and their no-nonsense methods of dealing with strikers, as told through the experience of two blackshirted brothers, Roberto and Mario.

The recently founded film journal *Bianco e Nero*, in a special issue dated August 1939, surveyed a group of Roman elementary school-children (of Leone's generation) to find out what they thought of *Scipione*. One replied: 'The film illustrates the courage with which the ancient Romans fought, and the valour they showed. Now our Duce has re-educated the Italian people about love of country and the spirit of sacrifice.' Another child, referring to the climactic battle sequence, reportedly said: 'When you see the battlefield at Zama and a soldier says, "Troops, we have conquered Cannae!", I thought about our Duce, who said "Let's conquer Adua!"' The journal's introduction, written by Giuseppe Bottai, the minister for national education, concluded with great satisfaction: '*Scipione l'Africano*, despite its technical and artistic flaws, has fulfilled its aims. Why? The children put it best . . . for its sense of epic spectacle, for its accuracy in depicting an historical period which has so much to do with our own.' Even though *Scipione* was not a success at the box office, the minister was determined to prove that it had succeeded in enthusing young minds for 'our African adventure' – his stirring reference to Italy's conquest and occupation of Ethiopia in 1936–7.[12]

Viewed today, the most noteworthy features of *Scipione L'Africano* are its Fascistic trappings: the emphasis on massed crowds and regiments, the anthems and salutes to the leader, the prominent display of the *fasci*. Some of the military extras had already been conscripted for the Ethiopian campaign, and it shows. The set-piece battle, with elephants charging at the Roman infantry, the clash of cavalries filmed by a mobile camera, and fast-cut hand-to-hand fighting, has been justly described as one of the most authentic 'ever put on film'. So it is not surprising that the schoolchildren of *Bianco e Nero*'s sample were bowled over, and it is likely that the eleven-year-old Sergio Leone, whatever his subsequent recollections of institutionalized lies, was equally impressed. Leone would later describe the atmosphere of his school as a somewhat limited choice between 'the lugubrious rites of the ecclesiastical world', and the 'masquerade of Fascism'. But that, again, may well have been with the benefit of hindsight. At the time, the Salesian Fathers' concern with tales of ancient Rome (and to a lesser extent Egypt and Greece, as preludes to Rome) appealed to him considerably, with their combination of 'philosophy, geography and history' – even though he was not a fan of 'dead languages'.

At least Leone's schooling provided him with a set of cultural resources, which would be of considerable use to him in planning his first films as a scriptwriter and director. *Viale Glorioso* would have the obligatory classroom sequences. And in time he would raid the annals of both Greek and Roman history. As he later admitted to me, with a broad grin on his face: 'I remain convinced that by far the greatest writer of Westerns was Homer, for he wrote fabulous stories about the feats of individual heroes – Achilles, Ajax and Agamemnon – who are all prototypes for the characters played by Gary Cooper, Burt Lancaster, Jimmy Stewart and John Wayne. Homer's stories are the great mythological treatments of the individual hero, as well as being prototypes for all the other Western themes – the battles, the personal conflicts, the warriors and their families, the journeys across vast distances – and, incidentally, providing the first cowboys: the Greek heroes entrusted the short span of their lives to their dexterity with lance and sword, while the cowboys entrusted their survival to the quick drawing of a pistol. Basically, it all comes down to the same thing.'[13]

In the end, it was not until the mid-1960s that Leone finally abandoned the project of realizing the autobiographical project of his youth. He told an interviewer, 'I found again, in my bottom drawer, a scenario written nearly twenty years before which I'd called *Viale Glorioso* . . .

Alas! Someone had had the same idea, and had already made an excellent film out of it: Federico Fellini's *I Vitelloni*.'[14] Fellini's 1953 film concerned the listless lives of a group of five youths in the seaside town of Rimini: posing in the streets, lounging in the local café, visiting the music-hall and the *palais de danse*, walking to the pier and staring at the Adriatic, picking up girls in the summer season; and, of course, going to the cinema. Eventually the Fellini figure, Moraldo, leaves Rimini to try his luck in Rome, and imagines his fellow gang members stuck in their usual routines. The contrast between these deadening routines and the dreams or distractions of 'the spectacle' is at the heart of Fellini's film. As Italo Calvino noted, 'Behind all the wretchedness . . . I recognize the unsatisfied youth of the cinema-goer, of a provincial world that judges itself in relation to the cinema.'[15]

Leone recognized his own preoccupations in the film, and finally lost heart in his own project, though by then he had the consolation of other projects, such as a fruitful collaboration with one Clint Eastwood. But fragments from the world of *Viale Glorioso* kept on turning up in his films, even though their subject-matter was very far from 'the facts of everyday life'. Childhood pastimes, moments of movie magic, the picaresque spirit of the *pupi Siciliani* puppet show with its noisy, brutal and colourful re-telling of the old stories – these would recur.

During script conferences about the childhood sequences of *Once Upon a Time in America*, for example, Sergio Leone would 'speak of my own childhood, of the Viale di Travestere, and of several elements which came from my apprentice script *Viale Glorioso*'. When he was preparing the sequence in *Giù la testa* (or *A Fistful of Dynamite*) where the peasant bandit (Rod Steiger) thinks he is robbing the bank at Mesa Verde but is in fact liberating the political prisoners kept in the vaults, Leone had in the front of his mind the sequence in Charlie Chaplin's *Modern Times* where Chaplin picks up the red flag in the street by mistake and is immediately pursued by socialist demonstrators. A visit to this Chaplin film by the Viale Glorioso gang in Rome was also to have been part of his earlier script.

Where the puppet shows were concerned, there is usually a clown-like figure in his films (such as Tuco in *The Good, The Bad and The Ugly*, Cheyenne in *Once Upon a Time in the West* and Juan in *Giù la testa*), who eats heartily, swears mightily, boasts too much, is the butt of everyone else's jokes and whose plot function it is to play Sancho Panza to someone else's Knight of the Rock-hard Countenance; on the subject of whom there is also an *Arlecchino* figure (such as the Man with No Name and the Man with the Harmonica), who is the hero because he is better at being a trickster than anyone else around, and who would be a knight errant but is too grown up, too worldly wise to believe in chivalry any more. He is only as straight as his nature, and his experience, will allow him to be. *Arlecchino* himself doesn't have family ties (although they once meant a great deal to him), but the other characters in the stories tend to put loyalty to their own families or clans before all other loyalties: just like in those Southern Italian villages and towns visited by the *pupi Siciliani*. And *Arlecchino* sometimes has to contend with corrupt or weak professional men (sheriffs, army officers, doctors), who resemble the 'Dottore' figure in the *commedia dell'arte*. Commenting on the presence of a 'picaresque spirit' in his films, and especially *The Good, The Bad and The Ugly*, Leone liked to explain exactly why such traditional forms were useful to him: 'Directors are scared of letting the audience laugh – of allowing a picaresque spirit to intrude on tragic adventures. The picaresque genre isn't *exclusively* a Spanish literary tradition, you know: there are also equivalents in Italy. The picaresque and the *commedia dell'arte* have this much in common: they do not have true heroes, represented by a single character.'[16]

Screenwriter Luciano Vincenzoni recalls being puzzled by Sergio Leone's insistence that their film *Giù la testa* should begin as a peasant urinates on a large ant's nest inside a tree. But finally an explanation was forthcoming: 'It was a game that he used to play as a child. In the spring, he would go with his friends, beneath the trees where there were colonies of ants, and they used to play a game to see who could hit the greatest number of ants while they were pissing. The story he *didn't* make into a film, *Viale Glorioso*, begins in this way – with small children who go to the top of a public staircase, piss down planks of wood, and then run as fast as they can to see whose piss will arrive first at the bottom of the staircase.'[17]

Bernardo Bertolucci, who would contribute to the original treatment of *Once Upon a Time in the West* in 1967, also formed a strong impression of what motivated Leone at work: 'For him, it is just like playing at cowboys and Indians when one is growing up. Regressive. When I went to see him, at his home in the suburbs of Rome, he spent a lot of his time asking me, "When you were a kid, how did you like to shoot? Like that [at arm's length] or that [at waist-level] or that [fanning the hammer]?" So, at times, this man of the West was completely like a child who has access to the dynamics of the imagination.'[18]

In fact, play-acting became one of the linchpins of Leone's directorial method. As his one-time assistant Tonino Valerii remembers, 'Sergio had a very limited English vocabulary when he was directing. And yet, perhaps fortunately for him, he started by directing English and American actors. He'd learned the phrase, "Watch me". He said to me once it was the only thing he'd learned in English – "Watch me!". And he mimed the actions the actors had to do – "You go from *this* to *this*"– and he made them see how they should move, and what they should do. He'd say, "Clint! Watch me! You go *this*, you go *that*, then, immediately – BANG BANG!"'[19] 'He's a short, heavy fellow,' Eastwood would comment, 'but when he acts out his roles, you can see what he wants. And you know that he really feels himself tall and lean, a gunfighter.'[20] (The 'watch me' approach sometimes led to misunderstandings: on the set of *The Good, The Bad and The Ugly*, Lee Van Cleef was once asked by his director to 'eat the minister' instead of 'eat the soup'.)

The exhibition *Omaggio a Sergio Leone*, which opened at the Galleria d'Arte within La Teatro La Scaletta in central Rome in December 1991, featured a series of stills showing his distinctive method of directing American actors: enthusiastically demonstrating to Lee Van Cleef how to holster his gun, handle forwards; getting down on his knees to explain to Eli Wallach how best to kiss his priest-brother's belt; sitting on an oil-drum raft, and excitedly showing Clint Eastwood how to blow up a bridge; acting out, for Jason Robards, how to get someone to shoot through his manacles; riding an aged motorcycle through rough terrain, for the benefit of James Coburn; carefully pointing the barrel of a gun into Larry ('Fat Moe') Rapp's mouth: 'Watch me!'

When *The Good, The Bad and The Ugly* was first released, Sergio Leone seemed literally to be giving the game away, when he went on record about why he was drawn to the genre he was in the process of transforming: 'The attraction of the Western, for me', he said, 'is quite simply this. It is the pleasure of doing justice, all by myself, without having to ask anyone's permission. BANG BANG!' On the face of it, this was a strange thing for a man in his mid-thirties to be admitting. He elaborated on this notion a few years later, in the Italian film journal *Bianco e Nero*: 'Naturally,' he said, 'it was not my business to write or make history – in any case, I had neither the inclination nor the right. So I made *Fistful of Dollars* starting from *my own* history – a history of fantasy ... Nevertheless, it was necessary to present a *very precise* historical debate, thoroughly documented, in order to address this problem ... Within this debate, I could look at human values which are no longer around today. It was a little like going *à la recherche du temps perdu*.'[21]

In all the best childhood games, the magic to a great extent depends on all the participants suspending their disbelief in the game they are playing. If they start to feel silly or self-conscious, the game will not claim their attention for very long. So a lot of detail, and a concerted effort to make the game look as realistic as possible, may well be required. This was also the case with Sergio Leone's cinema. But, crucially, it is almost a trademark of Leone's films that there will be a moment when the magic spell is broken: when the viewers are abruptly encouraged to stay at arm's length from the story, and are made aware that they are watching a game – that the film is someone's 'fantasy'. In *Fistful of Dollars*, it comes when Silvanito the saloonkeeper observes the antics of the Man with No Name, and says, 'It's like playing cowboys and Indians'. In *Once Upon a Time in the West*, it comes when little Timmy McBain mimes his father's actions as he shoots partridges: 'Bang-ba-ba-bang-bang!' This is a deliberate, and distinctly risky, strategy on Leone's part. He wants us to believe in his fables, goes to considerable lengths to ensure that we do – and yet he doesn't.

Leone the puppeteer often illustrates his version of Hollywood history, Italian-style, by introducing us to the strange spectacle of grown-ups playing with toys. Consider the Man with No Name, 'arranging' the corpses as if they were marionettes in *Fistful of Dollars*; El Indio's wooden model of the safe in El Paso, in *For a Few Dollars More*; Tuco taking pot-shots at a row of one-dimensional wooden Indians, in the shooting-gallery sequence of *The Good, The Bad and The Ugly*; Brett McBain's wooden model of a train, which symbolizes the Irishman's 'dream of a lifetime'; Mr Morton's metal model of a man standing before an iron horse, which symbolizes the 'small obstacles' which his employees must remove 'from the track' in *Once Upon a Time in the West*; the wooden toy train, called the 'Johnny and Johnny Express', pulled on a piece of string by an angelic boy, which helps Juan and Jean blow open the bank of Mesa Verde in *Giù la testa*; the model of a vat of bootleg alcohol, which is intended to rise from the bottom of the East River to the surface, and which the boys demonstrate to the Capuano brothers in *Once Upon a Time in America*. In most of these examples, the toys are presented as embodiments of lifelong dreams, as if cherished since childhood, when everything seemed possible. And, as it transpires, in most cases, the dreams go tragically wrong as they begin to come true. Again, Leone wants us to dream, and yet he doesn't; to take the fantasies seriously, and yet consider them ironically. Leone's 'fairy-tales for grown-ups' usually end in tears, rather than 'happily ever after'. Children in his stories tend to have a short life expectancy.

So why make Westerns at all? This question was put to Sergio Leone in 1979, after an Italian survey of *Il Western* had noted in perplexity that, 'In his films, we are in the West, but at the same time we're in a personal imaginary world'. Leone answered by citing a famous passage from Karl Marx's *Grundrisse*: ' "A man cannot become a child again unless he becomes childish. But does he not enjoy the artless ways of the child, and must he not strive to reproduce its truths on a higher plane? Is not the character of every epoch revived, perfectly true to nature, in the child's nature? Why should the childhood of human society, where it obtained its most beautiful development, not exert an eternal charm as an age will never return?" I believe that a film director who is on the point of shooting a Western must bear in mind, above all else, this truth. So, I haven't chosen the West as physical, historical *evidence* of anything, but rather as representative, or as emblematic, of these artless ways of the child.'[22]

The immediate context for Marx's reflections was, in fact, a discussion of the artefacts and myths of ancient Greece, and why they still provide for us a source, even a model, of aesthetic enjoyment: 'Looking at it from another side: is Achilles possible side by side with powder and shot? Or is the *Iliad* at all compatible with the printing press or even printing machines?' Or indeed, he might have added some forty years later, with the apparatus of the cinema? At the same time as Leone was citing Marx, this question was being tackled head-on by a number of cultural theorists, who had adopted the methods of structural anthropologists in order to 'read' popular artefacts (among them, Western films) as myth; part of a folk culture as much as an entrepreneurial culture. Marx's conclusion – that the artefacts and myths of ancient Greece exert 'an eternal charm' – was treated by most commentators in the late 1970s as a little too sentimental to be of much value as a tool of analysis. Surely, they contended, in today's world 'the artless ways of the child' have been left behind? Surely today people expect far more complex problems to be resolved through their art and their myths?

Leone, for one, strongly disagreed: 'I believe it is a good thing to help audiences dream – by recovering these "artless ways", and looking at them again in a more mature way. If, as I also believe, one of the primary functions of all art is this "catharsis", then perhaps through it – or by means of it – even the most difficult of problems and contradictions will seem more easy to resolve. Fable and myth are still the most suitable means of getting there: their loss would be irreplaceable . . . So it is with Westerns . . . To take one example, probably the most obvious – *High Noon*: it isn't only about the dialectic of time and destiny, or the more specific dialectic of time and fear, it is also about something more concrete which was buried in the reality of America during the McCarthy years. The fear of power, and of ostracism towards those who don't want to be involved in it, who reject it.'[23]

To the end of his life, it was very rare for Leone to discuss his films without introducing Charlie Chaplin into the conversation at least once, and to talk of Chaplin's perception that 'America itself is a world of children'. Leone often implied that, for him, Chaplin was a key influence. This cinematic love affair – which had lasted since the late 1930s – reached its consummation in *Once Upon a Time in America*: 'Like the scene of the child and the charlotte Russe on the stairs. It is a homage to Charles Chaplin. Not imitated from one of his films, you understand, not citing a sequence that he shot. But simple evidence of a love for him. And I dare to think that he might have filmed that situation in exactly that way.'[24]

Moreover, Leone contended, his Western fables provided him with 'a formal "mask" for a more subjective need to express myself'. Autobiographical elements continually made their way into his films; not least his memories from the period of the Second World War. For instance, in *Once Upon a Time in the West*, the sequences featuring Sam (Paolo Stoppa) and his heap-of-bones horse Lafayette, as they transport Jill (Claudia Cardinale) through Monument Valley, were based on Leone's memories of an incident that occurred in 1941, when he was twelve. He had travelled from Rome to Naples to join his father, who was working on a film project there. 'It was a time of acute food shortages and famine in Naples, but there was always "the Neapolitan temperament" to help carry them through. When I arrived, my father hired a horse-drawn carriage for us, but the horse didn't move very quickly. His condition was lamentable. You could see the ribs sticking out from under his skin. We proceeded on our way very slowly. My father wasn't too happy about this. He shouted at the coachman to speed up. In vain. As my father continued to repeat the order, "Speed up!", the coachman turned round to face us. He looked at my father and said, "But sir, what do you expect? My horse is running on water." '[25]

As Leone admitted, some of the set pieces in *Giù la testa* (the killing of Juan's children, the reprisals against Mexican insurgents, the German colonel in his armoured car at the head of his mounted troops) were about both the Mexican Revolution of 1910–20 *and* events that took place in Italy in the latter part of the Second World War: 'The massacre of the people in the Grotto, that was based on an historical incident: it actually took place in Italy. Part of a campaign of reprisals by the occupying Germans: they shot 300 people at one time, women, children, Jews and politicians, indiscriminately. The executions in the long trenches or ditches by the railway station, with the soldiers lined up in ranks along the edges, that was also the "Fosse Ardeatine". The Colonel, well, he looks like a Nazi officer, doesn't he?'[26] There is a big betrayal in *Giù la testa*, as in most of Leone's films. Usually it is the result of torture, and the victim discovers that talking will not save him.

For the fourteen-year-old Leone, as for countless others, the German occupation of Rome from September 1943 to June 1944 was a turning point. The living conditions were bad enough. There was a lack of electricity, clothing, food, even water, at times, aerial bombardments, which Mussolini had said would never happen, sudden brutal skirmishes on the streets, round-ups of young men to work on Nazi armaments. Driven home amid this horror was the realization of what a Fascist regime really entailed: 'When we came face to face with the Nazis, it made us discover in no uncertain terms that, under all the masks and the uniforms and the theatre, lay a much more menacing and frightening prospect.'

With the collapse of the Italian army from July to September 1943, and the arrival of the war on Italian soil, German troops and administration had poured into Rome. Although Mussolini had ordered his Fascist regime to be anti-Semitic as early as summer 1938, with bombastic speeches about the 'Levantine' characteristics that had entered Italy through the slaves bought by the Roman Empire, it took the Nazi occupation of 1943–4 to make the rhetoric come true. The Gestapo Headquarters on Via Tasso masterminded round-ups of Roman Jews, for deportation or despatch to the secret concentration camp at San

Sabla near Trieste, run by both Fascists and Nazis. Leone's reference to the 'Fosse Ardeatine' concerns an event that occurred in the spring of 1944 when, as a reprisal for a partisan bomb attack which killed thirty-three SS officers, Hitler ordered the summary execution of ten Italians for every German dead. Since a round-up of Jews, partisans and their families, and a cull of criminals from the Regina Coeli prison could not provide enough victims for this purpose, scores of people were grabbed from off the street as well, to be led to the caves known as the Fosse Ardeatine, at the end of the Via Ardeatina parallel with the Old Appian Way, near the largest of the Christian catacombs. There, the condemned were shot in the nape of the neck, five or six at a time to make the agony last, and piled up in the caves. The entrance was then dynamited. But word got around, and a few weeks later, after the Nazis had retreated, the corpses were dug out and most of them identified: 100 Jews, 12 foreigners, a boy of fifteen, doctors, teachers, electricians, workers, 335 civilians in all (no women). So Hitler had his appointed 330 victims, plus an additional five picked at random by Gestapo chief Herbert Kappler. This terrible massacre succeeded in politicizing more Roman civilians than any other single act of the war.

*Giù la testa* is set during the Mexican Revolution, but, like Pasolini's *Salò*, concerns the death-throes of a Fascistic regime, and its accompanying extremes of violence and decadence. The peasant Juan Miranda stands in the grotto amid piles of corpses: among them, his children. After muttering, 'All of them, six, I never counted them before,' he throws away his wooden crucifix. His last words to his children had been 'May the Good Lord watch over you.' His conversion at that moment to the cause of the Revolution is also a reference to Alcide Cervi of the Italian resistance, whose seven sons were butchered by the Nazis.

Even *The Good, The Bad and The Ugly*, with its picaresque story of three characters riding in and out of the American Civil War, managed to include an explicit reference to 'the Nazi concentration camps, with their Jewish orchestras which drowned the cries of tortured prisoners', as Leone explained when discussing the sequences set in 'Betterville Camp'. His father Vincenzo Leone had worked during the war for an organization in Rome which tried to save Italian Jews from being deported to Germany: 'One of them', Sergio Leone recalled, 'had been taken by the Nazis. My father intervened in the affair, by claiming that the man was his nephew. This was very dangerous, because the Gestapo could have made further inquiries – and the whole family would have found themselves in a camp. But he was determined. He even went so far as to put the man up in our house.'[27] The fact that 'Leoni' is sometimes a Jewish surname (originating in Spain), Leone added, also 'caused us problems at times', even though his family had, as far as he knew, always been 'Christian and Italian'. When his father was away from Rome for extended periods, filming in the south, Sergio would sometimes stay with a young Jewish family in Trastevere. His memories of that household were to come in useful when he was researching *Once Upon a Time in America*.

At the age of fourteen, during the 'groundswell of social and ideological movements which were to come into the open during the liberation', Sergio Leone, together with a group of Roman schoolfriends, 'resolved to join the resistance against the Nazis. We made preparations to join the partisans in the mountains.' But he was persuaded by his mother to stay at home. 'She would have died of grief if anything had happened, and of worry if it hadn't.'[28] Among his generation of film-makers, several did make this journey, and would later weave their experiences into their films; including a few Westerns of the 1960s.[29]

From all this, it is surely clear that, to a surprising extent, film-making for Sergio Leone was indeed 'a little like going *à la recherche du temps perdu*'. It is no accident that his films usually feature an elaborate flashback, which only comes into focus, piece by piece, as the story progresses. 'The function of the flashback is Freudian,' he observed in 1973. 'The Americans had been using it in a very closed way, too rigorously and literally. This was a mistake: you have to let it wander, like the imagination, or like a dream.'[30] Leone's flashbacks tend to be stimulated, not by the taste of a charming little piece of patisserie (as in Proust), or by the plot demands of a police investigation (as in Hollywood *films noirs*), but by a sound: a chiming watch, or the wail of a harmonica, or the incessant ringing of a telephone. Although Sergio Leone could never sing in tune, he was, he claimed, 'musical inside', and very sensitive to natural sounds.

Shortly before he died, Leone talked of a new opening sequence for *Viale Glorioso*, one that would bring his first script right up to date. It came to him as he entered one of his favourite restaurants, a specialist in traditional Roman cooking called *Checcho er Carettiere*, on the Via Benedetta in Trastevere. This establishment has on its wall a fading school photograph in a wooden frame, dating from 1937. The school-children of class 5A of the elementary level of the Instituto Saint Juan Baptiste de la Salle di Viale del Re – forty-nine of them – are all dressed in high white collars, floppy bow-ties and dark smocks, and they are sitting outside the school building in the leafy courtyard. Among the names which have been inscribed in capitals on the photograph – Savini, Masciardelli, Mancini, Grisanti, Paolucci, D'Aguanno, Salvini and Pinci – are 'Leone S' and 'Moricone', two grinning children who were together in the fifth grade. The restaurateur, Pippo Porcelli, had been at school with both of them.

The new opening would involve a fifty-eight-year-old film director arriving at this restaurant for a class reunion. He is early, so he orders his customary bottle of sparkling Cannellino and, beneath the fading school photograph, looks at all the empty chairs around the table, as the soundtrack mixes from contemporary Rome to the late 1930s, and the echoing noises of excited children. The camera moves in towards the bespectacled eyes of the middle-aged director, as he conjures up his schoolfriends from the past: their lessons, their street fights, their rites of passage, in a masculine world of adventure and bravado. Part of this memory, said Leone, would be about the dreams and images and fabrications of America which the children shared: abstract dreams, since none of them actually knew much about what America was really like. These would be contrasted with their first experiences of real-life Americans, when in 1943 the war intruded on their lives, and life was still in black and white.

Until then, their knowledge had been confined to images from the movies and comics, and (for some of them) letters from elderly relatives who had emigrated to the States earlier in the century. He and his classmates, Leone said, had grown up in 'the capital of the imperial Mussolinian melodrama ... a dead neighbourhood of the provinces that was cultivating ridiculous and dangerous dreams of grandeur ... Lying newspapers, cultural connections with Tokyo and Berlin, one military parade after another, leaps into the circle of fire. But mine was an anti-Fascist family, above all devoted to the cinema, so at least I didn't have to share in every aspect of the ignorance. Films opened windows on to the world of play, of liberty, of adventure. But the America of my infancy was not just Hollywood – or rather what filtered into Italy from Hollywood through the gaps. Also novels, the songs of Bing Crosby, jazz, reports of the flight of Felice Balbo to Chicago, poetry, history books, redskins and as many stories as I could listen to told by families which had been to America.'[31]

All of this, Leone claimed, made a welcome change from white telephones, radio parodies of *The Three Musketeers*, spectaculars by Blasetti, local competitions organized by the regime, and Salgari's nationalistic popular novels. But Leone's America was still in the abstract: 'As Pavese justly observed, American culture allowed my generation to look at a collective drama as if it was being projected on to a gigantic screen. The problem was that we could not openly take sides in the drama, the fairy-tale, so we studied American culture like we studied earlier centuries, Elizabethan drama or *Stil Novo* poetry. We secretly read Dos Passos, Hemingway, Scott Fitzgerald, Chandler, learning to love this utopian America which was socially fluid, shiny and ambitious, but nevertheless sealed, like a genie in a glass bottle, by our youthful desire for transgression. "Who's afraid of the Big Bad Wolf?", Disney's song, was a sarcastic comment on Roosevelt's New Deal, which also chimed with the difficult days of our own "depression". The American Dream hid itself from us in different disguises, and America remained a country of children, who pointed an accusing finger at the old world, the world of adults. The "Keep Smiling" ethos offered by the USA, with its upbeat music and edifying visions, was opposed in Europe by the sad, pained gaze induced by totalitarianism and warfare.'[32]

Direct contact with real-life Americans, following the invasion of 1943–5, was something else – another form of betrayal, even: 'In my childhood, America was like a religion. Throughout my childhood and adolescence (and I am by no means sure that I have grown out of that stage even now), I dreamed of the wide open spaces of America. The great expanses of desert. The extraordinary "melting pot", the first nation made up of people from all over the world. The long, straight roads – very dusty or very muddy – which begin nowhere and end nowhere – for their function is to cross the whole continent. Then, real-life Americans abruptly entered my life – in jeeps – and upset all my dreams. They had come to liberate me! I found them very energetic, but also very deceptive. They were no longer the Americans of the West. They were soldiers like any others, with the sole difference that they were victorious soldiers. Men who were materialist, possessive, keen on pleasures and earthly goods. In the GIs who chased after our women, and sold their cigarettes on the black market, I could see nothing that

I had seen in Hemingway, Dos Passos or Chandler. Nor even in Mandrake, the magician with the outsized heart, or Flash Gordon. Nothing – or almost nothing – of the great prairies, or of the demi-gods of my childhood.'[33]

Leone's dreams could hardly survive contact with the reality. As his widow, Carla Leone, puts it, 'This fairy-tale image was what fascinated him. And at the time, he really came to believe in these characters who represented American justice and loyalty and honour. Then he had to start doing business with them in the flesh, and that was that.'[34] Leone himself remembered that to begin with he 'admired the Americans on the screen a lot – their style, their way of speaking and their way of wearing hats'. But 'after a while, I began to realize that America belongs to a worldwide patrimony and that the American people have only rented it. The Americans have the horrible habit, among other habits, of diluting the wine of their mythical ideas with the water of the American way of life – a way of life, incidentally, which isn't of interest to anyone who has a head on his shoulders. Take Doris Day. There is a vision of America in her films, which is totalitarian and quasi-Soviet! A world without conflict, Abel without Cain. While America itself, on the other hand, like every other society is really about conflict and truth competing with untruth . . . I wanted to show the cruelty of that nation, I was bored stiff with all those grinning white teeth. Hygiene and opti-mism are the woodworms which destroy American wood. It is a great shame if "America" is always to be left to the Americans.'[35]

In that imaginary prologue to *Viale Glorioso*, the middle-aged dir-ector would be waiting in the restaurant for classmates who had shared with him the powerful fantasies projected on to gigantic screens. As they too entered *Checcho er Carettiere*, he would have difficulty recognizing them and matching their faces to the fading photograph on the wall. Though Leone's autobiographical film was never realized, the class reunion did in fact take place: a press photograph of the assembled men, fifty years on, now hangs next to the original. The reunion was the idea of a journalist working on *Messagero*, another of the class of 1937, who covered the story. Sergio Leone is standing in the shadows, looking uncharacteristically reticent, next to his very old friend Ennio Moricone. He does not look a healthy man.

But since we are by now well into the second reel, it is time for the flashback to start coming into focus.

# 2

# Bob, Son of Robert

It was pleasant inside the cinema, warm and comfortable. A warm cathedral, as rich as possessions. Not a moment lost. You plunge straight into an atmosphere of warm forgiveness. You only have to let yourself go to feel that the world has at last become indulgent. Already you almost think that. Then dreams waft upwards in the darkness to join the mirages of silver light. They are not quite real, the things that happen on the screen, they stay in some wide, troubled domain of dreams and dead men. You have to hurry to stuff yourself with these dreams so as to endure the life which is waiting for you outside, once you've left the cinema, so as to last through a few more days of strife. You choose from among these dreams those that will warm your heart the most.
   Louis-Ferdinand Céline, *Journey to the End of the Night* (1932)

Sergio Leone was born on 3 January 1929, in Rome. Some sources state that he was born in Trastevere, others that he came from Naples. In fact, he was born in Via dei Lucchesi, in Palazzo Lucchesi, near the Trevi Fountain; but he spent most of his childhood and youth (from the age of two to twenty) in Trastevere. His father Vincenzo was nearly fifty years old, and his mother Edvige Valcarenghi – whose stage name was 'Bice [short for Beatrice] Walerian' – had married him thirteen years previously. Sergio was the first and only child of the marriage, and as he recalled, 'the event was treated by both of them as if it was a miracle'. His mother had almost given up hope.
   Neither of Sergio's parents originated in Rome. Vincenzo was born in Torella dei Lombardi, in the province of Avellino near Naples, on 5 April 1879. His family owned a small estate in the Irpinia. Sergio Leone liked to say that 'my ancestors come from the *campagna* – the area around Naples'. Edvige's family came from Friuli, and her father was proprietor of the Russian Hotel (no longer in existence) in the Piazza di Spagne, linked to the church of Trinita dei Monti by the Spanish Steps, part of the most elegant quarter of Rome. So she was Roman 'by accident', born there in 1886. She met Vincenzo in 1912, when they were both given contracts by Aquila Films of Turin: he as an 'artistic

director' and actor, she as an actress. They married in 1916, and 'Bice' retired from the screen a year later to devote her energies to setting up home. She never worked as an actress again.[1]

Vincenzo Leone was educated at the College of the Salesian Fathers at Cava dei Tirreni (one of his lay teachers was the well-known language scholar Italo Zingarelli), and he proceeded to read law at the University of Naples – where he had his first experience of amateur theatricals. His son was to recall: 'This was at a time, before the First World War, when the town of Naples was one of the cultural centres of all Italy. In parallel with his legal studies, my father was drawn to the artistic milieu. He found many friends there. Important figures such as Eduardo Scarfoglio, the great – and powerful – writer and journalist . . . and poets and playwrights such as Italo (Roberto) Bracco. He knew Gabriele d'Annunzio well – they had been to school together . . . While he studied for his degree in jurisprudence, he worked as an actor and director with an amateur theatre company.'[2]

Naples was still – albeit only just – the sophisticated city it had been before the unification of Italy began to shift the sophistication further north. It supported several theatres: mainly repertory companies specializing in everything from the classics to popular dialect comedies and music-hall. In 1905 Bracco and the actor Amleto Novelli introduced Vincenzo to Roberto Talli, the manager of one such company, Talli-Dramatica-Calabresi (T-D-C), which, from a home base in Naples, toured productions around the whole country. After graduating Vincenzo joined the company as a performer. He used the stage name 'Roberto Roberti', in imitation of the famous actor Ruggero Ruggeri who had also worked for T-D-C before going on to higher things. Sergio Leone was to explain: 'His family thought that my father was practising as a barrister in Turin, but in fact he was a member of a touring theatre company . . . it became difficult to work under his real name. The family would have learned the truth. And they would have disinherited him, broken off all contact. You must remember that at that time, the theatre was really taboo in a family such as his. If he'd said he wanted to be an artiste, they would have treated him like Pulcinella.'[3]

After a stint with Roberto Talli, 'Roberti' spent some time with the Eleanora Duse Touring Company – or so Leone family folklore claims: no documentary evidence for this has yet been unearthed. In 1911, when he found himself acting *jeunes premiers* in Turin, he met a lawyer called Lino Pugliese, the administrator and partner of textile magnate Camillo Ottolenghi, who four years previously had founded the small film production house Aquila Films. Pugliese persuaded Roberto Roberti to appear in his début film. It was a melodrama (Aquila's speciality) called *La Bufera* (*The Storm*); the 'artistic director' was Carlo Alberto Lolli, and it opened in December 1911, to lukewarm reviews. The Turin film journal *La Vita Cinematografia* concluded, 'the sole redeeming feature, amid all the improbabilities and the poor scenario, is the assured performances of *sigg*. Achille Consalvo and Roberto Roberti'.[4]

It was boom time for the Italian film industry, with production companies springing up in Turin and Rome, usually run by lawyers, with backing from Northern industrialists who enjoyed the confidence of the big banks. By 1914, there were twenty-two of them, and their fortunes waxed and waned in cycles of boom and bust. For his part, Lino Pugliese was keen to build up a stock company of actors from the world of theatre, alongside technicians on yearly contracts. But Roberti preferred to return to the live theatre, rather than be tied down to a contract with a film company. For the spring season of 1912 he appeared at the Teatro Mercadante in Naples, but the theatre company folded shortly afterwards when its star actor died. Thus, out of a job, he contacted Pugliese to say that he was now 'free and ready to accept Aquila's offer and move to Turin', at a starting fee of 1,000 lire, high for the time. He was engaged as 'lead actor' and 'artistic director'. (It wasn't unusual at that time for there to be two directors on each project – one 'artistic' and the other 'technical'.) Several other performers were contracted to Aquila at this time, all of them trained in classical theatre, including the comedy actress 'Bice Walerian'. Her contract with Aquila stipulated that she would play both dramatic and comedic parts. She, too, had adopted a stage name, derived from the surname of her ex-fiancé Prince Walerian. When she joined Aquila and met Roberti she broke off her engagement with Walerian, but retained his name. What the hapless Prince thought of this, history does not record.

The year 1912–13 was an *annus mirabilis* for the industry, with the international success of Enrico Guazzoni's blockbusting version of *Quo Vadis?*, produced by Cines of Rome, and at nearly two hours the longest and most spectacular film ever made. First published in 1895, Henryk Sienkiewicz's novel had been filmed in France, in considerably shorter versions and without the benefit of copyright clearance, in

1901, 1902 and 1908. But Guazzoni was the first to acquire the rights to the novel formally and, a painter and designer by training, he gave it the full treatment. If *Quo Vadis?* still looked as though it was filmed from the front stalls of a theatre by a static camera, it nevertheless managed – through sheer scale, and Guazzoni's visual imagination – to look like a piece of epic cinema. Elaborate scenes – such as the terrified citizens rushing through the streets of burning Rome while Nero played his lyre and sang on the balcony of the palace – helped to lay down the ground rules for countless historical epics in the future. Its international success prompted critics to write of a distinctively 'Italian' contribution to world cinema, and encouraged even small operations like Aquila to emulate the sales tactics of the larger production houses, by delivering longer films in an identifiable style. Product differentiation was now the name of the game. *Quo Vadis?* had cashed in on a wave of popular nationalism, following the conquest of Libya in 1912. The film was also presented as a prestige 'educational' production. Aquila, however, set its sights somewhat lower.

The style chosen by Lino Pugliese (derived in part from German and Danish films then appearing on the home market) was melodramatic and passionate: 'sensational stories set among the upper classes', presented in serial form, with titles like *The Golden Cycle*. The 'artistic direction' credits for these *grand guignol* productions were to be shared by Roberto Roberti and Achille Consalvi, who also acted the leads in each other's films. Roberti's films during this period included *La Contessa Lara* (1911, a spy film, with Bice Walerian); *Un sogno* (*A Dream*, 1912, co-directed with Consalvi); *La folgore* (*Lightning*, 1913, which Roberti directed, and in which he also played the lead); *La regina dell'oro* (*The Golden Queen*, 1913, directed by Consalvi); *L'ultima vittima* (*The Final Victim*, 1913, with Bice); *Il suicida n.359* (*Suicide number 359*, 1913); *La torre dell'espiazione* (*Tower of Expiation*, 1913, with Bice, directed by and starring Roberti); *L'assassina del ponte di S. Martin* (*Killer from Saint Martin's Bridge*, 1913, with Bice) and *La vampira indiana* (*Indian Vamp*, 1913, again with Bice). Most of these films have not survived, other than in the form of press stills and fragments, so all historians can do is to try to reconstruct them from trade journals and the reactions of critics.

Film historians Aldo Bernardini and Vittorio Martinelli conclude, mainly from written sources: 'With these works, Roberto Roberti became a force to be reckoned with, in the Italian production of full-length films at that time . . . The public seemed to like the Aquila type of film – partly because it dealt with daring, transgressive subjects and scenes, which challenged social conventions and commonplaces. But the critics and the censor were not so happy with them, and tended to denounce them whenever they could. Which may be why some of Roberti's films were not easy to distribute, and why they did not stay in circulation for long. They were a bit too strong for the market, and critics referred to them as "somewhat vulgar" or "incoherent": but these same critics usually praised the production values, the quality of the artistic direction and the virtuoso acting of the protagonists.'[5] Whatever the critics chose to write, Aquila films remained popular at the box office, when they could find distribution. The establishment might have preferred the new medium of film to concentrate on 'refined subjects' and educational ambitions, but the paying customers did not always agree.

It is interesting that the pace of Aquila's (and Roberti's) productivity accelerated in the years 1913–15, for this was a time in which Italian cinema came to dominate the continental European market, in both qualitative and quantitative terms. They were also the years when well-known playwrights and novelists began to shed their scruples (or snobbery) about working in a mass-production industry. Emilio Ghione was a prominent actor-director of the period, later a Fascist sympathizer with strong views about the emergence of Italy's national cinema. He was to write: 'The beginning of the First World War helped Italy greatly in the conquest of foreign markets: for France, Germany and Austria halted their output, and America had still not realized what cinema was about; hence Italy was the cinematic ruler of the world.'[6] Hollywoodland was still a real-estate company when Guazzoni fed his Christians to the lions. By 1915 there were no fewer than 500 cinemas nationwide, and eighty production companies in the four 'film capitals': Turin, Milan, Rome and Naples. Film was also beginning to be taken seriously by serious critics, a fact that helped Vincenzo Leone's family (from the lesser aristocracy) to come to terms with his chosen profession. But still he held on to his stage name.

In the light of future developments, Roberti's *La vampira indiana* (1913) is particularly interesting. It wasn't the first Italian 'Western' worthy of the name: that honour (if such it be) goes to Giacomo Puccini's opera *La fanciulla del West/The Girl of the Golden West*, which, with Caruso as the hero, premièred at the New York Metropolitan in

1910. But it was the second. There had been plenty of other *European* Westerns made before 1913: for instance, several short Lumière films, such as *Repas D'Indien*, shot by Gabriel Veyre in 1896. But, as Sergio Leone was understandably delighted to recall, 'this was the first *Italian* film Western, and it was directed by my father, with my mother playing the Red Indian'. It opened on Christmas Eve 1913. A surviving press still shows bejewelled Bice Walerian, attired as a Red Indian princess, sitting on a white horse being led by a Big Chief in full warpaint and a feathered war-bonnet. She plays the vamp of the title, who commits a series of crimes, including murder, to help her brother. An innocent man is condemned for these crimes, and his daughter tries energetically to clear his name; eventually coming face to face with the Indian princess herself. From the evidence, *La vampira* appears to combine parts of the story of Cecil B. de Mille's *The Squaw Man* with the kind of 'vamp' who was fashionable in late nineteenth-century poetry and symbolist paintings.

The critics at the time were not greatly enthused by *La vampira indiana*. *Il Maggese Cinematografico* (Turin), on 10 January 1914, set the tone: 'The mise en scène is decorative, the photography good. The subject is just about acceptable, if rather far-fetched. Let us accept that a Red Indian woman commits all these crimes to help her brother. But that she does these things all by herself seems a bit too much to swallow! . . . There's no denying she has great talent. She enters and exits from the palazzo at will and does exactly what she pleases. She kills, telephones, and a poor innocent is condemned in her place.'[7] By February 1914, the film was being hailed as 'a success for Aquila'. With such a heady mixture of war-bonnets, horses, telephones and a palazzo, not to mention a duel between the two leading ladies, it could hardly fail.

Roberto Roberti made seven more films with Bice Walerian, most of them with an emphasis – in one critic's words – on 'fairy-tale and sentiment rather than blood and thunder': *Il barcaiulo del Danubio* (*The Boatman of the Danube*, 1914); *L'istrione* (*The Ham Actor*, 1914); *La principessina di Bedford* (*The Little Princess of Bedford*, 1914); *Il Bandito di Port-Aven* (*The Bandit of Port Aven*, 1914); *La piccolo detective* (*Little Girl Detective*, 1915); *La vampa* (*The Vamp*, 1916); and *La cavalcata dei Sogni* (*The Dream-Ride*, 1917), in which the names of 'Roberto Roberti' and 'Bice Roberti' make their final appearances amongst the acting credits. Clearly the surname Roberti and the business of setting up a home were by now more important to Bice

Walerian than a career in films. When her husband began to work exclusively as a director, she pulled out of the business altogether. Shortly after *La cavalcata*, Aquila Films went bankrupt, the victim (like a lot of the early, under-financed, small Italian production companies) of inflated costs, over-production and shrinking wartime markets.

Roberto Roberti had not been called up to the Italian army in 1915: his medical examination judged him to have a weak heart. When Aquila closed down, he could well have been unemployed for the duration. But, perhaps because of his theatrical background and his experience of dealing with strong-willed actors and actresses, he was approached in 1917 by Giuseppe Barattolo, an advocate from Naples, to join his Caesar Film in Rome as an artistic director. Caesar, founded in April 1914, had since built up a repertory company of technicians, directors and actors around the company's 'prima donna' and prime asset: twenty-nine-year-old Francesca Bertini (real name Elena Seracini Vitiello). In 1917 Caesar had just signed a contract with La Bertini for a series of films called *Sette peccati capitali (The Seven Deadly Sins)*, guaranteeing her a special retaining fee of 200,000 lire, on top of her regular salary. Bertini's contract guaranteed that she would have 'full creative control' over her work at Caesar. Whoever her directors turned out to be, they would need to be blessed with very long fuses. Roberti was engaged to direct the diva in *La piccola fonte (The Little Fountain*, 1917), based on a 1905 play by Roberto Bracco – the same Neapolitan dramatist who had launched him on his theatrical career. Sergio Leone was happy to recount a suitably exaggerated tale of Bertini's egomania which he heard from his father: 'One day, the actor Febo Mari gave her some lip. He was a highly regarded actor . . . He had the ability to cry, with real tears, to order. And so, during one scene, Febo Mari asks Bertini if she can cry. She agrees. And she asks for onions or menthol. Febo Mari protests. He declares that an actor should be able to cry "from within". Without artificial aids. He concentrates. And demonstrates his skill. He begins to gush, like a fountain. At this point, Bertini shows the whole crew what he is doing. And she says, "Do you know why this man is crying? It is because it has just struck him that he will *never* earn two million lira per film!" '[8]

It may have been Roberti's friendship with Bracco that prepared the ground for the Caesar contract, or it may have been his track record with Aquila. Either way, *La piccola fonte* turned out to be a one-off. By early 1918 he was back in Turin, as artistic director of a 'Maciste' film

SERGIO LEONE

for the ltala Company, an organization co-owned by Giovanni Pastrone. The ever-popular muscleman hero Maciste (loosely based on the
character of Ursus in *Quo Vadis?*) had first appeared in Pastrone's epic
film *Cabiria*, produced by Itala in 1914. In that film, Maciste played a
Roman noblewoman's trusty bodyguard, who endeavoured to rescue
her from Carthaginian priests determined to sacrifice her to their god,
Moloch. In the film's best-known sequence, Maciste led his mistress
down the face of a huge open-mouthed effigy of an animal deity, while
being chased by spear-waving soldiers (a dramatic precursor of the
Mount Rushmore sequence in *North by Northwest*, and, thus, of the
battle sequence in Sergio Leone's later *Colossus of Rhodes*).

*Cabiria* boasted, among many other attractions, a script partly written by Gabriele d'Annunzio, soldier-poet of the radical right, of whom
Pastrone was a fervent admirer. According to d'Annunzio, the name
'Maciste' was 'a very ancient surname of the demi-god Hercules', and
his script was 'inspired' by Flaubert's *Salammbò*. In an essay on
*Cabiria*, d'Annunzio stressed the appropriateness of cinema as a
medium for spectacularly showing off the muscular male body in
athletic or gymnastic poses: Maciste makes his first appearance in the
film standing on a rock, his huge arms folded, looking out to sea –
an overweight classical sculpture come to life, and heir to the tradition, founded by photographer Eadweard Muybridge, of using the
photographic image to exhibit statuesque male nudes in motion. In
d'Annunzio's version, Maciste is a mixture of historical artefact,
contemporary superman, circus performer, bodybuilder and object of
contemplation: a trophy for the masses.[9] Some, in the late 1920s, were
to note the striking facial resemblance between the actor who played
Maciste and an equally heavy-set superhero who liked to fold his arms
for the newsreel cameras: Benito Mussolini. Maybe the dictator based
his act on the movies.

*Cabiria* also featured the eruption of Mount Etna, Hannibal crossing
the Alps, the blowing up of an entire fleet, and the most publicized
tracking shot in early film history, whereby Pastrone showed off to full
advantage the huge Carthaginian temple of Moloch he had designed,
complete with stone elephants. But despite all this spectacle, as Pastrone
would subsequently admit, it was 'the character of Maciste who was
largely responsible for the film's success. I trained that actor myself.
Bartolomeo Pagano was not a professional; he was a docker in Genoa
when I hired him.' Still later, Sergio Leone liked to claim that it was in

fact his father who discovered Maciste, in the formidable person of Pagano (born 1878). It is possible that Roberti brought this huge figure to the attention of Pastrone, who then lured him away from his native Genoa and 'trained' him to become the blacked-up, balding muscleman in a loincloth who made his name at the age of thirty-six in *Cabiria*. But there is no confirming evidence.[10] Pastrone always claimed that Pagano was discovered by two of his 'faithful associates', Domenico Gambino and Luigi Romano. When Leone made *his* claim, the character of Maciste had reappeared in no fewer than twenty-three 'peplum' pictures, produced in Rome between 1960 and 1965. (The word 'peplum' is a Latinized version of the Greek 'peplos', meaning a short tunic or dress worn in ancient times, and the term was coined to describe the 'sword and sandal' historical epics so popular at the time.)

Maciste was to become the most resilient of all home-grown Italian superheroes of the cinema. His popular success in *Cabiria* sparked a boom in screen musclemen which lasted from 1914 to 1926 and included no fewer than 181 films in Italy alone. Maciste would be rivalled by Samson, Atlas, Ajax, Hercules, Galaor, Saetta (a 'futurist' version, apparently) and the giant *Buffalo* who was always teamed with the diminutive *Bill*. The muscleman hero in Italian cinema became the male equivalent of the diva – originating in the docks or the gymnasium, rather than the classical theatre. The first spinoff, *Maciste* (1915) came from a script by Pastrone. Thereafter, Bartolomeo Pagano referred to himself, on credit titles and in public, by that pseudonym alone. This led to the inevitable 'series' from Itala. A contemporary critic, writing in *Cinema-Star* of 6 February 1927, concluded: 'None of the various cinema Goliaths can compare with Bartolomeo Pagano, whose morphology – complex, harmonious, powerful – is really worthy of the Hercules of mythology ... The masses – the collective, primitive, soul – love goodness which is powerful; that is why they prefer, above all the heroes of the screen, our Maciste who, in anatomy and character, is Latin.'[11] In the summer of 1928 Pagano retired to his specially built 'Villa Maciste' in Liguria for a well-earned rest. He had demonstrated the triumph of the torso in nineteen Italian films. Carlo Campogalliani (known abroad as Charles Campana) directed and acted in a 'Maciste trilogy' starring Pagano in 1920. In 1941 (the heyday of Fascist cinema), he made the big man an offer he thought he couldn't refuse: a role in 'an adventure film – with patriotic inspiration' which he hoped might 'launch the unforgettable Maciste to new generations of spectators'.[12] Pagano turned him down. He had fallen out with Campogalliani after the 'trilogy', accusing him of hogging the limelight. He was also suffering from arthritis. But Campogalliani was not so easily deterred. In 1960, thirteen years after Pagano's death, he relaunched Maciste in the person of bodybuilder Mark Forest (real name Lou Degni), in the stirringly titled *Maciste in the Valley of the Kings*, a follow-up to the same director's *Goliath and the Barbarians*.

Roberto Roberti returned to Turin at the beginning of 1918 to direct *Maciste poliziotto (Maciste the Detective)*, starring Bartolomeo Pagano. Like most of Maciste's post-*Cabiria* adventures, it had a contemporary setting. The strongman finds himself employed in the household of industrialist Mr Thompson, at a time when nasty labour agitators are planning a strike in the Thompson factory. The ringleaders turn out to be three of the factory's employees. Because they are not having much success at provoking the workers into strike action, they kidnap the boss's daughter Ada and hold her to ransom. So, as the *Rivista del Cinematografo* (Milan) related: 'The Herculean Maciste goes looking for her, tracks down the ringleaders, hits them a lot, is captured by the ringleaders, then escapes, then is captured again, then escapes again, then slugs it out with all the delinquents in a large room, where they have gathered to force Thompson to sign this agreement which will harm his business interests.'[13] *Maciste poliziotto* was released while news of the Russian Revolution, and unrest in Germany, was hitting the headlines in Italy. It suggests that the 'Breaker of Chains' had taken several steps rightwards in the four years since his lumbering début, and was well on the way to earning a black shirt. *Maciste poliziotto*, part of a trilogy with *Maciste atleta* and *Maciste medium*, was then recut to become a sequence of episodes in the American serial *The Liberator*, released in November 1918. And while it was the only film Roberti made for Itala, it can at least claim the distinction of being the first 'Leone' action film distributed in the USA.

Towards the end of 1918 Roberti rejoined Caesar Films in Rome, this time with a longer-term contract; and, after directing a couple of spy films for them, resumed a partnership with Francesca Bertini (fourteen films, between 1919 and 1925) which at last placed him centre-stage in the postwar Italian film industry. Following the armistice, European markets had opened up, and in yet another attempt to compete with American and German imports, Giuseppe Barattolo had made history by giving his diva her own production house. In 1920 she signed a two-year contract that guaranteed her eight films a year and a total of 4 million lire. This contract caused a sensation, since the accountants, other producers, and rival divas all spotted its inflationary potential. Nevertheless, Barattolo, who by then had a controlling interest in the Unione Cinematografica Italiana (UCI) and enjoyed the temporary confidence of some of the largest banks, was convinced that the future of the industry lay in the foundation of a star system. Indeed, his deal with Bertini has been said by some film historians to have enshrined such a system for the first time. Bartolomeo Pagano had never been treated so well.

Although several signed stills from their films together have survived, (on which Francesca Bertini wrote such sentiments as 'To dear Roberti, a million thanks'), it seems that this working relationship took a while to settle down. Roberti wanted to be treated as more than just a jobbing director hired to promote an overpaid diva. But these initial tensions were overcome during their first film together: somehow, Roberti managed to keep his cool while all about him were losing theirs. Most of their films together were melodramas expressing extreme and violent passions, and in all of them Bertini played a distinctively Italian version of the femme fatale. With her expressive face, exaggerated and balletic hand movements and large features, she seems today like a Neapolitan version of Greta Garbo – although she originated, in fact, from Florence. In her book *Passion and Defiance*, Mira Liehm writes: 'In *La Serpe* [*The Serpent*, 1920, directed by Roberto Roberti], the heroine (Francesca Bertini) is literally torn apart by her passion. She wants to kill her lover, a musician (another stock figure of Italian movies), in order to avenge her father's death. She kills herself at the end, though, confessing her great love for him.'[14]

Roberti's other films with La Bertini were basically variations on this theme, freely adapted from French authors such as Alexandre Dumas, *fils* (*La Principessa Giorgio/Princess George*, 1920), Octave Feuillet (*La Sfinge/The Sphinx* and *L'Ombra/The Shadow*, both 1920), Henry Bataille (*La donna nude/The Nude*, 1922) and Georges Ohnet (*La Contessa Sara/Countess Sara*, 1919 and *Lisa Fleuron*, 1920). In *La Contessa Sara*, Bertini plays a beautiful gypsy girl, who inherits a fortune and has to choose between an elderly general (who is besotted with her) and a young romantic; she chooses the general (and a title), but 'abandons herself to her passion' with the young Pietro as well.

Eventually, haunted by remorse for having betrayed a man who is 'like a father to her', she slips away from the general's castle, runs to the sea and hurls herself into the waves. Sergio Leone later recalled, of this famously weepy final sequence: 'I have in my possession a letter that the actor Amleto Novelli wrote to my father, to let him know that he had just seen *Countess Sara* with [the film director] Carmine Gallone. According to Novelli, in the silence of the cinema all you could hear was a single phrase, repeated over and over again by Gallone as he sobbed: "She's reviving; she's coming back from the dead." '[15]

The critics were less convinced. They now complained that Bertini's performances were becoming repetitive and stereotyped, that the femme fatale motif was ossifying into a formula. They even coined a damning neologism (*Bertineggia*) to describe this tedious process. Bertini's decline was mirrored in the industry as a whole, with its increasingly overblown remakes and sequels: *Quo Vadis?* in 1924–5, a German–Italian co-production with Emil Jannings as Nero, which led to the closure of the UCI studios (and during the filming of which an extra was actually eaten by a lion); and *Gli ultimi giorni di Pompei* in 1926, co-directed by Carmine Gallone (the *fifth* Italian version since 1908), made at a cost of 7 million lire, a film which was justly re-titled by Emilio Ghione 'The Last Days of the Italian Cinema'. Total production was plummeting (415 films in 1921, 130 in 1922). When the financiers began to pull out, and even the larger production houses such as Itala and Caesar began to fail, directors and actors began to look for work abroad – especially in Berlin and Hollywood. Bertini signed a contract with William Fox, for a million dollars, then – in a classic example of life imitating art – fell madly in love with Paul Cartier, a Swiss banker who was cousin to the Parisian jeweller. They were married in August 1920. She broke off her Hollywood deal, and managed to persuade Giuseppe Barattolo to absolve her from complet-ing that much-publicized contract with Caesar. Reducing her output to one or two pictures a year, she then went into affluent semi-retirement, first in Florence and then in Paris. She died in Rome in 1985 at the age of ninety-three, having lived long enough to see Roberti's son become a director of films which commented on the typecasting of mega-stars, of which she was a very early example.

Meanwhile, Roberto Roberti, whose career had become dangerously linked to the fortunes of a failing star, and who had become famous for the kind of film it was becoming impossible to finance, had reached a professional crisis. In autumn 1922 he was offered work in Berlin, to replace Ernst Lubitsch (who had emigrated to Hollywood) on a series of films with Pola Negri. He had earned a reputation (like George Cukor's in the 1940s and 1950s) as a 'woman's director', who worked like a patient theatrical producer. But, according to Sergio Leone, 'My mother said she had no wish to leave Italy. So my father didn't sign a contract with Pola Negri, and I was born in Rome.'[16] Having abandoned her career to make a home in Trastevere, Bice Walerian wasn't keen on going back to being a 'strolling player', as she had been before settling down with Roberto. Instead, her husband directed two very different films for EFA in Rome: *Fra Diavolo* (1925, a swashbuckling adventure which he also co-wrote) and *Napoli che canta* (*When Naples Sings*, 1926).

*Fra Diavolo* or *The Devil's Brother*, was based on the exploits of a patriotic Robin Hood figure of the late eighteenth century, who masqueraded as the Marquis de San Marco in order to 'rob the great lords of their gold and their wives of their hearts'. Roberti's version stressed the bandit's patriotism as he fought against the French General Hugo and his men, as well as the Lady Caroline, sister of Marie Antoinette, for control of the Kingdom of Naples. Eight years later this tale was to be more famously parodied by 'Stanlio and Olio' (actually playing characters with those names under Hal Roach's direction), in an ironic version of Auber's operetta. To judge by reviewers of the mid-1920s, Roberti's *Fra Diavolo* – dubbed 'un grandiose film Italiano', and a parable about 'liberta' and 'dominazione' – was a little deficient in irony. *Napoli che canta* was a short, silent, all-singing location piece, based on traditional *canzonette* (or little songs). When it was screened at the Belmont Theatre, New York (known as 'the only Italian motion picture house on Broadway', intended mainly for immigrant audiences), the poster promised 'There's a thrill in every scene – You will enjoy the picture tremendously even without understanding Italian . . . HOW THEY SING IN NAPLES!!!' How they sung at all when the film was silent, the audience had to find out for itself. Released at a time when Neapolitan production had virtually ground to a halt, *Napoli che canta* was treated by the film cognoscenti as a very pallid reflection of a once-thriving film culture.

After completing *Napoli* Roberti worked briefly for Barattolo again, on a low-budget remake of *Assunta Spina*, the pioneering film in which Bertini had made her name fourteen years earlier. But the critics deemed it no more than a piece of cheap sentimentality. Thereafter, Roberti did not make another film for ten years. Apart from the general decline of the industry until the mid-1930s, there may well have been political reasons for this uncharacteristic period of inactivity. Sergio Leone often speculated about these, in interviews: 'My father enrolled fairly early in the Fascist party, because he believed in what they said they would do. He was a Neapolitan, and a romantic by temperament. But after three weeks they told him he would have to re-enrol, to get another card, because the treasurer of his local section had run off with all the subscriptions. He refused to renew his subscription, saying that he was no longer prepared to carry the card, and little by little they began to insinuate that he must be a communist. They said (correctly) that he had proposed to the minister for the arts, Giuseppe Bottai, that the industry should form co-operatives as a way out of its problems, and this proposal was called "a communist solution". He was only saved from being banned from work altogether, or exiled, because another minister, Roberto Forges Davanzati, who was a childhood friend and an honest man, said he was prepared to stand as guarantor of his behaviour. So he narrowly escaped exile, but was constantly being harassed by the regime. He had become President of the Italian Guild of Film Directors, a key position in the industry, so it was difficult for them to touch him.'[17]

Leone continued, 'One incident which was to have an important effect on his career was when he was offered a project by the Unione Cinematografica Italiana, to adapt for the screen the book *Claudia Particella – The Cardinal's Lover*, a short piece of fiction written by the young Benito Mussolini. My father was approached directly by Mussolini himself, to offer him the job. But when my father read it, he said loud and clear that he thought it was terrible and that he didn't want to know. Bottai, who was one of Mussolini's most consistent and loyal supporters, continually persecuted him: the result was that my father could not find any work.'[18] The book in question was written in 1910 when Mussolini was still a struggling journalist and editor of a weekly newsletter called *La Lotta di Class* (*The Class Struggle*). It belonged to a phase in his career when he was an angry young socialist, much given to peppery attacks on the established Church. In his newsletter Mussolini had written of priests as 'black microbes' in the pay of the capitalist system, and about a supposed love affair between Jesus Christ and Mary Magdalene. *Claudia Particella*, a tale set in the seventeenth century, was serialized in the daily newspaper the *Popolo*, published in the Austrian province of Trentino. It was not published in Italy until after Mussolini's execution. According to Denis Mack Smith, it was 'a violently anti-clerical book, and its villain a lecherous cardinal ... The book earned him some notoriety, and though he himself called it trash, he obviously understood popular taste and knew how to cater for it. Eventually the book was translated into several languages.'[19]

Recently the film historian G.P. Brunetta unearthed a copy of the script of *Claudia Particella* written early in 1923, and it is clear from the evidence that the story of its adaptation into a screenplay could not have happened as Sergio Leone later remembered, or as his family folklore passed it on.[20] The title-page of the complete script (written on UCI notepaper) which Brunetta reproduces in his book *Storia del cinema italiano 1895–1945*, reads in typescript:

Claudia Particella
Azione Cinematografica
dal romanzo di
BENITO MUSSOLINI.

Next to the words 'dal romanzo di', someone has written the word 'anonimo', and below the words 'BENITO MUSSOLINI', Mussolini himself has written, in pen, the words 'A cura di Leone Roberto Roberti'. So Roberti *did* write the script, and Il Duce continued to take a professional interest in the project after the adaptation had been completed.

This new evidence presents various possibilities. Since the script appears to have been written shortly after the March on Rome, but before Mussolini consolidated his regime, it may be that what had seemed a good idea early in 1923 had since become a political liability. If so, then it was Mussolini who decided not to proceed with the film, maybe because its fierce anti-clericalism was incompatible with his newfound respectability as leader and statesman. He had begun to think twice about his outspoken views on the priesthood even before the March, and his very first speech as Prime Minister in November 1922 ended with the words 'May God help me bring my arduous task to a victorious end.' From 1923 onwards, he began to court the Vatican (for instance, agreeing to restore the crucifix to schools and canteens); a process that began to pave the way for the 1929 Lateran Pact with the Holy See. So, having commissioned the piece, perhaps he then withdrew his own approval.

Or it may be that Roberti agreed to write the script, completed it, and subsequently had a change of heart. Or – the most intriguing possibility – perhaps Roberti remained committed to the project; too committed, at a time when Mussolini was in disavowal. Perhaps it was Roberti's continuing support for *Claudia Particella* that made him Giuseppe Bottai's 'marked man'. Roberti's refusal to become a card-carrying Fascist, second time round, was very unlikely to have caused him that much trouble. It has been estimated that until 1932 there were never more than about one million actual party members (or about 2½ per cent of the Italian population). Even within the film industry, membership was by no means compulsory at this time.

We know that from the mid-1920s, Roberto Roberti gravitated towards left-wing circles (including some of the writers he first got to know in Naples at the turn of the century), and that he liked to spend time, especially on Sundays, in the Aragno café in Rome – where intellectuals of the left would meet, in suitably stylish fashion, in a 'Red Room' decorated with scarlet drapes. Sergio Leone remembered being taken there as a child and being told by his father that they were likely to be followed on the way by plainclothes policemen. By the late 1930s, Roberti – in reaction against the shallow rhetoric of Fascism during and after the Ethiopian campaign – was beginning to turn towards Communism, which he would later give his full support. And we know that he was unable to find work – despite his senior administrative position as head of the Italian Directors' Guild – from winter 1929 until summer 1939, the first ten years of his son's life. Beyond these facts, we can only surmise why, unlike so many of his contemporaries, he never managed to adjust to the era of the so-called *telefoni bianchi*. Sergio Leone tended sometimes to offer over-dramatized reasons, and to talk of his father's 'house arrest'. Screenwriter Luciano Vincenzoni asked, 'Did his family suffer? Not really . . . *My* father was killed by the Fascists.' In any event, his father's unemployment meant that Leone grew up in Trastevere with both parents at home for most of the time. 'I knew that he had once directed films,' Leone recalled, 'but this was an abstract idea to me.' At least Roberti had made a great deal of money from the Bertini films, which kept the family going. He had also made a collection of fine antique furniture (a passion inherited by his son), which was sold off, bit by bit, to supplement his bank balance.

But in 1939, out of the blue, Roberti was approached by Giuseppe Barattolo to direct a modest comedy film called *Il socio invisibile* (*The Invisible Partner*, released December 1939, co-written by 'Roberto L. Roberti'). Barattolo was back in business, following the absorption of his company in 1938 by Scalera Films of Rome and his appointment as director of production there. He let it be publicly known that his deal with Roberti was based on an agreement signed before the Fascist era. Part of the arrangement was that Roberti would work with Barattolo's repertory company. *Il socio invisibile* tells of what happens when a poor man from South America invents a well-off business partner called 'Walter Davis', to obtain the financial credit that has up to now been denied him. Eventually, the invisible partner becomes an obsession with him, so he decides to reveal the truth. The trouble is, no one will believe him, so he burns down his office, claims that 'Davis' is dead, and – when he is told what a dreadful man his late partner really was – resolves to start a new life. Giuseppe Isani in *Cinema* (25 December 1939), while unimpressed by the piece as a whole, nevertheless observed, 'It is good to see that Leone Roberti, a veteran director of the silent era, has resurfaced after a gap in his work of nine [in fact ten] years.'[21] One of the lead actors in the film was Carlo Romano, who over twenty-five years later would be chosen by Sergio Leone to dub the voices of Eli Wallach and Jason Robards into Italian.

Two years later, with Italy at war, Roberti returned to Naples with twelve-year-old Sergio in tow, to do location filming for *La bocca sulla strada* (*Mouth on the Road*, released October 1941). This was a comedy written by the larger-than-life journalist, playwright and film critic Guglielmo Giannini, who in 1946 was to found a political party called the Fronte dell'Uomo Qualunque (Common Man's Front), backed by disillusioned ex-Fascists, which polled a million votes in the South by attacking *everything* that annoyed 'the average Italian'. This short-lived, and for a time surprisingly successful, party added a new term to the Italian political lexicon: 'qualunquista', meaning 'a total cynic'. Sergio's memories of riding through famine-stricken Naples in a horse and carriage date from this shoot. 'At last,' he recalled, 'I understood what my father *did*.' He also discovered, to his amazement, that his father (who had lived in Turin and Rome for most of his adult life, and always spoken standard Italian) conversed fluently in the Neapolitan dialect with all the locals.

*La bocca sulla strada* concerns the illegitimate young daughter of a

Neapolitan aristocrat, the Marquis de Fermo. After her father's death in a duel, the girl is brought up by the porter employed in the ancestral home ('in accordance with the nobleman's wishes'). A new-money industrialist from Milan and his family move into the chateau twenty years later, and eventually (after various comic misunderstandings) his son and heir marries the girl. Exteriors were filmed in Naples, interiors at Cinecittà in Rome. This was to be Sergio's first encounter with the artificial world of a sound stage: 'I was about twelve or thirteen years old when I first entered Cinecittà. My father took me there, to see him at work. Despite the "purification" of Fascism, he had managed – in a very strange way – to find a producer for *Mouth on the Road*. Then he found out that the producer was in fact a spy, working for Ovra [the secret police]. In my childish way, I was madly in love with the prot-agonist of the film, the beautiful Carla Del Poggio. And I was con-stantly running away from my father. I wandered on to the set of *La corona di ferro* (*Iron Crown*) and inspected the leather riding boots of the director Blasetti, whose uniform resembled that of a director/grand duke. I wandered, too, on to another set where Mario Camerini was trying to assemble the actors in *I promessi sposi*. I can still conjure these flashes of memory. It was that entrance, as the son of a director who "wasn't working any more", which first opened the door into the fairy-tale world of cinema. I would return as a man to the set of that first film, which I had experienced at one remove, as if in a reflection.'[22] Carla Del Poggio, for her part, recalled in 1979 that 'Sergio Leone followed his father around while that film was being made'.[23]

As for the critical response to Roberti's comedy, Filippo Sacchi, in *Corriere della Sera* (Milan, 18 October 1941) reckoned that it 'abounds in the things our cinema does *best*: Neapolitan dialect comedy com-bined with a good old weepy'. 'Director Roberti', he claimed, 'holds the film together by sustaining a sad, rather passive atmosphere.'[24] More recently, critic Oreste de Fornari has followed Sergio's lead in asserting that the film was thought by many to be 'very impolite to the Fascists and the police spies'. Yet the reviews of the time interpreted the piece as having more to do with Giannini's cynical 'me ne frego' ('don't give a damn') views on life in the South; the deferential world of the aristocrat and the brash world of the nouveau riche are presented as equally unsatisfactory alternatives.

Roberti's final film – another Neapolitan comedy, partly shot on location – was started during the last months of the war, shortly before

Rossellini commenced *Rome, Open City*. The film was called *Il folle di Marchechiaro/The Madman of Marchechiaro*, and featured Aldo Silvani in the title role, playing opposite Polidor, a veteran comic actor and mime from the silent cinema. Together they wandered around the bombed ruins of Naples, looking for the 'madman's' long-lost love in streets such as the Via Petrarca, by now 'buried in cement'. The sixteen-year-old Sergio Leone was hired as an unpaid assistant. He had the chance to observe his first complete shoot from close up; and also to appear on screen in one sequence as a very young American G.I. *The Madman* crept into distribution in 1951, by which time misty-eyed films harking back to the silent era were firmly out of fashion with critics and public alike. It ran for two days at the Galleria Umberto Cinema, a flea-pit in Naples, and then disappeared from circulation.

At the age of seventy, Vincenzo Leone had made his final film. After this sad ending to a long and fairly distinguished career, he retired from Rome to his native town of Torella dei Lombardi in 1949, where he died a decade later. During his declining years, he struck up a friendship with Tomaso Smith, the leading light in *Paese Sera*, and spent a lot of his time attending debates and discussing politics with writers and thinkers associated with the Italian Communist Party (PCI) of the *campagna*. The new film establishment seemed to have forgotten all about him, and, as Sergio Leone remembered, 'the neo-realists completely ignored him'. Sergio himself stayed in Rome.

Sergio's memories of his relationship with Vincenzo at the start of his own career, when he stood most in need of paternal advice and support, were tinged with regret that he never really got to know his father as a person or as a professional. As Carla Leone recalls: 'Sergio was very proud of his father and of what he had achieved. But there was a problem: he really wanted there to be a meeting of minds, in the full sense of the phrase. But his father had stopped work, and was an old man by then. He was also disenchanted with life. So the image of his father – the achievement and the man – was something that really made him suffer. He loved him a lot. Only once did he admit to me that it was sad, where his family life was concerned, that his father had become so rigid and dogmatic in his political ideas, his ideas of life. So inflexible. He only said it once, but I knew.'[25] Sergio Leone's assistant on *Fistful* and *For a Few*, Tonino Valerii, adds: 'Sergio's relationship with his parents was very unresolved. He adored his father, absolutely adored him – looked upon him as if he was a saint and desperately wanted to impress him.'²⁶

Where Bice was concerned, the distance was perhaps even more pronounced. She had retired from the film business to become a homemaker. In 1943, she had begged the fourteen-year-old Sergio not to join the partisans against the occupying Nazis. Family and home in Trastevere, and her only son, born thirteen years into her marriage when she was forty-three, were clearly the most important things in her life. And yet, as Carla Leone notes, Sergio seldom talked of her, because 'something didn't "click", didn't work well between Sergio and his mother. She was an actress, a professional actress who was much older than her son Sergio, so probably she did not feel comfortable after her career on stage and screen to have a child so late in her marriage.'²⁷ Whether it was the age difference, or a certain feeling of resentment, or the fact that she had wanted to have more than one child (Sergio's birth had been treated as 'a miracle', and his memories of her were usually associated with Bice being overprotective), they were never close. Vincenzo Leone died, near where his family had owned a small estate, in 1958. Bice Roberti then went to live for a time with Sergio in an apartment in the Via Paolo Emilio near the Vatican. Having suffered a stroke in the late 1950s, she was deprived of the power of speech for the last ten years of her life, and had even more difficulty communicating with her son. She died in 1969 at the age of eighty-three.

Tonino Valerii met Bice Roberti in 1964 just as *Fistful* was becoming a popular hit in Italy, and he recalls witnessing 'a very revealing scene . . . I was at Sergio's home, which was in a semi-popular area of Rome – a nice residence, small. One morning, I caught sight of some kind of a ghost wandering around the house. A tiny woman; really very petite. Her face was identical to Sergio's. I gathered that she must be very ill. This woman was staring, and I tried to interpret her look. What made the deepest impression on me, though, was that when Sergio arrived a moment later, he caught sight of his mother and pushed her – "pushed" is the right word, because he did it with very little tact – to make her sit down somewhere else. Out of sight. Sergio's personality was, I think, affected profoundly by this lack of a relationship with his mother. Profoundly and negatively . . . Maybe he felt guilty that his mother retired from acting because of him. Maybe!'²⁸ Sergio Donati, who by this time had known Leone for many years, and who was to become one of his key scriptwriters, recalls: 'With Sergio's mother, the ending was very, very difficult.'[29]

By the time Sergio was old enough to start making career choices, Roberto Roberti had come to believe, like his father before him, that film-making was not a worthwhile career. Instead, he encouraged his son to study law at the Lycée, as vocational training. Sergio dutifully obliged, until he was twenty. As he recalled, his father 'had become frightened of the world of cinema. It had become too different from the world he knew in the 1920s. A totally different ambience. Even if Fascism hadn't happened, he would have had increasing difficulties working as he wished, in the way he knew how. It's understandable. He was a man from the beginning of the century, who was used to making verbal agreements based on trust, and sticking to them. In his day, people in the industry were loyal. A handshake was as good as any signature. After the Second World War, things had become very different.'[30]

Film-makers of the old guard and ambitious young radicals were jockeying for position in an unsettled and competitive postwar world, where the USA and its financial aid were beginning to play an increasingly important part. Roberti's circle of friends and acquaintances mostly belonged to the old guard. 'When the Duce was killed', Sergio was to remember, 'I went out with my father to Rosati's. We were with the directors Augusto Genina and Mario Camerini. We were chatting about the death of Mussolini. And who should walk in but Alessandro Blasetti! He had argued forcefully in favour of Fascism, and we were curious to know what he would say. He wasted no time in giving us his opinion: "It's dreadful! I was so wrong. What terrible mistakes we've made over these last years! Fascism dragged Italy down into darkness and tragedy. The priority now is to get our country back on to its feet again. Our sole hope is that a man will come along who knows how to take things in hand. A strong man, with a great brain and a lot of guts." Then my father interrupted him to ask, "Someone like Mussolini?" Without thinking, he replied, "Yes, yes." Then he went pale. Tried to correct what he'd just said. Made light of it. But what had just happened was happening all over Italy. No one actually wanted another Mussolini, but, deep down, many people wanted the same old confidence trick all over again. They'd learned nothing. And it took two or three years to recover from this tragedy.'[31]

At precisely the same time, the *Commissione per l'epurazione delle categorie registi, aiuto registi e sceneggiatori del cinema* (the hastily convened commission for the purging of directors, assistants and screenwriters, reporting to the High Commission for Purges) was in the process of discussing what to do about those members of the industry who had been too deeply embroiled in Fascism. This commission aimed to be 'tolerant' rather than vindictive, and to sever the industry's links with the past regime as painlessly as possible, so that the 'rebirth' of Italian cinema, preferably with government funding, could happen sooner rather than later. The opening words of its report were 'severity from above, indulgence and forgiveness from below'. It included among its members Mario Camerini, Luchino Visconti and Mario Soldati. As a result of the commission's investigations, three directors were 'suspended from all cinematic production' for a period of six months: Carmine Gallone, Augusto Genina and Goffredo Allessandrini. Roberto Rossellini was mentioned in the commission's unpublished reports, because of the three war films he had directed in 1941–2: *La nave bianca*, *Un pilota ritorna* and *L'uomo della croce*, which used (and this was the troubling bit) some of the cinematic techniques he was to develop in the left-wing *Roma città aperta*.

So, when Roberto Roberti, a communist sympathizer, went out to dinner with Genina and Camerini, he was dining with a film director who was in the process of being temporarily 'purged' by an industry commission, and a film director who was among those doing the purging. No wonder Sergio Leone remembered this as a baffling time.

Sergio had got to know well several senior figures in the Italian film industry when he was growing up in Rome. Mario Camerini was his godfather. Mario Bonnard, prolific director of historical films and romantic comedies, was his father's closest friend. Carmine Gallone (who made *Scipione l'Africano*) was also a family friend. So Sergio Leone was thoroughly networked into the industry when he decided to change direction, as his father had done, from a career as a barrister to a career in show business. It was Gallone, on his return to film-making, who gave Sergio his first opportunity as a paid assistant, and Bonnard who gave him his first chance to direct. However unfashionable these purveyors of 'le cinéma de papa' became, they nevertheless continued to hold influential positions within big-budget popular cinema. Above all, Sergio was the son of a director who had helped to create the cinema's first star, and who had worked for forty years in most of those popular genres which were to remain the backbone of Italian cinema.

Moreover, Roberti's visual style (in those films that Sergio managed to see) evidently made a deep impression. Carla Leone recalls him enthusing about a scene in one of the Bertini films: 'It was a dinner-party sequence, where the light wasn't directed on to the faces of the diners, but on to the white plates which were on the table. The people were in half-shadow. Sergio was bowled over by this.'[32]

There were to be other legacies. In time, Sergio too (like Roberti with Bertini) would experience some initially prickly relationships with the stars he was directing. He was sensitive about not seeming to be the boss on his own set. He worked within genre cinema, again like his father, but was always keen to stress that he had somehow managed to make 'personal films' under the circumstances. He was highly suspicious of political dogmatism, from the left or the right, and often spoke about how his father's dreams had been shattered by the compromises of postwar Italian politics. Why had Roberti bothered to stick his neck out in the 1930s? To pave the way for the Cold War and consumer boom of the 1950s, when the heroes of the resistance were steadily squeezed out of serious politics? And where did Roberti's socialism get him? It had simply turned him into 'a director who wasn't working any more'. Leone also inherited from his father a love of antique objects, and an almost obsessive fascination with the look and texture of things, which he carried over into his films. He also acquired a sentimental attachment to Cinecittà, as symbolized by that first visit to the 'fairy-tale world'. It is tempting to relate his 'very unresolved' relationship with his mother to his adult absorption in an exclusively masculine world of adventure and physical action. But that may be to over-personalize the Italian cultural context within which Sergio Leone was working. His family is, understandably, much more comfortable talking about the paternal legacy. Andrea Leone recalls that 'my father spoke of my grandfather with the greatest admiration. But when my father was born my grandfather was forty-five or forty-six years old, so my father suffered from this great age difference. He was born into the cinema, and his greatest sorrow was that he was acclaimed at a time his father could not share in it. His father had died too soon.'[33]

'My father died a broken man,' Leone would remember. 'In a magnificent part of the world, his native land, which is that same Irpinia which was rhapsodized by Virgil in the *Pastorals*. He fell ill there, and died very soon after, and when he looked at me – almost for the last time – I read in his eyes the deepest regret that I'd decided to abandon my legal studies, and to turn towards the cinema. In my mind, though, my chosen career seemed like a debt I was paying to both my parents.'[34] Sergio wanted very much to impress them both. It was in acknowledgement of this 'debt' that he would choose as his pseudonym for his first international success as a director – *Fistful of Dollars* (1964) – the name 'Bob Robertson'.

# 3

# Hollywood on the Tiber

*Operation Cinderella* is about the occupation of a small town in Italy. It has always been occupied – by the Romans and the Goths, the Saracens, the Barbary pirates, and then by the Germans and the English. Peace finally, and then suddenly a long line of trucks comes up the road. Who is it *now*? Hollywood! It is the story of the occupation of this town by a movie company. The population divides between the collaborators – those who play along with the movie company – and the underground which tries to get rid of them. Great part for Anna Magnani as the Passionaria of the underground . . . Nobody has any rights. You can't cross the street because they're shooting pictures; you can't get home, you can't go anywhere. So the underground gets organized, and the townspeople, who've been working as extras, go on strike and refuse to work, in this great knights-of-old sort of battle that has to be fought in the film. Subs are bought in from the next village. The two towns have hated each other for seven hundred years – and now there's a real battle between the home team in civvies and the strikebreakers in armour. They make a catapult out of a movie crane . . . meanwhile, the Hollywood crew has broken the statue of the town's patron saint. So every time they're ready for a shot, just on the cry of 'action', one tiny little cloud appears right in front of the sun. The Cinderella is a local girl they've picked up. At the end she's leaving with them on the bus – going to Hollywood to be a big star.

Orson Welles, reminiscing about an unrealized film project of the early 1950s

There is a scene in Vittorio De Sica's *Bicycle Thieves* (1948), where a small group of seminarists of the Propaganda Fide, attired in clerical garb, run across the deserted market at the Porta Portese in Rome and shelter from the torrential rain under an overhanging cornice. These seminarists stand near Antonio Ricci and his son Bruno for a few moments, and they chat in German. The Italians listen, but cannot understand a word; one of the students smiles at Bruno, but he doesn't respond. Then, as the rain begins to clear, they walk away. In the middle of the group is a young, bespectacled man. He was played by the nineteen-year-old Sergio Leone.

Although De Sica and his scriptwriter Zavattini had meticulously planned and scripted most of the 'accidental' sequences shot on the streets of Rome (which became seminal scenes in the history of neo-realism), this particular scene was, according to Leone, an unusual spur-of-the-moment invention by the director. It was raining at the time, and De Sica wanted to take advantage of the visual effect of 'rain and summer light – using it to create an aura around those young seminarists, all dressed in red'.[1] A friend had introduced Leone to De Sica, who, 'when he learned that I was the son of Roberto Roberti', had taken him on as an unpaid fifth assistant. If Sergio was prepared to act as well, he could even be given a modest fee. He was put in charge of finding extras for the seminarists' scene: 'I remembered some friends of mine who were dutifully continuing with their legal studies at the Faculty. Someone went to hire them, and came back (after a breathless tram-ride) with about a dozen law students – and De Sica arranged them in the square as a procession of theology students. I was proud to be placed at the head of the file.'[2] But his wardrobe proved problematic: 'Under this clerical costume, I was wearing a brand-new yellow pull-over . . . with all the rain, the dye from my red robe stained the wool of my pullover . . . They described me as "the Roman oriflamme", because the city's colours are yellow and red. As for me, I didn't find it at all funny. My pullover was ruined and De Sica didn't want to reimburse me for it. It took lengthy discussions to sort everything out. In the end, they paid me.'[3]

It was a fascinating experience, Leone later recalled, to be 'an actor taken from the street, to participate in Bicycle Thieves': sheltering under that cornice, 'while the light was being reflected in the puddles, chattering away in an incomprehensible language, and making the nightmare of the poor builder in his dripping hat even worse than it was already'. More fascinating still was the experience of eavesdropping on a script conference between De Sica, Cesare Zavattini and Sergio Amidei: 'Maybe I owe to those screenwriters my own pedantry where script revisions are concerned, a habit which has made me a little unpopular with the writers who have worked with me. I remember Zavattini was reflecting, in a Northern Italian accent, on a certain scene. Amidei was also there – he was still involved in the film, at the time – and De Sica was standing with his back turned to everyone else in the room, looking out of the window with his arms crossed, his head tilted to one side. His mind seemed to be on other things. "The poor builder", says Zavattini, "exits from the house with a mortadella sandwich in his hand, and", he adds significantly, "the sandwich is wrapped up in a newspaper, on which you can clearly make out the word *Unità*." A long silence. Then Amidei starts swearing and protesting that *Unità* [a communist newspaper] has nothing whatever to do with it: you should just be able to make out the letters *tà*, he says. Another silence. De Sica, still standing with his arms folded and his head on one side, continues to look at the city through the open window ... Then, without turning round, he says in a very calm way – as if he has been visited by an angel, as if he is whispering to the clouds in the sky – that in his opinion, the builder ought to exit from the house eating a nice apple. A *red* apple, he explains to the rooftops of Rome. No, not a red apple, but a multi-coloured one. Half red and half *sfumate*. The builder will bite this apple and will start on his journey towards disaster. Honestly, I was listening to all this with the sensation of being able to *eat* that apple. De Sica could conjure it up, before our very eyes, like an *ex voto* miracle. The cinema, for him, was all about attention to details such as this.'[4]

Sergio Leone worked as an assistant to various directors during holidays while he was still at the Lycée. He also began to play truant from his courses in jurisprudence in order to devote 'more time to the cinema', which also meant seeing as many of the backlog of Hollywood movies as he could. He later claimed 'It was a period of great indigestion ... a time when dreams at last seemed to come true for Roman adolescents. The great return of the American cinema [after the post-1941 boycott]. The cinemas were full to capacity every day. Not to mention the bookshops ... full of comics which contained four years of adventures of our favourite heroes ... Also, the discovery of the great authors of the *noir* school.'[5] The back numbers soon established a commanding position in the Italian market. By 1948, a mere four years after the fall of Mussolini, only 11 per cent of all films screened in Italy were Italian products, while 73 per cent were American or British. The critics might rave about 'neo-realism', but in strictly economic terms the impact was marginal. *Rome – Open City* and *Bicycle Thieves* had been popular hits, but commercial distributors seem to have treated them as the exception rather than the rule. While De Sica was shooting on the streets of Rome, the city was already becoming Hollywood's bridgehead to Europe. The tastes of Italian audiences in this period are reflected in Visconti's *Bellissima* (1951), as Anna Magnani watches Howard Hawks's *Red River* in a backstreet cinema in Rome, and waxes eloquent about the cattle being herded by John Wayne through a river: 'Look! The cows are all getting wet! Isn't it *marvellous*!'

There were, however, some attempts to establish a solid commercial base for Italian film-making during the early period of Marshall Aid, and Sergio Leone gained his first professional experience as an assistant on two of them. His career began with a formal introduction to sixty-two-year-old Carmine Gallone, who was no longer simply a family friend but a potential employer. Back in business, Gallone was preparing a series of filmed Italian operas for Titanus, and he gave Sergio the opportunity to help out with 'buying the cigarettes, fetching the coffee', and assorted logistics, in recognition of which his name appeared on the credits as 'assistante alla Regia'. These films included *Rigoletto* (1947, with Tito Gobbi), *La leggenda di Faust* and *Il trovatore* (1949), *La forza del destino* (1950, with Gobbi and Nelly Corradi, who sang but did not appear), *Taxi di notte* (1950, again with Gobbi) as well as some shorts.

According to Gallone, in an article he wrote for a promotional brochure in 1951, opera films, with Italian singers playing or voicing the leads, could contribute significantly to the 'diffusion of Italian film abroad'; so it was 'almost a duty to renew our efforts in the field of musical films as soon as the war ended'. Fifteen years earlier Gallone had been writing of the glories of Roman history; now he was writing of the glories of the Italian film industry.[6] The problem was how to make these films satisfying both musically and as pieces of cinema. Clearly, Gallone contended, filming operas exactly as they were mounted on stage was not the answer (although in his 1947 *Rigoletto* he had done just that). But how much adaptation was permissible? Several important critics of the day pondered the question. For Bela Balasz, an acceptable 'film opera' had to be thought out as a completely new creation, with some small measure of stylization (but not much). For Siegfried Kracauer, virtually any departure from the conventions of photo-realism was liable to create bad film art and to strain the credibility of the audience. Gallone might have claimed to be extending, even subverting, the conventions of opera, but to discerning viewers, he succeeded only in photographing opera badly. But as historian Gian Piero Brunetta writes of the 'cineoperas' of this period, they found a popular audience, 'one which had the sensation of acquiring, at low cost, a knowledge of all the main Italian operas'.[7] And stars such as Anna Magnani, Gina Lollobrigida, Amedeo Nazzari and Sophia Loren (whose *Aida*, made in 1952 by Clemente Fracassi, particularly infuriated the music critics) attracted attention to themselves through this unusual route, as did screenwriters Mario Monicelli, and Age and Scarpelli.

The cycle was launched in 1946 by Carmine Gallone's comeback movie *E avanti a lui tremava tutta Roma/And Before Him all Rome Trembled*, in which resistance fighter Anna Magnani struggles to play Tosca (dubbed by Onelia Fineschi), at the end of the Nazi occupation. Police chief Scarpia (Tito Gobbi) was presented as a Fascist functionary, and his henchmen wore Il Duce's uniforms. Gallone evidently saw this film as a way of rehabilitating his reputation following his expulsion from the industry; at the same time he was courting the scale of audience he had become accustomed to in the 1930s. But the 'cine-opera' cycle of 1946–56 (twelve major films in ten years), the first of the home-grown commercial cycles of the postwar era, had at least attempted to research the differences between stage and screen. Gallone's *La forza del destino*, with Sergio Leone eagerly assisting the director, is a characteristic example. A voice-over tells the more complicated parts of the story; about half the screen time is devoted to location sequences; and the libretto and music are edited down to 100 minutes. Where possible, Gallone uses tracking and crane shots to add dynamism to the location work. The characters, regardless of whether they are played by singers, are dubbed to studio recordings, giving the soundtrack a curiously disembodied quality. But such films made the operatic baritone Tito Gobbi into one of the most popular movie stars of the immediate postwar era.[8] Among young Sergio Leone's most prized possessions was a collection of personally signed photographs of Gobbi and Gigli.

Sergio Leone's role in all this was to be at the director's side whenever he snapped his fingers: 'Carmine Gallone was martial, severe, a man with a short fuse . . . I was around all the time, trying to make myself as useful as I could. I ran errands and commissions, prepared the coffee – basically, whatever *signor* director asked me to do; but I was really spending my time looking at each gesture of the cameraman and the operator, as if they were part of my devotions. Gallone manoeuvred a hundred people on the set – like troop movements. He managed to regulate their movements like the mechanism of a clock.'[9] Leone's Westerns were later to be dubbed by the critics as 'operas of violence' (and by Clint Eastwood as characteristically Italian 'operacizations' of the Western), in reference to their careful orchestration of music, movement and visual image. But Leone never accepted the label. Wasn't it significant, he was asked in the early 1970s, that his Westerns emerged from the land which invented grand opera? 'No,' he responded, 'people talk about Italy as if it were a country of people who are music-mad; that's entirely false! The percentage of our population that listens to serious music is lower than that of Greece: about three per cent . . . We are one of the most under-developed countries in that area.' Surely, the interviewer persisted, Leone himself *must* be an opera lover, with all those post-Puccini scores he commissioned from Ennio Morricone? 'Me? I detested opera on film when I worked as Gallone's assistant and I still do today. I've been offered operas to direct, but I simply couldn't do it. I'd be laughing too much. When I see an actor singing on a horse, and he falls out of the saddle to become his noble self again, while continuing all the while to belt out his *bel canto* at full volume – I just fall about laughing. It's too silly for words.' The only credible way of presenting opera on film, he added, was to use professional movie actors against authentic backgrounds, and 'do play-back with the best singers, like in Preminger's *Carmen Jones* . . . You absolutely need real actors: you can't make a *film* with someone like Placido Domingo in it.'[10] He was offered *Carmen* on film and *The Girl of the Golden West* on stage, but turned them both down.

Another postwar scheme for promoting distinctively Italian film abroad was to hark back to the prewar style of Enrico Guazzoni, and remake the popular late Victorian novels that were the foundation of the epic genre: Edward Bulwer Lytton's *The Last Days of Pompeii* (1834), Henryk Sienkiewicz's *Quo Vadis?* (1895), Raffaello Giovagnoli's *Spartaco* (1874), Lew Wallace's *Ben-Hur* (1880) and Cardinal Nicholas Wiseman's *Fabiola, or the Church of the Catacombs* (1854). This revival hit its expansive and expensive stride in 1947, with the 165-minute *Fabiola* (or *The Fighting Gladiator*), directed by Alessandro Blasetti (he of the unfortunate dinner-party conversation with the Leones) at the recently reopened Cinecittà studios. Sergio Leone was an uncredited assistant director.

Adapted by fourteen screenwriters (eight of them credited) from a bulky novel concerning the conversion of a Roman noblewoman (Michele Morgan) to the new faith of Christianity in the era before the rise of Constantine, *Fabiola* centred on the love affair between a gladiator and the heroine, and became famous for its spectacular and gory sequences in the arena. According to the characteristically bulked-up publicity, these involved 7,000 extras and 200 French and Italian athletes, not to mention Massimo Girotti (the tarnished hero of Visconti's neo-realist *Ossessione*) in the first of many epic characterizations, as the martyr Saint Sebastian, shot by the troops of Marilius Valerian (Paolo Stoppa). A scene involving nude females being fed to the lions had to be excised from American prints of the film: another, involving topless dancers at a Roman orgy, survived. The logistics facing Leone's department, with three other assistants, must have been horrendous. Cinecittà had been bombed by the Allies in 1944, occupied by the Nazis shortly afterwards, and then transformed by the Allies into a refugee camp. By 1948, the damaged sound stages and back-lots were back in business.

Writing about *Fabiola* for the same promotional brochure that featured Gallone's article on film opera, Blasetti was unrepentant about working in such a critically unfashionable (and ideologically tainted) genre. The film sided with the oppressed early Christians, he said, *against* the persecuting Romans with their eagles and *fasci*. Blasetti attributed the hostility of younger critics to 'a rather superficial prejudice on grounds of taste' towards a class of film that could yield 'spectacular success in world markets' . . . The purpose we aimed at in making *Fabiola* was to open up again for Italy the successful path of the historical film, making the most of neo-realistic teachings and endeavouring to abandon the policy of the spectacle as an end in itself, of sets aiming at the colossal, of people looking like classical statues . . . We believe that neo-realism is a good road, but we also believe it can exhaust itself into a formula monopolizing any imaginative effort.'[11] Blasetti was unquestionably right in one respect. The critical dismissal and commercial success of *Fabiola* in America matched that of Cecil B. de Mille's *Samson and Delilah*, and laid the foundations of the Italian peplum boom of the 1950s and early 1960s. The road these films took was not towards neo-realism, however. They favoured demonstrations of physical prowess, orgies, dark temptresses and fair ladies (both with hourglass figures), plus ever-increasing doses of irony and irreverence. The road from *Fabiola* to Pietro Francisci's *Hercules* (1958) would take a decade – as memories of the Fascist epic, and indeed of abstruse debates about neo-realism, faded into the cinematic past.

Sergio Leone, for his part, could take or leave neo-realism: 'I was aware of the importance of neo-realist films . . . They were necessary films. They put over just causes, which was healthy after twenty years of Fascism. But it wasn't the kind of cinema I preferred.'[12] He continued to spend time with some of his friends from the Viale Glorioso, 'even though I was no longer a *vitellone* – a lout– that stopped when I was about fourteen years old'. But his main social network had become the crews and actors of the films on which he worked, and his further education had become a visual and technical one. 'I became an adult very quickly,' he recalled. Others might have signed their names to the various political petitions from 'young cinema' that were doing the rounds, but Leone, despite his father's political interests, was more interested in getting on with any work he could find.

The definitive break with his studies, and the prospect of a career in the law, came in 1949, when his parents moved out of Rome to Torella dei Lombardi. Sergio stayed behind, to work full time in the film business. Again, it was family connections which gave him the opportunity: one of his first projects as a paid assistant was with his fifty-five-year-old godfather Mario Camerini, working on *Il brigante Musolino* (1950, *Musolino the Brigand* or *Mara, fille sauvage*). The stars were Amedeo Nazzari and Silvana Mangano; Leone immediately fell 'madly in love' with Mangano and 'worshipped her from afar'. As he remembered, 'I was a green young boy, rather like the initiate Nick Adams in *The Killers* by Hemingway who watches in amazement as the hired assassins track down the Swede. And I ventured with enthusiasm, unmatched by experience. So I dutifully lit cigarettes for the adults, and smoked a lot myself.'[13] But Leone held his employer in high regard: 'Camerini had been the director of "white telephones", and was one of the true maestri of our cinema – although dismissed by film critics of the later 1950s and 1960s, who would only rate a director of "the regime years" if he happened to make *Das Kapital* by Marx; if he'd made *The Great Dictator*, that would not have been considered holy enough. If Camerini had gone to Hollywood instead of Cinecittà, he could well have become a second Capra, or another Lubitsch. His "white telephones" actually contained a lot of truth, compassion and irony – if only those critics had looked at them.'[14]

Camerini then introduced Leone to Luigi Comencini, for whom he worked on *La tratta delle bianche* (1952, *The White Slave Trade*), a contemporary story about a girl (Eleonora Rossi Drago), who is rescued from 'this sordid trade' by her boyfriend, Ettore Manni, who in turn proceeds to turn the traders over to the police. Comencini provided Leone with an entrée into the productions of Dino De Laurentiis, the backer of *La tratta delle bianche*; and Leone worked for Dino on *Jolanda la figlia del Corsaro Nero* (1952, *Iolanda, Daughter of the Black Pirate*), directed by Mario Soldati, loosely based on an Emilio Salgari novel, with May Britt as an icy but glamorous buccaneer; and *I tre corsari* (1952, *The Three Pirates*), directed by Soldati and based on another Salgari tale, the story of three buccaneer brothers who avenge the death of their aristocratic father.

Aldo Fabrizi, the actor who had played the tragic priest in Rossellini's *Rome – Open City*, had since graduated to direction, and Sergio Leone next assisted him, on a trio of films which helped to launch the *commedia all'italiana* boom of the late 1950s: *La marsina stretta* (*The Tight Raincoat*, 1954, a segment of the portmanteau Pirandello movie *Questa è la vita*/*This Is Life*); *Hanno rubato un tram* (*They've Stolen a Tram*, 1954, a film begun by Mario Bonnard but completed by Fabrizi, based on a story by Luciano Vincenzoni); and *Il maestro* (1957). Between these, Leone assisted Mario Bonnard on *Mi permette, Babbo!* (1956), in which Fabrizi played opposite Alberto Sordi. Twenty years later, Fabrizi was interviewed about being both a director and a comedic actor in the mid-1950s. He recalled: 'Well, the assistant director was Sergio Leone, but he wasn't yet even contemplating a time when he would be able to direct Westerns; come to think of it, he wasn't even thinking about becoming a director. He was really an assistant of Mario Bonnard at that time, living in Bonnard's house.'[15]

Veteran director Mario Bonnard (born 1889) had been a close friend of Roberto Roberti. He had known the family from the time when he was, in Leone's words, 'the Italian Rudolph Valentino', right up to his greatest critical success as a director, with 'the first neo-realist film, *Campo di fiori*' (1943). Bonnard's biography, like Vincenzo Leone's, almost paralleled the story of the Italian industry. In Bonnard's case, he had been a matinée idol in the 1910s; a director specializing in literary adaptations (Stendhal's *Le rouge et le noir*; Manzoni's *Promessi sposi*) in the 1920s; unlike Vincenzo, he had made the trip to Berlin in the 1930s, to make 'mountain films'; and having flirted with neo-realism, he found himself to be one of the dependable workhorses of Italian popular film-making in the 1950s. Vincenzo Leone had retired hurt: Mario Bonnard managed to keep going. So it was perhaps predictable that Leone would work regularly with Bonnard as an assistant from the early 1950s onwards: on *Il voto* (1950, *The Vow*), *Friné cortigiana d'oriente* (1953, *Phryné, the Oriental Courtesan*), *Tradita* or *La notte delle nozze* (1954, *Betrayed*, with Brigitte Bardot in a minor role), *La ladra* (1955, *The Thief who Was a Woman*) and *Mi permette, Babbo!* (1956, *Allow Me, Daddy!*). Leone was credited as 'assistant director' on all these films. Several were Italian–French co-productions. Today, the best-known is *Phryné*.

Set in ancient Thebes and Athens around 500 BC, it tells the story of a slave-girl called Afra (Elena Kleus) who becomes a wealthy courtesan, and model of Aphrodite for the sculptor Praxiteles. She spends the second half of the movie defeating a conspiracy hatched against her by the elders of Athens, and avenging the indignities she has suffered. Eventually, she proudly displays herself 'in all her nude beauty' to the Theban senators, a sequence which purports to show the first authenticated striptease in history. Sergio Leone made an uncredited contribution to the script, which contains the seeds of many of the evergreens of the late 1950s sword-and-sandal boom: sculptor and model, political conspiracy, avenging woman, and discreetly shot disrobing (with cut-aways of ogling, obese senators). As the posters helpfully put it, 'Phryné – pure of soul and generous of body'.

Leone spent a lot of time with Mario Bonnard throughout the 1950s. Between 1949, when he left home, and 1960, when he got married, he lived in a self-contained apartment in Bonnard's house on the Via Paolo Emilio, in the Prati district of Rome. 'I liked Mario Bonnard a lot,' Leone was to recall. 'There was a special atmosphere on his shoots. Something very lively . . . He was not a very cultured man; pretty naive. Had an obsession with melodrama. A solid artisan, although he was very backward-looking in stylistic terms. Almost like a conservator where his technical language was concerned . . . With him, the shoots often turned into epic performances. We began at eight in the morning and were expected, without fail, to wrap at three in the afternoon. With no breaks. This was so that Bonnard could go to bed at half past three. He'd have a sandwich and then sleep it off until six o'clock. Then he'd go out to work again until two in the morning.'[16]

'Something bizarre happened once,' Leone remembered, 'when we were shooting the exteriors for the comedy *Il voto*. We were preparing a scene during which a boat left the quayside, while a crowd shouted and cheered it off. For once, we had permission for a short lunch break. We knew that Bonnard loved to eat little shellfish that were very complicated to shell. Knowing that he couldn't resist this kind of food, we

ordered a huge plateful. He immediately realized that this was a conspiracy to extend the lunch-hour. As he was eating, he mumbled and
cursed, "You bunch of bastards, do you take me for an idiot? While I'm
feasting myself, all you have to do is lay a camera track along the quay,
and set up the shot. It'll be the last in daylight. When we've got it in the
can, I'll go home." After coping with the pile of shellfish, he arrived on
the set. I explained to the extras in the crowd how to play the scene:
those who had to cry, those who were to blow kisses, those who were
to chat amongst themselves . . . But Bonnard interrupted me, shouting
that we had to get the shot immediately. The cameraman protested. He
announced that he didn't know what the hell he was supposed to be
doing. He needed a rehearsal to be sure of the tracking shot. Bonnard
slagged him off. He ordered him to get the camera rolling, and start
tracking. Now, the entire crew began to panic. I explained that I hadn't
finished telling the extras what to do. Bonnard sent me packing. He
yelled, "There's nothing at all to explain." He took a handkerchief, and
waved it in front of the crowd. "Look at me, I'm the boat! . . . Roll
camera. Settled? Action! . . . Look at me, I'm the boat!" He walked
right to the edge of the quay. But he didn't see one of the tracks. And,
still saying, "Look at me, I'm the boat," he stumbled and fell into the
water. He couldn't swim. His face reappeared on the surface. He spat
out some sea-water and said, "Look at me, I'm a complete idiot." And
then he sank. We had to dive in to save him from drowning.'[17]

In the early 1950s, according to Leone, Bonnard was the most com-
petent and experienced director working in pepla. Directors Riccardo
Freda and Vittorio Cottafavi were around, and churning them out, but
hadn't yet found their own voices. In addition to assisting Bonnard
during the day, Leone would help him doctor some of his screenplays,
in the evenings at home: 'I had a hand in the screenplay of his *Phryné*,
though you won't see me on the credits of that one. I didn't give a damn
about credits in those days. I often tinkered with scripts when I was an
assistant. Where Bonnard was concerned, I seemed to fire his imagination. Stimulated him. I learned how to get things down on paper in the
proper order. I noted what should be kept in, and what it was better to
cut. I wouldn't call it the work of an author. I restricted myself to
suggesting ways he could get what he was after. However, I did put my
name to *Aphrodite, Goddess of Love* [or *Slave Women of the Orient* –
for Bonnard, several years later in 1958, which was really a recycled
version of *Phryné*].'[18]

In 1952, Leone was second assistant director (with Lucio Fulci) on *L'Uomo, la Bestia, la Virtù* (*Man, Beast and Virtue*, derived from Luigi Pirandello's minor farce about adultery). The director and screenwriter was Stefano Vanzina, usually known as 'Steno'. It was the story of a humble country teacher (the revered variety artist and film comedian Totò) who tries to save the marriage of a brutal sea captain, the 'Beast' of the title (Orson Welles), and his neglected wife ('Virtue', played by Viviane Romance), although the teacher has had an affair with this wife, and made her pregnant. Welles was later to describe both the film and its production as deeply incoherent ('None of the dialogue made any sense at all. Complete non sequiturs.')[19] Even at the time, he made it clear that he was not happy with the production; and when it shut down for five days, because of problems with the Agfacolor stock, Welles asked Leone, out of the blue, if he would help out on 'a film he was going to begin the next day'. At that stage in his career Welles often rented out his name and his well-known face to popular films made in Italy, to help finance his own 'independent adventures', which were always running out of money. On this occasion, he agreed to forgo his five days' salary if Dino De Laurentiis would agree to lend him the technical crew, and one of the assistants, for his own purposes. Much of Welles's *Othello* had been pieced together this way, filmed bit by bit in five different towns in Italy and five different towns in North Africa. On the set of Henry King's *Prince of Foxes* (where Welles played the scheming Borgia, opposite Tyrone Power's romantic lead in leotards), Welles's wiles had even become a running gag: 'I tried to hide,' Welles admitted, 'and wait until Henry King started to scream, "Where is he? I *know* the son of a bitch is away in Venice shooting that goddamn Shakespeare!"'

Leone's first task for Orson Welles was to 'find an actor who has the most villainous face imaginable'. He responded by introducing Welles to a young acquaintance who bore a strong resemblance to Mussolini – save for a serious skin problem. 'Perfect,' said Welles. Then, in short order, Leone had to find ten policemen, and a working locomotive. The sequence, it seemed, was about a robber, pursued by the police, who jumps on to a moving train to Naples at night. While directing it, Welles was dressed in a red and blue magician's cape, and wore a blue beard. 'The shooting of this sequence lasted three evenings,' Leone remembered. 'Take one. Take two. Take ten. Take twenty. After each take, Welles asked the villain to run closer to the train. Closer! Closer!

After the third evening, the actor came over to me, shaking with fear. "Signor Leone, do me a favour, will you? . . . Tell Mr Welles that I work in films to live, not to die!" [20] Welles never divulged what the film was about – if indeed he really was intending to use the sequence in a feature. He had various travelling projects on the go at the time, but the only one that remotely fits this description was *Operation Cinderella*, the story of 'the occupation of a small town in Italy . . . by Hollywood'. Even more mysteriously, despite his outlandish outfit, Welles never once appeared in front of the camera. When Leone asked why this was so, Welles would only say, 'You never know. Maybe I'll do a close-up of myself. When the time comes. Maybe.' A press still, taken on the streets of Rome during the shooting of *L'Uomo, la Bestia, la Virtu*, shows an irritable-looking Welles, smoking a cigar, in dark glasses and a huge overcoat; a studious Sergio Leone, peering owlishly at a page of the script through his spectacles, sits in the background. Welles looks as though he wishes he was somewhere else. Leone looks as though he is trying very hard not to appear impressed.

In this period, Leone made his first professional contacts with several behind-the-camera people with whom he would work, sometimes regularly, ten years later: editors Nino Baragli and Roberto Cinquini; screenwriters Age and Scarpelli, and Luciano Vincenzoni; and cinematographer Tonino Delli Colli. Delli Colli, who was to photograph *The Good, The Bad and The Ugly*, *Once Upon a Time in the West* and *Once Upon a Time in America*, first met Leone when they worked together on Bonnard's *The Vow*. 'He was like a son to Bonnard,' recalls Delli Colli. So he worked hard to impress the older man with his efficiency: 'preparing the scenes in advance, choosing the secondary actors and so on'. [21]

Luciano Vincenzoni, a key contributor to most of Leone's finest Westerns, also met the young assistant at this time when 'believe it or not, he was thin like a plucked bird, timid and introverted'. Vincenzoni was twenty-five in 1954 when he sold his first story to the movies: *Hanno rubato un tram*, directed by Bonnard and filmed in Bologna. But in 1984, the writer recalled, 'As Bonnard was already old and ill, I think that half of the film must have been put together by Leone. I remember him in Gigi Fazi's restaurant where all the film people gathered, sitting at a table with Bonnard, Fabrizi and the screenwriter Maccari; he was silent, very self-effacing and listening intently to everything that was said. They'd send him to do menial tasks, and he'd agree.

61

Maybe he was more than a little bored with the company of these much older men, and would have preferred to be with people his own age – maybe with a girl; but he was there, because it was his work, this was how he earned his living. As a young man, he must have put up with a lot of boredom and humiliation among the older generation, but both of these helped him build his character: and also gave him the confidence – in time – to make his own presence felt, to impose on others . . . This period in his life – when he put up with a lot – turned him into a hardened professional, apprenticed and trained like few other directors.'[22] Concerning Vincenzoni's assertion that Leone took over as director after Bonnard became ill, the reference books claim it was Aldo Fabrizi who completed *Hanno rubato un tram*. Fabrizi himself made a point of saying that Leone 'wasn't even thinking about becoming a director' at that time. But Leone may well have helped out. If so, this was his first work as a director.

Sergio Donati, who was to become the main scriptwriter of *Once Upon a Time in the West*, and who co-scripted *Giù la testa* with Vincenzoni, was a fledgling writer of detective stories when first he met Leone. In 1983 he told Oreste de Fornari: 'My earliest work in the cinema was a collaboration on the script of *Trust Me*, directed by Riccardo Freda and based on a novel by James Hadley Chase. During the shoot, a hungry-looking young assistant director, who used to drive around in an old Fiat 600 [it was a Multipla – the large, egg-shaped version], came up to me: it was Sergio Leone. He suggested that I should write a horror film, set in a snow-bound hotel. I'd met a hotel owner, who was curious about the exciting, behind-the-scenes world of the cinema, so wrote a treatment. But nothing happened. And in any case, snow is supposed to be unlucky in the cinema. My thrillers were translated into many languages, but I still couldn't live off the income they earned, so once I'd finished my studies in law I went to Milan to work in advertising as a producer, and stayed there for six years . . . Leone used to telephone me every now and again from Rome, with unlikely offers.'[23]

When I spoke to Donati in 1998, I put it to him that Leone seemed to have spent a lot of time with an older generation of film people – his father's network of contacts – rather than with his peers: 'Absolutely. This was I think the problem of his professional life. He had some kind of bitterness and frustration, because Bonnard and Fabrizi – these cynical old men – they would send him off to buy cigarettes and to find girls as well. He knew where to buy both. And he developed some bitterness and some tightness with money, which came from this experience . . . He was famous, also, because he would put a box under the camera with "For contributions towards cigarettes" – for him – written on it. As a joke? Well, he did always smoke other people's cigarettes, even when he was rich. This was very typical of Sergio . . . Sergio already seemed very sure of himself and behaved as if he was one of the Lumière Brothers – which was the same when he was nobody. When I met him as an assistant director, he was already the inventor of the movies. How do you explain that? When much later I worked with De Laurentiis and Vincenzoni in Los Angeles, one day Vincenzoni told me, "I want you to meet a young director, very interesting." And they introduced me to a young Neapolitan kind of guy, with a white Rolls-Royce and red leather seats, and he talked *exactly like the young Sergio Leone* . . . And the name of the guy was Michael Cimino – who has many things in common with Sergio.'[24]

Tonino Valerii, who was later to become Leone's assistant, reckons that it was Sergio's apprenticeship with American crews, rather than with Italians, which was the decisive factor in shaping his later career. Critics of the Italian *pepla* and Westerns of the late 1950s and 1960s were later to argue that their emphasis on fast-moving action sequences, which in Hollywood films would have been handled by second units, grew out of the experience of Italian directors apprenticed on Hollywood epics in Rome. The Italians didn't have so much experience of dialogue scenes, and this may have given them a low boredom threshold. Moreover, the action sequences were the ones that most appealed to Italian cinema audiences. Whether or not the observation is true, there is little doubt that Leone's flair for handling the logistics of large-scale set-ups, and investing smaller set-ups with a sense of scale through framing, cutting and a hyperactive soundtrack, came from this source. As Valerii has recalled: 'He had worked long and hard, as an assistant with American crews, learning some very important rules and precious information, which wasn't always available in the Italian industry. That whenever you film a sequence, you must do a "master shot" first, then the details, from all points of view and with different lenses; that you must move from one sequence to another by use of some indirect memory; that you make up for the lack of true acting ability by making sure that the characters' personalities come out in their clothes, their gestures, their outward appearance, their "tics", and by using extreme close-ups for details of their eyes and other parts of the body. A good editor will always be able to salvage something presentable from this assemblage of material.'[25] Vincenzoni disagrees: he reckons that Sergio Leone learned a lot more from the Italians.[26]

Leone's first experience as an assistant on an expatriate Hollywood production was in 1950. The film was Mervyn Leroy's version of *Quo Vadis?*, the first Cinecittà-based American production with an ancient Roman setting. It paved the way for *Helen of Troy* (1954), *Ben-Hur* (1957) and *Cleopatra* (1961), the series of gigantic spectaculars that helped to fuel the minor 'economic miracle' in Rome-based leisure industries from the mid-1950s onwards. For US companies the attractions of Cinecittà were many. Costs were lower, and they could use up some of their frozen assets (a proportion of the income from Hollywood films in Italy, which, since the introduction of Giulio Andreotti's formula in 1947, had to be recouped or spent where it was earned). Moreover, they could take advantage of the favourable exchange rate, and mobilize a workforce, inexpensive by Los Angeles standards, which had a long track-record of reconstructing the artefacts of the ancient world on back-lots just outside Rome. They could also hand on costumes and props from film to film and make use of colourful seaside and desert locations near by.

Where the Italians were concerned, according to Leone, some of the main beneficiaries were 'the technicians, the craftsmen, the electricians, the studio maintenance people, and of course the extras – at one time or another, just about all the students in Rome were working as casual labour'. The main disadvantage was that American and Italian crews tended to work in very different ways, and at different paces. As Leone remembered of the Americans: 'When they arrived, it was like an army on the move. The commander-in-chief was the producer . . . Everything was systematically compartmentalized, to an extreme degree . . . If I asked the assistant props man in charge of weapons for a sword, he couldn't give it to me without getting the permission of the chief props man. So someone had to find the chief. When they'd found him, he came to see me. I asked again for the sword. He gave it to the weapons man, so *he* could entrust it to me. A process which took more than an hour!'[27] As Leone could not speak English (he was never, in fact, to learn more than the rudiments of the language), and required an interpreter to communicate, a great deal of patience and gesticulation was required on both sides. The 'family' atmosphere of the Bonnard sets must have seemed a very long way away. On the epics, the assistant was confined to a life of shouting at crowds of talkative extras, of varying abilities, through the megaphone, as well as whistling for all he was worth, to try against all the odds to get some silence just before the director called '*Azione!*'

The Americans' chief problem was that Cinecittà still operated from a comparatively low technological base. *Quo Vadis?* was the biggest Technicolor film ever to have been made in Italy, and the Cinecittà power supply was too meagre to run the hundreds of arc lights essential for clarity of image on insensitive stock. Five huge generators had to be borrowed from MGM in England, and one from the recently decommissioned Italian battleship the *Vittorio Veneto*. According to the usual publicity ballyhoo, the production had assembled 63 lions, 7 fighting bulls (none of them actually used in the arena, where Deborah Kerr was to be terrorized by a chloroformed black cow whose udders were carefully masked from the public), 450 horses, and 2 cheetahs which were trained to be fondled by the equally slinky Patricia Laffan as Nero's wife Poppaea. All this, plus the largest cast ever – 32,000 people, 250 of them in speaking parts. So it was essential that they could be seen clearly from the front stalls. As the posters, showing Rome in flames, put it: 'This is the big one.' The publicity also stressed that the production was making good democratic use of a moribund Fascist studio (originally built to compete with Hollywood), and referred to the Marshall Plan's reviving effects upon the European economy. The film itself would preach a rhetorical lesson on the history of Western civilization; about how even Imperial Rome, 'an undisputed master of the world', could be brought low by corruption. As guardsman Vinicius (Robert Taylor) frets in a portentous epilogue, 'Babylon, Egypt, Greece, Rome . . . what follows?' 'A more permanent world, I hope. Or a more permanent faith,' replies his comrade Fabius. In the context of post-Fascist Italy, as the publicity made clear, hopes of permanence were vested in Marshall Aid and the American way.[28]

As became industry standard, British actors of the old school played the decadent Romans; Robert Taylor and other Hollywood actors played the good centurions who had converted to Christianity; a nice English rose played the gentle Christian girl; while the hundreds of extras were largely Italian, Spanish and Turkish. Peter Ustinov (Nero) recalled, 'Let me not forget Mervyn Leroy's inspired instruction to a couple of mountainous wrestlers, one Italian, one Turkish, who were supposed to kill each other with savage grunts and groans for my pleasure, as I nibbled at larks and fondled my favourites: "Action! And make every word count!"' Leone's very junior role in all this was a share in the marshalling of the Italian extras. He had to brandish a large wooden stick with a coloured card stuck on top of it, wave his hands, blow a whistle, and negotiate with his Italian-speaking superiors. During the entire shoot he never once met Leroy, or indeed any of the principal actors, just 'crowds and soldiers and martyrs, who had to be told where to stand'. The sequences that involved him, in this lowly capacity, were the ceremonial entry of Marcus Vinicius and his Fourteenth Legion into Rome (filmed in a style that echoed Riefenstahl's *Triumph of the Will*); the mass baptism of Christians by St Paul in the catacombs; crowds rushing in panic through the streets of Rome while expensive sets supplemented by miniatures collapsed and burned behind them; the massacre of Christians in the arena (Leone had to help co-ordinate the Roman salutes and 'thumbs down' signs of the fickle crowd); and the seizure of power in the arena by Vinicius and the Praetorian Guard, who stand in a circle to protect Lygia and Ursus from overexcited Roman citizens. Another of Leone's chores was to make sure that the crowds and soldiers were not wearing wristwatches – which in *Spartacus*, ten years later, they clearly did, and gym shoes too. After the Hollywood people had left, having conspicuously consumed their nine million dollar budget, it was back to smaller-scale productions where Sergio Leone not only met the director on the set, he had known him for years, lived in his house and spoke the same language.

It was during this era of Hollywood on the Tiber that the bars, open-air cafés, nightclubs and hotels of the half-mile Via Veneto began to seem like Rome's equivalent of the better end of Sunset Strip. Hollywood stars (often past their best but still treasured by a loyal Italian audience) would rub ample shoulders with producers and financiers, showbusiness reporters and photographers in the American Bar, the foyer of the Excelsior Hotel, the Café Doney and the Café de Paris. They could be readily gawped at by Romans and tourists, and photographed by a new figure on the movie landscape, the freelance paparazzo (named after a character in Fellini's *La Dolce Vita* [1960], who makes a nuisance of himself scooting around on his Vespa and snapping Anita Ekberg). According to Walter Wanger, the paparazzi, who often hunted in packs, began to develop 'a perverse kind of pride, since Fellini saw fit to take notice of their existence'.

Early in 1955 the cast and crew of Robert Wise's *Helen of Troy*
descended on Rome, bearing the usual gifts, to shoot a film that had
been on the drawing board for nearly three years. They were preceded
by a much-hyped search for the Most Beautiful Woman in the World, as
Wise rejected the option of using a Warner contract star to play the
lead. Eventually, the twenty-year-old Italian actress Rossana Podestà
was selected. Wise's *Helen*, made at Cinecittà, hoped both to be 'modern in terms of the acting and delivery of the scenes' and simultaneously
to 'reflect the times and life of the period'. But inevitably it was the
action (such as the duel to the death between Achilles [Stanley Baker]
and Hector [Harry Andrews], and of course the delivery of the gigantic
wooden horse) which far outshone the overwritten dialogue scenes,
dubbed into Old Vic English, and strictly run of de Mille. Perhaps most
banal was the moment when Priam and his court catch their first
glimpse of the Greek armada arriving, at night, on the shores of Troy:
'Hundreds . . . Five, six hundred . . . More!'; 'No less than a thousand
ships!'; 'See what you have brought upon us – the face that launched a
thousand ships!'

Robert Wise was in charge of the main unit, while stunt director
Yakima Canutt ran the second unit. But shortly after shooting began, a
fire at Cinecittà during the lunch break ruined the entire Trojan set
(designed by Edward Carrere with Ken Adam at a cost of $95,000),
which led to cost overruns and an extended schedule. Raoul Walsh flew
over from Hollywood to help Robert Wise finish the film (uncredited),
and to take over some of the big scenes. Sergio Leone was initially
employed as one of Walsh's assistants, and then moved over to Wise's
main unit. Leone assisted Walsh as he helped to film the disembark-
ation of the Greeks, the siege of Troy, and the final night-time battle
around the wooden horse. He eavesdropped on sessions when the logistics were discussed ('Walsh wanted them to be authentic, to put over a
sense of what they must have been like'), and when the details of the
Greek encampment, with its troops and huge wooden machines of war,
were planned. He was also present at meetings about the delivery of the
horse, which, unlike the finely sculpted creature in Piero Fosco's silent
*Fall of Troy* (1910), had to look as though an army of Greek soldiers
had knocked it together out of planks and deck-boards. And, together
with Yakima Canutt, Leone was at conferences where they plotted how
details of the battles (soldiers hit by spears and flaming arrows, raiding
parties trapped in burning towers or caught scaling the ramparts,

panic-stricken horses) would intercut with the Cinemascope panoramas of troops on the move. Shooting on such a vast scale required
all the professionalism Walsh could muster, particularly since the crews
were now against the clock. According to Leone, a misunderstood
command led to the deaths of two of the extras. Benito Stefanelli (then
a very junior stuntman, later a trusted Leone collaborator) found it an
exhausting, dangerous, but in the end valuable experience as he fell
from the tower at Cinecittà carrying a shield and sword when someone
shouted the number 'five'. A whole generation of Italian stuntpeople,
he noted, learned their trade from American stunt directors on films
such as *Helen of Troy*.[29]

Despite the language barrier, Leone was keen to let Walsh know just
how much he admired his work. He recalled: 'He was aware of his
great reputation, but preferred to appear indifferent about it. Didn't
seem to give a damn. But, working closely with him, I realized what a
true professional he was. While we were shooting, he announced – and
he meant it – "I'm just earning my living, that's all." Outside working
hours, he liked to burn the candle at both ends. Alcohol, women,
brawls. But whatever happened the night before, you'd find him back
on the set, at exactly the right time in the morning. Always in focus.
Always effective.'[30]

During lunch breaks an eager but shy Sergio Leone would endeavour
to generate multilingual conversations with Walsh on the subject of his
past accomplishments: 'Walsh had been a master of the Western. I
admired his work very much [*They Died with Their Boots on*, *Pursued*, *Colorado Territory*] and I wanted to take full advantage of my
time with him on *Helen of Troy*. Alas! Whenever I brought up the
subject, he always replied, "The Western is finished" . . . I had to watch
all these Hollywood cinéastes, like Walsh and Wyler, sacrifice themselves to the taste of the moment by making peplums. And I was their
assistant, the victim of some curse. I was more in love with the idea of
America than anyone you could imagine; I had read everything I could
on the conquest of the West, already building up a huge archive on the
subject, and I was obliged to spend my time making films set in tatty
versions of antiquity, directing Roman circuses in pasteboard Colos-
seums. While I organized chariot races, sea battles between triremes
and explosions on galleys, I was silently dreaming of Nevada and New
Mexico.'[31]

Leone later claimed that, once he had been seconded to Robert

Wise's main unit, he 'struck up quite a friendship' with the director. Apparently, Wise was never at ease during his many months in another town, and his main concern was to minimize the amount of time spent standing around. 'We talked a lot together,' Leone remembered thirty years later. 'He spoke French, and was keen for me to learn English. He wanted me to continue as his assistant on his next films, and proposed that I should accompany him back to America. He wasn't misty-eyed about it, though. He recognized that he needed me to sort out many problems with the large cast. To begin with, these people spent all their time arguing among themselves, and generally screwing things up. Total lack of discipline. When I was transferred, I insisted on having carte blanche with them. The production agreed. Two days later, things had become more organized . . . You see, at that time I was much in demand as an assistant. Working all the time. And I had strong views about those extras who stirred the shit. They knew that if they made trouble, I might disown them and they would never work with me again. This concentrated their minds.'[32]

This reminiscence, like many of Leone's concerning his status and authority at this time, has a prickly quality to it: as if, even in retrospect, he is a little too keen to remind the listener about who was boss. Maybe this was another example of Leone behaving 'as if he was one of the Lumière Brothers', to give himself the status he thought he deserved. After he had made his name, for example, he maintained that it was his idea to put Robert Wise in touch with the young French actress who had played a small part in Mario Bonnard's *Tradita*; that he persuaded the American director 'to give her the role of Rossanna Podestà's handmaiden'. As a result, Brigitte Bardot worked for eight days on *Helen of Troy*, prior to making her first film with husband Roger Vadim (who until then was also an assistant at Cinecittà). So, Leone 'discovered' Bardot. This story is unlikely, to say the least.

But it is certainly true that by the late 1950s, Leone's reputation as the kind of assistant who saved money by getting things done (indeed, who was exceptionally careful with money) was well known by the liaison people working for the Rome offices of Hollywood studios. He could work with Italian or (plus an interpreter) American casts and crews; and, as he put it, 'when Wise and Walsh said they were happy with the results I got, word began to get around the American community'. However, he was never tempted to take employment in Hollywood. His network of professional and familial contacts all centred on Rome. By the time he was contacted by the Warners office to assist on Fred Zinnemann's *The Nun's Story* in 1958, he was one of the highest-paid assistants in the business.

*The Nun's Story* was filmed at Cinecittà, and on location in Bruges and Stanleyville (now Kisangani) in the Belgian Congo. It was the story of Sister Luke (Audrey Hepburn), who, having learned the three virtues of 'poverty, chastity and obedience' under the stern but benevolent guidance of her Reverend Mother (Edith Evans), is posted to a bush station in the Congo, where she practises tropical medicine with the cynical Dr Fortunati (Peter Finch). Eventually, after seventeen years in her missionary order, she decides to leave ('obedience' has always been a problem for her), to join the Belgian Resistance against the occupying Nazis. Fred Zinnemann came to Rome because the studio could accommodate a facsimile of the large convent church of La Bylke in Ghent (he couldn't get permission to film in the actual place), and because the Vatican, with its technical advisers, was just down the road. Sergio Leone's role was to assist on the sequences filmed in the Congo, and to liaise between Rome and Stanleyville. Again, he was working with a director whose work he much admired, in particular *High Noon*: 'the way in which unities of space, time and action were handled, in those scenes at the station, was a triumph'. He was also working with the Hungarian-born Alexander Trauner, one of the great film designers, best known for his collaborations with Marcel Carné, Billy Wilder and Orson Welles (for whom he had constructed suits of armour out of tin cans, because the *Othello* budget could not run to the real thing). Trauner enjoyed the challenge of recreating an entire convent, complete with sculptures and stained-glass windows, and also of building a bush station in the real landscape. And Sergio Leone was deeply impressed by Trauner's eye for detail: 'He was much, much more than a set decorator. He was a documentarist. He had analysed in detail just about every church in Belgium, to reconstruct one in the studio . . . Trauner was a genius.'[33]

Leone was also struck by Zinnemann's conscientiousness, if not his decisiveness: 'He exposed 350,000 metres of stock, for two little hours on screen. When he worked on a set-up, he filmed every single detail from every single angle – walls, objects, hands, ceiling, floor. He never missed *anything* out.' Leone also found that Zinnemann, rather than talking about his films, preferred the main topic of conversation to be a controversial moment in nineteenth-century Italian history: 'Fred Zinnemann is Austrian. And he never ceased asking me when Italy would return the South Tyrol to Austria. He brought up the subject every day. I ended up by saying that, if it was up to me, he could have his South Tyrol right now. Sadly I wasn't in a position to make that decision. And I added that I really didn't give a damn.'[34] When I asked Zinnemann whether he recalled any of these bizarre exchanges, he replied: 'I don't remember the details, but I'm quite sure that must have happened . . . I remember working with Sergio Leone with great affection and some amusement. Because Sergio was not a man who was cut out to be an assistant, and as a result he used to dance most of the night, and sleep much of the day – discreetly, away from the set. Fortunately, there were other Italian assistants who took up the slack. But he was a charming man and I liked him very much. If there was an excellent restaurant somewhere in the Congo, I feel sure he'd have found it.'[35] While Zinnemann was clearly struck by the epicurean aspect of his assistant, he also recalls that Leone 'was certainly ambitious'. He added that he somehow 'managed to miss' Leone's film *Once Upon a Time in the West*, with its opening homage to *High Noon*, and much preferred not to comment on his attitude to Italian Westerns.[36]

Leone and Zinnemann were in complete agreement about one reminiscence of the filming of *The Nun's Story*, and that is the atmosphere of racial tension that surrounded the set, arising from the contrast between the affluence of the whites and the poverty and disease besetting everyone else. A curfew meant that 'the blacks weren't allowed near the European area after dark', and both Zinnemann and Leone had the sensation – which neither reckoned to be the product of hindsight – that the status quo was rapidly becoming insupportable. A year after the crew left the Congo, the revolution took place: the Belgians were driven out, several of the missionaries with whom the crew had worked were killed, and Patrice Lumumba (whom Leone briefly encountered, when Lumumba was still a post office clerk in Stanleyville) became head of state.

But the story that Leone most loved to recount at dinner parties had nothing to do with politics. It concerned a trek through the jungle, scouting for locations, with cinematographer Enzo Barboni, who assisted the second-unit cameraman: 'We were lost in the jungle, and came across a clearing. But our path was blocked by a huge man, like Mandrake's side-kick, only twice his size . . . He was in full tribal rig, with a row of lion's teeth around his neck. We couldn't get past him. I said to Enzo, "You ask him to move." "No, you," he replied. And so we went on. Eventually, to make conversation and ease the situation, I spoke to him in French. "Do you speak French?" He nodded. There was a long pause. "Are you a hunter?" He nodded. Then, an attempt at bonhomie: "Did you kill the lion with your own bare hands?" Quick as a flash, the huge man replied, "Me? You must be kidding, duckie." '37

Shortly after *The Nun's Story* wrapped, Leone was hired as first assistant in one of the second units working to William Wyler on the $15 million MGM production of *Ben-Hur*, a show that had rented the entire Cinecittà complex, back-lot and all. Thirty-four years previously, Wyler had been an assistant in the second unit responsible for the chariot race of the 1925 version of *Ben-Hur*. That sequence lasted nearly eight minutes, involved ten chariots hurtling around the arena, and became the major selling-point for the film. Perhaps because of bad memories, Wyler insisted on a clause in his 1959 contract absolving him from any direct responsibility for the race itself. Yakima Canutt was to stage-manage the chariots and teach the actors how to drive them. ('Chuck,' he said to Charlton Heston, 'you just drive the chariot, I guarantee you'll win the damn race.') Andrew 'Bundy' Marton was to help direct the sequence, and Leone was part of the Italian team supporting him, with special responsibility for retakes. Leone also had some liaison with Wyler over props. The giant Antioch Circus set had been constructed at Cinecittà, complete with Herculean sculpted figures, seating for 2,000 extras, Pontius Pilate's ceremonial box plus a rehearsal track to the side. After nearly two months' rehearsal, filming of the race took place between the end of May and the beginning of August 1959. No miniature or process shots were to be used this time. On the first day of shooting a sequence with dialogue, William Wyler observed the assistant directors trying to get a huge crowd of extras in order by frantically waving flags and said, 'I wonder which one of those guys'll direct the *next* remake.' Sergio Leone was among them. Charlton Heston, meanwhile, caught sight of Leo Genn's costume from *Quo Vadis?* on the back of an elderly extra.38

*Ben-Hur* was uncommon among 1950s Hollywood epics of the Roman Empire in that it did not centrally concern a conversion to Christianity; the Romans were not presented as decadent psychopaths (although they *are* all played by Englishmen); there were no set-piece land battles or sieges, and no gladiators or martyrs in the arena. But there was a spectacular sea battle, and, of course, that chariot race, a virtual rerun of the 1925 version, in Technicolor, 70 mm and stereo sound, with eight chariots this time and lasting just under nine minutes. The main differences are the addition of sharpened blades to Messala's chariot wheels, an absence of dialogue, a lot more gore, more subjective shots, and a series of minor collisions rather than the almighty five-chariot pile-up (frighteningly real, by the look of it) which climaxed the 1925 race. According to Leone, the second unit was expected to watch the Niblo version repeatedly, to psyche themselves up: 'I was the first assistant in this second unit; we had two months to prepare the horses, and more than three to shoot the actual race. During that time, I must have seen the first *Ben-Hur* made by Fred Niblo one hundred times, for there was a screening of the film every single evening and the whole unit had to go and watch it.'[39] But Wyler was an uncompromising task-master: 'The second unit was entirely responsible, and Wyler had to be shown the results, as rushes. If anything did not satisfy him, we would do it again and again until he was satisfied.'[40]

And yet, from the moment Wyler's *Ben-Hur* was announced, all showings of Fred Niblo's version were suppressed by MGM (the owner of both). A film historian tried to organize a rival première of the Niblo film (the abridged 1931 version, with a Movietone soundtrack) but was raided by the FBI. Andrew Marton, one of Wyler's credited second-unit directors, did not remember a single screening of the Niblo film for the second unit. But he did acknowledge that the urge to compete with the original version was on the unit's mind. 'Producer Sam Zimbalist said to me in pre-production, "You know, this is a very tricky task. Number one, everybody who's never seen the old film will say, 'Oh, the race was much better in the old film.' " '[41]

Following the international success of his Westerns, Leone was happy to exaggerate his role in the chariot-race sequence. 'The second-unit director', he claimed in 1977, 'was too old for that kind of sport! That was how *I was able to direct the famous "shock sequence" of the film.*' Ten years later he sang the same tune: 'Wyler said to me, "Have you seen the chariot race in the Ramon Navarro *Ben-Hur*? I want to go one better. We will rehearse and shoot the sequence until we have reached perfection." Officially, Andrew Marton was in charge of the operation. But he simply saw it as a way of paying the rent. I, on the other hand, *adored* doing it.'[42] In fact, the fifty-five-year-old Marton, working in partnership with Yakima Canutt, appears to have been very much in control, and very enthusiastic about the job in hand. As the man himself recalled to an interviewer from the Director's Guild of America: 'With those heavy 70 mm cameras in the race, I don't think there's a single scene that is shot at the normal twenty-four images per second . . . We had six different hands working on the cameras – the people who were doing this had to be strapped to the camera-car. We didn't want to lose any assistants and have them trampled to death by the horses following. Strapping them in also enabled them to use both hands for focusing, changing speeds and changing shutter openings.'[43] The camera-car had a customized low-slung arm attached to its back, to enable the crew to film the horses from below. According to Leone, who commissioned this piece of equipment, 'if a cable snapped, we would have fallen under the horses' hooves and the chariots' wheels'.

Despite the scale of the operation, Sergio Leone did get to be in the same room as Wyler, during discussions about props. Wyler had just finished cutting The Big Country, and Leone, no doubt, wanted to edge forward and talk Westerns with him. Instead, at his first meeting with Leone present, Wyler opened the conversation in French by asking if the Romans walked barefoot or not. Leone, speaking with some authority as a veteran of Quo Vadis?, replied that as far as he knew they wore sandals. '[Wyler] was certainly a perfectionist, but he didn't seem to know much about history. He had ordered his props and costumes from Hollywood. Everything was prepared down to the last detail. But still he had his doubts. So he invited an historian, a specialist in the Roman Empire period. I was charged with showing her everything: arms, costumes, decorative details and models . . . At the end of the day, she let him know that everything was very beautiful and would no doubt look very spectacular on screen. Wyler interrupted. He wanted to know if everything was faithful to history. The woman looked at him, amazed. Wyler became impatient. "What do I have to do, to bring things closer to historical accuracy?" The specialist shook her head. Then she muttered, "I would burn the lot, if I were you!" '[44]

William Wyler had decided to cast Charlton Heston as Judah Ben-Hur while he was still filming The Big Country. But even after his arrival at Cinecittà, Wyler was not quite finished with his previous opus. Leone enjoyed recounting an incident he witnessed three days into the Ben-Hur shoot, on 22 May 1959: 'Wyler had finished The Big Country . . . but one particular shot was troubling him. He decided to reshoot it while we were working on Ben-Hur. So we saw Charlton

Heston arrive, dressed as a cowboy, in the middle of the Roman circus. Wyler filmed him for several hours, until he got the exact shot he was after. Then, he edited it into all the completed prints . . . It's incredible, but true. That shows the extent of his power at that time.'[45] This was the first opportunity Sergio Leone had had of seeing a Western, or a fragment of one, being filmed. Tall as the tale may sound, Heston confirms it: 'Wyler wanted to do a retake of a close-up of me at the end of the fight scene with Greg Peck. A close angle. I don't think I even needed to have the pants on, but they flew over the shirt and the make-up man put on 1885 sideburns because my sideburns were shaved short for *Ben-Hur*. I lay on the ground, in the arena, and tried to get back inside the ranch foreman I'd played nine months before!'[46]

In his autobiography, Charlton Heston is dismissive of Leone's Westerns, arguing that 'Americans are the only ones who can make them,' and going on to say, 'No, Sergio Leone is not the exception; Clint Eastwood and Henry Fonda lent his spaghetti Westerns what validity they had.' When I spoke with Heston, he stood by that view ('Leone's films are good, but I don't think without Clint Eastwood and all those guys they would be'). But Heston, having starred in *Major Dundee*, had a lot of time for Sam Peckinpah; and he now concedes that Leone did at least create a climate which made possible Peckinpah's work of the late 1960s ('Yes that's quite true. It was unfair of me to ignore that').

*Ben-Hur* marked the end of Sergio Leone's apprenticeship as an assistant director. In the eleven years between 1948 and 1959, he had gained experience of all levels of the Italian film industry. Like his father before him, he was clearly most at home at the more commercial end of the spectrum, where the project had a large audience firmly in its sights from the planning stage onwards. After working 'on about fifty Italian and American films', Leone summarized the lessons he had learned from the standpoint of a hardened Cinecittà professional: 'If you are an assistant with ideas of your own, it is better to work with several directors – for, if you work with one, and particularly if he is one you admire, you eventually lose your own identity. I cannot say that working with the great American directors was a dazzling experience. For one thing, the Italians I worked with were professionals of the old school, who knew their job well. For another, it is easier to make films as the American directors do, if you have vast budgets, kilometres of film footage, several cameras, and several crews who often do all the hard work.' He elaborated, 'I think that to become a good director, it is better to work with the "mediocre talents" than with the "film geniuses". With the latter, you have all the facilities you could ask for, for their goal is perfection, with the "mediocre talents" you have to use your brains, to learn from all the imperfections, as a way of shaping your own experience and finding your own voice. Necessity is the mother of invention.'

Leone contrasted his long apprenticeship with the rapid ascent of his successors: 'Today, everyone wants to become a director from the outset. And it has become feasible to do so. In those days, assistant directors had a very different attitude. Elio Petri, Francesco Rosi, Franco Zeffirelli and I, we all belonged to a different school. Firstly, we were scared of making a film which didn't do well, for there was no way we could go back to being assistants again after that. Secondly, we had strong scruples vis-à-vis our producers. We didn't want to ruin them by directing a first film which was unsuccessful ... Anyway, I reached a point where I was being paid on a level with directors, in those cases where the producers knew that I had actually shot certain sequences [in Bonnard's films].'[47] The experience had given him a 'repertoire of techniques' to fall back on, in case his first film was a failure.

Having served time assisting certain Italian masters, Leone was pleased to pay tribute to them, by contrast to the American interlopers: 'Take Vittorio De Sica's attention to detail. Nothing of this kind would have been possible in America, where the stratification of the industry suffocated the director's intuition under three layers of ultra-professional dust. I learned more from De Sica, in a few working weeks, than from being a paid assistant, in the following years, for the big American directors who were descending on Italy from a great height to reveal to us the miracle of the great historical and mythological films, which incidentally went down like stodgy food.'[48] Nevertheless, when Leone was asked in 1984 whether he had participated in 'the fascination of Italian intellectuals for America in the postwar period', he replied: 'Let's be frank: I was impatient to get away from neo-realism. For me, cinema is imagination. It can say things by using the resources of the fable. The doctrinal sort of film never appealed to me ... So the encounter with Wise, Walsh and Zinnemann was essential for me, above all to understand how a certain kind of cinema was constructed. I mean the technical side ... I believe this experience helped open certain windows on a kind of cinema which could have thoughts, and at the same time be spectacular.'[49]

But Leone also contended that his experience taught him a great deal about what *not* to do when directing: 'I made fifty-eight films (*sic*) as an assistant – I was at the side of directors who applied all the rules: make it, for example, a close-up to show that the character is about to say something important. I reacted against all that, and so the close-ups in my films are always the expression of an emotion. I'm very careful in that area, so they call me a perfectionist and a formalist, because I watch my framing. But I'm not doing it to make it pretty. I'm seeking, first and foremost, the relevant emotions.'[50] He had watched at close quarters the classic Hollywood way of telling a story, and had developed an interest in 'allowing the camera to move about on its own'.

Leone tended in later years to describe the Hollywood Greats on whose shoulders he stood with words such as 'tired', 'compromised' and 'safe'; and their work in Italy as 'dull', 'predictable', 'too senti-mental' or 'like an inaccurate history lesson'. They descended on Italy, 'from a great height'. Worse, they were extravagant. The outstanding exception in Leone's great reckoning was the production designer Alexander Trauner, whose obsession with the tiniest visual details chimed with his own, and whose reputation originated with his European work. But above all else, Leone had developed a lasting respect for the 'old men' and the professionals of Cinecittà, and had thoroughly networked himself into their world. This was Leone's 'film school'.

Pasolini was to write of Cinecittà as 'the belching stomach of Italy'; and the Northern Italian intelligentsia of film did look down on those Romans who were trained in and aspired to produce 'pulp' films, usu-ally pitched at a thrill-seeking home market rather than at discerning international festivals and art houses. But as Leone was often to point out, this was only the most recent example of a longstanding North/South divide in Italian culture, and he was, in any case, just as much a product of his regional origins as they were. The most famous 'art house' directors we associate with Italy in the 1960s all originated from the same region of the North: Antonioni (Ferrara), Bertolucci (Parma), Fellini (the Romagna coast) and Pasolini (Emilia-Romagna). All of these film-makers returned to their home landscapes, and to the pro-vincial societies in which they grew up, to use them as settings for their films. Some of them (notably Fellini and Bertolucci) subsequently built bridges between their biographical origins and the cinema of mass appeal. Pasolini tried to become Roman by adoption. Leone, as we have seen, often returned to his childhood and adolescence in Rome and Naples for nourishment, albeit in an indirect way. But his regional origins were also about growing up in and around Cinecittà, and around the people who worked in a sophisticated industry, located in the capital city of the Italian countryside.

The Northern intelligentsia also tended to deride the 'industry professionals' for their lack of political engagement and social responsibility, and there is no doubt that at an early stage Leone developed a cynicism about formal politics, which would surface time and again in his mature films. Usually, he would attribute this disillusionment to his family background: 'My father eventually opted for communism, but I tended more towards socialism . . . Since then, as a socialist I have seen *so many* deceptions and compromises'; 'My father was exiled from the industry for his principles – and, looking back, *for what*?' Sometimes, though, he attributed it to the ways in which the Italian 'economic miracle' had happened in an atmosphere of greed rather than planning, without any thought as to its social consequences (especially where Rome and points South were concerned). His films, Leone said, related 'to everything my generation has been told in the way of promises. We have waited, but we are still waiting!' Their pessimism was not the pessimism of the 1860s and 1870s, when his Westerns were set; but that of 100 years later.[51]

It is characteristic of Leone the man that, while Pasolini and others might write analyses of Palmiro Togliatti's 'historic compromise' with parliamentarianism and consumerism, and his attempt after 1956 to develop a distinctively Italian style of communism, Leone preferred to compare Togliatti with Charlie Chaplin, and then move on to another topic of conversation. 'Me? I'm a *Roman*,' he asserted, 'therefore fatalistic and pessimistic . . . We have historical evidence of our empire scattered all through the city, as permanent proof of our errors and stupidities.' Leone saw the visual image as more powerful than the word, and he associated political optimism with the 'grand narratives' of Hollywood. His oft-repeated put-down of the Hollywood films on which he worked was that they had too starry-eyed an interpretation of history. Whilst he admired films that conveyed ideas in a spectacular way, he professed to find Hollywood a little thin on imagination. Yet various visual 'moments' from Hollywood spectaculars dating from the era of the economic miracle would later turn up in his own films, as traces of his formative years. The exchange of hostages in *Fistful of Dollars* closely resembles a scene where, in an equivalent atmosphere of mistrust, Helen of Troy is handed over by Hector to Menelaus. Those circular arenas in which the final 'settling of accounts' take place in all of Leone's Westerns from *For a Few Dollars More* onwards bear a strong family resemblance to the Antioch Circus of *Ben-Hur*. Leone's apprenticeship certainly provided him with an arsenal of visual resources, as well as a cynicism about Hollywood's preferred manner of mounting a big story. But it was the next phase of his career that would teach him how to transform all of these resources into his own 'fairy-tales for grown-ups'.

# 4

# Economic Miracles

It was as close as movies got to a cultural lineage, this process of spirals by which you got the myth (the real, original Italian epics, *Cabiria* and *Quo Vadis?* and *The Fall of Troy*, that took America by storm in 1914) and the myth of the myth (the improved and homogenized American epics, *Intolerance* and *Ben-Hur* and *The Queen of Sheba*, which in turn found their way back to Italian screens) and then, beyond computing, the myths of the myths of the myths, as each photographed the other's photographs: the Fascist historical epics with their perfect emulation of Hollywood gloss (*Scipio Africanus*, *The Crown of Iron*), the fifties Hollywood spectacles that took advantage of cheap Italian backdrops and extras (*Helen of Troy*) and the Italian spectacles that took advantage of Hollywood stars (Kirk Douglas in *Ulysses*), the even cheaper Italian imitation of those spectacles (*Hercules, Hercules Unchained, The Loves of Hercules*) that turned unemployed bodybuilders from Muscle Beach into authentic European stars and ultimately – by way of drive-ins and neighbourhood chains – back into authentic American anti-stars ... For one long interval – the Age of Dress Up – it was as if a relatively young child with a propensity for storytelling had been cajoled into spinning out a single open-ended tale, an adventure without beginning or end, while a team of screenwriters took notes. To the child's basic outline were added few adult touches: literary references and a hint of decadent sexuality.

Geoffrey O'Brien, *The Phantom Empire* (1993)

Since the beginning of the 1950s, Italian cinema had depended for its economic wellbeing on a series of hit-and-run film cycles: such as the opera film (1946–56), the film-*fumetto* or sentimental 'weepy' (1950–54), and the dialect comedy (1955–8). An occasional windfall success would prompt an avalanche of cheaply made films, financed either by guarantees from distributors or help from abroad. Then, just as suddenly, the assembly-line would re-tool for a different product, triggered by another hit which was thought to be repeatable. This approach did not lead to stability: every four or five years, Italian newspapers would write of a 'crisis' or 'slump' in the industry. But it did lead to the production of a lot of films, which seemed less like freestanding productions than episodes in a long-running serial.[1]

From Blasetti's *Fabiola* (1949) through to Guido Brignone's *Le schiave di Cartagine* (*The Sword and the Cross*, 1957 ), there had been one or two 'epics' a year. But not since the silent era of Maciste and friends had these amounted to a fully fledged cycle. The trigger-year was 1958, when Pietro Francisci directed and co-wrote *Le fatiche di Ercole* (*Hercules*), a Franco–Italian co-production, inspired by the success of Hollywood epics made in Rome, but also harking back to the silent musclemen. The film starred Steve Reeves, a bodybuilder who had been Mr America in 1947, Mr World in 1948 and Mr Universe two years later ('It must have been my sympathetic face,' Reeves remarked). Francisci's daughter had seen the Hollywood musical *Athena* (1954) dubbed into Italian, and spotted Mr Universe in a small role. Until Reeves stumbled on to the scene, the female star had traditionally been the centre of the action in Italian 'epics'. From 1958 onwards, heroes with outsized pectorals dominated proceedings. Between 1958 and 1964, Reeves was to revive the triumph of the torso in ancient settings eight more times, also playing Goliath, the Giant of Marathon, Glaucus in *The Last Days of Pompeii*, Aeneas (twice), Romulus, and the Son of Spartacus. He also appeared as Morgan the Pirate, the Thief of Baghdad, Sandokan the Great and Murad the White Devil: Reeves did like it to be known that he was keen to avoid typecasting.

*Le fatiche di Ercole* showed only two of Hercules' labours (the lion and the bull), and then retold the story of Jason and the Argonauts, but with the strongman, rather than Jason, at the helm. It began with the usual homily, brought Hercules right down to earth, and placed him in a series of increasingly outlandish settings, photographed by Mario Bava. The combination of domesticity and myth proved a winning one on the home market: the film grossed 900 million lire. But the breakthrough happened when Boston film impresario Joseph E. Levine bought the American distribution rights for a song, and proceeded to spend $1.2 million (over five times the film's original budget) publicizing his product. Levine produced eight different television trailers and placed ads in 132 publications, prior to the film's simultaneous opening at 600 cinemas.[2] He cleared over $4 million in profit on the deal. Francisci's follow-up *Ercole e la regina di Lidia* (*Hercules Unchained*, 1959) made even more money both in Italy and America. Following Levine's lead, American film companies began to take an interest in these films, partly as a way of filling up their distribution slates at a time of spiralling domestic production costs. The 'peplum cycle' had well and truly begun. Even *Scipione l'Africano* was dubbed into English and shown on television as *The Defeat of Hannibal*.

'Peplum' is a Latinized version of the Greek 'peplos', meaning a short tunic or dress worn in ancient times; and the term was first coined by Parisian critics who saw all sorts of hidden depths in some of these films. Other critics called them 'epics', but this may perhaps have been a distant relic of their classical education and the cultural prestige they attributed to ancient times. If Hopalong Cassidy did it, then it was a Western; if Hercules was doing it, then it had to be an 'epic'. 'Pepla' was nearer the mark, for this was simply to describe these films as a form of costume drama. From 1958 to 1963, around 170 'pepla' were made. They were cheap to produce, on eight-to-ten-week shooting schedules; and even superstar Reeves earned only $10,000 a week. They used reach-me-down props left behind by Hollywood, the sets could be re-dressed from film to film, and the cataclysm footage was easy to recycle since the main characters were usually somewhere else at the time. Maciste and Ursus, the home team, made their comebacks in 1960, Samson in 1961, the fearless Gladiator and the Rebel Slave in 1962. By 1963 the musclemen were joining forces and being pitched into battle against assorted Moon Men, Mole People, Vampires, Stone Age Monsters, Lizard Folk, Mongols, Aztecs, Saracens, Sheiks, Tsars, and popular comedians of the day. Steve Reeves resigned from the Hercules role after two efforts, and was succeeded by an assortment of American bodybuilders (or actors who had 'bulked up' in the gymnasium), whose names alliterated with his own: Mark Forest, Ed Fury, Brad Harris, Gordon Scott, Kirk Morris, Dan Vadis and Rock Stevens. British bodybuilder Reg Park even took a turn, as did the Italian actor Sergio Ciani, who became 'Alan Steel'. According to *Newsweek* (29 August 1960), Italian bodybuilders, or 'fusti', became so angry that Americans were nearly always cast in these roles that they formed a pressure group called 'The Society to Protect Italian Musclemen'. If muscles rather than acting ability were the deciding factor, they said, then why not cast Italians? Not a bad point.

At the beginning of *The Ten Commandments* (1956), Cecil B. de Mille had cited his sources in footnotes. He even appeared in a prologue, before a plush red curtain (giving a touch of theatrical class to the proceedings), and hymned the film's historical credentials. The

Italians had a far more flexible and irreverent attitude towards history and myth. The moral lessons pronounced in schoolbooks ('Nothing to excess', 'Proportion in all things') were treated as a load of baloney. Among all the settings in which the 'pepla' placed their superheroes, they tended to avoid the Bible, except for the very occasional scrap with the Philistines. The Vatican was, after all, only a stone's throw away. When Samson appeared, he was transposed to thirteenth-century China, or King Solomon's mines. In one film, his frozen body was reanimated to take on the Tsar of Russia. The Italian emphasis was instead on virility (often tested in sporting events), the fair lady versus the dark lady, sensuality rather than spirituality, and the corruption of the city and its squabbling politicians versus the pleasures of the country. The audience would be treated to a cabaret turn or two (usually dancers at a feast, or well-oiled wrestlers or acrobats) observed by balding patricians fondling grapes in more or less suggestive ways. Other staples were a torture scene often involving an elaborate implement; a slapstick-style punch-up; and a set-piece battle permitting our hero to perform extraordinary feats.

While the leading men were busy pumping iron, the film-makers were seizing upon the old classical stories, half-remembered from schooldays, and frantically pumping irony into them. Vittorio Cottafavi, director of the superior *Ercole alla conquista di Atlantide* (1961), called these films 'big, noisy and colourful machines constructed in the vein of strip cartoons'. The theatricality, sentiment and nationalism of the silent era, some of it shading into Fascism, had made way for knowing nudges and winks at the expense of high culture and the extravagant pomposity of Hollywood. Most of the Italian film journals and newspapers, when they bothered to notice Maciste, Hercules, Ursus, Samson or Goliath, took the view that sword-and-sandal adventures were so bad they were almost good. At least they had shed the cloying aspects of their silent forebears. They were touchingly naïve in their re-presentation of simple stories for the benefit of a mid-twentieth-century audience. They were not for *us*, you understand, but for *them* – the less demanding punters queueing up outside the Roxy Calabria.

In January 1965, shortly after completing *Maciste Against the Mongols*, *Hercules Against Spartacus*, *Hercules and the Tyrants of Babylon* and *Goliath at the Conquest of Bagdad* – all in one year, and probably on the same sets – veteran director Domenico Paolella replied at length to such lofty judgements, in an article entitled 'La Psicanalisi dei Poveri'.³ A type of film, he began, which accounted for two-thirds of all the revenues earned by Italian films in 1962–3, and which attracted seven out of every ten cinema-goers (albeit often in *terza visione* houses with cheaper ticket prices, rather than the more upmarket *prima visione* houses in the big cities) deserved much more serious attention. Paolella then attempted to explain its social significance: 'Those who visit the upmarket cinemas to see their "art films" clearly have other needs, other forms of satisfaction. It is the humblest in society who are attracted by mythology: the victims, the least mature, those who have been wounded by life and its confusions. And, sad to say, they are the vast majority. The "fantasy film" is the psychoanalysis of the poor.'⁴

In Italy, Paolella argued, the 'mythological film' had triumphed at the box office at a time of great social change: the drift to cities, increased mobility, the spread of consumerism, the loosening of family bonds, the development of technology, and the diffusion of 'city' sophistication among the less developed regions: 'The films are full of images which are part of the language of dreams, and hidden within them, in symbolic form, are all the obstacles encountered in everyday life. The monsters are the factories or workshops, the towns, the offices; the enemies are other people; the elaborate weapons of the adversary are complicated machines; the rivers of fire, the no less dangerous streams of traffic which choke our towns. And, in the middle of this hostile and confusing world, full of traps and snares (or, in other words, reality) there is the individual with his extraordinary muscles who can only in the end count on himself. Such films re-awaken the sense of individuality, and confront the individual with decisions and responsibilities, and also confidence and hope.'

Other critics, bemused by such inflated claims, mounted a counterattack: in France the pepla were called 'a seven-day wonder in rural zones, *Cahiers du Cinéma*, the Near East and Latin America'. In other words, they represented an attempt to invade Third World markets with a very basic and ephemeral form of mass-marketing. Regardless of language, the heroes could easily be identified by their short tunics, their muscles, and their musical themes on the soundtrack. The action scenes came thick and fast, for those with a low boredom threshold, and the emphasis throughout was on instant gratification and a proletarian interpretation of the classics.⁵ Christopher Wagstaff, who has made a study of Italian cinema-going habits in the 1960s, confirms at least some of this when he characterizes the typical (male) visitor to a *terza visione* cinema: 'He would not bother to find out what was showing, nor would he make any particular effort to arrive at the beginning of the film. He would talk to his friends during the showing whenever he felt like it, except during the bits of the film that grabbed his (or his friends') attention.'[6]

Sergio Leone's father had directed one of the few original Maciste films to be exported to the United States. Leone himself knew all about how to shoot action sequences, Hollywood-style. He had a feel for the Italian system of making popular films, and was ready to direct one of his own. Yet he resisted the many offers of cheap 'pepla' which came his way at this time. For one thing, he said, the pictures weren't prepared properly. Writers and directors usually threw them together in a matter of weeks, and it showed. Maybe the cycle had originated in a popular success, but it had long since turned into what Leone called 'a con trick' on a vast scale, chucking bread and circuses at *terza visione* customers. 'Perhaps the most serious debate on the subject of ancient Rome', Leone claimed, 'was made by Kubrick in the film *Spartacus*: the other films have always been cardboard fables, superficial in every way.'[7] As usual with Leone, he placed a high premium on 'surface realism' in deriding lesser efforts: 'They were kidding themselves if they imagined they could make a film in this genre which was historically accurate. It would take a lifetime to research the authenticity of everything, to study the period and be certain of getting the look right. Nevertheless, at the end of the 1950s the peplum became the most sought-after cinematic genre in the world: the Chinese, the Arabs, the Americans, the French, the Germans . . . everyone bought this kind of film. And inflation set in. A huge number of stupidities and howlers began to accumulate, in all these productions. Personally, I had no wish to take part in this idiotic rat-race. Unless it was to turn it inside out, and send it up. To throw it all up into the air, a little like John Boorman was later to do with the thriller in *Point Blank*. To try to reach a point of no return, an auto-da-fé of the entire genre.'[8]

As Leone remembered of the muscleman heyday, 'I certainly wasn't short of offers. Producers would telephone me. I warned them that if they so much as mentioned the word "Maciste" I would spit – there and then. But they always ended up admitting that they were, after all, preparing one of those dreadful con-tricks. Even if they argued that I could approach them in a different way I always told them to get lost.

There seemed to be nothing else but Maciste on the screen . . . It had become impossible: Maciste in China, in Hell, in Africa, in Scotland, in Egypt, in Mongolia, among the head-hunters and even against Zorro!'[9] Leone's preferred argument was that, for a cinematic fable to work, it must convince its viewers that it is really happening. One way to achieve this was to be fiercely attentive to details. 'To this extent and to this extent only,' said Leone, 'I am a child of neo-realism.' By abandoning this precept, the peplum cycle, according to Leone, was displaying an arrogant attitude towards its audience. Leone's criticisms, like his pronouncements upon the Hollywood legends for whom he worked, suggest a kind of pedantry in his approach to film-making at this time. Given the genesis and development of the Maciste cycle – its disdain for the cod-reverential atmosphere of the Hollywood epics, in favour of more playful modern myths à la Jean Cocteau – it seems strange to criticize the films for their shortcomings as history. True, the Italian countryside didn't resemble Greece, and the rocks were unmistakably made of expanded polystyrene or papier mâché. But, as director George Roy Hill replied, when told that the 'Bolivia' of his *Butch Cassidy and the Sundance Kid* bore no resemblance to the real thing: 'Well, it does now.'

So, from 1958–60, during the headlong rush towards the golden fleece, Leone continued to work as Mario Bonnard's assistant. Quite possibly, he lacked the confidence to stand on his own two feet. Certainly, he understood just how important his first effort as a director could be: 'We were scared of making a film which didn't do well.' Some sources claim that in 1957 Leone directed a short film set in Rome, called *Taxi . . . signore?* But he did not feel ready for a feature. Meanwhile, after years of tinkering, he finally signed his name to a Bonnard scenario: *Aphrodite, dea dell' amore* (1958, *Slave Women of Corinth* or *Slave of the Orient*). The credits acknowledged 'Sceneggiato da Ugo Moretti, Mario Bonnard, Sergio Leone, Mario di Nardo' and 'Assistenti Regio Sergio Leone/Romolo Girolami'.

Though released in the same year as Francisci's *Hercules, Aphrodite* was billed in subtitle as '*Un episodio della storia Greco-Romana*', and like a lot of 'pepla' with Roman rather than Greek settings, it is solid, conventional, a little pedestrian, owing more to self-important 1950s epics than their wilder and more imaginative offspring. Actually, it was a rewrite in a new setting of the old *Phryné* story of 1953. Its main interest lies in its central theme of art and politics, and use of a hallowed ancient artefact to symbolize a brutal political struggle (providing a link with Leone's *Colossus of Rhodes* of three years later). *Aphrodite* is set in Corinth in the year AD 67, shortly after the Great Fire in Rome and Nero's subsequent persecution of the Christians. Antigono, governor of the province, is in the process of building a canal across the isthmus. Paid for by punitive taxes on local merchants and farmers, it will cut through the holy site of Aphrodite's temple. Demetrio (Antonio de Teffé), a gifted young sculptor from Rome, is commissioned to make a new statue of the goddess, as a way of promoting the city and the regime, and he has to choose between two real-life models: the blonde Lerna (Isabelle Corey), a Christian slave-girl, and the dark Diala (Irene Tunc), a pleasure-loving Phoenician courtesan. The court promotes Diala, while Demetrio is fascinated by Lerna; so at one point he attempts a compromise by sculpting Diala's body and Lerna's face in clay. After pondering the alternative options, Demetrio falls in love with the slave-girl ('Your eyes have a different look – a brightness of purity. That may be what I seek'). There is a busy background of court intrigue, persecution, massacre, plague, famine and wild (well, wild-ish) orgies; Diala performs the obligatory dance of the seven veils. Finally, Demetrio and Lerna manage to survive until the death of Nero, and the succession of Galba, to be reunited on the streets of Corinth during a purifying rainstorm. Together, they examine the image of the Goddess Aphrodite, modelled after the now-dead Diala.

Demetrio may have had a problem finding his model, but it is clear throughout where the model for the film came from: Mervyn Leroy's *Quo Vadis?* Demetrio, like Robert Taylor, is torn between duty to Rome and the spiritual attractions of Christianity; Lerna, like Deborah Kerr, is imprisoned for her beliefs; Diala, like Patricia Laffan's Poppea, dresses in exotic colours and poisons the Governor's mind against the Christians. Such connections might suggest that the script for *Aphrodite* had been lying around for some time. Leone implied as much by always mentioning *Aphrodite* in the same breath as *Phryné, the Oriental Courtesan*. Where Leone's personal contribution might be detected, there is more emphasis than in *Phryné* upon the physical details of brutality: Roman horsemen attacking farmers, archers firing burning arrows at hapless martyrs, panic-stricken prisoners trapped in a burning jail. And one action sequence – Demetrio riding his horse down the side of a mountain to head off the pursuing Roman posse, and warn the

Christians that they have been betrayed – was to reappear almost shot-for-shot in *Fistful of Dollars*, with Clint Eastwood in the saddle.

All in all, the experience of working on *Aphrodite* can't have done much to progress Leone's career, although he helped to shoot one or two sequences. But it did provide him with an after-dinner story he enjoyed telling, with embellishments, for many years to come. Carla Leone recalls it vividly: 'They were filming the scene where the prison burns down. The designer had designed the prison to look like marble, so it wouldn't have been realistic for it to burn. So Sergio scattered straw everywhere. The idea was that the shot would begin with a flaming torch, pull away to the man holding the torch, the torch would light the straw, and the prisoners trapped inside would be terrified. Well, when they tried it, the whole prison went up, and so did part of the studio. There was only one fireman and one hose, but he did his best to quell the flames. Meanwhile, the man who held the torch, a burly Roman, kept interrupting Sergio over and over again, tugging at his sleeve, and excitedly saying, "Do you want me to do it again?" Eventually, Sergio said, "Yes, yes – but not the bit where you burn the studio down, okay?"'[10]

Nevertheless, Leone's stock continued to rise: 'I had helped with, or doctored, scenarios before,' Leone later recalled, 'and everyone in the profession knew about it. So producers began to ask me to write for them officially.' Later in the same year, Leone contributed to the screenplay of Guido Brignone's *Nel segno di Roma* (1958, *Sign of the Gladiator*). The credits, set against an imposing red curtain, read 'sogetto e sceneggiaturi di Francesco Thellung, Francesco de Feo, Sergio Leone, Giuseppe Mangione, Guido Brignone'. Publicity referred to Leone as 'Roberti Sergio Leone'. It was and is a convention in Italy for the names of all contributing writers (from treatment to finished screenplay) to appear onscreen; hence the impression of so many cooks. *Segno* was an Italian–French–West German co-production, unlike the all-Italian *Aphrodite*. Locations were shot in Yugoslavia. The editor was Nino Baragli, later to edit all of Sergio Leone's films from *The Good, The Bad and The Ugly* onwards. The battle sequence was directed by Riccardo Freda.

Guido Brignone was another grand old man of the industry. He had been responsible for four of the original silent Macistes (at the tail-end of the cycle, in 1924–6). In the Fascist era, after making the second-ever Italian sound film, he had specialized in costume dramas and senti-

mental comedies with an opera setting. Towards the end of the shooting schedule of *Nel segno di Roma*, Brignone was taken seriously ill.
The film was completed by, of all unlikely people, Michelangelo Antonioni. He was short of cash, because of the time and money he had
spent on theatre work with Monica Vitti in the late 1950s, and so
agreed to make uncredited contributions to a couple of other people's
films, including *Segno*. Since Antonioni came from such a different
cinematic and intellectual background, a few critics have since speculated that his involvement must have been uncomfortable, to say the
least: a case of mystery and introspection meeting flamboyance and
gaudiness. Leone knew Antonioni socially, though they had no direct
contact during the shoot. All seems to have gone smoothly, though, and
to schedule: 'He finished the film . . . and was very conscientious about
it. Every day, when Antonioni had completed shooting, he'd sit by
Brignone's bedside. He'd report in detail exactly what he'd done during
the day. Then he would ask him for instructions for the sequence to be
shot the following day. This was a very Milanese attitude. Antonioni
was absolutely scrupulous about it. He did not want in any way to
betray Brignone's vision for this film. He was quite happy to implement
what the original director wished. But it has to be acknowledged that
the result was still not very impressive.'[11]

*Nel segno di Roma* (literally, *With the Blessing of Rome*) is set in
Syria in AD 217, during the reign of Emperor Aurelius, where the
defeated Roman Consul Marcus Valerius (George Marchal) has been
enslaved by Zenobia (Anita Ekberg), feisty queen-goddess of the desert stronghold of Palmyra. Valerius manages to escape from forced
labour, with help from Decurion Julian (Jacques Sernas), and gains
admittance to Zenobia's bedchamber. There, he claims to have turned
against Rome, and so begins to win her confidence. Later, he overhears
a plot to overthrow Zenobia, by her chief minister and trusted adviser
Semanzio (bulky Folco Lulli) and dark-haired temptress Erika (Chelo
Alonso), who aim to form an alliance with the Persians. He reports this
to the Queen, and becomes her right-hand man. They fall in love, but
Marcus is torn between his duty to Rome and his duty to himself.
Eventually, when the Consul Marcellus invades at the head of two
Roman legions, Marcus betrays the Syrian battle plans to him, and the
ensuing battle leads to a rout of Zenobia's forces. In a fit of pique, the
Queen hurls a javelin through the chest of her erstwhile lover. But
Marcus is possessed of 'exceptional strength: it would have been fatal

to anyone else', and recovers in time to beg for Zenobia's life before the Roman Senate. The Senate's verdict is 'LA VITA' ('Let her live'), and she retires to married bliss as a private citizen with Marcellus, whom she has forgiven. Meanwhile, benevolent rule under the blessing of Rome is re-established in Palmyra, under the more pliant Queen Bathseba.

The main interest of this stolid piece of costume drama was its introduction of Anita Ekberg to the genre, in the year before Fellini's *La dolce vita*. From her first appearance, in a gold tasselled lime-green chiffon gown with a plunging neckline, to her last, in an off-the-shoulder black evening number as she stands before the understandably impressed Roman senators, she effortlessly runs away with the show. Those garments are, she tells Marcus, 'typical Palmyrian attire'. (They were designed by Nino Vittorio Navarese, something of a specialist in Egyptian-style glitz, later the costume designer of Mankiewicz's *Cleopatra* (1963) and Stevens's *The Greatest Story Ever Told* (1965).) The art direction by Ottavio Scotti is also distinctive, in its visual contrast between a land of palm trees, pastel colours, camels and leopard-skins, and the usual well-scrubbed Rome beneath impossibly blue skies. There is plenty of action and gore: the last section of the film consists of an elaborate battle, with hundreds of extras, huge mobile wooden catapults, flaming arrows, booby traps in the sand, and Zenobia observing it all clad in a preternaturally protruding green and gilt breastplate with golden helmet. There's the obligatory orgy, where Cuban dancer Chelo Alonso (in her first peplum role after leaving the *Folies Bergère*) does a flamenco cabaret act which ends with her stroking an outsized pink marble pillar. But the plotting is very slack, and only the fast-paced editing of the battle sequence (horses' hooves; zip-pans from general skirmishes to details; an impressive array of weapons) would have provided Leone with useful experience for the future. Otherwise the film is a minor-league version of the old holiday romance between Mark Antony and Cleopatra. Age has certainly withered it, and it wasn't so very varied in the first place.

*Nel segno di Roma* was, however, one of the first pepla to be bought, distributed and exploited by drive-in specialists American-International Pictures. They retitled it *Sign of the Gladiator*, which was odd, since there were no gladiators (or even signs) to be seen. But, in a double-bill with *Goliath and the Barbarians*, it performed sufficiently well for AIP to give the same treatment to scores of others over the next seven years.

The *New York Times* called the film 'unmitigated junk'. *Variety* added that 'the deepest thing about the film is Anita Ekberg's cleavage'. Having immortalized said cleavage in *La dolce vita*, Fellini was then to turn Ekberg into a 'huge symbol of eroticism' when she stepped down from a billboard advertising the joys of drinking milk, in order to stalk the miniaturized streets of the EUR in Rome, in *The Temptation of Dr Antonio*, a segment of the four-part *Boccaccio '70* (1962). This film both satirized and celebrated the assembly-lines of Cinecittà, by showing a film crew on location for a muscleman movie: the movie is so cheap that Hercules is expected to pick up a papier mâché rock, rescue a temple virgin, and carry her (with some difficulty) to safety, on a pavement near a shopping centre.

However much they derided it in print, the peplum craze evidently fascinated the 'Northern intelligentsia' of the film world. Fellini adored Cinecittà, and the circuses that came to town on its sound stages. Pier Paolo Pasolini didn't; and in the *La Ricotta* segment of the portmanteau film *Ragopag* (1962), he cast Orson Welles as the long-suffering director of a tacky Crucifixion movie being shot near a housing estate on the outskirts of Rome. The Crucifixion sequence itself (shot in colour by Tonino Delli Colli, while the rest of the film is in monochrome) takes the form of a static devotional tableau, which eventually collapses in a fit of giggles when the actor playing Christ falls over during the Deposition. *La Ricotta* caused Pasolini to be given a prison sentence for blasphemy. Shortly after this, Jean-Luc Godard (who had no time at all for Cinecittà's circuses) had Fritz Lang directing a costly Italian–American co-production of *Odysseus* for producer Jack Palance, in *Le Mepris* (1963). Palance is constantly trying to get Fritz Lang to turn his abstract meditation on Man's Fate into an exploitation movie, complete with naked mermaids. He cites the success of '*Totò Against Hercules*' and boasts, 'Whenever I hear the word culture I reach for my cheque-book.' Godard's contempt is plainly directed at the commercialism of international spectaculars, and the shallowness of artists who 'sell out' to them. Those Hollywood veterans who took the Cinecittà dollar often had newly minted reputations as 'auteurs' to protect, and so they would publicly dismiss such productions as lucrative blips on their *curricula vitae*. On Italian prints, they shared directorial credit with an Italian counterpart. In the States, there was nowhere to hide: they were lumbered with full credit.

In 1962, Vincente Minnelli, a darling of the *Cahiers* set, made *Two*

*Weeks in Another Town,* his disillusioned companion piece to *The Bad and the Beautiful,* in which drying-out Hollywood actor Jack Andrus (Kirk Douglas) and washed-up Hollywood director Maurice Kruger (Edward G. Robinson) find themselves at Cinecittà shooting a second-rate costume drama set at the time of the Risorgimento. Andrus is given a crash course in the Roman way of making films. 'We don't use her voice, just her charms,' explains Kruger, referring to a temperamental Italian starlet who can't speak dialogue in any language. Later, Andrus is offered a Maserati and a suite at the Excelsior on expenses, and Kruger counsels, 'You've got to make these people feel you're important – otherwise they'll walk all over you.' Kruger peruses a magazine called *Now,* with a picture of the Trojan Horse on the cover, which describes him as a 'prototype of the obsolete Hollywood talent now flourishing in Rome', and Cinecittà as 'a museum of directorial clichés'. So while the Italian film factory was being rubbished on the festival circuit, it was also being patronized in Los Angeles as an elephant's graveyard for expatriate talent. The tensions between intellectuals and jobbing directors, and between Americans and Italians, were beginning to become palpable.

In 1959 Leone again assisted Mario Bonnard, and helped with the script, on *Gli ultimi giorni di Pompei/The Last Days of Pompeii.* It was an Italian–Spanish–West German co-production, largely funded by Procusa of Madrid, and underwritten by Opus Dei, a promotional wing of the Roman Catholic Church. United Artists distributed it worldwide. *Pompeii* was shot in the Andalusian countryside, with most of the interiors filmed in Madrid. The credits acknowledged 'Screenplay by Ennio de Concini, Luigi Emmanuelle, Roberti Sergio Leone, Duccio Tessari and Sergio Corbucci', and each of the contributing production companies insisted on a name above the title to represent its interests and protect its investment: Fernando Rey (who played the evil high priest of Isis, and who, according to Leone, 'came with the Spanish money'), Annemarie Baumann and the then little-known Christine Kauffman ('an amazing young German actress I found'). The story, a credit noted, was 'freely adapted from the novel by Bulwer Lytton'.

Bonnard's *Pompeii* was the eighth cinematic version of Lytton's lumbering but best-selling novel, first published in 1834 and mightily promoted by the convenient eruption of Vesuvius just before publication. Set against the background of the eruption of August AD 79, the novel told the love story of Athenian gentleman Glaucus and Greek girl

Ione, interrupted by nasty Egyptian priest Arbaces who murders Ione's brother and falsely accuses Glaucus of the crime. When the volcano finally erupts, a blind flower-girl called Nydia, infatuated with Glaucus, rescues him from being fed to the lions in the arena, takes the two lovers to a rescue ship, and then drowns herself, leaving Glaucus and Ione to sail to Athens and convert to the new faith of Christianity. Lytton's 'metaphysical novel' was an example of a widespread fascination among English painters, philosophers and writers of the early 1830s with great natural catastrophes and the moral lessons to be learned from them. There was no firm historical evidence of the existence of a Christian community in Pompeii, but this proved no impediment to Bulwer Lytton.[12]

Cinematic versions before 1959 had clung to the eruption of Vesuvius, the Christian punchline, the lions in the arena and the villainous high priest, but jettisoned much of the rest. Paolo Moffa, co-director (with Marcel l'Herbier) of the dull 1949 version, was producer of Bonnard's effort which, following *Hercules Unchained*, had the chance to breathe life into old tissue, with the added box-office advantages of Eastmancolor and a widescreen process called Supertotalscope. This was money for old chains, so to speak. Leone recalled that early script drafts were 'in old-fashioned, classical style', a rewrite of the 1949 film as put together by the prolific Ennio De Concini, contributor to several Macistes and Goliaths. Leone was impressed by his track record, but less than impressed by the way De Concini worked: 'He was far better at improvising stories live, in front of producers, than at writing them down ... One day, he announced that he had an idea for a peplum called *Jupiter*. And he sold this idea for a lot of money. He went home to begin writing down the actual script. He took a blank sheet of paper and began: Olympus. Exterior. Day. He paused. The penny dropped: Exterior? *Olympus?* It just couldn't be done. So he gave up.' Leone also considered the screenwriter to be something of an opportunist: 'De Concini had been quite happy writing Fascist songs before discovering he was a communist and a poet. Well, a part-time communist, at any rate.'[13]

About a fortnight before shooting began, Moffa triumphantly announced that Steve Reeves had signed up for the lead role of Glaucus. After back-to-back *Hercules* films, Reeves was ready for a change, and reckoned that *Pompeii* might be a step up in the world. Glaucus would now be a Roman centurion, rather than an Athenian gentleman, as befitting the Reeves persona. Lytton's novel receded even further into the distance. 'Bonnard had imagined the character as a sort of James Bond figure,' Leone was to remember. 'An intelligent, thoughtful man, who was also a man of action . . . We had to change everything at top speed for Mr Muscle Culture. Scenes in his style had somehow to be integrated into the story: a fight with a crocodile, a sequence where the column of a temple is lifted up and destroyed, etc. Lamentable! However, Steve Reeves turned out to be a gentle sort of fellow. He applied himself to flexing his muscles. He applied himself a lot less to exercising his brains. When he got on a horse one side, he fell off the other. His physique created a certain problem of balance. But he was manageable as an actor. Not at all pretentious. No real strength, though. He had to have stunt doubles for everything.'[14]

As soon as the crew arrived in Spain for the exteriors, Bonnard was taken ill with a serious liver complaint. He never enjoyed working away from his home base in Rome. So Leone found himself in charge of the production, a role he was manifestly ready for. While Bonnard convalesced, his assistant hastily assembled a team to complete the picture. First, he phoned his close friend Sergio Corbucci in Rome, and invited him to direct the action sequences. Corbucci's career was going through a lean patch, following the commercial disaster of a melodrama called *I ragazzi dei parioli*, and he was quite content to become a second-unit director again. Since Corbucci spoke good English, he would be well equipped to handle 'Mr Muscle Culture'. Leone then appointed Duccio Tessari, who had done some uncredited script work for De Concini in the past, as his own assistant. The cameraman on the second unit would be his longstanding associate Enzo Barboni; Franco Giraldi would shoot the interiors.

It was the first time in his professional life that Leone had been surrounded by a team of youngish cinéastes: ex-critics Corbucci and Giraldi were born in 1927 and 1931 respectively, Tessari in 1926. Only Barboni belonged to a network like Leone's, having been a camera operator for the Instituto Luce during the war, subsequently working in second units for Zinnemann, Walsh and Wyler. Corbucci had made a few low-budget features, Tessari had assisted Gallone and Cottafavi, but the experience of working together on *Pompeii*, and its subsequent box-office success, would launch their careers. Later in the 1960s, Leone, Corbucci, Tessari, Barboni and Giraldi would, between them, direct over thirty Italian Westerns. They were the founding fathers of the genre.

Sergio Corbucci was later to insist that *Gli ultimi giorni di Pompei* sowed the seeds from which the Western grew: 'I saw that in Spain there were these magnificent horses, these extraordinary canyons, this desert landscape which looked a lot like Mexico, or Texas, or rather, like we imagined them to be. So when we were shooting *Pompeii*, we often said to each other, "Hang on a minute, we could make an amazing Western here, couldn't we?" '[15] Moreover, Corbucci reckoned that many of the characteristics of the peplum (the stylish superhero, the desert settings, the flamboyant visual style, the ritualized duels, the ironic relationship with Hollywood) were to be carried over into Cinecittà's next great commercial cycle. But Leone, who later tended to downgrade most aspects of his involvement in the peplum craze, was not so sure: 'We really amused ourselves a lot on that film, but ... I believe the Westerns could well have happened without the mythological films. They were something different.' He could not remember the conversations with Corbucci about making 'an amazing Western', saying 'Spain was certainly beautiful; the only problem was that it was full of policemen. We did talk all day long – from morning to night – and drink sangria, which would even have loosened the tongue of one of the heroes of my Westerns! Frankly, I cannot recall anything else.'[16] Certainly, Leone had been fantasizing about making a Western since long before the peplum cycle took off; hence his discussions with Walsh and Wyler. But it is quite possible that the experience of working on *Pompeii* made the idea seem practicable for the first time. What was new was the concept of making one in 'the extraordinary canyons' of Spain, with interiors filmed in his own backyard.

*Gli ultimi giorni di Pompei* was unusual among pepla, in that it combined the exuberance of the Hercules/Maciste theme (in the person of Steve Reeves) with the story and production values of a minor Hollywood epic about Romans and Christians in the era after Nero's death. Much care was taken, by production designer Augusto Lega, to recreate the marketplace, cobbled streets and villas of the city of Pompeii, which were duly trounced in the last reel. And the American publicity stressed the spectacle of the film, rather than just the dimensions of the hero's pectorals: 'SEE the yawning jaws of the flesh-ripping alligator death pit – the martyred Christians thrown to the gaping fangs of crazed lions – the Centurion Colossus, in battle with the blood-hungry beasts – the shameless orgy as drunken Pompeii abandons itself to the Goddess Isis – the pillaging, plundering black-hooded death riders . . . THE VERY SUMMIT OF SPECTACLE.' Admittedly, viewers were required to stretch their imaginations in order to supply most of these attractions, but at least *Pompeii* made an attempt to put the co-producers' money up there onscreen; and United Artists was well pleased with the result.

*Pompeii* does indeed begin with some 'plundering black-hooded riders', as they set fire to a villa, massacre its inhabitants, and paint a Christian cross on the wall before they leave. Glaucus (Reeves) has returned from active duty as a Roman centurion, to 'home and the sea' near Pompeii in AD 79, only to find his family murdered and his villa looted – apparently by an underground sect of Christians. He rescues the Consul's daughter Ione (Christine Kauffman) when her two-horse chariot goes out of control (shades of *Ben-Hur*). In the marketplace of Pompeii, Glaucus then saves a young slave (Angel Aranda) from a brutal whipping by Roman soldiers (who shout 'Murdering Christians!' as they administer the blows). After witnessing a rather tame orgy, hosted by the High Priest (Fernando Rey), Glaucus traces the massacre to an organization based in the sacred Temple of Isis, where the priest and the Consul's Egyptian mistress Julia (Annemarie Baumann) are raising funds to finance an uprising against Rome. After the Christians, including Ione and her blind maidservant Nydia, have secretly gathered in some caves to worship, a gang of armed riders bursts in and announces that Christianity has become a capital offence. The Christians are then tortured (with whips, racks, wheels and red-hot irons), while Glaucus listens to their protestations of innocence.

Julia murders the Consul Ascanius and puts the blame on Glaucus, who has begun to thwart her plans. He falls through an elaborate trapdoor in the temple, placed in front of an effigy of the Goddess Isis, and finds himself in a waterlogged underground chamber wrestling with a crocodile (not an alligator, and there isn't any flesh-ripping either). Though he wins that fight, Glaucus is condemned to death with the Christians. As the martyrs are whipped into the arena, singing hymns, Glaucus manages to pull his chains from out of a lump of rock, strangle a hungry lion and spear two gladiators, before joining a band of bowmen as they open fire on the royal box. Just at that moment, Mount Vesuvius erupts; cue scenes of panic, looting, falling masonry, and the effigy of Isis collapsing on to Fernando Rey as he counts his gold. But

Glaucus swims through a burning harbour to rescue Ione and sail away towards the open sea.

As well as *Pompeii*'s numerous debts to previous Hollywood epics, Leone enjoyed describing the last-minute attempts to integrate Steve Reeves into the plot. As the synopsis suggests, the many exhibitions of his muscle power seem imposed on the action as afterthoughts. But his big scenes lack the *brio* of the Hercules and Maciste films which were being mass produced at the time. Only the set-piece action sequences seem well planned and stylishly directed. Of those, Leone himself was responsible only for the hooded riders and the anthology of tortures; Corbucci directed the rest. Though all concerned recalled the fun they had on the shoot, *Pompeii* is bereft of humour. The involvement of Opus Dei in the production perhaps explains the ponderousness of the scenes with the Christians: the catacombs and the condemned cells, in particular, resemble a Sunday school pageant. Nevertheless, *Pompeii* was a runaway commercial success, making 840 million lire on first release (just 70 million shy of the record established the previous year by *Hercules*). In the early 1980s it was re-released in France on video, as 'directed by Sergio Leone'; and, following Leone's death, as 'directed by Sergio Corbucci'. Now that Corbucci has died as well, perhaps video versions will revert to the original credit 'directed by Mario Bonnard'.

When asked about his involvement, Leone replied that though he had directed the main unit throughout the shoot, he in no sense identified with the finished product. It was just a job, and the film belonged to Bonnard: 'Some critics have written that my first film as a director was *Gli ultimi giorni*. But it wasn't . . . I didn't plan it or conceive it. I held it together and line-managed my two assistants Corbucci and Tessari. Besides, I was told in no uncertain terms by the producer that my name would not be appearing on the film, which would be presented as entirely Bonnard's work. This was fine by me. I was thirty years old and couldn't have cared less.'[17]

However, it was the success of *Pompeii* that gave Leone the opportunity to direct his first credited film, *Il colosso di Rodi/The Colossus of Rhodes*, and to break away from the drudgery of taking orders from veteran directors who knew his father. Despite Leone's many later attempts to distance himself from *Pompeii*, his directorial debut has much in common with it. It shares some of the same actors, such as Angel Aranda, in similar parts; the same basic scriptwriting team of Ennio De Concini plus Tessari and Leone; the same Italian and

Spanish co-production partners (Cineproduzione and Procusa, this time with French rather than West German interest as well); the same director of photography (Antonio Ballesteros), costume designer (Vittorio Rossi) and composer (the prolific Angelo Francesco Lavagnino); even a suspiciously similar story. A wandering warrior encounters an elaborate conspiracy, reluctantly joins a band of patriots, is captured by the villains and imprisoned in a giant statue (the Colossus this time, rather than the Goddess Isis), and escapes from a climactic earthquake. As Leone was to concede: 'The direct model for *Colossus* was indeed *Pompeii* . . . But the difference was that I used these "givens" as a starting point this time. Getting beyond them, I could imagine everything. I respected the structure of the genre, the better to turn it inside out.'[18] The result was to show that old habits did not die so easily. The stunt director on *Colossus* had been one of Charlton Heston's doubles in the chariot race of *Ben-Hur*.

It was Paolo Moffa, working on behalf of Procusa (Madrid), who first suggested the idea of *The Colossus of Rhodes*. He knew that Leone had proved on *Pompeii* that he was able to cope with big-budget action. Moffa showed Leone an article in an illustrated popular history magazine, *The Seven Wonders of the Ancient World*. One of these Wonders was the statue of Apollo that stood next to Rhodes harbour between 280 and 224 BC, before being destroyed in an earthquake. It could be the basis for a script, and Leone started working on the idea. He reduced the lifespan of the statue: his story begins with its unveiling in 280 BC, and ends with an earthquake a few weeks later. He added a plot about a tyrannical King of Rhodes confronting Greek freedom fighters; and turned the 110-metre Colossus (actually, it was about 30 metres high) into a secret political prison and torture chamber. He incorporated set-piece scenes in the circus arena, and on the streets of Rhodes during the earthquake. And he invented a jaded central character who is visiting the island on holiday, and becomes unwittingly involved in these complications. Leone then handed this outline over to seven other writers (including De Concini and Tessari), who made it even more complicated.

The development of the script gave Leone the opportunity to 'amuse myself with some little ideas'. The Colossus, with its metal torch, would become a symbol of tyranny, and a satirical reference to the Statue of Liberty. 'This statue didn't welcome the huddled masses,' he explained, 'it protected the most important port in the Mediterranean by showering fire and brimstone on to attackers.' The central character would be based on Cary Grant in Hitchcock's *North by Northwest*: 'a spoiled child, a little tired of it all, who finds himself involved in a series of events he doesn't understand, and has to spend all his time looking for ways to escape from everyone'. Hitchcock's celebrated Mount Rushmore sequence would be echoed in a sword-fight where the soldiers emerge from the statue's ears, and balance on its arms ('I asked the designers to think of the Colossus as if it was the faces of the presidents in Hitchcock's film'). The laid-back manner of the Greek hero on holiday would be contrasted with the seriousness and formality of members of the Rhodean court. There would be a series of sudden *coups de théâtre* (the prisoners being revealed as Phoenician invaders; the heroine becoming a betrayer in the last reel), and a lot of elaborate, bizarre tortures.

Towering over the story, and the harbour, would be the Colossus itself. Two full-sized 30-metre sections were built: feet to knees, and bust to top of head – so that the sword-fight could be filmed without trickery. Leone's original plan had been to put Mussolini's face on the Colossus, so that it 'would appear as Benito's twin brother', with his hands on his hips. Finally he contented himself with a sculpture 'in arte Dux', looking a little like one of the sixty statues of the Stadio dei Marmi (Stadium of Marble) within the Foro Mussolini by the Tiber. (The original plan for the Foro had in fact included a 100-metre statue 'representing Mussolini as the new Colossus of Rhodes', which would have competed with St Peter's for dominance of the skyline of Rome. In the event it was relocated from the Monte Mario to a less prominent site.) Leone's Colossus was 'in the style of' (as the director put it), rather than an explicit reference. Mount Rushmore and the Foro Mussolini were not, in his view, a million miles apart.[19]

While this huge prop was being built, and just before the Spanish part of the shoot was to begin, Paolo Moffa's associate had a meeting with Leone to check up on how the budget was faring. Clearly, in all the excitement, Moffa had omitted to tell his associate about that article on *The Seven Wonders of the Ancient World*. 'He rubbed his hands together with glee as he said, "Tell me, Leone, who is going to do the Colossus?" I was somewhat surprised at this question. But I replied, "The architect, of course." His eyes opened wide. "Which architect?" Not to be thrown by this, I explained, "The architect who constructed the statue." The other man was getting more and more anxious. "But

... which statue?" I explained again, "The Colossus of Rhodes. It was a statue." At which point he panicked. *"What do you mean, a statue? Isn't the Colossus a mighty man, with huge muscles? Like Hercules?"* I repeated calmly, "No, it was, and is, a statue." Then he began to shout: "I am ruined. RUINED. To put so much money into a film which is just about a statue! You are all mad, you people. We could have Steve Reeves and you are talking *statues*!" He choked. He was passing out. I tried to reassure him. I proposed to him: "You can have action sequences without the hero being Samson or Maciste." Nothing doing. His despair only got worse as I spoke. "Would you like the Colossus to walk on the water and over the harbour? And to crush people under its feet?" A dim light began to shine in his eyes. He sighed with relief and said, "You're a GENIUS. We are saved!" After that conversation, they gave me *carte blanche*.'[20]

Although Leone now had a substantial budget, a spectacular location (the Spanish port of Laredo, in the Bay of Biscay), and *carte blanche*, he was expected to co-ordinate the production in double-quick time. 'With two months' extra preparation,' he would lament, 'I could have made a much more personal film.' Worse, in this his long-deferred directorial début, he seems to have had some difficulty in establishing his authority. Pre-production, although rushed, at least gave him the impression that he was on top of the project. He was working with trusted colleagues (such as assistant director Michele Lupo, from *Nel segno di Roma*), and many of the technical people from *Pompeii*. He originally intended to shoot the film in sequence, 'without stopping, day after day on the set'. But circumstances then intruded, firstly due to the logistical problems of working in Spain, which Leone should have known well from the *Pompeii* experience – but as employee rather than employer: 'It really is the worst place in the world to work. They keep saying, "Tomorrow – we'll see about it tomorrow." And then nothing happens. Yes, the Colossus was built. But not the sets. I had to film all the panoramic shots from one side only. Then I had to wait several weeks to film the other side ... The shooting schedule had to go completely haywire and I was forced to improvise as I went along. All my careful advance preparation counted for nothing.' Secondly, Leone came face-to-face with his leading man, and was thoroughly rattled by the experience.

The producers had signed John Derek to play Dario, and were delighted to have secured the man who had played the swashbuckling stonecutter Joshua in Cecil B. de Mille's *The Ten Commandments* five years previously. True, he had been listed seventh in the cast list, and hadn't done much of note since, but in peplum terms his casting was something of a coup. The problem facing Leone, though, was that Derek was now in the process of transforming himself into an actor-director. From the moment Derek arrived in Madrid, Leone managed to convince himself that the leading man was after his job. As usual, he hid his own insecurities behind a show of bravado. 'I know', he later admitted, 'that this shouldn't have concerned me – because I'd prepared things in advance so that if I was replaced, everything would have to be reshot. But it *did* concern me . . . I brought the crew together to organize some rehearsals with the master at arms. Derek did not want to demean himself by taking part in these rehearsals. He said that he'd been a stuntman, that he was in peak condition. I insisted, diplomatically, that I'd love to see how the scene played with him in it. He interrupted me, saying, "I much prefer to improvise as we go along." Patiently, I played modest, "I am incapable", I said "of inventing a battle scene without preparing things down to the most minute detail. It gives me the chance to think precisely about camera positions." He gave way and promised to go to the rehearsal.'

Leone continued, 'A few hours later, I happened to be passing the studio. And I saw Derek in the shade of the set. He was framing with his fingers as if they were a viewfinder, calculating the movement of the camera between two columns. I crept up behind him and took hold of his fingers, turned them towards his eyes and snapped, "You're supposed to be in front of the camera, not behind it." He made light of the incident, told me he was simply testing to see if the camera could pass between two columns. In his opinion, there wasn't enough room. My reply to him took the form of simply moving a column – with the reminder that this was a set, so such things were possible. I added that the question of "who was director" wasn't within his remit. It was *my* way of earning a living, not his. He smiled, and affirmed that of course he had complete confidence in me. But the problems were by no means over.'[21] Leone was still bitter about this incident in the 1970s and 1980s.

The next crisis came during rehearsals of the battle scene. John Derek was, apparently, 'waving his sword around all over the place' and making fun of the hapless master at arms, who lodged an official complaint with his director: 'I called the superstar over to me and said "You have just made the man whose job it is to help you rehearse look ridiculous. But in fact you are making *me* look ridiculous. If you don't like the man who is rehearsing you, you come and tell *me* and demonstrate to me that he is incompetent. Right? But you have no grounds to complain that he is incompetent. It is about time you understood a few things around here. *I* am the director. If I say I want you with a beard, you put one on. If I change my mind five minutes later, and say you should be clean-shaven, you take off the beard. If I think you look better with half a beard, you put on half a beard. If I think about it for an hour and decide after all that you should have a full beard, you put it back on. You DO IT. And I am in a position to make you put on and take off that beard all day if I feel like it. I make the decisions. Savvy? Right now, you tell me you are one of the greatest actors in the world. In which case you need to find the greatest director in the world, which isn't me, I can assure you. I'm going to send a message to MGM and Procusa – the message being that, in my opinion, you have screwed things up. If you are still here tomorrow, then I'm off." And I phoned the production office to give them until the following day to replace John Derek. If not, I would catch the 12.30 plane for Rome. I hung up and went back to the hotel.'

Despite a last-minute attempt by the then Mrs Derek (Ursula Andress) to intercede, Leone stuck to his guns. And the man who had worked with Cecil B. de Mille was fired from *The Colossus of Rhodes*. By 11.30 the following day he had been replaced by Rory Calhoun, who happened to be in Rome and was ready, willing and able. He arrived on the set while Leone was rehearsing a scene with Lea Massari, playing Diala, the heroine who turns out to be a villainess. Leone later recalled: 'As he didn't know who I was, he began by embracing everyone – thinking they were me. Finally, when he discovered where I was, he fell into a swimming pool which was between us. Then he burst out laughing. From then on, everything went marvellously. In addition to which, he was more suited to the character than John Derek had been. Rory Calhoun was a sort of proletarian Cary Grant. And that was just fine.'[22]

In the script, Dario is constantly bemused by the fact that he is involved in a series of complicated plot developments which he doesn't understand. At fraught moments, he is prone to utter the classic line from countless Westerns, 'I'm a stranger here myself.' Calhoun seems to have understood the comic potential of these from the outset. He and

Leone decided to contrast Calhoun's languid performance (a fixed grin, and slightly sozzled expression throughout) with the serious histrionics of the other principals: especially Georges Marchal as Peliocles, the intense leader of the rebels, and the volcanic Roberto Camardiel as Serse, sporting an outrageous curly red wig and beard. Dario arrives in Rhodes on vacation, gets involved despite himself in various political machinations, dresses 'Greek' (as distinct from the fussy Rhodeans), and tries to keep at arm's length from any emotional entanglement. 'I command you', says Diala, 'to say something beautiful'; to which he replies, 'Being so close to you I've lost my voice.' Thus, almost by accident, Leone stumbled on the central character, and the contrasting performance styles, of his Westerns. As he later remembered, 'This contrast added to the ironic edge of the film, and Calhoun brought a lot to it; he had that tired nonchalance which I was to find in Clint Eastwood as well.' But Dario doesn't work for money and he wears a short tunic rather than a Greco-Indian poncho. And his curtain line ('Yes, there's a lot of work to be done here') implies that he will settle down; almost as if the Man with No Name had decided to stay on and rebuild the community of San Miguel.

In retrospect, there's no doubt that the film contains some distinctively Leonian 'little ideas'. At times the director's bizarre sense of humour struggles through the generally ponderous proceedings. An elderly patrician wears earplugs in bed, to shut out the noise of a storm; so he doesn't hear a fistfight which is going on in the very next room, involving pots, pans and sculptures smashing against his wall. He only wakes up when one of the freedom-fighters pushes him into a gong by mistake. The same patrician says to Dario, 'At your age, you only suffer for women. At mine, you only suffer because women don't make you suffer any more.' Serse shouts, 'Let's have some *life* around here', just before he gets an arrow in his chest. There's an emphasis – unusual even for a peplum – on elaborate tortures. The freedom-fighters have acid poured over them through holes in the ceiling of the torture chamber, and their leader Thar has a large metal bell placed over his head, which is then struck several times by a leering torturer. During the arena sequence (which takes place at night, by torchlight), a slave is strung up above a pit full of hungry lions, while a warrior shoots arrows at the ropes which hold him there – just as Blondie would later shoot at the rope which hangs Tuco by the neck, in *The Good, The Bad and The Ugly*.

The film is full of *trompe l'oeil* effects: such as when Rory Calhoun takes an evening stroll along the deserted jetty, while a whole shipload of freedom-fighters tries to land just beneath his sight-line. Or when the slave-girl Norte suddenly comes across a dead horse in the stone desert, and discovers that Thar's followers have been massacred. There are surprising visual moments, too, such as when the Colossus's head opens up, and boiling lead pours out of it; or when – this the most effective sequence – five soldiers crawl out of the Giant's ear, to chase Dario along its shoulder and arm only to be driven into the sea by the Athenian's swordsmanship; or when the gigantic work of art turns out to be a political prison. It was these moments which Leone himself was to recall with the most affection: 'It was the first film in which "playing with appearances" became important in my work. An approach which favours irony. I wouldn't have made the film at all if I hadn't had at least some chance to practise this kind of game. I enjoy juggling with illusion and *trompe l'oeil* – it's no coincidence that I love the paintings of René Magritte, and loved them at the time as well.'[23]

But such 'little ideas' never amounted to the 'auto-da-fé of the genre' which Leone subsequently claimed to be attempting. The spectacular set-pieces and the many contrived ironic reversals in the plot seem predictable and mechanical – almost as if Leone was overly concerned with 'respecting the public who enjoyed these films'. There's no attempt to create a credible or involving relationship between any of the characters. We don't care enough about the victims of these various disasters because we don't know enough about them. The dialogue is full of cod solemnities ('Let us hope that all Olympus will be on your side'). The Supertotalscope visuals (again using an anamorphic lens, with a 2.35:1 aspect ratio, as developed by the ATC laboratory in Rome) are far more sophisticated than the verbals. Not surprisingly, the Italian critics spent most of their column inches praising the pretty location, the energy and drive of the piece, its sense of scale and weight, and Leone's visual imagination. But at 142 minutes (127 in Britain, 128 in the USA) most of them agreed it needed more than a few 'little ideas' to keep at bay the audience's sense of déjà vu. Nevertheless, *The Colossus of Rhodes* was a giant success at the home box office: 657 million lire, not in the *Hercules* league, but ahead of the Macistes, Samsons and Goliaths. Over the next few years, the inevitable spinoffs would appear – from *Colossus of the Stone Age* (1962) to *Colossus of Rome* (1965): in both of these the Colossus did, indeed, become 'a mighty man with huge muscles'. Sergio

Leone's verdict on the film, in retrospect, was: 'It's not bad – in particular, all the kitsch aspects of the design and the costumes, which added to the parody of the peplum. The accumulation of such bad taste enhanced its fascination: a film made of stucco and fake jewellery.'

Leone tended to treat the film, like all his pre-*Fistful* work, as a potboiler. He would claim to have made it 'for bread and butter, to pay for my honeymoon in Spain'. It certainly generated a rash of work offers: 'I was obliged to turn down about six "Macistes" a day. When they offered me two of these films, I had only 200,000 lire in my current account. I put off signing the contract until the next day. Carla, my new wife, said to me: "If you really don't feel like doing them you should refuse. Something else is bound to turn up." What turned up was a film script.'[24.]

So it was that Leone next contributed, with six others, to the screenplay of *Le sette sfide* (abroad, known variously as *The Seven Challenges*, *The Seven Revenges*, even – in France – as *Ivan the Conqueror*). The film was directed by Primo Zeglio, and released in 1961. Leone had worked with Zeglio a couple of years before, as an assistant on *Il figlio del Corsaro Rosso/Son of the Red Corsair*, inspired by yet another Emilio Salgari novel. An Italian–Yugoslavian co-production, with location shooting near Zagreb, *The Seven Challenges* begins with the Great Khan attempting to end tribal warfare by forcing chieftains to settle their accounts through individual hand-to-hand duels. Ivan (Ed Fury) duly fights six duels with his enemy Amok, but is tricked into defeat on the seventh. He retires hurt, but resolves to get his own back on Amok, who in the meantime has murdered his beloved Tamara (Elaine Stewart). In the final marathon challenge Ivan and Amok both die, and Ivan's brother Kir takes over the leadership of his tribe. The *Rivista del Cinematografo* reckoned that 'the best part is the first, dedicated entirely to a series of duels: interesting, violent and ingenious; the second part belongs more to the world of serial novels, constructed as it is around the usual vendetta'. The setting of the film, the era of Genghis Khan, was to become popular during the final phase of the peplum boom, partly because Yugoslavian locations seemed to provide credible backgrounds for the Mongol hordes. Zeglio's film made 419.6 million lire at the box office.

Then Leone conceived the idea for another peplum, this time to be set around 763–753 BC, the era when, according to folklore, Romulus founded the city of Rome. Surprisingly, no one had thought of this before; even though the story of Romulus and Remus provided an excellent opportunity to cast two bodybuilders as the twin brothers and rivals, and the setting (wood, leather and forests) offered a welcome respite from stone columns, togas and market squares. Leone quickly registered the title *Romulus and Remus* (in America *Duel of the Titans*) and worked up a detailed treatment. The opening and closing sequences were to have virtually no dialogue – just music, natural sounds and images to evoke the legend.

The opening shows a woman in a green cloak, placing two screaming babies on a little wooden raft, folding two medallions into their swaddling clothes, and watching them float down the Tiber. Horsemen arrive and surround the woman, as the babies disappear from view. The raft becomes stuck in some reeds, and a she-wolf hears the babies' howls of terror. The wolf turns the raft on its side and sniffs it. Dissolve. A shepherd minding his flock with his dog sees a wolf on the horizon, and shoots an arrow, striking the animal in the side. This shepherd finds the two babies in a cave, surrounded by wolf-cubs, their cries mingling with the cubs' growls. He carries them out. The wounded she-wolf looks on, panting.

The closing sequence has Romulus making a single long furrow in a fertile valley, with two oxen and a plough. Soldiers and pilgrims stand around him, in a large circle, and watch. 'In the name of the immortal gods,' cries Romulus, 'I proclaim myself king of this city.' As the pilgrims step forward to acknowledge Romulus, a lone horseman appears on the distant hillside. He rides across the valley and directs his horse to trample through the furrow. As his horse wheels round, Romulus says, 'It's you who wanted this, Remus,' and they begin a hand-to-hand duel before the circle of onlookers. There are various shots of the duel, through different points of the circle, accompanied by drumbeats. First fists are used, then stones, then the horns of the oxen, then short swords. In the end Romulus reluctantly stabs Remus, and a helicopter shot shows (successively) Remus' corpse lying across the furrow, Romulus standing over him, the circle of pilgrims and soldiers, the furrow bisecting the valley, and, at the edge of the valley, a semicircle of mounted Sabine troops. As these troops advance, the inner circle gathers around Romulus, who looks up to the sky. The music (now orchestral) builds to a crescendo. 'This', intones the voice-over, 'is the end of the legend, and the beginning of the story of the greatest city in the world, the eternal city – ROME!'

Between these two highly rhetorical sequences, the story of *Romulus and Remus* was fleshed out with a subplot involving the King of the Sabines, his warriors and his beautiful daughter Julia (the fair lady, contrasted with the dark lady Tarpeia). Rivalry develops between peace-loving Romulus and macho Remus; Romulus is tortured, tied to a revolving wheel and flogged, then goaded into an arena with a hungry bear. A wagon train of pioneers sets off towards a mythical 'city beyond the mountain of fire, in the valley of the seven hills', only to be harried by Sabine cavalry (Indian-style) before splitting into two parties (*Covered Wagon*-style). One of these, under Romulus, takes the forest route, while the other, under Remus, tries to cross the mountain of fire but is smothered for its pains in molten red lava. There is a battle with the Sabines at a bridgehead across a ravine. The valley is discovered and Rome founded.

Leone had a hand in the script, which was developed by the *Pompeii* team of Ennio de Concini, Duccio Tessari and Sergio Corbucci, plus Luciano Martino (from *Colossus*) and Franco Rossetti. Enzo Barboni was signed on as principal director of photography, Franco Giraldi as director of the second unit. The stunt director was Benito Stefanelli. The cast was a strong one, with Steve Reeves and Gordon Scott (the peplum's best known musclemen, in their only film together) as the two brothers, Massimo Girotti as the King of the Sabines, Jacques Sernas as the slippery henchman Cursius, and Virna Lisi as Julia, who bathes beneath a sylvan waterfall in a mini-peplum. Only the dancing girls were conspicuous by their absence: since Rome had yet to be founded, evidently they were waiting in the wings. But the prospect of directing *Romulus and Remus* did not appeal to Leone: 'Since Corbucci had backed me up so effectively on *Pompeii*, I asked him to do it in my place. It was my gift to him. From then on, his second career as a director really took off.' Leone's 'original story' credit wasn't an empty one, though. For *Romulus and Remus* turned out to be one of the most effective contributions to the entire cycle, making 712 million lire. As Derek Elley notes in his study *The Epic Film*, the screenplay 'imaginatively retains the story's legendary character ... Visually the film is careful in early Roman period detail.'[25] The design was by a young architect, Giancarlo Simi.

Leone was by now thirty-one years old, an experienced assistant director who had directed two major films (one credited, one not) and a short. He had proved himself repeatedly as a dependable and obedient second-in-command who could, when the need arose, deliver projects of his own, on time and on budget. According to Sergio Donati, Leone was, 'at this time, highly rated in the Italian business for his qualities as a technician'. Luciano Vincenzoni adds, 'he was an obstinate young man . . .'[26] Leone had also contributed to, or originated, several scripts. So it is surprising that he should resist all offers of directing assignments, and continue working on scripts that happened to 'turn up'. He had been an aggressive assistant director, and the John Derek incident showed that he could display a fierce temper when cornered. He liked to show off his knowledge of films to Italian colleagues. Maybe he felt ill at ease working on pepla. Maybe he was not settled in his mind about the direction his career should take. He certainly found it difficult to cut the umbilical cord. Whenever he was out on his own, and in a position where the buck stopped with him, he seems to have wanted to return to the arms of his extended family.

Just before commencing *The Colossus of Rhodes*, Leone married Carla Ranalli. He had first met her over ten years earlier, when he was nineteen years old and she was a teenager small for her age: 'She was sixteen at the time, but looked no more than twelve. One of my childhood pals was going out with her then. I told him that there must be something wrong with him, to want to court such a tiny little girl. He argued that she wasn't that small. And in any case, she had successfully resisted all his advances. And I lost track of this Carla for the next ten or eleven years. Then, one evening, I was on my way to some function or other with a blonde starlet on my arm . . . A car came to pick us up at Cinecittà. The driver of the car happened to be none other than Carla. I didn't recognize her. But she remembered me, and what's more reminded me of our meetings all those years before. I was amazed. So I abandoned the pretty blonde, and spent the whole evening reminiscing with her. Not that I knew it yet, but the story of our life together had begun. And when I told my childhood friend that I was going to marry Carla, he was thoroughly gobsmacked.'[27]

Carla herself remembers their first acquaintance well: 'I must admit I didn't like him, because he was "playing cool" all the time. Wearing the latest line in brightly coloured shirts and posing. He was beginning to work in the film business, and kept on reminding everyone of the fact. I didn't like the film business any more than I liked his image. I was training as a dancer, in classical ballet. Then we met again at a party, at a friend's house. I had to drive around and collect everyone in my car, and take them to the party. And I picked Sergio up outside one of the big newsstands on the Via Veneto. Everyone got into the back of the car, but he sat on the front seat beside me. After a little while, I said, "I'm sure I know you – haven't we met somewhere before?" He stared out of the windscreen, and didn't turn towards me . . . I said, "I seem to remember that you are an assistant director. Is that what you still do?" He kept on staring in front of him, without looking at me, and I kept on talking and talking and asking questions . . . Then eventually I said, "I think your name is Sergio." And he turned to me, and began to show some interest. He had come to the party with a stunningly beautiful starlet who was at least twice my size – in every way. But we spent the whole evening together, chatting away on a sofa. He was full of self-deprecating humour, and irony, jokes against himself – and I loved this a lot. The first thing we had in common was this sense of humour and quizzical attitude to life. A sense of the ridiculous. He was *molto simpatico*. A great storyteller. And he had a lot of stories to tell.'[28]

While they were going out together, Sergio went to see Carla's performances in the classical ballet repertoire on stage in Rome. Given his outspoken views on the subject of opera and ballet, this had to be a sign that things were getting serious. Carla recalls: 'He had a wonderful ear for sounds. Not a musical ear – he always sang out of tune. But he was hyper-sensitive to everyday sounds. He didn't have much time for the classical repertoire and its conventions, though. After we met again, he would come and see me perform at the Rome Opera. But then he'd make it clear, "Let me know when your entrances and exits are, so I don't have to hang around for the rest!"'[29] In fact, Carla Ranalli's name is to be found on the credits of *The Colossus of Rhodes* as choreographer of the various dances that entertain the Rhodean nobility. 'My training came in useful there,' she says. But, according to Sergio, the 'misfortune' of her height had meant that her career on the stage would never progress very far: 'At that time, to become a star of the classical ballet, you just *had* to have the height of a model.'

Between first meeting Carla and the beginning of their 'life together' in 1959–60, Sergio had gone out (for several years, 'off and on') with a woman chosen as 'Miss Somalia' in the early 1950s: the daughter of an Italian father and a Zanzibarian mother. At first, he enjoyed the spectacle of young Romans wolf-whistling as the couple walked by in the streets, or on the beach. But finally, it began to get on his nerves. He had also dated assorted starlets and film people, usually as escorts to film evenings or dinners, but none of these relationships was serious. The family archive includes various photographs of Leone dancing with pretty actresses in Roman night-spots. After he and Carla met again, they decided quite soon to settle down permanently together. But, as in most aspects of Leone's life, it was important to him that his father granted his approval. Vincenzo hadn't approved of his choice of career, but perhaps things would go better this time. Vincenzo was by now a very sick man, in the last year of his life. Carla never did get to meet him, but she remembers that, 'shortly after Sergio and I met again, he went to visit his father in the South of Italy, near Naples, a place called Torella dei Lombardi in the Avellino district. When he got there, Sergio nervously showed his father a photograph of me, and said, "I met this girl and I like her very much." Vincenzo replied, "Yes, she's got an intelligent look about her. I agree with you!"'[30] He may have been relieved that his son was at last showing signs of making up his own mind.

Shortly after they were married, Carla joined her new husband on location at the Bay of Biscay for the shooting of *Colossus*. They then set up home together in the Via Gaetano Capocci in Rome, before moving, about seven months later, to the Viale Jonio, where they stayed for the next five years. Since Sergio had been living in Mario Bonnard's house ever since his father retired to Avellino in 1949, this was, in a sense, the first time he had definitively left the parental home. And it happened just at the time he emerged professionally from under Bonnard's wing as well. His domestic life was now his own, and he had made his directorial début proper. On 26 November 1961 Sergio's and Carla's first daughter, Raffaella, was born. Marriage to Carla introduced Sergio to her brother-in-law Fulvio Morsella, who would later become his business adviser and producer. Morsella had lived in America for several years, and was a translator of technical books as well as a professional interpreter. From now on, he would be Sergio's 'English voice'. Morsella's first impression of Sergio Leone was that 'his particular gift was to make things seem spectacular, in every aspect of his life. He was – I don't know whether the word is acceptable in English – but he was a "spectacularizer", in his films, and at home.'[31]

But in 1961, Sergio took a surprising career step backwards, by agreeing once again to become a second-unit director. The film was *Sodom and Gomorrah*; the great attraction this time was that he would be working with Robert Aldrich. 'Aldrich adored *The Colossus of*

*Rhodes*,' Leone recalled, 'and so he asked me to direct the second unit and all the battle sequences.' These were to be shot in Ouav Zazate and Marrakech, Morocco, the main unit being based at Titanus Studios in Rome. Here was a chance to work with the man who had made the great 'double-cross' Western, *Vera Cruz*, the freewheeling, picaresque cactus-and-crucifixes adventure which, according to François Truffaut, had introduced irony into the genre. More recently, Aldrich had made *The Last Sunset*, featuring one of the great 'settling of accounts' sequences, in its final duel between tortured, black-clad Kirk Douglas and angry nice guy Rock Hudson. Leone had also admired Aldrich's films of the mid-1950s: *Kiss Me Deadly*, *The Big Knife* and *Attack!*[32]

Goffredo Lombardo, of Titanus Productions (Rome), had been trying to get *Sodom and Gomorrah* off the ground for years. First with Robert Siodmak, then with Carlo Bragaglia, who had several pepla to his name. More recently, Lombardo started negotiations in Hollywood with Joseph E. Levine, who had made a fortune by bringing *Hercules* to the USA. Levine was so struck by the title alone that, on the spot, he had raised 80 per cent of the first million dollars required by Titanus to get the production moving. He also upped the ante by suggesting Stewart Granger and Pier Angeli for the leads, and decreeing that Bragaglia be ditched. Thus was Robert Aldrich summoned to Italy, but his initial meeting with the scriptwriters went badly, as script doctor Alessandro Continenza recalled: 'He said that the proverbial affluence, the glittering majesty of Sodom, was probably subjective and not objective – because to the Jews, a poor, nomadic pastoral people, anything that contrasted with their poverty *seemed* like affluence. So I said, "Okay, fine. But what's the point you are making? We're not talking *neo-realism* here are we?" In any case, I'd already read this idea over and over again in about twenty of the thirty scripts I'd waded through, so I added, "the film is scheduled to begin shooting soon, so you'd better decide what you want to do".' In the end, the screenplay was signed by Giorgio Prosperi, who had a contract with Lombardo.[33]

Aldrich then contacted Sergio Leone, for two reasons. First, he wanted Leone to take charge of the second unit: an assignment which already threatened to be both complex and costly. Second, he wanted Leone to agree to accept a credit as 'co-director' and 'collaborator'. The latter request came about because of a technicality in the Italian state-subsidy system under which the film was to be made. If Italian counterparts were employed, in name if not in fact, for important production jobs, then *Sodom and Gomorrah* would be eligible for a substantial Italian government grant. So Leone was to be 'director of the Italian version', and on the original Italian posters the credits read 'Una film di Robert Aldrich. Regia di Sergio Leone'. In fact, Leone worked on the film for a grand total of eight weeks as second-unit director: two weeks to shoot the battle sequence that concludes Part One of the film, the rest 'waiting around with a thousand riders and a crew of seventy people for the costumes and the weapons to arrive'.

Sadly, as had happened so often in the past, the experience of working with one of his great cinematic heroes turned out to be something of a let-down for Leone: 'From the moment we met, the scales fell from my eyes. He stated that he was going to make *La dolce vita* – an ancient version. Alas! This idea reached the extent of its audacity when the brother of the Queen sucked his sister's finger. For Aldrich, apparently, this was the epitome of perversion. From the start, we were positively swimming in lunacy. The head of the Italian production side was a man called Borgogni. He was an elder statesman in the industry and a man of great culture. After reading the final script, he rushed round to Aldrich, who asked him his opinion. Borgogni replied, "I think a small error has crept into the film's basic concept. Signor Aldrich, Sodom and Gomorrah were in fact two separate cities. Not one city with a double-barrelled name. But in your shooting script, Sodom and Gomorrah have become one and the same city." Apoplectic with rage, Aldrich made him leave the room.'[34]

In the finished film, we are clearly supposed to imagine that all sorts of erotic excitements go on at the Sodomite court, to judge by Queen Bera's (Anouk Aimée's) suggestive glances offscreen at her favoured handmaidens, and the faint suggestion of incest in her relationship with brother Astaroth (Stanley Baker). As Aldrich later confessed, 'You expect just by the nature of a picture about Sodom and Gomorrah to have some oblique, you hope tasteful, references to deviant moral behaviour . . . but if someone then says, "Where is the sin of Sodom?" and there isn't any, they have a right to complain.' And that is precisely what most of the critics did when the film opened. *Time* magazine opined that '*Sodom and Gomorrah* is the first motion picture that ever tried to tell the story of sodomy to kiddies'. There was nothing to justify the mushroom cloud with which Aldrich insisted on destroying the twin cities of the plain at the end. Just the usual peplum tortures, but on a bigger budget.[35]

Leone was responsible for filming the large-scale sequences which involved the charging cavalry of the fierce and nomadic Helamite tribe. In the story, the Helamites under their chieftain Segur (Daniele Vargas) are plotting with Astaroth to overthrow Queen Bera and take control of Sodom-and-Gomorrah. The Hebrews, who have agreed to rent the Valley of the Jordan from Bera for seven years, and thus provide a buffer against the Helamites, eventually find themselves in the front line of this conflict. Following the immortal opening line of the film, spoken by the Helamite chieftain ('Be careful of Sodomite patrols'), the black-clad horsemen appear in three separate sequences, all of them shot by Leone. In the first, the Helamite cavalry lays on an elaborate 'display of our marching and horsemanship' for the benefit of Astaroth. In the second, the cavalry thunders towards the camera, graphically illustrating the chieftain's boast, 'Do you see any lack of spirit there?'

In the third, by far the most exciting and visually ambitious sequence in the entire film, the Helamite cavalry attacks the Hebrews in the Valley of the Jordan. This sequence, filmed to a storyboard drawn for art director Ken Adam, begins with the Helamites being sighted in the distance during a Hebrew wedding ceremony. The Hebrews retreat to their prearranged positions around the dam which they have built to irrigate the valley. The Helamites, led by their chieftain in his war chariot, spears at the ready, ride in formation into the Hebrew camp, to find it deserted. The frustrated chieftain issues the order – 'No prisoners will be taken. The word of the day is KILL' – and leads his men full pelt across the valley, straight into the Hebrew trap. A wall of flame, across the entrance to a canyon, boxes in the cavalry. Lot (Stewart Granger) orders his sons to break open the dam at the head of the canyon. The Helamite troops retreat in disarray; most of them, including the chieftain, are drowned, concussed with stones fired from sling shots or hit with arrows which whizz into the air, *à la Henry V*. The opening of the dam has revealed huge deposits of salt, which give the Hebrews just the economic advantage they have been waiting for. 'Open up shops,' exhorts Stewart Granger. 'Give honest weights, fair measures. The Sodomite tyranny is ended. SALT!' End of Part One.

Many critics praised the charge of the Helamites, which does appear to have included a cast of at least a thousand, and combines helicopter shots, a specially dug runway, a camera-car in the thick of the action (tyre tracks are clearly visible), and close-ups of hooves, faces, spears, all edited in accelerating rhythm, until the charge comes to a dead halt when flames stretch out across the desert. The sequence seemed to be self-contained and dispensable, and it didn't take the story anywhere: but it was at least dynamic and spectacular. And, according to Leone, 'Those action sequences certainly gave me a few ideas – the bare bones – for the bigger scenes in my later films.'[36]

Leone's unit was based fifty kilometres south of Marrakech on locations approved by Aldrich, because they gave the twin cities and surroundings a certain lived-in quality. Quite apart from the physical difficulties of working in daytime temperatures of over 110 degrees (freezing at night), these locations created huge communications problems for the producer, as well as putting constant strain on the budget. Alessandro Continenza recalls that 'this big American film-maker had a private aeroplane to visit Morocco, and every two or three days he was coming to see the material that had been shot – backwards and forwards, Rome to Morocco, as if he was looking after his private vegetable garden'.[37] Once, Aldrich would claim, the director dropped in unannounced on Leone, and discovered the Italian wasn't doing his job 'quite the way I had envisaged': 'I was greeted with the sight of five to six thousand people, all of whom were taking a three-hour lunch break. I waited for three hours at the top of a sand dune; nothing happened. Then *another* three hours: still nothing. I called him over and said, "Get your air-ticket and go back home, you're through." '[38] Of course, Sergio Leone enjoyed tucking into a good lunch, but he had already evolved a work pattern of getting up at dawn, stopping at siesta time, then resuming. Whatever the truth of the matter, Leone hotly disputed Aldrich's version of events: 'I worked on that film for eight weeks. Robert Aldrich didn't understand why I quit. *He wanted me to stay on.* With nothing to do except collect my salary and so contribute to the financial ruin of the producers. Me? I was too fed up with everything about the project to stay on . . . there was no question of continuing to associate myself with such a disaster.'[39]

It is difficult now to disentangle what actually happened amid all the bad feeling and mutual recriminations. The budget soared from $2 million to a staggering (at the time) $5 million. Lombardo fell out with Aldrich, who in turn fell out with Joseph E. Levine, who never involved himself personally in a peplum again. 'The Italians', said Aldrich, 'were ready to kill all of us.' Goffredo Lombardo felt that Aldrich was out of control, 'making more and more exorbitant requests', and that he forced the financiers to throw good money after bad. For the cavalry-charge sequence, the director apparently ordered a thousand riders from Morocco, and 'brought them all to the desert; to the point where you couldn't see a thing because the horses' hooves churned up the sand and created a staggering amount of dust'. Aldrich's solution was to stop shooting and demand 'barrel after barrel of water, in the desert, to make the sand wet and stop the dust from rising! Naturally, this water, after half an hour under the blazing sun, fifty centigrade, quickly dried out. So at this point we had to call in special technicians, who solved the problem with a mixture of petrol and water – which fortunately stayed put for four or five hours. This little episode cost the film five hundred million lire more. And there was more, much more, of the same.'[40]

Such extravagance ensured that *Sodom*, though a moderate success in Europe, could not possibly recoup its costs. But since Leone was supposed to be responsible for the cavalry charge, as director of the second unit, the question remains: was it Aldrich's fault or Leone's that the sequence went so wildly over budget? Leone, for his part, was in no doubt about who was the villain of the piece: 'Aldrich's aim was to gain complete control of all aspects of the production of the film. He even tried to enlist my support in his plot to get rid of Lombardo. Since I wasn't prepared to play ball, and Lombardo resisted as well, Aldrich decided that the next best thing was to ruin Lombardo. So he did everything he possibly could to demolish him, financially. To give an example: after I left, he hired an American director whose sole job it was to film inserts which showed in detail the wounds sustained in the battles. That's all he had to do. This man stayed for six months to work his contract. And he was paid at the top rate ... While I was still working on the film, I'd written a letter to Lombardo asking him to come to the location and help out on the spot. See things for himself.' What the letter actually said was: 'Instead of fishing in the South Seas, could you come back at once with a machine gun? And when you land at Marrakech, don't worry too much, but just shoot. Whoever you manage to hit will be one of the guilty ones, since this is a criminal organization: they're *murdering* you over here.'[41]

The longer-term legacy of the whole debacle was to confirm certain sections of the Italian film community in their deep cynicism about mercenary American film-makers abroad. As Lombardo put it at the time: 'They treated us with a certain disdain, as if we were underdogs, from a lower caste. When Italian film culture started to show signs of life, they did all they could to kill it stone dead – and I have to say they are succeeding.'[42] Maybe Lombardo was biased. After all, the *Sodom and Gomorrah* fiasco, together with the equally disastrous international reception of Visconti's *The Leopard*, had driven his company Titanus into the ground. The major banks had stopped lending money to film clients, who had seemed gilt-edged during the *Hercules* boom. 'Economic conditions', Leone remembered, 'made it virtually impossible to shoot a film in Italy.' The sound stages at Cinecittà, he added, were like deserts, surrounded by unemployed technicians and extras. Meanwhile, Robert Aldrich found himself fighting in the Italian courts over whether he or Lombardo had the right to decide how long the final cut of *Sodom and Gomorrah* should be. His original version ran for over four hours. Leone, for his part, reckoned that at any length the film was still a piece of garbage. What mattered to him most in the summer of 1962 was that one of his cinematic idols, the man who shot *Vera Cruz*, should in real life prove to have been such a wreck of a human being: 'My illusions were thoroughly shattered.' The most expressive actor in the film, he added, had been the pillar of salt.

In the meantime, Leone worked for a week or two as a substitute director for Giorgio Bianchi, 'to get the producer [Aldo Panilia] out of trouble', on an Italian–French co-production, *Il cambio della guardia/ The Changing of the Guard/En avant la musique*. The film was set in the little Italian town of Ardea at the time of the Battle of Anzio, and told of the rivalry between two mayoral candidates (one a known anti-Fascist) whose children are about to get married. The Fascist authorities intervene in the election, there are arrests, demonstrations and confusions of identity; and in the end the American troops arrive, to put both Fascists and Nazi hostages to flight. The anti-Fascist candidate becomes the new mayor and the town of Ardea lives happily ever after. *Il cambio della guardia* was an attempt to repeat the success of the *Don Camillo* series of the 1950s, borrowing its stars Gino Cervi and Fernandel. Filming began on 2 April 1962, in Anzio, and on one much publicized occasion Elizabeth Taylor and Richard Burton visited the set. When the film was finally released, *Image et Son* (May 1963) concluded: 'Artistic result: zero . . . We would not recommend it to our friends.' Leone did not like talking about his involvement in *Il cambio della guardia*, even as an excuse for one of his celebrated put-downs: 'It was a ridiculous project, this film which was adapted from a novel,

*Avanti la musica* by Charles Exbrayant. The Italian characters in it were caricatures for tourists. I tried to organize things as best I could. But I was in no sense "author" of the project.'[43] Some sources claim that Leone did more than this: a French biography of Fernandel even claims that 'a certain Giorgio Bianchi . . . was the future Sergio Leone', a surprising conclusion since Bianchi had already directed thirty-two films!

But Leone was, he added, in no sense author of *any* project at this stage in his career. He now had the experience, the contacts and above all the motivation to make his own films. With *The Colossus of Rhodes*, he had put his signature on a genre film. He had outgrown the American cinematic heroes of his youth, as well as learning from them. He had even come across the Spanish locations he would later use. All the elements of a successful career in mainstream Italian film-making seemed to be in place. And at precisely that time, the bottom had fallen out of the film economy.

Sergio Leone's entry in the *Annuario del Cinema Italiano* for 1961, the year of *Sodom and Gomorrah*, was a brief one:

LEONE ROBERTI SERGIO
Assistant director, treatment writer, screenwriter. C.V.: story and script in collaboration: *Nel segno di Roma*. Script in collaboration and direction: *Il colosso di Rodi*. Script in collaboration: *Le sette sfide*.[44]

He had been in the film business for thirteen years.

# 5

# Fistful of Dollars

The entrepreneurial film-makers who have acclimatized the Western to Italy have been faced with a problem of expression which is quite different from their American counterparts. There's no West in Italy, no cowboys and bandits on the frontier; no frontier for that matter, no goldmines or Indians or pioneers. The Italian Western was born not from ancestral memory but from the herd instinct of film-makers who, when young, were head over heels in love with the American Western. In other words, the Hollywood Western was born from a myth; the Italian one is born from a myth about a myth . . .

The dominant theme is no longer the struggle between the lone, intrepid individual and the negative forces of nature and society: the dominant theme is the scramble for money. The main characters are everyday delinquents who were in the background of American films but who, in Italian ones, have invaded the foreground and become the protagonists. The qualities which make them attractive, in the eyes of our public, are not generosity and chivalry but guile, street wisdom and 'ingenuity' . . . These misanthropes, this scramble for money, this guile contrasts radically with the grand settings and epic tone of the Western genre. So you find yourself asking this question, and often: 'After all those stories – then what? Just a fistful of dollars? Or is there more?'
Alberto Moravia, January 1967

Late in 1963 the lighting cameraman Enzo Barboni was coming out of the Arlecchino cinema in Rome when he happened to bump into Sergio Leone. Barboni had just seen and enjoyed Akira Kurosawa's *Yojimbo*, and thought the film would appeal to Sergio. The film was about a footloose samurai (Toshiro Mifune) who offers his services as bodyguard to two rival factions, silk merchants and saké merchants. Largely out of boredom, Mifune plays one faction off against the other, and watches the ensuing mayhem from a wooden fire-tower overlooking the village's main street. Barboni felt this tale had just the combination of 'adventure, ritual and irony' that Leone would enjoy.

Leone went with Carla to see *Yojimbo* the following evening.

Like most of his colleagues in the Italian film business, he had been under-employed for about eighteen months, and had plenty of time on his hands. Even though pepla were proving much more difficult to finance, he'd been picking away, off and on, at the script of yet another one, called *Le aquila di Roma* (*The Eagles of Rome*). It was 'a sort of *Magnificent Seven* set in ancient Rome'.[1] He had also contributed to the screenplay of *Le verdi bandiere di Allah* (*Under the Flag of Allah*), an *El Cid* derivative recently released in Italy. The film was directed by Guido Zurli and Giacomo Gentilomo, the script co-written by Leone, Zurli and Umberto Lenzi. Set in sixteenth-century Spain, this Italian–Yugoslavian co-production told of an evil politician who tries to incite the Christian community against the Muslim community. Ultimately, he is thwarted in his masterplan by two knights, one from each faith, who manage to prevent an all-out war. Leone's heart just wasn't in the piece.

But Carla Leone recalls his passionate response to Kurosawa's film: 'Sergio was restless, looking for something he really wanted to make. I remember going to see *Yojimbo* with him, and he got the idea of turning it into a Western there and then. He loved it; it made his brain work overtime. He always tore at the edges of a cigarette box, or any piece of cardboard which happened to be lying around, with his fingers, when he was thinking hard. Or bit at a piece of card. Well, by the time he got home from the cinema, he was tearing away at a piece of cardboard, and saying excitedly, "You know, the original story of *Yojimbo* comes from an American novel, and it would be wonderful to take it back to where it originally came from." '[2] The following morning he phoned his colleagues – fellow directors Duccio Tessari and Sergio Corbucci, scriptwriter Sergio Donati and cinematographer Tonino Delli Colli – and urged them to see *Yojimbo*. Corbucci had already seen it, on Barboni's recommendation. Donati, who had been sent on several 'wild goose chases' by Leone in the past few years, 'didn't trust his judgement on this one', and didn't go; a decision he was later to regret. But Tessari, whose career as a director also seemed to have reached a dead end at the time, shared Leone's enthusiasm.[3]

The Italian film industry had experienced bad times before, but even in retrospect, none seemed as bad as 1963. Annual ticket sales were falling fast: about 680 million that season, compared with 820 million in the mid-1950s. After the fiascos of *Sodom and Gomorrah* and *Cleopatra*, the Americans had pulled out of Italian studios. Worse, they were also in the process of reducing the amount of product they could offer the Italian market; the main companies were now operating through agents, rather than in situ. The trade papers were full of references to 'the crisis' in the industry: a crisis of confidence (where investors were concerned), of productivity (where distributors were concerned) and of creativity (where popular film-makers were concerned). There were too many cinemas, not enough product to keep them going, and an almost complete lack of stimulus at the lower end of the market.

Carla Leone remembers, 'We had to be very careful with money, because we were still living off the proceeds of *Sodom and Gomorrah* and a few other things, and looking after our first child.' So Leone knew that he couldn't wait for ever for the right project to land on his desk. Big-budget films were out of the question; but then cheaper alternatives suggested themselves, as Leone was to recall: 'The Germans had launched the idea of the European Western, with a series of films which were like very, very bad television – the "Winnetou" series based on the writings of Karl May. But at least these films showed that the West still had some magic left in it, and that the frontiersman was a hero who still lived in the hearts of European cinema audiences.'[4]

The first 'Winnetou the Warrior' film, *The Treasure of Silver Lake/ Der Schatz im Silbersee*, had been made in 1962, produced by Rialto Film of Hamburg and Jadran Film of Zagreb, and directed by veteran Austrian Dr Harald Reinl. It was adapted from one of a series of books written in the late nineteenth century by Karl May, chronicling the adventures of 'Old Shatterhand', the Teutonic pioneer, and 'Winnetou', the noble chief of the Apaches. May's books indulged his curious views on Christian fellowship, ecology, 'the cultural degeneration of the Indian nations' and the proper behaviour of the *Ubermensch*. But the film versions shifted emphasis towards comedy, lively action sequences and stunts (usually filmed near Split, on the Adriatic), and widescreen Eastmancolor panoramas of the Yugoslavian landscape. Lex Barker, who played Tarzan in Hollywood between 1948 and 1955 before emigrating to Italy in 1960, became the buckskin-clad Shatterhand.

*The Treasure of Silver Lake* was followed, in short order, by *Winnetou the Warrior* or *Apache Gold* (1963), and a cycle was born. Stewart Granger joined the team in 1964, playing 'Old Surehand'. The cosmopolitan repertory company for the rest of the series included Klaus Kinski, Charles Aznavour, Herbert Lom and one 'Terence Hill' (appearing under his real name of Mario Girotti, usually as a tongue-tied, blue-eyed Romeo). At the height of the new Karl May craze, German pop singers were to be heard offering 'Der Wind der Prairie', and a newspaper helpfully featured a 'Wild West ABC', elucidating the meaning of terms ('as used in the West') such as 'thounderation', 'the deuce', 'zounds' and 'hang it all'. Stewart Granger reckoned that by 1964 the Winnetou films were making a cool $2 million each out of German, Austrian, Dutch and Scandinavian markets alone; which inevitably led to the production of rival German Westerns, such as *Hot Was the Wind* and *The Inexorable Sheriff from Santa Cruz* (both 1964).

But it was the success of the Winnetou films in Italy and Spain that encouraged Italian producers to invest. Westerns had, of course, been made in Italy before: beginning with Vincenzo Leone's *La vampira indiana* in 1913. *Buffalo e Bill* had made the first of three appearances in 1917. The inimitable William Cody had been a well-known figure in Italy for over twenty-five years, ever since he brought his Wild West show to the Arena di Verona. Andrea Uccellini's *La reginetta dei butteri* (*Queen of the Cowboys*) had been filmed in 1922, featuring a cast of real-life Italian cowboys, or *butteri*, who looked after the buffalo herds of Tuscany. In the 1940s some Italian Westerns had been distantly derived from Puccini's opera *The Girl of the Gold West*, such as *Una signora dell' Ovest* (1942) and *Il fanciullo del West/The Kid from the West* (1943). 1948 saw the first Italian publication of *Tex*, a Western comic-book by Bonelli and Galeppini. According to critic Oreste di Fornari, it favoured 'baroque villains in the style of Cagliostro, lots of violent deaths and very few women characters' (and it is still being published today).[5] Tex was an ex-secret agent who had learned that it was safer to take the law into his own hands. A rival comic, Benito Jacovitti's *Cocco Bill*, was drawn in the hyperactive slapstick style of Warner Brothers Looney Toons, and featured a clean-shaven, square-jawed hero of the Zane Grey tradition, who preferred a lassoo to a gun. These, together with the success of the Winnetou films, support Leone's view that the frontiersman hero still enjoyed currency with European audiences.

Hollywood, meanwhile, was producing fewer and fewer Westerns. As a percentage of all North American releases, Westerns had decreased from 34 per cent in 1950 to a mere 9 per cent in 1963; from about 150 films to about 15. And, as *New Yorker* critic Pauline Kael pointed out, those Westerns that were being made staked their appeal less in the vitality of the stories than in the veteran movie actors wheeled out to embody them. On the whole, cinema-goers appeared to turn out for Westerns only to reassure themselves that James Stewart and John Wayne could still get on a horse. As Kael wrote in her review of *Yojimbo*, audiences had become 'saddle sore', bored with a played-out Hollywood genre that had about as much relevance to modern life as the Elizabethan Pastoral: 'In recent years, John Ford, particularly, has turned the Western into an almost static pictorial genre, a devitalized, dehydrated form which is "enriched" with pastoral beauty and evocative nostalgia for a simple, basic way of life. The clichés we retained from childhood pirate, buccaneer, gangster and Western movies have been awarded the status of myths of our old movies. If, by now, we dread going to see a "great" Western, it's because "great" has come to mean slow and pictorially composed. We'll be lulled to sleep in the "affectionate", "pure", "authentic" scenery of the West . . . or, for a change, we'll be clobbered by messages in "mature" Westerns like *The Gunfighter* and *High Noon* (the message is that the myths we never believed in anyway were false).'[6]

Kael concluded that a film-maker such as Kurosawa, operating outside the Hollywood myth-factory, was in an excellent position to exploit the conventions of the Western genre, while debunking its morality. Kurosawa himself had conceded that his *Yojimbo* was originally born, in part, out of a love for the Hollywood Western, and particularly for *Shane*: an incredibly popular film in Japan and an unusually self-conscious piece of myth-making. 'Westerns have been made over and over again', he said, 'and in the process a kind of grammar has evolved. I have learned from this grammar of the Western.' But, he had added, he had no intention of making any kind of a 'pastiche' of George Stevens's movie.[7] After all, the 1950s Western had become a global text; the one enthusiasm which Josef Stalin, Ludwig Wittgenstein and Winston Churchill had in common.

Leone's judgement was that the early Italian spinoffs from the German craze were a fairly sorry sight: 'They all had stolen titles. The names and credits were all Americanized to hide the identities of Spanish directors and tenth-rate Italian writers. They were often co-productions between Germany, Italy and Spain to split the risk three ways, and they were thought by everyone to be "B" movies, releases dumped on the Italian market of American TV programmes.' (The Americanized pseudonyms were intended to reassure mainly Southern Italian audiences in *terza visione* houses that American product was still coming off the assembly-line.) Yet, however slipshod these productions might be, Italian Westerns made sound financial sense as long as they were co-produced and shot on location in Spain, which had the landscape, the sound stages and laboratories (in Madrid), assistants, technicians, wranglers, horses, costumers and beefy actors who made great Mexican heavies – all geared up and rearing to go.[8]

Following the stabilization of the peseta in 1959, independent producer Samuel Bronston had succeeded in bringing together Spanish facilities and crews, and American directors and stars, for a series of mega-productions. He couldn't have afforded to make them unless they were based in Spain. Bronston had rebuilt Jerusalem, at the extensive Sevilla Film Studios, for his *King of Kings;* followed by the Cathedral of Burgos for *El Cid;* the Imperial City of the Dowager Queen and a section of the Great Wall of China for *55 Days in Peking*, on a vast site at Las Matas twenty kilometres outside Madrid; and the entire Roman Forum – next door – for *The Fall of the Roman Empire*. That last effort cost $28 million, and its box-office failure toppled the Bronston empire, too. But there were various important legacies. A whole generation of Spanish technicians had been trained to the highest Hollywood standards; local pueblos had come to depend on regular employment in the film business; and parts of the Las Matas studio complex could now be rented out to production companies making low-budget films. In the wake of Bronston – between 1961 and 1964 – came about ten co-produced Westerns, marketed as entirely American films: among them, *Savage Guns* (1961), made by Britain's Hammer Films, which used some of the locations in Almeria that Leone would later discover for himself. These Westerns provided work for Hollywood actors going through a lean period, and for American directors who had fallen out with Hollywood.

Spain had produced a few Westerners of its own, most prominently the director Joaquín Romero Marchent, whose films included *El Coyote* and its sequel *La justicia del Coyote* (1954), *Zorro the Avenger* and *The Shadow of Zorro* (1962) and *Three Good Men* (1962). Critic Carlos Aguilar justly calls Marchent 'the pioneer of the Spanish Western'.[9] As Marchent told me: 'Alberto Grimaldi, later to become Leone's producer, first decided to invest in films as a result of the success of my *Zorro* and put money into *Taste of Vengeance /Gunfight at High Noon* and *Hour of Death* in 1963–4, for Centaur Films. José Calvo, who played the bartender Silvanito for Leone ten years later, was in my *El*

*Coyote*. And indirectly I helped to find the location for *Fistful of Dollars*. Where do you think all that furniture, those Western houses and stables and stagecoaches came from? From my *Zorro* films.' Marchent denies that the legacy of Samuel Bronston led directly to those Spanish Westerns: 'Money and sets, yes, but I didn't need Bronston to teach *me* anything.' Marchent reckons that the Spanish contribution to the European Western has been unjustly neglected; in fact he is still quite angry about it.[10] So, although Sergio Leone liked to present his idea of adapting *Yojimbo* into a Western as an inspiration from out of the blue, it is evident that Westerns were already on the menu of Italian producers who did deals with Spanish and German colleagues in cafés on the Via Veneto. Moreover, John Sturges had already adapted Kurosawa's *Seven Samurai* as *The Magnificent Seven*: a smash hit in Italy.

When Leone's first Western was released in 1964, critics tended to compare it with the classic Hollywood variety, and noted the most obvious points of difference: the personal style of the hero; the distinctive art direction and dusty Spanish locations; the music and sound editing; the action-packed plot made up of a series of noisy climaxes, sometimes garnished with ultra-violence; the drift towards irony, surrealism and wry humour. But a comparison with earlier Italian and Spanish Westerns is equally telling. They were reach-me-down American-style Westerns, which were, in the words of Sergio Donati, 'worse than "B" movies; they were "C" movies!'[11] So how did the transformation from 'copyists' to 'Italianizers' come about? Leone would explain: 'I thought up the treatment in five days. With Duccio Tessari. [It was called, shrewdly, *Il Magnifico Straniero*/*The Magnificent Stranger*]. Tessari didn't quite understand what I was doing. He spread it around Rome that I had gone a bit strange. Then I made the adaptation, alone, in about a fortnight. Sitting in my apartment in Rome.'[12] Carla Leone adds: 'There was a lot of tearing of bits of cardboard going on. Sergio didn't rate Tessari very highly as a writer, but he was a good friend and Sergio wanted to share his ideas with someone. They used to play gunfights together – bang, bang – as they wrote. His fascination with the gunfighter character and his passion for Western films were rekindled during those weeks.' According to Duccio Tessari, Leone would arrive in the morning and excitedly say, 'Last night I dreamed three words. You must put this idea in the film.'[13]

Sergio Corbucci contends that Leone spent much of his time 'slaving away at a moviola machine and copying *Yojimbo*, changing only the setting and details of the dialogue'. Leone conceded that he made a copy of 'the dialogue of *Yojimbo*, translated from the Japanese', but only 'in order to be sure not to repeat a single word. All I retained was the basic structure of Kurosawa's film.'[14] But there were still close affinities between the two scripts: at one point, the stranger even wields a machete as if it was a samurai sword. On another occasion, Leone stated somewhat defensively: 'The resemblance was only mentioned because I myself drew attention to it . . . and I drew attention to it in order to explain the reasons which had encouraged me to take such risks in the first place. Reasons which had to do with being provocative, as well as expressing my own, personal ideas. What stirred my curiosity, when I was doing the adaptation, was a piece of news in the paper which accompanied the Italian release of *Yojimbo*. In it, the writer noted that Kurosawa's film had derived *its* inspiration from an American thriller – Dashiell Hammett's *Red Harvest*. Kurosawa had rearranged the story, by adding the grotesque masks and the martial code of the samurai. What I wanted to do was to undress these puppets, and turn them into cowboys, to make them cross the ocean and to return to their place of origin. That was the provocative bit. But there was another thing. I had to find a reason *in myself* – not being a character who had ever lived in that environment. I had to find a reason within my own culture.'[15]

Above all, Leone wanted to put into practice a lesson he had learned the hard way from all those years as an assistant: 'I had learned always to put myself under the skin of the most demanding member of the audience,' he later said. 'When I go to the cinema, I'm often frustrated because I can guess exactly what is going to happen about ten minutes into the screening. So, when I'm working on a subject, I'm always looking for the element of *surprise*. I work hard to sustain people's curiosity . . . On first viewing, people experience the aggression of the images. They like what they see, without necessarily understanding everything. And the sheer abundance of baroque images privileges surprise over comprehension. On second viewing, they grasp more fully the discourse which underlies the images.'[16] The 'discourse' of Leone's Western debut, he was to claim, concerned nothing less than 'an historic break with the conventions of the genre. Before me, you couldn't even make a Western without women in it. You couldn't show violence because the hero had to be a positive-thinking sort of person. No question, then, of playing with a kind of realism: the main characters had to be dressed like fashion models! But I introduced a hero who was negative, dirty, who looked like a human being, and who was totally at home with the violence which surrounded him.'

Leone made various changes to the scenario of *Yojimbo*. The location was shifted from provincial Japan to the Mexican–American border, with its Hispanic system of values. The masterless samurai who shrugged his shoulders, chewed on a piece of wood and was quick to draw his sword became the mysterious stranger who wore his hat over his eyes, smoked a cheroot and was quick to draw his Colt. Two big scenes were added: a massacre at the Rio Bravo Canyon, and a shoot-out in a cemetery, where two dead soldiers are used as decoys. Another key scene was removed: the arrival of 'the county inspector', who had revealed that there was a political and social world going on beyond the confines of the story. *Yojimbo*'s subtle distinction between the patriarchs who ruled the two factions and their brutal employees went completely, to make way for a corrupt world where, Leone wrote, '*everyone* has become very rich, or dead'. And, instead of being presented as an episode which might have happened in nineteenth-century Japan, *The Magnificent Stranger* was signalled as a piece of theatre, introduced by a 'chorus' (the crazy bell ringer Juan de Dios) and ending at the final curtain with an overhead shot of the corpse-strewn stage (as the coffin-maker takes his bow). 'When I was preparing my first Western', Leone recalled, 'it occurred to me that William Shakespeare could have written some great Westerns – just as he wrote some great Italian romances, without ever having been to Italy.' For good measure, Leone chucked in a reference to *Hamlet*, as the bell ringer greets the stranger in San Miguel.[17]

The 'puppets' on the stage certainly belonged more to Leone's culture than to Kurosawa's. There were numerous references to the New Testament: the stranger riding his undernourished mule into San Miguel like Christ entering Jerusalem (or John Ford's *Young Mr Lincoln* entering Springfield Illinois); his 'crucifixion' on the wooden sign outside the Cantina; his involvement in the Last Supper of the Rojo clan; his death and resurrection; a profusion of crosses, cemeteries and coffins. Leone referred to the stranger as 'an incarnation of the Angel Gabriel' – an exterminating angel, whose story deliberately resembled 'a parable'. There were important references, too, to the *commedia dell'arte* and the carnivalesque tradition. These could be discerned in the chorus, the trickster-hero, the unusually detailed emphasis on eating and drinking, the mockery of death, the larger-than-life gestures of the Hispanic characters, the grotesque realism of the bandits' faces, the presentation of hallowed moments from popular culture (here, the Western) as if they were part of the liturgy and a profusion of double-crosses which helped to keep the audience guessing. All of this amounted, in literary critic Mikhail Bakhtin's famous phrase, to 'the use of the rich world of *laughter* to oppose the official culture, the serious, the religious and the hierarchical'. Instead of *Christ Stopped at Eboli*, it was 'Eastwood Looked in at San Miguel'.

And there were references to the American Western. Leone recalled that *Shane* (1952), the story of another mysterious stranger who arrives from nowhere and finally returns thence, was 'particularly important' to him during the gestation of his first Western script. Though not greatly enamoured of Alan Ladd's performance, Leone considered *Shane* 'an abstraction, a walking piece of myth'. He also admired Wilson (Jack Palance), the professional gun who wears a tall black hat and one black glove, and who gets off his horse 'very, very slowly and stylishly'. And he relished the shooting sequence outside the Grafton store, which showed 'what really happens when a bullet hits someone'. Leone also admitted having in mind Edward Dmytryk's *Warlock* (1959), the overwrought film in which Anthony Quinn refers to towns-people waiting for a gunfight as 'little boys waiting for the circus parade'; John Ford's *My Darling Clementine* (1946), 'with the gunfight in the dust, whipped up by the stagecoach'; Howard Hawks's *Rio Bravo*, 'where Wayne and Martin take one side of the street each, on their so-careful night patrol'; Fritz Lang's *Western Union* (1941) with its 'marvellous shootout in Joe's barber shop between the half-shaved badman and Randolph Scott'; Anthony Mann's *Winchester '73* (1950) with its iconic rifle, and its hero purging himself of and through violence; and John Ford's *The Man Who Shot Liberty Valance* (1962), because it was 'at long last, a work of disenchantment'.[18] According to Luciano Vincenzoni, 'Sergio's all-time favourite around this time was *Warlock*; he had that one printed in his head. The interaction of the characters impressed him a lot.'[19]

Disenchantment was certainly one of Leone's 'basic mechanisms'. The town of San Miguel has nothing going for it. The puppet stage is revealed to the audience through a curtain of dust, and the puppets chase after the almighty dollar not in order to invest it but because it is the *prize*. It was while writing this script that Leone claimed to have first realized the 'strange fraternity between the marionettes of the traditional Sicilian theatre, and my friends of the Wild West ... Of course the decors and details were different ... But the motivations of human beings are simple, and the situations do not change.'[20]

Leone's town of San Miguel is ruled by two notably vicious extended families or clans, the Rojos and the Baxters. At the centre of the town is a bell-tower or campanile: and *Campanilismo* (or 'bell-tower patriotism') is the nearest thing to civic awareness that exists in this isolated, listless place. It is characteristic of Leone's regard for 'family' that he placed a version of the Holy Family (Julio, Marisol and little Jesus) at the centre of his action, unlike the equivalent family in *Yojimbo*.[21] The single moment when the Stranger admits to a past and a personal ethic arrives when he is asked by a grateful Marisol, 'Why do you do this for us?' He replies, ''Cos I knew someone like you once and there was no one there to help.' (In the first draft, this cryptic comment referred to an explanatory prologue, later ditched.) The Stranger's attitude to the Holy Family reveals that he is really a good man; just as the Rojos family's attitude to Jesus (they take pot-shots at him) underlines their evil. Still, in the final reckoning, the family is forced to pick up and settle elsewhere; San Miguel is no place to bring up children.

The Stranger, of course, prefers always to go it alone. Esteban Rojo tells him that, if he wants to belong to the clan, he is expected to 'sleep here with us'. Blowing cigar smoke into Esteban's face, the Stranger replies, 'That's all very cosy, but I don't find you men all that appealing.' Indeed, 'you men' turn out to be a bunch of sadistic thugs, who enjoy beating up the Stranger while laughing uproariously, as Esteban rubs his hands gleefully between his legs. It is Esteban who shoots Consuelo Baxter as she mourns her husband and son: an act which shocks even his psychopathic brother Ramon. The Stranger's relationships with Consuelo (the matriarch of the rival clan) and Marisol seem to imply that the women, too, are to be treated as 'chaps'. The Stranger creeps up behind Consuelo in her boudoir, as if to attack her, and then proceeds to tell her a story that begins, 'Once there was a wagonload of gold that the soldiers were taking to the border'. The first time he meets Marisol he punches her in the face by mistake. At these moments, Leone was evidently writing for the boys in the audience: boys with a short attention span who chatted through the romantic bits in traditional Hollywood Westerns, and who still lived at home with *mamma*.

The Stranger is like an adolescent who cannot bear to touch anyone or reveal his feelings.

A comparison of a key sequence from Leone's script and the equivalent sequence in *Yojimbo* serves to point up the many similarities, and the many differences. In Kurosawa, the *Yojimbo* informs the watchman and the cooper that he's happy to stay in town, happier still if he can profitably ply his trade: 'Listen, I get paid for killing. It would be better if all these men were dead.' He then decides to provoke a fight with the saké merchant's men. He ambles pensively over, scratches his head, and issues a challenge in wisecracks: 'What gentle faces. Anger makes you even sweeter.' When his victims finally stir, Mifune whips out his sword, cuts an arm off, punctures a gut, then formally replaces the weapon in its scabbard – all within a few seconds. He walks over to the cooper and orders 'two coffins'. On reflection, he adds, 'maybe three'.

Now, the Leone version: the Stranger is insulted by the Baxters, who also spook his mule and nearly topple him from the saddle. So he coolly offers his services to Don Miguel Rojo, cautioning 'I don't work cheap'. Then he decides to provoke a fight with the Baxters. Approaching them slowly, he passes the coffin-maker, who hums loudly to himself as he planes a piece of wood: 'Get three coffins ready.' He reaches the Baxter residence, where the men who earlier insulted him lounge aimlessly on the corral gate. They taunt him, laughing: 'We don't like to see bad boys like you in town. Go get your mule.' Head down, the Stranger retorts: 'You see, he got all riled up when you went and fired those shots at his feet.' He raises his face to stare meanly at the gang – no more jokes: 'You see, my mule don't like people laughing. Gets the crazy idea you're laughing at him. Now if you'll apologize, like I know you're going to . . . I might convince him that you really didn't mean it.' This is enough to get the Baxters spitting and twitching. The Stranger's eyes narrow and the Baxters go for their guns – but not before the Stranger draws and fires four fatal rounds. Sheriff John Baxter immediately confronts the Stranger ('You killed all four of them. You'll pay all right. You'll be strung up'). The Stranger merely tells him he had 'better get these men underground'. He turns and walks away, reaching the sidewalk outside the Cantina, where he sees the coffin-maker: 'My mistake. Four coffins.'

It is the flamboyance and the *rhetoric* of Leone's treatment, plus the knowing references to innumerable other confrontations in Hollywood Westerns, that support his argument that he was 'translating' into

Italian, rather than executing a 'a carbon-copy of *Yojimbo*'. The Stranger's personal style – a mixture of technical skill, hard dialogue and tight-lipped silence when it is needed, rather like the *omerta* of the Mafiosi, is half a world away from Kurosawa's shambling, itchy samurai.[22]

Having completed his 'adaptation' by the end of January 1964, Leone looked for a producer. Tonino Delli Colli suggested his wife's cousin, Arrigo Colombo, and even considered investing in the project himself before withdrawing 'because I wasn't sure it had the potential'.[23] Leone then took it to Franco ('Checco') Palaggi, an executive producer at Colombo's 'Jolly Film' company, and acted out the story for him, playing all the parts himself. Palaggi agreed that there would be little problem in attracting West German and Spanish finance, provided there were members of the cast from both countries, and provided the film kept within a low budget of about 120 million lire, each country chipping in 40 million. 'I already had good relations with the Germans and the Spaniards from peplum days,' Leone reckoned, 'and so I was naïve enough to hope that all the contributions would come in without too much trouble.' The German investor was Constantin, which had done best out of the Karl May adaptations. Palaggi then recommended the project to Arrigo Colombo and his partner Giorgio Papi, whose Jolly Film had already participated in a Spanish–Italian Western called *Duello nel Texas/Gunfight in the Red Sands*.[24] Papi had been in the business since the early 1940s, and had produced eight feature films; he had a hand in Jean Renoir's *French Can-Can* (1954) and had produced some Italian versions of Hammer horrors in the early 1960s. Colombo was more of a newcomer, with *Maciste Against Hercules* (1962), among others, to his credit.

After an initial meeting in the Excelsior Hotel on the Via Veneto, Papi and Colombo treated Leone to a screening of *Duello nel Texas* in a viewing theatre. It starred muscleman Richard Harrison, then under contract to Jolly, was co-scripted by Albert Band, photographed by 'Jack Dalmas' (real name: Massimo Dallamano), and scored by 'Dan Savio' (Ennio Morricone). When the lights came up, while the lyrics of the closing ballad receded ('Keep your hand on your gun, don't you trust any one . . .'), Leone was, for once, at a loss for words. 'It was the sort of film', he later remarked, 'where an actor fell to the floor before the pistol-butt actually made contact with his head.' It was also the sort of film where the buckskin-clad hero, called Gringo, having galloped into town to tell the authorities that his father has just been shot, coolly strides into a barbershop, has a wash and brush-up and a shave, then announces, 'I must find the sheriff now. Someone's just killed my father.'

But Papi and Colombo now had the capital, they said, to invest simultaneously in two more Westerns – or, at least, one and a half. The first already had a title (*Bullets Don't Argue/Le pistole non discutono*), a script and a director (Mario Caiano, alias 'Mike Perkins'). If Leone was prepared to work within a tiny budget (less than 40 million lire from Jolly, in exchange for 'an i.o.u. of 45 million – so they made a nice profit whatever happened'), and the guarantee of a six-week schedule, Papi and Colombo would also back *The Magnificent Stranger*, as a way of 'using up waste material'. Their offer involved using the same locations, most of the same crew, the same costumes, the same kind of screenplay, and even some of the same actors. One big difference would be that Rod Cameron, the Canadian star of *Bullets Don't Argue*, would be paid more than the whole cast of *Stranger* put together. Leone, who two years previously had been in the big league, was back in Poverty Row with a vengeance. Even then, there was a problem, as Tonino Valerii recalls: 'The producers didn't want Leone to direct the picture, because they didn't have much faith in his abilities, or hold him in very high regard. He had a reputation for being manic on the set, not sure of himself and full of costly ideas. But it was Palaggi who succeeded in convincing them that Leone *had* to be the director.'[25]

Originally Leone was due to share the designer selected for Caiano's film, Alberto Roccianti. But, as Valerii recalls, 'One day the architect Carlo Simi came into the Jolly offices – he was in the process of redesigning producer Colombo's apartment in Rome at the time – and caught sight of the set designs scattered on Leone's table. He said, with a smile, "Is this supposed to be a Mexican interior?" "Why?" Leone asked anxiously. "Could you do it any better?" Without replying, Simi took a pencil and sketched an interior with a huge ceiling held up by enormous pillars of wood and heavy-duty supports. Leone's mouth fell open with amazement, and he immediately made sure that Simi replaced Roccianti as the art director. Simi would go on to do the sets, the costumes and the props in all his films.'[26]

It wasn't by chance that Simi happened to know about the architecture of the Wild West. As he told me, 'I'd already studied the buildings of that era for Sergio Corbucci, who had asked me to design an

Italian Western called *Minnesota Clay* – which had just fallen through, for lack of money. One evening I was visiting Franco Palaggi, a friend of mine. He was having a meeting with a certain Sergio Leone, whom I only knew by name and reputation . . . Sergio made a big impression on me. He spoke in a tone which dared you to reply to him, and dominated everyone. I was near a table, on which were the drawings for the film . . . I have to say I found them unacceptable. And I made the gaffe of expressing this opinion rather loudly. Sergio asked: "Can you back up what you're saying?" "Sure, I'm a qualified architect." "Well go and get some drawings, to show me what you're capable of. I'll wait here" . . . So I came back with the designs for *Minnesota Clay*. Sergio studied them, asked me to go up a floor to the office of Arrigo Colombo, then blurted out to his producer: "I don't want the designer I've been assigned any more. I want this man." Colombo at first claimed there wasn't time for a change, then altered tack and agreed on condition that I did the designs and costumes for two productions simultaneously – *The Magnificent Stranger* and *Bullets Don't Argue*. I had an enormous amount of work to do in a short time . . . and then, would you believe, they decided to make *Minnesota Clay* as well.'[27]

Carlo Simi's set designs and costumes for the film, and for many other key Italian Westerns, would be stylish and original. Director of photography Massimo Dallamano (another Jolly recommendation) also had a key contribution to make, as Valerii remembers: 'He was the first person to understand that the new widescreen format for Techniscope – the "2P" or two perforations format – would mean that you'd need a new kind of close-up, a sort of *very* close-up, which would frame the face from the chin to the bottom part of the forehead, in order not to lose too many of the small details of the features . . . Another key collaborator was Franco Giraldi [alias 'Frank Garfield', later to direct such Italian Westerns as *Seven Guns for the Macgregors* (1965)] an underrated second-unit director.'[28]

Leone gladly accepted the offer of the main location: a 'Western main street', originally built in Sierra Madrid for Marchent's Zorro films in 1961–2, and since used for one or two early Spanish–Italian Westerns. The exact site was called Hojo de Manzanares, close to La Pedrizia di Colmenar Viejo in the San Pedro region, thirty-five kilometres north of Madrid. The Zorro set consisted of one side of a clapboard main street, an adobe church, and a two-storey building with a circular fountain linking the two of them. When Sergio Leone first went to see the location, 'it already had the abandoned look of a ghost town, which was just the effect I wanted. I had to persuade the Spanish proprietors *not* to renovate it'. He also accepted a riverside location, to be his 'Rio Bravo Canyon': in *Bullets*, it did service as the banks of the Rio Grande. A third location on offer was the 'Casa de Campo' in Madrid, a museum of traditional rural life and folklore which included houses, courtyards, an inn and a cellar, and which, according to Simi, 'had been chosen by Colombo to save construction money'. This became the Rojo residence. 'The big house for the rich and powerful Baxters' was specially designed, 'and Sergio was enthusiastic about its "baroque feel", as he put it.'[29]

The *Bullets Don't Argue* unit would move into Colmenar first, followed by Leone's unit at the end of April 1964. To shoot scenes that were supposed to take place in the surrounding scrubland, the *Stranger* unit would return to 'a piece of desert I'd found [while shooting *Pompeii*] in Almeria, much further south. No telegraph poles, no electricity wires, a place where you could pivot the camera 360 degrees if you wanted to. With small adobe houses which seemed to belong to an earlier age.'[30] According to Tonino Valerii: 'Leone didn't actually spend any time at all in Almeria, during the shoot. Franco Giraldi shot the famous scene at the Rio Bravo Canyon, the night-time sequence when the Baxter house burns down, and the key exteriors in the desert.'[31] Giraldi himself recalls that he was appointed at the last minute, when the crew was already in Madrid, 'because they hadn't realized till then that they would need a second unit at all'.[32] Leone restricted himself to shooting the Stranger's scenes and cutaways. But he did help to recce the location, and found a cobbled courtyard, with a well and adobe dwellings, at Cortijo El Sotillo, some five minutes from San José to the east of Almeria town. These belonged to a wealthy local landowner, and were ideal to serve as the outskirts of San Miguel in the film's all-important opening. Leone also looked at the two 'ramblas' (dried-up river beds) at the base of Los Filabres mountains above Tabernas, which could double as canyons through which Mexican heavies hurtled on their horses. But these were not very accessible at that time. There was no airport to speak of at Granada or Almeria, so the desert was a long train-ride from Madrid or an even longer car-ride from Malaga. Moreover, the surrounding region had little in the way of facilities, Almeria being the least developed region of Spain. Some claimed that Franco had deliberately punished Almeria for its fiercely Republican sympathies in the Civil War by not offering any central or regional government support. But since parts of David Lean's *Lawrence of Arabia* were filmed there in spring 1962, the Almerian desert had become increasingly appealing to international film-makers.

On a recce in Madrid, Leone met stunt director and actor Benito Stefanelli. As Stefanelli recently recalled: 'I'd already done two comic Westerns in a reconstructed village in Cinecittà ... Sergio was very interested, since he was getting ready for a Western himself, with Papi and Colombo, and wanted to know where we'd got the pistols and costumes from. He told me the storyline, and I threw in a few suggestions from time to time. At the end of the chat he asked me to be stunt co-director for the film. I replied that he should ask the one he'd done *The Colossus of Rhodes* with. Leone insisted and finally we began the film, which was made on the rebound.'[33] Stefanelli would work with Leone on all his Westerns, over the next seven years.

Leone's leading man had to be American; and Papi and Colombo really wanted him to cast their big asset, Richard Harrison, an ex-contract player for American–International Pictures, who had bulked up for roles in such offerings as *The Invincible Gladiator* (1962) and *Perseus the Invincible* (1963). But Leone turned him down: 'Harrison cost only $20,000, but he still didn't appeal to me.' Leone originally had Henry Fonda in mind as his Stranger. He envisaged this as a great piece of casting against type, a *surprise* an audience would cherish; moreover, Fonda was a hero of Leone's cinephile youth 'in dark and dirty movie houses in Trastevere'. So the script was sent to Hollywood, in an English-language version; but Fonda's agent didn't even bother to show it to him, replying by return that his client 'couldn't possibly do it'. Next, Leone thought of two younger actors of the strong, silent type who had made their mark as 'specialists' in *The Magnificent Seven*: James Coburn and Charles Bronson. Coburn agreed to play the part for $25,000, 'which was too much for the producers'. Bronson thought the script was 'just about the worst I'd ever seen', and turned Leone down flat. ('What I didn't understand', Bronson later admitted, 'was that the script didn't make any difference. It was the way Leone was going to direct it that would make the difference.'[34]) According to Sergio Donati, Leone also 'seriously considered Cliff Robertson; he was an actor he had in mind, but would have cost as much as the whole movie'.[35] Papi and Colombo then thought about offering the part to fifty-four-year-old Rod Cameron who, at a pinch, could do both films back to back. But even he would have stretched the budget too thinly; and in any case he was all wrong. The man who had begun his career as Buck Jones's stunt double was not quite the character Leone had in mind.

At this point Claudia Sartori, who worked in the William Morris Agency in Rome, contacted Jolly Film to let them know that she had just received from America a 16 mm copy of episode 91 of the long-running CBS television series *Rawhide*. A 'young, lanky actor who appeared in it' might possibly be of interest. Tonino Valerii, who was at that time head of post-production for Papi and Colombo, recalls how Leone responded to Claudia Sartori's proposal: 'Sergio said to her, "I hear what you're saying, but it won't work. You know I want James Coburn." [I replied,] "You have to be realistic, Sergio, if you ever want to get your film made." So we went to a viewing room near the office, where there was one moviola machine, to view this film.'[36] The episode, first aired on American television on 10 November 1961, was called *Incident of the Black Sheep*, and it concerned the traditional 'cattlemen versus sheepmen' conflict that had been at the heart of countless feature Westerns (including *Shane*).

The herd (on its way from San Antonio, Texas, to Sedalia, Kansas) stampedes when it scents sheep on the trail. Driver Jim Quince is injured when his horse falls on him. Trail boss Gil Favor (Eric Fleming) asks sheepman Tod Stone (guest star Richard Baseheart) to move the sheep on, but he refuses. And so the task falls to the herd's ramrod, Rowdy Yates (Clint Eastwood), who cannot understand 'what sheep are doin' on a cattle trail' and feels 'sick to my stomach' whenever he smells them. Yates tries to spook the sheep, fails, and gets into a fistfight with Stone, who falls and seriously injures himself. Favor orders the ramrod to eat humble pie, by escorting Stone in a covered wagon to the nearest doctor. In town, a couple of cattlemen take Yates for a sheep-man and rough him up; which, iniquitously, lands Yates in jail. Thus, he learns a much-needed lesson about the perils of 'sheep-hating' in particular, and prejudice in general: 'Look,' he says, 'I'm an American citizen.' 'You're nothin' – you're a sheep herder,' is the reply. Along the way, Eastwood has a few gritty exchanges of dialogue, and a couple of moody double-takes. But for most of the show, he wasn't 'rowdy' at all – just wholesome, likeable in a puppy-dog sort of way, dressed in a checkered calico shirt and leather chaps. He was introduced behind the opening credits ('Clint Eastwood as Rowdy Yates') stripped to the waist, smiling self-consciously as he sipped a ladle of water.

Of the viewing session, Valerii recalls, 'About halfway through, Sergio stood up and walked out. So we all left. Then Sartori sent some stills which had been taken from the film, and Sergio looked at them. He said, "This man, with a vacant look on his face, in an unwatchable film about cows?" But Claudia Sartori replied, "Look, this actor is on the way up in America. Maybe by the time the time the film is over, he will be worth a lot more." At the time, Eastwood was worth $15,000. And it was this which convinced the producers that he must be just the right person for the job. Coburn wanted a lot more. Leone had been told by Papi and Colombo that he had to start to make the film now or he never would. I don't recall that Leone ever actually said "Yes" to Clint Eastwood.'[37] So Leone, 'with some reluctance', was swept along by the idea of casting the clean-cut, thirty-four-year-old actor who played the ramrod in that film about cows.

'What fascinated me about Clint above all', Leone told me nearly twenty years later, 'was his external appearance and his own character. In *Incident of the Black Sheep*, Clint didn't speak much ... but I noticed the lazy, laid-back way he just came on and effortlessly stole every single scene from Eric Fleming. His *laziness* is what came over so clearly. When we were working together, he was like a snake, forever taking a nap 500 feet away, wrapped up in his coils, asleep in the back of the car. Then he'd open his coils out, unfold, and stretch ... When you mix that with the blast and velocity of the gunshots, you have the essential contrast that he gave us. So we built his character on this, as we went along, physically as well, giving him the beard and the small cigar that he never really smoked. When he was offered the second film *For a Few Dollars More*, he said to me, "I'll read the script, come over and do the film, but please, I beg of you, one thing only – don't put that cigar back into my mouth!" And I said, "Clint, we can't possibly leave the cigar behind. It's playing the lead!"'[38]

Although Leone was joking (nasty Eastwood gags being one of his party-pieces after they parted company in 1967), it is certainly true that the 'props' surrounding the character of The Mysterious Stranger (named 'Joe' in the original script) played a key part in that character's success: the light growth of beard, the poncho, the sheepskin waistcoat, the cigars, the brown suede boots, the shrunk-to-fit jeans. The role had been written for a much older man, and part of the process of building the character involved customizing it to Eastwood. Leone specified: 'Clint was a little sophisticated, a little "light", and I wanted to make him look more virile, to harden him, to "age" him for the part as well.'[39] And so the traditional Western hero, with his psychology, his history, and his morality, became a 'physical *presence*', an embodiment of Latin machismo rather than American toughness. As Leone later liked to put it, 'The story is told that when Michelangelo was asked what he had seen in one particular block of marble, which he chose among hundreds of others, he replied that he saw Moses. I would offer the same answer to the question why did I choose Clint Eastwood, only backwards. When they ask me what I saw in Clint Eastwood . . . I reply that what I saw, simply, was a block of marble. And that was what I wanted.'[40] Such are the benefits of hindsight.

Clint Eastwood had first been told about Leone's script by the William Morris Agency in Los Angeles. The agency had been telephoned by its Roman branch following the screening of the *Rawhide* episode: 'The man at my agency suggested I read a Western script to be done in Spain as an Italian–German co-production, and my first instinct was, "Absolutely not." And he said, "Well, would you just read it? You might have some comments for the office in Rome." '[41] The agency was simultaneously negotiating with another of its clients, Henry Silva, who specialized in playing short-fused gangsters. So they may have been going through the motions when they asked Eastwood to look at the script. In the event, Henry Silva wouldn't cross the ocean for less than $16,000. But Clint Eastwood agreed to glance at the script, which arrived the following day. He found it an unusually thick document (a carbon copy on onion-skin paper), full of clumsily translated English ('He is buried in the hill of boots') and lengthy stage directions: 'It was in English, but very strange English, because it had been written by an Italian group of people who didn't speak English that well; especially English with a Western kind of slang.'

'But the moment I got into it,' Eastwood was to recall, 'I recognized something – the chance to design another type of character – and I researched and found that this director hadn't directed but a couple of toga movies before that, and heard that he was considered talented in terms of Italian cinema, that he was a very humorous man . . . I'd already realized this reading the script.'[42] At that stage, the humour wasn't always intentional. It was the first appearance of Joe, the mysterious stranger, which particularly stuck in Clint Eastwood's mind:

'Usually the hero rides into town, sees a horse getting beaten, sees the schoolmarm, rescues the horse, and you know who he's gonna get hitched with at the end – and it isn't the horse! But in this, he rides into town on a mule and wearing a black [actually brown] hat, sees a kid being shot at and kicked about, sees the maiden in distress, and then he just turns and rides away. You're never really sure if he *is* the hero until about halfway through. And then you're not sure because he's only out to get whatever he can.'

Eastwood tried the script out on his wife Maggie, to test her reaction. She, too, was intrigued by 'this story of a loner', and fancied the idea of a six-week holiday in Italy and Spain during the early summer break from the *Rawhide* schedule. Eastwood took this professional risk without having met the producers, the director, or indeed anyone directly involved in the production. Further, he chose to ignore all the horror stories he'd heard around Hollywood about working in the volatile Italian film business. 'I didn't see any risk, though, because I still had to go back to do more segments of *Rawhide* [he'd just signed for the seventh season] and if for some reason it didn't work out – well, at least I'd had a vacation in Spain.'[43] Eastwood had, in fact, been complaining for some time, and in print, about the restrictions under which CBS expected him to work. 'I haven't been allowed to accept a single feature or TV guesting offer since I started the series,' he had told the *Hollywood Reporter*. 'Maybe they figure me as the sheepish nice guy I portray.' He was very keen to get away from the 'Mr Good Guy' image, and to see his name above the title of a feature film in America: 'A lot of Italian-made Westerns had been shown throughout the world, but none of them had been shown here in England or the United States, or to an English-speaking audience . . . I really did want them to be shown in these other countries, as almost everyone who has done a television series would.'[44] He had appeared in ten features between 1955 and the start of *Rawhide* in 1958, but usually as a walk-on. His film career had actually been in decline when the television opportunity first came up.

The relationship between Eastwood and Leone got off to a shaky start. Leone was so unsure about the lead actor he had signed in near-desperation that he sent Mario Caiano to Fiumicino airport to meet Eastwood in his stead. At least Caiano could speak English. The actor arrived, dressed like an 'American student' with a suitcase containing, among other props from the CBS store, the gun-belt and wooden pistol grips (adorned with metal snakes) he had worn in *Rawhide*. These he brought for luck. Tonino Valerii recalls: 'Caiano had to make his apologies. "Sergio Leone is not feeling very well," and so on.'[45] Finally, actor and director met at Eastwood's hotel in Rome, where Leone seemed fidgety, 'gruff' and diffident, over-keen to remind the actor of who was boss. He later admitted that he felt 'intimidated' by the encounter and hid the fact in his usual way. The following day, the American actor Brett Halsey met Eastwood outside the hotel, and invited him to a party. They knew each other, and Halsey already had experience of working in Italy. At this party, one guest advised the Eastwoods to be very careful of the *Magnificent Stranger* project, because it had been off and on for some months, and on the stocks for much longer than that. This wasn't true, but could well have thrown the new arrivals. Eastwood recalls that he replied, 'It may have been around a long time, but I like it. I think it will be fun to do.' In any case, it was too late for second or even third thoughts.[46]

Leone later claimed that the props associated with Eastwood's character were his idea: 'I gave him a poncho to broaden him out. And a hat. No problem.' He even remembered getting hold of one of those black-and-white stills supplied in desperation by Claudia Sartori, and inking in a beard, a toscano cigar and a poncho. Eastwood disagrees. He told English critic Iain Johnstone: 'I went down to a wardrobe place on Santa Monica Boulevard, and just purchased the wardrobe and took it over there. It was very difficult, because for a film you always have two or three hats of the same sort, two or three jackets of the same kind, in case you lose a piece of clothing or something gets wet and you need a change. But for this film I had only one of everything: one hat, one sort of sheepskin vest, one poncho, and several pairs of pants because they were just Frisco-type jeans. If I'd lost any of it halfway through the film, I'd have really been in trouble.'[47]

When I put it to Eastwood that Leone's recollection of events was appreciably different, he replied: 'He didn't accept that? Well – I guess I heard that too, and I heard stories where people would say that he would lay a rope down the line on the ground where I should walk. All that stuff. And I thought, "Funny, he's the only one who ever had to do that." But I guess it's normal for him. All of a sudden I go back to America, and he does several films in the same vein and then drops out for a while, and he sees me going on to do other things and maybe that affected him. Who knows why a person says different things?'[48]

Actually, Carlo Simi's original drawing of the Stranger's poncho has survived, so that item of wardrobe at least seems to have been part of the Italians' production design.

Whoever originated the 'look and style' of the Stranger, Eastwood agrees that the character's visual appearance was a radical change from Alan Ladd's fringed buckskins in *Shane*: 'You ask most people what those films were about, and they can't tell you. But they tell you the "look" [he mimes throwing the poncho over his shoulder] and the "da-da-da-da-dum" [he hums the opening bars of *The Good, The Bad and The Ugly*] and the cigar and the gun and those little flash images that hit you.' In time, *Fistful of Dollars* would even be credited as the origin of 'designer stubble'. Eastwood isn't so sure ('When a person's out on the prairie like that there's no way you can shave'). And Leone, for once, agreed: 'It wasn't an invention for that film. I consulted historical documents and I can assure you that the drifters in the West were much more dirty in reality. As to their faces, they were incredible – much more scarred and pockmarked than those of any of my actors!'[49]

One of Clint Eastwood's conditions for accepting the role was that he would have the opportunity to change some of the dialogue, as well as rethink the talkative central character: 'I always felt that if the character explained everything as per the original script, we wouldn't have had any mystery at all to him.' Thus, Eastwood became one of the very few actors in film history to fight for fewer lines. Leone remembered giving Eastwood every encouragement to pare his dialogue. Eastwood remembers that Leone, unsure of himself, at first stood by his script. The pages were 'tremendously expository', the actor remembers, 'and I just cut it *all* down. Leone thought I was crazy.' The prologue plus three whole pages of dialogue were pruned to become 'I knew someone like you once and there was no one there to help'. Eastwood found that conveying this to Leone was a complicated business: 'He didn't speak any English, I didn't speak any Italian, so we had a little communication problem to begin with, but then, with a lot of hand waving, we both sort of came to an agreement . . . Our interpreter was a Polish lady, Elena Dressler [Constantin's representative in Rome], who spoke six or seven languages. She'd been in a German concentration camp and was liberated by the Americans. One of the assistants [in fact, Benito Stefanelli] spoke English and would give me all the necessary instructions.'[50]

Eventually, Eastwood remembers, he and Leone came to an

agreement over his performance: 'Sergio understood what I was doing, but when the producers saw the rushes, they thought I was doing nothing, that it was a disaster. When the film was cut together, they changed their minds. It was fun working with Sergio after *Rawhide*, where the stories were so conventional ... Maybe Sergio's methods and ideas weren't very orthodox, but they helped me discover another point of view. He was a great admirer of the masters of the Western, Hawks and Ford. But he had his own vision of what a Western should be, and some of his ideas were truly crazy. Sometimes I'd have to intervene to keep the ship on course.'[51] Eastwood's moods weren't helped by those cigars. He kept stubs of various lengths lying around the set, so he could put them in the corner of his mouth without actually having to light them. But sometimes he did have to spark up; and then, 'If I had to be in an unpleasant frame of mind, I took a couple of draws and boy, I was right there.'

Once shooting was under way – first in Rome, then Colmenar, then Almeria – Leone began to 'relax' into the project. He would turn up on the set in a cowboy hat, Western boots and spectacles (looking, according to Eastwood, like 'Yosemite Sam'). He would proceed to agonize about the tiniest details, acting out everyone's part while shouting 'Watch me!', alternating between overexcitement and fury at the frustrations of low-budget film-making. Since the script was available in English, Italian, German and Spanish, Leone's talents as a mime were tested to the full. Franco Giraldi reckons that one of Leone's big contributions emerged from this: 'he managed to synthesize the Roman rogue, a villain but a sympathetic one, with the Western hero who had become too pure and stereotyped ... When Sergio acted things out on set, he turned the character into a little Roman figurine.'[52] Eastwood felt that 'he loved the joy of it all. I know he had a good time when he wasn't getting furious.'[53] The actor perceived that Leone's bluff exterior masked 'a very nervous, intense and serious guy ... he was very volatile, very tense; he would wring his hands and he would get nervous, but he was just keeping his focus'.[54] Leone was approaching the project with all the excitement of a child playing with an elaborate new toy: 'He had this childlike way of looking at the world', and he wanted to re-create for adult audiences in the mid-1960s the magic of going to the cinema in Trastevere when he was a small boy. His 'fairytales for grown-ups' would be watched by adults as if they were children. The American Western had made its heroes and villains too mundane: now he would re-mythologize them. 'The West', Leone liked to say, 'was made by violent and uncomplicated men'.

A central feature of the film was the contrast in acting styles between the quiet American and the European supporting cast. In particular, Leone had to prevent the Italians from indulging in what Eastwood characterizes as the 'Hellzapoppin' school of drama'. Gian Maria Volonté was a particular offender in this respect. He had graduated from the National Academy of Dramatic Art in Rome in the mid-1950s. He played Romeo in the Arena di Verona, made his name with an Italian television version of Dostoevsky's *The Idiot*, and appeared in a few low-budget films in the early 1960s. But this was his first significant 'international' part, and his first villain. Volonté felt that his theatrical training was of limited value on the Wild West set. When he had difficulty thinking himself into the part of the vain and sadistic Ramon Rojo, 'Leone told me to practise scowling a lot'. The director also added a leather killing glove to his wardrobe, to make him seem even more villainous, and gave him a few more nasty lines. By the time they filmed the final duel, Volonté told the press that he was getting the hang of it: 'I made Clint Eastwood fire three extra bullets at me before I stepped down. I was so caught up in the part I just felt too mean to die!'[55]

But, according to Leone, Volonté tended to play to the gallery rather than the camera: 'He's the histrionic type, who theatricalizes everything . . . For the first Western, this shortcoming proved helpful to me. It emphasized the character – a spoiled child.' Volonté, for his part, was later to recall that, 'In his genre of film, Leone knows how to do things . . . his own perspective is that of playing games' but that the Western is 'a tiring genre in which I personally do not have much interest'.[56] One big attraction, where Papi and Colombo were concerned, was that Volonté was prepared to work for only 2 million lire. Franco Giraldi recalls that Volonté spent much of his time on the set 'reflecting about the politics of our situation – in Franco's Spain, in a miserable village in a bizarre film'. Volonté even tried, unsuccessfully, to engage Clint Eastwood in a debate about Italian politics.[57] The Spanish actors, Leone confirmed, were chosen 'for their faces – blemishes and all'. Mario Brega, who played a fat Mexican slob called Chico, was 'a friend from Rome' who had already appeared in one or two early Italian Westerns. Margherita Lozano, who played the statuesque and powerful Consuelo Baxter, was noticed by Leone in Luis Buñuel's *Viridiana*. Marianne Koch (Marisol) had spent a little time in Hollywood in the mid-1950s (*Four Girls in Town*; *Interlude*), and had recently been voted the most popular film actress in West Germany by *Film Echo*: 'I did not want her to read the script', said Leone, 'but I told her that it was a small, almost wordless part and that if she agreed to have confidence in me, she would make quite an impact. I was right.' The part of the coffin-maker was offered to Josef Egger, an Austrian music-hall comedian, largely because Leone just 'loved his way of grimacing, while making his beard go up in the air. He looked like a Western "character".'[58]

Meanwhile, Clint Eastwood's influence extended well beyond the details of his own performance and 'look'. By his account, 'we had to change all the wardrobe when we got over there, because they had Davy Crockett hats and all kinds of things that didn't fit into a Mexican situation'.[59] This account somewhat undercuts Leone's claim that he, a card-carrying Western buff, had amassed a 'substantial archive' of photographs and documents on the look and feel of the American frontier. As he was fond of saying: 'I began in the business during the neo-realist period. I love the *authentic* when it is filtered through imagination, myth, mystery and poetry. But it is essential that, at base, all the details seem *right*. Never invented. I think a fairy-tale captures the imagination when the story is a fairy-tale but the setting is extremely realistic. This fusion of reality and fantasy takes us into a different dimension – of myth, of legend.'[60] Again, Eastwood disagrees: 'Sergio doesn't really know *anything* about the West. He's just a good director. I mean he has his own ideas, and I think the fact that he doesn't know too much about the West is what works for him . . . I think his very open, adolescent-type approach to film – I don't mean this in a derogatory type of way – gave to the film a new look . . . He did things at the time that American directors would have been afraid of in a Western.'[61]

Some of these innovations happened, Eastwood believes, because Leone was not acquainted with the Hollywood rule-book. For instance, the Hays Office had long stipulated that a character being struck by a bullet from a gun could not be in the same frame as that gun when it was fired: the effect was too violent. 'You had to shoot separately, and then show the person fall. And that was always thought sort of stupid, but on television we always did it that way . . . And you see, *Sergio never knew that*, and so he was tying it up . . . You see the bullet go off, you see the gun fire, you see the guy fall, and it had never been done this way before.'[62]

Another innovation was Leone's extraordinary use of close-ups, not as the traditional 'reaction shots' or 'reverse shots', but as a series of portrait-studies of faces staring at one another: Andalusian gypsy faces, scarred Italian actors, an American with two weeks of stubble. Gargoyles. He also favoured close-ups of eyes which revealed 'everything you need to know about the character', as Leone put it: 'courage, fear, uncertainty, death, etc.'.[63] Or, in the case of the Eastwood character, complete impassivity: his eyes, like his aphorisms, give nothing away. Those close-ups belonged more to the world of Sergei Eisenstein, with his ideas on 'faces as types', than to Hollywood. Fellini might have been another precedent. As Eastwood remembers, 'Leone believed, as Fellini did, as a lot of Italian directors do, that the face means everything. You'd rather have a great face than a great actor in a lot of cases.'[64]

The filming itself was equally unpredictable. With a shoestring budget, things were pretty basic: 'Everyone went behind trees, you know,' recalls Eastwood. 'There were no facilities.' At the start of each day's shooting, Leone had a very clear idea of where he wanted to place the camera, but he was forced to print 'lots of the same shot – they were always having problems; the lab scratches one; they've lost three others'. And the rushes were in black and white, which didn't help. When he viewed them, Leone became increasingly 'paranoid' and hyper-cautious. Eastwood remembers that Colombo (whom he did not get on with) once peered at the day's rushes and exclaimed to the assembled company: 'Jesus, this is a piece of shit!'[65] Back in Rome, Carla Leone kept watch over the packages of rushes which were dispatched from Colmenar and Almeria to the processing lab, and she would call Sergio if there were any major problems. Unlike Clint Eastwood, she does not remember too many. Since she was carrying their second child (another daughter, Francesca), she was unable to join her husband on location, much to her frustration. But she did get to watch Sergio shoot the interiors in Rome. The sequence she remembers most vividly was the first to be filmed. 'It was the interior of the house of the three Rojo brothers, where Eastwood checks in after shooting Baxter's gunmen – and from which he slips away.' Carla also witnessed the sequence where Eastwood recuperates from his brutal beating-up by the Rojos in a mine-shaft. These and other Italian interiors enabled the production to qualify for a modest government subsidy.

Tonino Valerii was the first to view the material arriving from the locations, in his capacity as head of post-production at Jolly: 'The

Techniscope process allowed you to save fifty per cent of the cost of negative film, by printing two frames for the price of one. But when you first saw the raw film, unless you realized this, you just saw two frames at the same time: two Clint Eastwoods, two Gian Maria Volontés, two mules, four guns. And you had to make the mental adjustment – as well as adjusting the equipment. When the first material arrived, I immediately thought Eastwood's performance – and his presence – were extraordinary, so I called the producers over. They looked at the two frames and just laughed. Nobody seemed to have any faith in the production, or any sense that Leone knew what he was doing.'[66]

Leone didn't improvise his set-ups. But a lot of improvisation had to happen in other departments. When he was shooting Eastwood's entrance into San Miguel at Cortijo El Sotillo, he decided he would like Joe the Stranger to ride past a solitary tree in the desert, with a rope and noose hanging from it. But there weren't any trees in that part of the Almerian desert, and, after much animated discussion, Leone drove off in his cowboy hat to find one. Eventually, he came across exactly the kind of leafless tree he wanted. The only trouble was, it happened to be growing in someone's farmyard. So the following day, he returned with a truck and some technicians, with the intention of making an elderly Andalucian farmer an offer he couldn't refuse. As Eastwood remembers, 'He goes banging in there and he says, "We're from the highway department. This tree is very dangerous, it's going to fall down and someone's gonna get hurt. We'll take this tree right out for you." This old guy's standing out there and before he knows what's happening there are these Italians sawing his tree down.'[67] So Leone *was* in Almeria, after all.

Cash-flow problems, too, forced everyone to take one day at a time, literally, as the deal between Jolly Film, Constantin and Ocean proved to be full of holes. If the week's money failed to turn up, it was always the fault of the other two. Tonino Valerii remembers vividly that 'Leone's percentage – thirty per cent of the film – was tied to the fact that he had bought in the Spanish co-producer who had promised to put thirty million lire into the pot. Very little, in fact. And after the first week's instalment, he no longer paid anything. So one day Leone went to the location at Colmenar and all the doors and windows had been taken away. A Western street without doors and windows! Which meant they couldn't shoot. So they called Papi and Colombo, and at a time when it was prohibited to export currency from Italy, the diminutive Arrigo Colombo set out for Madrid with thirty million lire in his briefcase – in cash – risking arrest at the border. Luckily, no one tried to stop him. He insisted on recouping the Spanish co-producer's quota because of this, and with it most of Leone's percentage.'[68]

This instability permeated the set, and seemed to confirm the warnings Eastwood had been given before he started filming. It cannot have helped Leone's self-confidence. During the preparation of the sequence where Joe crawls away from his heavy punishment at the hands of the Rojo clan, Eastwood remembers that: 'I scuffed around in the dirt all morning waiting for the director and crew to quit arguing. The talk was all in Spanish and Italian and I didn't understand a word, but I could tell there was a violent discussion going on about *something*. I hoped they'd get it straightened out before we blew the whole morning without getting one shot. Finally, Sergio called me over. "Okay, Clint, you can start making up," he said through his interpreter. What the heck, I decided. They were always at it . . . The scene called for a lot of make-up because my face was to be badly swollen from being beaten up by a whole gang. I came out feeling hot and uncomfortable, and headed for the set. I was literally the most alone man in Spain. The set was deserted. No producer, no director, no crew. Only the big arc lamps standing there like Spanish vultures. It seems the crew hadn't been paid for two weeks . . . With one eye sealed shut by make-up and all the other junk on my face, I'd had it . . . I told them they could find me at the airport. Fortunately Sergio caught me before I left the hotel. He apologized and promised it wouldn't happen again. Things ran a little smoother after that.'[69]

As Eastwood sensibly reflected, 'I wouldn't have been in Spain at all if they'd had a lot of money. I'd still have been back in Hollywood with Maggie waiting for the breaks . . . so I figured I'd have to put up with the disorganization.' Things did run a little more smoothly for a while, until the final week of the shoot, when, as Leone remembered, the money finally ran out altogether. Papi and Colombo were all for 'cutting out the remaining expensive bits' and ordering the crew back to Rome. Instead, they soldiered on in Almeria with a select band of three actors and fifteen technicians, and managed to persuade the San José landowner to put them all up, on credit, for the necessary week's filming, along with use of his electricity supply. The film could not have been completed without him.[70]

Luckily, editor Roberto Cinquini was skilled at making the most of the footage which came back from the lab in one piece. Tonino Valerii recalls: 'The famous sequence of the Baxter massacre, with all those close-ups of Mexicans who smile or laugh as they shoot, is part of [Cinquini's] contribution.' (In the Italian version of the film, this sequence is considerably longer, with a series of close-ups of Mexicans laughing orgiastically, their faces reflecting the flames of the Baxter house as it burns to the ground.) 'Cinquini also made sure that as many as possible of the takes that had been rejected were printed and made copies of lots of the good takes as well. He was a maestro at this. He knew how to use the same set-up four or five times, always using a different moment to start from. I myself made several contributions to the dialogue, during post-production. Leone came back from Spain without the most up-to-date copy of the script. He'd lost it! I used the original screenplay, changing a number of things, because during the editing stage, the story had been changed quite a bit. And I actually shot a couple of detailed close-ups which were needed: a burning fuse, for example.'[71]

But perhaps the most nerve-racking moment occurred three-quarters of the way through the shoot, when word came down from Jolly Film in Rome that Sergio Leone (and everyone else for that matter) 'should refrain under any circumstances from mentioning the word *Yojimbo*'. 'The rights had not been cleared yet,' Eastwood has recalled. But they were all assured that this was a technicality, and 'the problem would be solved in the next few days'. It wasn't. Whether because Jolly were too mean to stump up the ten thousand dollars needed to secure remake rights (as Leone claimed), or because Leone just forgot about *Yojimbo* in all the excitement (as others have claimed), or because Jolly contacted Toho Films in Rome and didn't get a reply (as Tonino Delli Colli claims) or because Leone genuinely thought he wasn't in fact remaking Kurosawa's film (just returning the story to its 'place of origin'), the question of securing the necessary permission had somehow been put on the long finger. The directive to avoid all mention of Kurosawa's title would suggest that *someone* was trying *something* on. Fulvio Morsella's version is that it wasn't Sergio Leone: 'He was taken in by his producers . . . he screened *Yojimbo* for them and said, "If you can get the rights for a remake, I'll make the film." Well, they told him they'd got the rights but actually they hadn't. And he went ahead and made *Fistful of Dollars*. And some litigation started with Kurosawa, who was in the right.'[72] Tonino Valerii remembers the subsequent plagiarism case as 'not at all jolly ... Papi and Colombo had first viewed *Yojimbo* with Sergio, very early on, at a private screening in a secret location. As head of post-production, I had the invoice for this screening in my possession. When the court case began, I still had this piece of paper. Remember I was being paid by Papi and Colombo and I was by then friends with Leone. So I adopted the only correct position in the circumstances. I went back home and tore up the invoice.'[73]

But there was to be another, more serious piece of paper: a formal letter signed by Akira Kurosawa and the scriptwriter of *Yojimbo*: 'It was addressed to Sergio and it said, "Signor Leone – I have just had the chance to see your film. It is a very fine film, but it is my film. Since Japan is a signatory of the Berne Convention on international copyright, you must pay me." Now Sergio was so naïve that he waved this letter around to everyone. The letter was really offensive, with its accusation of plagiarism, of copying Kurosawa's film, but he didn't seem to realize it. He couldn't get beyond the fact that the great director Kurosawa had written to him, and called his work a very fine film. He was so thrilled about this. When anyone tried to get him to put the letter away, he kept asking, "Why?"'[74]

The lawyers representing Jolly Film and Leone reckoned that the best means of defence was attack, and tried to build a counter-claim: 'They said to us, "We will certainly lose this case unless we can demonstrate that it was in fact *Kurosawa* who copied from an earlier literary work, and preferably an Italian one" ... I was the person responsible for finding this wonderful piece of literature. I happened to see an advertisement for a performance of Carlo Goldoni's play *Arlecchino servitore di due padrone*, produced by one of our most eminent stage directors. So I phoned my friend Gastaldi, the fortunate possessor of a copy of the *Bompiani Dictionary of Literature* in his charming library, and asked him to look up *Arlecchino* among Goldoni's plays, and read the plot over to me. That same afternoon, I took my piece of news to Giorgio Papi, a little bit ashamed of the irreverence of what I was doing. I said, "I've found the piece of literature Kurosawa stole *Yojimbo* from. It's called *Arlecchino*!" He referred me to the lawyers, who were sceptical at first but said, "Okay, let's go with it." I even got thousands of lire as a reward. So it was, I'm very much afraid, in this way that Goldoni became the inspiration for the Italian Western.'[75]

The 'Goldoni' defence was not a bad one, given the cultural changes that Leone had introduced when adapting *Yojimbo* for Italian con-

sumption. It didn't work, but at least it provided the basis for a negotiation. According to Valerii, 'Until then, Kurosawa had us up against
a wall, but now at least we could talk about things, and a compromise
agreement was reached.' Kurosawa and Kikushima, deemed to be the
authors of *Yojimbo*, were compensated for the obvious resemblance
between the two stories by being granted exclusive rights to distribute
the film in Japan, Formosa (now Taiwan) and South Korea, plus 15
per cent of the worldwide box-office takings. Leone's lawyers had
agreed that the author's royalties for both films should have been paid
to the estate of the (very late) Carlo Goldoni. The published noveliz-
ation of the film, when it later came out, had to state that it was 'based
on the screenplay of a Jolly film, Rome . . . by permission of Kurosawa
Productions Ltd, Tokyo'. Giorgio Papi flew to Japan and sealed the
arrangement.

One side-effect of the case was that, much to Clint Eastwood's disappointment, distribution in America and Britain had to be delayed for
over two and a half years. Suddenly, it looked as though he had backed
a loser. Another side-effect was that a built-in distribution mechanism,
and a demand, had been created in the 'Far East territories'. Many
years later, at the Cannes Film Festival of 1990, Clint Eastwood finally
met the eighty-year-old Akira Kurosawa during the opening-night
party, and they talked (through an interpreter) about *Yojimbo*: Leone
forgetting to clear the rights, and the fact that Eastwood owed his big
career break to a piece of plagiarism. The two men had a good laugh
about it. At the time, it hadn't seemed quite so funny. Leone's own
acerbic conclusion was that 'Kurosawa was entirely correct to do what
he did. He is a businessman and he earned more money from this
operation than from all his own films put together. I admire him as a
cinéaste very much. I only ask myself if his ideas about *hara-kiri* have
something to do with the success achieved by the remakes of his films.
Already, John Sturges's *The Magnificent Seven* had pulverized the box
office.'[76]

Papi's flying visit to Japan, according to Valerii, had been the last
straw where Leone was concerned: 'First, they'd taken away the percentage which came with the Spanish co-production, and now Papi was
giving away 15 per cent of his film.' They then, according to Leone, proceeded to sell their assets to another company, which discovered that
'the coffers were empty'. By the time Leone had prepared a legal case
against them, there was, magically, no money left with which to pay

him. For a man who was always very careful with his own money, this was an ominous start to his career as an 'author'. Leone's reaction, twenty years later, was still, understandably, very bitter indeed: 'Even today, *Fistful of Dollars* is the only one of my Westerns which earned me nothing. Worse still, it cost me a great deal of money. After that experience, I resolved to produce my films myself.' In the end, the director was compensated 'with the Mexican rights, the one place the film has never done well because the Mexicans are the bad guys'.[77]

Whoever the story originated with, it was the *experience* of *Fistful* – the look and the sound – that was really distinctive. As Eastwood reflects, 'I think Sergio's films changed the style, the approach to Westerns. They "operacized" them, if there is such a word. They made the violence and the shooting aspect a little larger than life, and they had great music and new types of scores.' Eastwood also acknowledges Leone's innovative use of sound design: 'A film has to have a sound of its own, and the Italians – who don't record sound while they're shooting – are very conscious of this in the post-production department. Sergio Leone felt that sound was very important, about 40 per cent of the film . . . Leone will get a very operatic score, a lot of trumpets, and then all of a sudden, "Ka-pow!" He'll shut it off and let the horses snort and all that sort of thing. It's very effective.' Sergio Donati adds the distinctive sound of gunshots to the list: 'Sergio enjoyed playing with the design of the sound. They had a lot of meetings to discuss it. He hated silence. For instance, the revolvers are in fact Winchesters, and the Winchesters are little cannons. They sent the sound man off to a valley near Rome, where there are no roads or distracting noises. Sergio sent the man, who came back with "ping-pong-pung", ricochets and echoes. It wasn't electronic. It was recorded in a natural setting, because he wanted air and atmosphere.'[78]

When he returned to America, Clint Eastwood had recorded a cue track, as was the Italian custom, and left decisions about the sound to the post-production department. Later, he would post-synchronize his own voice in a dubbing studio in Rome. For the Italian version of the film, the voice would be that of actor Enrico Maria Salerno: a deeper and richer-toned voice than Eastwood's, which would make the central character seem much more 'heavy', much less detached and cool. Italian audiences were used to that: the voice of Emilio Cigoli, which had dubbed John Wayne's for years, was also a full-bodied, theatrical kind of voice.

Under pressure from Papi and Colombo, Sergio Leone showed composer Ennio Morricone a rough-cut version of the film. He had originally wanted Franco Lavagnino to write the music; they had worked together on *Pompeii* and *Colossus*. But Jolly Film, who had commissioned Morricone to score *Gunfight at the Red Sands*, and were in the process of using him for *Bullets Don't Argue*, begged Leone to go and see him. He went, and was greeted with a surprising piece of news: 'I'd scarcely entered Ennio's house when he announced that we had been at school together. I thought he had to be bluffing, that this was some kind of a joke. Not at all. He showed me a photograph of the class of the *terza elementare* [just before secondary level], and I had to agree that we were both in it. This was a nice touch, but not quite enough to persuade me to employ him! I said, being frank about it: "Your music for *Duello nel Texas* was just about as unoriginal as it could be. A watered-down version of Dimitri Tiomkin." To my astonishment, he concurred: "I couldn't agree more. But they *commissioned* me to write a watered-down version of Dimitri Tiomkin. So that's what I gave them. A composer has to earn a living." I saw that he was on the level about this. So I gave him a chance.' Morricone reminded Leone that whereas Sergio preferred to play cops and robbers in the playground of St Juan Baptiste de la Salle, *he* always preferred football. And that they were both 'very lively children ... We reminisced together about the games we used to play, about the photos we had kept, and the mutual friends we still had from that school. Because we hadn't met since we were eight or ten years old. Twenty-five years before.'[79]

Ennio Morricone was born on 10 November 1928, on the Via S. Francesco a Ripa in Trastevere, so the two men were roughly the same age and, as it happened, from similar backgrounds. Morricone senior was also in show business, although Mario Morricone's career as a trumpeter in night-clubs and music halls was less lucrative and stable than Vincenzo Leone's. Mario taught Ennio various instruments at an early age, notably the trumpet: 'I began composing', he recently recalled, 'when I was six. My father taught me the G clef. We were on holiday and I wrote some silly bits of music. They were hunting themes, things I'd heard on the radio. I destroyed them. I was inspired by Weber's *Der Freischutz*, and wrote down the overture I'd heard. Perhaps these hunting themes helped me to write for Westerns ... The great outdoors, I suppose it could have been that. Because those themes do have some link with the music I wrote for Sergio Leone's Westerns.'[80]

While Leone was registering at Law School, Morricone entered the Santa Cecilia Conservatory in Rome, to specialize in trumpet, harmony and composition, under the close supervision of composer Goffredo Petrassi: 'everything from Palestrina and Monteverdi to Stravinsky, Stockhausen and Luciano Berio'. It was very unusual for a trumpet specialist to go on to study composition, and he combined his daytime researches with evening work helping out his father. In 1943, at the age of fifteen, he even deputized for an unwell Mario in 'Costantino's Band'. These experiences, according to Morricone, encouraged him to treat music as 'an experience rather than a science'. In 1954 he received his Diploma in Composition with a mark of 9.5/10 and left the Conservatory. Under Petrassi's guidance, in the mid- to late 1950s he composed a series of pieces: a cantata, a sextet, five variations on a theme by Frescobaldi, an 'invention' for piano, a clarinet trio, a concerto, three studies for flute and a 'distanze per violino, violincello e pianoforte', some of which were noticed by the International Society of Contemporary Music. In the evenings he 'continued to play trumpet in a night-club to make ends meet'.

Following his marriage to Maria Travia in October 1956, and the birth of a son the following year, he was confronted by the difficult decision of whether to continue composing contemporary music 'on a very meagre income' subsidized by a teaching salary, or whether to pursue more commercial employment. Morricone decided to 'start working as an arranger for radio, television, theatre' and then for record companies. So, while his concerto was being performed at the Fenice in Venice (1960), and his 'Distanze per violino' at the Ateneo Theatre in Rome (1962), he simultaneously arranged Neapolitan evergreens such as 'Funiculì, Funiculà' and 'Santa Lucia' for Mario Lanza, right up to Lanza's death in 1959. Morricone worked so diligently at this time that he became known in the trade, somewhat to his chagrin, as 'the father of modern arrangement' rather than as a composer. He also did arrangements for RAI Television variety shows, until his friend the film composer Mario Nascimbene asked him to direct a few pieces of music, and write a little, incognito, for Franco Rossi's *Morte di un amico* in 1959 and Richard Fleischer's *Barabbas* in 1961. His formal introduction to film music came through Luciano Salce, whom he met in a television studio. Salce wanted a composer for two plays he was directing in Rome, and chose Morricone. He also recommended Morricone to Dino De Laurentiis for the job of scoring *Le pillole di Ercole*, but Dino turned him down on the grounds that he was 'an unknown'. A year later he secured his first credit when Salce asked him to score *Il Federale/The Fascist*. He had scored three other Salce pictures, plus a couple for director Camillo Mastrocinque, when he was reunited with Sergio Leone.[81]

In some ways, the careers of director and composer had run along similar lines. But there were important differences. Most evidently, Morricone's professional life had followed a single trajectory since leaving the college which trained him, while Leone had several false starts. It was a relationship that would, in Leone's words, turn into 'a marriage like Catholics used to be married before the divorce laws': tempestuous, but devoted. As Morricone puts it, 'Sergio was almost tone deaf, but our relationship was intense and very creative, and I felt very tender towards him. When he wanted to refer to a theme, Sergio would say, "You know, it's the one which goes da-da-da", in a vague way . . . It was a huge effort on my part to understand which theme he was referring to.'[82]

As they began their collaboration on *The Magnificent Stranger*, Leone was especially preoccupied with thoughts about music for the two set-piece sequences: the exchange of hostages, and the final show-down. 'The south of Texas', Leone later recalled, 'is a passionate, over-heated place. There's a mixture of Mexico and America there. This gives a particular tone and atmosphere to their funerary rites and their religion. Just the setting I needed for my dance of death. For my first Western, I asked for a score which was like the *deguello* which Tiomkin used in *Rio Bravo* and *The Alamo*. It's an old Mexican funeral chant.' Leone and Cinquini had hummed the tune together while rough-cutting the sequence on a moviola machine. But it did not have the lineage Leone ascribed to it. The *deguello* was specially written and arranged by Tiomkin for *Rio Bravo*, as a dirge for Sheriff Chance (John Wayne) and his raggle-taggle team of deputies standing guard over the town jail. A Mexican saloon band incessantly plays the mournful trumpet air, with mariachi guitar backing. Colorado (Ricky Nelson) explains: 'They call it the *deguello*, the cut-throat song. The Mexicans played it for those Texas boys when they had them bottled up in the Alamo.' The atmosphere of doom and the collision of two cultures were what Leone was after. But Morricone was not at all keen to plagiarize the piece. Whether or not it had been based on an 'old Mexican' tune, Tiomkin had put his name to the score, and it had been published as sheet music for piano. It was a question of professionalism.

Morricone recalls: 'I had to say to Sergio, "Look, if you put that lament into the film, I won't have anything to do with it." So he said to me: "Okay, you compose the music but do it in such a way that a bit of your score *sounds* like the *deguello*." I didn't take very kindly to that either, so I took an old theme of mine, a lullaby that I'd written for a friend, for a theatre version of three sea dramas by Eugene O'Neill [*I drammi marini*, 1960/1]. The lullaby was sung by one of the Peters Sisters . . . Make no mistake, the theme was certainly far removed from the lament. What brought out a resemblance was its performance in a semi-gypsy style on the trumpet, with all the *melismas* – the flourishes played around single notes of the tune – which are characteristic of that style. But the theme itself was not, repeat not, the same thematic idea as the *deguello*.'[83] Clearly, the question of attribution was, and still is, a sore point with Ennio Morricone. (The confusion was compounded in 1965, when Morricone wrote an arrangement of Tiomkin's *deguello*, complete with vocals and chorus, and issued it on an album in Italy.) Morricone is insistent: 'Yes, I recaptured the musical atmosphere of Hawks's film, an atmosphere which suited the Mexican ambience, but I did it through the interpretation and *performance* of the piece on the trumpet. The piece itself was completely original.'

Both he and Leone agreed from the outset that they did not want the music to be 'inspired in any way by the American Western'. In Morricone's view, Hollywood Western scores tended to have too much 'symphonic music' in them. He believed that they over-orchestrated simple folk tunes to the point where they sounded lush and sentimental, and were 'too full of redundancy', bearing little or no relationship to the wild prairie tales they were accompanying. At a technical level (Leone was apparently obsessed by this), the sound mixing of concert-like music with naturalistic effects meant that 'the human ear could not take it all in'. Moreover, to Leone's mind, it wasn't prominent enough, because characters clogged up the soundtrack with a surfeit of dialogue: 'The producers laid so much vocalizing on top of the gunshots and the hoof-beats that they lost sight of what the Western stories were all about. All those voices! They superimposed the most positive and reassuring values of the day on to a brief period of American history which was in reality amazingly violent, what I've called the rule of violence by violence. But you wouldn't know that from the films.

Talk, talk, talk.'[84] Morricone and Leone hoped to achieve 'much more interaction between music, sounds and visual images' than was the Hollywood standard, as they believed that 'in each scene, each silence and each sound of any kind should have a *raison d'être*'. Ideally, Leone suggested, the music should be written *before* a foot of film was shot, so that it could be integrated into the story at script stage, and so that the director could conjure up mental images of its impact in advance. But their current project was too far advanced, and too sparsely budgeted, for such an innovation.

In early meetings, composer and director, completely in synch about what they didn't want, set their minds to what sort of music *was* appropriate. Since, under the Italian method of post-synchronization, the entire soundtrack could be 'designed' from scratch, the question was bigger than it looked. Morricone recalls that they worked 'very closely together in using music to "complete" certain characters on the screen, to complete them as *types*. For example, I tried to underline with music the *ironic* aspects of certain characters. Leone never really shared the American psychology, to which he manifestly preferred a more Italian reality – a down-to-earthness. Leone was born in Rome, like me. Certain characters in his films, the bad ones in particular, are very Italian, and even very Roman. But with stetsons on their heads. Nothing to do with American history, really, and to underline the irony and craziness of these Italian characters, I created an "Italian" sound.' Partly this was achieved through use of distinctive musical instruments which were unusual in a Western setting: 'I wanted to hammer out a kind of music which was more pressing, more troubled, more of a direct experience. So I used the Sicilian guimbard and the maranzano ['jew's harp'], a Mediterranean instrument which is also played in North Africa and Asia.'[85]

Morricone also enjoyed 'using instruments which resembled the human voice, like the flute and the violin' and 'using the human voice itself, solo and choral, as if it was a musical instrument [like in some forms of nasal folk-singing] because it is for me the most beautiful instrument of all with a sound attached to life itself'. Both the guimbard and the folk-singing were associated with the 'music of remote places', which again was appropriate to *The Magnificent Stranger*. 'When I began to compose for Leone', says Morricone, 'I didn't think about it as writing specifically for that kind of film. With reference to the American Westerns which were the available "models", I wanted simply to use the idea of the escape to the prairie or desert and the expression of solitude. I wanted to put all this in music: isolated locations, a long way away from the noise and bustle of towns; I tried to re-create in my music this sense of wildness.' This is why whistling – as an 'expression of solitude' – seemed so appropriate.

Sergio Leone shared these ideas, but he needed something more to feel that the score was as distinctive as the film he had just shot. Morricone continues: 'Sergio heard an arrangement I'd made for an American folk piece a year or two before, an arrangement where I'd deliberately left out some of my musical ideas. The ideas, or layers, I'd left out in that arrangement were to let people hear for themselves, behind the musical theme, the nostalgia of a character, Mr X, for the city . . . So, as if a city was being heard from a distance, I could use city sounds from far away . . . Sergio listened to this, liked it very much, and wanted it as the arrangement of one of my themes.'[86]

The piece, a Woody Guthrie song called 'Pastures of Plenty', was arranged by Morricone in 1962 for American tenor Peter Tevis, and released in Italy as an RCA single in 1962. His arrangement consists of a strong vocal line accompanied by an insistent rhythm, whip-cracks, bells, hammers, and a brief scale of sixteenths on a flute. For the chorus ('We come with the dust, and we're gone in the wind'), there are strings and a male-voice choir. In addition, one verse is played loud on a Fender Stratocaster rather than on the traditional Spanish guitar. The chorus is *identical* to the *Fistful of Dollars* theme (barring the latter's incomprehensible lyric), as are the strange instrumental sounds. 'Leone wanted that exact arrangement with a melody put over it,' says Morricone. He didn't want Peter Tevis's overdramatic vocals, though: they had already 'irritated' him in *Duello nel Texas*. He asked Morricone to hunt out the master track minus the human voice, which Morricone managed to do. Listening to this, Leone remembered, 'I was absolutely smitten. So I said, "You've *made* the film. Go to the beach. Your work is over. *That's* what I want. Just get hold of someone who is good at whistling." The man for the job was thirty-nine-year-old Alessandro Alessandroni, whom Morricone had known as a singer, pianist and guitarist since his teenage years playing in Roman night-clubs. Alessandroni now led a well-known vocal group called the Cantori Moderni, which Morricone was also to use for vocal and choral effects. 'Alessandro', he said, 'is an extraordinary chorus-master, and I've never heard a better vocal group than his . . . He can also whistle, as if this was a musical instrument like any other.'

So Alessandroni provided and prepared the choir, played the guitar and did the whistling. As he told me, proudly clutching his beaten-up 1961 brown and white Fender and displaying an assortment of Italian folk instruments in different keys (including a maranzano and a ceramic arghilofono): 'Nobody in the company at RCA believed in that film, so they wouldn't spend much money on the soundtrack. And when we saw some sequences to which Morricone had to put music, we were laughing because there were so many deads [sic] – a lot of deads lying around . . . Sergio came often, sitting in the booth and he'd sometimes joke with me. He was so big, you know? "So you have to whistle the best you can this morning – understand?"' Alessandroni appreciated Morricone's desire to experiment with the instrumentation, and was able to contribute: 'I knew every quality of my choir, each single voice, so he would ask me what was possible.'[87]

The arrangement, in Leone's words, 'substituted for the usual monotonous accompaniments the audacious invention and use of natural sounds, the cries of birds and animals, extraordinary sound effects'. It had actually emerged from Morricone's ongoing research into the idea that all noise belongs to the realm of music. He had attended a seminar in Darmstadt in 1958, led and demonstrated by John Cage, and had since made contact with an informal group of avant-garde musicians and composers who called themselves Gruppo d'improvvisazione Nuova Consonanza. This group had come together in the late 1950s to give occasional concerts to specialized audiences in Rome, and was to become a fully fledged band in 1964. Morricone denies 'a direct line' from his experiences with Nuova Consonanza to his film scores, but accepts that there may be some elements in his mainstream film scores 'which are appropriate to the group's researches'. Such elements include the innovative use of natural sounds and extraordinary effects for Leone's Westerns: 'Sergio's films did suggest to me a certain way of thinking; the insertion of everyday sounds into this body of Westerns seemed to give new life to these film compositions.'[88]

It is no coincidence that all of *Fistful*'s most striking ingredients have since been the subject of disputes about originality: the *deguello* theme (Morricone versus Tiomkin), the appearance of Joe the Stranger (Eastwood versus Leone) and the relationship with *Yojimbo* (Kurosawa versus Leone). If they hadn't contributed to the film's success, then maybe no one would have bothered to argue about them. It used to be said of

Steven Spielberg's films that the only one which did not involve some sort of litigation about originality was *1941*.

The first critical responses to the film slightly irked Leone, because they ignored the 'Italianizing' elements: 'The newspaper reviewers accused me of trying to copy the American Western, from the very start. Later, the critics wrote that I was trying to create a form of "critical cinema". Both were missing the point, in their different ways. Because in fact I brought to the Western some strict conventions of my own. And obviously, there's a culture behind me that I can't just wish away.'[89]

Some of these conventions were visual ones, though these weren't nearly so apparent in *Fistful of Dollars* as in subsequent films. The final shootout around the fountain of San Miguel is a case in point. Joe strides towards Ramon Rojo and his henchmen. It looks as though this will turn into a traditional, linear confrontation. But, as the resurrected Stranger stumbles from side to side (when bullets hit his metal chest-shield), Leone intercuts close-ups of the faces of the Rojo gang, one by one. An entire circle is thus described; and as Ramon dies, a series of blurring subjective shots perform circular motions against the sky. So instead of the traditional main-street confrontation, the shootout turns into a circular event, like attending a *corrida* or watching a roulette wheel. As Leone put it: 'A *theatricalized* duel . . . in the arena where the moment of truth takes place. Not face to face! The last chance of living is played out in the circular arena. It is the moral of the fable . . . The duel in *Fistful* reverses all sorts of conventions. There's the phrase, "When a man with a .45 meets a man with a rifle, the man with a pistol will be a dead man." And I amused myself by proving the contrary . . . The true West had nothing at all to do with the Western. I prefer to mix games with a documentary feel. When Volonté's rifle is empty, Eastwood places his pistol on the ground. The duel begins. We follow his technique of picking up his firearm and loading it. We also follow his opponent's technique. The rifle takes longer. So: Volonté loses.'[90]

Another of Leone's 'strict conventions' was to take visual moments from the classic Hollywood Western and film them in a deliberately expansive way. The duel involves an unusual emphasis on external appearances: close-ups of boots or weapons or nervous tics, as the protagonists jockey for position. In an earlier shot, Leone and Giraldi show the arrival of Silvanito the bartender and Joe the Stranger at a ledge overlooking Rio Bravo Canyon; the focus is adjusted as the two men dismount, then the camera cranes up and over the ledge to reveal a group of wagons (Ramon's gang) and a detachment of cavalry, riding across the river beyond. Later, Leone intercuts the two rival clans shooting it out in a cemetery, while at the same time the Stranger explores the Rojos cellar. As the Stranger taps the various wooden barrels with his pistol, his every action is matched by simultaneous events in the cemetery: four taps – four shots, and so on. It is a piece of cinematic rhetoric, which draws attention to itself as a visual and aural gag, and it makes the old clichés seem fresh again. Sometimes this kind of rhetoric satirizes the conventions of the American Western; sometimes it celebrates them; and sometimes it undercuts them.

Leone argued that he was reacting against the laziness of American directors of Westerns, who had lapsed into a 'repetitiveness' and a 'lack of attention to detail'. To Leone, these were almost cardinal sins. As he confessed to me: 'Remember *Shane*? I'm thinking of the scene where Jack Palance challenges the little man outside the saloon. When the little man is shot, he staggers six yards back into the mud. It is a very realistic presentation of death. And it is the result of careful thought . . . When you think of all the Westerns you've seen, I'm sure you'll agree that as a rule the producers shied away from a realistic approach and turned the whole thing into a pre-packaged formula kind of entertainment which paved the way for the empty clichés of television.'[91]

On *Fistful*'s budget, a certain 'attention to detail' in design could – just about – be afforded. In case we expect the bad guy to wear black, Ramon first meets the Stranger in a milk-white shirt, and white pieces of fluff float across the scene, almost suggesting a snow effect. During the exchange of hostages, this white gives way to a softer autumnal brown (leaves on the street, sand, dust, horses, costumes) against which Ramon's dark Spanish-style outfit and the child's white smock stand out. But more money would clearly have helped: the townspeople only appear in two short scenes, which look as though they were shot on the same day; and colour-matching is poor (particularly for dusk or night-time sequences, most of which seem to have been shot in daylight). This may be part of the reason why Leone had difficulty, at first, in market-ing his film: 'Before *Fistful*, about twenty-five Italian Westerns had been made. When I finished the film, a Roman businessman who owned a chain of at least fifty cinemas didn't even want to attend a private screening, because it had already been established that the Western genre in Italy was completely finished. These Westerns had been released, but the critics had not noticed them . . . Nobody had noticed, because they all had "stolen" titles, because they were thought to be "B" films.'[92]

*The Magnificent Stranger* certainly had a 'B' budget, and its producers had been responsible for two of those early Italian Westerns. It would need some top-drawer marketing to separate it from the herd. The first step was to re-christen it *Fistful of Dollars* – a nod to the hero's preferred mode of payment, and perhaps a reference to the famous statement made by Emiliano Zapata during the Mexican Revolution in 1911: 'Many of them [the Maderistas] so as to curry favour with tyrants, for a fistful of coins, *por un puñado de monedas*, are making the blood of their brothers spurt forth.' A fistful of coins, like Judas.

The next stage was to commission some eyecatching credit-titles from Luigi Lardini: bits of action footage rotoscoped against a black, red and white background, with the main title theme turned up to full whack. Finally there was a poster courtesy of graphic designer Sandro Simeoni, which showed, in classic American Western style, a gunfighter in a red shirt, kneeling on the ground and shooting a comic-book baddie in the stomach. This poster contains no likeness of Clint Eastwood (who was an unknown quantity) and no reference to the visual style of the film. It could have been advertising any of those early Italian Westerns. The only unusual feature was that the gunfighter was pointing his pistol straight at the viewer. The upright lettering (in blue and red) informed potential punters that the director was 'Bob Robertson'. The villain was played by 'John Wells' (Volonté = will = wells), and the co-star was Marianne Koch. Since Ms Koch had only one line of dialogue in the entire picture, her billing as the female lead was questionable. Only when the punters had bought their tickets would they discover that the film didn't in fact have a female lead. Benito Stefanelli became 'Benny Reeves', a name he chose 'in memory of having worked in four or five films with Steve Reeves'.[93]

With impeccably Americanized credentials, *Fistful of Dollars* was taken to the annual film-market in Sorrento, only to find no takers. Westerns were yesterday's event. After one screening, the owner of a chain of cinemas in Tuscany congratulated Bob Robertson: 'I enjoyed your film a lot. Lots of new things. Bravo.' 'So you'll take it then?' enquired Leone. 'No. It can't possibly be a success, because there are no women in it.' Leone then tried to persuade the distributor that some of the most successful American Westerns (*Gunfight at the OK Corral* or *High Noon*) had been ruined by the Rhonda Flemings or Grace Kellys of this world: 'Even in the greatest Westerns, the woman is *imposed* on the action, as a star, and is generally destined to be "had" by the male lead. But she does not exist *as a woman*. If you cut her out of the film, in a version which is going on in your head, the film becomes much better. In the desert, the essential problem was to survive. Women were an obstacle to survival! Usually, the woman just holds up the story.'[94] But the distributor was unimpressed. In fact, Sergio Leone had substituted for the old-style heroine a Madonna-figure complete with Holy Family who did not so much 'hold up the story' (she wasn't on the screen long enough) as help make at least some sense of it.

What happened next has been told so often in Italian film histories, and around the Leone family dinner table, that it achieved the status of myth long ago. One of Sergio Leone's versions went like this: 'I will never ever forget that month of August 1964. I went to Florence for the first screening on the 27th. It was stiflingly hot: in Italy, to release a film in August is to kill it stone dead. In this downtown cinema, it was to kill it and bury it as well. The cinema was in a kind of alleyway. The wooden fixtures and fittings dated from 1908 and the invention of cinematography! In my worst nightmares, I'd never lived through such a dismal scene. Naturally, the producers – discouraged by comments at the film market – hadn't invested a single lira in publicity. My film was simply announced in the listings columns of the newspapers. It was as if it did not exist, had never existed.'[95]

After below-average takings at the box office on the Friday and Saturday, Leone returned home to Rome. But when he called the manager on the Monday, he heard a very different story. Monday's takings were double Sunday's: 'It was a unique happening in the history of contemporary cinema. With the minimum of publicity, without a single criticism, the film took off by itself, in that doubly unknown cinema – and took off with a vengeance. The famous "word of mouth" which people talk about so much and in which no one really believes had happened. Tuesday, Wednesday – people were turned away. I still ask myself how these people even found out the address of the cinema.'[96] Six months later, *Fistful of Dollars* was still running in Florence. The manager, Leone enjoyed telling everyone, had refused to surrender the print. Two weeks after the Florence opening, a second 'world première engagement' took place at the huge Supercinema on the corner of the

Piazza del Viminale in Rome, attended by many of the business people who had rejected *Fistful* at Sorrento. Between November 1964 and December 1965, the box office all over Italy (but especially in Rome, Milan, Turin and Naples) went into orbit.

Tonino Valerii tells this 'sleeper' story a little differently: 'The cinema was in a semi-central position – not in the real city centre, not a first-run house, shall we say, but not a flea pit either . . . The commercial director of Unidis, who distributed the film, was responsible for the fact that every day tons of tickets were bought up to prevent the film from being withdrawn from the programme. On the Monday, a miracle occurred: the cinema was magically filled with spectators who had really paid . . . One fact which cannot be ignored when explaining "word of mouth" was that the cinema was situated near the railway station and was generally frequented by travelling sales reps who liked to kill two hours while waiting for their trains. Sales reps are of course good at spreading the word.' Valerii continues: 'They had to make many more prints, and in double-quick time. This is a beautiful story. The film was printed at Technicolor. One negative in yellow, one in red, one in green; then all combined. There was so much demand for copies that, without realizing it, they sent out some copies printed with only one matrix – all red. There were some theatres in Italy which actually screened these copies, and one gentleman went up to Leone and said, "Signor Leone. Ah, beautiful film. Very beautiful. All red!" "*What do you mean, all red?*" Leone demanded. "The picture was beautiful. Such a clever idea." '[97]

Sergio Donati has yet another version of the story: '*Fistful of Dollars* was a success due to the stubbornness of Sergio. It was released among other "B" Western movies and like them would have stayed on for only two or three days and then over – except that the owner of the cinema in Florence enjoyed the movie and kept it on for two weeks. And so Sergio went to Florence and convinced the owner to keep the movie for a month. Then he went to Rome and said, "In Florence, it is a huge success." '[98]

In Florence, the film drew only a few short critical notices. In November 1964, though, *Fistful* was reviewed in the Roman press as if it was a new release. Dario Argento, a young critic writing for the left-wing *Paese Sera* at the time, recalls the initial reaction amongst 'the intellectuals . . . My reaction to the first Sergio Leone picture was enthusiastic, but the other Italian critics mainly said this was a terrible

picture. Too crude in every way . . . I went to the Supercinema in Rome
to see it with three young friends. We were surprised. Surprised because
this was a Western we dreamed of seeing – the historical Western was
not so inventive, not so crazy, not so stylish, not so violent.'[99] Another
critic who bucked the trend was Ageo Savioli, who also worked for
*Paese Sera*. This was particularly ironic, because as one of the co-
screenwriters of *The Colossus of Rhodes* four years earlier, Savioli had
seriously fallen out with Leone. Leone, by his account, had been so
unimpressed with the results that he had told Savioli he could keep his
name on the credits, and continue to draw his salary, but that he should
stop even trying to write: 'If we don't play it that way, we will both be
wasting valuable time: you by writing and me by reading what you
have written.' It would be their little secret. So Leone was amazed to
read Savioli's glowing review: 'The day after *Fistful* reopened in Rome,
one of the reviews really got to me – because it was written by my
enemy. It was a thoughtful review, which even suggested connections
between *Fistful* and the works of John Ford . . . I picked up the telephone and said to him, "I'm touched, truly touched by your support.
Thank you so much. I'm so glad you were able to bury our disagreements." And this was his reply: "But what on earth have *you* got to do
with *Fistful of Dollars*?" It was then that I understood that he was the
only critic in town not to have found out that behind the name of Bob
Robertson was Sergio Leone. Since then, with monotonous regularity,
he has always panned my films.'[100]

Meanwhile, in America episode 151 of *Rawhide* was being aired on
network television, and Clint Eastwood was well into his seventh season: a particularly stressful one. He had read a paragraph in *Variety*
which stated that Italian Westerns, after a brief success on the European
market, 'have finally died out here [in Rome]'. Then, in a subsequent
issue, he learned that a low-budget Western called *Fistful of Dollars*
had become a surprise success at the box office. Since no one had
taken the trouble to inform him that his film was no longer called *The
Magnificent Stranger*, this comment meant nothing to him. 'The producers hadn't bothered to write to me since I left,' he later recalled, 'to say
thank you or go screw yourself, or whatever.'[101]

And then, on 18 November 1964, *Variety*'s correspondent in Rome
reviewed a film he had just seen at the Supercinema: 'Crackerjack
western made in Italy and Spain by a group of Italians and an international cast with James Bondian vigour and tongue-in-cheek

approach to capture both sophisticates and average cinema patrons. Early Italo figures indicate it's a major candidate to be sleeper of the year. Also that word-of-mouth, rather than cast strength or ad campaign, is a true selling point. As such it should make okay program fare abroad as well . . . This is a hard-hitting item, ably directed, splendidly lensed, neatly acted, which has all the ingredients wanted by action fans and then some.' The show-stopper, where Clint Eastwood was concerned, was that the reviewer went out of his way to praise the performance of one Clint Eastwood, who 'handles himself very well as the stranger, shaping a character strong enough to beg a sequel for admirers of this pic'. So *The Magnificent Stranger* had become *Fistful of Dollars*, and its lead actor had somehow become a superstar in Italy. *And* there was talk of a sequel. Maybe those six weeks in Europe hadn't been a total waste of time after all.

# 6

# For a Few Dollars More

The charm of a child lies to a great extent in his narcissism, his self-contentment and inaccessibility, just as does the charm of certain animals which seem not to concern themselves about us, such as cats and large beasts of prey. Indeed, even great criminals and humorists, as they are represented in literature, compel our interest by the narcissistic consistency with which they manage to keep away from their ego anything that would diminish it. It is as if we envied them for maintaining a blissful state of mind – an unassailable position which we ourselves have since abandoned.

Sigmund Freud, *On Narcissism, An Introduction* (1914)

Sergio Leone's immediate reaction to the success of *Fistful of Dollars* was to agonize about whether he could possibly hope to repeat it in a sequel. Deep down he was, as Clint Eastwood has observed, the sort of personality who 'was afraid to go to the post' and yet wanted very badly to do just that. Certainly, everyone Leone knew in the business expected him to proceed swiftly to a second Western, in traditional Cinecittà style. The more people pressurized him, though, the more he cast around for a completely different project: 'There was pressure from all sides to reveal the exact location of a second goldmine, and I felt less and less in the mood to give in to it. My success, finally, led me to a kind of creative paralysis. I read everywhere that the man who made *Fistful* would never be capable of directing a film in a different genre. They were challenging me . . . So I pulled *Viale Glorioso* out of the bottom drawer.'[1] But, apart from the fact that Fellini's *Vitelloni* had already covered much the same ground, no one seemed interested in backing an autobiographical tale of 'everyday life' in late 1930s Trastevere; at least, not if it was to be directed by Sergio Leone.

He also contemplated a remake of Fritz Lang's *M*, possibly with Klaus Kinski (admired for his theatre work at that time), in the Peter Lorre part of a Dusseldorf child murderer. At the same time he contacted Sergio Donati, asking him to write a script for another Papi and

Colombo production. It was a thriller about a diamond heist, called *Ad ogni costo/Grand Slam*. Donati recalls: 'He was supposed by contract to do something like ten movies in a row for [Papi and Colombo] . . . I was even ready to go to the location. I had the ticket to Egypt, and Sergio called me in Milan at the last minute and said, "Don't go, don't go." '2

By his account, Leone eventually settled on *For a Few Dollars More* out of sheer bloodymindedness. Papi and Colombo had let it be known that Leone might be able to get his hands on some of his 30 per cent cut of the *Fistful* profits, if he 'cross-collateralized' with a further film for them: another Western, of course. According to both Donati and Luciano Vincenzoni, Leone had, in his desperation to get *The Magnificent Stranger* off the ground, signed a very unwise contract. By law, he owed them at least one sequel. But Papi and Colombo's behaviour over *Fistful* had, in Leone's view, absolved him from any further obligations to them: 'The behaviour of Jolly made me sick to my stomach. So I went to see the two producers. I told them that the way in which events had turned out in fact *pleased* me . . . Because it meant that I would never have to make any more films with them. I was going to institute legal proceedings and I didn't want to see them ever again. Out of that came the seeds of my revenge. I said to them, "I don't know if I really want to make another Western. But I'm going to. Just to make you feel bad. And it will be called . . . " At that moment, the title came into my head – *For a Few Dollars More*. Of course, I had no idea at that stage what on earth it would be about.'3

Carla Leone confirms that 'Sergio called it *For a Few Dollars More* just to upset Papi and Colombo,' and that, at around this time, he met another potential producer, a Neapolitan lawyer with an office in Rome. Sergio liked to say of him, 'He was a small-time lawyer who sometimes worked for United Artists, and who speculated on the side with low-budget Spanish productions which he sold to Italian distributors.' In fact, he was one of the top entertainment lawyers in Italy, he worked for Columbia and Twentieth Century–Fox, and he had produced – uncredited – seven Spanish Westerns, including three with Joaquín Romero Marchent. He even claimed to have 'invented the Italian Western, following some market research which revealed that 80 per cent of viewers loved Westerns, while the Americans were producing hardly any. It was a simple question of supply and demand.'4

'The lawyer's name was Alberto Grimaldi,' Carla Leone continues, 'and they met because someone had told Sergio that he wanted to get more deeply involved in films – that he was looking for a big break. *Not* because Grimaldi was his lawyer in the Jolly case, as some have said. Sergio met him at dinner at an agent's flat. They had a long chat . . . And Sergio said, "Well, I have in mind this film *For a Few Dollars More*." And Grimaldi made Sergio a terrific offer.'[5]

Grimaldi's terms were indeed exciting: 'expenses, salary and 50 per cent of the profits'. Since any profit from *Fistful* now seemed highly problematic, and since his second daughter Francesca had just been born, this seemed like an offer Leone could not refuse. Donati reckons that Grimaldi was 'a very clever man, not a great producer . . . but he did have this intuition of a great producer to go to Leone at just the right moment with a contract which gave him fifty per cent participation: it was a great big infusion'.[6] Now, Leone would just have to get out of his 'creative paralysis' and get on with the job.

Part of the 'pressure from all sides' Leone was then feeling came from the many rival attractions that had been rushed into pre-production the moment *Fistful* began making serious money. For Sergio, this was a dubious honour. Maciste had been bad enough. The gradually massing army of Italian gunfighters, bounty-hunters, avengers and comedians was, in his view, even worse. They had an assortment of names and personal styles, following the lead of Leone's Joe and Sergio Corbucci's *Django*, the second most popular (named after the wild gypsy guitarist Django Reinhardt who had showed American jazz bands that he could do it too, but in a European all-string style). The roll-call would eventually read: Amen, Apocalypse Joe, Arizona Colt, Blade, Buckaroo, Cemetery, Chuck Moll, Clint the Stranger, El Diablo, Django, Djurado, Durango, Dynamite Jim, Gringo, Halleluja, Holy Spirit, Indio Black, Joe the Implacable, Gentleman Jo, Joko, Holy Water Joe, Johnny Hamlet, Johnny Texas, Johnny Yuma, Kitosch the Man from the North, Matalo, Minnesota Clay, Navajo Joe, Pecos, Piluk, Providence, Quinta, Quintana, Ramon the Mexican, Ringo, El Rojo, Roy Colt and Winchester Jack, Sabata, Sartana, Shango, Silence, Sledge, Sugar Colt, Trinity and Veritas. And those were just the ones whose names were featured in the title.[7]

A couple of years later, the phrase 'Spaghetti Westerns' was coined to describe such films, and it irritated Leone at first. He told me that when first he'd heard it, he took its meaning too literally: 'I thought it was quite subtle – maybe the spaghetti had replaced the lassoo.' Then, he realized that the word 'spaghetti' was simply being used as a synonym for 'Italian'. Leone considered that 'there was nothing malicious about the phrase. Just a way of defining national origins, taken up by the Americans. It was some Europeans who took this label in a critical spirit to stigmatize an entire genre.' In fact, it *was* to be used as a put-down in America. But whatever its intended meaning, Leone was keen to distance himself as far as he could from the 'entire genre' which was about to spew off the assembly-lines: 'When they tell me that I am the father of the Italian Western, I have to ask, "How many sons of bitches do you think I've spawned?" There was a terrifying gold rush after the commercial success of *Fistful of Dollars*, and I felt and continue to feel a great responsibility for this phenomenon. It wasn't as if the Italian Western had been taken up by many serious producers or directors. Most of them built their castles in the sand instead of on rock. The foundations just weren't there. A stampede! Imagine the affection with which people must have viewed my first film, when they were prepared to put up with four hundred more as they searched for the same thing.'[8]

Alberto Moravia wittily suggested that the 'gold rush' had something to do with an unconscious fear on the part of Italian audiences of over-population: the solution to the problem was more and more massacres. Luciano Vincenzoni takes a more positive view: 'Sergio Leone did a thing which created jobs for ten thousand people for ten years. In a way, he was a saint!' There was some method in all this apparent madness. It was a 'stampede' which, from the distributors' point of view, served three main purposes: to counter the continuing fall in ticket sales (683 million in 1964, as compared with 819 million in 1955); to fill the hole left by American distributors who had pulled out during the 'crisis' of 1962–4; and to keep the huge number of Italian cinemas fed with noisy and attention-grabbing product. Since most of the cheaper Westerns (and a lot of them were very cheap indeed) were financed by distributors' guarantees, and the distributors had managed to convince themselves that Westerns were gilt-edged investments, then Westerns it would have to be.

Sergio Leone's favourite story about the hit-and-miss atmosphere that surrounded the making of those rotgut pictures destined for *terza visione* cinemas goes like this: 'A film was being financed week by week. They'd show the first week's rushes to the investors who would then decide whether to pay for the second week, and so on. Everyone was expecting to be fired at any moment. Well, during the last of these tense weeks, the leading man walked out because he hadn't been paid

. . . Since they were about to shoot the final sequence, the director was in serious trouble. The sequence was to be about the leading man riding into an Indian encampment, either to make peace or to have a show-down. Which would it be? Well, the director was told the bad news of the leading man's departure: "Give me half an hour," he said to the producer. "I'll come up with something." Half an hour later he returned. "You know the old man who cleans the floor of the studio?" I should say that he wasn't referring to Cinecittà, but to something much more downmarket. "Well, put him in a cowboy costume, quick as you can." In the revised script, which they began shooting immediately, the old man drives in a buggy to the Indian encampment and says, "My son couldn't come, so he sent me instead" . . . That's what it was like in the heyday of the Italian Western.'[9]

By the time Leone started planning *For a Few Dollars More*, his friends (and rivals) Sergio Corbucci, Duccio Tessari, Franco Giraldi and Enzo Barboni were all directly involved in the stampede. Corbucci's *Minnesota Clay* had been released, the first Italian Western to be 'signed' by an Italian director under his own name; Tessari's *Pistol for Ringo* was in pre-production, as was Giraldi's comedy *Seven Guns for the MacGregors*, co-scripted by Tessari, for Papi and Colombo of Jolly Film; while Enzo Barboni had already photographed *Massacre at Grand Canyon/Red Pastures* (co-directed by Corbucci when he was still 'Stanley Corbett'). This 'pressure' from fellow professionals undoubtedly influenced the direction which *For a Few Dollars More* was to take. Leone somehow had to keep ahead of the field. Against all odds, he had to produce something original.

In autumn 1964, Clint Eastwood invited his friend Burt Reynolds, another American television actor trying to make the transition to the big screen, to view a print of *Fistful of Dollars* at Review Studios in Hollywood. Eastwood wanted to test Reynolds's reaction; so Reynolds took time off from playing a half-Indian blacksmith in the seventh season of the CBS series *Gunsmoke*. Reynolds recalls in his auto-biography, 'As those corny little titles came up, and that strange music played, I wondered how in the hell I was going to tell him the picture was very, very strange. Then all of a sudden came that opening shot . . . The look was totally unique, the music suddenly was like nothing I'd ever heard before, and I was in love with it. At the end, I said, "This guy Sergio Leone is brilliant. He gives every actor the greatest introduction of any director I've ever seen . . . The guy has big *cojones*."' Shortly afterwards, Eastwood introduced Reynolds to producer Dino De Laurentiis, who signed him up for a hastily packaged Western, Sergio Corbucci's *Navajo Joe*. Reynold recalls: 'Dino gushed, "But-a, this-a picture, it's going to be-a so big-a. I tell you-a, in order for *Fistful of Dollars* to make-a the money it made in Italy, the average Italian had to see it thirty-five times-a. But-a, we're going to be bigger. Clint killed 100 people. You're going to kill 245 people. We'll-a be-a two times as big-a!" Here was a thinking man, I thought.'[10]

Leone had a title. Now all he needed was to find a subject. Tonino Valerii, shortly to become Leone's assistant director, was close to him at this time: 'A treatment turned up on Grimaldi's desk, written by Enzo dell'Aquila and Fernando Di Leo and called *The Bounty Killer*. Sergio really liked this treatment, so Grimaldi purchased it for him. It was bought for a relatively high sum . . . on condition that the two young authors would renounce any right to appear in any form on the credits of the film: they'd originally wanted to make their reputation with this piece of work. Maybe Leone was too much of a snob to make a film written by two unknown authors. Maybe Luciano Vincenzoni said, "I will write the script if it is only me on the credits." Whatever, the screenplay, based on the treatment, was written by Vincenzoni, with Leone. The role of the bounty-hunter was slotted for Clint Eastwood from the outset, but Papi and Colombo were busy conspiring to take him away from Leone.'[11]

By the time scriptwriter Luciano Vincenzoni joined the project, a revised treatment had been derived from the original document, by Leone and his brother-in-law Fulvio Morsella. Vincenzoni had first met Sergio ten years before, when he wrote the original story for Mario Bonnard's *Hanno rubato un tram*. His first screen commission, it was a comedy about the friendly rivalry between the driver of a tram and his inspector. Vincenzoni had subsequently become a much-respected screenwriter, specializing in what he called 'commedia all'italiana', sometimes with a political twist. For Mario Monicelli, he wrote (with Age and Scarpelli) his breakthrough film *La Grande Guerra* (1959). It concerned two unlikely rogues (a conscript from Rome, another from Milan) who become heroes, despite themselves, in the First World War. He had also, inevitably, been sucked into the peplum boom, providing a treatment for Ferdinando Baldi's *Orazi Curiazi /Horatia and Curatii* (1961), starring an ageing Alan Ladd. The previous year he had written a play based on the 'Sacco and Vanzetti' case, the Roman production of which starred Gian Maria Volonté as Sacco and Enrico Maria Salerno as Procurator Katzmann. Sergio Leone was particularly drawn to Vincenzoni's combination of 'documentary realism and an urbane sense of humour'.

Vincenzoni claims credit for transferring Leone's sense of humour to his Westerns: 'I didn't take the movies seriously. Not because I was intellectually trying to inject a flavour of comedy. It is the critics who think like that. I came up with some humour because ... I found it ridiculous that an Italian, or a Venetian like me, should be writing a Western ... I wrote them with my left hand, so to speak, just as a joke. I have written movies that won prizes at Cannes and Venice with Mario Monicelli, Pietro Germi. These were screenplays for which we suffered on paper for months. Do you know how long it took me to write *For a Few Dollars More*? Nine days.'[12] He has since added, 'I had a bit of a snobbish attitude to the film, at that time.'[13]

Vincenzoni recalls that Sergio Leone had come to his apartment, knocked on the door and nervously said, 'Good day, *Dottore*.' He replied, 'What do you mean, *Dottore*? We're friends. We haven't met for years but we're friends. Come in, Sergio.'[14]

Vincenzoni continues: 'The first thing he told me about, in order to get me to do the film, was the duel between Clint Eastwood and Lee Van Cleef, when they tread on each other's toes, kick each other and generally pull each other's hair out. I was a bit perplexed by this. Okay, it was intended to be ironic, but I just can't see John Wayne kicking Henry Fonda – it doesn't make me laugh, and I must say I found it a bit infantile. But when Sergio told me about the whole sequence, he convinced me. Basically, it's a game between argumentative children, which works very well when applied to characters who are so instinctive. He maintained that the success of the Western worldwide was due to the fact that the tomfoolery of the Western hero – Richard Widmark or John Wayne – is identical to that of someone from a Roman suburb, or from Trastevere ... Sergio grew up in Trastevere, and he played with these macho bullies, these arrogant and physically strong children, who will kick you and provoke you. And he had transferred these childhood memories into the Western.'[15] But Vincenzoni, too, was 'passionate about the American Western', and he particularly appreciated the potential for irony in Leone's approach. It was clear in the way Leone acted out all the characters in the story specially for him. In the sequence in question, it took the form of three children watching the antics of the two bounty hunters from under the boardwalk, as they dirty each other's boots, punch each other, and shoot each other's hat off, before having a friendly drink together. 'It's like the games we play,' the kids conclude. Fulvio Morsella remembers this performance as a good example of Leone 'managing to make things spectacular . . . When he had some fictional events in mind, he would call a scriptwriter and discuss with him the whole thing he had in his head. Act if out for him. And they would prepare the film together. However, it must be noted that Sergio had very bad grammar – he wrote very badly – and so he had to rely completely on the scriptwriters to get things down on paper.' [16]

Meanwhile, another game was being played by Papi and Colombo. Arrighi Colombo had been in touch with Clint Eastwood, by letter and phone, asking if he would be interested in making a 'sequel' for Jolly Film. Colombo was understandably vague about the story of the new project, of course, while Eastwood's first reaction was to ask, 'When can *Fistful of Dollars* be released over here?' Colombo made the customary noises about the copyright dispute with Kurosawa. But Eastwood had scarcely concluded his conversation with Colombo when a representative of Grimaldi's company in Rome came on the line, and reported that Sergio Leone had definitively split with Jolly Film. [17]

Tonino Valerii remembers vividly what happened next: 'Clint Eastwood was very loyal to Sergio and telephoned him: "Do you know that all this is going on? Don't worry, I won't accept until I've heard from you." So Sergio had to leave right away. And this was his very first trip to the land of his dreams, America . . . He was not at this point rich, and had not learned the lesson that money makes people immortal. He was scared of flying, of aeroplanes! So he asked me to drive to Fiumicino airport, to bring Carla back home with me after takeoff. At the airport, he was shaking like a leaf. I can still remember the definitive farewell atmosphere which hovered over this parting scene. In a sepulchral tone of voice, as if he was speaking his last words, Sergio said, "What can you do?" He looked like someone who'd been condemned to death. But at least he had company. He was travelling with Fulvio Morsella, who spoke much better English.' (In fact, Leone remained very apprehensive about flying, even after he became accustomed to it. He would invariably settle into his seat, place a magazine on his lap and touch his testicles for good luck.)[18]

Leone and Morsella didn't yet have a script – just the rejigged treatment. But this wasn't about to deter them. According to Richard

Schickel, Clint Eastwood's mother clearly recalled a long meeting in the living room of her son's house, during which she and Clint watched Sergio Leone tell the story of *For a Few Dollars More*, miming all the main scenes. Eastwood himself describes 'Sergio coming over, sitting with me and telling me the plot line'. This was followed by a restaurant meeting with a lawyer and people from the William Morris Agency, during which Leone and Morsella tried hard to seem relaxed as they urged Eastwood to sign a contract there and then. After dinner, in the parking lot, one of the Italian party suddenly pulled out an envelope containing at least half the proposed fee – over $25,000 in cash – and tried to put it in Eastwood's fist. But the actor tactfully said, 'There's no hurry on it': he would wait for the final script, and a properly drawn-up contract, before signing. Carla Leone's version of the story is simpler: 'Papi and Colombo tried to muscle in on the project, but Clint said, "In Italy, I just work with Leone." '[19]

Back home in Rome, the development of the script became top priority, and Leone started collaborating in earnest with Vincenzoni, who was to write all the dialogue. *For a Few Dollars More* had become the story of two bounty-hunters. 'Clint would be the young hero,' Leone knew, 'and beside him would be the same person at the age of fifty, so there'd be a contrast, and there'd also be the different life experiences of both characters.' They are chasing the same prey: the psychopathic Mexican bandit Indio. After various double-crosses and displays of prowess, the two men join forces 'for a few dollars more', and operate in an uneasy partnership to wipe out Indio and his entire gang. The older man rides off into the sunset, having avenged a family death; Clint just keeps the money. If the key Hollywood influence on *Fistful* was *Shane*, the model this time round was *Vera Cruz* (1954), the dreaded Robert Aldrich's story of two mercenaries (Gary Cooper as a mature Southern Major, Burt Lancaster as a gun-fighting confidence-trickster) who team up to escort Emperor Maximilian's gold through Juarista territory in 1860s Mexico. The freewheeling structure, the setting (cacti and crucifixes), the cynicism and the theme of older-versus-younger hired guns all contributed significantly to the tone of *For a Few Dollars More*. Another important influence was Henry King's *The Bravados* (1958), in which black-clad Gregory Peck tracks down four convicts whom he thinks killed his wife and child, and shows them a picture of his wife, in a pocket-watch, just before he executes them.

In Leone's retrospective view, the generational antagonism of his two leads was central to the script: 'One is a colonel – an older man, cultivated and refined. He behaves with premeditation and care, to accomplish his revenge. The other is just a professional. He does his job pure and simple. He's cynical . . . Almost a robot. It appears that only money interests him. And that's the greatest violence there can be: money as the motive force of the action. But we discover that maybe money isn't so important after all, because he can die at any moment . . . At the end, he will save the colonel instead of taking all the money for himself. And he'll do it with a sporting gesture: he will give his revolver to the colonel. He will allow him to earn his life, by competing on level terms with Indio. Until then, the colonel has survived on his wits and intelligence. He calculatedly makes use of distance, of the limited range of his opponent's gun, which gives him time to adjust his sights and get the advantage. A technician more than a professional. In the final duel, Clint obliges him to prove his professionalism, once and for all, at the moment of truth. He gives him his chance, but the colonel must move fast because Indio is quick on the draw! And Clint will not help him in this closed situation. He'll remain a spectator. If the colonel is beaten, then he will avenge him. But the essential thing is to preserve his colleague's moment of truth. This is much less banal than a saloon duel.'[20]

To oppose these two professionals, Leone had need of a villain who was considerably larger than life. Assistant director Tonino Valerii played a small part in this: 'The character played by Gian Maria Volonté in the earliest version of the script was called Tombstone, and was just an ordinary bandit. He wasn't at anywhere near the same level as the two heroes. Leone asked me to think about some ideas for this character, and I transformed him into "El Indio", a bandit of Mexican–Indian origin, a drug addict, who kills while he is undergoing withdrawal symptoms, and who, while he is taking marijuana, remembers the time when he had – practically – killed the sister of Colonel Van Cleef.'[21] Indio was to become the first villain in mainstream cinema to smoke pot. Valerii and Leone persuaded themselves that 'drugs were a form of daily bread in poor countries such as Mexico or Bolivia'; and they enjoyed the idea that 'they were taboo in the cinema at the time, especially in the Western'. But in all the excitement, they don't seem to have done much research into the real-life effects of marijuana, which up to then had been confined in cinematic terms to shock–horror exposés like *Reefer Madness* or cheap horror movies. Thus, every time

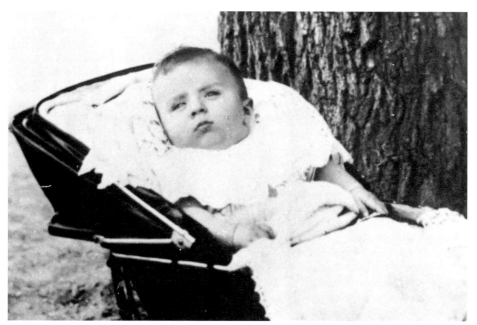

1 Sergio Leone aged three months, April 1929

2 Edvige Valcarenghi (later to be known by her stage name Bice Walerian) in the Borghese Gardens three years before she met Vincenzo Leone, 1909
3 Sergio Leone with his father Vincenzo (stage name Roberto Roberti) in the mid-1930s

4 School photograph of class 5A at the Instituto Saint Juan Baptiste de la Salle in 1937, showing both 'Leone S' and 'Moricone'

5 Reunion of class 5A at the Trastevere restaurant Checco er Carettiere, in the late 1980s: Morricone and Leone are second and third from left

6 Studio portrait of Sergio Leone, at the time of his first communion
7 Sergio Leone in his early twenties, with Sophia Loren on his knee

8 Director Mario Bonnard (left) with assistant Sergio Leone (in dark glasses), on the set of *Tradita* in May 1954

9 Assistant Sergio Leone (left) watches director/actor Aldo Fabrizi rehearsing a tracking-shot for *Hanno rubato un tram*, 1954

10 Sergio Leone directs Rory Calhoun (Dario) for the earthquake sequence of *The Colossus of Rhodes*, 1960

11 Leone mimes the effect of a spear in the small of the back for the arena sequence of *The Colossus of Rhodes*, 1960

12 Sergio Leone introduces daughter Raffaella to a Westerner's horse, on the 'White Rocks' set of *For a Few Dollars More*, May 1965

13 Leone directs Clint Eastwood (Blondie) in *The Good, The Bad and The Ugly*, May 1966

14 Leone directs extras dressed as Union troops at Calahora, just outside Guadix, for the railroad sequence of *The Good, The Bad and The Ugly*

15 Eli Wallach (Tuco) watches, while Clint Eastwood rehearses slapping director Sergio Leone, at one of the Spanish 'Western Villages' of *The Good, The Bad and The Ugly*

16 Rehearsing the 'blowing up the bridge' sequence, at Covarrubias near Burgos, with Clint Eastwood and Eli Wallach

17 Leone enthusiastically shows Lee Van Cleef (The Bad) how to holster his gun on the set of *The Good, The Bad and The Ugly*

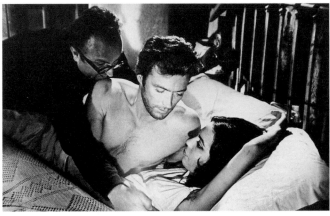

18 A bedroom sequence (later deleted), involving Blondie and an uncharacteristic female partner, is directed by Leone

19 Leone cracks the whip, while Tonino Delli Colli films a shot and Eli Wallach observes, on one of the 'Western Village' sets of *The Good, The Bad and The Ugly*

Indio lights up a reefer, there is an electronic whirr on the soundtrack, and the screen goes red.

Leone recalled that he had 'certain problems with the Italian censor' concerning both the drugs and the violence. Indio becomes more aimless as the film progresses, setting his followers against one another, and leading them all to mass destruction in a place called Agua Caliente ('hot water'). His brutality was pruned by two minutes for international prints. In the original version, he baptizes his gun in holy water before shooting the prison governor in the face, and emptying four further rounds into him. Colonel Mortimer's sister takes Indio's gun and shoots herself, just after he has raped her. And he bursts into fits of manic laughter as Eastwood and Van Cleef are savagely beaten up by his henchmen. But even in international prints, El Indio's evident *enjoyment* of homicide came over loud and clear. Vincenzoni considers Indio's savagery among Leone's more 'heavy, stupid' ideas, evidence that 'he always went too far'. He was especially offended by the scene in which Eastwood's character receives a beating, having been caught in the act of theft by Indio's gang: 'You see the close-ups of faces. Everybody laughs crazily. I said to Leone, "Please, what is this? Some people punch, and others laugh as if they are at the carnival of Rio." We have thirteen idiots all punching and laughing, minutes and minutes long without any stop. Besides it is not realistic – because if a man is punched by thirteen other men in that way, in two minutes he is gone for good.'[22]

In *Fistful*, Eastwood had ridden into a single town and made money out of the two clans ruling it. In *For a Few Dollars More*, he would cross the path of a fellow professional as he rides through several towns – White Rocks, El Paso, Agua Caliente – in pursuit of a single bandit clan: from one hero and two villains to two heroes and one villain. Apart from the geography and scale of the story, one basic difference between *Fistful* and its follow-up is that in the first film Eastwood was a saddle-tramp, just passing through: a masterless warrior. In *For a Few Dollars More*, he is a professional bounty-hunter. This is where Leone's researches into the history of the Wild West came in: 'The character of the bounty-hunter, the bounty killer, is an ambiguous one. They called him "the gravedigger" in the West. He fascinated me, because he demonstrates a way of living in this land, and at that time. A profession which substitutes for official justice. You must kill to exist.'[23]

In preparing the first two *Dollars* films, Leone claimed to have studied some 'sixty eye-witness accounts' of what it was like to live in frontier communities, and two texts in particular seem to have stuck in his mind: Mark Twain's *Roughing It* (1872), a series of tall stories emanating from mining towns around Nevada Territory; and a related primary text, Thomas Dimsdale's *The Vigilantes of Montana, or Popular Justice in the Rocky Mountains* (1866), an account of the chase and capture of Henry Plummer's band of bloodthirsty road agents.[24] Twain quotes Dimsdale repeatedly, and both sources make much of one 'Captain' Jack Slade, who was employed as an agent in the early 1860s by the Overland Stage Company, to ensure that coaches and attached livestock were protected on the route from Julesburg, Colorado Territory, to Salt Lake City, Utah. 'He was supreme judge in his district', wrote Mark Twain, 'and he was jury and executioner likewise – and not only in these case of offences against his employers, but against passing emigrants as well.' Twain had met him at Rocky Ridge, Wyoming, in August 1861 and found him 'so friendly and so gentle-spoken that I warmed to him in spite of his awful history'. But he 'politely declined' Slade's offer of a cup of coffee: 'I was afraid he had not killed anybody that morning and might be needing diversion.'

The tall tales which stage drivers and swing-station people liked to tell about Slade usually concerned his cunning, ruthlessness and prowess with a gun. Twain heard several versions of these tales from several people, 'and they evidently believed what they were saying'. But Jack Slade was better known for a series of incidents that occurred near Julesburg in 1863. He had been commissioned by the Company to get rid of a fellow professional, the French Canadian ex-agent René Jules (or Jules René), who was suspected of being in league with a band of horse thieves. 'War was declared', Twain notes in characteristically amused fashion, 'and for a day or two the two men walked warily about the streets, seeking each other, Jules armed with a double-barrelled shotgun and Slade with his history-creating revolver. Finally, as Slade stepped into a store, Jules poured the contents of his gun into him from behind the door. Slade was pluck, and Jules got several bad pistol wounds in return. Then both men fell, and were carried to their respective lodgings, both swearing that better aim should do deadlier work next time. Both were bedridden a long time, but Jules got on his feet first ... and fled, to gather strength in safety against the day of reckoning.'

Eventually (for Slade was 'not the man to forget him'), Captain Jack's men captured Jules and tied him to a fence-post in the middle of a cattleyard in Rocky Ridge. Slade carefully examined his victim's bonds then retired for the night, in the knowledge that he would enjoy the luxury of killing him slowly upon rising: 'In the morning, Slade practised on him with his revolver, nipping the flesh here and there, and occasionally clipping off a finger, while Jules begged him to kill him outright and put him out of his misery. Finally Slade reloaded, and walking up close to his victim, made some characteristic remarks and then dispatched him. The body lay there half a day, nobody venturing to touch it without orders, and then Slade detailed a party and assisted at the burial himself. *But first he cut off the dead man's ears and put them in his vest pocket, where he carried them for some time with great satisfaction.*' Prior to his eventual lynching in Virginia City, Montana, Slade was reportedly seen using Jules's shrivelled ear in various bars as 'mock payment for a drink'. The other he used as a watch fob.[25]

Having written the story of 'a true desperado', Mark Twain considered his behaviour 'a conundrum worth investigating'. Leone, in turn, found the Jack Slade legend 'fascinating': the skill, the cunning, the coolness. But it was the detail of the ear which really made him stop and think: 'Was he a sadist? A madman? Not at all. A man just like any other, who was scared – like everyone around him. For the West was dominated by fear . . . The ear signified, for all to see, "Careful, leave me alone, I am dangerous."' Leone was especially drawn to Slade's bravura display of that severed ear in saloon bars: 'The bounty killer did not make this exhibition in order to boast. He wanted to show that he was ready to kill the first person who even *tried* to shoot him in the back.'[26] If tales of Slade's escapades were tall in the first telling, they grew some more when Leone recounted them. Sometimes his preferred punchline to the saloon story was that Captain Jack flipped the ear clean across the bar: at which point the pianist stopped playing, the card-players stopped talking, the tarts stopped giggling, and the Captain's drinks were henceforth on the house.

Similarly, Leone had another favourite yarn, which demonstrated the ruthless violence of the West, and acquired fresh detail each time it was aired. One version runs: 'When he was nominated sheriff in a small town, Wyatt Earp decided to go and provoke a petty criminal into a duel. This was a duel which obeyed the rules – a rare thing. Wyatt's opponent found himself in the dust. But wait a moment! At the end of the duel, hearing a sound behind him, the new sheriff thought that one of the dead man's friends had come for his revenge. He turned round, drew his gun and fired . . . at his own deputy, a man he had appointed that same day. He killed him with a bullet between the eyes. Life in the West was not pleasant . . . The law belonged to the most hard, the most cruel, the most cynical. After that, one form of violence was replaced by another: the killers of the West were succeeded in America by those of the Mafia, by the anonymous society of crime.'[27] Clearly, Leone had a cavalier, 'spectacularized' view of American history. He always relished a one-liner, told to him by an American businessman, to the effect that, 'The Constitution, which appears so democratic but which is in fact tremendously evasive, was drafted by criminals.'

Sergio Leone was drawn to the more bizarre details of life on the frontier, which he unearthed with glee in historical sources; or persuaded others to unearth on his behalf. Luciano Vincenzoni accompanied Leone on a visit to Washington, and claims of some 'Leone' discoveries, '[they were] the research I carried out in the Library of Congress . . . Leone was with me, but mainly stayed in the hotel. I was in the Library, working.'[28] Leone liked stories of particularly violent, unpredictable, dishonourable behaviour, and he took them not as isolated examples, but as representative moments of the epoch. Mark Twain's account of Jack Slade, shrewdly aware of its own status as folklore, did not go quite far enough for his taste. By Leone's account, Slade's sadism was just 'like everyone around him'. Shooting people in the back became 'the way people were killed in the West'. The 'Wyatt Earp' story, if it happened at all, happened to 'Wild Bill' Hickock in 1871: not in a 'small town' but in Abilene, Kansas; not while the lawman was dealing with a petty criminal, but during a gunfight on the main street; not with a deputy 'he had appointed that same day', but with his trusted deputy Mike Williams. It is said that Hickock was most upset by Williams's death, and proceeded to burst into tears. No matter. The 'Wyatt Earp' version made just as good a story, and it also carried Leone's argument: life was violent; lawmen had no special moral authority; duels which obeyed the rules of chivalry were rare; gunfights tended to turn into gun-downs.

So, print the legend. John Ford explained what he meant by this punchline to *The Man Who Shot Liberty Valance*, in an interview with Peter Bogdanovich: 'We've had a lot of people who were supposed to be great heroes, and you know damn well they weren't. But it's good for the country to have heroes to look up to.' However, Sergio Leone's embellishment of the facts was intended only to bear out the 'you know damn well they weren't' part; and to impress the hell out of his listeners. It does seem clear that he amassed a fair amount of material to support his Hobbesian view of 'that brief period of American history'. It was just that the material had nothing to do with the gospel according to Hollywood, and precious little to do with the interests of professional historians in the mid-1960s. Leone liked to 'read' the West as if he was a kind of reverse alchemist, turning gold into base metal. And there was plenty of raw material to choose from.

Leone knew that the formal face-to-face duel was a rare thing, and yet he treated the rules as if they were part of the liturgy. He also knew that the handguns of the period were far from accurate; and yet, in *Fistful*, Eastwood manages to kill four members of the Baxter gang with as many bullets. And he must have known, as contemporary researchers were showing, that violence in the cattle towns and on the open range was as nothing compared with big city violence, even in the historical era of the classic Western, between the Civil War and the official closing of the frontier. So it was evidently not a question of making a neo-realist Western. It was rather a question of a making 'a fairy-tale for grown-ups', where the 'documentary basis' provided enough verisimilitude for the audience to suspend its disbelief. If 1960s audiences (especially in Italy) liked to believe that most contemporary politicians, officials and policemen were on the take, then in the new-style fairy-tale, the sheriff (as in *Fistful*) would be a member of one of the corrupt ruling factions or (as in *For a Few Dollars More*) in the pay of bandit Baby 'Red' Cavanagh, whose 'wanted' poster is nailed to his office wall. 'Is the sheriff supposed to be courageous . . . and above all honest?' asks Eastwood. 'That he is', replies the crestfallen sheriff of White Rocks; at which point Eastwood pulls the tin star off the man's chest, throws it into the street, and tells the townspeople, 'You need a new sheriff.' In the kingdom of the bad, the bounty-hunter is king.

Bounty-hunters in postwar Hollywood Westerns were usually presented as cowardly punks who rode into town with high-priced corpses strapped to their saddles. Anthony Mann's *Naked Spur* (1952) and *The Tin Star* (1957) had attempted to explore their motivation. In *Spur*, the embittered James Stewart character wants to earn enough money to buy back the ranch he lost unfairly in the Civil War. But in the last reel, he realizes the self-destructive nature of his chosen calling, which had led him to treat his quarry as 'not a man but a sack of money'. In *The Tin Star*, the embittered Henry Fonda character resorts to bounty-hunting after the death of his wife and baby son, when the townspeople refused him a loan to cover medical expenses. But he rebuilds his life by supporting an inexperienced young sheriff (Anthony Perkins) and looking after his widowed landlady and young son: a substitute family. So both Stewart and Fonda become bounty-hunters because they are damaged people, frustrated by injustices they have experienced. There *has* to be a justification for their unsavoury way of earning a living. They do *not* become bounty-hunters because of greed or ambition. And they reject the trade when personal relationships become important to them again. Bounty-hunters are loners: normal people are married people, preferably ranchers. André de Toth's *The Bounty Hunter* (1954), which was made in the wake of *The Tin Star*'s success, retells this moral tale. Jim Kipp (Randolph Scott) brings the corpse of thieving, murdering Ray Burch into town, to collect a $500 reward. Eventually, Kipp explains to the local doctor's daughter Julie (Dolores Dorn) that he originally took up the game because his father, a small grocer, was shot and killed by two outlaws. But through his admiration for Julie, Kipp comes to realize that there is more to life than making money and getting his own back on 'every murderer I can get my hands on'.

Leone had evidently seen all these films, and there are references to them in *For a Few Dollars More*. The opening sequence of *The Bounty Hunter*, wherein black-clad Randolph Scott rides across desert scrub while an outlaw shoots at him from the rocks above, is very similar to the opening sequence of Leone's film, though the roles are reversed. In *The Tin Star*, Henry Fonda strides over to the town's sole hotel, watched by the townspeople, only to be told in no uncertain terms that all rooms are booked; he walks out, meekly, and rides away. There is an equivalent sequence in Leone's film: Eastwood is similarly spurned, only he refuses to take 'no' for an answer. The climax of *The Tin Star* involves Henry Fonda overseeing a gun duel between the young sheriff (Perkins) and a baddie called Bogardis (Neville Brand). Shotgun in hand, Fonda makes sure that there is fair play. The duel at the end of *For a Few Dollars More* strongly resembles this; only it is the older man who duels with the baddie, and the younger man, rifle in hand, who referees. *The Bounty Hunter* includes a sequence where Randolph Scott, alerted that one of his victims is staying in a hotel room on the upper floor, breaks into the room just as the outlaw exits by the window and jumps from the balcony into the street – very like Colonel Mortimer and Guy Calloway in *For a Few Dollars More*. Leone occasionally mentioned *The Naked Spur* in interviews, and seems to have appropriated from it the trauma in Mortimer's past which turns him from a respected officer in the Civil War to a cold and calculating bounty-hunter. But while making these references, Leone retained his own perspective, as encapsulated in the words that appear onscreen at the beginning of his film: 'Where life had no value, death, sometimes, had its price. That is why the bounty killers appeared.' *The Bounty Hunter*, by contrast, begins with the words, 'They made themselves both judge and executioner in some lonely court of no appeal. They were called Bounty Hunters.'

The distance between them is also illustrated in the contrast between Leone's anti-heroes and the heroes of the 'Ranown' cycle of low-budget Westerns directed by Budd Boetticher between 1956 and 1959. Boetticher was a director much admired by Leone, a taste he shared with the *Cahiers du Cinéma* critics. He particularly enjoyed the films' combination of pessimism and good humour, and the contrast between the granite-faced stoicism of the hero and the colourful, well-drawn villains. But while Boetticher had touched on the connections between bounty-hunting and revenge in *Ride Lonesome* (1959) – where dependable Ben Brigade (Randolph Scott) appears to be turning in outlaws Sam Boone (Pernell Roberts) and Wid (James Coburn) for the prices on their heads – the story was really about Brigade's search for Frank (Lee Van Cleef), the man who hanged his wife. As a critic has justly written of Boetticher's heroes, 'life goes on with no meaning other than the sense of worth and purpose that strong individuals bring to it'. In Leone's *For a Few Dollars More*, as the prologue makes clear, life has no value beyond the sums of money printed on wanted posters. Leone's violent, uncomplicated individuals have no purpose other than to collect the reward in great style. Clint Eastwood has no qualms at all about killing his prey. In *Ride Lonesome*, by contrast, Pernell Roberts makes the definitive Boetticher statement: 'There's some things a man just can't ride around.'

Predictably, Anthony Mann and Budd Boetticher were not too enthusiastic by the sierra Leone-style. Of *For a Few Dollars More*, Mann observed: 'In that film, the true spirit of the Western is lacking. We tell the story of simple men, not of professional assassins; simple men pushed to violence by circumstances. In a good Western, the characters have a starting and a finishing line; they follow a trajectory in the course of which they clash with life. The characters of *For a Few*

*Dollars More* meet along their road only the "black" of life. The bad ones. And the ugliness. My God, what faces! One or two is all right, but twenty-four – no, it's too much! The shoot-outs every five minutes reveal the director's fear that the audiences get bored because they do not have a character to follow. In a tale you may not put more than five or six minutes of "suspense": the diagram of the emotions must be ascending, and not a kind of electrocardiogram for a clinic case.'[29]

Boetticher was to experience the contrast first-hand when one of his noble heroes, a professional gunslinger called Lucy (who turned bad only because he'd lost everything that made sense of his life) was transformed into a less traditional Leone-style anti-hero in Don Siegel's *Two Mules for Sister Sara* (1969). When Boetticher saw the finished film and watched the early sequence where Hogan (Clint Eastwood) lights a stick of dynamite with his cigar, coolly slinging it in the direction of three drunken heavies, he realized that his script had been 'turned by someone else into another Eastwood thing. The character had really become the man without a name . . . My men become *tough for a reason*.' Eastwood was tough just because he was tough. Nevertheless, when Leone and Budd Boetticher finally met, at a film festival in Milan which Leone was chairing in the late 1960s, they found they had a great deal in common. As Boetticher told me: 'I was a little apprehensive. Anyway, I was going up the stairs and he came bounding down there saying, "Budd, dear Budd, I stole *averything* from you!" ' Subsequently, there was talk of Sergio Leone producing *A Horse for Mr Barnum*, Budd Boetticher's planned comeback movie, about a Spanish horse in the wild southwest. But for the time being Hollywood producers were no longer interested in old-style Western directors, and the talk amounted to nothing.[30]

There was no doubt in Leone's mind that the younger of his two bounty-hunters had to be played by Clint Eastwood. But this time his role would be more explicitly ironic, thanks in large part to Luciano Vincenzoni; and he would introduce that trademark smile. For *Fistful*, he had been paid a $15,000 flat fee and a standard-class air fare. This time, he would earn $50,000, a first-class fare and a small percentage of the box-office gross. There was a minor problem, though. 'He had to have a cigar constantly in his mouth when he did not know how to smoke.' The cigar in question would continue to be a toscano, a particularly hard type of Italian weed which was a challenge to light. The locals were used to cutting them in two with a penknife. Eastwood was expected to bite the end off and spit it out. He spent most of his scenes lighting his cigarillo rather than smoking it.

For the Colonel, Leone again pursued Henry Fonda, but he got the same response from Fonda's agent as he had received for *Fistful*. His second choice was Charles Bronson, who passed, again. He then decided on either Robert Ryan or Lee Marvin. In Leone's view, Marvin had been 'terrific as the badman with a whip in *The Man Who Shot Liberty Valance*', and he even made an oral agreement with Marvin's agent. But a few days before filming was scheduled to begin, Leone learned that Marvin had signed a contract to play an over-the-hill gun-slinger, and his vicious tin-nosed brother, in *Cat Ballou*. Leone would have to fly to Los Angeles again, and find another Colonel, at very short notice. He went with his production manager Ottavio Oppo and the usual briefcase full of American cash. Moreover, he was armed with a photo he had torn out of the reference book *Academy Players*. 'It was a very old photo', he recalled, 'in which the actor resembled a young hairdresser from the south of Italy. But he also had a hawk-like nose and the eyes of Van Gogh. I had no idea what he looked like in 1965.' This was Lee Van Cleef. Carla Leone explains: 'From the moment Sergio arrived, he kept bumping into an actor who had dressed up as a cowboy to show him that he could play a role in this film. But he just pointed at a photo of Lee Van Cleef and said, "This is the face I want."'

As Leone would tell it: 'I made a calculation that he must have been about 40 then, so now he would be about 48, 49 or 50 – just the right age for the Colonel. [In fact, Van Cleef had just turned forty.] When I got to Hollywood, he seemed to have completely vanished. Finally, after a lot of running around, we managed to find an agent called Sid. This agent told me Lee Van Cleef was no longer an actor, that he was a painter, and that he had been in hospital for a long time, because he had been in a head-on car accident in a canyon at Beverly Hills [in autumn 1958; he had shattered his left kneecap and the operation had left him with a bad limp which had subsequently healed. He sometimes needed a stepladder to get on a horse, and he still could not run]. He had decided to take up a new profession . . . But I said, "Well I must see him at all costs because physically when I think of this character I picture him." And a few hours before my plane left, Lee Van Cleef [with his agent] came to this small hotel on the outskirts of Los Angeles where I was staying. It was a drive-in, motel kind of place. Canyon Dry, or something like that.'[31]

From what Carla Leone was told, the actor cut an impressively rugged figure at this meeting: 'Lee Van Cleef was wearing long black boots, a worn-out shirt and a long trenchcoat – all stained. His face was so strong, though – so powerful. Sergio said, "We'll sign the contract, and tomorrow we'll go to Italy. Would you accept ten thousand dollars?" I forget the exact amount. He said, "Yes, but I've got to finish this painting first. I've promised to deliver it to a client, and I've been paid an advance." Two days later, they were at Cinecittà together. They *had* to have Lee Van Cleef immediately because the set was built.' At first, Lee Van Cleef had thought that Leone was teasing him, and became abusive. But the bartender intervened and all was well. Leone judged 'his physical appearance was just right – like an eagle, grizzled, black and grey', and he clinched the deal there and then. 'I gave him the script . . . so he could read it on the flight to Rome. When we got there, a car came to collect us and take us to Cinecittà, where we had to start shooting the first set-up right away. Straight down to business, without even a couple of hours' rest. Anyway, he read the script, and when he'd finished, I came up to him on the plane and asked, "Well, what do you think of it?" And he said with a smile, "It's Shakespearean." He was so shaken by events that he hadn't understood it too well.'[32]

Lee Van Cleef had begun his film career as Jack Colby, one of the three gunmen waiting by the railroad for the arrival of Frank Miller in *High Noon* (1952). Since then, his 'beady-eyed sneer' (as he liked to call it) had been featured in numerous Westerns, but somehow he had never managed to survive until the last reel. As he wistfully recalled, 'In just about every film I ever made I was killed off by John Wayne or Gregory Peck or Gary Cooper.' He'd been shot in *High Noon*, hanged in *The Tin Star* (1957), knifed in *Gunfight at the OK Corral* (1957), gut shot and left to die in *Posse from Hell* (1961) and pushed over a cliff by Angie Dickinson in *China Gate* (1957). In *The Bravados* he'd been hunted through the tall grass by the obsessed Jim Douglas (Gregory Peck), who proceeded to show him a photograph inside a pocket-watch to jog his memory before shooting him dead. Van Cleef had not made a film since 1962. But these Westerns had lodged in Leone's mind: he could recite whole passages from *The Bravados* as if they were performance poetry.

Van Cleef was delighted with Leone's deal: 'Hell, my *per diem*, just the living expenses they gave me, was as much as I made on my very first picture. His production manager opened an attaché case containing *thousands* in greenbacks. I shelled out ten per cent to my agent and went home ... We were living on TV royalties and unemployment, and what my wife made as a secretary. I didn't even have money to pay the phone bill, and it wasn't all that big.'[33] He was impressed that this Italian film director knew so much about *High Noon* and *The Bravados*, but did not appear to notice that the Colonel's chiming watch, with his sister's photograph, was directly derived from the latter film. Characteristically, Leone had chosen Van Cleef for visual reasons, and cinematic associations. He'd been prepared to sign him up without even hearing the actor speak: the kind of 'audition' only possible in the land of post-synchronization. (Lee Van Cleef's Italian voice was to be much lighter and higher in register, altogether more friendly, than his real-life gravelly snarl.)

Lee Van Cleef was also taking a risk. A complete stranger had given him a caseful of dollars in a motel car-park. 'All I had in my pocket', he admits, 'was the promise of a movie, and two weeks' advance pay.' Leone may have been starry-eyed, but he only parted with a down-payment and (had Van Cleef but known it) a somewhat insubstantial one at that. But this casting would ensure for Van Cleef a successful second career in Italy and Spain – twelve Westerns in nine years. In Italy, he became a name above the title: a status he had never achieved back in America. When *High Noon* was re-released in Italy in the late 1960s, the posters somewhat optimistically read, 'Starring Gary Cooper and Lee Van Cleef'. Leone recalled that, on a later visit to New York, he was invited by Van Cleef to a 'marvellous Chinese restaurant with his wife Joan, who had also been his nurse in hospital ... I said to her, "What a beautiful fur coat," and she smiled at me: "We owe it to you. Two years ago we were having trouble settling the electricity bill." '[34]

Nevertheless, at first Van Cleef found his work with Leone an unsettling experience, to say the least. Upon arrival in Rome, he was swiftly kitted out with a large flat-brimmed hat, a black cape, a frock-coat and a pair of black knee-length boots. Then he had to get to grips with the language barrier. 'I understand that when Clint made the first film he and Sergio conversed hardly at all. Well, I can't say that on this they managed to string too many words together in conversation, but Clint assured me that Sergio was speaking better English than he had done a year before. Although we managed to get by during filming, I had to wonder how they managed to get the first film made if Sergio's English, and Clint's Italian, had been even worse.' In one particular scene, as far as Van Cleef could hear, 'there were five languages spoken: Greek, Italian, German, Spanish, and a Cockney Englishman that I couldn't understand any better than I could understand the Greek! But I got along in it because I knew what everybody was supposed to be saying in English by my script. So when they'd stop speaking, then I would say something.' Eventually he became adept at this game: 'The simple trick of it, of course, was just to memorize everybody's dialogue.'[35] Leone's English may have improved, but not *that* much – as Fulvio Morsella remembers: 'It wasn't that he refused to learn English. He didn't like English. He used to call it "this damned type of language with these strange sounds". So he would deliberately say English words that sounded funny – I don't remember any one in particular – but he'd be very funny indeed when he tried to speak English. Specially with American actors. And yet, here's the paradox, he was fascinated by America and the West.'[36]

Carla Leone saw an amusing side to Van Cleef's perplexed progress: 'He spent the whole of the first day just doing the glances, the looks out of the window of the hotel through a telescope when he watched Indio's gang from above. Just staring out of the window, all day long. Sergio told him, "Again, again." Sergio was also laughing like crazy, thinking about this poor guy! "I went to America, he agreed to do a film, he doesn't even know what it is about, he doesn't know me. He's flown to Italy, he hasn't had time to sleep, he's just had a sandwich and he doesn't speak a word of the language. And there he is, behind a window." '[37]

Vincenzoni remembers that despite the language barriers, on the set Van Cleef entrusted himself entirely to the director. The long-term effects of his accident created one or two problems: he wasn't able to run, he had to ride a docile, high-stepping circus horse and he needed a fair amount of liquid refreshment. But Van Cleef's drinking was always under control. Vincenzoni recalls: 'He was an angel. He went along with everybody, would have gone along with King Kong. He was so sweet. He liked to receive orders. Sergio told him, "Now you have to be very serious, and after that you have to laugh." He imitated perfectly what Sergio Leone said.'[38]

Clint Eastwood had worked the previous season on two episodes of *Rawhide* in which Lee Van Cleef also appeared, well down the cast list. In the second, *Piney*, he had shot Rowdy Yates off his horse before being killed himself. Six months later, Van Cleef was his co-star in

Rome. Eastwood recalls that, when the newcomer arrived in April 1965, he figured that Leone was 'completely crazy'. But Eastwood advised Van Cleef to see *Fistful of Dollars* in Italian as soon as he possibly could, to get the hang of things. Van Cleef went to a cinema in Rome and came out saying, 'Now I see what you mean; the script element is important but definitely second to the style.'[39] Although there was a 'Babel of monoglot actors' (in Anthony Burgess's apt phrase) among the smaller parts, this time at least the Americans could talk among themselves: Eastwood recalls that Leone cordially asked everyone on set to speak English if they possibly could. This was harder for some than for others. On *Fistful*, Gian Maria Volonté had been looped by a different voice for the English-language version. Now he was contractually obliged to do it himself, and he spoke no English.

The budget was 200 per cent higher than that of *Fistful of Dollars*: about $600,000, which 'sounds a great deal', Leone said, 'but which wasn't much considering that the film was longer and much more complex'. Alberto Grimaldi had brokered a co-production deal between his own European Associates (Rome), Arturo Gonzales (Madrid) and Constantin (Munich) which did at least enable Leone to indulge his passion for detail, and let the narrative breathe in a looser, more leisurely and less linear way. In fact, the main plot (the Stranger and Colonel Mortimer versus Indio and his gang) takes about twenty minutes of screen time to get going. *For a Few Dollars More* begins with offscreen sounds. While we *look* at a lone horseman in the desert, we *hear* some whistling, the lighting of a toscano, the inhaling of smoke and the cocking of a rifle. There is a single rifle-shot and the horseman falls into the scrubland. Cue main title music. Thus, *Fistful* aficianados are apprised that the mysterious stranger ('Monco' or 'the one-handed man' as he was called in the script and, occasionally, in the film) is on the ledge overlooking the desert. His traits (the whistling, the cigar) announce him; he doesn't even need to make an appearance.

Then we see a leather-bound Bible, which is lowered to reveal the face of Colonel Mortimer: a 'reverend' on his way to Tucumcari by train. So Lee Van Cleef appears before Clint Eastwood. 'Monco' is first seen from behind, riding into White Rocks, wearing his hat and poncho in a torrential rainstorm. For his first close-up, the brim of his hat slowly rises to reveal his unshaven face. He lights his toscano with his left hand, leaving his gun hand free: the hand that matters. We first glimpse the bandit El Indio (Volonté) waking up on a bunk in the territorial prison. These three main characters will then be visually linked: Monco stands before a Wanted poster for 'EL INDIO: 10,000 dollars'; then Mortimer does likewise; followed by rapid cross-cutting, punctuated by metaphorical gunshots, of details of the faces of the three protagonists: face, mouths, noses and especially eyes. They do not meet physically until much later in the film. But Sergio Leone was evidently getting into his stylistic stride and, perhaps for the first time as a director, beginning to enjoy himself.

There is much more of the carnivalesque in *For a Few Dollars More* than in *Fistful*. El Indio reveals his plans to raid the bank at El Paso from the pulpit of an abandoned baroque church: 'To help you understand what I mean', he tells his twelve disciples, 'I would like to relate a nice little parable. Once upon a time, there was a carpenter . . .' His disciples have already signalled their arrival by shooting excitedly at the church's bell. Round these parts, the priest has no more authority than the sheriff, and nobody trusts anybody. After Mortimer has advised Monco to go north with Indio's gang, they both (as if by magic) manage to meet in the cantina at Agua Caliente, which is neither to the north nor the south. How could the Colonel possibly have known which direction Monco would take? The answer is an hilarious example of professional wariness: 'Easy. When I told you to tell Indio to go north, I knew you'd tell him just the opposite, and he, being suspicious, would go a different direction altogether. Since El Paso's out of the question, well – here I am!'

For the first time in a Western, Sergio Leone was able to indulge his crude, earthy sense of humour. A bounty-hunter bursts into a hotel room and, discovering a naked woman in a bath, mutters, 'Pardon me, ma'am.' Another forcibly ejects a resident from a hotel bedroom which overlooks the bank, and throws the hapless man's long-johns down the stairs saying, 'I don't wear 'em.' The diminutive, ratty hotelier calls the bounty-hunter an 'animal', but his vast and blowsy wife replies, 'He's tall isn't he?' The vignette of the wife was apparently based on 'the real-life wife of a producer who had not behaved entirely correctly towards Leone'.[40] An old prophet (akin to the coffin-maker in *Fistful* and played by the same actor) does funny things with his beard. A baddie appears covered in shaving cream, with half his beard shaved off. There are chickens all over the streets of Santa Cruz, and the telegraph office is full of eggs. Monco leaves a calling-card in Alamogordo (the desert site of the first atomic bomb test) in the form of some sticks of dynamite. Minor functionaries who get in the way (a travelling salesman, a railway guard, a sheriff, a bartender, a telegraph operator) are the butt of increasingly elaborate insults. In a scene that induced hysterics in Leone and Morricone when projected in rough-cut, Colonel Mortimer is extremely rude to a hunchback called 'Wild', played (with much eye-rolling and twitching) by Klaus Kinski. Wild recognizes the Colonel and says, 'If it isn't the smoker. Remember me?' Mortimer continues eating: 'No.' 'El Paso.' 'It's a small world.' 'Yes, and very, very bad.' Wild turns to offer his back to the Colonel, saying, 'Now you light another match.' 'I generally smoke just after I eat. Why don't you come back in ten minutes?' snaps the Colonel. By now twitching hellishly, Wild snarls, 'In ten minutes you'll be smoking in hell. Get up!' Wild draws, but Mortimer produces a derringer from his sleeve and kills him, a show of skill which earns the interest of the watching Indio. In the same sequence, we see Mortimer relishing a simple meal of vegetable soup and plain white bread in a seedy cantina. Evidence of the pleasures of eating would become a staple of Leone's film-making from now on.

Sergio Donati was summoned to Rome by Leone to sharpen up the script, 'paid but uncredited'.[41] Vincenzoni was not informed. Donati came up with Mortimer's line 'This train will stop at Tucumcari', the scene with the old prophet, and the line which he thinks of as the finest of his career. The joke involves Monco totting up how much he has earned from the killing of Indio's disciples, as he heaves their bodies on to a farm-cart. 'Ten thousand, twelve thousand, fifteen, seventeen, twenty-two . . . twenty-two.' He pauses, realizing that he's been short-changed; then one of the wounded bandits appears behind him and tries to shoot. Monco beats him to it and says, with relief, 'Twenty-seven.' Mortimer, riding off into the sunset, shouts back at him: 'Having trouble, boy?' 'No, old man.' Monco removes his toscano from his mouth. 'Thought I was having trouble with my adding.' Such deadpan grotesquery, here conceived by Donati, is at the heart of Leone's film. It is also the model for the celebrated catchphrases ('Do you feel lucky?'; 'Make my day') favoured by Eastwood once he had hit his stride in Hollywood.[42]

Another first was that Leone's fascination with the surface texture of the past had at last become affordable, and was evident in the cluttered bar-rooms, banks and prisons, and the locomotive with period carriages. Luciano Vincenzoni recalls how Sergio Leone was 'concerned with everything' on this film, 'every tiny detail' from set construction to the fine distinctions between models of the Navy Colt: 'He's a man who loves objects. He collects eighteenth-century Roman silverware, he collects furniture and paintings, and he's had a great visual education. So he's one of those rare directors for whom you will write a scene where you can see ten potential ways of doing it, and he'll give it back to you with a hundred ways. And when you see the film, you ask yourself, "My God, did I really write *that*?" After having worked with lots of "cowboy" directors [in the sense of cowboy builders], I understand Sergio's great quality: he really believes in what he is doing.'[43]

For the sequence of the saloon in White Rocks where Monco discovers Red Cavanagh playing poker, Leone was determined to get away from the well-scrubbed and over-lit look of Hollywood. He wanted a dirty, overcrowded place, filled with the smoke of cigars and wood-burning stoves: courtesy of several smoke machines at full throttle. When the smoke had dispersed a little, so it looked credible, the technicians switched off the machines. 'No, no!' he yelled. 'We need *more smoke*. It has to look as though a man could choke in there.'

Leone confirmed that on this film he was able at last to develop 'an authorial voice' and invest himself totally in his material as well as in 'the application of my documentary obsession to the myth'. He gave the example of gun lore: 'The lives of the two bounty-hunters depend on a perfect knowledge of the tools of their trade: guns. I couldn't invent imaginary objects. I needed to be *exact* from the technical point of view, so I prepared my documentation . . . Among other things, I found exact descriptions of all the types of weapons of that period. I ordered them to be remade for the film, and was surprised to discover that manufacturers of these guns were still working in Northern Italy – in Brescia. There's a workshop in each house where they construct revolvers of the last century. They supply the American market . . . But authenticity wasn't enough. I had to be precise about ballistics and range as well. To nourish my fairy-story with a documentary reality.'[44]

When Mortimer is first put through his paces, he waits until his victim Guy Calloway is just out of pistol range, and casually unbuckles his saddle-cloth (accompanied by a loud 'twang' on the soundtrack) to reveal a Buntline Special with detachable shoulder-stock, a Colt Lightning pump-action rifle, a Winchester '94 and a double-barrelled Lefaucheux action pin fire.[45] He attaches the shoulder-stock to his Buntline, and shoots the wanted man (value: $1,000) squarely between the eyes. Monco still favours his simple Colt 45, with snakes on the grips (courtesy of CBS props department). According to the Italian guns and ammo magazine *Diana Armi*, the Western craze was to do wonders for those craftsmen working in the Brescia-based replica fire-arms industry: 'the single-action pieces used in the various films shot in Italy, Spain and Yugoslavia are identical to those we can buy from any respectable gunsmith, except for the barrel which is faked – it is a simple tube, without rifling'. By the late 1960s some gunsmiths, as well as manufacturing replicas, specialized in the restoration of firearms damaged during the filming of Italian Westerns. They were regularly requested to straighten rifle or pistol-barrels that had been bashed against rocks by overenthusiastic Mexican heavies. Replica Reming-tons of 1858–65 were for some reason favoured by most Italian props people rather than the Colts of the American Western. The title of the magazine *Diana Armi* (fusing mythology, sex and guns) says a lot about the gun culture in Italy, and helps contextualize Leone's fetish-ism. The details in his films may not always be quite right, but that isn't the point: he is into realism, not reality. While preparing *For a Few Dollars More*, he would leaf through pictorial catalogues of Wild West firearms with Carlo Simi, who recalls that 'Sergio knew everything about them – period, model, make.'[46]

Simonella, a props company which had made a good living out of supplying chariots and temple fixtures and fittings for sword-and-sandal films, was used for street furniture, interiors and stagecoaches. This was a step up from the Zorro discards which had been used for *Fistful*. Pompeii, which had previously supplied countless pairs of Roman sandals, now tooled up for leather cowboy boots. Over the next few years, both would do very well out of the Italian Western boom.

One reason why the budget was not as large as it sounded was that 'an entire Western town' (designed by Carlo Simi) was constructed near Tabernas, about twelve kilometres from the seaside town of Almeria. The lead actors were put up in the four-star Grand Hotel next to the Palace of Justice. Leone's favourite room was 532, to which he would return whenever he was filming in the desert. The hotel has not changed much since the 1960s. A hotel clerk with a long memory still recalls that Lee Van Cleef spent an appreciable amount of time in the bar, and sometimes had to be helped back to his room after too many whiskies. The 'Western town' still exists; it is now called 'Mini-Hollywood'. It consisted of the traditional wooden frontier buildings on either side of the main street: a two-storey saloon, an hotel, a sheriff's office, an undertaker's parlour, a telegraph office, a barbershop. To these was added a large adobe structure now labelled 'First City Bank'. At either end of the street were the granite-coloured mountains, the sage and cactus and olive trees of the Almerian desert. For the film, it became El Paso and White Rocks.

Carlo Simi recalls that Leone asked at an early stage for 'the finest Western village in the world, which must be like a protagonist in the story; the bank must be like a character in itself. Since the town was El Paso, I designed an old Spanish fortress with parts of the building destroyed, all by itself in a sunny square. The other buildings had to be some way away, to allow room to shoot the attack of El Indio and his men. Much of the film was made in my Western town, including interiors of the hotel and saloon. Sergio and Grimaldi were pleased with the results, and let me play the part of the director of the bank in the film. The town was to have been built at La Pedrizia, north of Madrid, but it was snowing there when we recced it, so we chose Tabernas instead, where we could rely on the weather.'[47]

A few kilometres away were the other main locations. The adobe village of Los Albaricoques (The Apricots) on the Sierra de Gata, with its cobbled street and rows of single-storey dwellings, became Agua Caliente; which, El Indio claims, 'looks just like a morgue'. The ridge overlooking the desert, used in the pre-credits sequence, was just off the Guadix–Tabernas road about fifteen kilometres short of the Tabernas turning, with a view of the Los Filabres mountains in the background. The crossroads in the desert where the Colonel meets Monco was in the hills just above Simi's set. The place of palm trees where El Indio's gang shot at the El Paso safe was known locally as El Oasis, just down the road from the main location along the Rambla de Tabernas. The palm trees had been planted by the set dressers of *Lawrence of Arabia* three years before. The church interior where El Indio makes his headquarters was filmed at the sixteenth-century church of Santa Maria, at Turrilas: a steep and windy drive south from Tabernas. The building was semi-derelict at the time (it has now been carefully restored). Leone and Simi were only permitted to fill it with baroque angels, 'spanishizing things', curly columns and a wooden pulpit because Luis Beltran (stuntman and local casting director) was friendly with the Mayor. Beltran recalls the detailed instructions Leone gave him: 'All the facial characteristics were written down: "blond and blue-eyed for the Americano . . . dark, gypsy face for the Mexican". There was a lot of competition to appear in these films. I was stabbed, twice, in the stomach by gypsies, in disagreements about who was in and who was out. [He proudly shows his scars as if they were war wounds.]'[48]

Assistant director Tonino Valerii scouted certain locations, supervised the choice of secondary actors, and prepared the backgrounds. He recalls that this proved a delicate task, 'because we started filming some interiors in Rome, then Madrid, back to Hojo de Manzanares near Colmenar, then Almeria and Guadix. To film the locomotive scene with an adapted local train, we went to the Guadix–Almeria railway.' The prison holding Gian Maria Volonté had its interior in Rome, and its external steps at the Almeria bullring, 'plus a bit here, a bit there'. Scouting around Almeria, Valerii found a photogenic area surrounding a disused goldmine called Mina Rodalquilar. He also recalls that 'above Tabernas in the Ramblas, overlooked by the mountains, I came upon dried-up riverbeds which proved very useful for desert sequences'.[49]

This time, Valerii adds, Leone was much in evidence at the Almeria locations. His wife Carla, meanwhile, acted the on-set diplomat: 'Sometimes Sergio would begin to get upset or hot under the collar about something, like a slow-burning fuse. Trivial things, little things. I had the role of "the woman who straightened out the rough edges". Little fights amongst members of the crew, things which were triggered off for no reason. I fielded them and enjoyed this role very much because it got me involved in his world. Francesca had a small part as a crying baby, and when the train arrived at the station, Raffaella was supposed to sit there and play with some stones. But every time the train pulled in, she was so scared she would run away and couldn't do it. And Sergio was getting upset with this three-year-old girl. He used sometimes to treat his children as if they were grown-ups.'[50] On one occasion, he was seen telling an educational bed-time story to one of the little girls: 'The first thing to learn', he said, 'is never put a cent of your own money into a picture.'

In the 1991 exhibition Omaggio a Sergio Leone, there were two stills of Leone with his children on Carlo Simi's main set for For a Few Dollars More. One finds him sitting on the steps outside 'Jackson's Store', on the spot where Eastwood throws the sheriff's badge into the dust. He looks rather apprehensive, in straw cowboy hat and glasses,

Raffaella in period costume next to him. The other shows him sitting on a horse, with Raffaella in a 'tomboy' outfit on the saddle in front of him, as he 'poses' on his Wild West street as if for a holiday snap. In both stills, he looks more like a father playing cowboys and Indians with his kids than a film director in the process of spending a budget of over half a million dollars. Leone was growing accustomed to life in the saddle. This time, there were no mass walkouts or pay disputes. But Leone still turned up in a cowboy hat, acted everyone's part for them, and listened to everyone else's opinion on what he was trying to do. There were tensions between him and Gian Maria Volonté, as he tried to reduce the size of Volonté's performance. According to Luis Beltran, these culminated in the actor walking off the El Paso set in a huff, while Leone shouted after him that he 'couldn't expect to get a lift from the production'. Volonté hitched a ride across the desert, but was found there a few hours later, by which time he had cooled off.[51] Maybe the politics were getting to him. But it was on this production, according to Fulvio Morsella, that Leone first discovered his talent for mobilizing a high-commitment, purposeful set: 'He would always have time to listen to other people's suggestions, provided they didn't collide with what he had in mind.' He was tense and liable to become overexcited, but firm. Did he tend to the child-like in himself, in such circumstances? Carla Leone concludes 'more *buffo* than child-like. He had a strong sense of the ridiculous, of the comedy in everyday situations. He did like the honesty and directness of children, and he trusted them.'[52]

Sergio Leone and Ennio Morricone were used to being frank with each other; and when they went to see *Fistful of Dollars* together, during its successful first run at the Quirinale Cinema in Rome, they both realized 'it could have been made much better'. They recognized that some of their shared ideas about music and image had been 'left unresolved', and that they could have achieved a more powerful impact on an audience in a full cinema. Since *Fistful*, Morricone had become a more experienced film composer, with nine new films to his credit. Because *For a Few Dollars More* was made so soon after *Fistful*, there was still no question of recording the music in advance. But Morricone was at least 'involved before the filming started'. Director and composer had a series of lengthy meetings. As Leone was to remember: 'I did not ask him to read the script. I told him the story as if it was a fairy-tale. Then I explained the themes I wanted. Each character had to have his own theme. But I spoke Roman-fashion, with plenty of adjectives and comparisons, making sure that everything was clear. Then, he worked at the composition and brought me some very short themes, one for each character. He played them to me on the piano . . . This would continue, often for some time, until he'd composed a piece which inspired me – because it was me the music had to inspire, not Ennio! When a passage pleased me, I'd say, "That's the one!" '[53]

Morricone confirms that Leone was becoming increasingly meticulous: 'Sergio asked for simple themes, easy on the ear, tonal, popular themes. He falls in love with the music and wants more from it. I'm an indifferent pianist, but if he likes it on the piano he'll love it in orchestration.' Morricone didn't compose at the piano, though. He composed 'at my desk', and when he orchestrated he wrote 'directly on the score'. Leone preferred to try out his 'short themes' on an ordinary household piano rather than on a concert Steinway. That way, he said, if the results were not 'inspiring' enough, the composer couldn't possibly blame it on the instrument.

This time the main focus was on the themes or *leitmotifs* which would be associated with each of the main characters. These were: a brief high-pitched scale on the flute or single twang on the maranzano for Monco; a flute scale in a lower register for Colonel Mortimer; church bells and amplified twelve-string guitar for El Indio. According to guitarist Bruno D'Amario Battisti, who did the recording of the Indio theme, 'the guitar would be very dramatic and aggressive, with a very big sound . . . I'd play normally and Ennio would say, "No, stronger. *Encora*. More." '[54] When the themes came to be recorded, Alessandroni again whistled and directed his choir, though he left his guitar at home this time.

The musical themes would be more than just illustrative. They would also 'comment' on the behaviour of the characters, like a form of musical punctuation: an electronic whirr for El Indio's drug habit; a trill to release the tension after some tough dialogue, and to accompany the movement of Eastwood's cigarillo across his mouth; a tuba making burping noises for the confrontation between Mortimer and the hunchback. Musical instruments would be used in unusual ways. For the robbery of the bank at El Paso, for example, piano wires were treated as if they were percussion. And there was a surprisingly lyrical oboe theme called 'Goodbye, Colonel', in which musicologist Sergio Miceli sees the seeds of one of the next phases in the Leone–Morricone partnership: 'Breaking the pattern of the "dog eats dog" story of

Leone's Westerns, the Colonel Mortimer character refuses his share of the bounty at the end, having satisfied his revenge. This scene justifies the piece "Goodbye, Colonel", with its new orchestral colouring, and the character inspires a new style – with a richer, more blended orchestral sound and a more refined, less raucous, use of the chorus, for the rhetoric of boundless horizons. This kind of music, which entertained the international market of film-goers and record-buyers ... was to become from here on a characteristic of Morricone's soundtracks, regardless of the genre of films.'[55]

In keeping with the carnivalesque atmosphere, at one point Morricone misappropriated a well-known classical theme, while 'quoting' it in a recognizable way. Following *For a Few Dollars More*, this irreverent use of hallowed moments from the history of music was to become something of a trademark for Morricone and Leone. But Morricone is keen to distinguish between 'citations' of this kind, which make a point within a certain context, and the tendency of some film composers to derive their ideas, unacknowledged, from classical music. In *For a Few*, the scene in question (which troubled the British censor) involved the bandit El Indio provoking Tomaso (the man who informed on him, leading to his jail sentence) inside the de-consecrated church. El Indio orders that Tomaso's wife and baby (framed as if they are a traditional icon of Madonna and Child) be shot and killed. He gives Tomaso a pistol and flicks open a chiming pocket-watch: 'When you hear the music finish, begin.' Chunks of Hispanic baroque architecture are strewn about the church. The two men face each other in the main aisle.

From the outset, Morricone had decided to bring an organ into his arrangement because of the church setting. This particular scene seemed to him to be 'almost out of Michelangelo. I didn't want there to be an arbitrary use of the organ, so I "quoted" the Toccata and Fugue in D minor by Bach. The theme of the trumpet, which takes up that of the organ, begins with that la-so-la. The bell was a distortion of the prolonged sound of the bell which was incorporated into Lee Van Cleef's pocket-watch. As in the case of the harmonica in *Once Upon a Time in the West*, what we were using – to adopt Sergio Miceli's term – was *internal* music, born from within the scene. The soprano voice of Edda dell'Orso was already used in *For a Few Dollars More*. In *Once Upon a Time*, her voice was to become one of the characters.' Sergio Donati was there when the 'organ' idea was first mooted: 'I remember Leone and Morricone seated at a moviola, and Morricone had a notepad and wrote down absolutely everything, and Leone would say, "Stop here." "It's just an empty road." "We will put here birds crying and all the noises *à la* Sergio." And I remember exactly when he said, in the scene of Volonté in the church, "I want here something religious." And Morricone said, "J.S. Bach, huh?" Sergio replied: "But also with the *deguello* on the trumpet, Ennio!" '[56]

On paper, this progression from musical box to amplified twelve-string guitar with castanets, to church organ with all stops pulled out, to solo mariachi trumpet backed by a choir seemed 'horrifying'. Played with the visual image, as Sergio Miceli notes, it not only works, it shows how a composer can 'undertake experiments . . . within the framework of a decidedly codified production. For Ennio Morricone, Westerns are something more and something less than an historical-geographical frame for a "period". They are first of all a state of mind, composed of sentiments and sentimentality, of sunsets and garishness, of subtle explorations of musical materials and vulgarity of sound, of the simple whistling of a man passing by, minding his own business, and the shameless blast of an organ.'[57]

According to Leone, he took the watch/musical box to Morricone, at rough-cut stage, 'as a point of departure', and asked him to adapt the la-so-la theme to blend with it: so its repetitive melody became at the same time 'a sound effect, a musical introduction *and* a concrete element in the story'. As with Charles Bronson's harmonica in *Once Upon a Time*, it also unlocked the flashback which took Leone 'to the rock-bottom of my characters'. In the case of *For a Few*, the flashback happens inside El Indio's head, but the music of the pocket-watch links it with Colonel Mortimer and his traumatic memories. Carla Leone remembers that Sergio would sometimes refer to the film as *Carillon*. 'The function of the flashback is Freudian,' Leone argued. 'Until then, the Americans had been using flashbacks in a very closed way, too rigorously. This was a mistake: you have to let them wander like the imagination or like a dream.' So the three flashbacks in the film, triggered by a repetitive melody, provide missing pieces in the puzzle; the ways in which the melody is woven into other motifs on the soundtrack indicate the importance of memories – vague, unfocused, intriguing – at key moments in the development of the story: 'One had to "discover" it bit by bit . . . part of my search for the element of surprise, the unexpected . . . Even within the flashback, the tension does not relax.'[58]

El Indio's memories tell us that he once watched a young couple making love: he shot the young man, but the girl committed suicide immediately after being raped by the bandit. The fact that El Indio remembers this particular incident, amid all the mayhem and butchery of his subsequent career, shows that the trauma goes deep. At the beginning of the first flashback, he is a voyeur. By the end of the final flashback, we get the sense that he has probably become impotent as a result of the girl's self-slaughter. Colonel Mortimer remembers the incident (which makes sense of his motivation throughout the film), because the girl was his sister. His chiming watch has a picture of her in it; so does El Indio's, which was stolen from the bedroom that night. All of this is hinted at, from Indio's very first appearance, through musical references on the soundtrack.

And the 'watch' theme is taken up in the final reel, when Mortimer and Indio meet for the final settling of accounts, in the first of Leone's *corridas* or bullfights. This time, instead of the main street of San Miguel, the duel takes place in a circular space: an arena of stones just outside the adobe village of Agua Caliente. It is a cobbled circle, one of the threshing yards often found behind farmhouses in Almeria. Carlo Simi recalls that 'Sergio had said we must find a circular space. He didn't say why, though.'[59] Mortimer and Indio move into their allotted places with all the ritual and formality of a bullfight, while Monco referees the proceedings with a circular chiming watch in one hand, a rifle in the other. The 'prolonged sound of the bell', first heard when El Indio is passing the time in his jail cell, finally leads to a resolution in the *plaza de toros*, where its sound is taken up in the form of a *deguello* by a mariachi trumpet again. This is at the same time the melodramatic climax of Mortimer's vendetta *and* a parody.

At moments like these, says Bernardo Bertolucci, Morricone's music becomes 'almost a visible element in the film: Sergio and Ennio were so complementary'.[60] It was after watching *For a Few Dollars More* that Gillo Pontecorvo asked Ennio Morricone to write the score for *The Battle of Algiers*. He, too, believed strongly that music was not 'something joined, tacked on to the work unjustifiably' and preferred to have music played on the set to create atmospheres. On *Algiers*, he played Morricone's drumbeat theme (recorded in advance with the finale in mind) during some difficult rehearsals of the pivotal sequence, where three Algerian women remove the veil to turn themselves into sophisticated Frenchwomen.[61]

When the soundtrack was being laid, Clint Eastwood and Lee Van

Cleef flew back to Rome for a series of dubbing sessions at the RCA Italiana studios. According to Sergio Donati, it was at this stage that Eastwood's vocal performance began to change and his trademark 'movie voice' began to emerge: 'When he heard Enrico Maria Salerno dubbing him and he took the same part in the second movie, I think he started to talk like Salerno. If you look at *Fistful of Dollars* and *For a Few Dollars More*, in the second one you can notice he talks slowly, more "Clint Eastwood". It was Salerno did that, I'm convinced.' Sondra Locke, Clint Eastwood's future wife, has written that the voice was inspired by a very different source: '[Eastwood] told me how he had developed his way of whispering in his performance during the "Dollar" films. He said he'd noticed Marilyn Monroe's breathy whisper and he thought it was very sexy. And since it had worked so well for her, he decided he'd do a male version of it himself.'[62]

Before he returned home from the dubbing, Eastwood was offered a part in a five-segment portmanteau movie called *Le Streghe/The Witches* which was being assembled by producer Dino De Laurentiis, each segment a showcase for his wife Silvana Mangano in a different role. For agreeing to appear as a boring businessman who becomes a fantasy cowboy in the segment *Una sera come le altre/An Evening Like the Others*, directed by Vittorio De Sica, Eastwood was offered by De Laurentiis either a fee of $25,000 or $20,000 plus a Ferrari. He chose the latter, partly because 'there's no 10 per cent on that Ferrari'; and he had the car shipped to New York after filming.[63] During the shoot, De Sica and his actor went to Paris for the French première of *For a Few Dollars More*. De Sica introduced Eastwood to the audience with the words 'He will soon be one of the biggest stars in the business; the new Gary Cooper'. By then, *For a Few* was breaking all box-office records in Italy, and *Rawhide* had finally ground to a halt with the last episode on 7 December 1965. *Fistful of Dollars* had alerted producers to the investment potential of the Italian Western, but *For a Few Dollars More* defined the style of an entire sub-genre. At the Sorrento trade fair, it had been sold to twenty-six countries in a single day. The film earned $5 million in the domestic market alone (as compared with *Fistful*'s $4.6 million) between 1965 and 1968 – a time when the number of cinemas was in significant decline. This made *For a Few Dollars More* the most successful film ever to have been made in Italy, beating *La dolce vita* by a factor of 50 per cent. On the domestic market, it was the film which sold the highest-ever recorded number of tickets, and it remained in that position until 1971 (with *Fistful* a close second).

Both achievements led to an avalanche of co-productions (by the late 1960s, half of all Italian film-making involved co-production money), a further proliferation of production companies, and the return of Hollywood company offices rather than agencies. The vast majority of spinoffs would be low-budget derivatives destined for *terza visione* cinemas and the home market. This was encouraged, indirectly, by the Legge Corona of 1965 which made it easier for production companies to attract subsidies and grants, and to raise credit from the Banca Nazionale del Lavora; thus a cheaply made Western could earn a respectable profit *and* be protected from making a loss.[64] Together, *Fistful* and *For a Few* activated and restructured the industry, in much the same way as Francisci's *Hercules* had done in 1958 – only on a grander scale. *Fistful of Dollars* had made the transition from flea-pit in Florence to *prima visione* cinemas. With *For a Few Dollars More*, Leone would definitively distance his work from the vast bulk of popular Italian film-making – even though the roots of his success, and some of his aesthetic attitudes, lay there. Another indirect result of his success was that Leone now had to attend 'a lot of meetings with executives'. Although his case against Jolly Film was still going through the courts, he was becoming a rich man. Amongst the livelier young film critics, Leone's stock continued to rise. Dario Argento, for one, was again struck by Leone's invention and apparent 'love for technique': '*For a Few Dollars More* was even better than *Fistful of Dollars* and we were annoyed that he had managed to surprise us even more.'[65]

1965 had been a pivotal year in Leone's life. *For a Few Dollars More* had been filmed between mid-April and the end of June, and had opened spectacularly in the autumn. He had moved to an upmarket area called AXA on the outskirts of Rome, ten minutes away from Ostia and closer to the sea. There was no name on the street then, but it is now called Via Lisippo, and the number would have been 23. His mentor Mario Bonnard had died at the age of seventy-six: in a career which went back to 1909, Bonnard had directed or co-directed over a hundred films, the last in 1961. Sergio Leone had assisted him on eight of them, had shot his first sequences under his aegis, and had lived in his house for over a decade. Symbolically, 1965 was also the year in which Sergio shed the pseudonym 'Bob Robertson' and proudly issued a film under his own name. At last.

# The Good, The Bad and The Ugly

Sancho's fat belly (panza), his appetite and thirst still convey a powerful carnivalesque spirit [heir to the grotesque tradition of the Middle Ages]. His love of abundance and wealth have not, as yet, a basically private, egotistic and alienating character. Sancho is the direct heir of the antique pot-bellied demons which decorate the famous Corinthian vases. In Cervantes' images of food and drink there is still the spirit of popular banquets. Sancho's materialism, his pot belly, appetite, his abundant defecation, are on the absolute lower level of grotesque realism of the humorous bodily grave (belly, bowels, earth) which has been dug for Don Quixote's abstract and deadened idealism. One could say that the knight of the sad countenance must die in order to be reborn a better and a greater man. This is a bodily and popular corrective to individual idealistic and spiritual pretence. Moreover, it is the popular corrective of laughter applied to the narrow-minded seriousness of the spiritual pretence; it is a regenerating and laughing death. Sancho's role in relation to Don Quixote can be compared to the role of medieval parodies versus high ideology and cult, to the role of the clown versus serious ceremonial . . . The humorous principle of regeneration can also be seen, to a lesser extent, in the windmills (giants), inns (castles), flocks of rams and sheep (armies of knights), innkeepers (lords of the castle), prostitutes (noble ladies), and so forth. All these images form a typical grotesque carnival. Such is the first, carnival aspect of the material bodily images of *Don Quixote*. But it is precisely this aspect which creates the grand style of Cervantes' realism, his universal nature, and his deep popular utopianism.

Mikhail Bakhtin, *Rabelais and His World* (1940, translated 1968)

When *For a Few Dollars More* followed *Fistful of Dollars* into the Supercinema in Rome, it broke the existing box-office record for a single film by a factor of three. And it was at the Supercinema – with Luciano Vincenzoni and some representatives of United Artists in the audience – that Leone's next Western, *The Good, The Bad and The Ugly*, was born. *Fistful of Dollars* had been inspired by a visit to a Japanese movie; *The Good, The Bad and The Ugly* was inspired by a visit to a Sergio Leone movie. For Vincenzoni, in addition to writing the script and the dialogue of *For a Few Dollars More* was contractually 'involved with the film's overseas sales'.

As Vincenzoni explains: 'I telephoned the vice-president of United Artists in Paris, my friend Ilya Lopert, who came to Rome with all his staff. I took them to the Supercinema, and fortunately it was one of those days when they continued to smash all records. It was a sell-out. There were three thousand people in the audience. The United Artists people saw the film amid all the laughter and applause, and afterwards wanted to go to the Grand Hotel to sign a contract – there and then. The minimum sum they guaranteed to pay was over three times higher than the most optimistic forecasts of the producer. As is typical of the Americans when they're doing business, the first thing they said when the contract had been signed was "now let's cross-collateralize, let's compensate profits and loss with the *next* film. Oh, by the way, what *is* the next film?" Well, we hadn't got any plans. So with the tacit agreement of Leone and Grimaldi, I began to invent things. "It's a film," I said, "about three rogues who are looking for some treasure at the time of the American Civil War – in the same kind of spirit as *La Grande Guerra/The Great War* which you distributed in America." And they immediately replied, "Okay, we'll buy it. How much will it cost?" Without any script having been written – just on those few words.'[1] Actually, the negotiation with United Artists was a little more complicated than that. Sergio Donati explains: 'Grimaldi was ready to sell the rights of *For a Few Dollars More*, in the United States and Canada. And at exactly the same time Luciano Vincenzoni was working with Ilya Lopert and was a great friend of Arnold and David Picker of United Artists. They were in Rome. He convinced Lopert to bring the UA people to a big screening of *For a Few Dollars More* . . . And Luciano really sold the movie to United Artists and had ten per cent of the profits of all this and a percentage of the next one, *The Good, The Bad and The Ugly*, as well.'[2] Vincenzoni's deal with United Artists (of which he owned a slice) was far more attractive than the deal which Grimaldi was negotiating at precisely the same time. So Grimaldi flew back from New York, to meet the UA people in Rome. Lopert's offer for *For a Few Dollars More* was, it has been estimated, one million dollars minimum guarantee.

Vincenzoni takes up the story: 'When Mr Lopert asked how much the new film would cost, I turned my head to Leone and asked, "How much?" Leone said, "*What*'s how much?" I said, "The movie I just sold them." Honestly, it was a miracle, without a story, just a little act. Grimaldi and Leone, asked me, "What did you tell them?" I said, "A story around the Civil War with three actors; tell me the number." Grimaldi said, "Well, what about eight hundred thousand dollars?" I said, "Make it a million." I turned to Lopert and said, "One million dollars." He told me, "It's a deal."³ From then on, according to Vincenzoni, his relationship with Leone began to turn sour. Leone believed fervently in the mystique of the director, and he seems to have felt himself diminished, 'usurped' by his writer. 'And all because I sold the movie.' Moreover, Vincenzoni now owned a piece of it. United Artists agreed to advance half a million dollars up front for the new film; their full investment would be exchanged for 50 per cent of the box-office takings outside Italy. The total budget of *The Good, The Bad and The Ugly* would ultimately be $1.3 million.

Predictably, Sergio Leone's own account of the origins of the film was very different. By the late 1960s he was presenting it to interviewers as an organic, 'authorial' progression from his previous two Westerns; and all his own idea: 'I didn't feel pressurized any more', Leone would assert, 'to offer the public a different kind of film. I could now do exactly the kind of film I wanted . . . It was while I was reflecting on the story of *For a Few Dollars More* and what made it work, on the different motives of Van Cleef and Eastwood, that I found the centre of the third film . . . I had always thought that the "good", the "bad" and the "violent" did not exist in any absolute, essential sense. It seemed to me interesting to demystify these adjectives in the setting of a Western. An assassin can display a sublime altruism while a good man can kill with total indifference. A person who appears to be ugly may, when we get to know him better, be more worthy than he seems – and capable of tenderness . . . I had an old Roman song engraved in my memory, a song which seemed to me full of common sense:

| | |
|---|---|
| *E'morto un Cardinale* | [A Cardinal is dead, |
| *che ha fatto bene e male.* | who did good and bad things. |
| *Il mal l'ha fatto bene* | The bad, he did well |
| *e il ben l'a fatto male.* | and the good, he did badly.] |

This was basically the moral I was interested in putting over in the film.'⁴ In fact, the film was not originally to be called *The Good, The Bad and The Ugly*. The title *I due magnifici straccioni* (*The*

*Two Magnificent Tramps*) was changed just before shooting began.
Vincenzoni dreamed up the new title (literally) and Leoni loved it.

At an early stage, Leone agreed with Vincenzoni that the story
would mix the tragic historical events of the Civil War with a 'picaresque spirit': a series of chance encounters between cunning tricksters
in the dusty Southwest. The picaresque and the *commedia dell'arte*
were useful reference points, he felt, because 'they have this in common: they do not have true heroes, represented by one character'.
With Vincenzoni's 'three rogues in search of some treasure' to build
on, the conferences began. As Leone explained: 'What interested me
was on the one hand to demystify the adjectives, on the other to show
the absurdity of war ... The Civil War which the characters
encounter, in my frame of reference, is useless, stupid: it does not
involve a "good cause". The key phrase of the film is the one where a
character comments on the battle of the bridge: "I've never seen so
many men wasted so badly." I show a Northern concentration camp
... but was thinking partly about the Nazi camps with their Jewish
orchestras.'[5]

Andersonville Camp in Confederate Georgia, and the atrocities that
had occurred there (slaughter, starvation, even cannibalism) were well
known in the historical literature, if not in the movies. Documentation
had been examined by scholars, to fathom exactly what went wrong.
Was it lack of supplies and support, confusing policy directives, the
Union decision to abandon exchanges of prisoners, or just plain cruelty
on the part of the officers concerned, including Camp Commandant
Wirz? When John Ford had featured a refugee camp for native Americans in *Cheyenne Autumn* (1964), he had placed it under the command
of a methodical German officer (Captain Oskar Wessels, a proto-Nazi
played by Karl Malden) as if that was enough to explain everything to
the audience. Asked by an army surgeon if he will take responsibility
for locking the Cheyenne in a warehouse and starving them during a
Nebraskan winter, Wessels responds: 'I am responsible for nothing. I
have simply been the instrument of an order.' To which the surgeon
replies: 'You say that as if you'd memorized it.' At the end of the earlier
*Horse Soldiers* (1959), based on the historical Grierson Raid 300 miles
into rebel Mississippi, Ford had explicitly referred to Andersonville.
The cynical but humanitarian Union surgeon (William Holden) tells
hard-nosed professional soldier John Wayne that he will risk staying
behind Confederate lines, and parting company with the troops, saying,

'Medicine's where you find it.' 'Even in Andersonville?' Wayne asks. 'Even in Andersonville' is the reply.

But the subject seemed to bear a Hollywood taboo. Even *Escape from Andersonville*, a fifteen-minute Kalem production of the silent era, simply concerned six Union prisoners who manage to flee the camp in a stolen locomotive. It had been rumoured in the 1950s that producer-director Stanley Kramer was planning a film version of Mackinlay Kantor's monumental novel *Andersonville*. Columbia subsequently announced that they were doing the project, and it would be directed by Fred Zinnemann. But when the estimated budget rose to over $12 million, it was abandoned. In Leone's *The Good, The Bad and The Ugly*, not only was the 'Betterville' Camp to be associated with the *victorious* side; the war itself was represented by a series of shocking details, involving both sides, indiscriminately. We see a one-armed Union soldier, and a legless Confederate 'half-soldier'; a field hospital in a mission at San Antonio, where the Franciscan friars are completely out of their depth; a Confederate spy, strapped to the cowcatcher of a Northern troop train, and a looter of 'supplies and equipment' who carries his coffin to a wall before being shot against it; wounded civilians trying to evacuate a bombed-out town under intense mortar fire; unburied corpses strewn all over the countryside; and a huge military cemetery in the middle of nowhere.

Leone said, 'I wanted to show human imbecility in a picaresque film where I would also show the reality of war. I had read somewhere that 120,000 people died in Southern camps such as Andersonville. And I was not ignorant of the fact that there were camps in the North. You always get to hear about the shameful behaviour of the losers, never the winners. So I decided to show extermination in a Northern camp. This did not please the Americans ... The American Civil War is almost a taboo subject, because its reality is insane and incredible. But the true history of the United States was constructed on a violence which neither literature nor the cinema had ever properly shown. As for me, I always tend to defy the official version of events – no doubt because I grew up under Fascism. I had seen first hand how history can be manipulated. So I always question what is propagated. It has become a reflex with me.'[6]

Betterville Camp consists of a stockade with watch-towers made of logs, a deep trench in which to bury the dead, and a small orchestra of Confederate musicians who play a sad 'ballad of a soldier' ('How ends the story?/Whose is the glory?') to drown the cries of tortured inmates. There is no shelter for inmates, though: only for Union officers. The design was based on steel engravings of Andersonville, made in August 1864 when the camp contained 35,000 prisoners of war. Why Betterville should be located in Texas is never explained. Perhaps it was because Leone's and Vincenzoni's knowledge of camps run by 'the North' (which Leone tended to present, conspiratorially, as if it was secret information) in part came from such films as Robert Wise's *Two Flags West* (1950), concerning Union prisoners in New Mexico, and Sam Peckinpah's *Major Dundee* (1964), where as often as not the setting was the arid Southwest. Historically, most of the action in the Civil War happened east of the Mississippi. When Hollywood produced 'Westerns' set at the time of the war, the stories tended to concern gun-running, horse-trading shipments of gold or the gathering of intelligence.[7] Supply-lines, in other words, rather than battles; and certainly not concentration camps.

According to Leone, however, there was an historical justification for the setting as well: 'American authors depend too much on other screenwriters and don't go back enough into their own history. When I was preparing *The Good, The Bad and The Ugly*, I discovered that there had only been one battle in Texas during the Civil War, which was really about the ownership of goldmines in Texas. The point of the battle was to stop the North (or the South) from getting their hands on the gold first. So, when I was visiting Washington, I tried to get some more documentation on this incident. The librarian there, at the Library of Congress, the biggest library in the world, said to me, "You can't be right about this. Texas, you say, signor? You must be mistaken. There's never been a battle fought over goldmines in America, and in any case the Civil War didn't reach Texas. Come back in two or three days and I'll do some checking for you. But I'm quite certain you are wrong." Well, I returned after two or three days, and this guy looked at me as if he'd seen a ghost. "I've got eight books here," he said, "and they all refer to this particular incident. How the hell did *you* know about it? You read in the Italian language, so how did you manage to find out? *Now* I understand why you Italians make such extraordinary films. Twenty years I've been here, and not a single American director has ever bothered to inform himself about the history of the West." Well, I've got a huge library myself now – they'll photocopy a whole book for you for eight dollars in Washington!'[8]

Leone had made use of bizarre anecdotes about the Wild West in his previous films. But this time, his perverse version of American history would colour the entire story. The Good, the Bad and the Ugly may all be self-serving bums, but the Civil War through which they ride is an inferno of needless destruction and cruelty. And if the film would question and make arbitrary each of these labels (in the context of the Western, where they were usually fixed as 'absolutes'), it would at the same time question the received, popular version of historical events. Leone, who had started in the business with the mythologies of Roman baths, now found himself grappling with the *Mythologies* of Roland Barthes: 'As always, I took conventional cinema as a base. Then I set about demolishing the codes in order to play with appearances, while presenting a "comedy of murders" to sweep up all the untruths attached to the historical context. But I tried all the while to hang on to documentary reality . . . It was fascinating to demystify the archetypes and the adjectives. And I emphasized this principle in each situation of the film. Always a deceptive play on appearances, as in the scene where the dust covers the blue uniform of the Northerners to make them appear as grey as the uniform of the Southerners. It was a manipulation of the signs, which chimed with all the other ingredients in the film.'[9]

The scene in question begins with Blondie (the Good) and his compadré Tuco (the Ugly), both clad in stolen grey Confederate uniforms, catching sight of a detachment of troops in the distance. 'Blue or grey?' asks Blondie. 'They're grey like us,' replies Tuco, 'let's say hello to them and then get going.' As the troops draw nearer, Tuco shouts, 'Hurrah for the Confederacy. Hurrah. Down with General Grant. Hurrah for General . . . What's his name?' 'Lee,' prompts Blondie. 'Lee. God is with us because he hates the Yanks too.' 'God's not on our side,' says Blondie, peering more closely at the now-stationary troops, ''cos he hates idiots also.' We then zoom in on the sleeve of the officer in charge as it is brushed clean of desert dust: he is in fact wearing a blue uniform. The confusion is reminiscent of the equally cynical short story *One of the Missing* by Ambrose Bierce, based on the author's experience in an Indiana regiment during the Civil War. It finishes with the young hero, a Union private, lying dead in the rubble, 'so covered with dust that his clothing was Confederate grey'.[10]

The Civil War had long provided scriptwriters with a credible setting in which to explore issues of commitment and 'destiny' at an individual rather than a national level. In Hollywood terms, the North was about progress, industry, the city, and the triumph of the national government from 1865 onwards. The South was about feudalism, moonlight and magnolia, 'the good old cause', slavery, and plantations exclusively given over to cotton growing. In Selznick's *Gone with the Wind* (1939), or Edward Dmytryk's *Raintree County* (1958) or John Ford's segment of *How the West Was Won* (1962), the question of which side the protagonists support is the moral touchstone of the movie. Even in *Great Day in the Morning* (1955), directed by Jacques Tourneur (whose work Leone admired), the central character, Pentecost (Robert Stack), is unusually cynical about the upcoming war. Finally, like the bounty-hunters of contemporaneous Westerns, he realizes the value of commitment and personal responsibility, through the love of a saloon girl who sacrifices herself; and he decides to enlist in the Confederate army. (This is so out of character that he is asked, 'What made you change your mind? Did someone play Dixie?') And yet Hollywood had largely steered clear of the war itself. While taking time out from his own war effort, Leone ran into Orson Welles at a restaurant in Burgos. Welles told him he was certifiable to make a film about the Civil War. Barring *Gone with the Wind*, the subject seemed to be box-office poison. Maybe the war between the states was too traumatic a subject: a war for the soul of America which was also the first 'total' war of modern times, involving civilians as well as brother against brother.

On these terms, *The Good, The Bad and The Ugly* was particularly heretical. In Leone's film, there is no moral touchstone – just a lot of dust. The Civil War is something very nasty happening in the background, against which the surreal adventures of the central characters can be played out, and to some extent judged. It is someone else's war; like the Second World War must have seemed to the adolescent Leone, growing up in Rome. It is refracted through anti-heroes who are as suspicious of idealism as they are of rhetoric; again, like Leone during the political compromise of the postwar period in Italy. The Civil War is not an obstacle to the long march of progress, an aberration. On the contrary, in Leone's film, the Civil War contains the seeds of the 'rule of violence by violence' which followed it, in the Wild West.

'The Good' steals a Confederate uniform, rides with a gang of Union renegades, helps a Union captain blow up a bridge, and gives a last puff on a cigar to a dying Confederate officer. 'The Bad' enlists in the Northern army as an NCO following a tip-off from a starving

Confederate sergeant, becomes a concentration camp official, deserts when he feels like it, and is prepared to shoot anyone of either persuasion if the reward is high enough. 'The Ugly' also steals a Confederate uniform before enlisting with the North; but he isn't even sure what the war is supposed to be about. All three of them have the same motivation: they want to find the gold, which is buried in the tomb of an unknown soldier, a tomb with no name. So Vincenzoni's hastily improvised tale of 'three rogues who are looking for some treasure' endured as the spine holding the film together.

With a splendid sense of construction, the war enters the narrative to *save* the lives of Blondie and Tuco on various occasions. A mysterious Confederate coach, marked 'CSA Headquarters 3rd Regiment', appears from nowhere, in the middle of the desert, to distract Tuco's attention and protect Blondie from being shot. A mortar shell smashes the floor and prevents Blondie from being hanged. As Tuco is being thumped by the slobbish Sergeant Wallace, a Northern train pulls into Betterville station and spares him for the time being. Tuco cuts through his handcuffs by draping the chain over a railway line; a Northern troop train does the rest. Confederate mortar fire provides a convenient smokescreen, from behind which Blondie and Tuco can systematically pick off members of the Bad's gang. The battle for Langstone Bridge provides a means of crossing the river and at last reaching the gold. Sad Hill cemetery hides the prize they are all after.

The set-piece battle itself, as Leone and Vincenzoni intended, refers to the trench warfare of the First World War; just as Betterville refers to Auschwitz. Their purpose seems to have been to create a living picture of war, to chime with a contemporary audience weaned on Bob Dylan's 'With God on Our side' and Joseph Heller's *Catch-22*. His larger budget gave Leone the opportunity to stockpile an extraordinary selection of Civil War weapons along the valley overlooking the Langstone Bridge: mortars, Gatling guns, Whitworth field guns and rifles, some of them borrowed from the Museo del Ejercito in Madrid. This museum, just off the Paseo del Prado, had in its display cases (in addition to the sword belonging to Rodrigo Diaz de Vivar, 'El Cid') a Navy Colt, an Adams rifle-revolver, a range of nineteenth-century Spanish mortars, an engraving of an 1878 15-mm cannon, an 'organ-pipe' cannon of 1836 and several models of wooden pontoon bridges dating from the Peninsular War up to 1939. All of these were to appear, in one form or another, in Leone's battle. The museum did not exhibit a

Gatling gun, but there were plenty of Hollywood films and reference books from which to copy one. Carlo Simi's drawings include a mortar and two mobile cannon 'del museo delle armi di Madrid', plus pictorial references to *The Frontier Years* by Mark H. Brown and W.R. Felton. No matter that the big cannon and the metallic-cartridge Gatling were not available until after the American Civil War. No matter that Blondie meticulously cleans and reassembles the working parts of his Navy Colt (a percussion pistol) only to fill it with metallic .45 cartridges. The point was only to create a cluttered 'peep-show' of history. Leone was evidently delighted to have the opportunity to zoom in on the Army Museum's collection of destructive technology, as transported to the countryside near Burgos, and then show its effects. Real museum exhibits stood side by side with specially made cannon – such as the huge Rodgers battery – designed by Simi from historical illustrations.[11]

The credit titles of the film, designed by Luigi Lardini, would make stills of the action look like sepia prints by the celebrated photographer Matthew Brady – albeit with garish colours splashed over them, Andy Warhol-style. Brady would even make a fleeting appearance, amid the mayhem of a wartime railway station, taking a picture of tidied-up Union officers proudly posing around a mortar in their Sunday-best uniforms. According to Lee Van Cleef, Leone often referred to archive photographs when setting up shots such as these: 'The prison camp that Sergio had built didn't have much to it – just a few houses and lots of fences. And it was overcrowded, but you had the feeling that it was how it must have been in the Civil War. It was like pictures I'd seen of Andersonville . . . just like a Brady photograph.'[12]

When it came to the grandstanding sequence in which a 200-yard wooden bridge was to be dynamited, the special-effects team accidentally destroyed it before the cameras were ready to roll, in an all-action version of the old 'Ready when you are, C.B.' gag. It has been suggested that this must have been the result of one of the ever-gesticulating director's arm movements. It wasn't, as Eli Wallach recalls: 'There were three cameras set up, one very close and another far away. The man who had arranged the explosives for this scene was a captain in the Spanish army. The special-effects man had told him what an honour it was to have him helping out on the set, and therefore the honour of pressing the button to blow up the bridge should be his. The captain said, "No, I don't want to do it," and the special-effects man said, "Sure, just listen, and when I say '*Vaya!*' (which means go), press the button." As this was going on, one of the assistants said, "You want me to put up one of the small cameras over there?" and he answered, "Yes, *vi*, fine." The captain heard the word "*vaya*", pressed the button and the bridge was blown up by accident. Leone was furious. "I'll kill him!" he was saying. "I'll fire him on spot. He's fired!" He told the captain all this, and was told, "I'll rebuild the bridge, just don't fire that man." '[13]

It took several days to rebuild, even in balsa wood, giving Clint Eastwood and Eli Wallach plenty of time to reflect on the sequence. It seems that Leone became so overexcited that he tried to get both actors to run and hit the ground, dangerously close to the bridge, during the actual explosion. A shot of the Good and the Ugly protecting themselves from flying debris, the bridge blowing up in the background, would, Leone thought, be unbeatable. Leone had made large-scale action sequences before (in his own and other people's pepla), but he had never been in personal charge of so many resources: it was, in Orson Welles's famous phrase, like having his own toy train set. Clint Eastwood watched as the charges were reset and asked Leone, 'Where exactly are Eli and I going to be?' Leone explained just how he saw it. Eastwood looked at the short distance between the bridge and cover, and said, 'Sergio, where are *you* going to be?' 'I'll be right behind the camera waiting for you,' he replied. 'Well, then, I'll do it.' Now Leone looked apprehensively at the exact distance between bridge and camera. After rehearsal, Eastwood couldn't help noticing that two stunt doubles had appeared unannounced, dressed as the Good and the Ugly, and that a shallow trench, protected by sandbags, had been dug for them to jump into. An assistant explained to Eastwood that Signor Leone had now decided to retreat to higher ground, and watch the proceedings from a better vantage. It was a clear case of a bridge too near. This change of plan in fact led Leone to an unusual but forgivable continuity error: Blondie and Tuco light the fuse, swim away, and are suddenly a quarter of a mile away from the action. Recalling the incident in the late 1970s, Leone shrugged it off, saying, 'bridges tend to get blown up in my films'.[14]

Of course, this study of 'human imbecility' and brutality was made with the tacit blessing of the Franco regime and with technical help from the Spanish army. At an American Film Institute seminar in 1973, Eastwood was asked if the production had any trouble with the authorities. 'In Spain', replied Eastwood, 'they don't care what you do. They would care if you were doing a story about Spaniards and about Spain. Then they'd scrutinize you very tough, but the fact that you're doing a Western that's supposed to be laid in Southwest America or Mexico, they couldn't care less what your story or subject is.'[15]

Leone's previous Westerns had demonstrated something of a pre-occupation with brutality. His third entry in the genre juxtaposed the violence of his treasure-hunters with the mindless and impersonal carnage of war. In developing this theme, Sergio Leone later claimed to have had in mind 'one of the finest films I know', Charlie Chaplin's *Monsieur Verdoux*, made in 1947 and based on an idea by Orson Welles. 'This film looked at the chaotic and absurd aspects of an era in which a hero who has murdered several women could say, at his trial, "I am just an amateur compared with Mr Roosevelt and Mr Stalin, who do such things on a grand scale." Verdoux is the model of all the bandits, all the bounty-hunters. Put him in a hat and boots, and you have a Westerner.'[16] At the end of Chaplin's film, Henri Verdoux tells the French court: 'As for being a mass killer, does not the world encourage it? Is it not building weapons of destruction for the sole purpose of mass killing? Has it not blown unsuspecting women and little children to pieces, and done it very scientifically? As a mass killer, I am an amateur by comparison.' There are interesting affinities between Chaplin's 'comedy of murders' and Leone's film: the idea that killings could be organized as 'a strictly business enterprise'; the humour of mixing the languages of business and murder ('You must have made a killing'); the changes of dress and uniform (Verdoux's different disguises); the structure of the film (built around the murderer's train journeys across country from one wealthy victim to another). But Luciano Vincenzoni waspishly denies the inspiration, saying, 'I wrote *The Good, The Bad and The Ugly* in eleven days, and I didn't have time to refer to anything. I mean I have too much respect for Charlie Chaplin to involve him with Sergio Leone Westerns.'[17]

Leone liked to tell interviewers (especially if they were French) that the central theme of *Monsieur Verdoux* reminded him also of Louis-Ferdinand Céline's semi-autobiographical novel *Journey to the End of the Night*. This, he said, was a favourite book, about 'the contradictions of living in the modern world' which he had first read when he was twenty; it was 'the sort of book which marks you for the rest of your life'. Céline's novel, his first, written while he had a piece of shrapnel lodged in his head, was published in 1932. It recounts in episodic picaresque style the adventures of the narrator Ferdinand Bardamu and his 'shadow' Robinson through the First World War (Flanders, the Ardennes, Meuse country), a French colony in Africa, New York, Detroit and finally the industrial suburbs of Paris. A series of absurd and often violent incidents reinforce the bleak moral message that the only value in existence is to survive, and to reject all pretensions to higher values. Céline himself had joined the French cavalry in 1913, and was wounded in the head during the first months of the war, in an action for which he was awarded a decoration. After being invalided out, he took a medical degree and became a staff surgeon at Henry Ford's assembly-line in Detroit before returning to Paris. The style of *Journey* was partly based on his excellent ear for French working-class uses of language, partly on his reading of such novels as Joseph Conrad's *Heart of Darkness* and Proust's *A la recherche du temps perdu*, and partly on his very dark sense of humour.

Céline's mixture of knowing literary references, colourful language, chance encounters, absurd incidents, an epic sweep and a belly laugh amid all the gloom would seem to have strong affinities with Sergio Leone's view of the world. Céline's profound distrust of authority figures (officers in the war, colonists in Africa, the super-rich in New York, the bosses in Detroit), who are cowardly and cruel when they aren't corrupt, may also have chimed with Leone's political attitudes. But Leone's screenwriters deny that he brought his admiration for Céline to the writing of *The Good, The Bad and The Ugly*. Sergio Donati goes further. He denies that Leone ever in fact read the book: 'For a man who had read very few books, Sergio was very clever ... *Voyage au bout de la nuit* was the bedside reading of Luciano Vincenzoni. He knew it by heart and he used to read extracts from that book to Sergio – who had never read a word of it. Absolutely. Vincenzoni kept quoting and quoting and quoting it to him. From 1968 onwards Sergio was treated by cinéastes in France as if he had an honorary doctorate of letters, and when he was asked, "What is your bedside reading?" he always said, "Céline, *Voyage au bout de la nuit*". "Oh," said the interviewers.'[18] Vincenzoni agrees with this: he recalls seeing Leone clutching a copy of the book on a French television programme in 1968, and gasping in disbelief.

Fulvio Morsella was in the best position to know about this. He would read whole books to Sergio, when they had been published in

English, translating them into Italian as he went along. Sergio Leone often told interviewers that his great ambition was to film Céline, but that he did not want to compromise the integrity of the novel: it was too important to him. Was this true? 'No, that was just a snobbish attitude. Because it wasn't for him – that kind of film he couldn't have made. It wasn't his type of vision. So he just talked about it all the time and never did it. I didn't, in fact, introduce him to Céline. It was published in Italian. In my view it was the title that fascinated him. He liked that.'[19] Plus the fact that it was Jack Kerouac's favourite book. There is a strong flavour of Céline's book in *The Good, The Bad and The Ugly* – as there had been, six years previously, in *La Grande Guerra*. In both instances, Luciano Vincenzoni probably put it there.

According to Leone, his battle sequence was also partly inspired by the similar scene in Buster Keaton's *The General* (1926) where a Civil War locomotive steams on to a burning trestle bridge, which then collapses spectacularly into the river below. Keaton, too, had endured a false start when preparing this scene, and at a cost of $42,000 the shot was to become, according to film historian Kevin Brownlow, 'the most expensive single shot of the silent era'. It had stuck in Leone's mind, since he first saw it in the Mussolini era, as both magical and spectacular. His screenwriters are happy to confirm 'the Keatonian echo': nobody has ever attempted to deny Leone's encyclopedic knowledge of cinema.

To add to the eclecticism, the Union captain's weary speech about how whisky is 'the most potent weapon in war – the fighting spirit is in this bottle' was apparently based on a passage in Emilio Lussu's book *Un anno sull'altopiano/A Year on the Plains*, another disenchanted novel about the First World War. 'In that book', Leone recalled, 'a captain says, "One must drink. Get plastered. It is our best weapon. Without alcohol, no one will reach the end." That was the speech I put in the mouth of the character played by Aldo Giuffré – a Neapolitan actor-comedian who was a pupil of De Filippo.'[20] Leone especially enjoyed placing the speech during the 'battle of the bridge', he added, because in John Ford's *Horse Soldiers*, John Wayne *refuses* a slug of whisky at an equivalent moment during the battle for the Southern trestle bridge just outside Baton Range.

When developing Vincenzoni's original idea into a script, Leone also turned to the comedy-writing team of Agenore Incrocci and Furio Scarpelli (known as Age–Scarpelli), who had made their collective name with a series of Totò films in the early 1950s, and had since attracted international attention with two films for director Mario Monicelli: *I soliti ignoti/Big Deal on Madonna Street* (1958) and *La Grande Guerra*, co-written with Vincenzoni. Sergio Donati interprets Leone's decision as an example of 'disloyalty' towards Vincenzoni. The man himself is more calm about it: 'We developed the screenplay with Sergio Leone, myself and Age–Scarpelli. We used to chat, and after that I wrote, he read and sometimes he asked me for some changes. The progress was a normal one.' In fact, it was Vincenzoni who *recommended* Age–Scarpelli.[21] When Leone approached Age and Scarpelli, they were working on *L'armata brancaleone*, a medieval romp with a carnivalesque atmosphere which mocked the pretensions of grandees, priests and knights. It even had *two* collapsing bridges. The match must have seemed perfect. But it did not work out that way.

As Leone recalled, the contribution of these writers was 'a disaster. There were jokes and nothing else. I couldn't use a single thing they'd written. It was the grossest deception of my life. I had to take up the script again with some ghostwriters.'[22] Sergio Donati was to become the main ghostwriter, and his recollection of the 'collaboration' with Age and Scarpelli for once matches Leone's: 'There was next to nothing of them in the final script. They wrote only the first part. Just one line. They were so far from Leone's style. It was typical of him to bring them in. He had to try something new. And we suffered. Age and Scarpelli wrote a kind of comedy set in the West rather than a Western.'[23] After his eleven days' work on the movie, Vincenzoni remembers that 'my relationship with Leone got somewhat colder, and so I agreed to write two other films, *A Professional Gun* for Sergio Corbucci and *Death Rides a Horse* for Giulio Petroni. Because with these two other films I was earning twice as much and I didn't have arguments all the time with the director.'[24]

Age and Scarpelli, for their part, had been looking forward to working with Leone. Scarpelli explained, with the benefit of hindsight: 'In our profession, we must have a certain curiosity and be attentive to the films of others – how they work, what's going on in them. It was the moment of the two Westerns of Sergio Leone. In all film people, there's a secret and infantile passion for the Western, so we agreed to collaborate on this film . . . He had always wanted to remake *La Grande Guerra* as a Western. But the encounter with him turned out to be fatal.'[25] The collaboration misfired, as Leone saw it, because Age–Scarpelli didn't appreciate his vision. He didn't want to make a slapstick comedy of a Western. He wanted to make an *epic* Western, where different 'levels of irony' would be applied to each of the main characters. This would be clear from the opening sequences.

Tuco is introduced to us leaping angrily through the glass window of a saloon, a half-chewed joint of lamb in one hand, and a gun in the other. He has just shot three saddle-tramps who interrupted his meal. (They look as though they are about to confront each other, but are in fact all gunning for Tuco.) A mangy dog has just padded into the saloon – a portent of the mutt that shows up in the final sequence, as Tuco himself digs for gold, dog-like, with his hands. Freeze-frame: The Ugly.

The Man in Black was known in the script, and in the Italian version of the film, as 'Sentenza', meaning 'sentence' or 'judgement'. In the English-language version he was 'Angel Eyes'. Lee Van Cleef remembered this idea as originating on-set with Clint Eastwood. We are introduced to the Man in Black in a darkened bedroom, visiting an elderly and sick man called Baker who has employed him to get some information from a farmer. The farmer has given the Man a thousand dollars, hoping to save his skin: 'I think his idea was that I kill you.' The two men laugh nervously. 'But you know,' says the Man, 'once I'm paid, I always see the job through.' Baker stops laughing, as the hired gun covers the old man's face with a pillow and shoots him through it. The Man smiles. Freeze-frame: The Bad.

Blondie is introduced while riding into the desert, leaving a furious Tuco to fend for himself. They have had up to then a business arrangement, whereby Blondie (perhaps in a nod to W.C. Fields's and Mae West's *My Little Chickadee*) turns Tuco in for the reward, then shoots through the rope with which the townspeople are endeavouring to hang him. Now, Blondie has decided to take the whole reward rather than accept a cut. Tuco shouts after him: 'If I ever catch you, Blondie, I'll rip your heart out and eat it.' Blondie reins in his horse and slowly turns round: 'Such ingratitude', he spits, 'after all the times I've saved your life.' Freeze-frame: The Good. (The freeze-frame, incidentally, came from the title designer during post-production: Leone liked the idea and approved it.)

So the man labelled 'The Good' is quite capable of being vindictive and mean. The man labelled 'The Bad' is very, very bad. And the man labelled 'The Ugly' can be charming and funny. According to Leone, the distinction as it developed was partly autobiographical: 'In my world, the anarchists are the truest characters. And I know them best because my ideas are closest to theirs . . . I am made up of all three of them. [Sentenza] has no spirit, he's a professional in the most banal sense of the term. Like a robot. This isn't the case with the other two. On the methodical and careful side of my character, I'd be nearer Blondie: but my most profound sympathy always goes towards the Tuco side . . . he can be touching with all that tenderness and all that wounded humanity. But Tuco is also a creature of instinct, a bastard, a tramp.'

So Leone was spreading himself between three roles – harlequin, *picaro* and villain – a fact that Clint Eastwood noticed when first he read the script. His immediate response was: 'In the beginning, I was just about alone. Then, there were two. And now there are three of us. I'm going to end up in an entire detachment of cavalry.' *Rawhide* had finished at the end of 1965, just five days short of a seven-year run. It had been cancelled mid-season, for which Clint Eastwood was paid (according to the trade press) $119,000 in compensation by CBS, because of his long-term contract. For the last thirteen episodes Eastwood enjoyed solo top billing, following his promotion to Trail Boss when Eric Fleming was sacked. Asked for his reaction, Eastwood apparently replied, 'Why should I be pleased? I used to carry half the shows. Now I carry them all – for the same money!' Eastwood's Italian work still awaited release in the USA, and Eastwood had the double disadvantage (where Hollywood was concerned) of being associated both with television and the slightly dubious Italian industry. Nevertheless, when Leone offered him a third outing, he was still anxious that this, the only big film on offer, might not do his hard-won image any good at all. Leone recalled: 'He nearly did not play the part of Blondie. After reading the script . . . he found, in effect, that the role of Tuco was too important, was the better role of the two. I tried to reason with him: "The film is longer than the other two. You cannot be all alone. Tuco is necessary to the story, and he will remain as I wanted him to be. You must understand that he is your water-carrier . . . And the moment you appear, it is *the star* who is making his entrance." '[26]

But Clint Eastwood needed a lot more persuading than that, and so Sergio and Carla travelled to California. Carla remembers it well: 'Clint Eastwood, with his wife Maggie, came to our hotel . . . I explained that the fact that he was surrounded by two great actors as well would only enhance his stature. Sometimes even a big star playing a smaller part together with other big actors could derive advantage from the situation. Less was sometimes more.' While the 'two wives negotiated', Carla watched the discussion turn into a clash of male egos, during which tension about 'who did what' surfaced for the first time: 'Eventually in the discussion Sergio said, "If he plays the part, I'm very glad about it. But if he doesn't – well, since I invented *him*, I'll just have to invent another one like him tomorrow." Such tactics always seem to work with Americans. Eye to eye, like a matador with a bull.'[27] A couple of days after the California visit, Clint Eastwood agreed in principle to sign, on the basis of the treatment. But he certainly drove a very hard bargain. This time, his cut would be $250,000, plus 10 per cent of the net profits from Western territories; a 400 per cent rise in one year. According to both Donati and Vincenzoni, Leone resented this deeply.

Eastwood's performance was more relaxed and good-humoured than in the first two films. He was called 'Blondie' throughout, in blithe disregard of his natural colouring. But he looked as though he was having a good time. He managed to appear credibly humane as well as untrustworthy, while gently sending up his 'Mysterious Stranger' persona. Notwithstanding the results, though, the relationship between Eastwood and Leone seems to have remained strained. Eastwood found the shooting schedule (over three months) to be unreasonably protracted. Although he joked about them in retrospect, he found chaotic incidents like the 'bridge' disaster to be tedious in the extreme. It must have taken him about five seconds of watching Eli Wallach's performance to realize that Wallach wasn't about to be his 'water-carrier'. He was Wallach's feed-man; and he couldn't help observing that Leone was trying with this film 'to be more David Lean than Sergio Leone'. As Richard Schickel has put it, 'Leone would use Clint iconographically in his grand design rather than as a compelling figure in himself. Or to put it another way, as the landscapes of Leone's films expanded, Clint could see that his place in them was contracting.'[28] The two men didn't row on set, but Leone must have realized that this would be the last time they would work together. Eastwood certainly did. Sergio Donati accompanied Leone to the USA to record Eastwood's dubbing track for the American edition, and was present when these tensions turned combustible. The immediate trigger was that tendency of Italian filmmakers to have not one but three scripts: one to make the deal, one to shoot and one to dub.

The dubbing of the other actors had been supervised at a Broadway theatre in New York in October/November 1967 by American actor Mickey Knox. A friend of Eli Wallach, Knox had appeared in Raoul Walsh's *White Heat* (1949) and Nicholas Ray's *Knock on Any Door* (1949). But he had fallen foul of the House Un-American Activities Committee in 1951, and had been forced into the more anonymous professions of dubbing and translating in Paris and Rome. He was a close friend of John Derek, but that didn't put him off working with Leone, after Wallach had championed his cause. Knox recalls, '[Sergio] had a very poor translation from the Italian, and in most cases the American actors changed the dialogue when they were doing it . . . I knew what they were supposed to be saying, because I had the Italian script . . . But I had to find out the right dialogue, not only in terms of moving the story along, but also to fit the lips. It's not an easy thing to do. As a matter of fact, it took me six weeks to write what they call "the lip-synch script". Normally I would have done it in seven or ten days for a movie. But that wasn't a normal movie.'[29] Out of this process came 'a lot of translated Italian quips' which turned into the American phrases 'there are two kinds of people in the world', 'it's no joke, it's a rope' and 'shoot, don't talk' – a version of the Italian saying 'when someone is talking he's unlikely to shoot you.' Wallach found the New York dubbing sessions a demanding experience. After all, he had the fastidious Leone at his shoulder, and his part was unusually vocal: 'We worked for seven straight days . . . it was a very difficult thing to recapture the outdoors, the shouting, the battle sequences.' But Clint Eastwood, being otherwise engaged, was not dubbed with the others in New York. So Leone laid off Mickey Knox, who commented, 'Sergio Leone was so goddamned cheap . . . He thought he could manage Clint's dubbing himself, without paying me any salary and living allowance. Clint was the last one, and by that time Sergio, who was the tightest man in the world, felt he was going to save a few bucks by getting rid of me.'[30]

Finally, Eastwood was summoned to discharge his duty by United Artists' vice-president Chris Mankiewicz, son of Joe. 'By this stage', Sergio Donati recalls, 'Sergio had come to dislike Clint Eastwood, I think because he had asked for so much money for the last film; both of them said they were responsible for the other person's success. Anyway, Eastwood turned up in the dubbing studio at eight-thirty in the morning, with his old copy of the shooting script, and, in order to provoke us, he put it on to the lectern and demanded to read that one – not the new version of the dialogue. There was a scene ... [Chris Mankiewicz] had to intervene and threaten that unless he co-operated, Clint would never make any more movies in America. Americans can make the most terrible threats in a completely deadpan manner.'[31]

Clearly, a large element of professional jealousy had crept into the Leone–Eastwood relationship. Tonino Valerii, one of Leone's assistants, was to recall that 'Sergio wasn't very good at recognizing the contributions of other people'. Perhaps Leone realized that Clint Eastwood had ambitions to become a film director himself, ambitions which went back to *Rawhide* days, when he directed 'some trailers and various coming-attraction things'. Leone had found it difficult to cope with John Derek when he came to a similar realization. The problem, as ever, was whether he could keep up his career momentum. Here, he was determined to extend his cinematic range, and enter the international league – possibly at the expense of Eastwood's 'presence' in the film. Vincenzoni reckons that Leone resented the fact that 'the critics and the audience identified his movies as Clint Eastwood movies'. For his part, Eastwood no longer had his *Rawhide* safety net. Whatever his asking price, he *had* to make an impact on Hollywood with this picture.

On the same trip to Los Angeles which secured Eastwood's services, Leone also called upon Eli Wallach and Lee Van Cleef. He had worried about 'carrying over' Van Cleef, since he didn't want to be accused of copying himself, and wasn't wholly convinced of the actor's range. Again, Leone had considered Charles Bronson for 'the Bad', and this time Bronson had agreed. But the contract he had just signed with Robert Aldrich for *The Dirty Dozen* meant that he was not available. So Leone came round once more to the man whom he had propelled to Italian superstardom: 'I said to myself that Van Cleef had first played a romantic character in *For a Few Dollars More*. The idea of getting him to play a character who was the opposite of that began to appeal to me.'[32] As 'Angel Eyes', Van Cleef summoned considerable menace, through the empty smile, the slow, gravelly delivery, the hollow laugh. He even managed to dismount his horse more slowly and threateningly than Jack Palance had done in *Shane*. In the first dialogue scene, this sinister delivery was particularly effective: 'Is that your family?' he asks the farmer, indicating a sepia photograph on the wall. '*Nice family.*'

Many other parts in the film were filled by members of Leone's

'Western' repertory company. Mario Brega (Chico in *Fistful*, Nino in *For a Few*) was the overweight and brutal camp guard Corporal Wallace: a Roman actor in a Union hat. Spanish actor Aldo Sambrell (one of the Rojo gang in *Fistful*, one of Indio's henchmen in *For a Few*) was Angel Eyes' carpet-bagging sidekick. Luigi Pistilli (who made his debut as Groggy, the last of the bandits to die in *For a Few*) now became Tuco's brother Father Ramirez. Trusted stunt director and interpreter Benito Stefanelli reappeared as a small-time baddie. New faces included veteran Spanish character actor Antonio Casas, as the farmer shot by Lee Van Cleef at the beginning of the film, and Canadian actor Al Muloch – in the part of a one-armed gunslinger, originally slotted for Jack Elam. The farmer's wife was played by Chelo Alonso, who had acted for Leone as a sultry temptress in his peplum days. Even Leone's stills photographer Angelo Novi took a turn before the camera, as a Franciscan friar.

But the casting coup of *The Good, The Bad and The Ugly* was Eli Wallach. Originally, Leone considered Gian Maria Volonté for the part, but decided that 'we needed instead an actor with natural comic talent'. They also needed an actor who wouldn't be quite such hard work. Leone had selected Eli Wallach not because of his distinguished Actors' Studio credentials, or for his work on *The Misfits*, or even for his performance as the Mexican bandit leader in *The Magnificent Seven*. He chose Wallach because of a moment in 'The Railroads', the George Marshall segment of *How the West Was Won*, where Wallach's badman Charlie Gant threatens the children of Jeb Rawlins (George Peppard) by pointing his two index fingers at them, miming the firing of two guns, and enjoying their nervous flinches. For Leone, that moment of mime had clinched it: 'People said to me, "Keep away from him – he comes from the Actors' Studio," but I would not listen to them. I just *knew* he would be a great clown.'[33] Wallach's performance as Tuco Benedicto Pacifico Juan Maria Ramirez, first and most memorable of Leone's *picaro* figures, more than justified his perception.

In the first two 'Dollars' films, through Juan De Dios the crazy bell-ringer and the equally crazy old prophet, Leone had introduced minor characters from popular Spanish or Italian literary traditions, as adapted by the Renaissance from late medieval models. Umberto Eco compared Leone's Westerns with the 'godless nostalgia' of feisty Renaissance writers for the Middle Ages. But in Tuco, Leone created a fully fledged character who couldn't *possibly* have emerged from

Hollywood: an 'amoral familist' and trickster, who comes on like the *Nofriù* figure in the repertoire of the *pupi Siciliani*: funny, childish, cunning, uninhibited and surprisingly tender; dressed in Mexican–Spanish rags, and dedicated to the pleasures of life. Tuco eats messily, belches, chucks whisky down his throat, talks too much, and pisses out of railway carriages. He yells elaborate and convoluted insults at the top of his voice: 'You're the son of a thousand fathers, all *bastards* like you'; '*Hijo de una gran puta*' (Son of a great whore); 'You know what you are? Just a dirty son of a bitch.' Sometimes these curses segue into shrieking vocal lines on the soundtrack, like Burt Lancaster's curses in *Vera Cruz*, which were interrupted by full-volume trumpet fanfares. Leone loved characters like Tuco. Wallach's performance, complete with Chico Marx accent and a sly grin on his face, is the Method gone way, way over the top; and he dominates the entire film. His acting style is deliberately set against the under-playing of his poker-faced American colleagues, who seem almost robotic by comparison. Sancho Panza to Clint Eastwood's tarnished knight. In Simi's drawings, he looks like a down-at-heel clown on horseback.

When Leone had first met Eli Wallach in Los Angeles, the actor had taken some convincing that this was the right career move for him: 'I was thinking to myself "Spaghetti Western?" That's like Hawaiian pizza.'[34] Wallach had recently written an article entitled 'In All Directions', about the difficulties experienced by an Actors' Studio graduate on film sets where thespian preparation and rehearsal are subordinated to technical logistics. He argued, 'I like to work with a director who is able, not to superimpose a performance on me, but to say, "Please, let me hear this type of melody, so that it fits in which the rest of the song." '[35] As Wallach confessed, 'My roots are basically stage', so he'd been fortunate that his first experiences in the film business had been with Elia Kazan (*Baby Doll*, 1956) and John Huston (*The Misfits*, 1961), directors who understood how to coax a performance out of actors by attention and discussion. Wallach had been less lucky with 'old-style, old-time directors'.

One of the dangers of working in films, he went on, was typecasting: 'Strange thing happens: in movies the initial imprint made on the screen for me was *Baby Doll*. I became a black figure, a dark figure, a foreboding, villainous figure, moustachioed vengeful Latin. But the first imprint sticks: from then on I was offered rather villainous roles. Then after *The Magnificent Seven* [1960], where I was the bandit chief with gold

teeth and a beard, I was offered more bandits, all kinds of bandits.'
Hence his sneering badman Charlie Gant in *How the West Was Won*
(1962). And hence the offer of a sequel to *The Magnificent Seven*, in
which Wallach was to play the uncle of the bandit who'd died at the end
of the original – an offer he refused.

To Wallach's mind, another danger of this kind of role was the over-
emphasis on violence: 'In *The Line Up* [directed by Don Siegel, 1958] I
killed five people. I think "Oh my God." It seems to me that films place
a good deal of stress on bullets, weapons, guns, violence and violence
and violence. And as a result of doing this film I felt I had to get out of
movies.' He returned to the Broadway stage, and lectured on the
Method. Eventually, he recalled, 'I was ready to go back to films. So
when I get enough villainy out of my heart in films, then I return to the
good, the shining knight, on the stage – which may explain why I shunt
between both parts.' So Wallach's initial meeting with Leone must have
pressed all sorts of alarm bells: another Latin villain, in a film directed
by someone who didn't speak English, and who had a reputation for
placing 'a good deal of stress on bullets'. Leone begged him to watch
'one minute of one of my movies', and screened the main title sequence
from *For a Few Dollars More*. And Wallach said, 'When do you want
me?'[36]

Although Sergio Leone had told Clint Eastwood that the character of
Tuco would remain as written, once Wallach and Leone got together in
Rome and Almeria, some script changes inevitably began to happen. As
Wallach recalls: 'When I first saw him in Rome he was wearing suspenders *and* a belt and I thought, "My God, that's a sure way to hold
your pants up." And I said to him, "I'd like to use that for the character
of Tuco." "Fine," he said.' Leone, too, remembered how they enjoyed
firing each other up on the set. They seemed to share both a craftsman's
approach to the task in hand and a bizarre sense of humour: 'Wallach
proposed the sign of the cross, which Tuco performs so clumsily: he
signs himself to exorcize ill fortune. He doesn't *really* believe, but you
can never be quite certain.' Wallach felt comfortable enough to joke
with Leone about his method of directing. 'I responded', Leone
recalled, 'by stage-managing some surprises. For the finale, it is Tuco
who discovers for us the cemetery where the gold is hidden. I asked him
to enter it with reverence and gravity. And also with hope and tension.
In the most perfect silence. And just as we started shooting, without
warning him, I had a dog start running towards his legs. I then filmed

his natural response – surprise. And this wasn't just a gag. I had to break the dramatic tension to avoid slipping into melodrama.'[37]

Eli Wallach recalls the negotiation between the two men about the details of the part as 'one of the best times I've had in the movies'. Despite Leone's lack of English, it transpired that he was open to discussion: 'We communicated in French, mostly . . . The script girl was very good, and she understood enough English to get me through. I asked him if I could have a gold tooth [like Calvera in *The Magnificent Seven*] and wear this hat, and he said, "Okay." With him, the actor felt like he had some input into the film and was allowed to use his creativity rather than being a puppet on a bunch of strings. When it came to a holster he told me he wanted me to wear the gun on a rope around my neck. I told him, "Yeah, yeah, and I suppose you want me to dangle it between my knees?" When he tried it, the gun hit him in the groin! After that, he said, "Forget it, just carry the gun in your pocket." '

Though Wallach initially detected a fair amount of chaos on the set, he came to realize: 'Sergio Leone knew exactly each shot he wanted . . . The Italians are innovative, unafraid to dare and try, and they are fun to work with. You mustn't be disillusioned if you ever watch a film being put together by the seeming anarchy, the seeming aimlessness and the lack of organization. The real man with his hand on the tiller in Italian films is the director . . . And Leone is an all-movie man. He sleeps it, he eats it. He's a nervous man. His hands are open and shut constantly while he's filming. He's tense, but he has some kind of magical touch. All I know is, as an instrumentalist I enjoyed having him wave the baton.'[38]

Lee Van Cleef recalled that both he and Eastwood were well aware of the director's affection for the character of Tuco. Leone and Wallach, it seems, spent a lot of time together: 'Tuco is the only one of the trio the audience gets to know all about. We meet his brother and find out where he came from and why he became a bandit. But Clint's character and mine remain mysteries . . . it was clear the public would go for the Wallach character.' Eli Wallach's main memory of working with Lee Van Cleef is that he had just become the proud owner of a new Mercedes. But Eastwood helped Wallach to understand the trials and tribulations of working on a seemingly anarchic Italian set. He 'took me by the hand and guided me through it all', for instance warning Wallach to take a particularly close look at any stunts and special effects. They flew together from Rome to Madrid (after interiors had been shot), and drove together to Burgos in northern Spain for the battle sequence.[39]

'I was very grateful to Clint,' says Wallach. 'He came up with ideas and bits of business that made my character even better . . . He didn't talk much on the set, but he was very bright and observant. He said this was his third movie in Italy and he was going to go back to the States and focus on his career there, which he did.' If he still felt sore about the fact that he had been demoted to guest star in what should have been *his* film, he certainly didn't show it to Wallach. On the contrary, his advice came in very useful. For the sequence where Blondie gallops up behind Tuco (who has his hands tied behind his back, and is running as fast as he can) and pulls him up on to the saddle, he advised Wallach to use a stunt double who wouldn't be noticed, because the camera would be placed behind the actors. Wallach agreed, but Eastwood performed his part of the stunt himself.[40]

There were other dangers, though, as Wallach still remembers only too well: 'I had thrown the guard [Mario Brega] I was handcuffed to from the train, and the only way I could get away was to put the body on the tracks and have the train run over the handcuffs. These hand-cuffs were made of very soft lead. Leone wanted me to do the scene, where I'm watching the train come, then turn my head so the audience could see my face and see it was really me, not a stuntman. So I watched the train come and at the last second turned my head like he wanted, but as the last car went by, I saw each of these cars had a set of steps on the end. Sergio wanted me to do the scene again and have me raise my head a little more. If I had raised my head just a little higher, I would have been decapitated. Leone said, "Do it again," and I said, "No." But we did it again, this time digging a little deeper hole in the tracks, and I kept my head down. Leone said, "Please, one more time." I said no, so we used the first take.'[41]

The filming of *The Good, The Bad and The Ugly* made the Broadway stage seem like a safe house in comparison. If Elia Kazan had been there, even he would have had to shout to make himself heard: 'You had no union rules over there, so you filmed from sun-up to sundown. Also, some of the camera equipment was old, and they had to keep changing the lenses. Like the scene in the cemetery. The camera would go to my waist, then down to my gun, then up to my waist again [then right into his eyeballs] . . . It was dangerous working with the Spanish horses. The scenes where I was about to be hanged and Clint shoots the rope – the prop man put a little charge of dynamite in the rope so it would break when Eastwood shot it. The horse I was sitting on was a little jittery when he heard the shot so I suggested to Sergio that he should put some cotton in the horse's ears! He said he'd never heard of that. I told him that in Hollywood they had a lot of shooting in Westerns, and they put cotton in the horse's ears to calm them down. But Leone wouldn't do it. Sure enough, when the horse heard the shot he got scared and took off with me on him, running like a bat out of hell.'[42]

On another occasion, they were filming one of the set-ups after Blondie and Tuco finally discover the gold, buried in eight leather pouches. Wallach remembers that 'they used a certain acid to weaken the pouch where the money was ... the idiot prop man had put the acid, by mistake, in a little bottle of Spanish lemon soda I liked drinking from.' Wallach was lucky: 'As soon as it hit my mouth I knew it was acid and spat it out.' After this succession of near-misses, Wallach must have questioned at times whether the director really *did* have his hand on the tiller.[43]

The character of Tuco represented a radical new departure in Leone's Westerns: as Richard Schickel has put it, 'he is a figure who, for all his depredations, offers us a full range of emotions with which to identify'. His 'amoral familism' emerges most strongly in the sequence where he visits his brother, Padré 'Pablito' Ramirez (Luigi Pistilli), at the mission of San Antonio. Pablito tells Tuco of the deaths of their mother (a long time ago) and father (a few days ago): 'Only now do you think of them.' Tuco responds by reminding his brother that when he was training for the priesthood, *he* had to look after the family and he first turned to banditry to make ends meet: 'You chose your way, I chose mine. *Mine was harder*.' At this point, they start scrapping like little children – while Blondie secretly looks on. 'Please forgive me, brother' says the thoroughly ashamed Padré Ramirez. Tuco walks out, without turning back, then boastfully tells Blondie: 'My brother, he's crazy about me ... even a tramp like me. No matter what happens, there'll always be a bowl of soup.' Blondie replies: 'Well, after a meal there's nothing like a good cigar.' Tuco wipes away his tears and proceeds to eat the cigar – a broad grin returning to his face. For Leone, this scene 'defined' the character of Tuco, as he explained: ' "Between you and me," Tuco says to his brother, "it is me who is the better person." And his brother understands, as a good old-fashioned Christian. He even apologizes. Then Tuco sets off again, with this marvellous, inflated idea of the family in his head. He tells Blondie that his brother is a wonderful man. At that instant, he becomes *really* touching.'[44]

So Tuco has moments of vulnerability, though he is pretty adept at exploiting the trait in others, as in the sequence just before the conversation in Padré Ramirez's cell. Blondie is convalescing after exposure to the desert sun, and Tuco seeks to ingratiate himself in order to find out exactly where the gold is hidden: 'Do you have parents, Blondie . . . A mother? Not even a mother . . . No, you're all alone . . . like me, Blondie.' On the whole, though, he feels much more at home in a world of dog eat dog, which inspires a series of strange translated maxims throughout the film, such as 'In this world, there are two kinds of people, my friend. Those with loaded guns and those who dig. You dig.'

Another such utterance comes while Tuco is enjoying his bath in a bombed-out hotel room. One of the saddle-tramps who appeared in the opening sequence (Al Muloch) bursts in: 'I've been looking for you for eight months . . . now I find you in exactly the position that suits me.' Four spurts of flame come from beneath the soapsuds. The saddle-tramp falls to the ground. Tuco slowly gets out of the bath clutching a soapy Navy Colt: 'When you have to shoot, shoot. Don't talk!' A while later, Blondie and Tuco find a note which has been left for them by Angel Eyes. Tuco struggles to read the words: 'See you soon Idi- Idio-.' 'Idiots,' suggests Blondie. 'It's for you!'

The filming of *The Good, The Bad and The Ugly* took thirteen weeks – in Rome (Elios Studio for the interiors), Tabernas and surrounding Almerian desert, Guadix, Madrid and Burgos. 'Northern Spain, around Burgos, is like Virginia,' said Leone. 'Southern Spain is like Arizona.' Carlo Simi's El Paso from *For a Few Dollars More* became a town full of retreating Confederate soldiers. The exterior of Ramirez's Franciscan friary was a nineteenth-century château, with chapel and outhouses attached, at Cortijo de Los Frailes (The Brothers), a few kilometres down a dirt track from Los Albaricoques: the interior had already been used in *For a Few Dollars More*, for the night-time scenes where Monco escapes from Indio's gang. Los Frailes was the house to which the unfortunate young couple fled in the real-life 1930s news story on which Lorca based his play *Blood Wedding*. It is now derelict. The hospital interior was filmed at the equally derelict Arlanza monastery near Burgos.

The 'miles of sun-baked sand', for the desert sequences, were filmed at a small area of sand dunes above La Almadraba de Monteleva near San José: the dunes have now been shifted, to create a beach. The derelict town, under mortar fire, was 'Aberdeen City' – a ready-made set at Colmenar Viejo. The railway station near the Northern prison camp was in fact Estación de Calahora, just outside Guadix, and Guadix itself served as the main junction for coping with the dressed-up locomotive and rolling stock. Carlo Simi specifies: 'The first "hanging" of Tuco was filmed at the Western village belonging to Elios in Rome; the second on my El Paso set and the third in a typical village near Albaricoques. The hotel where Blondie is nearly hanged was the saloon interior at Tabernas ... The opening sequence was filmed in a village specially constructed on a plain overlooking one of the *ramblas* near Tabernas, so that the horizon could be seen in the distance. All the exteriors were difficult to install or redress, because the materials were heavy and sometimes had to be transported by hand ... The other important scenes were filmed further north, especially on location halfway between Aranda de Duero and Burgos, in a place called Covarrubias (Red Grottos) where we did the battle, the trenches, the river Arlanza. The bridge was designed in wood, and I superimposed on it a stone bridge which had been destroyed. We had to put in a barrage to make sure the river had enough water since it dried up in the summer months ... Today, the whole area is covered by an artificial lake.'[45]

Leone's obsession with visual detail during the shoot was to turn into a piece of industry folklore. Luca Morsella, the son of Leone's business partner and adviser Fulvio Morsella, heard it doing the rounds: 'One day they were shooting a scene and the production manager [Fernando Cinquini] was very happy because they had done everything on time. Then Sergio said, "I've missed the detail of the spur; I'll do it another day." And the production manager said, "Yeah, don't worry about something as small as the spur – we can shoot it anytime." Eventually, the day came when on the production manager's schedule it said "Detail of the spur", so he went to talk to Sergio and said, "Shall we shoot it now?" And Sergio said, "Well, you know I need three hundred extras and stagecoaches and horses and rifles and everything." Because, yes, it was the "detail of the spur", but in the background he wanted to see the whole city living, with people walking and horses coming. And from that moment on, it became a folktale in this business. Whenever a director says, "I just missed one detail," they have to make sure that it is not like the detail of the spur.'[46]

Luciano Vincenzoni had one of his 'Did I really write this?' experiences when he saw onscreen the sequence where Blondie and Tuco discuss business arrangements in the desert. As written, the two men have just earned their reward money in the usual way: 'five for you, five for me'. But Tuco wants a new deal: 'There are two kinds of people in the world, my friend,' he says characteristically, 'those with a rope around their neck and the people who have the job of doing the cutting. Listen, the neck at the end of the rope is mine. I run the risks. So the next time I want more than half.' Vincenzoni saw what then happened to the scene: 'Sergio sent back the takes of this scene for several days, until the assistants had found him a place on a mountainous pass [above Tabernas, in Almeria] with a majestic backdrop which gave a great boost to the dialogue.'[47] Like all the desert exteriors, this sequence echoed the dustiness of William Wellman's *Yellow Sky* (1948), shot in Death Valley National Monument, with its seventy miles of sun-baked desert and wooden ghost town where coyotes howl, shutters flap and the wind whistles.

Tonino Delli Colli had taken over from Massimo Dallamano (or 'Jack Dalmas') as Leone's director of photography, a position he was to retain for the rest of the director's career: 'We had a single point of departure, and that was an aesthetic principle: in a Western, you can't put too many colours. We went for subtle shades – black, browns, off-white – because the buildings were all made of wood and the colours of the countryside were all fairly vivid. We're both fond of sand-coloured shades.'[48] Leone spent a lot of time (without storyboards) discussing framing, composition and the use of space with Delli Colli. They had some animated conversations about the huge and complex close-ups which were filmed at the end of the working day, after the master scenes and large production shots were safely in the can. With Leone, these took as long to shoot as the tiring daytime work and Delli Colli was not always amused by this.[49] As Clint Eastwood recalled in 1997, 'Tonino Delli Colli did not feel as enthusiastic as Sergio, maybe, because close-ups are not that interesting to shoot. But Sergio knew how to make a film look big and intimate at the same time.'[50] The landscape in *The Good, The Bad and The Ugly* was a mere backdrop through which the main characters prowl, with an urban sensibility; an effect emphasized by the Techniscope process. They would never turn the desert into a garden (like those farmers in their adobe cottages) or invest in the city (like those time-serving hoteliers and officials). The 'prize' is everything: they use the land entirely as a means to their own ends, and then they ride away, never to return. As if they were passing through city streets.

The cinematic space lacks any kind of unity: it is either too full or too empty. The film opens with a shot of the desert, which seems to go on for ever into the distance: suddenly, the pock-marked face of a saddle-tramp (Al Muloch) fills the frame, in extreme close-up. The film closes with a long high-angle shot as Clint Eastwood rides across the entire width of the screen and into the geology of Almeria. Originally, according to Eli Wallach, for this final set-up 'Sergio wanted very much to have a helicopter shot . . . leaving me as a tiny ant-like figure in the middle of this cemetery: well, he couldn't get the helicopter camera to really work because it shook . . . But he was able to make good with what he had.'[51]

Between these two sequences, Leone explores shapes and spatial relationships in expansive ways which make his previous work seem almost understated. For much of the film, the camera will simply not keep still. As gunslingers get off their horses, the camera starts below their stirrups, then rises to be level with their faces by the time they reach the ground. Panning shots explore horizontal shapes: a Colt's barrel, a Henry rifle. Objects appear from out of frame, originating *beneath* the camera's field of vision. Often, the camera 'reveals' things to us, startlingly, which the characters should have been able to see already. In classic Hollywood terms, these camera movements are entirely unmotivated, redundant. Other spatial shocks involve things the characters couldn't possibly have seen: Blondie and Tuco are walking, with their map, through a deserted landscape; suddenly the rifles and bayonets of Northern sentries appear at the bottom of the frame; equally suddenly the camera cranes over to a high-angle shot of the huge and crowded battlefield which was just on the other side of the hedge. Cinematic space in *The Good, The Bad and The Ugly* is full of surreal juxtapositions of this kind, to trick the eye and keep the audience intrigued.

Sergio Leone was upset when American preview audiences found some of these juxtapositions irritating, the camera movements mannered, and the desert sequences far too long and drawn-out. The rhythm of the film seemed to them to have slowed down since the first two 'Dollars' films to an almost hallucinatory pace: the dilation or stretching of time, followed by sudden interruptions. With Morricone's music, the experience was like a long evening at the opera, or maybe like taking hallucinogenic drugs. Was Leone *taking* something? This was the first of his films to be 'amputated', not for reasons of squeamishness but because of the pace. It was reduced from 182 minutes to 148 ('to increase the sales of popcorn,' said Leone with some bitterness). Out went a scene of Tuco piecing together a revolver in a gunsmith's shop and then proceeding to rob the shop with the aid of it (James Cagney reference, this time to *Public Enemy*); plus all the scenes involving the Betterville Camp Commandant. Out went Angel Eyes being given directions to Betterville, Tuco to the mission of San Antonio via Apache Canyon, and most references to the map – cuts which made the geography seem even more surreal. Leone was keen to defend the desert sequences. The shots of Tuco riding behind a parched and blistered Blondie, clutching a pink, frilly parasol to protect himself from the sun (in a parody of how blue-blooded aristocrats might behave if they were unfortunate enough to find themselves in similar circumstances) particularly appealed to Leone, who lamented: 'The worst thing was that [in America] they found the desert scenes too long. I adore them myself. Tonino Delli Colli photographed them in a way that was worthy of the great surrealist painters.'[52]

Since the early 1950s, Leone had been 'devoted' to the work of some Surrealist painters. It started with the paintings of Max Ernst, then Magritte, then Giorgio De Chirico. In Leone's estimation 'it was De Chirico who was the great turning-point. Without him, Salvador Dalí could never have happened. De Chirico represents the rupture in the history of painting: his inventions paved the way for Surrealism and Futurism.'[53] When describing his admiration, he tended to emphasize their games with perception, their use of illusion and *trompe l'oeil*, their bizarre juxtapositions, the fact that 'things are never what they seem'. De Chirico made extraordinary use of perspective, and of the relative scale of his objects and people, he said that his paintings had a hard-edged, high-contrast look to them, as if everything was being viewed in the noonday sun. If the Surrealists were important, Leone added, for the ways in which they explored the language of dream and illusion, the significance of the Futurists (some of whom his father knew) was 'ripe for reappraisal . . . the painter and poet Balla made an enormous contribution – and yet he was a minor figure compared with the sculptor Umberto Boccioni'. For Leone, the Futurists' celebration of technology, their fascination with extreme or violent acts, their rhetoric (in manifesto and on canvas), their attempt to find a visual idiom to capture the dynamics and surprises of a modern world, had not been given sufficient attention – especially by writers on cinema. Maybe it was because leftish film critics had been put off by the movement's associations with the rise of Fascism, which in Leone's view was a criticism that had been overdone.

Leone started collecting pictures in the late 1950s: 'I already possessed a few works salvaged from the wreck of our family patrimony. When I earned enough money, I bought according to my means. Very little, to start with. Then a great deal. But I have eclectic tastes: only things which touch me personally; never according to the dictates of fashion.' His collecting had begun in earnest when – according to Tonino Valerii – Leone inherited some works of twentieth-century Italian art from Mario Bonnard in 1965. Valerii recalled: 'Bonnard was like a surrogate father to him, and left him several of his most valuable pieces.'[54] About the time of *The Good, The Bad and The Ugly*, Leone purchased a small De Chirico canvas: it shows an urban arcade or colonnade in a deserted space, a female figure lying horizontally in the foreground and a 'Western' American locomotive – with smokestack and cowcatcher – in the background. The extraordinary use of perspective is there, as is the odd sense of scale: and the painting does look as though the light comes from the sun directly overhead. It could well have been one of the paintings Leone showed Tonino Delli Colli before they started shooting the film. Another De Chirico, showing a piazza with a statue in high-contrast light – with two arcades, one in the background and one to the side, plus some figures in silhouette – was purchased later. Leone also acquired a Miró painting, a simple, abstract image consisting of yellow teardrop shapes resembling a sunburst: this was dated 1966, the year *The Good, The Bad and The Ugly* was released.

Carla Leone did not always share her husband's passion for the Surrealists at this time: 'He adored Magritte, but I'm afraid I didn't allow him to buy them! I didn't understand them at all. He once wanted to buy a picture which was of a tree, but the design also made it look as though it was of a bird. And I can't stand birds. This was a bird of ill omen. There was an eye somewhere in the painting, too. I have no idea what it meant. It was probably wonderful but I didn't want to have it around the house.'[55]

Early on in the marriage, they started going regularly to private views in Roman art galleries, and spending Saturday afternoons mooching around expensive antique shops which specialized in the history of the decorative arts, especially the seventeenth and eighteenth centuries. Sergio Donati, who tends to be dismissive of Leone's claims to any literary sophistication, concedes that his 'visual education' was strong, and that he did turn to paintings for inspiration: 'Yes, that's true. And he owned beautiful things also – silver and furniture – and then every afternoon when we worked together in Rome we'd go to the Monte di Pietà, the state pawnshop, because he used to buy jewels at the auction. And I once said to him, "But those jewels are full of blood and tears." "I don't care," he said. He used to spend Sundays polishing these things with an old toothbrush and soap. I remember him saying, "If I were a woman, I would love these things." He loved the feel of things, absolutely. And he had this Carlo Simi who was his man to achieve this in the films.'[56]

Sergio Leone had already developed a passion for the Prado Museum, which he started visiting regularly when filming *The Last Days of Pompeii* in Madrid. His favourite paintings there were Velasquez's *Las meninas/The Maids of Honour* (1656) and Goya's *The 3rd of May in Madrid: The Executions on Principe Pio Hill* (1814). Leone believed that *Las meninas*, which shows the back of the painter's canvas and Velasquez's double-portrait (the King and Queen of Spain) reflected in a mirror on the back wall of his own gloomy studio, was as much about the process of image-making as it was about its ostensible subject matter. This 'painting as parable' helped to make Velasquez 'the greatest painter of his time'. But his themes and subjects ('the beggars, the infirm, the dwarfs') 'also influenced me, I must recognize that'.

'The dark Goya I love. Not the royal Goya. The *Naked Maja* has always given me indigestion. But Goya was the first to use a lot of techniques. He made a cinemascope image with his shootout. You only have to look at the way he places the rifles and bayonets, and the way he used light. I showed these tableaux to my director of photography Tonino Delli Colli. He was leaping with excitement when he said to me: "But this son of a bitch placed a 5,000-watt light behind the figures. For rear-projection. That must be how he got that extraordinary effect of clarity." '[57]

Again, Leone was drawn to a painter who contrasted, dramatically and sharply, dark and light tones (monochrome-style); and who used a palette of earthy, sandy colours: Goya also took a sensual delight in the textures (of fabric, stone, wood, earth) that he painted. In *The Disasters of War* and *The Capricos*, Leone observed, Goya sometimes showed grotesque peasant faces; but he showed them with evident sympathy; the bourgeoisie and the aristocracy were treated less sympathetically. Where social satire of this kind was concerned, Leone also rated highly the Weimar paintings of George Grosz ('a painter who left deep traces on me ... with his colours, his sense of the ridiculous and the grotesque') and 'the formidable Otto Dix' ('with that same terrible irony'). Surprisingly, given the frequent use of the word 'mannerist' to describe his films, Leone never enthused much about El Greco or Caravaggio.

Leone seemed to be looking at the history of art as a visual lexicon for a modern-day film-maker who shoots in widescreen and enjoys playing games of perception. As Eli Wallach put it, adding Vermeer and Rembrandt to the list, 'he's a man who leans on the painters'. But Leone's comments on Edgar Degas, another painter who by his own admission 'marked' his own aesthetic, show his particular way of seeing: 'I see Degas as if he was a great film director. The way he managed to capture the gestures of the ballet-dancers. Never in academic poses; always in spontaneous movements. All those moments which appear insignificant but which on closer inspection reveal the deepest truths of a particular character. Degas was extraordinary.' What particularly impressed Leone was the way Degas managed to capture the dancers in informal moments: washing, having a tutorial, exercising; rather than 'performing' on the stage. Also the way he used his figures to create perspective – with one dancer in the distance, and one in the foreground in extreme close-up, cropped by the side of the canvas; only the relative size of the figures showed the viewer how deep the plane was.[58] Leone, too, would see figures in this way, especially in desert scenes where there were no telegraph poles or railway lines to create lines of perspective. *The Good, The Bad and The Ugly*, from first sequence to last, is full of such 'threesomes' or trinities. In Leone's pictures, though, at least two out of the three are about to be shot. It is a dance of death rather than a *corps de ballet*. In *Once Upon a Time in America*, the sequences of young Deborah dancing to the music of a wind-up gramophone would be lit and framed in the style of Degas. Tonino Delli Colli recalls that 'Sergio didn't use paintings while we were actually shooting, but we discussed them during preparation as "axes of the work".'[59]

One major progression for Leone was that some of Ennio Morricone's music had been written (and partially recorded) in advance of filming: the budget was at last substantial enough to allow for this. 'In *The Good, The Bad and The Ugly*', said Leone, 'each character had his musical theme. And he was also a kind of musical instrument, who performed my writing. In this sense, I played a great deal with harmonies and counterpoints . . . I was representing the route-map of three beings who were an amalgam of all human faults . . . And I needed crescendos and spectacular attention-grabbers which nevertheless chimed with the general spirit of the story. So the music took on a central importance. It had to be complex, with humour and lyricism, tragedy and baroque. The music even became an element of the action. This was the case with the concentration camp sequence. An orchestra of prisoners has to play in order to drown out the cries of the tortured. In other parts of the film, the music accompanied sudden changes of rhythm, as when the phantom coach arrives from nowhere in the desert. I also wanted the music to become a touch baroque at times. I didn't want it to limit itself to the repetition of each character's theme – crossed over. Anyway, I had some of the music played on set. It created the atmosphere of the scene. The performances were definitely influenced by it. Clint Eastwood appreciated this method a lot.'[60]

Apart from anything else, this must have helped with the language difficulties. Morricone made a recording, with a few instruments, of some musical themes and key character motifs: Leone by his account then played the tape on set, and the 'actors acted to the music' or 'found correspondences with the music'. None of the main actors remembers this happening, however. Sergio Donati has 'a clear memory that the music for the "triello" at the end was written before and then rewritten. Maybe they had music during pre-production and then changed it.' Alessandro Alessandroni, too, remembers 'the director asking the composer to make a demo with a small orchestra, to prepare some sequences. And then on the demo – with Sergio Leone's later films – we put the big orchestra sometimes. All of it, for *The Good, The Bad and The Ugly*, was re-recorded to the image.'[61] This unusual procedure proved especially valuable, according to Leone, for the last twenty minutes of the film, in effect twenty minutes of mime to two Morricone themes, 'the ecstasy of gold' and 'the settling of accounts'; also for the Civil War sequences: whether or not the pre-recorded score was actually played on the set. There was no musical instrument featured in the plot this time, so 'internal music' was confined to the Betterville orchestra ('play that fiddle, son', snaps a Union sergeant to a distraught Confederate boy, as he accompanies the only song in a Leone film) and the end title theme, where Tuco's elaborate insult ('You know what you are? Just a dirty son of a . . . ') blends with yelling singers in a reprise of the film's signature tune. 'The ecstasy of gold' – a simple, insistent four-note theme played on the piano, punctuated by a clanging bell, which builds up to a soaring vocal line by soprano Edda Dell'Orso and is interrupted by a chorus of graveyard ghosts singing 'wah, wah, wah' – turns the sequence of Tuco manically running around Sad Hill cemetery, which must have looked like very little on the page of the script, into a highly dramatic piece of choreography and a tour de force of dynamic camerawork. It stops very suddenly, with a slight echo, and then there is silence. Leone had the music in his mind when he shot it.

Critics were to note the long silences in *The Good, The Bad and The Ugly*, and begin to make jokes about horse operas and convoluted plots. These were the silences of people who did not want to give anything away about themselves or other people; silences in a world where 'a man's life can depend on a mere scrap of information'. More to do, perhaps, with Machiavelli and the Mafia than with the Southwest of America. Leone was unrepentant: 'My Westerns have been compared with melodramas. If this comparison arises from the importance of music in my films, then I feel flattered. I have always limited the use of dialogue, so that spectators can use their own imaginations while they observe the slow and ritual gestures of the heroes of the West – in the middle of the mountains, or in the immensity of the prairies. If it is true that I have created a new-style Western, with picaresque people placed in epic situations, then it is the music of Ennio which has made them talk.'[62]

In *The Good, The Bad and The Ugly*, Morricone's 'insignia' took the form of phrases from the opening bars of the main title theme, played in different registers for each main character: treble for 'the Good', bass for 'the Bad'. The theme itself had been orchestrated in a bizarre way, as Morricone recalls: 'The coyote howls which give rhythm to the credits of the film are usually played by the clarinet, when I conduct the piece in concert. But in the original version, I proceeded in a much more inventive way. Two male voices sang in superimposition, the one crying A and the other E. The AAAH and the EEEH had to be eloquent, to imitate the howling of the animal, and evoke the savagery of the Wild West.'[63] These 'coyote howls' were heard throughout the film: sometimes on flute, sometimes on electric guitar, sometimes with shrieking voices. The AEAEA sound was mixed with simulated 'natural' sounds in an unusually complex piece of sound editing.

In the 'silent' opening sequence, for example, the main title theme gives way to the howl of a coyote, the whistling of the wind and the rustling of canvas, the crunching of boots on gravel, the cocking of weapons . . . then sudden silence. In the final sequence, the duel between the three protagonists at the flagstone hub of Sad Hill cemetery is punctuated by the cawing of crows and the laughter of ghosts: the musical theme, another of Leone's beloved *deguellos*, begins with Spanish guitar and castanets, and builds with a human chorus to a triumphant mariachi trumpet solo with syncopated backing, which becomes more and more insistent as the theme progresses. There's even a quotation from the musical box of *For a Few Dollars More*. For Leone, this 'triello' (rather than *duello*) was 'a sequence which gave me the greatest satisfaction . . . especially from the editing point of view. The picaresque journeys all come to a conclusion within it.' Virtually the whole film could be read in the eyes of the main characters: Tuco has the eyes of a 'rat', anxious, calculating, naive; Blondie has the eyes of a 'guardian angel', assured, intelligent, amused; Angel Eyes has the eyes of a 'robot', cold, collected, implacable. Vincenzoni reckons that the cemetery scene was 'the highspot of the movie', and helped to make up for 'so many ugly scenes' which preceded it. As Leone remarked shortly after the finished film was released in France, 'I always enclose the final sequence, the dénouement of my films, within the confines of a circle: it is there that Clint kills Gian Maria Volonté; that Clint, Eli and Lee confront each other . . . It is the arena of life, the moment of truth at the moment of death.'[64]

Setting up this arena at Carazo near Salas de Los Infantas, in the valley of the Arlanza, was a logistical nightmare. Leone wanted 'a cemetery which could evoke an antique circus. There wasn't one in existence. So I turned to the Spanish chief of pyrotechnics who had been in charge of the construction and destruction of the bridge. He lent me 250 soldiers who built the sort of cemetery I needed: with 10,000 tombs. Those men worked solidly for two days. And it was done. This wasn't a whim on my part. The idea of the arena was crucial. With a morbid wink of the eye, since it was the dead who were witnesses to this spectacle. I even insisted that the music signify the laughter of corpses inside their tombs . . . The first three close-ups of each of the actors took us an entire day. I wanted the spectator to have the impression of watching a ballet. And I had to accumulate shots of their cunning in action: their looks, their gestures, their hesitations. The music gave a certain lyricism to all these "realist" images – so the scene became a question of choreography as much as suspense.'[65] Finally Clint Eastwood rides off in his poncho – perhaps towards the San Miguel of *Fistful of Dollars*. 'So the game went on,' said Leone. And it was circular. The military cemetery was supposed to have been built around consecrated ground – with an obelisk and stone markers in the centre, but in the end Leone decided on an empty circular *corrida* instead.

Before they began shooting, Eli Wallach had a proposal for the director: 'I suggested to Sergio Leone a shot that I remembered from a film, *Great Expectations*, which I'd also asked Kazan to use in *Baby Doll*: that is, I became the camera as I was running around in that thing.' The shot at the beginning of David Lean's film shows young Pip going into a graveyard, and seeing a creaking tree with the wind blowing the autumn leaves off its branches: for a moment, the camera 'becomes' Pip. Of the cemetery itself, Lee Van Cleef commented: 'So there we were in the middle of this cemetery and Sergio was taking one close-up after the next of each of us, and taking close-ups of our hands wavering near our guns, and all sorts of unusual angles. I said to Sergio, "I could take Clint, you know. Shoot him down." "I know," said Sergio, "and that's why the audience will wonder just who will walk away from this gunfight alive!" He made that scene last, what, five minutes? And all we do is stand there and look at each other across this great circle, with the music blaring on the soundtrack. It's one of the most impressive scenes I've ever seen, let alone been involved in.'[66]

After the filming schedule of mid-April to mid-July 1966 was completed, *The Good, the Bad and The Ugly* had to be ready for Italian cinemas by Christmas Eve, and Leone was deeply involved in post-production right up to the last minute, with editor Nino Baragli, Sergio Donati and Morricone. Dario Argento happened to be in a dubbing studio next door, while Leone was mixing the soundtrack. He was to recall that: 'He was inserting the cries of a bird of prey into the setting of a valley: trying to find the exact sound and the exact moment. He tried so many, but he never seemed to be satisfied.'[67]

Nino Baragli, who had first worked with Leone fourteen years earlier, began to call him 'the pulverizer', saying 'he can reduce you to a pulp when the editing begins ... Sergio shoots a lot of footage, for several reasons: because he is determined to get the most out of his actors, and because he wants to cover himself. So there are a thousand ways of editing one of his films: some sequences can even turn out to be dramatic or ironic according to how they are edited.'[68]

One big pressure-point, during post-production, was the sheer length of the film. This was the first of many occasions when the running time of a Leone film would become an issue. United Artists had advised Vincenzoni in advance that they didn't want 'anything over two hours'. The first cut he saw was about double that 'so we had to fight and I must admit I was temperamental'. Sergio Donati's job was to try to find ways of abridging the film to a compromise 180 minutes. He recalled: 'Sergio prefers to take out entire chunks of story, rather than abbreviate sequences or alter the rhythm . . . I wrote a scene to create the necessary link. There was a not-very-useful scene between Lee Van Cleef and the soldier with no legs, the "half-soldier". They spoke of other things. And so we made the soldier explain what had happened in the part that had been cut.'[69]

Donati remembers the tense atmosphere at this time as another turning-point in Leone's career. Donati had left a reasonably lucrative profession in advertising, and spurned an offer from up-and-coming director Giuseppe Colizzi to work with Leone on this film. Leone had insisted on a close collaboration, and was, Donati remembers, 'a little upset, jealous' when 'his' writer scripted *La resa dei Conti/The Big Gundown* for Sergio Sollima and Alberto Grimaldi in the meantime. Later, as their intensive editing work neared completion, Donati found Leone plagued by self-doubt: 'Something happened in his mind. Maybe he was insecure. I don't know. But he looked like he didn't want that movie to be finished . . . At five in the morning, the twentieth remake, he was never satisfied. It looked like he didn't want to make the deadline, you know? He killed us . . . He had said, "So you are my writer." And so I was happy. I gave him my life. We slept in the dubbing room the last week, Baragli, Morricone and I . . . Jesus Christ, 23 December, there was that spirit of "We did it!" . . . The last mix. Up, down. And there was the production inspector ready with champagne, so we could celebrate in style. Everybody else was moved. "Okay," Sergio said. "Okay. Goodnight." And, dodging past the inspector, he went away. Thirty, forty people who gave their blood. "Goodnight" was all he said.'[70]

Leone had always been much less confident than he appeared, but during the editing of *The Good, The Bad and The Ugly*, the mask slipped. Donati elaborates: 'Until maybe the shooting of *The Good, The Bad and The Ugly*, he was the kind of director who enjoyed inventing and creating things. In the middle of the editing, he changed completely. Partly a fear of not living up to his own reputation. He was not a presumptuous man – in his heart of hearts he was aware of his limitations – and he was continually plagued by self-doubt. He tried to put off the release date of the film and became, frankly, pretty unpleasant at a human level. And from then on, he became very concerned about money, and then about making things which were bigger and bigger and bigger. I remember saying to him, "Sergio, stop . . . where will it end?" Well, that's Sergio.'[71]

Donati hoped he might at least see his name on the credits, after spending from July to December 1966 observing, writing and contributing to post-production: 'I remember of that time all the things I learned, which was a lot . . . but Sergio could be a mean son of a bitch. Insensitive, you know. For instance, I was almost divorced for that movie. I gave six months of my life to the editing, the dubbing and everything. And I expected Sergio would have told me, "Sergio, I put your name at least on the end titles." Nothing. I didn't ask. His thing was that I was paid. And also, I know this because I knew him very well, he was a little irritated by the fact that I wrote in the meantime for someone else.'[72]

When Sergio Leone said 'goodnight' to everyone in the dubbing room on 23 December, he hoped that he was also saying a long goodbye to the Western. He was quoted in the Italian press as saying, 'I do not want to make any more Western films. I have finished with that kind of film, that kind of story . . . I do not love them any more as I used to.' After three films in three hectic years, one after the other, his obsession had left him utterly drained. 'He had', recalls Carla Leone, 'been fantastically busy, and our lives had completely changed.'

Clint Eastwood wasn't so sure that he was moving forward. He had been offered the part of 'an Irish gangster' in 'a gangster movie', which Leone said he was vaguely thinking about, but had dismissed the idea. There was nothing on paper, and, besides, it would probably have been 'just a repeat of what I'd been doing'. So Eastwood stayed in California, in the hope of finding the right property to persuade Hollywood executives that, despite his eccentric curriculum vitae, he could become as big a star in America as in Europe. Of his work with Leone he later said, 'I could have gone on doing them for another ten years, but there's only so far to go.' Still, it would take Eastwood some time to find a credible way of domesticating his 'Magnificent Stranger' image for the consumption of American cinema-goers. From summer 1966 until summer

1967, he was searching for exactly the right script. When one finally came along, United Artists tried to market the resulting film, *Hang 'Em High*, as a home-grown continuation of the Italian saga, which it plainly wasn't. United Artists had invited Leone to direct; he immediately turned them down. Only in 1968, with Don Siegel's *Coogan's Bluff*, did Clint Eastwood succeed in bringing it all back home.

Eli Wallach, who considered Leone 'a beautiful person', returned to Italy and Spain in the next few years to make three further Westerns: *Ace High* (Giuseppe Colizzi, 1967); *Don't Turn the Other Cheek* (Duccio Tessari, 1971), wherein Wallach had a treasure map tattooed on his bottom, hence the American title, which he invented; and the unwatchable *The White, the Yellow and the Black* (Sergio Corbucci, 1974), the title of which, sad to relate, referred to an American, a Japanese and a sheriff called Black Jack.

The shooting and editing of *The Good, The Bad and The Ugly* had been shadowed by Giuseppe Colizzi, a forty-year-old writer and journalist who had published two novels based on his travels in the United States and South America, and who was a nephew of director Luigi Zampi. Now he was starting to specialize in writing and directing Westerns; hence the offer to Sergio Donati. His first, for his own production company, was *Dio perdona . . . Io no!/God Forgives, I Don't*, released some months after Leone's film. It told of the aftermath of a violent train robbery, and the adventures of a group of men who went on the trail of $100,000 in gold. Two of the men were played by 'Terence Hill' and 'Bud Spencer', a double-act of 'brain and muscle' (as the film put it) which Colizzi was the first to launch. While observing Leone's editing and mixing, he prepared the script for a sequel, which came to be called *I quattro dell'Ave Maria* or *Ace High*.

During the planning of his Westerns, Colizzi had come across a *série noire* book (or rather a *giallo*, since in Italy they had yellow covers rather than French black). By a crime journalist called Harry Grey, entitled *Mano armata* or *The Hoods*, the book had been translated into Italian and was available in paperback in Roman bookshops. Without asking permission, Colizzi 'lifted' a scene of a casino heist from the book, for *Ace High*. Colizzi also recommended the book to Fulvio Morsella and gave him a copy. Morsella promptly 'read literally the whole book in Italian to Sergio, who was fascinated'. Colizzi had told him 'this is a story for Sergio'.[73] He was right. Leone remembered, 'The book seemed to me nothing particularly special, but it had a lot of very curious details in it [the blurb on the cover of the book had said that *The Hoods* was 'the autobiography of a real-life gangster'] ... and I became interested in this character who was obviously a loser – this small-time character who lived gangsterism from his childhood onwards in a way that was almost anarchic.'

Harry Grey, whose real name was Goldberg, had originally published in 1952 his story of a gang of small-time hoods from New York's Lower East Side during the era of prohibition. He wrote it, he said, to set the record straight: the gangster films of the 1930s, and especially those with Cagney, Robinson, Muni and Bogart, had over-romanticized the gangster milieu, and Grey wanted to set against these images the authentic saga of a gang of small-time punks who belonged to a very different universe; punks who behaved like overgrown little boys obsessed with their guns, their cocks and their fast bucks. The book had finished with the repeal of prohibition in December 1933, and the flight of the central character (nicknamed 'Noodles') from the police and the Combination, having betrayed his three childhood friends. That this character was really Harry Grey was revealed in the final paragraph: 'Well, you see I am here, after all the years, to tell the story. But how I got away, where I holed up – that's another story and you will understand why I can't tell that now.'[74]

Sergio Leone later said that on first reading the book he was particularly struck by the fact that Grey believed he was 'telling it like it was' when in fact much of his fictionalized autobiography, particularly the 'adult' sections, was a rerun of the clichés of Hollywood gangster films. These films had so colonized his unconscious mind that Grey could no longer tell the difference, and this, Leone felt, 'could turn into something that belonged to *my* universe'. The 'episodes from his childhood', set on and around Delancey Street in the 1910s and 1920s, seemed to have more authenticity about them, before Grey's memories became hopelessly confused with the gangster films he had later watched as an adult. These episodes could become the starting-point for Leone's next film, which he told everyone who would listen was to be called *Once Upon a Time in America* or *Once Upon a Time, America*. 'Once Upon a Time' meaning the fairy-tale, Hollywood-inspired version of events; 'in America' meaning the reality of the interwar years and the childhood of the hoods.

'I went over to the States and had discussions with some of the most influential producers who, impressed by the commercial success of *The*

*Good, The Bad and The Ugly* [in Europe and Japan], agreed that I could do exactly what I wanted. But it wasn't true. They wanted me to remake a big Western, so they adopted a hard line: "Your new idea is beautiful, great . . . but, hey, listen, why not make us a good Western, and *then* we'll give you the chance to direct your project." I said to the producers, "The West belongs to everyone. To the Italians, like myself. To the Germans, who have made those Sauerkraut Westerns, to the French who are filming Camembert Westerns at Fontainebleau. Even to the Japanese. The *série noire* doesn't belong to you Americans any more, either. The story of Murder Incorporated is on the coffee-table of every screenwriter in the world." But they didn't want to know.'[75]

At this stage, the focus of Leone's story was to be on 'the earliest gangsters in the roaring twenties, a period before they sat behind a table and conducted their business affairs by telephone'. It would contrast the anonymous methods of organizations such as Murder Inc. with the pioneer hoods: immigrants 'who grew up on the streets, and died there'. And overlaid on this story would be the rags-to-riches dream of films such as *Little Caesar*, *Public Enemy* and *Scarface*, which were released after the first-generation gangsters had gone, mythologizing their lives. The big difference would be that instead of Irish (Cagney) or Italian (Robinson, Muni) hoods, his story would focus on Jewish gangsters who arrived from Eastern Europe and grew up in tenements around Delancey Street.

With this idea in mind Leone made a preliminary visit to New York, where he had business in any case, with Sergio Donati, who recalls: 'I did some early research for this film. I went to the archives of the *New York Times*, to soak up some of the atmosphere of the period, and we wandered around New Jersey together. Sergio was at his best during times like this. But I told Sergio that I had some concerns about the project. "If you want to do this book", I said, "it's an East Side Jew 'people' story. You don't know nearly enough of these people." It was not a gangster story, really, it was the story of young immigrants: the first part of the book, which was what interested him. It was such an American story, so East Side American, that I told Sergio, "It is very difficult for an Italian"– and Sergio was not so cultured himself. Just an exceptional cinematic culture: knew everything about films. Could Sergio deal with this story? It was as if an American director was trying to tell the story of Trastevere in the 1930s. The way he wanted to do it at the time was wrong. I'm still convinced it was wrong because he was going to tell a realistic story about a world he didn't know. Just a story of young people, as in the book. The great idea which came later was to widen the story – to make the "after" and "later", with the flashbacks. But not in 1967.'[76]

Leone might be trying to persuade the money people that the gangster picture had global appeal and belonged to everyone, but Donati was far from convinced. Firstly, *The Hoods* wasn't really a gangster story in the traditional mould at all; and secondly, the 'rules' of the Western genre were much more pronounced and recognizable than those of the gangster movie. Donati recalls: 'Leone realized that he would come up against a narrative style that was completely different from his own. Gangsters can't move like *pistoleri*; they can't take a quarter of an hour to get out of a car.'

Meanwhile, United Artists urged another Western upon Leone. But if he made another film for them he might (he recalled) 'have been obliged to cast Kirk Douglas, Charlton Heston and Gregory Peck' – a prospect which did not appeal.[77] Paramount seemed a more attractive option, providing access, at long last, to Henry Fonda. But, as Carla Leone recalls, he was only at this stage prepared to consider *producing* another Western: 'He agreed: "I'll do the script, with some other writers: I'll 'run' the film; I'll oversee everything – locations, costumes, actors, everything – but you will have to find another director." On mature reflection, though, that might mean "it would not be made according to my ideas". So, yes, all right: he would agree to direct after all. Provided he could make the film, as a writer-director, *exactly* as he wanted to.'[78]

Fulvio Morsella, Carla's brother-in-law, now became increasingly immersed in Sergio's career: 'After the success of *The Good, The Bad and The Ugly*, Vincenzoni said to Sergio that an American company – I don't know whether it was Paramount or United Artists or Warner Brothers – would give him $500,000 per picture. So Sergio said, "I'll sign the contract right away," and gave it to me to read. And I read it and said, "This is a fake. They'll give you $500,000 not as your compensation but for the cost of the whole picture." That was when our friendship started. He started having real confidence in me . . . I came to deal with all the contracts. And in this sense I became partly his producer and partly his English voice.'[79] This confusion over the contract, following Vincenzoni's negotiation with United Artists which had enabled *The Good, The Bad and The Ugly* to happen, on top of the row over the cuts to the film, cannot have assisted an early reconciliation between writer and director. Now he had been 'rescued' from a bad contract, as he saw it, which would have committed him well into the future, like his bad contract with Papi and Colombo. In such situations, Leone turned to people he could trust, people who did not have a professional axe to grind, and that meant family. Not writers who could be snobby with him.

Once Leone had allowed himself to be persuaded to direct 'a personal film', his first notion to distance himself from the 'Dollars' trilogy was to cast Clint Eastwood, Lee Van Cleef and Eli Wallach as three *pistoleri* at the beginning of the new film, and shoot them down behind the opening credits. 'I wanted to say farewell to them, and to the rules of the game which I had imposed.' Lee Van Cleef and Eli Wallach agreed, but Clint Eastwood declined. Leone said, 'It wasn't a question of expense. He just couldn't understand the joke. He doesn't have the greatest sense of humour, you know.' There was no point in using the other two, without the Mysterious Stranger.[80]

Meanwhile, *The Good, The Bad and The Ugly* had opened in Rome and, between December 1966 and February 1968, was to gross $4.3 million in Italy: as compared with *Fistful*'s $4.6 million and *For a Few*'s $5 million, thus causing a slight downward curve on the graph. Producer Alberto Grimaldi completed the negotiations that Luciano Vincenzoni had set in motion with David Picker of United Artists, for the American distribution of Leone's entire trilogy. He had purchased the rights to *Fistful of Dollars* from Papi and Colombo, and was keen to add this film to the deal. United Artists were excited by *The Good, The Bad and The Ugly* (in which they'd invested heavily), provided twenty minutes was cut out of it, but the studio apparently needed a little persuading that *Fistful of Dollars* merited distribution. In the end, it was agreed that all three films would appear in quick succession (the problem with Kurosawa having been settled), and they opened in the States in February 1967, July 1967 and January 1968. The marketing department at United Artists, fresh from promoting the British James Bond series, geared up to present the trilogy to the American public as a single package. And it was at this stage in the game that the 'Man with No Name' took centre stage.

In *Fistful* the Eastwood character had been called Joe; in *For a Few* Monco; in *The Good, The Bad and The Ugly* Blondie. Despite the occasional reference to these names in the English-language versions, it was felt that an anonymous hero, like Dashiell Hammett's Continental Op, would help in marketing the film to mid-1960s youth audiences. Just before *Fistful* was released, newspapers carried a teaser campaign, created by graphic designer Bernie Fuchs, which featured various key props associated with the Eastwood character. This was followed by an advance poster and flyers bringing the props together: 'This long gun belongs to the Man with No Name; this cigar belongs to the Man with No Name; this poncho belongs to the Man with No Name.' A week before the film opened, the advance material made way for the film poster itself: 'He triggers a whole new style in adventure' or alternatively 'He is, perhaps, the most dangerous man who ever lived' blared the copy over a comic-strip graphic of Clint Eastwood with all three props. 'This is the first motion picture of its kind. It won't be the last!' Then, for *For a Few Dollars More*, 'The Man with No Name is Back! The Man in Black is waiting.' For *The Good, The Bad and The Ugly*, there was a more realistic graphic of the three protagonists standing by a cannon, superimposed on a letter-box image of the battle of the bridge. It boasted in the new caption 'For Three Men The Civil War Wasn't Hell. It Was Practice!'

The campaign made history by inventing in retrospect the name, or rather the lack of it, of the central character. References to 'Joe' and 'Monco' were, however, left in American prints and press material, and the United Artists trailer for *The Good, The Bad and The Ugly* even succeeded in confusing who was who: Eli Wallach became 'the Bad' and Lee Van Cleef 'the Ugly', with the result that Van Cleef was saddled with the name 'Mr Ugly' in future American advertising campaigns for his Italian films. Predictably, Leone's films were panned by the critics in the States (as 'ersatz Westerns' with only their visual style to commend them) and extremely successful at the box office. *Fistful* grossed $3.5 million; *For a Few Dollars More* grossed $5 million and *The Good, The Bad and The Ugly* $6 million. The title of that last picture entered the vernacular when it was adopted by Bobby Kennedy during an election campaign. All in all, it was small wonder that the studios wanted Sergio Leone to 'remake a big Western'.

# 8

# Once Upon a Time in the West

Member of audience: 'You seem to talk about films, Mr Greene, as though they were entertainments, equivalents of what you call "entertainments" in writing. You seem to imply that the medium is out of control and we don't know what to do with it. And you suggest *Once Upon a Time in the West* as one of the best films of the last decade . . . Do you not really take film as seriously as you did once?'

Graham Greene: 'I take it seriously, and I take *Once Upon a Time in the West* seriously . . .'

Philip Oakes (interviewer): 'Could I just interrupt? Mr Greene saw it in France, which I think was a completely different version from the one we saw – ours was a much shortened version.'

Graham Greene: 'Yes, what irritated me when I saw the film, what irritated me about the criticisms I'd heard in England, in the English press, about it, was that it was criticized the whole time for being so slow. And I don't see why a film shouldn't be slow. I think you can have wonderful films which are quick in action, quick in photography, quick in cuts, whatever you like. But it seems to me equally valid that one could have a very slow and admirable film. And I love the almost balletic quality in *Once Upon a Time in the West*, especially the opening quarter of an hour or so.'

Graham Greene, at the National Film Theatre, 1971

Just before Christmas 1966, Bernardo Bertolucci went to see *The Good, The Bad and The Ugly* in Rome, at three o'clock in the afternoon on the first day of its run. 'Watching films', he later recalled, 'was a way of finding some comfort from the ones I was not then able to make myself.' He had directed two feature films: *The Grim Reaper* (1962), based on an idea by Pier Paolo Pasolini, and *Before the Revolution* (1964), which had been screened at the Cannes and New York film festivals, but which 'was almost determined not to find an audience'. Since then, Bertolucci's career had ground to a halt. He felt like a foreigner in his own country.

A happy surprise awaited Bertolucci at the screening he had chosen:

247

'Sergio Leone was actually in the projection booth, to oversee the projection of his film. Dario Argento was in the booth with him. Leone recognized me, and Dario made all the introductions.' The following day, Leone telephoned Bertolucci at home and asked if he had enjoyed the film: 'I said I did, but that was not enough. Sergio wanted to know why. So I replied with a phrase which I think he liked very much, which almost seduced him. I said I liked the way he filmed horses' arses. In general, in both Italian and German Westerns, the horses were filmed from the front and sides – in profile. But when *you* film them, I said, you always show their backsides; a chorus of backsides. Very few directors shoot the back, which is less rhetorical and romantic. One is John Ford. The other is you. He was completely knocked sideways by this! Went quiet for a few seconds and then said, "We must make a film together sometime." And he started to tell me the beginning of a story.'[1]

Dario Argento had been in the projection booth having a characteristically animated conversation with Leone about *mise en scène*. Like Leone, the twenty-seven-year-old Argento had grown up among jobbing film people in Rome: his father Salvatore was a top public relations executive with Unitalia, the Italian government agency dealing with film exports. One of Dario's earliest memories (a cherished one) was 'being bounced on Sophia Loren's knee'. After leaving grammar school he had worked as a film critic on *Paese Sera*, where he came to Leone's attention by raving about the first two 'Dollars' films: 'We spoke together a lot, and he was struck by my love for the cinema. Amongst the boys of my generation it was fashionable to go into politics and not many of my circle wanted to go into the business, or were interested in what a dolly is. Leone liked talking cinema with me, and of course I was mad about talking cinema with him. Not theory but concrete facts. I was still too naïve and he brought my feet down to the ground.'[2]

Bertolucci's father Atillo had been a poet and film critic of *La Gazzetta di Parma*, and Bernardo had lived in the Emilian countryside until the age of twelve, when the family moved to Rome. As a child, just after the Second World War, Bernardo would often go to one of the six cinemas in nearby Parma, to see previews of films before they went on general release: 'My friends didn't come to the cinema as often as I did. They were the sons of workers or peasants or *pendolari*. So I had to tell them the stories of the films I had seen in order to reconstruct them. We each took a part with the names of the characters in the movies. I was fond of *Stagecoach* by John Ford and naturally chose the part of Ringo for myself. I identified totally with John Wayne between the ages of seven and ten. I tried to imitate him in his walk and in his half smile.'[3]

By the mid-1960s, in the left-wing literary and cinematic circles to which Bertolucci was drawn, 'there was a suspicion of American cinema – a cinema which I liked a lot'. Similarly, there was suspicion of popular Italian cinema, on the grounds that 'much of it was a degradation of neo-realism down to the level of the *commedia all'italiana*, Italian-style comedy'. Bertolucci felt much closer to Godard and Resnais than to Italian directors, but he reckoned that Sergio Leone was 'the only one, apart from the four big maestri – Rossellini, Antonioni, Visconti, De Sica – doing something different'. He managed to reassure himself that 'there was no contradiction about our political views of the moment – in 1967 – and the great classic Westerns. At that time, anyway, the cinéastes of Paris all loved Hollywood.' 'Besides,' Bertolucci admits, 'I needed desperately to work. And I dreamed, even then, of doing a film which gave pleasure to everyone, in the sense of Roland Barthes's *Plaisir du Texte*.'[4]

After a period as a poet, and an assistant director to his father's friend Pasolini, Bertolucci had been inspired by the French new wave (Godard in particular) to explore the relationship between politics and personality, Marx and Freud, in his own films. Sergio Leone also came from a left-wing background, but he had long since decided to express his particular brand of disillusionment through popular cinema. Against all odds, these two found that they had a good deal in common. The Marxism of Bertolucci met the melancholy, and the cinephilia, of Sergio Leone: the point of contact was the kind of film that Godard had dubbed 'the most cinematographic genre of all'. Bertolucci recalls: 'I got on extremely well with Sergio, because our relationship with cinematic "models" was in some ways similar. In me, this arose through having read Bazin and French film theorists; in him, it was more direct – but basically the way I saw American Westerns, when I used to go by bike to Parma, couldn't have been very different from the way Leone saw them, in a cinema in Trastevere. The fever in our eyes must have burned at the same temperature.'[5]

Leone signed Bertolucci and Argento to write the story of his new film, *Once Upon a Time in the West*. Thus, the three men began a series of meetings at his house on the Via Lisippo. Carla Leone recalls that: 'This was a very unusual step for Sergio to take: Dario and Bernardo were young people, and they were very attracted to Sergio's way of talking about cinema.'[6] In order to have control over the project, Leone contracted the 'young people' to his new production company Rafran, a title taken from the first syllables of his children's names, Raffaella and Francesca. He had told Paramount that this would be a much more personal film than the 'Dollars' trilogy ('a film for myself rather than for the public, a *reaction* to my previous work'). There would be no question of 'using my old screenwriters', he informed the money men. There would also be as little trace as possible of the Cinecittà assembly-line. Leone had told the studio that he would 'make the new film in a framework that would allow me to prepare my project of *Once Upon a Time in America*'. Charles Bluhdorn, the Austrian head of Gulf and Western (Paramount's parent company), a flamboyant and short-fused businessman who didn't like being contradicted, was sufficiently impressed with Leone to leave him to his task.

Sergio Leone recalled, 'So we met, the three of us, and began to dream together. Very soon Dario Argento felt himself being overtaken. But Bernardo and I went further and further, always making reference to the American cinema we admired. And it became like a tennis match between him and me. Argento remained as a spectator, watching the exchanges between us. He gave good advice and was, above all, good company. I should say that at that early stage in the proceedings, I wrote nothing down. They were just conversations in the course of which I played the role of devil's advocate. I didn't want to turn the discussion into a draft, for fear of being too satisfied with the result. I preferred to have the freedom to question everything before committing myself.'[7]

According to Leone, this process went on for about two months. Bertolucci recalls three or four, Argento six. Argento was certainly fired up by the collaboration: Leone had 'understood that cinema was changing, and that there was a need for people who wouldn't tell you the same stories in the same old ways: in our treatment we put visual images and sensations rather than a lot of dialogue. Because we'd only just begun, we were overflowing with ideas from inside ourselves which had gestated over many years. There was a lot of talking, a lot of vague talking about a story . . . We spoke about this particular shot, that old film – all in order to get ourselves going.'[8]

Bertolucci remembers that Leone was also thinking about *Once Upon a Time in America* and smarting over the recent studio reaction to his proposal. The theme of Hollywood dreams and historical reality, which he had gleaned, in a vague way, from *The Hoods*, was very much on his mind. His conversation apparently veered from 'great sophistication to a very Italian kind of vulgarity – a combination which had never happened before in Italian film . . . Leone is strange – he has a double nature. He wants to be a kind of Visconti – part of an elegant, sumptuous, aristocratic world – so he shot a Western as Visconti might have done. On the other hand, his basic ideology is a completely child-like vision of life. So at times this man of the West was just like a child who has access to the dynamics of the imagination . . . And Leone is vulgar and genial like Visconti – even if one comes from the Lombardy aristocracy and the other from the Roman petit bourgeoisie.'[9]

Insofar as they were focused at all, the discussions seem to have been focused on the many meanings of the phrase '*C'era una volta, il West*', which means 'once upon a time, there was the West'. The project's central theme was to be the arrival of 'civilization' and 'progress' on the rural frontier, in the form of the transcontinental railroad. There was nothing particularly original in that: indeed, the writer Frank Gruber had categorized the 'Iron Horse' formula as one of the seven basic plots in the Western genre. But Leone's particular interest in the story was to explore the relationship between popular fictions ('Once upon a time . . .') and their historical basis ('. . . there was the West'), at the same time as lamenting the end of the golden age, and of the Western as fable. It was nearer the labyrinths of Jorge Luis Borges than the standard Hollywood treatment.

In John Ford's *The Iron Horse* (1924) the 'laying of the track' had been an epic story of American ingenuity and endurance, dedicated to Mr Lincoln. The railroad was a symbol of the new nation itself, bringing together Irish, Italian and Chinese immigrants, and the Americans who had fought for both Union and Confederate sides, in an inspiring common purpose. Cecil B. de Mille's *Union Pacific* (1939) had told a great American adventure story, involving runaway trains, spectacular crashes, attacks by Plains Indians, and a lot of penny-plain melodramatics, climaxing in a streamlined 1930s locomotive (symbol of modernity and progress) hurtling towards a rosy future. In the most recent treatment on an epic scale, the 'Railroad' segment of *How the West Was Won* (1962) directed by George Marshall and Henry Hathaway, the race between Union Pacific and the Central Pacific had been presented in three-camera Cinerama as an important stage in the winning of the land, 'from nature and from primitive man'. *How the West Was Won* concluded that the 'laying of the track' was yet another example of 'the way Americans have of acting out their dreams', and as such the gains and profits were manifestly destined to outweigh the losses.

Sergio Leone's starting point was very different: 'The basic idea was to use some of the conventions, devices and settings of the American Western film, and a series of references to individual Westerns – to use these things to tell *my* version of the story of the birth of a nation.'[10] 'My choice was provocation ... *Once Upon a Time in the West* began, under the pretext of a nothing story with conventional characters, as an attempt to reconstruct the America of that epoch, to see it live its last moments ... We placed these characters in an epic context, that of the first economic boom which was about to make the great romantic epoch of the West disappear.' So the story conferences started with debates about the confrontation between Western heroes ('an ancient race') and the new era of the railroad boom, and the survival through memorable images of childhood fairy-tales of cowboys and gunplay into the complex world of adults. The theme of 'the world we have lost' led them somewhat inexorably into Luchino Visconti territory, though Bertolucci recalls, 'Mine was the melodramatic Visconti, of behaviour which is taken to excess and also of a certain sensation of class guilt. While for Sergio, Visconti tended to be a reference point for elegant *mise en scène*.'[11]

In one of the best-known scenes of *Once Upon a Time in the West* as eventually filmed, the connection with Visconti was perhaps deeper. The climactic duel between Frank, the railroad hit-man who has ambitions to become a businessman, and Harmonica, last of the frontier individualists, is introduced by a solemn discussion about the golden age, shortly to be killed off by opportunists like the railroad baron Morton. 'Other Mortons'll be along, and they'll kill it off,' Harmonica states. This discussion is punctuated by shots of the railroad gang laying tracks, and has its visual counterpart in the shot on which the film finishes. As the train pulls out of the new town, Harmonica rides off into the hills with the corpse of the bandit Cheyenne in tow. Those whose destiny it is to make way for technological advance not only foresee their own fate; they resent it. The moment is redolent of Lampedusa's *The Leopard* (1958), in which Don Fabrizio, Prince of Salina, comes to realize that in a unified Italy, the feudal South must be undermined by Northern progress: 'We were the leopards and lions;

those who'll take our place will be little jackals, hyenas – and the whole lot of us, leopards, jackals and sheep, we'll all go on thinking ourselves the salt of the earth.' Harmonica is no aristocrat (at least, not in Visconti's sense), and his lament does not have the reactionary cast of Don Fabrizio's, but the sentiments are similar.

At times in conference, the Leone who collected paintings and fine antiques seems to have been centre stage. At others, the Western buff, the 'regressive' Leone took his place. 'Leone sometimes gave the impression', says Bertolucci, 'that preparing a film was like playing cowboys when one is a child.' Dario Argento recalls the importance of play: 'Sergio mimed. He's a big mime because he doesn't speak very well English but he says he imagines English. He explains things in mimes like guns and also us, like kids, we joked with guns like Americans.' For Argento, the spirit was infectious: 'I bought a gun, a Colt . . . a real one. I needed to feel the weight. So, alone in my house I would play with the gun, turning it around and around in my hands. I bought a cowboy's hat too, and I used to wear it in front of a mirror. It was all done to try to fit into the spirit of the thing.' Gradually, the work acquired rigour: 'Bernardo and I, we worked out a system to share the duty; and every one of us was choosing to write the things we were more "into" and then we amalgamated them. Sergio listened to us and sometimes said something to correct and because he was a maestro in that kind of game, we profoundly believed everything he was saying . . . Leone fascinated me a lot, when, for example, he was describing in advance *exactly* the camera movements that needed to be made for a certain scene: to me it was like Dante declaiming his verses.'[12]

At last, the story of *Once Upon a Time in the West* began to take shape. By now, Leone had visited the United States several times. He had made a recce in a hired jeep through the deserts of Colorado, Arizona and New Mexico. He had even taken a guided tour through Monument Valley, on the Arizona–Utah border, with Tonino Delli Colli, who still remembers 'Sergio excitedly telling me almost all the shots in John Ford's films: "He shot from this angle. He placed the camera here." And it was all in his head.'[13] His collaborators, however, had only celluloid to draw upon. Argento recalls: 'Our Western was sure to be different from the American models, because we are Italian and know Westerns only because of movies – because of John Ford and Tony Mann and Nicholas Ray.'[14]

For Bertolucci, cinephilia was an extension of the game: 'In those days, there was a cult of using quotations, and I used to say to myself, "Wouldn't it be wonderful if a director of Leone's talent would use quotations without knowing it, in all innocence – quotations which, rather than being intended, just happen?" It is possible that for a couple of quotations, I was successful in making him do this.'[15] What did Sergio Leone think of this, when he subsequently found out? 'He didn't like me saying that there were references in there which he didn't recognize!' Bertolucci, apparently, teased Leone and 'he became furious, saying, "I knew it was there!" "No," I said, "you didn't." "Did." "Didn't." '

The key films which kick-started this postmodernist game were Nicholas Ray's *Johnny Guitar* (1954) which Bertolucci had referred to in a celebrated critique as 'the first of the baroque Westerns', and which he recalls as 'one of the more explicit references in *Once Upon a Time in the West*'; John Ford's *The Searchers* (1956) which inspired the 'family massacre' at the McBain ranch; 'all those films about the building of the railroad, such as *The Iron Horse* and *Union Pacific*'; John Ford's *The Man Who Shot Liberty Valance* (1962) for the conflict between political pressures and the rugged individual of the West; Robert Aldrich's *The Last Sunset* (1961) which Bertolucci was later to reference in his own *The Spider's Stratagem*; George Stevens's *Shane* (1952) for its self-consciously mythic qualities, and its funeral sequence; and John Sturges's *The Magnificent Seven* (1960) which confirmed the choice of Charles Bronson to play Harmonica, and inspired Dario Argento to rewrite its story, twice, in subsequent scripts for Italian Westerns.[16]

But the movies were just the catalysts for a more wide-ranging debate. As Leone explained: 'For this "dance of death", I wanted to take all the most stereotypical characters from the American Western – on loan! The finest whore from New Orleans; the romantic bandit; the killer who is half-businessman, half-killer, and who wants to get on in the new world of business; the businessman who fancies himself as a gunfighter; the lone avenger. With these five most stereotypical characters from the American Western, I wanted to present a homage to the Western at the same time as showing the mutations which American society was undergoing at that time. So the story was about a birth and a death. Before they even come on to the scene these stereotypical characters know themselves to be dying in every sense, physically and morally – victims of the new era which was advancing.'

Leone's ultimate goal was nothing less than a 'cinematic fresco on the birth of America'.[17]

So at one level, *Once Upon a Time in the West* turned into an anthology of 'worn out' scenes and visual clichés which stood for the whole history of the Hollywood Western from the silent era right up to the 'psychological', 'neo-classical' and cult Westerns of the 1950s and early 1960s. It went beyond just Westerns, though. According to Bertolucci, the name 'Brett McBain' was 'made up from the crime writers Ed McBain and Brett Halliday: we had many, many obscure references like that, not just to Westerns but to American cinema in general'.[18] From the last scene of *Farewell My Lovely* came the line 'She made swell coffee, anyway'. From *Murder Inc*, the scene where a killer's hands gently take over the sharpening of a razor from those of an Italian barber. Frank at one point exclaims: 'How can you trust a man who wears both a belt and suspenders? Man can't even trust his own pants.' This is appropriated almost verbatim from Billy Wilder's *Ace in the Hole*. Sergio Leone himself, as Eli Wallach observed, was also one of those who couldn't even trust his own pants, which is perhaps why the line stuck in his mind. From Max Ophuls's *Letter from an Unknown Woman*, maybe, came the idea of a flashback or memory which 'appears in fragments' and which only makes sense during the final duel between the two main protagonists. And one of the great lines of *Once Upon a Time in the West* ('People like that have something inside', says Cheyenne to Harmonica, 'something to do with death') resonates with Raoul Walsh's *High Sierra*, in which Doc Banton (Henry Hull) says 'Remember what Johnny Dillinger said about guys like you and him – he said you were just rushing towards death. Yeah, that's it. Just rushing towards death.'

Surprisingly, the name 'Sweetwater', site of the McBain ranch, wasn't stolen from Victor Sjöström's silent epic *The Wind* – set in a desert waterhole of the same name: the team hadn't seen the film. Bertolucci recalls, 'Looking at a map of that part of the United States for a name which we could give to this place, I found one I liked very much, which was "Sweetwater".'[19] The fictional town of the story was originally to have been Abilene, Kansas, but once it had been decided to feature a buggy-ride from the train station to 'Sweetwater', *via Monument Valley*, the name was changed from Abilene to 'Flagstone' – a reference to Flagstaff, Arizona. It made no sense with reference to the map, but Jill McBain and Sam just *had* to ride past the red sandstone buttes in the valley which had been featured in ten John Ford Westerns, from *Stagecoach* (1939) to *Cheyenne Autumn* (1964). 'We watched Stagecoach for Monument Valley – yes,' says Bertolucci. Once that had been decided, it was a question of looking at the map to find a suitable destination: northeast of Monument Valley, on the Utah side, is a small village called 'Sweetwater', the name Bertolucci 'liked very much'. This 'creative geography' was something like the process by which Bertolt Brecht found the lyrics for his songs about 'America' in 1920s Berlin. According to Lotte Lenya, words such as 'Alabama' were chosen for their sound, and for the image they conjured up in the minds of radical young Germans, rather than for any *real* associations.[20]

Bertolucci chose 'Sweetwater' for ironic purposes: this is the site of McBain's 'dream of a lifetime', of the massacre of his entire family, and of the mixed blessings the railroad brings with it; to Sam it is a 'stinking piece of desert'; to Harmonica it has the makings of a 'beautiful town'. And, like Brecht's version of America, the story of 'Sweetwater', with its analogy between businessmen and killers, capitalists and hit-men, seemed to be as much about an unending struggle in capitalism between victims and predators as it was about the specific American Western conflict between 'barbarism' and 'civilization'. Brecht famously wrote that he found 'the principle negative character so much more interesting than the positive hero . . . because he is performed in a spirit of criticism'. The villain of melodrama showed the audience, through his larger-than-life gestures, that he was distanced from the character he was playing. In Leone, the chief badman who destroys McBain's utopian dream would become a classic exemplar of this strategy.

Bertolucci notes that the game of homage the scenarists were playing was also intended to put the question, 'What is cinema?' As Sergio Leone explained: 'We wanted that feeling throughout of a kaleidoscopic view of all American Westerns put together. But you must be careful of making it sound like citations for citations' sake. It wasn't done in that spirit at all. The "references" aren't calculated in a programmed kind of way, they are there to give the feeling of all that background of the American Western to help tell this particular fairy tale. They are part of my attempt to take historical reality – the new, unpitying era of the economic boom – and blend it together with the fable.' What of Bernardo Bertolucci's claim that Leone didn't always recognize the 'references' for what they were? Leone was characteristically prickly on this score. 'First of all, I'd like to say that Bertolucci remembers less clearly than he might. He worked on the story and *not* the script of the film. I made all the decisions as director, but he really did bring something personal to his work on the story. The script was prepared, after Bernardo had worked on the treatment with me for about two months, from his outline suggestions. I in fact wrote the script with Sergio Donati, very quickly indeed. It took less than a month.'[21] And, he added, although the explicit references to Hollywood Westerns were intended to amount to 'a kaleidoscopic view of all American Westerns put together', and although it was assumed throughout the film – via a process of intertextuality we would now call 'postmodernist' – that the paying customers would recognize the most obvious citations, part of the point of the exercise was to create the impression that the audience was watching a film they'd seen some-where before – only to jolt them with the realization that they'd never seen the story told in quite this way before. Again there was the mix of recognition and surprise, visual clichés and *trompe l'oeil*, which Leone reckoned was the key to keeping ahead of his audience.

Dario Argento took his own lesson from the experience: 'From Sergio I learned that cinema can basically be time and rhythm – and this has obsessed me so much since then that in my own films I stop-watch everything even if I don't necessarily use it in post-production ... I learned about the author as another character in the film – who is always on set and who always makes his presence felt – the thing Godard was searching for at round about the same time.'[22]

On one level, *Once Upon a Time in the West* is structured around a series of often ironic reversals of famous moments from the Hollywood Western. The three *pistoleri* are waiting at Cattle Corner Station for the hero (rather than the villain) to arrive on the noon train (which is, or course, running two hours late from Flagstone). The villain's name is 'Frank' as it was in *High Noon*. Little Timmy McBain goes hunting with his daddy, like little Joey Starrett with his wooden rifle in the opening sequence of *Shane*. But this time, instead of the white-hatted saviour riding into view between the antlers of a deer, both father and son are ruthlessly gunned down. A series of sinister portents – cicadas suddenly going silent, partridges flying away from the sage brush, sage hens squawking excitedly – herald not the arrival of Comanche war-riors at the Edwards ranch (as in *The Searchers*) but the appearance of a gang of hired killers employed by the Morton railroad company.

But the most important reversal, permeating the entire film, is of the visual grammar, and the ideology, of the Western films of John Ford. To that extent, *Once Upon a Time in the West* can be interpreted as a key contributor to a European cinematic 'moment' of the late 1960s, when cinephile film-makers evolved a form of critical cinema (a phrase Leone wasn't too fond of) that made reference to the work of Hollywood directors about whom they had written. The starry-eyed eulogies of the first *Cahiers du Cinéma* generation had made way for a more analytical perspective. As Claude Chabrol was to Hitchcock, Bertolucci to *film noir*, so Leone, in *Once Upon a Time in the West*, was to Ford: 'John Ford is a film-maker whose work I admired enormously, more than any other director of Westerns. I could almost say that it was thanks to him that I even considered making Westerns myself. I was very influenced by Ford's *honesty* and his *directness*. Because he was an Irish immigrant who was full of gratitude to the United States of America, Ford was also full of optimism. His main characters usually look forward to a rosy future. If he sometimes de-mythologizes the West, as I had tried to do on the "Dollars" films, it is always with a certain romanticism, which is his greatness but which also takes him a long way away from historical truth (although less so than most of his contemporary directors of Westerns). Ford was full of optimism, whereas I on the contrary am full of pessimism.'[23]

On his debt to Ford, Leone added, 'There is a visual influence there as well, because he was the one who tried most carefully to find a true visual image to stand for "the West". The dust, the wooden towns, the clothes, the desert. The Ford film I like most of all – because we are getting nearer to shared values – is also the least sentimental, *The Man Who Shot Liberty Valance*. We certainly watched that when we were preparing *Once Upon a Time in the West*. Why? Because Ford finally, at the age of almost sixty-five, finally understood what pessimism is all about. In fact, with that film Ford succeeded in eating up all his previous words about the West – the entire discourse he had been promoting from the very beginning of his career. Because *Liberty Valance* shows the conflict between political forces and the single, solitary hero of the West . . . He loved the West and with that film at last he understood it. Someone pointed out to me that *Liberty Valance* also has a "triello" like the ones in my stories – a three-way duel between Stewart, Wayne and Marvin.'[24]

Of his *Fort Apache* (1948), Ford had remarked, 'It's good for the country to have heroes to look up to.' But by the time he directed *The Man Who Shot Liberty Valance* in 1962, its newspaper editor's famous line – 'This is the West, sir. When the legend becomes fact, print the legend' – evidenced a much darker outlook. Senator Ransom Stoddard (James Stewart) has made a political career out of the fact that he was the man who shot the vicious outlaw Liberty Valance (Lee Marvin) and thus helped to tame the wild frontier. What actually happened was that 'solitary hero' Tom Doniphan (John Wayne) shot Valance while hiding in the shadows during the climactic duel between Ransom and Liberty. Throughout the film, which is constructed around one long flashback interrupted by the duel, Ford seems to be nostalgic about the old days even while celebrating the arrival of law and order in the West. It begins with an iron horse pulling into the town of Shinbone, belching black smoke, and ends with that same iron horse going back East; with Stoddard on board, musing about a new irrigation bill which will transform the landscape. His wife Hallie (Vera Miles) says, 'Once it was a wilderness. Now it's a garden. Aren't you proud?' When asked about why his vision of the West had become increasingly pessimistic over the years, John Ford replied, 'If our ancestors could see us now, they would be bitterly ashamed.' But Leone was wrong to suggest that this disillusionment had suddenly and inexplicably surfaced in *Liberty Valance*. It had been present since *The Searchers* (in 1956), if not before, and seemed to mirror Ford's increasing depression about the whole business of film-making.[25]

The sequence of *Once Upon a Time* where Sergio Leone most explicitly refers to Ford, and to the destruction of his utopian dream by the railroad, occurs when Harmonica and Cheyenne are examining the kit of wooden parts that has been delivered to Brett McBain's farm. They take the measure of what will become the train station. The Sweetwater farmhouse, centre of McBain's little community, is in the background. Harmonica figures out the Irishman McBain's stratagem. ('He knew sooner or later that the railroad coming through Flagstone would continue on West. So he looked over all this country out here until he found this hunk of desert. Nobody wanted it, but he bought it. Then he tightened his belt and for years he waited.') Cheyenne catches on quickly: 'Aha, he was no fool, our dead friend, huh? He was going to sell this piece of desert for its weight in gold, wasn't he?' To which the reply is, 'You don't *sell* the dream of a lifetime.' McBain is 'our dead friend', because agents of the railroad company have massacred him and his entire family – Leone's most extreme take on what really must have happened to 'the dream of a lifetime' and the utopian community which supported it in the films of John Ford.

By the close of *Once Upon a Time*, the 'worn-out stereotypes' of the Western have no further use. The railroad baron Mr Morton, who has tried unsuccessfully to adopt the methods of a gunfighter, never gets to see the Pacific: instead, he dies crawling like a snail towards a puddle in the middle of the desert – the urine of his own puffing and wheezing locomotive. His funeral dirge is the music played earlier when he looked longingly at a painting of the ocean. Frank never succeeds in making the transformation from gunfighter to businessman. At the death, he discovers that he is 'just a man', and also discovers exactly who his nemesis is; the harmonica, stuffed into his mouth, plays his death rattle. Cheyenne the romantic Mexican bandit asks Harmonica to turn away, as he dies, gut-shot, just out of sight of Sweetwater. John Ford's community square dance has turned into a dance of death. Harmonica rides off into the hills, away from the 'beautiful town', by now an anachronism. They were all part of the rhetoric of the American Western and they have all played out their roles on the desert stage, only to be destroyed by historical processes.

All, that is, except one – Jill McBain. Whereas the others strut their allotted roles then bow out, she at last has a useful, purposeful role to fulfil: attending to the thirsty railroad workmen. As the mythologies dissolve, she comes into her own. For the one and only time in his film-making career, Leone placed a female character at the heart of the action. The world of the 'Dollars' films, and their imitators, was exclusively male. With only one or two exceptions, women were restricted to the roles of whores, buxom hotel receptionists, *bandidos'* molls or silent Mexican widows living in adobe pueblos on the outskirts of town. Sure, the Italians had managed to make the old-style Western heroine redundant, a definite plus. But in the process they had merely scraped away, in critic Andrew Sarris's words, 'the thin veneer of Madonna worship' to reveal a misogyny 'never remotely approached even in the wildest of the Freudian Hollywood Westerns'.[26]

Leone had intended to show Clint Eastwood in bed with a Mexican woman, in a short sequence of *The Good, The Bad and The Ugly* – but although he filmed it and press stills were issued, the sequence was deleted from the final edit. The same happened with a sequence in *For a Few Dollars More* where Eastwood goes to bed with a hotel receptionist. It was as if the self-contained, iconic hero would be diminished if he showed his vulnerability in this way. Confronted by accusations of misogyny, Sergio Leone tended to reply that his films were mythic: Homeric, even – concerned with 'a simple world of adventure and of uncomplicated men – a masculine world'. He would contend that, in the real Wild West, 'the essential problem was to survive, and women were an obstacle to survival!' In all his comments on historical research, he never once mentioned the studies of pioneering women (the reprinting of memoirs, letters and diaries; the publication of women's histories of the frontier process) that were just beginning to emerge in the late 1960s. He regularly scorned the perfunctory presentation of female characters in the classic Hollywood Western: 'Ever since I was a small boy I've seen a lot of Hollywood Westerns where, if you cut the woman's role out of the film in a version which is going on in your own head, the film becomes far better.' Leone's daughter Raffaella defends the apparent indifference to women displayed in his films: 'When asked why women played such a small part in his films, he'd say, "Well there are three strong women at home – Carla, Raffaella and Francesca – and that's maybe the reason!"' Carla adds: 'Women had an essential role in his life, so in his films he couldn't just show them as props.'[27]

Since Leone was so set on bucking Western conventions, it was appropriate on this occasion to centre the film on a resourceful and powerful woman. 'Jill represents the water, the promise of the West, the plot revolves around her and she's the only one who survives.' But it seems Leone didn't 'invent' this aspect of the story at all. It was Bernardo Bertolucci: 'I'm still very proud of my contribution to that treatment. I convinced Leone to introduce the character of a woman, for the first time. To accept that character and take her seriously. I worked hard on that.'[28] He took Leone to see *Johnny Guitar*, a film that centres on two remarkable females. But it could still be an uphill struggle: 'I was talking to him about a scene [involving Charles Bronson, after he has recovered from the gunfight at Cattle Corner Station. It was filmed, but cut from the final version]. The hero goes into a small hotel, throws himself on to the bed, and says to the girl, "Take off my boots" (and she takes them off), "Massage my feet" (and she starts to massage his feet). This should have been the beginning of an erotic encounter. But Leone interrupted me: "Yeah, yeah. She massages his feet slowly, very slowly . . . and *he falls asleep*." He had a tendency to neutralize the possibility of a sexual relationship.'

In other respects, Bertolucci remembers, Leone didn't miss a trick. 'The treatment said that Claudia Cardinale "appears for the first time when she gets down from the train and she's wearing the latest fashions from New Orleans". Leone said, "The door of the railroad carriage opens. Focus on the steps of the train. You see the feet coming into view, then the camera gets covered by her skirt, and we realize that she hasn't got any knickers on." I think this is beautiful: a person who is immediately connoted, or delineated, by her sex.'[29]

As Bertolucci recalls, Vienna, Joan Crawford's character in *Johnny Guitar*, was the cinematic model for Jill McBain. Claudia Cardinale confirms this. Jill is the dark lady who develops into the fair lady. A stock figure in the classic Western is the 'dance-hall girl' (as postwar Hollywood coyly called her) who travelled out West to escape her past. She is usually alienated from the rest of the 'respectable' towns-folk, and thus more willing and able to understand the hero's moral conflicts, to offer sympathy and revive the hero's flagging commitment to his 'crusade'. Yet (unlike the hero, usually) she is deeply committed to town values. Jill McBain evidently grew out of this stock figure. She has come to Sweetwater from one of the finest whorehouses on Bourbon Street. At first she reacts to the threats she encounters by behaving as she would have done back in New Orleans: 'If you want to, you can lay me over the table and amuse yourself – and even call in your men. Well, no woman ever died from that. When you've finished . . . I'll be exactly where I was before – with just another filthy memory.' But, she confides to Cheyenne when she gets to know him better, she had hoped for better things. She describes meeting McBain, 'who looked like a good man. Clear eyes, strong hands. And he wants to marry you, which doesn't happen often, and he says he's rich, which doesn't hurt. So you think, "Damn you, New Orleans. Now I'll say yes and go live in the country. I wouldn't mind giving him half a dozen kids after all. Take care of a house. Do something, what the hell" ' . . . 'You deserve better,' replies Cheyenne. 'The last man who told me that is buried out there,' is Jill's reply.

During this long exchange, cross-cut with a discussion between Morton and Frank, it becomes clear that the rootless Cheyenne would desperately like to treat Jill as some kind of mother-substitute. As he prepares to leave, he sentimentally observes, 'You know, Jill, you remind me of my mother. She was the biggest whore in Alameda and the finest woman that ever lived. Whoever my father was, for an hour or for a month, he must have been a happy man.' At their final meeting, towards the end of the story, he approvingly confides, 'My mother used to make coffee this way – hot, strong and good.' By this time, Jill has overcome her initial disillusionment and decided to stay and make a go of things: she has changed from whore to pioneering woman, reluctantly believing in the promise of the new Western town.

Jill also becomes 'earth mother' to the hot and tired railroad gangs, working just outside her new home: a very Italian conceit. (Claudia Cardinale had appeared five years before as 'the young girl of the springs' who offers spa water to depressed film director Marcello Mas- troianni, helping to 'restore him to life' in Fellini's *8½*.) In truth, she is carefully groomed for this role throughout the film. Cheyenne helps her build and light a fire. Harmonica stops her from packing her bags and returning to New Orleans: he strips her of 'the latest fashions' she is wearing, leaving her with more practical clothes to fetch water from the Sweetwater well. This extraordinary sequence, which at one point seems to threaten a rape, also shows Harmonica to be Jill's protector: the stripping removes all traces of white lace from her dark costume, so she will not become a sitting target for Frank's hit-men. She is still wearing her practical working clothes when Cheyenne takes his final leave of Jill by gently patting her behind – a gesture which associates him with the workmen outside (her 'sons') who, he has sheepishly warned her, may occasionally attempt the same ('You can't imagine how happy it makes a man feel . . . Make believe it's nothing'). As the train pulls in, and both Harmonica and Cheyenne exit, the rail gang gathers around Jill, and history takes over.

Finally, though, whereas the behaviour of all the *male* characters impacts upon events, Jill McBain remains a rather passive, reactive figure. At no stage in the story, until the very end, does she take the initiative. But her function in the film is crucial: she brings into focus all the other 'worn-out stereotypes' and is the only character to survive and adjust to the modern world. Nevertheless, Leone was presenting her survival at the end with ambiguity: 'From one point of view, it is optimistic – in that a great nation has been born . . . It's been a difficult birth, but all the violence has made the greatness possible. From another point of view, it is pessimistic, undoubtedly – because the West has given way to the great American matriarchy, the worship of "Mom". America has come to be based on this, and the arrival of the railroad ushers in the beginning of a world without balls. The great force in American life – part of its formidable success story – is based on women with iron balls, so to speak. I'm pretty sure that Rockefeller's grandmother came from a whorehouse in New Orleans.'[30]

The final result of the many script conferences involving Leone, Bertolucci and Argento was a treatment, or story, consisting mainly of descriptions, suggestions for visual images, and stage directions. Bertolucci remembers it as 'huge . . . about three hundred pages long'. He was then offered the opportunity to direct a half-hour film about myths of theatricality, with Julian Beck and members of the Living Theatre Group. It was called *The Barren Fig Tree*, later retitled *Agony* as part of the portmanteau film *Love and Anger*. 'As I wanted very much to make a film of my own, I divorced myself from the team,' Bertolucci recalls. He proceeded to *Partner*, adapted from Dostoevsky's novel *The Double*, in which the style of mid-1960s Godard was allied to some of the camera movements of *Once Upon a Time in the West*.

Dario Argento went straight on to contribute to the scripts of several Italian Westerns. On one of these, *The Five Man Army*, he directed a few sequences; and, by 1969, he felt ready to make his solo directorial début, a Hitchcockian suspense film called *The Bird with Crystal Plumage*. It was, he now confesses, the experience of working on *Once Upon a Time in the West* which set him on course: 'I was lucky enough to work near Leone. I don't think he particularly wanted to be my maestro – he isn't the kind of person who surrounds himself with apprentices – but his knowledge transmits itself . . . When I started on my début film, I followed the lesson of Sergio and took on a lot of beginners amongst whom there was cinematographer Vittorio Storaro . . . However, for the music I called in Ennio Morricone. This was another thing I'd learned from Sergio.'[31]

The conferences took place from January to April 1967. Midway through this period, on 9 March, Carla Leone gave birth to a son, Andrea. It was fortunate that Sergio had already named his production company Rafran, because Andrea's name could also be incorporated into it – to join Raffaella and Francesca. Or maybe Leone had that in mind all along. Sergio Donati quipped that 'he had to call him Andrea; either that or change the company's name'.[32]

But Donati was by now feeling very bitter. He had spent months working uncredited on *The Good, The Bad and The Ugly* with the promise of writing the script of Sergio Leone's next film. But he had heard nothing since December: 'I refused every offer. And I waited –

January, February, March – near the phone . . . And then I understood that he was working with Argento and Bertolucci. But not a word. And then, at the end of April, ring, ring! Sergio said to me, "The two intellectuals, they abandoned work. How can we go and make a movie?" He seemed disappointed by them. I was very offended.'[33] This feeling deepened the more Donati heard Leone refer dismissively to 'my old scriptwriters' (Vincenzoni and Donati). As Donati saw it, Leone may have been 'aware that cinema was changing', that it was the time to be talking about Brecht and *Cahiers du Cinéma*, but that did not absolve him from his obligation to the writers who had helped to make his name. 'So I stayed with Sergio for two weeks, together, to make the skeleton, the outline, to tell each other the scenes very clearly. That was really a state of a farce. I never met Bertolucci and Argento at that time. The story they produced was not so gigantic. It was eighty pages. Then I wrote the whole script in twenty-five days, I think. Working like hell, scarcely getting up from my seat. And I had to rewrite just two things. If you read the shooting script, everything was shot exactly as in the script. Including the fly at the station.'[34]

The reason Sergio Donati emphasizes 'the fly' is that Dario Argento subsequently claimed this aspect of the opening sequence as his idea; and further that he had a hand in the 'screenplay' rather than just the initial treatment.[35] This still infuriates Donati, who observes that Argento couldn't even say with certainty what colour the cover of the screenplay was, because he never set eyes on it. 'I'm very angry about Argento's behaviour: Bertolucci, though, always told the truth.'[36]

So, what was the state of the treatment when Donati received it? 'All his intentions were in there, but it was slow and rhetorical . . . It was not Sergio Leone. There were very good intentions, but no substance.' Donati, whose early fiction reveals a fondness for the romantic, injected some of this flavour into the script. He had previously written a treatment for a Western, in which the protagonist, unbeknown to the audience or the townspeople, is slowly dying over twenty-four hours, due to a gunshot wound in the belly. This fate was reserved for Cheyenne in the new script. 'The best thing I did, I guess, was to give a meaning to the story of *Once Upon a Time in the West*. I mean, this railroad which unites one ocean to the other one is the end of the frontier, the end of adventure, the end of the lonely hero and so on. This was much of me. And I invented the man with no legs, this Mr Morton who wants to reach the other ocean.'[37]

'I put together the kind of script Leone likes – with interminable descriptions, allusive dialogue, long biographies of the characters, and many different suggestions on how to direct the sequences. He often said to me, "When you're writing a script, you should give me as many options as you possibly can." We always had to indicate three or four different possibilities, so he could choose which one to use when he was actually setting up the scene. I fought against many things which are still in the film – some of which turned out to be pretty good. For instance, the interminable scene in the saloon in the desert, where nothing happens. As for the final duel, I did manage to persuade Sergio to make it slightly shorter than the ones in his previous films – in fact I would even have left the duel outside the camera's field of vision, and just shown Claudia Cardinale's reactions to it.'[38]

Some elements of the treatment survived the transition, especially those that happen before the story gets going. When Bertolucci saw the finished film he recognized certain sequences: 'There was one part which was miraculously similar to what I had written. It was the part where the family is waiting for Claudia Cardinale to arrive, and they are putting cakes on some tables out of doors. (There was no dialogue. I wrote it thinking about *The Searchers*.) I remember some pages where with great detail I'd described the sounds of the cicadas which were interrupted by these very worrying silences – and then the white duster coats, and dust clouds, of the bandits who came out of the cornfields. I had written "cornfields" because I had brought the West into my Emilian countryside.'[39]

The unusual gestation of the story and screenplay might explain, in turn, why the finished film is so full of 'quotes from all the Westerns I love' – or, as Sergio Leone put it, such a mosaic made up of 'references to individual Westerns'. This can be seen as the first truly postmodernist movie, made by a cinéaste for cinéastes. It begins with *High Noon* and *The Iron Horse*, and moves on to *Shane*, *Pursued* and *The Searchers*. The characters in the early sequences include John Ford's statuesque black actor Woody Strode, the wall-eyed heavy of countless 1950s Westerns, Jack Elam, and a man playing a harmonica – like Silent Tongue in *Run of the Arrow* or, as Leone put it, 'Bronson's harmonica is also Johnny's guitar'. Once Henry Fonda has appeared on the scene – 'the glacial Fonda in my film is the legitimate son of the intuition which John Ford brought to *Fort Apache*' – and Jill has taken her buggy-ride through Monument Valley, the middle sequences refer to *Winchester*

'73 (the trading post), *Shane* again (the funeral), *Johnny Guitar* (the wooden model of the railroad), and *Warlock* (Cheyenne's search for a mother). The character of crippled railroad baron Mr Morton is derived from a succession of wheelchair-confined patriarchs who try to run their landholdings with a rod of iron in 1940s and 1950s Westerns. The debate about business and gunplay nods in the direction of *The Man Who Shot Liberty Valance*, while Jill's preparation for her role as water-bearer resembles the equivalent scene in *Man of the West*. Cheyenne's unusual way of travelling on Morton's train is from *Man Without a Star*, the auction again refers to *Liberty Valance* and Frank's cautious walk down the Flagstone street recalls *Rio Bravo*. Mr Morton's death is from *Western Union*, Cheyenne's conversation about Jill being patted on the behind is from *Jubal*, Harmonica whittling on a piece of wood is from *The Magnificent Seven* and the final duel is edited just like the last reel of *The Last Sunset*. The ending comes from the 'end of track' in John Ford's *The Iron Horse*. All in all, there were about thirty references to other Hollywood Westerns – confirmed by at least one of the participants in the pre-production meetings.

Amid the numerous citations, there was also to be an element of self-homage in the final duel: As Leone remembered, 'It is there that Lee kills Gian Maria Volonté in *For a Few Dollars More*, that Clint, Eli and Lee face each other in *The Good, The Bad and The Ugly* – there, too, that Bronson triumphs over Fonda. It is the arena of life, the moment of truth, and that's why I included the shot where you see all that rocky pass behind Bronson and Fonda.' Leone wanted even *more* extreme Techniscope close-ups than before; there was evidently not going to be a *rapprochement* with the classic Western on this score: 'It is because the eyes are the most important element to me. Everything can be read in them. When Fonda kills his adversaries on the street of Flagstone, helped by Bronson on the balcony, and he looks up at him, all his character, all his problems are in that look, and also the announcement of his end – for nothing will count from now on but to understand what Bronson wants.'[40]

Leone took time out from his work on the screenplay to play a part in an Italian Western – his first appearance in front of a camera since *The Bicycle Thieves* of twenty years before. He was invited to appear by his old friend the French actor Robert Hossein, who was directing and starring in *Cemetery Without Crosses* (1967, co-written by Dario Argento), and who aimed in the film to include some 'typically Leonian moments'. Carla Leone remembers how excited Sergio was about the project: 'Sergio loved him a lot, because Hossein was completely crazy. *Simpatico*, a fascinating man. His father André used to write music for movie soundtracks . . . Hossein asked him to be as bold as he liked with the role, although Sergio didn't participate in the making of the film.'[41]

*Cemetery Without Crosses* is about a footloose Mexican gunfighter called Manuel, who gets revenge on a wealthy rancher called Will Rogers for lynching his best friend – the husband of his beloved Maria (Michèle Mercier). The film owes a lot to *Johnny Guitar*, so Argento must have been taking notes. In one sequence, Manuel (Hossein) hitches up his horse and strides into a seedy Wild West hotel. The hotel clerk is a short, rotund man in wire glasses, white shirt, waistcoat and string bow-tie, with a short beard (plus a bald wig). This is Sergio Leone. He smokes a cigar, reads a newspaper, doesn't look up, even as he says offhandedly, 'That'll be a dollar for the room and fifty cents more if you're planning to take a bath.' A noisy row is going on upstairs ('I want my money'/'Go to hell'). Manuel looks up, but the clerk, oblivious, just spits, bites on his cigar and says, 'Pay me the money now.' But he then raises his eyes slowly, as a slap is heard in the upstairs room. 'That's all you're getting,' says a man's voice. 'Get outta here.' A furious girl rushes down the stairs shouting, 'Scum! Pig! His old man and brothers are all bastards!' The clerk gets the key and leads Manuel up the stairs, still ignoring the mayhem. As the girl meets him halfway, she says, 'I'll make him pay for this – I'll get him,' and a woman's coat flies out of the door, landing in the clerk's face. He looks up disapprovingly, removes his cigar and says, 'Go on now, I don't want trouble with Rogers.' The sequence lasts just over a minute, and is an explicit parody of the equivalent scene in *For a Few Dollars More*, which of course was parodic in the first place. No wonder *Cemetery Without Crosses* was dedicated to Sergio Leone. Leone's slow-burning performance gives an idea of how he liked such parts to be played. But he had no illusions about his acting talent: 'When I saw myself in the film', he said, 'I decided I would not repeat the experience: the horses acted better than I did.' He chose to conserve what thespian gifts he had in future for miming and acting out roles for the actors he was directing.

Meanwhile, Leone was busy distancing himself from the world of 'Spaghetti Westerns' as he negotiated with major Hollywood stars. In a television interview for a French news programme in spring 1967, dressed in a smart suit and tie, he told a reporter excitedly, 'We'll be

shooting in Monument Valley, with some scenes in Spain because we can use old trains and railroads there. It'll cost about $4 million and we have Italian actors Claudia Cardinale and Enrico Maria Salerno [the original Mr Morton] and also the Americans Henry Fonda, Charles Bronson, Jason Robards, Frank Wolff, Robert Ryan [the original sheriff], Jack Elam, Woody Strode and many others.' He pronounced Woody Strode as 'Woody Strody' and his hand was shaking. But Fonda was at the top of the list: 'To play the character of Frank, a very bad man, I wanted an unexpected actor. Frank is an outlaw with political ambitions: a totally ignoble assassin. And to act the part of such a bad man I needed someone who had always represented "the good". I needed Henry Fonda.'[42]

Of course, Leone had previously courted Fonda but had been unable to get around the actor's agent. Now he had an indisputable reputation, but there were still problems. Fonda had recently played the part of an ageing villain in *Firecreek* (1967), but Leone's script went much further in its presentation of 'the meanest man you ever saw'. The version Fonda received was written in stilted English, a direct translation of Donati's words: 'I didn't dig it and I turned it down. I told the fellas I was lunching with that some Italian producer was flying in to try to talk me into doing it. "Who?" they asked. "Sergio somebody." "Sergio Leone?" I said yes, and they all fell down. Seems Sergio Leone had made the three biggest box-office pictures to come out of Italy . . . Well, I went home and called an old, valued friend, Eli Wallach. I told him I wasn't wild about the script. "Pay no attention to the script," Eli told me enthusiastically. "Just go. You'll fall in love with Sergio. You'll have a marvellous time. Believe me!" '[43]

So Fonda agreed to meet Leone in person, with Eli Wallach's friend Mickey Knox as interpreter. He was sent a new translation of the script, prepared by Knox. Fonda's first words, as the director later remembered them, were 'I'm used to the old methods. I can always turn down a film offer. But if I accept, I like to give full authority to the director. That's how it is. Now, before I agree to anything I'd like to see your films.'[44] Leone was usually at his worst when meeting a charismatic actor for the first time, and his lack of confidence tended to make him seem abrupt and diffident. But this time, Fonda had pressed exactly the right button. Evidently he was an excellent judge of character. Whether or not Fonda actually offered to 'give full authority to the director', he had evidently sussed the best way of putting Leone at his ease. According to Mickey Knox, 'The meeting was very cordial.'[45] So, Leone recalled, 'Early one morning, in a private projection room in Hollywood, with the patience of a saint he saw without interruption *Fistful of Dollars*, *For a Few Dollars More*, *The Good, The Bad and The Ugly*. When he came out, it was already late afternoon. "Where's the contract?" was the first thing he said.'[46] In fact, Fonda stopped short after 'about half of the third one'. But by the end of this marathon, he was suitably impressed ('I had a lot of fun, all by myself. I thought they were funny and entertaining in every possible way.') and was satisfied that Eli Wallach had not been wrong.

Fonda described his preparations for the part at an American Film Institute seminar in autumn 1973: 'Now, I read the script again, and I know that the guy he wants me to play is a heavy . . . So I went over to a guy in the Valley, an optometrist, and I had myself fitted for contact lenses that would make my eyes dark – because I didn't think my baby blues would be the proper look for this heavy character. I grew a moustache which was little bit like John Booth's, who shot Lincoln.' Thus transformed, Fonda arrived in Rome. He recounts what happened next in his autobiography *My Life*: 'Sergio, who spoke no English, took one look at me and let loose a volley of rapid-fire Italian, gesturing wildly with his hands and arms as he spoke. An interpreter stood beside him and the first word in English I heard was "Shave!" And the next thing was "Throw away the brown eyes. Where are the big blues? That's what I bought." '[47] Leone was to remember that he got his way by more subtle means: 'I said nothing to him about it. I delayed the filming of his scenes. Each day, I suggested that he remove one of the elements which were masking him. First the thick black eyebrows. Then the moustache. Finally, where his eyes were concerned, I said that his contact lenses made his "look" vacant. He listened to all these suggestions without appearing to agree with them.'[48]

But in retrospect, both Fonda and Leone recalled that it was during the filming of the McBain family massacre that the penny finally dropped. This was not the first of Fonda's scenes to be filmed, but it was the first where he grasped Leone's intention. Until then he'd just been 'doing what he was asked to do'. 'There's this happy rancher and his family. They're getting ready to eat outside their cabin, smiling, laughing. A shot rings out and the eighteen-year-old daughter of the family falls dead with a bullet through her eye. Her father looks up and a bullet gets him right in the forehead . . . A sixteen-year-old youth comes out of the barn and bam! He's dead. That leaves a nine-year-old boy standing in the middle of the worst massacre you can imagine. The camera cuts to a long shot and from behind the sagebrush on the desert come five ominous figures, all wearing long gray [actually brown] dusters, black, wide-brimmed hats, and they're carrying rifles and side arms. Slowly, they converge on this little boy. Cut to him. Cut to the advancing men. Cut to the terror in the kid's eyes. Cut to the back of the central figure of the five desperadoes. Very slowly the camera comes around and that's what Sergio was going for all the time. The main heavy. "Jesus Christ, it's Henry Fonda!" '[49]

Leone elaborated: ' "Now I understand!" he said to me . . . The audience would be struck in an instant by this profound contrast between the pitiless character Fonda is playing and Fonda's face, a face which for so many years has symbolized justice and goodness.' He wanted to build on 'the intuition which John Ford bought to *Fort Apache*' when he cast Fonda as 'an unpleasant, authoritarian colonel who violates moral codes and treaties with the Indians'. *This* man Leone wanted as his smiling, blue-eyed child killer. As he liked to put it, with a measure of dramatic exaggeration, 'The vice-presidents of the companies I have had dealings with have all had baby-blue eyes and honest faces and what sons of bitches they turned out to be! Besides, Fonda is no saint himself. He has had five wives. The last one fell out of a window while trying to murder him. He stepped over her body and went to the theatre to act his part in *Mr Roberts* as if nothing whatever had happened.'[50]

From then on, Fonda became much more confident in his relationship with the director. As Leone noted with some amazement, 'He didn't behave at all with the temperament of a star, he was as docile as a child.' He seemed obsessed with the finer points of his craft: 'I was surprised by his requests for directions. If he had to hold a glass, he would ask me, "Do I use my right hand or my left?" It was the same with each shot . . . At one such moment, I called over the interpreter so we could clear things up between us. "Let Henry know that I've spent all my life worshipping him as an actor. Today, my dream has come true and I am directing him in one of my films. But he never stops asking me about completely futile details. Is he mocking me? I rate him so highly as an actor that I simply don't understand why he is asking me such utterly banal questions. He could easily resolve such problems without me." Then Fonda replied, "Leone is right, but he must understand that I've always been a highly disciplined actor. I think of myself as a soldier taking orders from a general who is the director. And I don't have the right to make the slightest mistake." '[51]

Leone remembered, 'Hank seemed uneasy, uprooted in his unaccustomed role, as if he were embarrassed at finding himself in this different kind of part and it seemed to me that he was reacting with a performance which was monotonous and undeveloped. Then finally I saw the rushes and it was my turn to say, "Now I understand!" He had created such a mosaic of subtleties in his expressions; he had designed a character so real and human that he ran the risk of having his personality overwhelm the other actors around him.'[52]

Sometimes Fonda's uneasiness comes over in his performance: but it fits his character's frustration at working for someone he doesn't respect. Still, other difficulties surfaced. Henry Fonda didn't like working with horses, least of all mounting them. He took some persuading that he was expected to act while a tape played Ennio Morricone's music, even though this helped to bridge language difficulties. And Leone had problems when dressing him: 'No matter what I put on him – even the most worn-out old rags – he always seemed a prince, with his noble walk and aristocratic bearing . . . his way of placing one foot in front of the other has an unequalled aesthetic effect.' Mickey Knox is still amused by the memory of these sessions: 'I'll never forget Sergio and Henry Fonda trying to find a proper hat for Fonda. I was with them. They tried hundreds of hats for hours.'[53]

Where Fonda was concerned, the main difficulty was that Leone worked all hours of the day and then some, so there was a danger he would become tired out. As Eli Wallach had also discovered, the sequences shot in Italy and Spain didn't seem to pay too much attention to union regulations. Mickey Knox, who was on the set as interpreter and translator of the English-language version, recalls that 'the normal working day was fifteen to seventeen hours . . . Leone hated to quit shooting at the end of a day. He always argued with the production manager, saying, "What are you talking about? We have only been shooting for eight hours. It's not finished yet." Well [Henry Fonda] didn't like it too much. He complained a bit, and Leone tried to make it easier for him.'[54]

'Normally', Leone recalled, 'I need few rehearsals for a take – four or five – to be sure the scene is good. With Fonda I could have done with less, but I always ended up taking a dozen. I never tired of it; yet it wasn't false adulation. I risked exhausting him [Fonda was sixty-three at the time] and tiring myself as well, but the temptation and the pleasure of working with him were so great.'[55] John Landis, who as a young man found himself in Almeria doing some stunts on the film, recalls overhearing a typical conversation: 'Sergio Leone made a long, long speech. "'Ank ... 'Ank," he said, "I want you to do *this* with your hands." To which Fonda replied, "Sergio, you say, 'Action', I'll draw the gun, and then you say 'Cut', okay?" '[56] After hours of this, the two men would sometimes discuss painting. Fonda's own paintings, Leone felt, 'reminded me a little of the Italian "magic realist" painters'. Their combination of meticulous technique and fantasy ('a kind of silent creativity without indecision') helped Leone to understand what made the actor tick. God, in both cases, was most definitely in the details.

While in Los Angeles wooing Fonda, Leone had made his pitch for the role of Harmonica, in inimitable style, to Clint Eastwood. Evidently the months following the dub of *The Good, The Bad and The Ugly* had made the heart grow slightly fonder. According to Eastwood, Leone delightedly acted out every single moment of the opening sequence for him. After some fifteen minutes, the actor interrupted him: 'Wait a second, where are we headed with this?' When he found out, he decided that *Once Upon a Time* was definitely not for him.[57] Leone made the same pitch to James Coburn, with a similar result. He also thought about Terence Stamp for the part. Early on in the project, the names of Rock Hudson and Warren Beatty were mentioned to him, but he was certain the audience would roar: 'What the fuck is going on? They're ruining the atmosphere!'[58] Leone finally decided that the face of forty-six-year-old Charles Bronson would provide a much more suitable climax to the opening sequence – even though the actor had never had a starring role before. Bronson was known as a character actor, specializing in ethnic tough guys. He had already played his fair share of native Americans: Hondo in Aldrich's *Apache* and the half-breed Captain Jack in *Drum Beat*, both in 1954; the Sioux Blue Buffalo in Sam Fuller's *Run of the Arrow* (1957) and the Mexican Indian Teclo in *Guns for San Sebastian* (1967). For *Drum Beat*, he had changed his surname from Buchinsky, which had an 'un-American' sound to it at precisely the wrong time in Hollywood. But in all this work, Bronson had been, by his own estimation, no more than 'the anchorman', his name always appearing after the leads'. As he told Leone when they met in Los Angeles, he was disillusioned with the work he was being offered, and had resolved to leave Hollywood for Europe.[59]

Leone's longstanding desire to cast Bronson hinged upon his physiognomy. As Jean-Luc Godard once wrote of Gary Cooper's face, 'it belongs to the mineral kingdom'. Returning to one of his favourite riffs, Leone reckoned of Bronson, 'He is Destiny . . . a sort of granite block, impenetrable but marked by life. I met many important people in the States – businessmen, heads of corporations – frankly, people who were even harder than the Bronson character. And they have exactly the same smile as Charles Bronson; menacing, unsettling.'[60] This was precisely what Leone required for the part: 'A face made of marble. A halfbreed who implacably pursues his revenge. A man who knows just how long to wait, before he kills the man responsible for the death of his brother. Since he is an Indian, he already hates the white man. And he will torture Frank with the names of all his victims. But he must always have an impassive look on his face. He doesn't talk much. He expresses his sadness with the harmonica. His music is a lament which comes from deep down. It is visceral – attached to an ancestral memory.'[61] As the last descendant of 'an ancient race', the character is identified only by that harmonica lament: he truly is a Man with No Name.

In 1967, Leone recalled, Paramount executives 'wanted to lock me up in an asylum' for suggesting Bronson's name in preference to 'all the stars on offer'. This had been one of the reasons he broke off negotiations with United Artists. But Paramount eventually agreed. Charles Bluhdorn was still keen to give Leone his head and his minions were too scared to contradict him. Once on board, Bronson was pleasantly surprised by Leone's evident intelligence, and his exhaustive knowledge of the Western, though he didn't necessarily share the director's grand design for the picture. 'It was never a question of showing Americans how to make a Western,' Bronson reflected. He felt that Leone's films were 'destined for a strictly European audience, and particularly an Italian one . . . Italians love violence and can laugh at it . . . Above all, these films amuse them.'[62] Bronson was tutored by harmonica soloist Franco De Gemini about 'how to put his hands around the instrument, how to breathe, etc.'[63] Most of Bronson's discussions with the director, though, were about how he should move. As a figure of 'Destiny', his presence is vaguely supernatural: always there, just out of shot, ready to appear when he is needed. At such times, he seems to slide into frame: from behind a railway carriage, or a post, or seen through a window. He is usually photographed in profile, and in extreme close-up. During the final duel, the camera zooms slowly into

Bronson's piercing blue eyes, and lingers for some twenty-two seconds, in the tightest close-up of any Leone film. Claudia Cardinale recalls of Charles Bronson's behaviour off-camera: 'He is a very solitary person. He sat around with his cap pulled down over his eyes so as not to have to see anyone and not to have to greet anyone. He always had a rubber ball in his hand which he would bounce continuously. It was difficult to get a smile out of him. We got along fine, though, maybe because I am an introvert too.'[64]

If Harmonica is presented to us as an avenging ghost, Cheyenne, the chaotic 'romantic bandit', usually appears within the frame of a doorway accompanied by the amplified sound of slamming doors. He is never truly at home; out of doors he is always on the run, indoors he moves very slowly. His most dramatic shift from one terrain to the other occurs when he flees the plush interior of Mr Morton's railroad carriage by using the lavatory's chain as a stirrup, the sound of the flush his departing fanfare. Leone had the forty-seven-year-old Jason Robards in mind from the outset: 'The part was tailor-made for him. The character is a mixture of several contradictory sentiments. At the beginning of the film, he doesn't seem very bright. But the scene on the train [where Cheyenne travels beneath the carriage, and later fires a gun which is hidden in his boot] demonstrates to us how resourceful and intelligent he can be. Even if he comes over in an almost grotesque way, he is filled with a kind of reality which reinforces his mythic status. He knows that he belongs to a world which has to perish. And Jason Robards was as close to him as anyone could be.'[65]

Like Leone, Jason Robards Jr was the son of an actor in silent films. Having graduated from the American Academy of Dramatic Arts, he made his name in two revivals of Eugene O'Neill, *The Iceman Cometh* and *Long Day's Journey into Night*, during the early 1960s reappraisal of O'Neill's work. His first film which attracted critical attention was a straightforward adaptation of *Long Day's Journey* where he played the heavy-drinking, self-destructive Jamie Tyrone. Leone first saw him on the Broadway stage: 'I was completely won over. He's an astonishing actor. He comes over as having an unsettling force of character inside him, combined with a romantic look. It is true that he looks like Humphrey Bogart but he could also play Leslie Howard roles, which Bogart couldn't.'[66]

Sergio Donati wasn't so sure that Robards would suit the part of Cheyenne, to which he felt particularly attached: 'Robards is a great theatre actor, someone whom the technicians applaud when he's finished filming a scene . . . He's one of those actors who, in the industry phrase, doesn't translate to the big screen. He hasn't got any eyes, I think that's his problem.'[67] And, for Leone, he would have to use his eyes a lot. Moreover, Robards had a reputation for being difficult to work with. Leone already had first-hand experience of the problems that might lie ahead: 'When we had our first interview, Robards arrived completely drunk. I was disillusioned. And so I left. His agent begged me to give him a second chance. I agreed, but added, "If Robards is ever drunk on set, I'll break the contract. And if that happens you, his agent, must undertake to pay for every single scene I'm obliged to reshoot with a replacement actor." But there was no problem at all. Even if he drank all night, Robards was always on the set, punctually and professionally.' On only one extraordinary occasion did Robards interrupt the shooting, as Leone remembers: 'We had learned about the assassination of Bobby Kennedy. Robards broke down and cried. He came to ask me if we would be continuing to work that day. It was one o'clock in the afternoon. I shut down everything until the next day. Honestly, Jason was an exceptional man: a thin skin, a disillusioned romantic and an actor of genius!'[68]

At the time of his casting, Robards had only one previous Western to his credit (the sedentary *Big Hand for the Little Lady* in 1966), but this inexperience proved useful to his character. At one point, Cheyenne's horse gallops away from Sweetwater before he is fully in the saddle, an uncool exit which contrasts with Frank's slow, deliberate style of horsemanship. In the shooting script Cheyenne is described on a Wanted poster as 'Manuel Cheyenne Gutierrez' but in the film, with his gravelly American voice, Robards never for one moment convinces as a Mexican bandit. Leone was to say he had a particularly soft spot for Cheyenne as 'the same type of person as Eli Wallach in *The Good, The Bad and The Ugly*: but there is more warmth in him, a humanity which, with a mixture of drollery and sadness, gives him a particular philosophy of life'. At one point Cheyenne says to Jill, 'I'll kill anything – but never a kid. Be like killing a priest; a Catholic priest that is.' Robards's style of acting – verging on self-parody even when he is being macho – reflects this. In the last reel, he stands outside the main action, looking at himself in a shaving mirror: the only bandit in a Leone film not to be a player in the final game. *His* duel with 'Mr Choo Choo' has taken place offstage, and has been a fumbled, almost accidental affair.

According to executive producer Fulvio Morsella, who oversaw some of the post-synchronization, Robards turned out to be 'one of the greatest dubbers I ever saw ... When you listened to the tape of the dubbing, which you had to many times, you couldn't recognize his voice because he changed it so often. "You want me to sound like this or like that?" he'd say. He could really use his voice.'[69]

The male leads were unusually mature for an Italian Western: Fonda was sixty-three, Bronson and Robards in their late forties. Spaghettis, post-*Fistful*, had become associated with youthfulness. But at least Leone had the twenty-nine-year-old Tunisian–Italian Claudia Cardinale: the woman described by David Niven, in typically suave style, as 'after spaghetti, Italy's happiest invention'. Nevertheless, Leone was relieved that she was not *too* Italian. At an early stage in the project, Carlo Ponti had been interested in participating, and unsurprisingly proposed Sophia Loren for the part. Leone said, 'I somehow couldn't see her as a tart from New Orleans.'[70]

Cardinale had made her first film appearances in France, after winning a local beauty contest. Introduced to Italian audiences in *Big Deal on Madonna Street* (1958), she had attracted critical attention, aged twenty, as the beleaguered teenage mother in Visconti's *Rocco*; then in Fellini's *8½*. Groomed for stardom following the departure of Gina Lollobrigida and Sophia Loren for Hollywood, she'd featured in multinational productions such as *Cartouche* (1962), *The Leopard* (1963), Samuel Bronston's *The Magnificent Showman* (1964), Blake Edwards's *The Pink Panther* (1964) and Richard Brooks's *The Professionals* (1966). Married by then to producer Franco Cristaldi, Cardinale had nevertheless not entered the Lollobrigida–Loren league, and was being cast largely to inject sophistication, to display a 'Latin' temperament, and to wear low-cut dresses. Her sex-goddess image was reinforced by Visconti who, in selling *The Leopard*, said of her: 'She is a splendid cat, stretched out on the vast couch, waiting to be petted – but watch out! The cat will become a tiger.' Still, Fellini had seen her potential as an earth-mother figure in *8½* and it was this very Italian combination which made her 'credible', in Leone's eyes, to play his tart-cum-water-bearer. She also represented, above the line, a star who would satisfy the Italian investors.

For Cardinale, Leone's huge, charismatic, trademark close-ups were a large part of her attraction to the piece, and she found him a generous employer: 'Sergio worked with me in an affectionate, intelligent way:

every time I had to act a scene, he would put on my music, the music for my character. And this really helped me to concentrate, to remove myself from the real world.'[71] Cardinale had already been introduced to the score when Leone called on her, tape in hand, to act out the part he wanted her to play: 'While he was speaking, we were listening together to the music of the film. And, while I listened, I understood every moment of the film, shot by shot, before seeing any of it on the screen.' They also shared an appreciation of the culinary arts. After a long day's shooting, Leone would talk film with her in a Roman or American restaurant: 'The pleasure of Sergio was watching me eat a huge number of things. He was watching me as I ate, happy because he was always saying that he couldn't. But then, he would be eating as well – and a lot.'[72]

Cardinale also found the locations helpful to characterization: 'When we went to work in Monument Valley, that majestic, beautiful place communicated a certain kind of emotion. We were staying in a motel [the Goulding Trading Post, where John Ford and *his* repertory company had stayed] in the middle of nowhere, practically the only people there. We didn't have much contact with the Americans: actually, we had more contact with the Navajo Indians when we went to film on their reservation – discreet people, silent, observing us from a distance. Sergio, in that kind of environment, felt it was his – he was really happy – like a small child, euphoric.'[73]

However, Cardinale's first scene (indeed, the first of the film to be shot, in April 1968) took her to Cinecittà. There, Leone was less in his element. It was the scene where Frank is lying on a suspended bed, on top of the naked Jill, who is desperately fighting for her life ('What a little tramp. Is there anything in the world you wouldn't do to save your skin?'/'Nothing, Frank'). It was an unusual scene with which to begin a long schedule. The set was closed to all but the fifty-strong crew, and the scene took two days to shoot. But Paramount's publicists had hyped it as 'the first true love scene of Henry Fonda's entire career', and called a press conference just before the cameras rolled. It was, said Cardinale, like being on a theatre stage in a very uncomfortable pose while an audience of not-very-interested strangers stared at you. Cardinale observed Fonda's evident embarrassment and was, she recalled, rather embarrassed on his behalf. 'Mr Leone introduced me to Henry Fonda. We'd never met before. We shook hands, said our polite "How do you dos" and soon after, there we were on the bed together and making passionate love in front of a camera.'[74]

Before shooting began, Cardinale had had a private discussion with Leone about whether it was absolutely essential for her to take all her clothes off: 'I said, "I think it is a bigger challenge to look sexy with one's clothes on, or at least some." Sergio replied, "It would look pretty silly for a girl to be making love on a bed with her clothes on, wouldn't it?" And we argued. Eventually, Sergio said, "Are you an actress or not? If you are the actress I believe you to be, you will not even notice you're nude once you begin acting the scene." And so he got his way.'[75] Following late 1960s movie conventions, Henry Fonda kept his shirt on; Claudia Cardinale removed her corsets. For the later scene, where Jill lounges in the bathtub of a Flagstone hotel room, they compromised on 'flesh-coloured panties'. 'I kept praying that the soap bubbles would not suddenly disappear ... and when I got out of the bath, clutching a towel and continuing to act, I kept wondering, "Am I properly covered?" It was a risky scene.'[76]

Leone was taking risks of his own. He was filming the 'first true love scene' of his career, too. If Henry Fonda looked embarrassed, Sergio Leone might have been feeling equally so. Cardinale remembers him 'betraying his tension by always playing with something in his hands, a pack of cigarettes, matches, whatever ... Sometimes I would come up behind him and block his hands!'[77] Leone was to concede that he 'did have some problems filming the love scenes, but Claudia helped me a great deal. She behaved as if she had a man of twenty-five lying on top of her instead of sixty-five – and he played the scene with his usual tact and discretion.'[78]

For Tonino Valerii, this film, like the 'Dollars' trilogy, continued to show that Leone 'didn't really understand the woman's psychology ... Look, the Claudia Cardinale character is taken identically from *Johnny Guitar*. The situation is the same, the character is the same. The big difference is that Claudia has to sleep with an old man who is Henry Fonda. This is misogyny, no? Leone had difficulty relating to women characters, probably because of his relationship with his mother. I heard him say once that the only relationships which interested him were masculine friendships. Always.'[79] But at least Cardinale was content that the film's events all revolved around her character; and she especially liked Jill McBain's 'grit, and her determination. She knows what she wants and she sticks to it until she gets it. You don't find many women's parts like that in Westerns.'[80]

For the boss of the A. and P.H. Morton Railroad Company, Leone eventually chose a distinguished stage actor, well known in Italian films since the Fascist era. Rome-born Gabriele Ferzetti had been a matinée idol in the 1950s, playing authorized versions of historical figures in *Puccini* (1952), *Giacomo Casanova* (1954) and *Donatello* (1956). He had become recognizable internationally via Antonioni's *L'Avventura* (1960), and was Lot in John Huston's *The Bible* (1966) but his film career was coasting. To theatre critics, Ferzetti was renowned for his 'patrician manner'. This was his first appearance in a Cinecittà-style movie, and, whereas the Americans in the cast were happy to follow Leone's lead and simply 'be', Ferzetti was evidently giving a 'performance'. At times, this gave the impression that Ferzetti was slumming it in an Italian Western, which, happily, fitted the character he was playing.

Sergio Leone knew (from his viewing of *The Iron Horse* if from nowhere else) that no single railroad company had ever attempted to lay tracks across the whole continent of America in the 1860s. Yet Mr Morton, the archetypal capitalist, starts his grand project in sight of the Atlantic, and hopes to see the Pacific before creeping 'tuberculosis of the bones' kills him. So, like all the other main characters in the film, he represents, as Leone explained, something which refers to history but is not strictly part of it. His name (like Mortimer in *For a Few Dollars More*) shows that he has something to do with death. In his case, this something takes the form of a trail of slime he leaves behind him, snail-like: 'two beautiful shiny rails'. Leone went on to explain that 'like Bronson, Ferzetti's character is centred on a single goal – to arrive with his train at the Pacific, and knowing as he does, like the others (more even than the others, because he is so ill), that he is condemned.'[81]

On set, Leone relied for atmosphere upon tapes of Ennio Morricone's main musical themes, which, this time, had all been written, performed and recorded in advance: 'Everyone acted with the music, followed its rhythm, and suffered with its "aggravating" qualities, which grind the nerves.'[82] Sergio Donati remembers vividly a particular instance: 'The music was played for the scene when Claudia arrives and there are the dead people laid out on the tables. It was in Almeria, it was sunset and everybody on the set was crying. Even the grips, the tough guys were crying.'[83] Morricone's music inspired Leone's choreography. The composer remembers, 'I believe Sergio regulated the speed of the crane which follows Claudia Cardinale when she comes out of the station, in time with the musical crescendo.'[84]

The music was slower in tempo than usual, more stately, with less variations; and there was much more of it. This time, there was no 'sproing!' of the maranzano, no grunting chorus, no whipcracks, pistol shots or bird cries to punctuate the driving rhythms. Leone was deliberately getting away from the riot of imagery in his earlier Westerns, and the music, which resembled a 1940s Hollywood score at times, matched this change of emphasis. The expansive main title theme summoned the wide open spaces, the arrival of the railroad and, with added glockenspiel, the character of Jill McBain. There was an ominous trumpet dirge, sometimes played on amplified guitar, with harmonica wails superimposed: this was called 'As a Judgement', and accompanied the McBain family massacre and the final duel (as well as appearances by Harmonica and Frank). Cheyenne's character had a casual clip-clopping piano and banjo melody. A rough-and-ready barroom stomp entitled 'Bad Orchestra', played on slide-whistle, tuba, banjo and violin, was prepared for the arrival at the fledgling town of Flagstone. Meanwhile, Morton was afforded an optimistic 'Pacific' theme, with piano rumblings breaking in with the sound of waves; and solo harmonica laments, played by Franco De Gemini, 'spoke' for Bronson's character. The harmonica was for Morricone 'a nostalgic campfire instrument that American composers have always associated with the solitude of the country', but for Leone it was 'more sinister', played with the hands cupped over the microphone in the style of a blues musician – only much, much slower. Morricone delightedly claimed that for this film, 'finally, we were just about liberated from the *deguello*'. And yet, the trumpet-dirge version of 'As a Judgement' still bears a family resemblance to the mariachi tune in *Rio Bravo*, as Henry Fonda rides past the railroad workers at Sweetwater.

Morricone remembers, 'The Cheyenne theme was born almost instantaneously, without discussion. We were in the recording studio, I started to play the piano, Sergio liked it and I wrote it.'[85] Leone differed somewhat in his recall. Initially, the Cheyenne theme was the one aspect of Morricone's work which didn't quite fit: ' "You'll see," Ennio insisted, "with instrumentation and arrangement it will create a different effect." I let myself be convinced, up to the moment when we reached the recording studio where eighty musicians were waiting, all professionals. Ennio stands at the podium, gives his instructions and begins to make the orchestra play. At the end of the piece he saw my face behind the glass – impassive, still unimpressed – and he understands that the music still doesn't appeal to me. "So what's going on?" he asks as he enters the booth. "Well, sorry, it's just that this music seems crap to me – just as it did four months ago. You told me that everything would be different with the arrangement but nothing has changed!" Ennio goes to the room next door, to the studio, and asks me to follow him, saying, "Come to the piano and explain to me once again what you want for your character, because I don't know what more I can do. I've already tried fifteen themes like this one!" Immediately I ask him: "Have you seen Walt Disney's *Lady and the Tramp*?" "Yes," he replies, "but what has that got to do with Cheyenne?" Then I explain. "Well, Cheyenne is the Tramp. He has at the same time intelligence and instinct, he's a bandit and a lout, a son of a bitch, but he has the capacity for friendship. So there shouldn't just be violence in Cheyenne's theme, but also a great tenderness, because he's a sweet, romantic character, proud and full of love." When he'd heard all these descriptive words, Ennio begins to play: "Tan, tan tan tan tan, tanti tan tanti tan." He's composed the music by instinct and I say to him "That's IT. That's the one." '[86]

Cheyenne's theme was the closest Morricone ever came, when working with Leone, to a straightforward musical cliché from the Western: the plodding horse, the campfire whistle, the lazy rhythm. The only unusual features were that it was also scored for electric piano, and it tended to break off – mid-phrase – just as the audience was getting used to its repetitions; like a *leitmotif* which stops dead. Alessandroni, as usual, did the whistling: at first, he adopted the shrill style of the 'Dollars' scores, but 'Ennio asked me not to do this kind of whistle, he wanted something soft and tired, with no vibration. Different. *Fistful of Dollars* was heroic whistling, *For a Few Dollars More* was aggressive, very strong, this was to be softer and more relaxed.'[87]

Morricone had also composed in advance a theme for the opening sequence, the long wait by the three *pistoleri* at Cattle Corner Station. It was to take four days to film, the last sequence to be shot in Spain (along the railway line near Estación de Calahorra, outside Guadix). The fly buzzing around Jack Elam's marmalade-coated growth of beard predictably took much longer than anticipated. A jar full of flies was produced by the prop man, but in the end, according to production manager Claudio Mancini, 'We managed to do it with just one fly.' The rusty water which drops on Woody Strode's head took three hours. But Ford alumnus Strode was happy to oblige for his egregious Italian director: 'The close-ups, I couldn't believe. I never got a close-up in Hollywood. Even in *The Professionals*. I had only three close-ups in the entire picture. Sergio Leone framed me on the screen for five minutes . . . That's all I needed. When I got home and saw Papa Ford, I told him, "Papa, there's an Italian over there that just loves the West, and he's not going to do another Western because they call them Spaghetti Westerns." I said, "Will you autograph a picture for him?" '[88]

While he was planning the sequence, Leone decided the music that had been written was not right; he would use a complex mix of amplified 'natural' sounds instead. Morricone recalls: 'There was something very important that I'd told Sergio. I had been, some time before, to a concert in Florence where a man came on to the stage and began, in complete silence, to take a stepladder and make it creak and squeak – which went on like this for several minutes, and the audience had no idea what it was supposed to mean. But in the silence, the squeaking of this stepladder became something else. And the philosophical argument behind the experiment was that a sound, any sound at all from everyday life, isolated from its context and isolated by silence, becomes something different that is not part of its real nature . . . I recounted this experience to Sergio, who already had these things in his blood, in his own ideas about silence. He made those extraordinary first ten minutes of *Once Upon a Time* from that idea. In my opinion, that was one of the best things Sergio did in this film.'[89]

So, at the mixing stage, the opening sequence became a symphony of exaggerated sounds interrupted by just one mumbled line of dialogue: the creak of a wooden door, the sound of chalk on blackboard, a windmill in serious need of oiling, the wind, crunching footsteps, the whimperings of the station agent, the fluttering of a caged bird (as one of the *pistoleri* makes angry cat sounds at it), the crowing of a cock, the windmill again, the slamming of a metal door – and all of this before the words A SERGIO LEONE FILM appear superimposed on a riveted door with 'Keep Out' painted on it. When he first saw the sequence, Morricone called the soundtrack 'the best music I've ever composed'. Carlo Simi remembers that 'Some little idiot tried to oil the mechanism of the windmill just before we recorded it. Sergio exploded, because he wanted that irritating sound at all costs!'[90]

Morricone reckons that Bronson's harmonica originated in early twentieth-century serial music: 'At the Conservatory, I studied the whole history of music, certainly, but with particular reference to Arnold Schoenberg and serial music. I use this kind of music very often, on screen, where I integrate it into the very heart of tonal fragments. In Bronson's harmonica theme, for example, I incorporated a little series of interior sounds, part of a tonal language. I've never been tempted to abandon serial music, in which I believe, and my researches with Nuova Consonanza have led me to transpose results such as these to the cinema.'[91] But the melodies remained simple to absorb, even if the orchestrations were complex and sometimes eccentric. 'For Harmonica, I used just three notes of the instrument, for a public which is used to a simple form of music, articulated, I'd say, as a physical force like a heartbeat.'[92] Mr Morton's 'Pacific' theme consists of just six notes descending a scale, while three-note citations of 'As a Judgment' accompany confrontations between Frank and Harmonica: simple, memorable and minimalist.

Crossover moments were scored after filming was completed. Leone had taken a great deal of trouble creating visual links between his big sequences: Harmonica getting up from the platform of Cattle Corner Station/Brett McBain's shotgun; Timmy's death/a locomotive's soundtrack and whistle; Jill making coffee/Mr Morton removing 'a small obstacle from the track', a toy figure; Frank in bed with Jill/Harmonica peering through some lace curtains. Many of Morricone's musical crossovers helped to reinforce them; 'to make spectators understand what dialogue couldn't explain', as Leone put it. These included a few bars of 'As a Judgment' for Harmonica's first appearance and of Cheyenne's theme for the bandit's arrival at the trading post; the 'Judgment' theme played lightly on strings for Harmonica's first meeting with Frank; the main title theme on solo violin for the scene on the hanging bed at the Navajo cliffs; piano played as if it was percussion for Frank's anxious walk down the street in Flagstone; and a reprise of Cheyenne's theme for the discussion with Jill about patting her behind – before 'As a Judgment' crashes in for the final, tightly choreographed, duel.

The score was recorded, as usual, at the Forum Studio, only this time with a larger orchestra, consisting of members of the Roman Union of Musicians: teachers from the Santa Cecilia Academy, musicians from the RAI and Theatre of the Opera orchestras, assembled specially for the project. Choral work was performed by Alessandroni and his

Cantori Moderni with soprano solos by Edda dell'Orso ('the human voice as musical instrument, vocalizing without a text'). The most lavish orchestration for a melody, which unkind critics were to liken to 'Oh, Sweet Mystery of Life', was devoted to Jill's theme. It is heard first, during the eighty-five-second track and crane shot showing her arrival at the town of Flagstone: in a single shot she walks from the train, followed by porters carrying her luggage, along the platform, into the station master's office where we can see her talking through a letterbox window; she then walks into the broad main street, as the camera rises over the roof tiles to reveal the entire wooden town of Flagstone and the desert beyond. This was the shot for which 'Sergio regulated the speed of the crane ... in time with the musical crescendo'. The tracking element lasts forty seconds, the crane forty-five seconds; the most flamboyant shot Leone had ever attempted. Edda dell'Orso's voice rises to a crescendo as the camera reveals the main street. The theme is heard last during the 140-second zoom and pan which concludes the film: the railroad workers gather round Jill as she distributes water to them, the locomotive reverses from the end of track, and Harmonica rides away to the right of frame with the body of Cheyenne slung over the bandit's horse. In the year Morricone recorded the final version of the score he also recorded twenty other soundtracks and served on the jury at the Cannes Film Festival. His career had progressed a lot since *Fistful* days.

Leone's 'cinematic fresco of the birth of America' takes place in four main settings. The isolated farm, the developing town, the railroad, the American desert: there would be far fewer settings than in the picaresque *The Good, The Bad and The Ugly*; fewer even than in *For a Few Dollars More*. But they would be unusually elaborate ones. 'I wanted to shoot the film on the actual locations, but found that this was impossible. There was no longer a wilderness that would look like it did in 1870. There were too many power-lines crossing the horizon, too many highways and billboards and far too many farms and ranches. Too much modernity in camera range.'[93] Also, more prosaically, 'Italy and Spain were better for reasons of economy: also I wanted to work with my own crew, and American unions can be very irritating indeed.'

The Sweetwater location was ten kilometres from Tabernas, thirty kilometres from Almeria, a few hundred yards from the N324 just before it meets the Almeria/Sabas road. By 1967, as a result of boom times for farmers, extras, stunt people, wranglers and construction workers in southern Spain (though not for technicians), there were two cinemas in the tiny village of Tabernas alone and one of its narrow streets had even been named 'Cinema Street'. If only there had been sound stages and post-production facilities as well, Almeria's gold rush would have been sustained: as it was, the locations were too far away from the studios and laboratories in Madrid. But Leone built his most elaborate sets there. A ranch-house, surrounding outhouses and stone well were built – to Carlo Simi's design – on this location: the two-storey ranch-house was constructed out of logs, with a sloping double-pitch roof covered in wooden tiles and a balcony above the entrance. It resembled a huge chalet (rather than the traditional log cabin) with behind it the greyish rocks of the Almerian desert and around it purple rosemary and sage with almond and olive trees – a very elaborate estab-lishment in which to bring up three children, particularly since there is no farm-land in evidence. In front of the house was placed a large tree-stump, the traditional explanation of how a wooden house happens to be there in the middle of the desert. Most of the set is still there: today it is known as 'Western Leone – *poblado del oeste*'. Carlo Simi recalls that 'Sergio originally wanted the house to be in America, and we recced the area around Las Vegas but couldn't find anywhere suitable ... he wanted the structure of the house to be very solid indeed, given the fact that it was supposed to have been built by a stubborn Irishman with a vision. The builder, a young Spaniard, got me a consignment of huge wooden logs which had been used in Orson Welles's *Falstaff*. Very sub-stantial, which is why it is still standing.'[94]

Leone constructed a railroad track down a shallow canyon leading to the Sweetwater set, and had the locomotive and rolling stock brought to the location on trucks: they were then craned on to the new railroad. He had been given permission to 'enlarge a pass, so I could bring my trucks along its side'; he could also hide the locomotive behind the hills. The production only had two locomotives: Carlo Simi decorated the Morton train with 'elegant elements, the passenger car-riage in Assyro-Babylonian style to display wealth and power', but the workers' train was more stripped down.[95] One of the locomotives was customized to look like an 1875 'Genoa' type, of the Virginia and Truckee railroad. The wooden sleepers which were laid for the film were to be subsequently reused to extend 'Western Leone'. The town of Flagstone was built a few hundred metres beyond the existing rail-road track at Estación de Calahorra, where some of the brick-built structures (the bank, the saloon, various stores and dwellings) still stand. Leone leased 100 acres of land around Calahorra. It was close enough to the mainline station at Guadix to control the logistics of moving the locomotive from one set up to another. In a siding near Guadix, there are still some rotting 'Wild West' carriages. The Flagstone set cost $250,000, more than the entire budget of *Fistful of Dollars* – and for that Sergio Leone was able to construct the 'new' wooden town of Flagstone, complete with its station, hotel/saloon, Bank of Abilene, stores, barbershop, stables, blacksmith's, theatre, offices, dwellings and side streets leading off the wide main street; with the Sierra de Baza mountains in the background. Parts of the town were completed, parts were just being started and parts were under construction – 'just', as Leone said, 'as it would have been at the time'. The interiors of the station, saloon, stables and barbershop were also constructed. In the finished film, the only time we see the entire town is when Jill arrives at the station and it is revealed from above.

Carlo Simi based Flagstone largely on archive photographs of El Paso, Texas, a town partly built of red brick, partly of wood. Simi recalls that 'We built the station, the platforms, and the town deployed beyond them. I put the saloon at its heart, which Sergio liked a lot. We were both after extreme realism where possible.'[96]

So it was Rome for some interiors (April 1968), then the provinces of Almeria and Granada for exteriors, then Monument Valley (July 1968) – roughly the same length of shooting schedule as for *The Good, The Bad and The Ugly*. One of the reasons Leone chose the Sierra de Baza and the Sierra de Los Filabres was because 'the area had a similar colouring to the red earth of Utah and Arizona', and when he was shooting interiors at Cinecittà, 'I was more meticulous and detailed than a Visconti; I even had brought that particular dust of that particular colour all the way from Monument Valley. I think a meticulous approach to the particular is a great help and support to the actor . . . Visconti has been criticized for being too fussy. You can't be.'[97]

Simi remembers dressing the set of Frank's Navajo hideout: 'I put adhesive on the wall and we sprayed it with sand. Sergio said, "Are you certain about the colour?" "Of course." "Hadn't you better fly over and get some, Carlo?" "Sergio, you're mad! How can I possibly do that?" "You're right. We'll find someone else." And he did.'[98] Monument Valley, the last location to be used, was *essential*, Leone said, for the twenty-five-second shot into the sun of the buggy passing West

287

Mitton Butte, East Mitton Butte and Merrick Butte on the Arizona side of the Valley, the thirty-second shot of the next stage of the journey deeper into the Valley, and the arrival of Jill and Sam at the specially designed trading post (with one of the Mittons in the background). It was also essential for the flashback, where the young Henry Fonda and his gang kill Harmonica's elder brother (played by production manager Claudio Mancini) by hanging him from an arch. This brick arch was built near a small airport about fifteen miles north of Monument Valley (on the Utah side), two miles from Highway 163 which links Gouldings Lodge and Mexican Hat. In the early 1980s the arch was still more or less intact, but by 1985 the central section had collapsed leaving only the brick supports.[99]

The arrival of the train at Flagstone reveals the fruits of Leone's love for detail. Out of the rolling stock come cattle, stock buyers, a soldier in uniform, a disabled child, a mother and well-dressed little girl, some black porters, a native American woman, some carpetbaggers, an elderly prospector with his burro and some 'redskin warriors'. Sacks of feed, tools, crates and barrels are unloaded – including one improbably labelled 'Olive Oil'. Cluttered interiors, too, revealed Leone's obsession with fact, detail and texture as well as his ambition to create an 'elegant *mise en scène*' Visconti-style: the fading family portraits, billowing curtains, cigar smoke, incense and dust of Visconti's *The Leopard* became the fading photographs, unused wedding bouquet, rosary-beads and drawers full of musty documents inside the Sweetwater ranch-house in *Once Upon a Time in the West*. For Visconti, the interiors of the huge Sicilian villa created an impression of elegant decay, an old world hanging on at a time of radical change; for Leone, the interiors of Sweetwater showed period clutter, gave carefully selected biographical information about Brett McBain and told the audience something about the woman who was rummaging through McBain's things. Sweetwater was credible and it told a story. The Leone sequence built to two moments which may well have been inspired by Visconti: Jill looks at herself in the dirty mirror, puckers her lips and brushes the hair from her face; in the ball sequence of *The Leopard* Angelica (Cardinale) does precisely the same thing. Then Jill lies on a four-poster bed and rolls on to her back as the camera zooms slowly, slowly down from above, filming her through the black lace canopy. Tonino Delli Colli was particularly pleased with this shot, even though he felt the change of focus was 'not quite perfect'. It is elegant and luxurious, but it also shows how, the longer Jill stays, the more she is in danger of becoming enmeshed in a spider's web of someone else's making.

Luciano Vincenzoni, whose relationship with Leone 'had soured a little', reckons that Leone's eye, and distinctive approach to visualization, came into their own with this film. 'Sergio can be heavy, exaggerated – as in certain of his violent scenes . . . but he is never squalid. Other directors are squalid, because that's the way they were born, and because they give in too easily to the demands of the production. If the producer says he can only give you two days for a scene, and Leone knows he needs six, he will ask for eight; another person would agree to do it in a day and a half. Leone is capable of going beyond the shooting schedule for twenty weeks – which costs six billion lire – and of shooting half a million metres even if on the screen you'll only see four and a half thousand of them. Someone who manages to impose himself to this extent is a very able director. *Bravissimo*. But then he finds he's got all these beautiful things he's filmed, and of course he doesn't want to throw anything away; every frame is like a child to him . . . Let's take the opening of *Once Upon a Time in the West*. You've got Leone's cinematographic memory – *High Noon* – with the three killers who are based at the station, and then there's this extraordinary "look". He constructed the planking with thousands of railway sleepers . . . This is a great *plastic* idea. Another director would have said in his place, "Well, there's some grass, there's some stones. Isn't that the same thing?" Or, alternatively, the huge drugstore in the middle of the desert. Leone wasn't worried that this should be credible: what was important to him was the fact that it should give a depth to the scene . . . For Leone always has to *make an effect*. Every time.'[100] Carlo Simi had agreed with Leone that 'the traditional little station made of commonplace wood was *out*: we wanted a non-construction, which had grown out of bits and pieces over time'.

Tonino Delli Colli prefers to describe the *High Noon* sequence as 'Leone setting up the theatre'.[101] A theatre where the costumes were deliberately past their best: 'I rummaged', Leone affectionately recalled, 'in the Western Costume warehouses in Hollywood among John Ford's and his friend's old cast-offs. Western Costume is a kind of department store of costumes, funded by the major American studios . . . Everything that has been made and used – collars to cuffs – eventually finishes up there. When I visited, they naturally showed me all the latest things, things which looked fresh and new that I had already seen in television films. But I explained I was a poor Italian film director with limited means at his disposal and was wondering if they had any left-overs lying around in the warehouse. And they replied that they had quite a lot of material in the basements, but that the costumes were practically in rags. This made my search very easy . . . after some time spent rummaging there with my costume designer, I managed to find exactly what I wanted.'[102] In future, Leone would always use Western Costume, as well as the Rome-based Pompeii.

Mickey Knox was very struck by the care Leone took over 'the look' he was creating, and contrasts it with his Hollywood experience: 'For example, those long coats called dusters they wear . . . In the American Westerns, they discarded that idea because they weren't attractive. You know, they had tight pants, gun belts and so on.' Leone proudly told me: 'When the Americans went on about the costumes in *Once Upon a Time in the West*, as they did, and asked where I had copied them from, I said, "I haven't invented anything – I've just gone back to the original." The "dusters" were a practical kind of garment, because they were the only protection a cowboy had, when he stayed away from town out in the desert for several days at a stretch – the only protection against the terrible dust of the desert in the daytime, and the down-pours of rain at night. And the dusters were good with whisky stains, too. Sometimes they were covered in buffalo grease, as a protective surface. So when the cowboys took them off they almost stood up by themselves! American authors depend too much on other screenwriters and don't go back enough into their own history.'

Mickey Knox was equally impressed by 'the interior of the inn where Charles Bronson first meets Jason Robards . . . That inn was very authentic because it was a very rough-hewn kind of place. Most other Westerns showed bars just like the bars today in the sense of lighting. But Leone's use of lighting was very authentic. It was very dimly lit. There was that magnificent moment when Jason Robards pushed the gas lamp towards Bronson, who was sitting in the dark. You start seeing his face when the lamp reaches it.'[103] (The 'inn' sequence also gave Knox the opportunity to chat with fellow blacklist victim Lionel Stander, the man who famously whistled the 'Internationale' in an elevator scene of *No Time to Marry*, a 1938 comedy, and who was thirty years later living as an expatriate in Rome.)

For Carla Leone, it all related to her husband's passion for looking at and collecting 'well-made things, in antique shops in Rome; he loved the feel of the materials themselves – the marble, finely carved wood, precious metal and inlay; the craftsmanship and the worked materials directly appealed to him'.[104] At around the time of *Once Upon a Time in the West*, she recalls, he bought a piece of seventeenth-century Roman furniture, originally designed by the architect Borromini as a 'prie-Dieu' or small prayer stool with ledge for prayer books and devotional literature: Leone was fascinated to discover that when Borromini delivered it to his client the piece had proved too cramped for kneeling purposes, so it had become a small desk in a cardinal's bedroom instead. He also 'admired very much the workmanship of antique silver – cutlery, plates, birds and animals. The way the material was worked by skilled hands in the past.'

Leone's melancholy epic seemed to dictate a certain pace as well as a meticulous look. As Leone told me: 'The rhythm of the film . . . was intended to create the sensation of the last gasps that a person takes just before dying. *Once Upon a Time in the West* was, from start to finish, a dance of death. All the characters in the film, except Claudia, are conscious of the fact they will not arrive at the end alive . . . And I wanted to make the audience *feel*, in three hours, how these people lived and died – as if they had spent ten days with them: for example, with the three *pistoleri* at the beginning of the film, who are waiting for the train and who are tired of the whole business. I tried to observe the character of these three men, by showing the ways in which they live out their boredom . . . So we had the fly, and the knuckles and the dripping water. They are bored because inactive.'[105]

Leone saw this stretching of time as partly inspired by Japanese cinema (Ozu, Kurosawa) with 'its utilization of silence, giving a pleasing rhythm to the films' and partly a reaction against the frenetic pace of 1940s and 1950s Hollywood films: 'My childhood and adolescence were lived under the sign of "speed". Then I noticed that all the directors I assisted were alike in their obsession with moving fast . . . They constrained the actors to accelerate their dialogue to the point where you couldn't hear the last syllables of one speaker or the first of the other. Never the slightest interval to show that a person might wish to think about it before replying. I didn't agree with this system. I found it too artificial . . . The sense of pondering a reply I could only find in Japanese cinema. And so I was influenced by it . . . I'd wanted for a long time to give this rhythm to a film. To make camera movements seem like caresses. Tonino Delli Colli was put out about it, at first.'[106]

Certainly the slow pace and elaborate technical set-ups made the film, from the visual point of view, seem a highly rhetorical exercise. All seemed to go well with the interiors shot in Rome, but when he was filming at Tabernas Sergio Leone suddenly panicked. If the film continued at this pace, he calculated, it would probably run for at least three and a half hours. Sergio Donati was contacted in Rome. Donati recalls that 'he had stopped the movie for a couple of days – covered by insurance – and phoned me, and he was very humbled at that time. "Sergio, I cannot do it . . . Come here and we have to cut twenty to forty minutes," he said. And I came by car with my wife and son and babysitter, it was in the summer and there was the French "events of May" – La Révolution – and I stayed for two or three weeks: when I arrived on the set, for the first time I saw Sergio in crisis, saying: "I was sure I could film it by altering the rhythm. But I'm not sure I can." So I stayed in Almeria and cut while he was filming.'[107]

Drastic action had to be taken on the run, which was not at all how Leone liked to work. Eight groups of scenes were cut from the shooting script – most of which had already been shot; and key lines of dialogue were then transposed to surviving scenes which hadn't. Some of the words between Jill and Sam in the Flagstone stables (a scene which went) were moved to the buggy-ride towards Monument Valley. A scene in the foyer of the Flagstone hotel, where Jill is given title deeds to the Sweetwater ranch by 'Signor O'Leary' from the bank, and recalls that Brett McBain once called that piece of earth 'a dream, a great and splendid dream', was cancelled and turned into Harmonica's later lines 'You don't *sell* the dream of a lifetime' and 'He got the rights to build it. I saw a document, it was all in order.' A scene in the Flagstone barbershop – just before the auction chaired by the County Sheriff – in which the barber tells Frank that there's a man outside 'and he's whittlin' on a piece of wood . . . I've got a feeling when he stops whittlin', something's gonna happen!' was cut and the lines given to Cheyenne as he turns to the camera and introduces the final duel. A scene where Harmonica knocks on Cheyenne's door in the hotel, and pauses 'with regret' as he pulls a gun on him was deleted, and became an exchange of glances at the top of the stairs in the auction sequence. A long sequence where Harmonica searches for Wobbles on a crowded passenger train went completely, and so did the sequence (to which Bertolucci referred) which had Harmonica being massaged by a Mexican woman before being beaten up by three deputies.[108]

These cuts, transpositions and rearrangements led Leone, inevitably, to some continuity errors in the finished film. Harmonica appears in Monument Valley and at Sweetwater bearing the scars from his beating by the deputies. Frank enters the Flagstone saloon looking clean-shaven, with his hair well groomed, for no apparent reason: originally he was to have gone to the saloon from the tonsorial parlour. Leone had often said that he 'reacted against the bad habit of having to simplify and explain everything', and so it was no surprise that the film had complexities that only became clear on second viewing. But the changes he had to make with Donati on the set because he had seriously mis-calculated the overall length were more serious than that. And they left their mark on his finished film. According to Tonino Valerii the signs were always there in Leone, and his pacing difficulties would dog him for the rest of his career: 'Sergio was very impressionable to ideas which were put to him – ideas which he then absorbed from his environment. He hadn't read anything – Tolstoy, Dostoevsky, Kafka – and if you don't read you don't know how to tell a story . . . Sergio was a fantastic visualizer, and he understood the dynamics of film so well. But he'd entered the film business too early in his life – before he had found a culture for himself. When someone starts in the business, he no longer has much time – no? It is most important that he has a culture before becoming a film-maker, as a resource.'[109]

Extraordinarily, the budget of *Once Upon a Time in the West* remained manageable throughout all these changes: 'It was a miracle,' Leone recalled, 'the way it happened. A Hollywood producer told me that "if it had been made by us at that time, the film would have cost us ten million dollars. Minimum." Remember we're talking about 1968. The cast above the line cost in the region of $1.5 million – but the total cost came to only about $3 million. So the cost of the film, less the salaries of the stars, was only just over $1 million. Which really is miraculous, given the cost of the main set. And for that Paramount allowed me to make a Western the way *I* wanted to make it.'[110] Mickey Knox reckons that 'Sergio was very lucky in that he was also one of his own producers [with Bino Cicogna, 'a very rich and noble man', following a break with Grimaldi] . . . So he could keep the budget in his mind fairly loose . . . He also had a very good relationship with the head of Paramount – a Gulf and Western company. [Bluhdorn] liked Leone a lot. Thought he was a great director.' So there was no interference from Hollywood. [111]

But, where money was concerned, Knox adds that Leone personally was a curious mixture of generosity and tight-fistedness: generous at giving dinner parties, tight-fisted with the production money, with paying bills and with giving credit where credit was due. In other words, a man with a mean streak: 'The crew had a great respect for him because they were scared of him. He knew what he wanted . . . He had always seen the picture in his head . . . But I've got to tell you that you could be dying of thirst and lying in the gutter, he'd step over you and walk away. He had very little concern about others. He was a very tough guy. That's an aspect of him I didn't like. To give you an example, we were staying in a motel in Monument Valley . . . During the evenings the whole crew always left good tips for the Indian waiters, because that's what these people earn to live. Sergio never left any tips for them. When I told him about this, he said the money he paid for the food already included a gratuity. I told him that it didn't leave them that much, and they needed it . . . I told him personally years later that "you were great as a director, however, as a human being you were a turd". I used the Italian term *stronso* because it is much better . . . and Leone laughed.' Knox concludes that when he was working Leone had a streak of 'ugliness in his character, actual as well as spiritual. He saw the movie in his head before he ever did it. Plus he was a great storyteller. Leone was shallow as hell; he was bereft of profound ideas. But nobody topped him in the technique of making a movie.'[112]

Just before the 'Cattle Corner' sequence was completed, Knox remembers, the actor playing 'Knuckles' – Al Muloch – committed suicide by throwing himself out of a hotel bedroom window, dressed in his full Western costume: 'Actually I was with Claudio Mancini in a hotel room and we saw the body coming down past our window. I guess he was a very troubled guy. Nobody knew what the hell was wrong with him, or why he did it. I think he was a Canadian. The interesting part was that we went down, and the body was on the ground. There was Sergio Leone over there. Claudio Mancini put him in his car and drove him to the hospital. But before that, Sergio said to Mancini, "Get the costume, we need the costume." The guy was dying there, and Leone was asking for the costume!'

Sergio Donati confirms: 'When we were editing *Once Upon a Time*, every time we looked at (Muloch's) performance, Leone would say, "Why couldn't he have died just a day later? I had one more close-up to do!" '[113]

Mickey Knox had been promised, or thought he had been promised, a single card credit at the beginning for 'original English dialogue' and 'Leone didn't honour the contract. He put my name on the list of technicians [at the end of the credits – Dialogue by Mickey Knox].' Maybe this was how he 'got his revenge'. But at least one sharp-eyed enthusiast noticed his name: 'Ironically, working with Leone is the one thing I am famous for. I was in Paris having dinner with a friend one time, later on, and at the next table saw Joe Losey sitting with someone I didn't recognize. "Mickey, how are you doing? Let me introduce you," he said. Joe introduced me to Graham Greene. I said, "Wow, what a pleasure to meet you. I've read a great deal of your work." Graham Greene said to Joe, "I'm sorry. I didn't catch the name." Joe said, "Mickey Knox." Graham Greene, said "Oh, yes, you wrote the English dialogue for *Once Upon a Time in the West*, didn't you?" '[114]

Another consolation for Knox was that Hollywood producer Harold Hecht – a very friendly witness in blacklist days, publicly revealing a list of all the communists he knew – asked him for a favour at the start of the shoot: 'Once day Sergio said to me, "Have lunch with me. Somebody's coming from New York, and you can translate for me." I said okay. So we went to the Cinecittà [studio] restaurant, and I asked who he was going to meet. He said something that sounded like "Harold Hecht". I said, "Harold Hecht?" He said, "Yeah, he has the rights to two Dashiell Hammett books, and if I agree to direct them, they are going to be produced." At this point, Harold was a producer. I said, "Oh, really?" He said yes. In walked Harold. He changed colour, from sort of gray to white, when he saw me. I did the translating and finally Harold left. Sergio asked, "What do you think?" I said, "Harold Hecht is a crook." Well, all you have to do is tell an Italian *that*. *That* they understand. So Sergio turned him down. A few days later, I got a call from an agent I knew in New York, saying Harold Hecht had called him and asked him to tell me that if Sergio Leone agreed to do these movies, there would be $20,000 in cash in an envelope for me. I said, "Why did he say that?" The agent said, "He feels you might oppose the deal for personal reasons." I said, "Oh, no, I would *never* do anything like that." [Laughs] That was my revenge on Harold Hecht.'[115]

Leone's 'farewell' to the Western had a mixed reception among

Italian audiences who were about to welcome Terence Hill and Bud Spencer into their hearts. As Leone later said, 'I can still remember, after the opening in Rome, one period in particular – a greengrocer who worked near the Piazza Venezia – coming up to me and saying, "Leone's gone crazy – he can't say a fucking thing straight any more. America must have had a bad effect on him." Eventually, though, *Once Upon a Time in the West* had the same kind of *succès d'estime* as Stanley Kubrick's *2001*. When they came out, both films had a rough ride in the first instance – and it was only after a few months that the word of mouth began to spread, among students and cineastes, in colleges and schools particularly in France and West Germany. Even in Australia. Critics began to appraise my earlier films, which I thought was hilarious.' Leone also remembered the earliest reactions to the film in Paris: 'There was a phrase going around Paris menswear houses, just after *Once Upon a Time in the West* opened. The phrase was "This year, the style is Sergio Leone." Somehow the French film-going public was better prepared for a kind of cinema which was slow and reflective.' One of Leone's favourite after-dinner stories was about the projectionist who worked in the cinema near the river Seine, at the end of the Boulevard St Michel. When Leone visited the cinema – where *Once Upon a Time* had run, uninterrupted, for two years – he was surrounded by young enthusiasts who wanted his autograph: all except one, the projectionist, who approached him and said, 'I kill you! The same movie over and over again for two years! And it's so SLOW!'[116]

Luca Morsella remembers going into a London bookshop and asking for a copy of *Halliwell's Film Guide*, to which the assistant replied, 'What do you want *that* for?' 'What do you mean?' he asked. 'Open it at *Once Upon a Time in the West* and see what you think of its judgements,' replied the assistant. Morsella dutifully opened the book and read: 'Immensely long and convoluted epic Western marking its director's collaboration with an American studio and his desire to make serious statements about something or other. Beautifully made, empty and very violent. This film has the longest credits of all . . .' 'See,' said the assistant. 'It *can't* be reliable.' When he got home Morsella told Sergio about the incident, and he sent a still from the film to the shop with the inscription 'To the defender of my reputation – Sergio Leone'.[117]

Except in France, however, the film did not do nearly as well at the box office as the 'Dollars' films. In Italy, it grossed $3.8 million (compared with *The Good, The Bad and The Ugly*'s $4.3 million). In Paris, it sold 5.5 times as many tickets as the preceding film and 5 times as many as *For a Few Dollars More*. It remains one of the most successful films ever to have been released in France.

In America, the film was withdrawn and recut after its lukewarm reception at New York previews. Out went the fourteen-minute scene at the trading post, the two-minute scene of Morton and Frank at their hideout in the Navajo cliffs, the seventy-five-second scene of Frank returning to Morton's railway carriage and discovering two corpses, and the four-minute scene of Cheyenne's death – following his run-in with 'Mr Choo Choo'. *Once Upon a Time* may have been, as one critic put it, 'an opera in which the arias are not sung but stared', but American audiences (and timid studio executives) just thought the film was too long and too slow. As a result, twenty minutes' worth of footage was removed – so that cinemas could at least squeeze an extra performance into the daily programme – leaving the main action sequences intact but destroying the overall shape of the work. Geographical and narrative continuity – difficult to follow in any case – was unceremoniously dumped on the floor. Perhaps the executives should have heeded the advice of composer Arnold Schoenberg when he once warned opera-house managers about the dangers of trying to reduce the length of Wagner's music dramas, however much they might be tempted to do so: when you try to shorten a long work by removing parts of it, he told them, you do not make it into a shorter work, merely into a long work that happens to be short in places.

Where *Once Upon a Time* was concerned, the decision to abridge the work just didn't have the desired effect. *Time* magazine headed its review of the *shortened* version (13 June 1969) 'Tedium in the Tumbleweed'. The review asserted, 'The fun is over. When the first Italian Westerns washed up on American shores . . . everyone assumed they were great satire and that Director Sergio Leone was either a big put-on or a superb conman. Leone's newest effort . . . proves that he is simply a serious bore . . . The intent is operatic, but the effect is soporific. The only thing capable of carrying this film is a stagecoach – the one headed out of town.'

It duly headed out of town, with a trailer – 'The widow, the landgrabber, the outlaw, the gunmen . . . in a new kind of Western' – involving two shots that had already been cut from the film: Frank revisiting

Morton's railway carriage, and a vertical shot of Frank facing Jill which, tilted sideways, became the two of them on the suspended bed. On the American domestic market *Once Upon a Time* made $1 million, one-sixth of the gross for the faster-moving, more heavily plotted, less talkative *The Good, The Bad and The Ugly*. As Henry Fonda succinctly expressed it, 'It didn't pull a dime.' Fonda was particularly amazed that whenever the film was shown on late-night television the commercial break occurred just at the moment he draws his gun – after the McBain massacre. The networks simply could not accept Henry Fonda killing a child. 'The decision to cut the film was particularly disastrous,' Leone admitted, 'because it was very carefully constructed like a geometric exercise – or rather, like a riddle taking the form of a rebus – with all the fine little components playing their part in the whole, and with all the component parts revolving around the centre. Like a labyrinth. It's a concept that appeals to me very much.'[118]

Leone's one consolation was that his favourite moment in the film – when the final flashback is *shared* by Harmonica and Frank, after the final duel – was still intact: 'The memory emerges in fragments, through the film. Like theatrical elements. The public doesn't recognize at once the person who is walking towards them. He comes from the depths of the image, just as he comes from the lower depths of memory. And the viewer doesn't recognize Fonda until the moment when Fonda begins to recognize Bronson. That is, during the duel. Frank is shot in the heart. Surprise makes him turn his back. He does not see his enemy. He doesn't know that he's just turned his back on him. He even tries to holster his gun as if everything could begin again. But it is the end of the flashback. And he dies.'[119] As Frank falls to the ground Harmonica returns to him the musical instrument which traumatized him as a child – and Frank nods, silently, as there appears a two-second slow-motion shot of the young Harmonica falling to the ground, Monument Valley in the distance. The two men are recalling precisely the same moment, without a word needing to be said between them. Just a death-rattle on the harmonica. And the rest is silence. It takes Frank two minutes to die, from the moment he is shot in the heart.

In expressing his disappointment at the American cuts, Leone later concluded that a general unwillingness to take the Western seriously enough may also have contributed to the executive decision. This may have been special pleading on his part: 'Nowadays, the audience is no longer so fascinated by the Western. Maybe this has got something to do with the use Hollywood and American television have made of this genre in the past. Or the fact that rural themes no longer appeal to an urban audience – but, against that, the backbone of audiences for the Western in its early days was immigrants in cities. Also, Westerns cost just as much as any other films – and sometimes much more these days, when everything has to be done from scratch. Howard Hawks or someone once said that you can't make a good Western without dust, rocks and actors who know how to have gunfights and get on a horse. That costs money. But in the long history of American Western films, there's never been one that's made a great deal of money. Unless you count *Gone with the Wind* (which I don't) or a Broadway satire like *Blazing Saddles*.'[120]

In the film-making community, *Once Upon a Time in the West* has continued to polarize opinion. The up-and-coming 'movie brat' generation, then at film school, rated it very highly indeed. John Boorman was a director much admired by Leone, and in his *Money into Light*, Boorman returned the compliment: 'The Western went into decline when writers and directors became self-conscious and introduced psychological elements. John Ford and others worked from the blood. Sergio Leone's "Spaghetti" Westerns revitalized the form because he consciously reverted to mythic stories, making the texture and detail real, but ruthlessly shearing away the recent accretions of the "real" West and its psychological motivations. Unfortunately this was not understood in Hollywood . . . Sam Peckinpah was the only American director to take the hint from Leone . . . In *Once Upon a Time in the West*, the Western reaches its apotheosis. Leone's title is a declaration of intent and also his gift to America of its lost fairy stories. This is the kind of masterpiece that can occur outside trends and fashion. It is both the greatest and the last Western.'[121]

Stanley Kubrick admired the film as well. So much so, according to Leone, that he selected the music for *Barry Lyndon* before shooting the film in order to attempt a similar fusion of music and image. While he was preparing the film, he phoned Leone, who later recalled: 'Stanley Kubrick said to me, "I've got all Ennio Morricone's albums. Can you explain to me why I only seem to like the music he composed for *your* films?" To which I replied, "Don't worry. I didn't think much of Richard Strauss until I saw *2001*!" '[122] *Barry Lyndon* could have been *Once Upon a Time in Georgian England*: the music, the choreography, the deliberate pace, the ritualized duels. Leone reckoned, though, that maybe Kubrick didn't quite have the common storyteller's touch to pull it off.

But Wim Wenders wrote of *Once Upon a Time* in the magazine *Filmkritik*, in November 1969: 'I don't want to see any more Westerns. This one is the very end, the end of a craft. This one is deadly . . . Leone's film is completely indifferent towards itself. All it shows the unconcerned viewer is the luxury that enabled it to be made: the most complicated of camera movements, the most sophisticated of cranes and pans, fantastic set designs, incredibly good actors, a gigantic railway construction site with all the trappings, built for the sole purpose that in one scene a buggy might drive through it. Yes, and Monument Valley, THE REAL MONUMENT VALLEY, not a pasteboard replica propped up from behind, no, the genuine article, in AMERICA, where John Ford shot his Westerns. It was at this point in the film, when the unconcerned viewer might feel reverence, that I became, when I saw the film for the second time, very sad: I felt like a tourist in a Western . . . when for the first time you see Henry Fonda's ghastly face; when Henry Fonda finally shoots down the boy; then it becomes clear why Woody Strode and Jack Elam are only there in the credit sequence. Their death is that of a genre and of a dream. Both of them American.' When I asked Wenders why he reacted quite so strongly, he replied, 'It was because it was the end of a genre, and because it turned the Western into an abstraction where the images no longer signify themselves.'[123]

Still, the students of May 1968 flocked to see *Once Upon a Time in the West*, half a mile up the boulevard from the Sorbonne. Brecht and the v-effect, Barthes and capitalism's reluctance to 'display its codes', and deconstruction (a freshly minted word) of Hollywood movies were all part of that season's haute couture. A new print of Sergei Eisenstein's *October* was circulating, to celebrate the fiftieth birthday of the Soviet Revolution, and *Cahiers* compared Sergio Leone's cinema – faces as types, the linkage and collision of images, rhythmic cutting – with Eisenstein's theory and practice of 'intellectual cinema'. Bertolucci, interviewed by a Parisian film magazine, said *Once Upon a Time* was 'Leone's film I like the best, even if it is a little too intellectual'. Umberto Eco later added, 'Leone's film represents the cinema of frozen archetypes. If a film contains one frozen archetype, everyone says it's terrible. But if it contains hundreds of them, it becomes sublime. The archetypes begin to talk among themselves.'[124]

Leone's writers were amazed at this turn of events. '*Intellectual?*'

explodes Luciano Vincenzoni. 'Do you imagine Sergio Leone with a *philosophy*? Come on! He was a primitive of movies. A great director on the set. That's it.' But in the wake of *Once Upon a Time in the West* Leone started giving interviews that created a very different impression: 'He was so surprised to be successful and he started to take himself too seriously. And there was a moment in which he supposed himself to be something between Bernard Shaw and Karl Marx . . . While I was sitting with him giving an interview, many times I had to stop him and say, "Please Sergio, slow down, don't say those stupid things." He discovered Sergio Leone through the journalists and critics. He discovered himself.'[125] Sergio Donati, equally flabbergasted that Leone should project himself as an intellectual to the cinéastes of 1968, confirms that the director began to remake himself in the image of the critics; also to become a celebrity, Hitchcock-style, which was something very unusual in Italian popular cinema: 'He started to build a personality for himself, no? He started to build a big belly as well, a beard of a prophet, and he gave interviews all the time which masqueraded his real ignorance.'[126]

Hence, the writers assert, the references to Céline and the attraction of using 'the two intellectuals' rather than his customary collaborators. Hence, too, his presentation of himself as 'the author' and tendency to downplay the contributions of other people. The critics wanted to believe in 'Leone' as a single, all-encompassing intelligence, and so he began to become that mythical person. From this point on, says Donati, Sergio Leone's public statements have to be divided by at least two and corroborated. From this point on, by the same token, his writers would become more critical, sour and even 'snobbish'– at first in private, then from the mid-1980s in public. The truth probably lay somewhere in the middle. Bertolucci's retrospective verdict is that: '[Sergio's] movies are good directly at the surface level. There are other layers, but I think Sergio was stronger as a pure talent of *mise en scène* – the relationship between the camera, the bodies of the people in front of it, and the landscape – than as a philosopher. [He sometimes talked] a bit like a super-critic, almost a philosopher of the cinema. That was the weaker part of him. He was generous with ideas about the camera and emotions and his extraordinary tricks. That's why I went to see *The Good, The Bad and The Ugly* on the first day at 3 p.m. And that's why I had to work with him.'[127]

Sergio Leone, meanwhile, announced to the world that his dream was to remake *Gone with the Wind* . . .

# 9

# Keep Your Head Down

*The Great Day*
Hurrah for the revolution and more cannon-shot!
A beggar on horseback lashes a beggar on foot.
Hurrah for revolution and cannon come again!
The beggars have changed places, but the lash goes on.
W.B. Yeats, *Last Poems* (1936–9)

MISS GILCHRIST: I always say that a general and a bit of shooting makes one forget one's troubles.
MEG: Sure, it takes your mind off the cost of living.
Brendan Behan, *The Hostage* (1958)

After the opening of *Once Upon a Time in the West*, Sergio Leone asked certain questions of himself, 'among them, the question of whether I shouldn't abandon my profession altogether'.[1] As far as Hollywood was concerned, he was a director of Westerns, which (with the exception of the last one) had made a great deal of money. Nevertheless, following a hectic four years of work, Leone seemed at last to have fallen out of love with 'the things associated with the West'. He did a lot of thinking aloud at this time. He was happy to be photographed standing in front of crammed bookshelves, especially if the accompanying article was to appear in a French journal. He sat on the juries of numerous film festivals, and at Cannes, in particular, he became a regular. There, in 1968, he was photographed while introducing Henry Fonda to a press conference; standing at the microphone, in suit and tie, he looked both proud and uncomfortable.

At this time he bought an apartment in the Via Garibaldi in Trastevere, while continuing to live in the Via Lisippo. The apartment was once part of a fifteenth-century convent; an architect had recently redesigned the interior. Leone recalled the first time he saw the place: 'Originally, my apartment had been the old washing area, with fountains in the courtyard. There were still some of the fifteenth-century timbers in place. The elderly owner was from Naples. He showed me round. There was a 360-degree view of all Rome, with Trastevere as the main axis. It was at the foot of the Gianiculum of my childhood. The owner puffed the beauty of this view. But I had taken more notice of the windows, where I could see murals of the Roman School made by Maffai ... The moment I saw those works in Cinemascope, I no longer heard the sweet-talking of the vendor. In my head, it was as if the apartment already belonged to me. I didn't even know what this man was doing next to me, as he bantered away. He was a visitor, an intruder ... But he was very kind to me. He let me know that John Huston had already reserved the apartment. But he preferred to sell it to me because I was Roman. And we clinched the deal within the hour.'[2]

It was, says Carla Leone, 'an apartment for the old days – a home to retire to'. Although Sergio was only thirty-nine years old, he was seriously thinking of leaving the film industry and pulling up the drawbridge. He had made himself (or been made into) a celebrity on the European cinema scene, recognizable by his ample girth and beard, his passion for Havana cigars (to which Luciano Vincenzoni had introduced him), and his prodigious appetite for good Italian food. Somehow, it was difficult to imagine him existing in any other sphere. Indeed, an interviewer later asked him how such a larger-than-life cinéaste spent his time when not preparing or shooting a film. He replied, 'I have to admit the horrible truth: I get brown in the sun, I go to the cinema and watch matches ... read books and screenplays, meet friends, go on holiday, play chess and mooch around the house, irritating my family with – and this is dire – my redundant comments and observations.'[3]

After *Fistful of Dollars*, the completion of each film had sent Leone into a serious dither about what he should do next. Could he possibly live up to the last one? Should he change course completely? Should he go out on a high and proceed to something else? Was he really as talented as some critics were saying? He would talk non-stop at dinner parties with industry friends, about stories that were on his mind. Profligate as ever with technical details and energetic hand-waving, Leone usually dominated the conversation until the early hours. Then he would ask for reactions; then he would get argumentative. Fulvio Morsella recalls: 'Sergio's "spectacularizing" thing was carried over into his private life ... [if] something did not go well with his ideas, he would holler and explode and send away the obnoxious person. I quarrelled with him a lot of times.'[4]

Tonino Valerii was accustomed to Leone's talk of early retirement, which he took about as seriously as Clint Eastwood's stated intention to 'settle down and possibly retire' in *For a Few Dollars More*. He'd heard it in the aftermath of *The Good, The Bad and The Ugly* when the American gangster project had failed to get off the ground. Above all, Valerii considered, 'He was afraid of a flop . . . He was always anxious about that. It started as a game; some remarks pitched at the French *cinemathèque*. But he really was afraid that the next one would ruin the reputation he had built up. He was a very unconfident man, despite the bluff exterior, the storytelling and the *bon viveur*.'[5]

Leone's imitators continued to proliferate. On the rebound from the success of *Fistful of Dollars*, well over two hundred and forty Italian Westerns had already been produced: at a very cautious estimate, in 1964, the year of *Fistful*, there had been twenty-seven; in 1965, the year of *For a Few Dollars More*, thirty; in 1966, the year of *The Good, the Bad and the Ugly*, forty; in 1967, seventy-four; and in 1968 – the peak year – there had been seventy-seven. For the first three years of the boom – once the imitation American phase had passed – most of these films had been *Fistful* derivatives, centred on a mysterious stranger, with titles beginning 'My Name Is . . .', or 'They Call Me . . .'. The man who didn't have a name had not yet been invented by Hollywood. The films – especially the low-budget ones, aimed at *terza visione* cinemas – had become increasingly ugly to look at and obsessed with elaborate weaponry, mad Mexicans, vendettas and sub-Morricone scores. Not so much violent as brutal: there was a general prudery about showing the impact of a bullet in too much detail. There had even been an Italian actor who called himself Clint Westwood, and a Spaghetti hero named Sam Wallach.

Some of the Leone spinoffs had been made by 'serious producers or serious directors', but most were simply feeding the insatiable demand for new product, notably in areas to the south of television's broadcasting limits. Now, following the extraordinary success of Giuseppe Colizzi (whom Leone liked to style 'my protégé') with the Terence Hill/Bud Spencer partnership, the emphasis was beginning to shift away from irony, melodrama and hyperactivity towards slapstick. Enzo Barboni's *They Call Me Trinity/Lo chiamavano trinità* was a hip version of Laurel and Hardy out West, with Terence Hill as the Northern brains and Bud Spencer as the Southern brawn. On the domestic market, it made half a billion lire more than *Once Upon a Time in the West*, for a fraction of the cost. 'The cycle ended with *Trinity*,' Sergio Leone said '[Barboni's] instinct was to take these stock characters from Italian Westerns, and present them to the same audiences who had sat through four hundred ugly films. Only this time round, he would spit in their faces, make fun of them and treat them badly. Then he would have a success with them again. Psychologically, the trick worked. But it was an easy game to play.'[6] There was a touch of jealousy in this, according to Valerii: *Trinity* had dislodged Leone from his position as Italy's favourite film-maker.

But his disillusionment went far beyond the world of popular film-making. It extended to the fashion for making 'political films', and beyond that to Italian political culture, post-1968. Leone commented: 'The riots emanating from the Latin Quarter didn't surprise me in the least. Any more than the entry of Russian tanks into Czechoslovakia or the renaissance of Fascism in Italy . . . These events simply confirmed my choice of a kind of anarchy, which I showed in my films. And when I saw a new cinematic genre emerge, called "political cinema", I didn't agree with it. I didn't believe in it. For me, militant cinema ought only to be shown to members of a party.'[7]

It was a time of great instability in Italian politics. There were major inquiries into police infiltration of political parties, and into the corrupt use of public funds or 'clientelism'. Terrorism (blamed on the left, but just as often the responsibility of the right) was becoming fashionable. Socialist parties could not make up their mind whether, or on what terms, to go into alliance with the Christian Democrats: the 'Italian road to socialism' seemed to be leading nowhere. Meanwhile, neo-Fascist and far-left groups, with a bewildering variety of names, were constantly in the news. Industrial and student unrest drew attention to the fact that the 'economic miracle' had not led to much needed social reforms, which were often blocked by the representatives of big business. The Vatican opposed any liberalization of the divorce laws. For seven months, in 1969, there was no credible government in power. Disillusionment with the parliamentary process was growing.[8]

In this climate, Leone felt certain that 'consciousness-raising films' simply preached to the converted. No one else bothered to see them. Surely, he challenged, the point was to make films 'which are not national and parochial, and whose meaning can be appreciated beyond the confines of a few people in Italy'.[9] Godard had argued for a way of making political films politically, of not being suborned by capital, which was, in Leone's view, to misunderstand the very nature of film-making: it was a mass medium or it was nothing. He believed that Charlie Chaplin's work in Hollywood, forty years before, had done more for socialism than either Palmiro Togliatti or 'my friend Francesco Rosi, who ... has 1,000 spectators who came to see his films, talk about them, and that is all'.

Certain 'political films' shared Leone's pessimism about the contemporary malaise. But he felt no kinship with them, and in discussing them, would often embark upon unstoppable diatribes: 'Politics no longer makes any sense in Italy! That's why I make the films I do. We believed in mankind and mankind has let us down. Sure, the situation is the same in other countries, but somehow we are the most unlucky. Our hypocrisy and our "politics of compromise" have put us into this permanent state of crisis. As intellectuals, we have resigned ourselves, tired of the battle. What else can we think of but death? After twenty years of Fascism, we are going to have to face it again. Isn't that the most unbelievable thing in the world? We are the only country in the world to live this absurdity. They are going to win and we act like a man who cuts off his balls to punish his wife. It's the purest madness! Me, I live apart and don't give a damn about anything.'[10]

Leone was fond of evoking the notion of gods that had failed: 'At the end of the war, like many Italians, I had illusions and dreams. I believed in revolution – in the mind if not in the streets. I dreamed about a more just and humane society, where wealth was more evenly distributed. I loved history, and tracing its broad lines of development. After all, my father struggled against Fascism, he'd created the Directors' Union, and I came from a socialist family.' Leone readily admitted his material detachment from the struggle, saying, 'You can't be a communist if you own a villa.' But he was keen to demonstrate a degree of engagement: 'Let us just say that I am a disillusioned socialist. To the point of becoming an anarchist. But because I have a conscience, I'm a *moderate* anarchist who doesn't go around throwing bombs ... I mean, I've experienced just about all the untruths there are in life. So what remains in the end? The family. Which is my final archetype – handed down to us from prehistory ... What else is there? Friendship. And that is all. I'm a pessimist by nature. With John Ford, people look out of the window with hope. Me, I show people who are scared even to open the door. And if they do, they tend to get a bullet right between the eyes. But that's how it is. Politics are never absent from my films. And in the films, the anarchists are the truthful characters. I know them well, because my ideas are close to theirs.'[11] Leone's continual elisions of politics and cinema, anarchism and Ford, are telling. He seemed much more at home talking about the latter than the former. As Luciano Vincenzoni was to put it, incredulously: 'Sergio Leone . . . *and politics*?!'

The second phase of the Italian Western (roughly 1966–9) had tried to infuse political debates into popular spectaculars. Sergio Leone didn't much care for those either. To interviewers, he freely exercised his cynicism, and seemed to relish making an effect: 'Of the so-called "political" – or was it just "intelligent"? – Italian Westerns, I think I only saw one – *La resa dei Conti/The Big Gundown* [1967], which owed its title to me, having taken it from a musical theme by Morricone. Franco Solinas's story was wonderful, but it was wrecked by a stupid film.' His considered opinion was: 'To mistake such films for political films is absolutely typical of the European mentality, and it's pseudo-intellectualizing.'[12]

The cycle of political Italian Westerns had begun two years earlier. In 1966, radical screenwriter Franco Solinas (of *Salvatore Giuliano* and *The Battle of Algiers* fame) had written a treatment about a young policeman in Sardinia, working for corrupt local government bosses, who tracks down an elderly peasant, a bit of a drunk, accused of molesting a little girl. This policeman comes to realize that the accused is innocent, and has been framed on account of his left-wing political activities; but he shoots him, just the same. The lawman's concern for the political establishment and his own advancement override his sense of justice. In the film as made, *The Big Gundown*, the policeman became Acting Sheriff Lee Van Cleef, the elderly peasant a wily young Mexican called Cuchillo (played with toothsome charisma by Cuban actor Tomas Milian), and the setting shifted from contemporary Sardinia to Texas in 1871. Following advice from Sergio Leone himself, the ending had been changed beyond all recognition. Thus, Sheriff Corbett joins forces with Cuchillo for a series of final duels with the corrupt capitalists, and, after much staring and reaching for firearms, most of the baddies eventually bite the Almerian dust.

Director Sergio Sollima had adapted the treatment with a lot of help from Sergio Donati, and to his mind, 'It could have been the story of an American Green Beret against the Viet Cong, or of an English officer against a native youth at the time of British imperialism in India. The two characters were "Western", of course, but the clash of opposites was also much broader in implication ... Cuchillo worked as a character because to the audience – and especially the young audience – he seemed "one of them", rather than a cold, remote superhero such as Clint Eastwood. He was of a social class that was never talked about in Westerns.'[13]

To writers and directors based in Rome, who had their ears to the ground, the fusion of Westerns and critiques of capitalism or imperialism seemed both interesting and commercially viable. At this heady moment, according to Jean-Luc Godard's collaborator Jean-Pierre Gorin, 'every Marxist on the block wanted to make a Western'. Shortly after the events of May 1968, student leader Daniel Cohn-Bendit went to Rome and started preparing a 'left-wing Western ... about miners on strike, who fight against their masters, about the boss with his gang of thugs who attacks the workers, the workers who take over the mine, and so on'.[14] But Godard reworked the project, and turned it into the very different *Wind from the East*, as much a deconstruction of the Italian Western as the American one. A fairly uncompromising version of Cohn-Bendit's story turned up three years later, as *La collera del vento* (or *Trinity Sees Red*), made by the up-and-coming Spanish director Mario Camus. Terence Hill played an assassin hired as a strikebreaker in Southern Spain at the turn of the century, who goes native and is himself shot by his employer's thugs. The film's retitling was intended to cash in on the Hill/Spencer craze; but audiences who went to see it must have had one hell of a surprise.

The political trend had actually started in 1966 with Damiano Damiani's *Quien sabe?/A Bullet for the General*. This modest film, whose box-office success surprised even its contributors, was about the cat and mouse relationship between a taciturn Gringo called Bill Tate (Colombian actor 'Lou Castel', or rather, Luigi Castellato) and an explosive Mexican bandit-revolutionary (Gian Maria Volonté), at the time of the Mexican Revolution. As the relationship develops, the Mexican begins to grasp the meaning of the revolution, while the Gringo reveals that he's only there for the dollars. Eventually, the bandit shoots the Gringo, gives his share of their ill-gotten gains to a passing peon, and tells him to buy not bread but dynamite. Franco Solinas, who co-wrote this script too, described *Quien sabe?* as a pop version of his more prestigious work with Gillo Pontecorvo, *Battaglia di Algeri* and *Queimada*. Left-wing critics in Rome and Paris were not quite so sure: they thought this change of direction might well be a mixture of opportunism (breaking into so-called 'Third World' markets) and a defusion of 'revolutionary discourse', turning it into a brutal and spectacular circus. All these films demonstrated, wrote one critic, was that 'the heart is more human than the robot', which was no substitute for political analysis. But in the process the phrase 'political Westerns' was coined.

Damiano Damiani, who began his career with neo-realist scripts for Cesare Zavattini, was at pains to dissociate himself from the genre, saying: '*Quien sabe?* is not a Western. Whenever the critics see a horse, they think they are watching a Western . . . *Quien sabe?* is a film about the Mexican Revolution set in the Mexican Revolution, and is clearly a political film and could not be otherwise.'[15] Damiani happily pointed up the structural affinities between his film and *Queimada*, both stories of an uneasy collaboration between colonizer and colonized, which acquires revolutionary significance when the colonized throws off 'false consciousness' and strikes at his oppressor. Another veteran of neo-realist days, Carlo Lizzani, took advantage of the cycle in 1967 by making *Requiescant/Kill and Pray*. The ubiquitous Lou Castel (in Mexican make-up) is the sole survivor of a massacre on land annexed to Texas, who tracks down the misogynist, racist Confederate patriarch (Mark Damon) responsible for the deed, and who is eventually converted to the revolutionary cause by a radical gunman-priest called Don Juan, played by Pier Paolo Pasolini. 'The idea of a Western', Lizzani recalled, 'really amused Pier Paolo.'[16] Pasolini, whose sunken cheeks are reminiscent of Jack Palance's, bashes a Bible most effectively as he tells Castel, 'Our plan is to free ourselves, and this Book will bring us freedom . . . Ideas, not cattle, are the most important things that have to be changed.' He also gets the curtain line, another comment on Leone's 'cold superhero': 'Unfortunately we need men like you, for you are the most expert killer of all.'

There were other surprises in store for Southern Italian audiences: according to Sergio Corbucci, one irate customer in Sicily was so upset by the ending of his 1968 picture *Il grande silenzio/The Big Silence* (where mute hero Jean-Louis Trintignant is slaughtered in the snow by bounty-hunter Klaus Kinski) that he started shooting at the screen during the final credits. But Corbucci's other main contributions to the cycle (such as *Il mercenario/A Professional Gun* (1968) and *Vamos a matar, companeros!* (1970)) were criticized by *Cahiers* for being insufficiently committed: jokey, comic-strip movies, which paid lip service to revolutionary themes, while demonstrating that 'the revolution is really there just for fun'. More Chuck Jones than Sergei Eisenstein.

The work of Franco Solinas was of a different order. Solinas himself remembered that the starting point for all his screenplays was 'an analysis of two conflicting forces motivated by contingent rather than idealistic terms'. And as a committed member of the PCI, the political context was for him a specific one: 'They were times when European politics were stagnating for two main reasons. First, the working class was thought of as completely integrated, it seemed non-existent in relation to the revolutionary cause. Second, a deep analysis of the political situation had completely ruled out the possibility of a revolution on our continent. You can understand how the explosions of colonial contradictions, the revolutions, the armed struggles that then were erupting in the entire geography of the Third World stirred up hope as well as interest. You had come to believe that capitalism, seemingly undefeatable at home, could have been defeated once and for all in its supplying bases.' And yet Solinas put together the original treatment of Corbucci's *Il mercenario*.[17]

Did a 'deep analysis' of the causes of revolution and social banditry survive all the jokiness and spectacle? Another question was how these films, with their anti-militarism, explicit references to Fascism, and condemnation of foreign interventions in Latin America, came to be made in Franco's Spain at all. Possibly, given the genre in which the films were cast, people were simply not looking very hard. (When I asked the veteran Joaquín Romero Marchent about this, he replied, 'Westerns? Radical? I don't understand the question.'[18]) The debate about the politics of the Italian Western brought in such luminaries as Jean-Luc Godard, Simone de Beauvoir, Glauber Rocha, the critics from *Cahiers du Cinéma*, and the Vatican. Some of the participants concluded that, compared with the diffuse unease of Hollywood's 'political' films (where it is always the fault of 'the system', 'the conspiracy', 'the organization'; never social structure or economic tendencies), these films, whatever their undoubted shortcomings, at least made an analytical case – especially if Solinas had anything to do with them. They certainly attempted to shift the point of audience identification from the 'cold superhero' to Frantz Fanon's wretched of the earth. One of their most obvious shortcomings, in retrospect, was their sexual politics: the Tomas Milian character usually has a Neanderthal attitude towards his women, and the gay baddies are invariably supposed to represent the last word in decadence.

Sergio Leone grew up in a highly politicized household. But in 1968, he had no time for the 'political' or 'intelligent' Italian Western. (Previously, he had demonstrated a little more tolerance. Visiting his old friend Corbucci on the set of *Django* at Elios Studio near Madrid, he surveyed the muddy streets, the ramshackle village, and the coffin the hero drags around with him throughout the story. He reflected for a moment and said to Corbucci and Franco Nero, 'I think you are on to a winner.'[19]) Maybe he resented Sollima's dismissive comments about a 'cold, remote superhero such as Clint Eastwood'. Maybe he felt a little jealous of directors who could refer back to their real-life experiences in the Second World War. Clearly, he was now keen to distance himself from run-of-the-mill Spaghettis. After all, he had acquired an international reputation and shot a sequence in Monument Valley; he could afford to be snide about Italian or Spanish films which were confined to the deserts of 'Mexico', Latino actors and a lot of gunfire. Moreover, he was very conscious of the movie myths which had been spun 'south of the border, down Mexico way'.

Mexico tended to be presented in American cinema as a place of escape, a refuge; a noisy, exotic alternative; a place for seeking lost ideals; and (its most characteristic role in silent movies) as a breeding ground for particularly vicious bad guys. The Mexican Revolution of 1911–19 routinely provided a colourful backdrop for footloose American heroes to discover for themselves that 'a man's gotta do what a man's gotta do'. In *Viva Villa!* (Howard Hawks and Jack Conway, 1934) it was a wisecracking journalist called Johnny Sykes, standing in for John Reed, radical author of *Insurgent Mexico*; in *Vera Cruz* (1954), set in the period when Juarez was rebelling against European colonialism, it was an unscrupulous gunman and a Southern gentleman, seeking adventure after the Civil War; and in the most recent example *The Professionals* (Richard Brooks, 1966), it was four American 'weapons specialists', commissioned to rescue a tycoon's wife from 'the bloodiest cut-throat in Mexico'. *Viva Villa!* was unusual in this company, in that the focus of attention was the bandit-revolutionary Pancho Villa himself (Wallace Beery). The captions which appeared at regular intervals throughout the film revealed that the makers were definitely of the romantic tendency: 'Starting with four men who joined him at the Rio Grande, Pancho Villa entered Mexico City three months later, as a conqueror at the head of an army of 60,000.' Villa was claimed as the maker of 'a new Mexico dedicated to justice and equality. The wild heart had not fought in vain.'

It was this sort of material which the Italian Westerns were challenging. Sergio Leone said at the time that he, too, rejected 'the romance of the sombrero' in Hollywood films, but because of his disillusionment with recent political and artistic developments in Italy, he found the cinematic rebuttals of this romance equally resistible. For a while, according to Sergio Donati, he pondered Ben Hecht's *Viva Villa!* script, and considered a remake, perhaps with Toshiro Mifune in the lead. Then Claudio Mancini acquired for Rafran a treatment called *Mexico*, about a disillusioned bandit-revolutionary. Donati conceived the first draft of a new treatment, and was summoned to conference on the Almerian set of *Once Upon a Time in the West*.

'Back in Rome, I wrote a first draft based on the treatment. And Sergio was editing *Once Upon a Time in the West*. On Sunday, I came to his house and there was Claudio Mancini and Fulvio Morsella, and Mancini's partner at the time, Ugo Tucci. Three or four people, who started saying things about the first draft – the sort of fiddly things that TV executives say about scripts. And I was looking to Sergio, but he didn't care anything about it – he wasn't into the movie yet. But I felt hurt, because they said such stupid things, and I looked at Sergio expecting him to tell them, "This is right", or "This is what I think." At the end of this meal I said, "Okay then." I took my script, I spent five days making a second draft with every stupid thing that was suggested, with Sergio not saying anything. But Sergio read it, and said, "What did you do?" And I said, "I did exactly what they suggested, and you didn't intervene . . ." And he started shouting at me, and so I said, "Fuck you." '[20]

The script was set at that historical moment, after the initial excitement of the Mexican Revolution (the early successes of Villa and Zapata, President Madero's land reforms), during the chaotic period when Huerta was trying to put the revolutionary impulse into reverse. Villa and Zapata are preparing a pincer movement in Mexico City from the south and north; Huerta's downfall is imminent. The central character was a naïve Mexican peasant, a born anarchist who believes only in his family and friends, who is on direct speaking terms with God, and who thinks the worst of those involved in the great changes which are convulsing his country. This Mexican would cross the path of a professional revolutionary with a guilty past, who uses the peasant for his own purposes. Eventually, this ill-sorted couple would come to depend on one another, as the revolutionary loses his illusions but comes to appreciate friendship, and the peasant is unwittingly swept up by the revolution.

Although Leone took his time to engage with the project, eventually it would chime with his ingrained pessimism. His concern was 'not *the* Mexican Revolution, but the Revolution as a symbol, only interesting in this context because of its fame and its relationship with cinema. It's a real myth.'[21] Once upon a time there was a fairy-tale, which too many people thought was a true story, idealizing it out of existence: Leone's story would confront it with the down-to-earth values of a simple man. He and Fulvio Morsella developed the idea 'of the friendship between a Mexican peon and a revolutionary who had belonged to the IRA'.[22]

As Donati remembers, Leone's advice had been, as usual, to 'think of all the dialogues in the "Romanesco". The attitudes of these characters – they are from Ostia, Spolati, they are really people from Rome.'[23] On the basis of Donati's draft script, Leone managed to assemble an impressive international package of investors: Rafran/San Marco, Miura and United Artists. (After their unforgivable treatment of his last film, Paramount was excommunicated.) At this point, Leone hoped to bow out of proceedings, and take only an 'overseeing' role behind the scenes. But the investors would only sign the contract if he became 'the official producer'. So, very reluctantly, he agreed to 'take responsibility for it', with Morsella and Mancini. Donati had written the part of Juan the peasant especially for Eli Wallach, but, the writer recalls, 'the film was going to cost a lot and the backers wanted a "famous actor" who would draw in the punters'. Donati was not impressed by the manner in which Leone conveyed this news to Wallach. (The actor has confirmed: 'Sergio Leone and I had a falling out as a result of *Giù la testa*. It's a contractual disagreement, and neither of us has gotten to the point. It's like the Israelis and the Egyptians – some outside party's got to bring us together.'[24])

Meanwhile, Leone let it be known in interviews that he was interested in various other projects, at least some of which seem to have been pure fantasy. There was the long-cherished remake of *Gone with the Wind*; the biography of Pancho Villa; an adaptation of Céline's *Journey to the End of the Night*; and a version of *Don Quixote*, set in present-day America, in which 'America would be represented by Don Quixote, while Sancho, a European finding out about that country, would be the only truly positive character in the film.' (From

Leone's comments, Sancho Panza would be another carnivalesque character, another Tuco.) Leone also vaunted a reconstruction of the last days of Mussolini in April 1945, when Nazis, Fascists, the Vatican, the National Liberation Committee, freelance Resistance fighters and the advancing American troops were all jockeying for position in Milan, around Lake Como and on the Swiss border. Of course, no script for the Céline was ever commissioned, although Leone later claimed that the writer's widow was keen for him to go ahead with it. The updated Cervantes seems to have gone to the treatment stage. The Mussolini film was abandoned, when it was discovered that the key historical source on which Leone hoped to base the screenplay had been purchased for Carlo Lizzani.

Meanwhile, Luciano Vincenzoni inherited the Leone/Morsella treatment, and Donati's draft script. He was, on the whole, pleased to be reunited with Leone on this project: 'The subject wasn't particularly original, but Leone managed to give it a dignified dimension, a certain scale. The difference between this project and *Il mercenario* was in the resources available to the production and the actors.'

Leone started looking for a director, and United Artists recommended an up-and-coming film critic turned film-maker, thirty years old, who had recently had a modest success with the low-budget *Targets* (1968). Peter Bogdanovich had worked in theatre off-Broadway, before masterminding some influential seasons of films (Welles, Hawks, Hitchcock) at the Museum of Modern Art, transcribing the most extensive interview ever with *John Ford* (1967) while preparing a feature-length documentary called *Directed by John Ford*, assisting Roger Corman on the biker movie *The Wild Angels* (1966), and directing his own first cinema feature. *Targets* had been an impressive début, combining a charismatic performance by Boris Karloff (as an ageing master of menace, Byron Orlok) with a story about a disturbed young gun collector from San Fernando who shoots passing motorists. Bogdanovich even squeezed in some found footage from Corman's *The Terror* (1963), and a bit of film buffery about Howard Hawks. The final sequence, where the sniper was confused between the images on the screen of a drive-in cinema and the real-life Boris Karloff, was right up Leone's street. Bogdanovich was a card-carrying film buff: he claimed to have seen 5,316 films and written index cards on all of them.

So Bogdanovich duly arrived at Fiumicino airport in October 1969. It promised to be a fascinating partnership. But the next three months were to show that producer and director had very little in common. According to Leone (who elaborated the tale every time he told it, making it increasingly scurrilous) the relationship started badly and went downhill from there: 'For the first two weeks of his stay, Bogdanovich spent his time organizing screenings of *Targets* for all the pseudo-intellectual aristocracy of Rome. And also for my cinéaste friends. Nothing wrong with that, but it didn't do much for our film! We had to wait until the third week to begin developing the script. Together with Vincenzoni, I would suggest things to him. His invariable response was, "I don't like it." Okay, so let's hear what you *would* like to do. He went pale and said, "I want Mother" – that's what he called his wife [the designer Polly Platt, who was also his creative collaborator]. He claimed he couldn't work without her. I agreed to let her take part. I had lent them a beautiful villa. But I insisted on having a story in a fortnight . . . Two weeks later, Bogdanovich and his wife bring me about a dozen pages written in English. I have them translated. I read them and *I* go pale. I think the translator must have got it wrong. I hire another one, to do the work all over again. The result reveals exactly the same disaster. That was enough. I had Bogdanovich sign each page of the English version and sent it to United Artists. I attached a letter to let them know that this was the work of the man they had recommended to me. Three days later, I received this telegram from the United States: "Arrange for return of Mr and Mrs Bogdanovich to New York. IN TOURIST CLASS" . . . I showed the telegram to Bogdanovich and gave him my best wishes, advising him not to show *Targets* too often in the United States.'[25]

Peter Bogdanovich's own account, which he turned into an amusing article for *New York* magazine, was different; and, allowing for ruffled feathers, perceptive on the subject of Sergio Leone: 'With assurances from United Artists that they would welcome radical changes of the first draft of the Mexican Revolution script I had received, and firm promises that Leone would really function only as producer and therefore leave me to make the film as I saw fit, and taking into consideration that it was a free trip to Italy, where I'd never been, and bearing in mind that I hadn't made a picture for well over a year, that three projects I'd been preparing had fallen through, remembering too that a baby had just made us three . . . I accepted, you might say reluctantly.'[26]

Bogdanovich's first impression of Leone wasn't particularly encouraging: 'In those days, Sergio didn't wear a beard [he'd shaved it off since *Once Upon a Time*, only to grow it again for the shooting of the next film]; in fact, he was a rather unimpressive-looking guy – medium height, pot belly (usually with a cashmere sweater pulled down tight over it), hardly any chin to speak of. But he met me at the airport with the majesty of a Roman emperor expending a bit of largesse on a worthy, if nonetheless decidedly inferior, underling. It was subtle, the feeling behind that first meeting, but the impression was confirmed in the weeks that followed. Actually, Sergio wanted me to believe he was a great director; *he* didn't believe it, which is perhaps why it was so important that those who worked for him did.'

Leone was never at his best in airport scenes with visiting Americans, and so he did tend to overact. It was as if he was trying too hard to prove a point, on behalf of himself and maybe even Italy. This time, the urbane Vincenzoni acted as go-between: '[Vincenzoni] and I got on famously right from the start, though his job was the not very appetizing one of being translator, mediator, arbiter and scenarist all at once . . . much of our time alone together was spent in his trying to get me to be more politic with Sergio. Our script conferences were usually called for 11 a.m., at which time I would arrive at Luciano's apartment and we would wait for Sergio. Around one o'clock he would call to say he'd be a little late, so why didn't we go out and have some lunch. About three o'clock, we'd return, and Sergio would arrive promptly at four-thirty for two hours of work. After a couple of weeks of this, Sergio inexplicably presented *me* with a watch (an old one of his) – presumably to keep *him* from being late.'

Those two hours were normally spent delving into the plot, with Leone living out every moment, as Bogdanovich explained: 'Sergio would begin each sequence with a rush of English and much acting, all of which he did in the middle of the room accompanied by dramatic gestures. "Two beeg green eyes!" he would invariably begin, one hand levelled above his eyes, the other below to indicate what we would be seeing on the screen – a shot I could easily picture, as I'd seen at least a score of them in every Leone movie. "Cut!" he would continue. "Foots work!" And all attention would now focus on his feet as they moved purposefully forward. "Clink, clink," he would say, providing the sound effects for the spurs. "Cut!" he'd *yell* this time. "Hand on gun!" he'd whisper, grabbing his hip. "Cut!" Hands would zip back to frame his face. "Two beeg green eyes!" and so on, until a burst of gunfire sent him reeling into an armchair, spent and panting, both from the physical exertion so soon after eating (in Italy, and particularly with Sergio, almost any time of day is soon after eating), and the pure inspiration of the sequence itself. He and Luciano would look at me for a reaction.'

Bogdanovich was getting the strong impression that his producer expected him to shoot the film exactly as he was acting it out, which wasn't at all the arrangement he had been promised. When Dario Argento had watched the equivalent performance two years before, he had likened it to the *Divine Comedy*. This time round, the American director was less star-struck. To him, the script conferences were beginning to seem more like purgatory. In particular, there was the matter of Leone's visual style, which was completely at odds with Bogdanovich's 'classical American cinema' way of seeing: school of Hawks and Ford. A key sequence in *Targets* had shown Karloff and Bogdanovich (as a young writer called Sammy Michaels) watching Howard Hawks's *The Criminal Code* (1931) on a hotel television: now *there*, said Bogdanovich, was someone who really knew how to tell a story: 'Sergio had just begun a fresh scene – "Two beeg green eyes!" – when I interrupted to say that I wished we could discuss the action instead of the shots and, besides, I didn't like close-ups anyway. When this had been translated, there was an amazed and deflated look on Sergio's face. A long pause followed. If I didn't like close-ups, he finally asked just a bit anxiously, what *did* I like? To which I perversely replied, "Long shots." Driving back to the city [from Leone's house near Ostia, an hour away], Luciano shook his head in wonder, saying, "I think you don't want to do this picture."'

As well as technical matters, Leone wanted to discuss theme. He would sometimes 'make a dramatic and terribly serious entrance' to remind the assembled company that 'the movie we were making was really about Jesus Christ'. This insight emerged, according to Bogdanovich, from some critical articles Sergio had been reading about the hidden religious symbolism in his films (amongst these might have been a piece by the present author). Henceforward, writer and director 'had to listen to a lecture on how the Irishman in this movie . . . was really a metaphor for Christ'. Vincenzoni's take on this is that 'the real idea was that Leone was supposed to be God and James Coburn to be his son Jesus Christ. You understand what I mean?'[27] In fairness, it has to be said that Leone had for some time been talking about the presence of religious references in all of his films since *Fistful* (which is what prompted my own article).

John Ford, whose *The Informer* (1935) was one of the main sources for the character of the Irishman, had 'crucified' his protagonist and given him a symbol-drenched 'transfiguration' scene; this being a trademark of screenwriter Dudley Nichols. But to Bogdanovich, virtually anything Ford did was holy writ, while most of what Leone did had 'no poetry in it'. It was simply a case of Leone swallowing what critics were beginning to write about him. Ford had in fact admitted to Bogdanovich, in the course of their long interview of 1967, that his main criticism of *The Informer* was that 'it lacks humour – which is my forte'. Leone wasn't about to let that be said about *his* new film. As Bogdanovich related: 'The times were spent watching Sergio act out his most cherished moment in the picture, which had to do with the Mexican bandit passing wind while holding a lighted match to his posterior. Sergio particularly relished making the sound both of the initial departure of wind as well as of the subsequent one caused by the meeting of visible match and invisible gas. After acting it out in splendid detail, Sergio would collapse in sad exhaustion in his chair, shaking his head about the pity of not being able to do this on the screen, at the same time threatening to do it anyway.'[28]

Peter Bogdanovich disputed Leone's version of events in nearly every particular. Leone talked as though *Targets* was as yet unreleased, when in fact it had done the rounds over a year before. By Bogdanovich's account, he was never hired as a writer, so never physically wrote a thing; Leone could not have rejected his draft treatment, because no such document was requested. And Leone did not 'fire' him – although he was probably poised to, when Bogdanovich ran for cover. But he certainly did recall Leone and Vincenzoni putting assorted ideas to him, to which he would indeed usually reply 'I don't like it'. His conclusion about these difficulties was that Leone really wanted to direct the film himself, but was too insecure to take full responsibility for it. Unconsciously, to be charitable about it, he was trying to engineer a situation where he would be forced to take the helm himself. As Bogdanovich explained it: 'If the picture then turns out to be a bomb, he has the excuse that it was not really his plan to make this one, and that he'd been forced to come in and do the best he could, at the same time postponing the major work he was preparing [*Once Upon a Time in America*]. When all those critics and people say you're good and you don't really believe it, at some point perhaps the thought of being found out becomes overwhelming and you would rather retire undefeated than face failure. Actually, if this perhaps presumptuous deduction is true, it is a considerable pity, because Leone is often a very good director.'

By the time Bogdanovich came on to the scene, the title of the project had changed from the original 'Once Upon a Time, the Revolution'. 'The Italian partners rejected my original title,' Leone recalled. 'I had to change it to *Giù la testa*, which means, "Keep Your Head Down", but also, "Get Out of the Way", so that the title takes on a very precise social connotation.' It was also a fair summary of Leone's own political credo in the late 1960s. As he was to tell Italian journalist Diego Gabutti: 'I really didn't want to make a eulogy to revolution as was presented for example in *Quien sabe?* by Damiano Damiani, filmed with a lot of passion but whose ideology suddenly seemed old and formulaic like the prayer of a medieval mystic. No. We had in mind a sort of social comedy, where a very unimportant character, almost naïve, is going through a different kind of story without knowing and without even seeing what is happening around him.'[29]

Leone hoped that audiences would discern 'the shadow of my humour and my own delusions'. He had planned an animated sequence under the opening credits: 'On the screen would be a big map of America, then a dizzying zoom would isolate the boundaries of Mexico, ringed with red fire. Desert, cactus, mountains. A peasant dressed in rags is working in the arid land, and behind him a white thread is moving like a snake across the fields. We follow this white thread with the camera, until we reach an enormous hand in huge close-up which plunges a detonator attached to the thread. "Giù la Testa, coglione," says a quiet voice out of frame. Then, "Boom!" There is a series of shattering explosions. The smoke envelops the cactus and the mountains, and when it clears, we see a completely flattened horizon. Then the peon comes out from behind a pyramid of stones, looks around in a stupefied way, shrugs, and starts again to move some earth with a plough as if nothing had happened.' This, Leone argued, would encapsulate the 'political message' of the film: 'You never know. You can't control events around you.'[30]

Instead, the finished film began with a quotation from Mao Tse Tung (cut from American and English prints), in capital letters on a black background:

> THE REVOLUTION
> IS NOT A SOCIAL DINNER,
> A LITERARY EVENT,
> A DRAWING OR AN EMBROIDERY;
> IT CANNOT BE DONE WITH
> ELEGANCE AND COURTESY.
> THE REVOLUTION IS AN ACT OF VIOLENCE

Mao's original quotation ended with the words 'by which one class overthrows another'. For fairly obvious reasons, Leone abridged it. After this preface, we see a colony of ants coming up a tree, and (from offscreen) someone urinating over them. There is a sound of flatulence, played on a bassoon, and a phrase from Morricone's musical theme, 'The March of the Beggars'. As the camera pans to the left, we then see two shoeless feet, and the silhouette of a man shaking his penis. Then, up to the face of the Mexican peasant Juan Miranda – and the noise of an explosion in the distance, to which he listens for a moment; an echo of whistling; and the main title theme 'Sean, Sean, Sean'. This is an anarchic variation on the children playing with scorpions and ants at the beginning of Sam Peckinpah's *The Wild Bunch*, with a hint of the friendship that will drive the film. The original version of the film ends with Juan turning to the audience, his plaintive voice-over exclaiming, 'What about me?': the words GIÙ LA TESTA emerge from his face, and loom large on the screen. Thus, 'Keep your head down' is the lesson; don't get involved. The title theme swells, the end credits roll. So the film opens with a poor peon who doesn't give a damn: it closes with a primitive rebel whose involvement in the revolution has destroyed everything he holds dear. 'The Irishman', Leone explained, 'has given a conscience to the Mexican, which makes him a lost soul for ever.'

Ironically, the Italian distributor thought Leone's original choice of title might cause confusion with Bertolucci's *Prima della rivoluzione*. However, it was retained for the French release. In England it became *A Fistful of Dynamite*. In America it opened as *Duck, You Sucker* and assumed the English title after poor box-office returns. Peter Bogdanovich had endless rows with Leone about that original US title: 'He said it was an Americanization of some well-known Italian expression: "Giù la testa, coglione" – meaning literally, "Duck your head, balls" which he wanted to use as the Italian title, only with the "coglione" bit left out. And he insisted that "Duck, you sucker" was a common American expression. I said to him, "They don't say that *ever*, Sergio, *anywhere* in America." "No. It is a big expression in America." Eye-block. He seemed to think I couldn't be a real American at all if I hadn't heard of it. "Dock You Socker," he kept on saying.'[31]

In conversation with me ten years after the event, Bogdanovich's comments revealed that his attitude to Leone (like that of the screenwriters) had hardened considerably: 'I'm not a big Leone fan, although I think he's a very good director. I think . . . he's as big a jerk-off as Spielberg or Lucas or any of them – all of whom are simply making movies they grew up with, over again.'[32]

Bogdanovich went further in his critique: 'Leone's pictures are cynical, which Ford never was. And there's no poetry in them. The problem is they do in a way reflect a change in American mythology: and they're rather Fascist in implication.' He felt they suffer from a fatal absence of Ford's concern for the maintenance and protection of family, home, tradition and future: 'In Leone's pictures, there is no future; it's just killing.' Of course, Leone often said (and even wrote) of Ford that his sense of community, albeit an isolated community, was the key to his films. Crucially, however, Ford, as a grateful first-generation Irish immigrant, took an optimistic view of the land. 'Oh, Ford understood what America was about before Leone was even born,' Bogdanovich claimed. 'And now, in his grave, he understands more than Leone will ever know.' What he finds most persuasive in Leone's films is their sense of humour, which he attributes to the contributions of Vincenzoni. What he finds least attractive is *Once Upon a Time in the West*'s riot of Western homages: 'That's the one I didn't like at all . . . I just *hate* "references" like that . . . it's completely arid. It's like critics talking to each other. And the film buffs don't make much of an audience.' Vincenzoni's retrospective verdict on the Leone/Bogdanovich affair was: 'I was in the middle because I was the diplomat, but it was impossible. After his enormous success, naturally Leone became a little arrogant . . . [Bogdanovich] is a friend. I wanted him to direct this film and I tried very hard. But, no way. It all happened at my house, actually.'[33]

After Bogdanovich's departure, Leone waited for United Artists to suggest a replacement, and Sergio Donati was brought back on to the team to help adapt Vincenzoni's version of the script. He recalls: 'Fulvio called me after about six months, and said, as usual, "With Sergio, it was a misunderstanding." "It was not a misunderstanding, Fulvio," I replied. "I can't stand this because I can't work this way." "No, come on, come on," he said. So I came back, despite the "fuck you" situation. And we stayed in this room with Sergio for a few days ... Having completed the final shooting script, I said, "Cheque, please." And he said, "Oh, what if you have copied the telephone directory?" I said, "Okay, maybe I have. Bye, Sergio." And I had deposited the script at the Italian Writers' Guild. I said, "If you want the script, it's there." He got the script from a lawyer. This was what we were reduced to at the end. So bad.' Donati reflects somewhat wistfully on this tempestuous collaboration: 'You see, when I told him of the first draft, and we had the bar-room brawl, and we got to the "fuck you" stage, six months passed for the work of Vincenzoni and Bogdanovich, and at the end he was unsatisfied, like with Argento and Bertolucci, and he called me back. And he knew that I was the guy. But he never was clever enough to understand that I needed him just to say, "Bravo!" Never once.' Maybe Leone needed Donati to say 'Bravo' as well, I asked him. 'Maybe,' he replied.[34]

By this stage, Leone was to say, with characteristic drama, the whole project seemed to be grinding to a halt, despite the fact that 'the time booked for shooting and construction was drawing closer'. Leone felt that United Artists were 'dragging their heels about choosing a director'. According to Bogdanovich, UA were now referring to Leone as 'Benito', albeit never to his face. And there were lengthy negotiations between Rome and Hollywood about casting. Eli Wallach was out. Jason Robards was in, as the Irishman Mallory, then out. Malcolm McDowell, of *If* ... fame, was in, 'because the men of the IRA were very young'. At one stage, as Clint Eastwood informed an American Film Institute seminar, he was offered a major part: it must also have been that of the Irishman. The producers were even prepared to 'shoot it in Mexico', if it made the project more attractive to him. But he declined. ('The film was nice,' said a film student at the seminar. 'Was it? I didn't see it,' replied Eastwood.)

'It was then', Leone recalled, 'that I joined Sam Peckinpah in London. We hit it off well. He was thrilled to be making a film which I would be producing. He gave me his agreement. I was delighted. I knew the impact our two names together would have on a poster. So I let United Artists know. To my surprise, they seemed put out. They didn't challenge the idea. But they wanted to have more talks.'[35] But Vincenzoni maintains Peckinpah never accepted in the first place, being too shrewd to accept another director as his producer: 'Especially if this producer is a man who is arrogant and uncultured like Sergio Leone . . . They would have killed each other.' According to Vincenzoni, Leone later expressed his hurt feelings about Peckinpah by placing his name on a gravestone in *My Name is Nobody*: 'He wanted to say with that scene, "Leone put Peckinpah in the grave, because Leone is better than Peckinpah." '[36]

As a fall-back, Leone even considered Vincenzoni as a possible candidate, but the writer sensibly declined, saying, 'Sergio, you would always be sitting on my shoulders.'[37] The Italian producers then had the idea of promoting assistant director Giancarlo Santi, who had worked closely with Leone on *The Good, The Bad and The Ugly* and *Once Upon a Time in the West*. According to Bogdanovich and Donati, Santi did in fact start to direct the film, but after a brief period of 'Leone's pushing buttons on his Italian surrogate, the stars refused to accept the situation'. Leone recalled Santi's directorial contribution as lasting for 'the first ten days', after which he took over extensive second-unit work on the big action sequences. Donati puts it at nearer one day. 'The first day the director was Giancarlo Santi – and then Rod Steiger came. Sergio said, "Santi is just like me – he's like I am behind the camera." And Rod Steiger said, "Okay then, tomorrow I'll send someone else in and explain everything to him, and he'll be just like me on the set." And he called Hollywood. And the day after, Sergio Leone began directing the film.'[38]

Leone's retrospective interpretation of all this palaver was that United Artists wanted him to direct the film from the outset: 'They were treating me like a puppet on a string, from the moment we originally signed our agreement.' He felt there was a secret 'plot' by all concerned to put him in a position where he had no choice but to accept: 'We were a week away from shooting; the crew had already gone to Spain when they told me that the actors had asked why I couldn't direct it. Even my family was involved in the plot.' Carla Leone, not surprisingly, denies any knowledge of a 'plot', saying, 'he really didn't want to direct this film; he was already thinking of a different kind of cinema. I think he meant it.'[39] The most likely scenario is that UA took the line of least resistance to save the project. Sergio Leone then found himself having to customize the script all over again, with Sergio Donati, to suit his particular way of working. His films since *Fistful* had been the result of meticulous preparation in advance. Now, he recollected, 'a couple of days before the start of the shooting, I found myself in a situation conceived for an American film-maker. I had to adapt myself as I went along.'

Nevertheless, Leone had been deeply involved in every stage of the scripting process, and as a result the screenplay was already full of his obsessions. As in *The Good, The Bad and The Ugly*, there were to be overt references to the two world wars, to expand the implications of the story well beyond its specific historical setting. As Leone explained: 'Mexico became a pretext to evoke wars and revolutions. In certain sequences, I signal events from other places and other times: the flight of the king [or Governor Don Jaime]; an 8 September [the Grotto of San Isidro, resembling the Fosse Ardeatine, where Juan's family is massacred]; the ditches and death pits of Dachau and Matthausen [where Reza's men under Huerta's orders slaughter hundreds of Mexican civilians]. I even chose a face resembling the young Mussolini and dressed him up in a uniform [the soldier who dresses up as a priest in order to desert and escape, but who is recaptured and shot against a wall, who was played by 'an engineer']. These are signs which are there to connote all wars and revolutions. Whether in Ireland, or Spain, or wherever. Here, the Mexican Revolution is only a symbol. Not the *historical* one. It only interested me in relation to cinema: Pancho Villa, *La Cucaracha*.'[40]

Other examples of historical cross-referencing include the reactionary and brutal Colonel Gunter Reza, who is presented like a Nazi tank commander; the cattle-wagon, belonging to the Ferro Carril de Mexico, clearly intended to look like the vehicles which transported Jewish victims to their doom in Poland; and the local revolutionary units, with their hit-and-run tactics and encampments in the hills, which refer to the Resistance of 1943–5. The behaviour of the agents of Huerta's regime, clinging on to power for dear life, mirrors the decadence and cruelty of the last days of Fascism (soon to become a cinematic mythology in itself, with Pasolini's *Salo* of 1975). 'But at the heart of the film, and my essential motivation, was the theme of friendship which is so dear to me,' revealed Leone. 'You have two men: one naïve and one intellectual (self-centred as intellectuals too often are in the face of the naïve). From there, the film becomes the story of Pygmalion reversed. The simple one teaches the intellectual a lesson. Nature gains the upper hand and finally the intellectual throws away his book of Bakunin's writings. You suspect damn well that this gesture is a symbolic reference to everything my generation has been told in the way of promises.'⁴¹

Céline's *Journey to the End of the Night* also seems to have had a decisive influence on the script; unsurprisingly, given Vincenzoni's involvement. Céline had written, of the anti-hero Ferdinand's visit to a New York bank: 'When the faithful enter their bank, you mustn't think they can take what they want for themselves as they please. Not at all. They communicate with Dollar, murmuring to him through a little grille; in fact, they make their confession.'

When Juan first describes the fabled bank at Mesa Verde to Sean, he gushes, 'You see it has the gates of gold like it was the gates of heaven – and when you are going inside, *everything* is gold.' He imagines that Sean has a halo hovering over him with the sacred words 'Banco Nationale Mesa Verde' written across it. He has built a votive altar inside the stolen stagecoach, where, beneath an effigy of the Virgin Mary, is a childlike drawing of the entrance to the bank. When Juan and family reach the bank (looking like snap-happy tourists), he imagines that the window above the entrance has turned into a golden version of the Exposition of the Blessed Sacrament, with the Host at its centre. But he doesn't kneel, and the nervous clenching and unclenching of his hands reveals he can't wait to get hold of all that gold. The Irishman's nitroglycerine which will help him he calls 'holy water'; and indeed Sean consecrates a drop of it on Juan's makeshift altar.

Céline had also written of the grotesque attitudes of the colonial administrators and businesspeople who are busy embezzling the profits of the trading stations in French Africa. Their chief topics of conversation seem to be the promiscuity of the natives, whether or not they happen to be cannibals, and their vexing ignorance of all things French. This section could well have inspired the early sequence of *Giù la testa*, set in a huge and luxurious stagecoach, where Juan is abused by the bigoted passengers: a cardinal, a landowner and his wife, a lawyer, and an American businessman from the deep South. The Mexican peasantry are royally patronized ('after all, they have won a revolution, or at least almost'), and execrated as lowly animals 'living in a heap, like rats in a sewer'. 'It was to benefit scum like this,' says one of the travellers, 'that the agrarian reform was imposed. And that ass Madero wanted to give the government and our land to idiots like this.' The visualization of this display of raw prejudice by a cross-section of the bourgeoisie is a montage of uncomfortable close-ups of faces, eyes, and mouths having food stuffed into them, such that the mouths come to resemble unwiped anuses. This is a cinematic equivalent of Céline's raw prose, which also owes a lot to Eisenstein.

As in *The Good, The Bad and The Ugly*, Leone reworked a scene from Charlie Chaplin. Juan attempts to rob the bank, only to discover that it is full of political prisoners; a reference to the scene in *Modern Times* where the tramp picks up a red flag which has fallen off a lorry and unwittingly finds himself at the head of a workers' demonstration. Juan dynamites himself into the street, where a crowd of the dispossessed rushes forward through the smoke to lift him shoulder-high and shout 'Viva Miranda!' 'You're a grand hero of the revolution now,' Sean laughingly informs him. 'All I want is the money,' he unsurprisingly responds. Another cinematic reference-point was *Viva Villa!* In that film, Villa orders a scribe to draw an image of him on a letter he is dictating to one of his many brides-to-be: 'You do as I tell you, you draw a great big bull.' This becomes a running gag (later he will steal a silver sculpture of a bull from the royal palace in Mexico City), and also gives particular irony to Villa's death outside a butcher's shop ('a funny place to die'). In *Giù la testa*, Juan speaks of Villa to Sean: 'The best bandit chief in the world – this man had two balls like the bull. He went into the revolution as a great bandit. When he came out, he came out as what? Like nothing like a general. That to me is the bullshit.' This prompts its own running gag about *cojones* and generals. Juan stays with his reckless Irish friend at the stone bridge in the desert, when all the professional revolutionaries think it is far too dangerous, because he has convinced himself it is really a test of his manhood ('You think you are the only man in the world who has the balls to stay. Well you are wrong'). In the final exchange between Sean and Juan, as the Irishman lies dying, Juan says, 'You leave me now and what's going to happen to me, huh?' 'They'll make you general,' replies Sean. 'I DON'T WANT TO BE NO GENERAL,' comes the retort.

Juan is unmistakably carnivalesque: he swears a lot, profanes sacred symbols, crosses himself and looks up to heaven just before machine-gunning people, shovels food into his mouth with both hands and introduces his extended family to one of the profiteers on the stage-coach with the words: 'You wanted to know my family? That's my sons, each of them from a different mother . . . My mother [who was a whore], she had the blood of the Aztecs, which was before your people.' This reminder that European colonization goes back a very long way is followed by a crude demonstration by Juan that he is just as well endowed as Pancho Villa. He asks the bespectacled landowner, 'Can you make a baby?' The man shakes his head. 'That's sad, but we'll fix that. SENORA!' The landowner's wife descends from the coach, and is led across a cobbled threshing circle towards a farmhouse: a reference to the very different 'settling of accounts' in earlier Leone films. Juan uses a stick to goad her into a cowshed. A cock crows. He looks her up and down, lasciviously. In the Italian version, he then exposes his penis (albeit out of shot), at which she stares in utter amazement. 'Just pretty good, huh?' he asks. As a cow moos on the soundtrack, he takes her decorated hat off and presses himself against her. She looks up at the roof and sighs, 'Oh Jesus! Help me! I'm going to faint.' 'No, you faint now and you miss the *best* part,' comes the reply. Cut to a naked male bottom in close-up, as Juan's children strip the inhabitants of the coach. The woman (who earlier fantasized about peasants 'living in such promiscuity', as she popped another cherry into her mouth) is about to have her worst fears (or secret fantasies) confirmed; and Juan is about to get his revenge. It is a difficult scene to watch. Yet Leone would explain his motive for the scene with perfect insouciance: 'I replaced a spectacle of heroes in the arena with a vulgar and trivial incident.'[42]

But as the story progresses, under the influence of Sean, Juan's attitudes change. In one of the pivotal sequences of the film, when he discovers that his family has been massacred in the grotto, he throws away the crucifix he has always dutifully worn round his neck and starts weeping. For once, he can't find the words: 'All of them. Six. I never counted them before.' In the Italian print, we don't see what he sees – only the reaction on his face, which makes the sequence all the more powerful. Juan then rushes out to face Reza's men, a machine-gun in his hand. This time, he doesn't look up to God. Later, when Juan is offered a case of jewels and money in exchange for the Governor's life, he will decide to shoot the Governor and show only a casual interest in the jewels – not an impulsive decision (he mulls over the massacre in his mind) but a considered one. Revenge, he has come to realize, is a dish best eaten cold. Throughout the film, indeed, the violence is carefully weighed up and, by Leone's standards, very restrained. Only in the combat sequences, and in particular the machine-gunning of Gunther Reza (trimmed in the American and British prints) is there the usual 'dance of death'. So Leone's customary *picaro* is an uncommonly complex figure here. He seems to be out of place wherever he happens to be: in the stagecoach, at Mesa Verde, in the revolutionary meeting. He only looks at ease with his family. But then he realizes that great historical events are not happening somewhere else. He builds a close relationship with Sean, and develops as a result of it. Through the serious trouble into which he is then led, he moves from stereotype to human being, from actor on the puppet stage to life-sized person. This makes him a first in Leone's cinema.

Sean, too, grows as a character. A cutting from *The United Irishman*, discovered by Juan on his motorbike, tells us (though not Juan, who is illiterate) that the British Government has placed a £300 bounty on his head. Juan happily assumes Sean is a fellow bandit, though the latter is diffident about the nature of the trouble he is in ('Oh we had a wee fart of a revolution in Ireland'). Sean is an explosives expert. So instead of the usual gun duel, there is much cat and mouse business involving dynamite and nitroglycerine. He carries his equipment – short fuse, medium fuse, long fuse – inside the lining of his long duster coat ('If you pull that trigger and shoot me, I fall, and if I fall, they'll have to alter all the maps. You see when I go half this bloody country goes with me. Including yourself'). However, he is a disillusioned rebel. He drinks too much: in the Italian version, he is so paralytic in one sequence that he is incapable of operating his detonator, so Juan has to blow up the mine-owner Aschenbach and his escort of soldiers by putting his foot on the handle. He also smokes dope, and behaves like a suicidal dilettante, saying things like: 'If it's a revolution, it's confusion' and 'When I started using dynamite, I believed in many things . . . finally I believe only in dynamite.'

For much of the story, he manipulates the naïve Juan. But unlike the double-crosses of the earlier films, this manipulation leads to personal tragedy, and Sean learns something from it. In a very touching scene in the cattle-wagon, he realizes the depth of Juan's grief, and begins to recall a time when he, too, was capable of experiencing the normal range of emotions. In the final slow-motion flashback, he fantasizes about an idyllic moment in rural Ireland, when he was young, in love, and with his ideals intact: Juan, who is somehow in synch with this fantasy, instinctively turns to look at his friend. The Irishman has just confessed to his Mexican partner, as he shows him the crucifix he has kept since the grotto massacre, 'Oh my friend. I did give you a royal screwing.' Juan shakes his head, as if to signal, 'No, don't say that.'

Sean, mortally wounded in the spine, then blows himself up, in a variation on Jean-Luc Godard's *Pierrot le Fou*, a film which Leone judged 'a masterpiece: when cinematic researches lead to such perfection and such emotion, I really am profoundly respectful.'[43] In *Pierrot*, Ferdinand (Jean-Paul Belmondo), having wrapped his face in multi-coloured sticks of dynamite and lit the fuse, then changes his mind and fumbles for the burning tip: 'how stupid!' are his last words. In *Giù la testa*, Sean takes a deep drag on his joint of marijuana which doubles as a detonator, smiles and relaxes into his idyllic fantasy just before the huge explosion. Ferdinand's gesture is impetuous and pointless: Sean's is calculated; he has been deliberately dicing with death ever since the two men met.

The betrayals in this story have serious consequences, such as that of Dr Villega (Romolo Valli), the intellectual strategist tortured by Reza into giving away his co-conspirators. This also marks a development in Leone. As he was to put it, Villega's action is not 'a farcical form of treachery like in *The Good, The Bad and The Ugly*. Sean's war consequently becomes an individual act, without political ideology. When Juan barges into Sean's suicidal gesture in front of the bridge, he unwittingly prevents him from dying alone. The very worst thing that could happen is that they will, as a result, escape death. And the people they are protecting will be exterminated! Because of an action which is completely mad. I love the dark irony of that.'[44]

Villega's betrayal leads to a firing squad in the rain, lit by candles and looking like Goya's painting *The 3rd of May in Madrid*. It also leads to the final stage of Sean's self-realization, as he forces Villega to atone for his guilt by taking part in another suicidal gesture. The intellectual is now expected to get his hands dirty by shovelling coal on a locomotive packed with dynamite which will collide with Reza's troop train. Villega senses his motive, and makes a desperate defence of his forced action: 'It's easy to judge. Have you ever been tortured? Are you sure you wouldn't talk? I was sure. And yet I talked.' His protests are angrily cut short by Sean, and as the locomotive hurtles towards its explosive destination, the Irishman urges him to bail out ('Just close your eyes and jump . . . For Christ's sake save yourself'). But Villega just closes his eyes.

The key to Sean's character is contained in a series of flashbacks to his time as a young IRA man. In the first he is motoring through the Irish countryside: a dark-haired colleen in the back seat takes off his hat, and they kiss, while their friend behind the wheel smiles approvingly. Then, the two men are busy distributing copies of a broadsheet called 'Irish Freedom' in a Dublin pub. Then (coinciding with Sean's recognition of Villega, 'that night in the rain'), Sean is drinking at a Dublin bar when a policeman and two British soldiers appear with the friend, who has been severely beaten up: the soldier points to various individuals in the pub, and the friend nods. Sean watches them anxiously in a mirror. He turns round, with a Lee Enfield rifle wrapped in newspaper . . . just as the Mexican firing squad opens fire.

At the moment on the locomotive when Sean tells Villega to 'shut up for Christ's sake', we are transported back to that bar: the two soldiers are shot, and the friend looks Sean in the eye and begins to smile. But he, too, is shot; as he collapses, we hear Sean tell Villega, 'I don't judge you . . . I did that only once in my life. Get shovelling.' The last flashback is that marijuana-stoked reminiscence, in which he fantasizes his younger self, the girl and his friend running happily through the Irish countryside: the girl leans against a tree and Sean kisses her, then the friend begins to kiss her too. His reverie is broken only by the huge, map-altering explosion, and Juan's shout of 'Johnny!'

Leone noted that, in many countries, the last flashback to 'the two Irishmen sharing the same woman' was excised, which irritated him considerably. 'This wasn't just libertarianism and free love; there was also a symbolic dimension. This woman represented the revolution everyone wanted to embrace. And Sean sees these images while smoking his strange cigarette. You don't know if he's dreaming, imagining or remembering . . . And I inserted the scene in such a way that Juan also sees Sean's phantasm . . . So they are together again, just before the Irishman blows up.'[45]

The cinematic origin of these flashbacks was, of course, John Ford's *The Informer*, in which the shambling drunkard Gypo Nolan (Victor McLagen) wanders through the expressionist fog of a studio-bound Dublin in 1922 and betrays his friend Frankie McPhillip to the police in exchange for the blood-money which will pay for his passage to America. Leone and Vincenzoni ran the film while working on the screenplay. *The Informer*, taken from a 1925 novel by Ford's distant cousin Liam O'Flaherty, was based on an actual incident of November 1923, during the Irish Civil War which followed the treaty with the British. Ford's film distils the novel into a simple morality tale with many sentimental songs; Nolan is presented as a confused simpleton who is 'as strong as any bull'. *The Informer*, famously, scarcely refers to the IRA, known throughout as 'the Organization'. Sergio Leone's reworking of Ford's film retains the theme of betrayal, but shifts the emphasis from the traitor to the avenger, one wholly devoid of forgiveness in him. Moreover, it is quite explicit about what exactly 'the Organization' is.

For the rural flashback sequences, *Giù la testa* raided Ford's later and more relaxed film *The Quiet Man* (1952), which tells of the return of another Sean (John Wayne) to a windswept cottage near the village of Innisfree, set in an impossibly green landscape and filmed in and around Cong, County Mayo. Leone borrowed the greenery, the name of Sean, and a dose of Fordian sentiment. He didn't hesitate, however, to take Ford to task for his 'shameful' attachment to a postcard Ireland ('He has the sentimentality of the Irish living in the United States who still believe in green prairies extending into the future'), and his historical oversight ('he made up a fairy-story where there was no reference at all to the IRA, and he shows that country as if it was a utopian paradise'[46]). In their excitement, Leone and his screenwriters seem to have forgotten that the IRA was not formed until 1919, when Michael Collins revived the almost moribund Irish Republican Brotherhood. Leone observed that 'the men of the IRA were very young': in 1913, they would have been very young indeed! In *Giù la testa*, events of 1922 are transposed to at least nine years earlier, in a visual set of references which are more cinematic than historical, and which perhaps chimed in the scriptwriters' minds with the 'troubles' in the North post-1968.

Since the script packed in such a cluster of Leone obsessions, it was wildly over-dramatic of him to claim that he had to 'rewrite everything' at the very last minute. His two writers confirm that the script had already been given a very large dose of Leone. As Vincenzoni recalls, he was most insistent that the carriage in which Juan is humiliated should be luxurious and authentic, a 'masterpiece of carpentry' stacked with 'original Louis Vuitton suitcases' and 'a lavatory, like in the old sleeper carriages'. Similarly, certain scatological details were to bear the Leone stamp: 'The idea of Juan pissing at the beginning of the film was one of Sergio's ideas; this is a game he played as a child . . . Another thing which Sergio was very attached to was the scene in which [Juan] is in the cattle-truck, and sitting underneath a bird's cage. At a certain point the bird shits on his head. He looks up at it and says, "But for the rich, you sing." '[47]

Sergio Donati joined Leone and Vincenzoni for a private screening of the final cut, and felt that it bore little resemblance to his first version. He and Vincenzoni 'wrote a ten-page letter suggesting cuts . . . and Sergio was very offended by the way we wrote'. As someone who felt considerable excitement about the political ferment of 1968, Donati viewed Leone's use of the celebrated Mao Tse Tung quotation with distaste; it was, he felt, 'a provocation . . . Sergio was a kind of "qualunquista", as we call it, and his film was full of rhetoric. Noncommittal. *Giù la testa* is a film I don't like very much.'[48] Vincenzoni adds that in the aftermath of *Giù la testa*, 'Leone and I had another fight, and after that we never worked together again'.[49]

Again, the main musical themes of the film were written in advance as a 'preliminary version' by Ennio Morricone. As usual, these were to be featured 'internally' in the film itself: Sean whistles a few bars from his tune (albeit offscreen) to signal to Juan that he is about to rescue him from Reza's firing squad – and Juan somehow recognizes it. The raid on the bank of Mesa Verde is edited to Morricone's 'March of the Beggars' – with 'quotes' from Mozart's *Eine Kleine Nachtmusik* every time Juan opens another door in the vaults to discover yet more political prisoners crammed inside. For the end titles ('After the Explosion') the soprano solo which up to then has been part of the arrangement of Sean's theme and the insistent choral refrain of 'Sean, Sean, Sean' have both gone, leaving just the orchestral backing which underpinned them: Sean's suicide thus has its musical equivalent. But there is far less of this than in *Once Upon a Time in the West*, which might suggest that the by-now customary partnership between Leone and his composer during the preparatory stages was less close this time round, perhaps because the project had not settled down.

In 1969–70, Ennio Morricone was a very busy man indeed: he recorded over twenty-five soundtracks. On the sleeve of the Italian disc of *Giù la testa*, Leone wrote a postcard to him on this topic: 'I have seen you sleep on benches at school. I have heard you snore on the editing table, but this music is so beautiful, these sounds so magnificent, I wonder when you could have composed them?' This was a tease which fast became a Leone favourite. He enjoyed informing interviewers and dinner guests, 'Morricone is a man who works very hard indeed. He gets up at six o'clock in the morning. Unhappily, he sleeps from nine in the evening. And sometimes in the recording studio.' He liked to add that on one occasion Morricone fell asleep during a recording session; Leone woke him by turning the console microphone up to

332

full volume, and booming, 'Ennio! Aren't you ashamed to be sleeping?' At which point Morricone was convinced he had heard the voice of God. Well, that was the story; to which the intense maestro Morricone has replied: 'The interviewer must have noted or translated the words "recording studio" wrongly – because I can't possibly sleep standing up while directing an orchestra! When this story happened, we were dubbing Leone's film. I could easily have stayed at home and slept in my bed.'[50]

There were fewer musical variations than usual in *Giù la testa*, and much more emphasis on Edda dell'Orso's voice and Cantori Moderni: the choir even sang words which mattered, while simultaneously turning them into 'sounds'. The main theme, associated with Sean, was lyrical and slow, with soft whistling by Alessandroni. It was played, against the image, during the sequence where the two men blow up the bridge, as if Sean was remembering the good old days back in Ireland. In forgoing a more high-energy musical accompaniment to this spectacular scene, Leone was saying that he no longer had to show off about his elaborate action sequences. The theme was also played for the flashbacks, and, according to Carla Leone, it was she who first suggested the words 'Sean, Sean, Sean' – rather than the original 'wah, wah, wah' – at one of the early conversations around the piano. Juan and his family are associated with the jaunty 'March of the Beggars', with bassoon, flageolet and military drum leading each verse. Morricone has recalled: 'For this march, because I had made use of some elements which were a little vulgar – for instance some farting sounds (the absurd thing was to put stomach sounds in a march that was supposed to be of hungry people) – because of this it seemed right to add something a bit more elegant like Mozart.'[51]

Brief quotes from the march were used in the first half of *Giù la testa* to punctuate visual gags involving the bad behaviour of the Miranda clan: it was played in full for the parade of the stagecoach party – stripped naked by Juan's overexcited boys – as they stumble towards a farm wagon which will be tipped up into the slurry of a pigsty (a punchline which was trimmed on international release); and for the raid on the bank of Mesa Verde, where, edited to match Juan's changing facial expressions – surprise, exasperation, rage – and building to a crescendo as the number of prisoners standing behind him swells to a total of 150, it represents the most successful fusion of music and (dialogue-free) image in the entire film. Musicologist Sergio Miceli related the 'incontinent humans . . . and mockery of quoting Mozart' to avant-garde Italian painting of the same period; Morricone acknowledged that some aspects of the score contained 'things that are appropriate to the activities of the Nuova Consonanza group'.[52]

Leone made some significant additions to the script as he 'went along' in filming. One was the discussion between Sean and Juan about 'revolution', in their tent at the rebels' encampment. Sean breaks off some reading to chide Juan about his indifference to 'this little revolution we're having here'. Juan erupts in indignation: 'I know all about the revolutions and how they start. The people that read the books, they go to the people that don't read the books – the poor people – and say, "Ho-ho, the time has come to have a change" . . . so the poor people make the change, eh? And the people that read the books, they all sit around the polished table, and they talk and talk, and eat and eat. And what happens to the poor people? They're DEAD! That's your revolution.' Sean reflects for a moment, considers the book he has been reading, and throws it into the mud outside the tent. The cover reads Michael A. Bakunin: *The Patriotism* (a careless translation, unusual for Leone). We cut to the wheel of an army lorry; then a soldier picks up the book from where it landed. He passes it on to his captain, who in turn hands it to Colonel Reza, who turns the pages with his gauntleted fingers. The people that read the books . . .

This exchange harks back to Juan's earlier outburst about Pancho Villa, but Leone wanted to expand the argument and so composed this fresh scene during filming. 'That is the moment where the real conflict between the two breaks out. When the naïve man gives a lesson to the intellectual . . . And I introduced the idea that the Nazi finds this anarchist book in the mud. And he knows who Bakunin is! This gesture of rejection shows all my disillusionment.'[53]

It also gives Reza a clue that he is on the right track; like Blondie's cigar stubs in *The Good, The Bad and The Ugly*. More importantly, it reveals Leone's mixed feelings about the 'intellectuals' of the film world – how he felt patronized by their ideas and, indeed, some of their films. He was determined to prove to them that one could be serious *and* popular, even vulgar, simultaneously. He had flirted with Parisian cineastes, and to some extent remade himself in their image. He was particularly sensitive about people saying of him (as they did) that he never read books. In the film, though, this exchange comes perilously close to an impassioned plea for ignorance. Not just an attack on cruelty, but a defence of 'qualunquismo'. As in Tuco's speeches to Blondie, it reduced the world to just two kinds of people.

Another set of late additions to the script, according to Leone, was more reference to Juan's and Sean's ambition to slip across the border to the USA, and change their names to 'Johnny and Johnny', the two great bank robbers. The entrance to the bank at Mesa Verde is blown up with explosives hidden in a wooden toy train labelled 'Johnny and Johnny Express'. In the cattle truck, Sean attempts to cheer Juan up with tales of America's bounty, of 'feed bags stuffed full of dreams'. Juan returns to this consolation as Sean is dying ('You leave me now and what's going to happen to me, huh?').

Evidently, Leone's American gangster epic was still at the front of his mind. He referred to *Giù la testa* as 'between the twilight of the fron-tier and the dark night of the city'.[54] In the first half of the film, Juan expresses the immigrant's fantasy of a land of milk and honey: not a land of self-improvement and evening classes, but one where there are plenty of juicy banks to rob. In the second half of the film, Sean feeds this fantasy – with increasing desperation – by reminding the depressed Juan that at least there is some place where all the streets are paved with gold: but both exits from the cattle truck lead back, inexorably, to the revolution. *Giù la testa* shows, in a rough-hewn way, the impulse that led to mass migration from Ireland, Italy, Spain and Mexico – all Roman Catholic cultures – to the Protestant-dominated melting pot of the United States, between the end of the Western frontier and the rise of the conurbations. It also shows how the ingredients in the melting pot might well remain separate from each other and everyone else.[55]

Leone recalled of this adaptation process, with a fair amount of post-rationalization: 'I wanted to bring one period of my work to a close. So I revisited some of the big situations in my earlier films, such as the attack on the bank, and the blowing up of the bridge. I pushed myself to treat them differently, while remaining faithful to my style. Then I took account of the fact that [*Giù la testa*] could become the second panel of a new triptych ... this one would push the story on to the second American frontier ... After that, I knew I would be ready to speak of my defining fantasies: my relationship with America, lost friendship and the cinema.'[56] It is possible, too, that some of the sight gags in *Giù la testa* – such as the three occasions where Leone creates a letter-box shape within the letter-box of the Techniscope frame, through a torn political poster and through the wooden slats of the cattle truck – were improvised on location: a self-referential joke about his own reputation for careful framing. Leone was working with a new director of photography on this film – 'Pasolini's man, Giuseppe Ruzzolini, because I wanted to liberate myself from all systems' – with Franco Delli Colli photographing for Giancarlo Santi's second unit. The latest video technology enabled them to see in advance the visual effects they were about to achieve – no longer having to wait anxiously for the rushes to come back from the labs in Spain. 'That is comforting. Previously, you'd ask after the "Cut!" if the take had been good and the cameraman, looking uncertain, would reply with a "Yes!" *That* was very distressing.' As with Tonino Delli Colli, Leone had preliminary discussions with Ruzzolini in which he used reproductions of paintings to suggest what he wanted: in this case, Goya's *Disasters of War* series was a key visual reference. Also shots from classic films, which he would, naturally, describe in detail.[57]

According to Leone, the principal casting happened fairly late in the day. Having rejected all his early suggestions (including the ones the parts had been written for, by Donati), United Artists advised him to go for bigger, more bankable names. And when the studio said they could secure the services of Rod Steiger, Academy Award winner in 1968 for his performance as the gum-chewing Mississippi police chief in *In the Heat of the Night*, Leone agreed. But with Steiger in place, Leone changed his mind about having 'a young and relatively inexperienced actor' for the Irishman. The forty-two-year-old James Coburn, who shared an agent with Steiger, fitted the bill. Steiger had a reputation for putting everything he'd got into a part, and Leone needed someone equally formidable as a foil.

Like Eli Wallach, Steiger was a graduate of the Actors' Studio, with its demanding emphasis upon motivation and 'the inner person'. Steiger rejected 'the Method' as 'a phrase of journalists', but was far more intense and improvisatory in his approach than Wallach. Steiger preferred the phrase 'representational actor' to describe the way he delved into his psyche to find his personal, highly charged performances. He liked to work on the spur of the moment. In film, he preferred the controlled environment of a studio, and a maximum of four takes; any more threatened a 'loss of spontaneity', a betrayal of instinct. Earlier that year, he had walked off the set of Sergei Bondarchuk's *Waterloo*, because the Russian director was shooting so many takes that the stock ran out. 'This is not a job, this is my life,' he'd said. His then wife Claire Bloom had appeared with him in Peter Hall's *Three Into Two Won't Go* (1969), and had marvelled at his tendency to go over the top in the first take, only to reach where he wanted to be by the third or fourth: 'Watching Steiger I realized you could as well start from the top and work your way down, as start from the most minimal twitchings and stirrings and keep grafting on to it.'[58] Sergio Leone's modus operandi – relying on post-synchronization, location work in wide open spaces, numerous takes, and the use of actors' faces as part of a grand design – could scarcely be further removed from Steiger's.

Since his début in 1951, Steiger had appeared in thirty-two films. His currency amongst cinephiles stemmed from the scene in the back of a car with Marlon Brando in Elia Kazan's *On the Waterfront* (1954). But he had also appeared in two cult Westerns (Delmer Daves's *Jubal* (1956) and Sam Fuller's *Run of the Arrow* (1957)) as well as Fred Zinnemann's *Oklahoma* (1957). Since the late 1950s, when his Hollywood career hit the doldrums, he had even worked on four films in Italy (one for Francesco Rosi set in the slums of Naples, another opposite Claudia Cardinale and Tomas Milian). At the time, Leone claimed: 'There were some small problems with Rod Steiger in the early stages of the shooting. He thought of the film as very serious and intellectual, and had a tendency to come off in the style of Zapata or Pancho Villa, but once he understood his mistake, everything went well.'[59] Fifteen years later, Leone felt himself at liberty to claim that the relationship had been much less happy: 'He thought he was pleasing me when he spoke in an Italian which sounded like Russian. He exasperated me. He wanted to construct a serious, completely cerebral character . . . I killed myself explaining to him that he was acting a simple peasant thief and bandit . . . I managed to keep my cool for a long week.' By Leone's account, he kept his cool to such an unusual extent that his trusted crew members, accustomed to a more volcanic maestro, ran to his wife, who was always on the set, dealing with the public relations side. In this particular case, Carla could offer no explanation for her husband's unusual restraint.

Leone began to see Steiger's habits rubbing off on Coburn's acting style. Finally, the inevitable explosion came. 'We were shooting on a mountain, about fifty kilometres from Almeria. I was directing a shot with Coburn. And Steiger came to interrupt. He said we ought to get back immediately if we weren't going to overrun the hours of a day's work. And he made a signal to Coburn to follow him. At that point, I burst out, "If I want to shoot for twenty-four hours I will do so. And I don't give a damn that your name is Rod Steiger and that you won an Academy Award *by mistake*. Because you are nothing but a piece of shit. And I cordially invite you to go fuck yourself, you and United Artists!" Then, according to his highly embellished account, Leone stopped communicating with Rod Steiger altogether. An assistant director acted as go-between, relaying such tactful messages as, 'Can he do it without wiggling his ears or palpitating his nostrils?' After four days of Leone's sulking, Steiger apparently came to apologize for all the difficulties he seemed to be causing on the set, and even offered to cancel his contract without legal redress if the director really thought he was so wrong for the part. From then on, the actor did as he was told, and, Leone claimed, 'after twenty-five takes, Steiger was too tired to get up to his Actors' Studio tricks. In the end, without his usual mannerisms, Rod is absolutely brilliant in the film.'[60]

Carla Leone supports her husband's account: 'Oh, Sergio sent him to hell. Steiger had just won an Oscar. He was pompous. He was an Actors' Studio graduate. Quite crazy from our point of view; we used to laugh about it a lot. The first day of shooting in Spain, he rehearsed the scene where he stops the coach. He used to walk away – over a kilometre – and we would look at him. We couldn't understand why he was going so far away. Then suddenly he would turn and start running. Saying to himself in Spanish, "My mother's not dead, my mother's not dead," to psyche himself up into the right frame of mind. Then he'd stop in front of the coach driver and say, "Senor, I need to go to San Felipe. My mother has died." All this running and self-analysis seemed out of all proportion to the simple line he had to deliver. The crew was really silent for once!'[61] Carla also remembers as the last straw Steiger's attempts to end a day's shooting, when they were doing the scene where 'Coburn blows up the coach': 'Sergio lost his temper. "*I'm* the one who's in charge here. Only I am allowed to say 'Action!' and 'Cut!' You broke my balls. If you don't like it, you can go to hell and I'll walk out tomorrow morning." From that moment on, the argument was *finito*. They both became like sheep. Coburn had a certain deference towards Steiger and allowed himself to be a bit led by him at first. But he came to understand that the less he was like Steiger the better for his performance.'[62] In her version, it was Leone, rather than Steiger, who threatened to walk out.

Leone liked everyone on the set to know that he, the director, was in the driving seat, no one else, and in any case he knew that much of the 'performance' would be constructed post-production. Whatever the precise details of the arguments on set, it is clear that something went seriously wrong and that Sergio Leone's own lack of confidence did not help to ease an already very difficult situation.

Luciano Vincenzoni, who was there, witnessed a scene that says a lot about the atmosphere on set at the time: 'We were in a big hotel in Almeria, in which there were three film crews with us . . . We were all sitting in the hotel lobby with cameramen and others. Suddenly, Rod Steiger came in. He had had a fight with Leone early in the morning. He passed by our table, and went to one ten tables away. He sat down, turned his head, and said, "Sergio, come here, I want to talk with you" – in front of 300 people. And Sergio Leone, like a puppet, stood up and went to his table . . . Rod Steiger started talking while he was sitting, and Leone was standing like a soldier. And after that he came back and told me: "This piece of shit just humiliated me." I said, "No, Sergio, you humiliated yourself."' Vincenzoni adds: 'You see, Sergio was shrewd as well; he knew exactly when to back down. I couldn't have done that.'[63]

At the time, Rod Steiger spoke very little, publicly, about *Giù la testa*. In *Photoplay*, September 1972, he was reported to have 'very little to say about his most recent picture *Duck, You Sucker*', other than fervently to hope that the title would change. But film columnist Barbra Paskin visited him in Almeria during the filming of the blowing-up of the bridge, and recorded a largely unpublished interview. Steiger remarked that the film was 'at best, only a kind of Western fantasy', devoid of 'any social significance', though he acknowledged, 'it does make a comment about revolutions'. (Tellingly, this was the first time Leone had cast an American actor who was 'personally not enamoured' of the Western.)

Steiger also complained about battling against noise on the set: he'd been led to believe in advance that he could record all his dialogue live, and was now confronting the Italian preference for post-synchronization. Of course, this kind of collision between working methods was part of the deal when you chose to work in Italy, and Steiger knew that. His big concern was that 'this wasn't an important picture'. Of Sergio Leone, meanwhile, he said little or nothing. There had been the usual tensions with the director, he said, but not nearly as many as there had been on the set of *Waterloo*.[64]

Twenty-six years later, Rod Steiger was re-interviewed by Barbra

Paskin for this book, and spoke a little more freely about the experience of playing Juan Miranda.[65] He also had a chance to weigh Leone's retrospective account of what happened on the set. 'Put it this way – I'd much rather work with a person of talent and a pain in the ass, like he could be, and I could be, than one who has no imagination . . . He had a wonderful sense of concept, and he got that picture in his head, and that was it. A big vision – and his ego matched it!'

He did indeed dislike the American title and 'begged them to change it' but, 'with Leone, you couldn't tell him much. He was used to being the maestro and he wasn't used to anybody suggesting anything.' What of the alleged explosion between them? 'Well, I remember we'd been up all day, shooting on top of a mountain in Almeria, and the sun was so hot . . . we shot about thirteen hours or something and he said, "Now we're going to do this." And I said to him, through a translator, "You see that Mercedes over there?" He said, "Yeah?" I said, "Well, I want you to watch me walk from here to there, and go home. It's been over thirteen hours." He started gesticulating – he had this thing with the hands – and he said, "You can't do that," and I said, "Watch me!" A tired imagination means there's no talent left.' Possibly, amid these gesticulations, Leone unburdened himself of some of the expletives he later claimed; possibly, his plain speaking was no more than what he wished he had said, in retrospect. Steiger did walk away, but only as far as the Grand Hotel in Almeria. After that, he has no strong recall of Leone driving him to submission with repeated takes.

Steiger does remember being unhappy about Leone's handling of an aspect of the battle scene, but not on his own account: 'He insisted on using the wooden-nosed bullets. And the nose on the bullet itself, I swear to God, was over an inch long . . . And we were pretty close to the camera, and they were putting half-inch plywood in front of the cameraman and the camera, to stop the bullets. I said to Sergio, "I don't think this is going to work," and he said, "Oh, sure it will." Sure enough, we did the scene, and one of the wooden bullets went through the wood and hit the cameraman, giving him a flesh wound through the leg. So that day was not a very pleasant day. I really got angry.'

Beyond this spat, Steiger remembers no running battles: 'I think frankly we were both very happy to leave each other alone.' Steiger was even content to make a small homage to his director's mannerisms: 'I put his hand gesture in the movie, when the Mexican and his little family see the bank. If you notice, I'm standing looking at the bank, and

I'm clenching and opening my hands. That's what Leone used to do all the time.' Steiger repeated this characteristic hand movement, in the scene where Juan faces the firing squad. It was particularly enjoyed by Sergio Donati, who confirmed, 'He makes Sergio Leone with his hands. *Si si*' – an affectionate gesture in the circumstances, by a man 'who did know he was not the actor Sergio really wanted'.[66]

Leone's personality remained something of a mystery to Steiger. His appetite, at least, was evident: 'He was like a compulsive eater. He set the corn muffin record at our house, I'll tell you that.' Steiger was certainly struck by Leone's perfectionism, which brought a certain stubbornness in its wake: 'He came on the set the first day, and said to me, "You see that stagecoach? That's exactly like it was built in the days they were using it." And it had four horses, solid wood and everything. So I looked down and noticed that the terrain was very like volcanic ash, very sandy. I said, "Well, isn't it going to be a little hilly with the sand?" "No," he said. Four horses, six horses, eight horses it took and a tractor behind. I think they had to rebuild it out of lighter woods. They lost a little time over that one ... That was the trouble with him. He was a very hard man to get to in many ways. Because he had proven himself and he figured his way was the right way.'

The business of post-synchronization, meanwhile, bothered him not a jot. Though the rest of the cast were dubbed, Steiger became the first of Leone's American stars to insist on using direct sound for his own dialogue: 'I told Leone that from the beginning. I said I'm not going to lose forty per cent of my performance through lip synching ... There was a noise problem in certain scenes. He was so busy with his visual effects that he didn't realize the effect this was having. But I didn't have to loop anything important. There were certain times when the best thing to do was cut as many lines as possible and shorten them. When there's going to be something like a big explosion, you know you're going to loop it, that doesn't come as a surprise. But I told Leone that I could not go back and loop the whole film.'

Steiger's account is altogether more sober and cordial than Leone's. So why would the maestro go around spreading such stories? The actor replies: 'I think because I wasn't kissing his shoes. I don't know. I just don't understand that.' He does remember that 'when Leone wasn't happy he was always mumbling in Italian to the crew, and James and I would look at each other because we never knew which one of us he was talking about. I had a hunch it was me most of the time.' And that he didn't want any music played when he was around: 'I don't need to follow a tune to play on scene!' But no explosions.[67] Clearly, and characteristically, Leone had exaggerated the tensions between them, to turn the story into a prize-fight between the maestro and the Actors' Studio, the maestro winning with a knock-out punch. It seems simpler and fairer to say that Steiger's hyper-conscientious approach occasionally irritated Leone, just as Leone's maestro act occasionally irked Steiger. But shortly after the filming, Rod Steiger gave a flattering talk in New York – which Martin Scorsese attended – about how Leone's *commedia dell' arte* style gave great prominence to actors and their physiognomies.

Both during and after the shoot, everyone seems to have agreed that co-star James Coburn went about his job calmly and sensibly, sometimes mediating between his overexcited colleagues. Leone was certainly pleased: 'With him, it's the star system: you explain the scene to him, he says, "Yes, sir," and off he goes and does it.' Of Irish–Swedish–Scottish descent, Coburn entered the business in 1959 with Boetticher's *Ride Lonesome* before his breakthrough as the lanky, slow-walking cowboy with a knife in *The Magnificent Seven*. Film buffs still tended to go up to him in the street and ask him to 'say the line', to which he would reply 'ya lost!', his throwaway at the end of the knife/gun duel.

Since then, he had worked for his friend Sam Peckinpah on *Major Dundee* (1964), with Rod Steiger in Tony Richardson's *The Loved One* (1965) and in a couple of James Bond spinoffs featuring *Our Man Flint* – where his famous shrug of indifference and endearing smile, plus his skills at karate, were harnessed to the US Secret Service.

Coburn had met Leone several times, most recently on the set of Christian Marquand's *Candy* (1968), partly shot in Spain, in which he'd played a demonic showbiz surgeon called Dr Krankeit. Of course, he had been offered the lead in *Fistful of Dollars* but, according to Leone, wanted too much money. As Coburn recalled in 1981, 'When I read the script I felt it wasn't anything great.' He also passed on *Once Upon a Time in the West*, somewhat to his chagrin later, as Charles Bronson shot to fame in his absence. 'Sergio and I didn't get it together until *A Fistful of Dynamite*, and the reason I did that was I was having dinner with Henry Fonda and I said, "How'd you like working with Sergio?" And he said, "He's the best director I've ever worked with in my life." I said, "You're joking". He said, "No, I mean it!" So I did the film and what happened? It opened in America as *Duck, You Sucker* and nobody went to see it!'[68] Predictably, Leone had wanted to work with Coburn ever since he saw the actor throw his knife in *The Magnificent Seven*. 'Coburn', he announced with a familiar needle, 'is a Clint Eastwood with more panache and humour.' Leone also reckoned that, when he wasn't trying to compete with Steiger, Coburn took direction well: 'I said to him, "The less you do in this film, the more you'll benefit. Rod grimaces. He wants to eat the lens. If you do nothing, you will be the one to collect everything." He gave me one of his sidelong glances. He had understood.'[69]

Like Steiger, Coburn was interviewed by Barbra Paskin on the Almeria set. Asked if the experience of working with Leone was proving worthwhile, he was laconic: 'Well I haven't finished it yet, so I don't know.'[70] But he was modestly upbeat about their progress: 'I think we've got a lot of really good stuff – I mean, for what it is. It isn't *A Man For All Seasons*.' The actor had already accustomed himself to Leone's rigour ('Serge knows what he wants, knows the area of what he wants and keeps working for it . . . Sometimes he gets it in two or three takes, sometimes he'll do as many as eighteen'). But he was somewhat perplexed by the business of making his character develop in a credible way ('There are a few points I have to get to yet. I still have to realize a certain affinity'). Coburn said enough to suggest that Leone's visual mannerisms were part of this problem: 'Serge sometimes likes little arbitrary movements and reactions. For his photographic scheme of things he needs to cut a look someplace where you really wouldn't look, and you have to work out ways of doing that to give him what he wants without losing what you were doing.' Clearly, Coburn was Leone's sort of actor. Okay, he wasn't everyone's idea of an Irishman – fair, laid back, detached – but that could be all to the good as well.

For Dr Villega, the revolutionary strategist and kitchen-table surgeon, Leone chose Ramolo Valli. Four years Leone's senior, Valli was a close personal friend who, after training as a medical student, had been a stage actor in the 1950s, as well as the artistic director of the Spoleto Festival for six years. He had since appeared as a character actor in various Italian films, including Visconti's *Il Gattopardo* (as the obsequious Jesuit priest attached to Don Fabrizio's house) and *Morte a Venezia* (as the fastidious manager of the Hotel des Bains on the Lido). Leone selected him early on, while the first script was still being drafted: 'There was an ambiguity about him which fitted well the character he was to defend in this film. Since I knew he had once been a doctor, I made him a member of that profession in our story. We even see him operating on someone [in the smoke-filled room behind the Café Carado, Mesa Verde, where his revolutionary cell holds its meetings]. From the beginning, I wanted to get rid of the mannerisms which came from his experience in the theatre . . . I asked him to unlearn everything he'd learned so far on the set, including with Visconti. This did not prove difficult . . . And James Coburn admired him a lot: they respected each other and remained friends.'[71]

The shooting schedule lasted from April to July 1970, about the same length of time as Leone's two previous films. The main locations were the mountains and *ramblas* of Los Filabres in Almeria, Almeria itself, Guadix, Burgos and Granada. The sequence where the coach stops, and the passengers are stripped, was filmed at a *cortijo* with outbuildings and threshing yard seven kilometres beyond Gérgal (towards the Tabernas turning) on what is now the main Guadix–Almeria road. The railway station of Mesa Verde was Almeria station; the firing squad, esplanade and church at Mesa Verde were filmed around the forecourt of the sixteenth-century church of Santiago in the old quarter of Guadix; the bank itself was a building in Burgos. The exploding bridge was five kilometres beyond Carlo Simi's El Paso set, up in the mountains: to reach the dirt track leading to the bridge the crew would have had to drive through the outskirts of El Paso. The stone foundations of the bridge are still there, on either side of the ravine, as are the gun emplacements once occupied by James Coburn and Rod Steiger. The spectacular sequence where firing squads execute civilians in a series of long stone ditches was filmed at a disused sugar factory called Azucareza San Torcuato (named after the first archbishop of Spain) just outside the centre of Guadix: the gullies were originally built for washing the sugar beet. Leone laid some extra railroad track beside the main factory building, and rerouted a locomotive from nearby Guadix station. By the time the *Giù la testa* unit arrived over 100 European Westerns had used locations in Almeria. The boom still had two or three years of life left in it. Interiors were shot at De Laurentiis Studio, Rome. And for the flashbacks Leone filmed around the vale of Glendalough and in the country house gardens of County Wicklow. Carlo Simi was not available to design the film. He was busy working for Alberto Grimaldi, designing his PEA offices, among other things. 'Sergio wanted me to do it, but I just couldn't,' he recalled. Ken Adam and Dean Tavoularis were considered, but the job went to Andrea Crisanti. Simi was very impressed with 'the firing squad in the rain and the slaughter in the station ditches'. As far as the rest of the film was concerned, he said, 'I would have designed some of it differently – but it doesn't matter.'[72]

David Warbeck, a New Zealand-born actor who until then had only appeared on British television and in a Hammer film, had the non-speaking part of Sean's friend and betrayer: 'Sergio was mad about *things*, like cars and gadgets. This is why his films are full of guns, old cars, wonderful machines and so on. For example, in the Irish sequences we did, while looking through a museum for the car, he found a wonderful 1930s bus and said, "We must work this into the film." I said, "How the hell are we going to do that?" and he said, "I know! It is a country bus going through the country and . . . (excited) yes! yes! It is full of virginal Irish schoolgirls going to school." So the hotel we were staying in was absolutely packed with virginal, miffed-looking schoolgirls and Sergio spent a lot of time shooting this bus going up and down. Of course this shot was never used. Oh, Sergio was a peasant . . . real, rough Roman . . . There was no question about the man's ability and visual flair, but the machismo thing was always a bit heavy going.'[73]

Leone's obsession with *things*, how they looked and felt, resulted in some unusual props: 'the film', he later said, 'is very precise when it comes down to certain details such as the armoured car (which was in fact the first model the Germans sent over to Mexico), the machine-guns, the train, the pistols which were originally manufactured in Belgium, Germany or America, the motorcycle, the colonial pith-helmets. Not for the sake of historical accuracy, but to make the fable more believable.'[74] One surreal side-effect of the search for an authentic 'look' was the sight of Rod Steiger and James Coburn sitting in the Spanish desert, surrounded by luxuriously padded furniture and Louis Vuitton luggage.

Like *Once Upon a Time in the West*, *Giù la testa* had a longish run in Italy, France and Germany, but again flopped in America, despite its calculating change of title. It grossed 1.8 billion lire on the domestic market, promoted by another Lardani trailer which showed a series of stills from the film, tinted and bleached, which burned like paper held over a flame. Among most French and Italian critics, it was Leone's best-received film so far: he was treated for the first time as a 'major film-maker' rather than a purveyor of rough-house entertainments, and his 'love of the possibilities of cinema, which is almost physical in its impact' was widely noted. Even Alberta Moravia found some good things to say about it. All those interviews, and Leone's makeover, were evidently paying off. But *Giù la testa* predictably caused a row among left-wing cinéastes in Europe who immediately saw its implications. Bertolucci called it 'a betrayal of [Leone's] childish, regressive vision: in trying to get grander he has lost his charm'. In Paris, Jean-Claude Guignet wrote for *La Saison Cinematographique* 'this time, Leone has gone a bit too far in his "I don't give a damn" approach . . . these two and a half hours of revolution do not have much worth seeing where real cinema is concerned'.[75]

Oreste de Fornari, realizing that part of the film's debate was with developments in *Italian* cinema, wrote: 'The structure of the film is almost diametrically opposed to the "populist" Westerns of Damiani and Corbucci. Corbucci, for example, concentrates his revolutionary message on the relationship between the two protagonists – and chucks in his massacres simply as *largesse* granted to the less "spiritual" tastes of the Italian public. Leone, showing less provincialism, downgrades the psychological aspects to comedy and melodrama – and instead *elevates* the scenes of action to the level of "historical spectacle". The Mexican Revolution was about taking land from the *latifondisti*, not just about defending oneself against the violent henchmen of Huerta.'[76] Leone's 'qualunquismo' had made the film uncomfortable to watch, and even patronizing in a 'falsely humble' way. Donati and Vincenzoni had predicted that this might well be the reaction.

Leone was very touched when, in a Paris restaurant, a couple of nights after the film opened there, a complete stranger sent a bottle of champagne over to his table and later joined the Leone party. 'Signor Leone,' the man said, 'I have two sons, of twenty-two and twenty years old. They were obsessed with politics – with views totally opposed to mine. We were constantly having violent rows, to the point where they both left home . . . They hadn't returned for many years, but because they went to see *Once Upon a Time, the Revolution*, they have now come back to us. Your film helped them see just how wrong-headed they had been. And they're going to stay at home with us from now on. Which is why I love your film so very much.' 'That', replied Leone, 'is worth more to me than the best review in the world.'[77] Strictly true or not, the story said a great deal about Leone's attitude to Italian politics at the time. His achievement had been to wean someone away from political discourse and back into the arms of the family. He did not feel any the less disillusioned for having made *Giù la testa*: 'I suffered a lot on that film. The shooting ... the plots ... the problems. And the editing which took such a long, long time. I'm attached to the film as one might be to a disabled child.'

At precisely this time, Leone – in a move that surprised many colleagues in the film world, not to mention his family – agreed to put his name to a short, anti-establishment 'film of counter-information' about the planting of a terrorist bomb on 12 December 1969 in the Banca dell'Agricoltura, Piazza Fontana, Milan, which resulted in sixteen dead and a hundred wounded. It was called *The Twelfth of December* or *Document on Giuseppe Pinelli*, and the co-signatories of the film included Luchino Visconti, Elio Petri, Mario Monnicelli, Cesare Zavattini and Tinto Brass. The purpose of this 'alternative newsreel' was to show that television coverage of the event had simply reinforced the official line; there was much more to say about it – and an effective way of achieving this, in the public domain, was for a group of established film-makers to put their weight behind some counter-images. The anarchist Giuseppe Pinelli had been arrested for the atrocity, but 'fell' to his death from out of the window of the Milan Questura during an interrogation by Commissar Luigi Calabresi. The socialist revolutionary group Lotta Continua publicly accused Calabresi of Pinelli's murder, and wondered what else was being covered up.[78]

Through its images, *The Twelfth of December* asked: did Pinelli really commit suicide when he fell from a window? Was there a cover-up? Were the anarchists behind the bombing? Why the rush to judgement? How deeply were the police involved? These questions also inspired Dario Fo's play *Accidental Death of an Anarchist* (1970) and Elio Petri's film *Investigation of a Citizen above Suspicion* (1969). The people that read the books were uniting with the people who made the films for the people that didn't read the books, to draw attention to the workings of the state apparatus. Perhaps this appealed to the anarchist in Leone. Or maybe he enjoyed having his name associated with the likes of Visconti and Zavattini. According to Luca Morsella, 'He never spoke of this film. It was very unlike him: he was not the type to get involved in "causes". Not at all.'[79] Nevertheless, in this case he might have found more fuel for his conviction that 'politics no longer makes any sense in Italy'.

# 10

## Entr'acte

'I enjoy working most,' said Monroe Stahr. 'My work is very congenial.'

'Did you always want to be in movies?'

'No. When I was young I wanted to be chief clerk – the one who knew where everything was.'

Kathleen Moore smiled.

'That's odd. And now you're much more than that.'

'No, I'm still a chief clerk,' Stahr said. 'That's my gift, if I have one. Only when I got to be it, I found out that no one knew where anything was. And I found out that you had to know why it was where it was, and whether it should be left there. They began throwing it all at me, and it was a very complex office. Pretty soon I had all the keys. And they wouldn't have remembered what locks they fitted if I'd given them back.'

F. Scott Fitzgerald, *The Last Tycoon* (1940)

Three dusty saddle-tramps ride into a shanty town, somewhere in the Wild West. In the foreground, a dog dozes in the shade, while several chickens pick their way across what passes for a main street. The saddle-tramps seem close to the camera, but an abrupt pull-back reveals that they are, in fact, at the far end of the street. The dog gets up, and ambles away. There is a close-up of the three faces, accompanied by the sound of an alarm clock and swelling guitar feedback on the soundtrack. A child, intrigued and anxious, watches these men from within a ramshackle barber's shop. A cock crows, as the *pistoleri* dismount in unison, and enter the barber's shop.

It is a rerun of the opening sequence of *Once Upon a Time in the West*. But this time, Leone is not at the helm. *My Name is Nobody* (1973) was based partly on his idea, and produced by him, but the director was his associate Tonino Valerii, who had assisted him in the 'Dollars' days. Nevertheless, *Nobody* is full of references to Leone's earlier films. As the opening sequence develops, the three *pistoleri* will try to remain inconspicuous, as they pass the time by milking a cow, brushing a horse and stropping a cut-throat razor – the sounds of

348

which will be amplified. The two protagonists take pot-shots at each other's hat, as part of a competitive ritual. An old and bearded prophet complains about the inroads of capitalism in the West. The behaviour of professional gunfighters is explicitly linked, several times, to children's games, carnivals and nursery rhymes. The central character is a man with no name, an Italian trickster who eggs on a Hollywood Westerner, and the final duel is an explicit parody (in front of an excited audience of townspeople) of the end of *Once Upon a Time*. This time round, these elements will be played mainly for laughs, affectionately sending up a series of Italian Western conventions which had been parodic in the first place. Steven Spielberg once called it his favourite Leone film. In Germany and France it was marketed as the new Leone picture, much to Valerii's fury.[1]

Peter Bogdanovich has suggested that Leone was yet again playing his complicated game of hide and seek: 'Sergio hired an inexperienced Italian fellow to direct another Western ... After a while, circumstances again forced Leone to take over, though finally I think that's what he wants.'[2] In fact, Tonino Valerii was far from 'inexperienced' – his signed output (six films as a director since 1966) was greater than Leone's. But he had earned his promotion to directing on Leone's recommendation. When the Technospresso laboratory developed an economical new film stock, 'Two P Techniscope' (so called because it had two perforations rather than the usual four), and sought to patent its invention, the firm was advised to produce a film making use of it. They settled upon a showcase Western, and approached Sergio Leone for his advice on who should direct. As Valerii gratefully recalls, his response was: 'I'm sorry to lose him as my assistant, but I think Tonino Valerii would do a good job for you.'

Thus, Valerii made his début with a bounty-hunter tale called *Per il gusto di uccidere/Taste for Killing* (1966); he followed up with *Giorni dell'ira/Day of Anger* (1967), starring Lee Van Cleef as a veteran gunfighter, which made 2 billion lire. Two more Westerns followed: *Il prezzo del potere/The Price of Power* (1969) and *Una ragione per vivere ... una ragione per morire/Massacre at Fort Holman* (1972). Valerii had also directed a couple of thrillers. Benito Stefanelli, who had cropped both in *Day of Anger* and *The Price of Power*, recommended the latter to Leone who went to see it with him at the Cinema Galleria in the Piazza Colonna, Rome. A while later, Valerii was approached for the *Nobody* job. He was conscious that Leone might favour 'a young man trained in the Leone school of direction', and aware also that Leone might be harbouring the conviction 'that he could influence me in a certain direction and make me do things *he* liked more than I did. In this game I could never win, because Sergio Leone for his début as a producer was not about to make a film which was too distinct from his style, his way of telling a story, his way of making a Western.'[3]

Like Van Cleef's Frank Talby in *Day of Anger*, *Nobody*'s lead character of Jack Beauregard was a gunfighter fighting the ageing process: 'He had the first signs of arthritis, that stiffness of movement which comes from age rather than from any real physical ailment.' Valerii acknowledges, 'the original idea for the film came from Sergio'.[4] Ennio Morricone remembers that, in discussions about the music for the film, the director was always accompanied by his producer – a situation which in other circumstances might have proved uncomfortable: 'It was his first production, so he was very particular about everything. He had to be, for by now he'd become an important director of Westerns . . . So Sergio insisted on being present at all discussions, and naturally supervised all the things we agreed.'[5]

Leone was still unable to find backers for *Once Upon a Time in America*, and 'couldn't get excited enough about any other project'. The gangster epic looked less realizable than ever, since his last two pictures had flopped in the USA. Offers of Westerns were still abundant, but Leone had now set his shoulders squarely against the genre. Hollywood was still calling, but not with anything that stirred his creativity. One such project was *The Godfather*. Late in 1968, when Mario Puzo's novel was still in typescript, Charles Bluhdorn of Paramount had sent a copy to Leone. Bludhorn liked the idea of an Italian making the film (it could head off potential image problems with the Italian-American community) and, despite the relative box-office failure of *Once Upon a Time in the West*, Bluhdorn – the man who succeeded Adolph Zukor at Paramount – still had a lot of faith in Leone's talent.

When the typescript arrived in Rome, Fulvio Morsella, as was his custom, read it out to Sergio, translating at sight. What happened next is still a matter for debate. According to Leone, he accepted Morsella's opinion that the book wasn't up to much. Thus, it was not until he read an Italian translation a few years later that he 'realized that a formidable film could be based on this story'; in particular, using the contrast between the youth of Don Vito Corleone as a petty thief on the streets of New York, and the Mafia wars of the late 1940s (which would be adapted into *The Godfather II*). 'But by then it was too late. Coppola had entered the scene.'[6] Fulvio Morsella tells a different story: 'I did everything I could to make him do it, but he didn't want to . . . He may have been sensible to do his own, rather than an Italian-American gangster film.'[7]

In other interviews, Leone took personal responsibility for turning down *The Godfather* and gave a variety of reasons. Another Paramount Mafia picture, Martin Ritt's *The Brotherhood*, had just flopped, he said. Also, he was well aware of the danger of presenting cliché Italians. 'I could never have avoided putting in a scene, for example, which involved plates of spaghetti. And I really didn't want to do that, because a lot of people were making a noise about Spaghetti Westerns. Sure, I eat spaghetti. But I eat it . . . in the same way Alberto Sordi does in *An American in Rome*: devouring a huge plate of it . . . In any case, *The Godfather* seemed to me a choral story. The protagonist was the family, the Mafia collective, not the single person or the characters who were the component parts. I'm much more interested in the isolated individual.'[8] Leone's preference was for 'punks on the street' rather than Murder Incorporated: 'When gangsters start sitting behind desks, I lose interest in them.'

Thus, Leone devoted himself to Rafran Cinematografica, in partnership with his brother-in-law Morsella and Claudio Mancini. Part of the attraction for Leone was his nostalgia for the work of Hollywood's 'creative producers' in the golden age of the studio system: such as David O. Selznick, or, lower down the scale, Val Lewton; not to mention Sam Spiegel, a favourite Leone example, who was then still working. Some scholars had argued that the films produced by these businessmen-artists bore their indelible authorial stamp, more so than any director who may have served time on them. By the Selznick–Lewton model, so many responsibilities were within the producer's remit (the choice of book or subject, the purchasing of rights, the commissioning of writers, the control over the adaptation, the influence over casting, and the appointment of 'an able technician to look after the shooting') that the 'creative producer' was ultimately responsible for the finished product.

Leone's exemplar for this process was, of course, a big and logistically complex film, one that he'd said he wanted to have a shot at remaking himself: 'Imagine if *Gone with the Wind* had not done well; the consequences would have been disastrous for Selznick – not for the half-dozen directors who happened to work on a film to which only Victor Fleming put his name. So by the same token, I originally went into the role of producer with this principle in mind: "a Sergio Leone film directed by someone else".'9 Of course, it had been the influence of the French New Wave, lionizing mavericks such as Orson Welles, Sam Fuller and Nicholas Ray, and which asserted the primacy of the writer-director or auteur over the old Hollywood hierarchies. Leone himself had been a significant beneficiary of the auteur craze. So his idea of hiring 'an able technician' to direct a pre-existing property on his behalf was, quite simply, out of date, even in the Italian industry.

Reflecting later on his efforts at producing, Leone considered that his own eminence had intimidated the directors he chose, and reduced the possibility of useful collaboration: 'Then I realized I had better go back to being a director because it was less tiring, more productive, less frustrating and, above all, less demanding – because, in the end, more is demanded of the producer-figure than of the director because you have to perform all the duties of a director plus at the same time those of a producer – going out to look for financing, setting up appointments, supervising everything.'10

In any case Leone's Selznickian aspirations did not sit well with his obsessive, confrontational personality, or his fear of failure. He was not good at giving credit to others, and on the set two was often a crowd. It was as if his 'nostalgia for those old American producers' had provided him with a mirror-image of his own experience since 1964. As a director he had sometimes wanted a figure to hide behind. But what if *he* was that figure? A figure, as he told his journalist friend Diego Gabutti, who would be 'un mogul di stampo franciscottfitzeraldiano'.11 A last tycoon, as 'larger-than-life' as he had once been when directing. Leone confessed to a 'certain romanticism' in his producing dreams, and the Fitzgerald echo would seem to confirm this.

For a man who wanted to 'distance himself' from the genre that had made his name, Leone certainly chose an eccentric subject for his first production – but then again, he had his public to consider. It was, after all, the calling card for a new phase in his career. The original idea for *My Name is Nobody* dated back to summer 1970 when Leone was cutting *Giù la testa*, as Sergio Donati remembers: 'I wrote a treatment, because the first idea was to do Homer. "My name is nobody", you see . . . The idea came from Fulvio Morsella, and it was to make *The Odyssey* into a Western. And it was Ulysses who is a captain of the Southern army and in a Yankee concentration camp. We had everything in there – Circe, the pigs, the Cyclops and even Penelope with the bad guys . . . And I went to New Mexico in 1972, with Piero Lazzari who was then to have been the producer. And I scouted the locations, I found the cemetery in the Navajo village – where there is the Sam Peckinpah reference. The Indians called it "city in the sky". Anyway, I did a treatment and then – everything took a long time.'[12]

So long, in fact, that Donati moved on. The final version of the script was by 'Ernesto Gastaldi, Fulvio Morsella from an idea by Sergio Leone'. Leone's basic concept, which had grown out of the Ulysses idea, was 'to confront the fantasy and vulgarity of the character of Trinity with the legend of the West, of the old Western, represented by Henry Fonda'. He resented the success of Barboni's two *Trinity* films, and, throughout the development of the project, he blew hot and cold about whether or not the Terence Hill figure should be sympathetic. Ernesto Gastaldi, it seems, did much of the writing. He had co-scripted about a dozen Italian Westerns (including the Sartana series) and was probably chosen because he had shared the scriptwriting credit with Tonino Valerii on *Day of Anger* and *Massacre at Fort Holman.*

Gastaldi's assessment of his working relationship with the producer had a very familiar ring to it. 'When I met Sergio for the first time', he was to recall, 'I was a conceited ass and I butted horns with him almost immediately. He used to humiliate people. Arguing about a scene of mine, he said to me "Questa è una scena da serie C!" [This is a scene from a low-budget 'B' movie!] I had a formidably strong voice, and so I shouted back, "Tu chi credi di essere? In serie A c'è Fellini, tu sei in serie B e ancora no hai vinto il campionato!" [Who do you think you are? Fellini is in the 'A' league while you are playing in the 'B' league and have yet to win your first championship!] I stormed out, slamming the door. Twenty days later, Sergio phoned me, as though we had parted only the day before, saying that maybe I wasn't completely wrong about that scene after all . . . Sergio was an uncultured genius, a son-of-a-bitch, but I loved him. I'll always prefer a son-of-a-bitch genius to a nice mediocrity.'[13]

*My Name is Nobody,* Gastaldi claimed, 'may have been the first movie that was filmed precisely as I had written it. Tonino Valerii was afraid of being criticized by Sergio, so he filmed my pages – shot by shot.' Previously, Gastaldi had always 'researched' his scripts with reference to 'thousands of American Westerns: I simply had to copy the atmosphere'. Only when working with Sergio Leone 'did I begin to read history books about the old West, to see original photographs from the Civil War, and so on'. At the heart of Gastaldi's story was a contrast between the classic Hollywood Western (embodied by Henry Fonda) and its hyperactive Italian counterpart. A veteran gunfighter at first refuses to accept his mythic status, while a younger man hero-worships him and is determined to engineer a mighty confrontation, which will enable him to step very publicly into the shoes of the legend. The film would show how Italian nobodies, who 'needed something to believe in' when they watched American movies in their childhood, had become somebodies after all. Every mythic hero, the story implies, needs a good scriptwriter and a receptive audience. And throughout the film the actions of Jack Beauregard and his style-conscious groupie are reflected in an assortment of mirrors; until, at the climax, they are frozen on to the sepia pages of one of those 'history books about the Old West'. The final duel, on a New Orleans street, is seen upside-down through the viewfinder of a photographer's camera, while local residents (well-dressed shoppers on one side of the tracks, poor blacks in straw hats on the other) behave like the crowd at a segregated baseball game.

The script would finish on Sergio Leone's *arrivederci* to the Western genre: an unusually wordy apotheosis. The bespectacled Jack Beauregard writes a valedictory letter to Nobody (who has at last become Somebody), from his cabin on the steamship *Sundowner*, which will take him to a well-earned retirement in Europe. Apparently, that is where civilized old Westerners want to go, before the last round-up. It is 1899, midnight for the nineteenth century: 'You can preserve a little of that illusion that made my generation tick. Maybe you'll do it in your own funny way, but we'll be grateful just the same. Because look-ing back, it seems to me we were all a bunch of romantic fools; we still believed that a good pistol and a quick showdown could solve every-thing. But then the West used to be wide open spaces with lots of elbow room – where you never ran into the same person twice. By the time you came along it was changed. It'd got small and crowded and you kept bumping into the same people all the time. But if you're able to run around in the West peacefully catching flies, it is only because fellas like me were there first. Yeah, the same fellas you want to see written up in history books – because people need something to believe in, like you say. But you won't be able to have it your own way much longer.

Because the country ain't the same any more and I'm already feeling a stranger myself. But what's more, violence has changed too: it's grown and got organized. And a good pistol don't mean a damn thing any more. But I guess you must know all this. Because it's your kind of time, not mine . . . This is why people like me got to go; and this is why you fixed that gunfight with me, to get me out of the West clean. Guess I'm talking like a damn preacher but it's your fault. What can you expect of a national monument!'

At this moment, lest we have forgotten the resonance of Henry Fonda, Hollywood's young Mr Lincoln, Beauregard looks up at a passing paddle-steamer called *The President. Nobody* is full of such knowing references. The opening and closing sequences set in barber-shops – where first Henry Fonda, then Terence Hill, sits down to be shaved, only to discover that members of the Wild Bunch are doing the shaving – refer to equivalent moments in Fritz Lang's *Western Union* (1941) and *Rancho Notorious* (1952) as well as Edward Dmytryk's *Warlock* (1959). The central relationship in *My Name is Nobody*, between Jack Beauregard and Nobody, mirrors the competition between Broderick Crawford and Glenn Ford in *The Fastest Gun Alive* (1956). Another key reference is to Sam Fuller's *Forty Guns* (1957) where the eponymous gunmen employed by Jessica Drummond (Barbara Stanwyck) hurtle through the countryside – just like the '150 pure-bred sons of bitches on horseback' in *Nobody*.

But in Valerii's film they are called 'the Wild Bunch', and one critic at the time referred to *Nobody* as 'an explicit, thoroughgoing critique of Sam Peckinpah's work up to 1970'. Indeed, there is slow-motion vio-lence (for the first time in a Leone Western), rookie soldiers chasing after a stolen train, a grave-marker in a Navajo cemetery which bears the name 'Peckinpah' ('That's a beautiful name in Navajo,' says Nobody), and an elderly gunfighter putting on his spectacles like Joel McCrea in *Ride the High Country* (1962). But Jack Beauregard will survive the mayhem, to 'go down in history'. Some, like Luciano Vincenzoni, felt that the references to Sam Peckinpah's work in this context were unduly superior. Leone referred at this time to 'the con-troversy about who influenced whom', and said that Peckinpah had been delighted to acknowledge his debt: Leone's films, Peckinpah apparently admitted, created the context which made *The Wild Bunch* possible. Game to Leone.

Beauregard's valedictory letter reads like a message from founding father John Ford, a reflection on what Sergio Leone had done to his genre, and on what has happened to the American Western since his retirement. Ford, who was dying of cancer, had recently moved 150 miles away from the film community in Hollywood to a ranch-style house in Palm Desert on the Old Prospector Trail, where his neighbours included Howard Hawks, Henry Hathaway and Frank Capra. Just before *My Name is Nobody* started shooting, President Nixon said of him, at a Hollywood ceremony during which Ford was made a full admiral and awarded the Presidential Medal of Freedom: 'As an interpreter of the nation's heritage, he left his personal stamp indelibly printed on the consciousness of whole generations both here and abroad. In his life and in his work John Ford represents the best in American films and the best in America.' Ford had recently gone on record as saying, 'Our ancestors would be bloody ashamed if they could see us today.' Beauregard's letter affirms that the spirit of Ford is incompatible with a world where 'violence [has] grown', where the good guys are constantly being cut down to size, where urban audiences tend to call the shots and where crime has become organized on business lines. The punchline of Beauregard's letter is that Ford is 'mighty grateful just the same'. The Italians, after all, had kept the Western alive – in their 'own funny way' – at a time when Hollywood had all but given up on them as big-screen entertainment. It is as if Leone wanted to settle his debt – yet again – to John Ford, and to prove to the great man, publicly, that he had become somebody. John Ford died, clutching his rosary, just after *My Name is Nobody* completed principal photography.[14]

The scenes where Henry Fonda (in this, his farewell Western) rides towards the sunset and the *Sundowner* have an unusually elegiac quality to them – visuals courtesy of painter Frederic Remington, music a Morricone variation on 'My Way'. The 'Nobody' scenes, by contrast, are shot in a zany, comic-strip style. The puckish stalker is seen to eat beans, belch, eat a whole apple in one go, drink a fifth of whisky without so much as flinching and stand in a public urinal while preventing an engine-driver *in extremis* from having a much-needed pee. At one point Nobody draws his gun and holsters it three times before his opponents even have time to draw once; this, while holding a saddle in the same hand. His carnivalesque behaviour is explicitly linked, this time, to a carnival – a street of fun peopled by dancers, dwarfs and fairground barkers, complete with sideshows, a hall of mirrors and a punching machine. Beauregard belongs to the wide-open spaces, but Nobody is more at home in an amusement arcade.

'The moral of this adventure attempts to show that people never attack a nobody. In the West as in life, the only person who is taken into account is the person who is thought to be unbeatable.'[15] And Leone's choice of title carried the message into the wider realm of mythology. Leone had often said in interviews that 'the greatest author of Westerns was Homer . . . and this dimension of the Western does not belong to the Americans but to the whole world, a universal fable which is filtered by each distinctive culture'. Tonino Valerii confirms that 'the title was supposed, a few years earlier, to have been the title of an Italian Western originally inspired by the adventures of Ulysses with Polyphemus'. But Leone appropriated it in order to show that the roots of the Western lay in the origins of myth itself, and the function of myth – from story-telling around a campfire to big-budget movies; from a folk culture to an entrepreneurial one – had not really changed that much. He also enjoyed the confrontation between the rash, quick-thinking Ulysses and the lumbering giant – one myth against another.

In Homer's *Odyssey*, Ulysses confronts the man-eating Cyclops, Polyphemus, saying: 'You wish to know the name I bear. I'll tell it to you; and in return I should like to have the gift you promised me. My name is Nobody.' The Cyclops vows to eat Nobody last, after the rest of his crew, but instead suffers the fate of losing his eye to an olive pole. After escaping from the Cyclops' cave, Ulysses cannot resist giving Polyphemus a piece of his mind, thus demonstrating to his crew and anyone else who is listening that he is a Somebody. This provokes Polyphemus' rage, and gentle remonstrance from his crew: 'Aren't you rash, sir,' they say, 'to provoke this savage?'

Beauregard is far from a lumbering brute, although he doesn't see too well. But the resonance in the face-off between trickster and national monument convinced Leone that *My Name is Nobody* was a great title. The Italian press picked up the reference immediately: elsewhere, nobody noticed; even though, at one point in the story, the trickster meets a giant – who turns out, on closer inspection, to be a dwarf on stilts.

Ennio Morricone came up with an unusually eclectic score – ranging from the variation on 'My Way' for the last round-up to an upbeat Europop melody for the main title to a parody of 'Like a Judgment' for the final duel – and evidently picked up on the jokey references to the greatest hits of mythology. Whenever the Wild Bunch appears, there are musical citations from Wagner's 'Ride of the Valkyries'. 'This wasn't a completely abstract idea,' he said. 'It created a concrete link between two elements. The idea was to make a parallel between the Valkyries – those amazing blonde women from the North who seem so manlike – and these masculine riders. This seemed to me a justified analogy in a comedy film, with elements of the grotesque and parody as well. And another thing that no one noticed. The theme of the Valkyries was at that moment played on car hooters. The frenetic energy of the Valkyries and the Wild Bunch seemed to me enough to suggest this idea, in a place where urban traffic did not exist.'[16]

According to Tonino Valerii, Leone was unabashedly competing with Enzo Barboni, since *They Call Me Trinity* (1970) and *Trinity is Still My Name* (1971) had 'knocked Leone from his perch as the maestro of the Italian Western. Moreover, these films were parodies which were very ironic at the expense of the clichés generally associated with this kind of film. So Leone was looking for *una vendetta artistica*.' Thus, the notion of casting *Trinity* star Terence Hill as a 'Nobody' had great appeal to Leone ('I must say there was a touch of malice in this operation'), though Leone had to introduce an uncommonly large number of comic scenes to induce Hill into the picture and get the best out of him. Valerii, though, was much more interested in the Fonda character, and in time he felt that Leone relaxed into the idea of Nobody as 'just a good boy who dreams of meeting the hero of his childhood, and when he does meet him finds that he is in something of a personal crisis and helps him to bow out of his career in a way that is fitting. Leone behaved very well over this change.'[17]

Even after the film was released, Sergio Leone could never resist harking back to those 'initial feelings of spite', and to the dynamic within the Italian film industry which helped to shape the screenplay. In particular, he did not like to think that audiences were being encouraged to laugh at the Italian Western, rather than with it – even if he did agree that most Spaghettis were rubbish. It made his own contributions seem superficial – a set of clichés which were all too easy to mock. 'Along came a film [*Trinity is Still My Name*] where pistol duels were replaced by slaps in the face! The audience felt liberated. It was a form of retaliation. They were delighted to see the bad guys from all these films having their ears boxed and their hats forced down over their ears. And this second *Trinity* was a colossal success . . . It was released at a very precise moment of exasperation with a genre which had run out of breath. When the film was later reissued, it had no success at all.'[18]

So, just as it was essential to Leone that Henry Fonda played Beauregard, Terence Hill had to play Nobody if the film was to make its point. The thirty-three-year-old Venetian actor, born Mario Girotti, (with 'the bluest eyes this side of Paul Newman', as Italian critics liked to say) was 'discovered' by director Dino Risi at a swimming gala, and made his first film, *Vacanze col gangster/Holiday for Gangsters*, at the age of twelve. His breakthrough role, which convinced him to become a full-time actor, was as the dashing young Count who courts Burt Lancaster's daughter in Visconti's *The Leopard* (1963). While shooting Giuseppe Colizzi's *God Forgives, I Don't* in Almeria, he married his dialogue coach, an American girl called Lori Hill, and changed his name. This picture teamed him with Neapolitan actor and garment designer Carlo Pedersoli, who also availed himself of a name change: 'Bud Spencer', 'Bud' because it seemed to suit his huge girth, 'Spencer' 'as a homage to the clothing industry' – presumably as in Marks and Spencer.

Success with subsequent Westerns (*Ace High* (1968) and *Boot Hill* (1969)) led Hill to the *Trinity* films. Of the top-grossing films made in Italy between 1956 and 1971, *Trinity is Still My Name* came first, *For a Few Dollars More* second. Leone, it seemed, had been 'knocked from his perch' by a loosely constructed comedy with an emphasis on slap-stick bar-room brawls in which stuntmen hurtled across the screen, in the style of Warner Brothers Looney Toons, from every direction. The character of Trinity was a footloose layabout in braces, always busy doing nothing, who performed an extended double-act with his bear-like brother Bambino: in French critical circles, they were compared with Asterix and Obelix or Laurel and Hardy; in Italy, more usual comparisons were with Don Quixote and Sancho Panza, or 'Northern guile and Southern brawn'. As a result of the second *Trinity* film, Terence Hill was voted in a readers' poll the fifth most popular star in the world, after Eastwood, Newman, Redford and McQueen. Leone advised Terence Hill to act the part of Nobody 'as if you were replaying Trinity, only in a more serious way'.[19]

Nobody's adversary Sullivan, the businessman who is manipulated by the Wild Bunch, was played by French stage actor Jean Martin. Martin was a friend of Samuel Beckett, and he originated the roles of Lucky in *Waiting for Godot* (1953) and Clov in *Endgame* (1957), before distinguishing himself onscreen as the sole professional in the cast of Pontecorvo's *Battle of Algiers* (1966), as Colonel Mathieu of the French Paras. According to Pontecorvo, Jean Martin was ill at ease on a movie set: 'I had more problems with him than with the people I found on the street. He may have appeared in *Godot*, but that doesn't automatically make him a good actor.'[20]

The different interpretations of the *Nobody* script by Leone and Valerii – at pre-production stage – might explain why the resulting film is so uncertain in its tone: the jokes go on for much too long; there is a jarring tension throughout between the lyrical 'end of the West' theme and the comic-strip antics of Terence Hill, who is allowed to do a series of music-hall turns which make the story grind to a halt.

It is clear that the maestro could not resist getting deeply involved in the actual shooting of the film, or rather the two films which were competing with one another. His attention to detail was undiminished, as Tonino Valerii recalls, not least in the case of Henry Fonda's wardrobe: 'I wanted to dress Henry Fonda in exactly the same clothes he wore in *My Darling Clementine*. Bravo, perfect. In my opinion, that *is* Henry Fonda. But Sergio had taken it into his head that he should wear a shirt with an enormous ruffle on the front, a lace ruffle. "Yes," I'd say. "Shirts like that are sometimes seen in Westerns, but this is a type of wardrobe more suited to an adventurer, or a professional gambler, or a minor character in the story."' Valerii let the maestro have his way. Some time later, Valerii was awoken in his chalet on a mountainous location, at an ungodly hour by someone saying: 'Mister Valerii – a call for you from Rome.' 'I was anxious,' he recalls. 'Maybe it was news about my family. I went to the phone and it was Sergio, who said, "What's that shirt you've put on Henry Fonda, with that horrible ruffle?" So much hot air! These are the contradictions of the man. Another director had been watching the rushes with him and asked him to make a note about this shirt, so wrong and so out of place . . . And just to keep *him* happy, we finally dressed him as I wanted.'[21]

A nine-week shoot began on location in America, before a second crew took over on a set near Guadix (partly, the *Once Upon a Time* set at Estación de Calahorra). The Navajo village was in Taco, New Mexico, the final duel and harbour scene in New Orleans. Sergio Donati claimed to have 'found' the Navajo cemetery. In fact, as Leone was later informed by Peter Fonda, 'the last Indian village was the same as the one where part of *Easy Rider* was shot'. Despite occasional interruptions, Valerii felt he was in control for this part of the schedule: 'Everything went very well in America – apart from disagreements between me and Armando Nannuzzi, the director of photography over there, who wanted to intervene in the film's direction without having the ability to do so.'²² Apparently, Leone had instructed Nannuzzi to 'help Valerii out as much as he could', which, of course, contributed to the tension. Fulvio Morsella recalled that the quarrels led to Nannuzzi's dismissal from the show; the production manager in the USA had already bitten the dust, because 'he started talking over Tonino's head all the time. And they quarrelled. So we had to hire different people for the Spanish side of the production.'²³

Towards the end of the American shoot, Leone arrived from Rome to check on progress. He let Valerii know that in Guadix there would be a replacement director of photography (Guiseppe Ruzzolini, who had shot *Giù la testa*), and a new crew waiting for him. 'But in Spain the sets had not yet been completed and the costumes hadn't arrived from America. We had to interrupt the work for a week, and since Henry Fonda had another commitment immediately afterwards, Leone offered to be the second-unit director – filming with Terence Hill, who was dying to be directed by the maestro – which is what they did for the saloon sequence with the glasses and the fiesta in the town.'²⁴ Leone filmed for about a fortnight at Guadix, also shooting the scene in the public urinal, and, according to Terence Hill, 'played a very large part' in the scenes where Nobody was centre stage. Valerii, meanwhile, shot the remaining Henry Fonda sequences and set up the big action set-pieces in the Almerian desert: again, according to Hill, Fonda was sensitive to Valerii, advising him 'to direct him as though he was an unknown actor'. The urinal scene was not in the script, recalls Valerii: 'It was one of Sergio Leone's spontaneous creations, and I leave it to others to judge its vulgarity.'²⁵

American actor Neil Summers had been cast in the saloon sequence (as Squirrel, the gunfighter with chattering teeth), after Leone had spotted him in John Huston's *Life and Times of Judge Roy Bean*. Summers was firmly under the impression that Leone was at the helm in Spain: 'Sergio directed most of the scenes I was in . . . On the first day I was on location there, we only rehearsed the action between Terence and myself, and we shot some of it the next day. It took over a week to shoot the fast-draw scenes with the glasses shattering . . . Sergio worked slowly and was constantly trying new angles with his camera and new innovative shots with his actors. I was also to do the house of mirrors scenes in Spain but they could not find enough mirrors to satisfy Sergio, so I was told I would have to go to Rome for the remainder of my scenes.'[26]

After the film was released, Leone publicly claimed that circumstances had 'obliged' him to direct 'the beginning [the barbershop scene], the battle [Beauregard versus the Wild Bunch] and the final duel'. Although Valerii vehemently denies that Leone had anything to do with the battle or the duel, there are photographs of him helping to direct both. And Leone did shoot the Terence Hill scenes in Spain, without ever admitting it. The most likely scenario is that Leone helped out on a duel, then took charge of second-unit work on 'the battle' (in Almeria), as well as directing the opening scene and the carnival section of the film. This might explain why some of the Spanish portions of My Name is Nobody seem so different, in style and tone, from the American portions. There is just a hint in Valerii's account that Leone deliberately created a situation where he would *have* to direct Terence Hill's big scenes. Whether or not this is so, it had certainly been the producer's responsibility to have the sets and costumes ready for Valerii's arrival in Spain. And they were not ready. Leone tended to vary his contribution, according to whether the interviewer was pro or contra: to one, he had the gall to say 'the film is my work . . . the burlesque scenes were a bit overdone, though'.[27]

Ernesto Gastaldi has an even more sinister interpretation: 'There is a vulgar, useless scene in which Terence Hill sings a stupid popular song in a street of the village [actually, it is a children's nursery rhyme, and it accompanies his actions on the soundtrack]. Leone added the scene only to make clear that this film wasn't one of the important serious films he had directed, because it was beginning to look every day more and more like it was going to be a very good Western indeed – maybe even better than his Westerns! And he couldn't bear it! After a while, he began to change his strategy, telling people *he* had been the real director!'[28] Tonino Valerii had been warned by Claudio Mancini of Rafran that 'if Leone shoots a single frame of film, everyone will say he made the entire movie', which is precisely what happened – not least because Sergio Leone's name appeared so often on the credits as 'Sergio Leone presents', 'from an idea by Sergio Leone' and 'produced by Sergio Leone', while the director's name appeared just once. Besides, the public was eager for a new Leone film. 'I didn't pay any attention to Mancini at the time,' Valerii remembered. 'Most of all, I didn't want Leone to suffer any financial penalty for overrunning ... But when the film came out, many critics wrote as if the real author of the film was Leone, and as if I was merely his amanuensis.'²⁹

For his first film as a producer, therefore, Leone had achieved his ambition of managing 'a Sergio Leone film directed by someone else'. He had also treated his director as 'an able technician to look after the shooting'. It had not been a particularly satisfying experience for anyone. He had overtaken *They Call Me Trinity* at the home box office: *My Name is Nobody* earned 3.63 billion lire (half a billion more than *Trinity*, about 1.3 billion less than its sequel). The film was also a huge hit in France and Germany, but did not do well in the USA, where Universal pruned it and did not put much muscle behind a lacklustre marketing campaign ('Nobody, but "Nobody", knows the trouble he's in!'). In retrospect Leone reckoned that 'the film was a bit disappointing. Valerii did not know how to give enough of a poetic dimension to this encounter.' Henry Fonda spoke of the film as a Western about which he felt indifferent. Terence Hill called his part 'the most mythic of my career – and the one I have the most affection for'. When asked later to assess Tonino Valerii's abilities, Leone tended to be sparing with his praise: 'He is intelligent and cultured . . . He became an efficient and correct director. Without genius, but with a lot of honesty.'³⁰ Tonino Valerii and Sergio Leone never worked together again.

Leone and family, meanwhile, took the opportunity to move house from the Via Lisippo out of town, to a large modern villa at 76 Via Birmania in EUR, next door to the Rafran offices. The villa was surrounded by a security fence and it was entered through an electronic gate. Sergio's next production for his company started life when he saw Bertrand Blier's *Les Valseuses* in Rome (1973 – the title was French slang for 'the testicles'). Blier's erotic farce, based on his own novel, told the story of two angry, unemployed suburban youths, Jean Claude (Gérard Dépardieu) and Pierrot (Patrick Dewaere) who join forces with Marie Ange (Miou-Miou), the mistress of a man whose car they have stolen, and con their way to the countryside. It was full of casual (usually brutal) sex, and quick thrills, with which the strange *ménage à trois* quickly becomes bored. Pierrot is shot in the testicles, unable to achieve an erection, and sodomized by Jean Claude; but, as the story progresses, he becomes more confident in his sexuality. Jean Claude is aggressive and macho, but becomes more mature and tender as a result of their adventures. Marie Ange, who is at first abused by everyone, discovers that sexual liberation can lead to personal liberation (she takes her clothes off at every possible opportunity). Critics couldn't make up their minds whether all this amounted to a misogynist rant or a feminist farce. Blier, for his part, claimed that 'I am not a misogynist; I show misogyny. My films are savage, but not only against women', and then went on to make the fantasy film *Calmos* (1975) which compared feminism with Stalinism. It was released during the first International Women's Year.

Leone's immediate thought was that this story of overgrown kids could be transposed into a Western setting, and he considered 'constructing a film for the trio from *Les Valseuses*', a *ménage à trois* between two conmen and an emancipated girl, drifting across Arizona and falling into a war between the US cavalry and the Indians. The kids would seem macho and callous, but would turn out to be on the side of the angels after all. 'But Bertrand Blier's film', said Leone, 'only did well in France – it wasn't even released to English-speaking markets' – so the decision was made to cast Terence Hill and Robert Charlebois (a thirty-year-old French-speaking Canadian singer) as 'the two boys' with Miou-Miou as the simple-minded girl in love with both of them. As the script by Ernesto Gastaldi and Fulvio Morsella developed, it left *Les Valseuses* behind and turned into a 'version of *The Sting*, only as a Western this time'.[31]

To direct it, Leone as producer selected Damiano Damiani, whose *Confessione di un comissario de polizia al procuratore della republica*/*Confessions of a Police Captain*, with Franco Nero and Martin Balsam, had been one of the hits of 1970, riding on the box-office successes of Costa-Gavras's *Z* and Elio Petri's *Investigation of a Citizen above Suspicion*. Leone had also been impressed by Damiani's Mexican revolution picture *Quien sabe?*; and Damiani had plenty of ideas to bring to the party: 'It is a *scherzo* on the formulaic clichés of the Western that differs from Leone's cinema – in that Leone really loves the formulaic aspects of the genre and strips them of all possible content. Leone is a great mannerist who sees in the Western a series of primitive struggles. It was a joy to be able to shoot in the place where John Ford made his films from *Stagecoach* onwards.'[32]

After a pre-credits sequence that shows a racist rancher being murdered by gunfighters dressed up as Indians (in the middle of Monument Valley), *Un genio, due compari, un pollo*/*A Genius, Two Friends and an Idiot* (1975) tells of a footloose saddle-tramp called Joe Thanks

(Hill) who performs gun duels in the street and then hands his hat around for contributions from the enthralled spectators (hence 'Thanks'). He is so quick on the draw that his gun comes out of his holster without him having to touch it. Joe meets his two associates, petty thieves Steam-Engine Bill (Charlebois) and Lucy (Miou-Miou), in a brothel, where they have been chased by an irate priest on the trail of his silver communion chalice. The trio then encounter some redundant workers from the Western Railroad Company who have been 'left high and dry' by their employers, also in Monument Valley. 'Where's the Pacific?' they ask. Joe persuades his two friends to take part in an elaborate sting: Bill will dress up as Colonel Pembroke (Jean Martin) and Lucy as his sister, so they can con crazy Major Cabot of the 5th Cavalry (Patrick McGoohan) out of $300,000 which rightfully belongs to the Indians. They cross the path of some gunfighters dressed up as Indians who, under their leader Mortimer, are causing mayhem in order to precipitate an all-out Indian war. On arrival at the fort, the scam goes badly wrong and Joe does a music-hall turn to cause max-imum irritation to the troops (to the strains of Rossini's *William Tell* overture). But the Indians are only prepared to negotiate with Pem-broke, so Cabot is forced to humour Bill and go along with the pre-tence. Eventually, a strongbox containing $300,000 is transported on a runaway stagecoach through Monument Valley, everyone chases it, the railroad workers are paid off and the Indians, now dressed up as set-tlers, are given the rest. The three friends embrace, and Lucy decides to settle for Bill – who has at last acknowledged that he is, in fact, of Indian descent. 'What the hell's going on?' asks Bill. It is a good question.

*Un genio* is full of references to Leone's films: the opening sequence is a rerun of the McBain family massacre, the Western Railroad Com-pany is an even more cynical version of Morton's operation, the chief baddie is called Mortimer and Terence Hill turns into Nobody about halfway through. When Joe challenges Doc Foster (Klaus Kinski) to a duel, he describes the conventional Leone routine: 'You know how these things work out in the West. Two fellas come out of the saloon and stand opposite each other. One of them's got his legs spread apart, and the people in the town get scared, and edge backward to a safe distance. And someone starts playing a funeral march on a bugle in the background [Joe starts imitating a Morricone *deguello*]. And then nothing – not a sound – only the whistling wind from the desert!' Only this time the duel will be a piece of performance art to impress the paying customers: 'Did you like the show?' asks the gunfighter in a duster, as he hands round his battered hat.

*Un genio* is also full of references to John Ford's work: the townspeople sing 'Oh my darling Clementine' as the real Colonel Pembroke arrives, Major Cabot tells the story of *Fort Apache* as a dinner-party speech, and there is even a reprise of Yakima Canutt's famous *Stagecoach* stunt. Superimposed – rather uneasily – on this network of film references is an ecological theme (the mountain in the way of the railroad is a sacred one), liberal attitudes towards the native Americans (the chief in all his finery is said to 'represent the past' – the important issue is how his tribe will earn a living in the modern world) and a fashionable streak of anti-militarism.

Blier's freewheeling *Les Valseuses* had turned into a chaotic film that tried much too hard to be clever. For Fulvio Morsella, part of the problem was the choice of director: 'It was an amusing script, directed by someone with no sense of humour at all. Giuliano Montaldo helped out by directing the second unit for Sergio, and some of it was shot by Sergio himself.'[33] After post-production, Morsella recalls, the worst of movie nightmares was visited upon the picture: 'Someone actually stole the original negative of the film, they kidnapped it and wanted a ransom for it in Rome . . . But being the managing director of the company, Rafran, I said, "I cannot pay you any ransom because I cannot justify it to the proper authorities as the manager of this company. So what you must do is find a person who can come and say I found this in a truck abandoned in this place; there is no other way." But they did not.' Fortunately, Leone had insisted on so many takes 'that we were able somehow to recuperate the film. The original negative was never found, and the entire film is made up of alternative takes. And they printed also a new negative from the positive of some shots.'[34]

'*Un genio* was not successful, also because people knew it was a recuperated film. Word got round, and we couldn't sell it very well.' It only earned 790 million lire in Italy (or 2.8 billion less than *Nobody*). In Germany *Un genio* was titled *Nobody's the Greatest* and in Portugal *Trinity and Friends*, which did not make a whole lot of difference. Oreste de Fornari called it 'a pretentious farce, where . . . the only relief is the emancipated smile of Miou-Miou'. Leone agreed with Morsella's verdict upon the director: 'I made a big mistake. Damiani excels in dramatic pieces, but he is not a humorist . . . The film disappointed me so much that I decided to produce no more Westerns.'[35] *Un genio* was indeed Leone's final encounter with the genre.

For a 'creative producer' who took risks, Leone seemed over-keen to distance himself from this project and shift responsibility on to the director he had chosen. He didn't, in fact, appear on the credits of *Un genio* – although his name appeared on French and German posters as 'Sergio Leone presents . . .'. And yet, the film was his original idea, and according to Terence Hill 'he was often present on the set'. Again because of a question of dates, Leone directed the pre-credits sequence, of the bigoted rancher in his isolated wooden ranch-house in the Valley who perishes at the hands of the 'false Indians'. As he runs away from imagined sounds in his head – it is as if the McBain massacre from *Once Upon a Time in the West* has become nothing more than a paranoid fantasy, a bitter joke. When the rancher falls to the ground it is not because he has been shot, but because he has caught his coat on a gatepost. Montaldo's second unit took charge of the subtitled sequences involving the Indians and their negotiations with the cavalry.

In future, Sergio Leone resolved to 'withdraw to the sidelines as a spectator'. His next production, his third for Rafran, emerged two years later: *Il gatto/The Cat/Who Killed the Cat?* directed by the sixty-one-year-old Luigi Comencini, whom Leone had assisted in 1952 on *The White Slave Trade*. 'I could be confident in choosing Comencini', he said ten years later, 'because . . . I knew him from experience to be a great professional.'[36] Leone called this gentle parody of Italian police films, which is also a comedy of manners, 'the story of a cat which leads to a series of murders'. Originally the script had been developed for comedian Alberto Sordi, but Leone decided that Ugo Tognazzi (as Amedeo Pegoraro) would make a better partner to Mariangela Melato (as Amedeo's sister Ofelia). Set in present-day Rome, the film concerned two middle-aged characters, both unmarried and both thriller addicts, who are offered one billion lire by an estate agent for their shabby genteel palazzo, which has been broken up into apartments. They decide to accept the offer, a decision which involves persuading the not-very-respectable tenants to leave. An opportunity to accelerate this process comes when their cat is killed. The owners go to the police and accuse all the tenants of being in some way implicated, and in the ensuing confusion they are all forced to vacate. The tenants include some prostitutes, a Mafia man, a priest, a CIA agent and a beauty queen from Yugoslavia. The investigation uncovers a mess of guilty secrets; including murder. Just when Amedeo and Mariangela think their problems are over, the story turns into a whodunnit. Mario Brega played a killer with a beard, and Ennio Morricone supplied a catchy theme tune – a sinister 'cat on the prowl' melody, arranged for xylophone, woodwind and mandolin, which sounds like Kurt Weill rearranged for a Roman café orchestra.

*Il gatto* did moderately well on domestic release (1.1 billion lire, considerably better than *Un genio*), and the humour was successfully exported to France where there was a solid market for dubbed versions of Italian domestic comedies. But it was scarcely seen by English-speaking audiences. When Leone went to Paris for the French première, an under-prepared journalist asked him if he had been tempted to give Luigi Comencini a few tips about how to direct the film: 'I replied that it was more likely that Comencini gave *me* advice. This incident showed the difficulties I was in, as a producer. If the critics thought that I had directed the productions which bore my name, the directors would begin to think so as well. And it would be impossible to avoid recriminations or silly compromises.' Fulvio Morsella remembers that 'Comencini knew his job well, so Sergio couldn't really interfere much.' Robert Benton's *The Late Show*, released the following year, had a similar plot and atmosphere to *Il gatto*.[37]

In 1979, the next Sergio Leone production did not 'bear my name' on the credits ('produced by Claudio Mancini and Fulvio Morsella for Rafran'). *Il giocattolo/The Toy/I'll Get a Gun* was directed by Giuliano Montaldo from a screenplay by Sergio Donati. It concerned meek security guard Vittorio Barletta (Nino Manfredi) who works hard for an industrialist called Griffo, until he sustains an injury in attending to a burglary, and is made redundant. His wife Ada (Marlène Jobert) is seriously ill and housebound. Vittorio's hobby is collecting clocks – the precision of the mechanisms appeals to his tidy mind. During his period of unemployment he becomes friendly with a policeman, and starts getting interested in guns. He joins a pistol club, and becomes a marksman. The pistol becomes his 'tragic toy' and he himself becomes a toy in the grip of violence. While having dinner with Vittorio at a pizzeria, the policeman recognizes a criminal and tries to arrest him, but gets killed in the process: Vittorio pulls out his gun and finishes off the murderer. His resentment against Griffo (years of petty oppression by a rich friend) and his bitterness about his wife lead him to contemplate revenge on his employer. But Ada tries to dissuade him and eventually takes the gun and shoots. Vittorio is mortally wounded. Critic Gianni Rondolino wrote of the film: 'This is not the usual "qualunquismo" which leads to fascism [like Michael Winner's *Death Wish* of three years before], but an exploration of violence in contemporary society . . . It is a shame that the film does not always avoid the temptation to become a conventional spectacle, and that Manfredi does not always avoid the unreal "mask" of a performance.' Morsella's recollection: 'Sergio had another strong director, and was less involved in this one.'[38]

Sergio Donati was extremely surprised to be working with Sergio Leone again, after the bad blood between them on *Giù la testa*: 'For a period, you can ask my agent, I had a clause in my contract under the heading "Sergio Leone". It stated: "If in the production of the movie Sergio Leone enters in any way, every sum of money must be doubled." I had that. Then I wrote a nice movie for Giuliano Montaldo, and Claudio Mancini produced. And at a certain point before the shooting, Sergio bought the share of Mancini's partner. And so I found myself with Sergio producing me. *Il giocattolo* was a great idea, ruined by the actor – Nino Manfredi . . . The finale of the movie was that this guy goes completely crazy, and his wife is ill and he decides to kill her, and she realizes that and waits in for him. It was intended like a Sergio Leone duel . . . Nino Manfredi said, "No, people see me as a good man, I can't do a thing like that." So there was a new finale. Sergio liked the original script very much. And I was very upset at first. But I must say he was a very good producer, defended the movie and so on.'[39] *Il giocattolo* was again edited by Nino Baragli and scored by Ennio Morricone (the main title theme, which begins and ends with a musical box, resembles that of *For a Few Dollars More*). The film earned 1.2 billion lire domestic, the tenth most popular Italian film of the year. After promoting it, Leone decided to 'put Rafran to sleep for a while – frankly I'd had enough'.

But he soon returned to the production side, for the company Medusa Cinematografica later in 1979. The film was *Un sacco bello/ Fun is Beautiful* (the title is slang for *A Sackful of Beauty*), the cinematic début (as actor-director) of twenty-nine-year-old Roman comedian and stand-up comic Carlo Verdone, son of film historian Professor Mario Verdone. Initially, Sergio Donati was expecting to be involved ('After *Il giocattolo* Sergio and I were friends again'), and suggested to Leone that in future collaborations, he would waive payment upfront for a stake in the 'back end' – 'like in civilized countries such as America'. A chance arose when Leone asked him about Verdone, and Donati enthused. The two went to see Verdone's stage show, and met him afterwards. Nine years later, Leone wrote an article about what had attracted him to Carlo Verdone when first he saw his performance: 'The ability to be many characters . . . a generous dose of "being Roman" (because his characters are always Roman), mixed with a credible cynicism and calculation. Carlo was "the man who uses his eyes" and this was the answer. And because of this I wanted to produce his first film while leaving the direction to him: his characters would not run the risk of being misinterpreted if *he* directed them.'

Donati recalls, 'I said, "Sergio, the thing that every producer would do is to take four characters played by Verdone, and make a movie. Why don't you do it? Four sketches, four characters." And I wrote a small story about a guy who falls in love with a girl, with other characters for Verdone to play. I worked with Carlo Verdone on the script.' Unhappily, shortly after completing a draft, Donati heard that Leone was touting his story to distributors, asking, 'What do you think?' Donati 'called Sergio and said, "What's this? This could happen with a shit of a producer, but not with *us*, surely . . .?" "Fuck you," again.'[40]

The script was then restarted from scratch, and developed by the team of Leo Benvenuti and Piero De Bernardi in collaboration with Verdone: these screenwriters were to become Verdone's regulars. *Un sacco bello* consists of three untitled parallel stories, each a showcase for one of the comedian's 'characters'. In the first he plays Enzo, a macho bully from the suburbs of Rome, who is looking for a friend to accompany him on a journey to Cracovia to pick up girls. In the second he is a hippy called Ruggero, a member of the 'Children of God' commune who is persuaded by his father (Mario Brega) to return home to his family, where he endures a series of homilies. In the third he plays Leo, a shy mamma's boy who meets a beautiful Spanish girl and fantasizes about a torrid love affair, before the arrival of the girl's fiancé shatters his illusions. Italian critics found some of these sketches to be 'a little dated', but praised Verdone's attempt to ring the changes on 'the tradition of Alberto Sordi', a tradition of *commedia all'italiana* distinct from the great Hollywood comedies, which, though very popular with home audiences from the mid-1950s to mid-1960s, was now in much need of a shot in the arm. Carlo Simi's production design, 'evoking a Roman suburban world with detail and sympathy', was also noted.[41]

*Un sacco bello* was Leone's most commercially successful production since *My Name is Nobody* (1.44 billion lire domestic) and turned Carlo Verdone into a major player in the Italian industry. The script included one or two in-jokes about Leone's own films: an idealized Spanish female called Marisol, a character called Sergio and Mario Brega playing an overweight traditionalist called Mario Brega. Verdone publicly acknowledged a debt to his producer: 'When Sergio decided to produce my film, the effect was to attract all the best collaborators to it. This was the début of a *jeune premier* and he helped me a great deal with direction, technique and editing. He supported me in all of these.' Sergio Leone was uncharacteristically modest: 'Verdone had never directed a feature – only one short documentary – so he felt apprehensive. Probably the fact that I was supporting him gave him the courage to go for it. I must say I stayed on the sidelines, and only gave some technical advice before shooting began – casting and then picking the right team to support him . . . The result was a hilarious film that did not seem like the work of a beginner at all. Actually, it appeared more technically sophisticated than it really was. I did the same thing with his second film, and then he really took off.'[42]

At about the time that he introduced Carlo Verdone to 'the trick of film', Leone made a brief cameo as himself, in Michael Ritchie's *An Almost Perfect Affair* (1979), a dark satire on the movie business, in which a young cineaste tries to get his first film, about the execution of murderer Gary Gilmore, screened at the Cannes Film Festival. It also featured Raf Vallone (taking off Dino De Laurentiis), Vittorio De Sica's son (as Vallone's son), plus uncredited appearances by Paul Mazursky, Marco Ferreri and other directors. *Affair* was partly filmed at Cannes in summer 1978, and shows how Leone had come to feel 'at home' in the festival environment as a regular jury member or visiting celebrity. He had bought a house in Paris in the mid-1970s. Cannes press photos show him as a member of the judging panel for feature films (1971), chatting with Italian film people (1974) and walking by Grand Beach (1978).

In the year after *Un sacco bello* was released, Leone helped to produce *Bianco rosso e verdone/White Red and Verdone Green* (a reference to the Italian flag) again for Medusa Cinematografica. Carlo Verdone continued to impersonate a variety of character types, all

371

motoring to their towns to vote in a general election: a bespectacled car buff from Turin who bores his wife and children to distraction with his incessant chatter; a vulgar Southerner in a too-small singlet who has emigrated to Germany; and an overgrown mamma's boy from Trastevere. Marketed as 'a portrait of Italy today', the film was one of the hits of the season in Rome, but *Variety* noted that its style 'plays so close to culture-bound humour that its exportability will probably be limited to other Mediterranean and Latin markets' – which is what happened. The sketches featuring the boy from Trastevere – in which Leone may well have had a hand, for obvious biographical reasons – were thought to be the most successful, not depending on 'crude stereotyping'; whereas the Southerner's struggles with a lavatory brush (he's never seen one before) and lavatory door (which he can't open) definitely came under that category. Luca Morsella was a third assistant on the film, and remembers Leone visiting a location near Fregene only to find that the background streets were deserted. ' "What happened here – did a bomb explode or something?" he asked. No one had noticed. It was very unusual to hear a producer wanting *more* extras! Verdone was his apprentice, sort of. But not to the extent Verdone sometimes claims.'[43]

Leone worked with Carlo Verdone again, five years later, on *Troppo forte/He's Too Much* (1986) – another episodic comedy in which Verdone plays Oscar (one of his television standbys), an overweight motorbike punk, who tries to impress everyone by styling himself 'the Rambo of Rome' and who auditions for an American action picture but is turned down because he cannot cut it as a tough guy. *Variety* criticized the film's 'tired, rerun look' and noted that Verdone's usual pathos and humanity were sadly missing this time; but the film had been a huge success in Italy 'thanks to younger viewers, especially'. Sergio Leone did not produce *Troppo forte*, but, according to his daughter Raffaella, who designed the costumes, 'he was sometimes on the set, helping out'. He even filmed (uncredited) a sequence involving a motorcycle race around Rome, his first directorial assignment since *Fistful* not to be scored by Ennio Morricone.[44]

In parallel with his career as a film producer, from 1974 onwards Sergio Leone directed around ten television commercials, mainly under the aegis of the French advertising company Télé Hachette: 'I had turned them down for a very long time. People approached me from all over the world and I always refused. That kind of work did not interest me. Finally, my entry into that milieu came through my friend Frédéric

Rossif [the French film director of *To Die in Madrid*, who had since become manager of Télé Hachette] . . . He promised me that the adventure would be amusing. Personally, I couldn't imagine what I could achieve in the space of thirty or forty seconds: in my films this was scarcely enough time for me to present a pair of hands clapping! But Rossif insisted. And I never regretted it – a fascinating experience to direct a half-minute film when one is more used to making productions lasting three hours. [When working on advertisements] I never agree to follow the images on a storyboard, conceived by individuals who are known – very paradoxically – as "creatives". It would be very unusual to find people with less creative ideas than these. Also, when I accept a commission, I insist on a certain freedom. They tend to agree to these conditions when there isn't enough time to find a more docile director. The slots have already been bought on television. Everything is scheduled. The advertisement has to be ready very quickly. In general I have only two weeks for conception, shooting, editing and mixing. And this pace pleases me, because the work is a distraction.'[45]

Of course, the financial rewards of such work were handsome in themselves, and Leone enjoyed mixing with French film people. His first commercial was broadcast in December 1974. It was photographed by Tonino Delli Colli, the music was Morricone's 'Valkyries' theme from *My Name is Nobody*, and the product was Gervais ice creams. A single helicopter shot shows the sand dunes of the Moroccan desert, over which a camel is being led by a female guide. An Arab sits on the camel, enthusiastically consuming a choc-ice. According to Leone, the woman was 'the Arab's wife in a state of slavery', but this subtlety is not apparent from the advertisement itself. Leone's next commercial was for the Renault 18. It was shot (again by Delli Colli) in Petra, Jordan, and showed the creation of the car in a temple. The machine, with an invisible driver, comes out of the darkness of the temple, down the steps and then seems to lose itself in the labyrinthine alleyways of Petra. A goddess appears and disappears, blocking its way – to which the car responds by flashing its lights, as if flirting with the veiled spirit. Eventually, the goddess releases the car and it drives on to a motorway. This was Leone's favourite among his advertisements: 'You feel that there is a breath of love between them; she makes a sign and the car leaves this sacred place to confront modern life and an autostrada.'[46]

Roland Barthes's *Mythologies* was a fashionable text among cinéastes at the time, and one of his essays concerns the launch of the Citroen DS (or 'déesse') at the 1955 Paris motor show: 'It is obvious', he wrote, 'that the new Citroen has *fallen from the sky* inasmuch as it suddenly appears as a superlative object.' The promotion of cars, Barthes continued, tended to present these machines as if they had magically appeared from out of nowhere, rather than from the assembly-line of a factory: hence the prevalence, in car commercials, of 'creation' imagery from the Bible; the car as Adam, shaped out of nothing. The codes of the advertisement masked the machine's real origins and enhanced its desirability. Whether or not Leone was consciously following this line of thought – highly doubtful – his Renault 18 commercial is a classic example of it. The car appears as if by magic, from within an ancient Jordanian temple. [47]

Leone then made another promotion for Renault, something of a parody of the Steve Reeves oeuvre, in which a diesel model appeared in chains in the middle of a small Colosseum, shot from above: the car struggles against the chains that restrain it, rears up and manages to break one of the huge links before shifting its own gears, spinning its wheels in the sand, and doing a lap of honour around the arena – all to the strains of Morricone's action music from *Un genio*. This one earned Leone a platinum 'Minerva': the Academy Award of European publicity. It was shot in the Roman arena in Tunis.

Leone's third commercial for Renault (the Renault 19) was photographed in February 1989 in Zimbabwe by Giuseppe Ruzzolini. It showed a biplane flying over an African village, with a herd of elephants below: four cars hurtle in formation out of straw huts at the start of a race, and the pilot tries to warn them about the elephants. To add to their problems a rickety bridge is about to collapse. Two of the cars manage to cross the bridge, while the other two jam on the brakes; their bumpers are chained to the bridge and they are driven very fast in the opposite direction. The bridge is saved by the combined power of the machines, just at the moment the elephants cross it. The cars are unhooked and driven away while the bridge collapses. As if to emphasize Leone's well-known penchant for destroying bridges, Morricone's duel music from *The Good, The Bad and The Ugly* plays on the soundtrack. According to Luca Morsella, who was the assistant, the crew arrived in the rainy season and had to wait around for some time to get what they wanted. Having shot some of the commercial, Leone lost patience, and left Morsella to complete it. Before he left, he asked a local cunning-man to pray for the rain to stop: the man replied that the community *needed* rain, but maybe he could arrange something for the following Tuesday – 'not Saturday to Monday, but something for Tuesday – don't tell anyone though; they'll kill me'. On the Tuesday it stopped raining, and Luca Morsella took over the advertisement. Then it started raining again. Needless to say, Sergio Leone enjoyed telling this tall tale whenever the opportunity arose. The shoot lasted a total of twenty-seven days.[48]

Other Leone advertisements in the late 1970s and 1980s included one for Galaxy washing-up liquid (1986, a thin veil is lifted from a table and blows out of the window, while a woman resembling Louise Brooks in *Pandora's Box* looks at the revelation of a spotless dinner service, and sees her boyfriend reflected in the wineglass); one for Euro-Assistance (also 1986, a young boy takes leave of his emotional family – at a crowded quayside – to go up the gangplank of a Marseilles–Trieste ship and point confidently at the Euro-Assistance badge on the sleeve of his bomber-jacket: 'dédans les banques et agences de voyages'); and one for Bonne Fournée bread mix (1985, a dramatically lit monochrome ad, in which a group of men leans over a bowl in the middle of a table, a long-haired hippy places a cloth over the bowl and takes the mixture to an oven, and there are cheers from his friends as the 'pain de campagne' emerges from this occult process: the table is on a raised stage, with curtains left and right, there is a Dali-esque desert backdrop and as the resulting bread is shared out the scene is set up to resemble the Last Supper). Leone also made advertisements for the Talbot Solara, Palmolive, J&B whisky and Lustucru rice at this time.

For a series of advertisements which Leone later claimed were conceived and made in two weeks flat, most of these were extraordinarily elaborate: locations in Morocco, Jordan, Tunisia, Trieste and Zimbabwe; helicopter shots and complex special effects; a crowded quayside and a specially built African village. According to Luca Morsella, Leone approached his commercials with his usual obsession about detail: 'For the Euro-Assistance one we had found a ship in Trieste, then just as we were going out to it, to film, he saw another ship he liked better so we had to negotiate for *that* one; for the Bonne Fournée commercial, I was sent to find an actor who looked like Jesus – and, yes, it was deliberately lit to look like a version of Dali – and when I came back Sergio said, "He *is* Jesus, so we can't use him," so he had to become a disciple instead.' Morsella adds, 'Sergio tended to choose his locations by deciding where the nearest good restaurant was' – one reason why, perhaps surprisingly, 'he actually enjoyed making a huge story in forty-five seconds'. That, and the fact that his good friend Carlo Simi designed most of them.[49]

All over Western Europe, the 1970s and 1980s were a period in advertising history when well-known but uncredited film-makers had the opportunity and the money to direct allusive commercials. These films were showered with awards at industry junkets, even though the products they were promoting were not necessarily successful in the marketplace. A kind of 'advertising for advertising's sake' seemed to be emerging, after the premium offers and glaring pack-shots of the previous decade (known in the trade as 'ad nauseam'), and cross-overs with the film industry, in both directions, were becoming more commonplace. The visual quality of billboards and commercials was undoubtedly improving. Where Leone was concerned, these little films were a chance to 'travel and experiment with things, and to put together some interesting syntheses . . . [Luigi] Comencini had a great line about today's television: some aliens land on our planet and ask what are those terrible films which distract them from looking at the commercials in peace and quiet.' It is clear from the results that Leone took a great deal more time and trouble over his commercials than he admitted. But he drew the line at rock videos. He was offered about a hundred of them, he said, but they did not interest him in the slightest.[50]

So commercials were a distraction – but from what? There were the productions for Rafran; there were various projects he half announced, only to abandon them. At the 1978 Cannes Film Festival Leone referred to a co-production deal between Italian television and the People's Republic of China to make a gigantic serial about the adventures of Marco Polo: 'the screenplay will have various episodes and will be filmed both for the small screen and the large. The Chinese themselves suggested my name as director . . . If I accept, I will shoot the exteriors in China for six months; interiors in a studio in Italy.' In the event, the series was eventually directed by Giuliano Montaldo and Franco Giraldi, with backing from America. There was to be another television series, on the life of Garibaldi; a joke going around the business was that if Leone told the story of the hundred red shirts, 'it would rapidly turn into two hundred or more'. There was a possible Steven Spielberg production, and an offer from De Laurentiis to direct

*Flash Gordon* ('I turned it down when I discovered that the project had nothing to do with Alex Raymond's original drawings').

As a producer, Leone said he was very tempted to work with Theo Angelopoulos and Alexandro Jodorowsky. Leone approached RAI with the idea of a ten-part adaptation of Gabriel García Márquez's novel *100 Years of Solitude*, but it fell through, either because Márquez 'asked a million dollars for the rights' or because RAI considered the wheeze a good deal less commercial than *Garibaldi* and *Marco Polo*. He contemplated 'the true story of the Nun of Monza', based on documents recently released by the church establishment, and thought it 'a great temptation as a film'. Plus there was the story of the anarchist Gaetano Bresci, assassin of King Umberto I in July 1900. And he continued to talk about Céline; and sometimes Pancho Villa; not to mention *Don Quixote*. When Leone went public about these projects, he never sounded entirely convinced, or convincing. He had something else on his mind.[51]

The years between *Giù la testa* in 1970 and *Once Upon a Time in America* in 1984 have been called Leone's 'wilderness years'. For those who were looking forward to the next stage in his development as a director, he seemed to be marking time. Leone *was* going through something of a crisis of professional confidence. He wanted to direct and he didn't. He wanted to be a 'creative producer' and he didn't. He was drawn to bigger and bigger projects, but had to content himself with supervising small ones. He dithered, and in public. Fulvio Morsella confirms that the role of producer really did not suit his 'spectacularizing' temperament. In one respect, he was unusually effective in the role: he was very careful about spending money. But Morsella parted company with his brother-in-law in the mid-1970s, 'because he would not pay me something that was due to me and so I quit . . . It's a long story. In certain things he was very generous. But in other things he wasn't.'[52]

His screenwriters, so accustomed to disputes with the maestro over money or contracts or credits, are more outspoken – bitter, even – on this score; Vincenzoni particularly. 'He used to buy just two dollars' worth of gas for such a hungry car [a Maserati] instead of a full tank, and he always ran out of it in the middle of a journey. He was waiting for somebody to give him a lift, and he used to say, "Well, the car ran out, and I have no money in my pocket." So, you had to buy him a full tank. This is the sort of man he was.'[53] For his Western writers, it was ironic that Sergio should want to be a 'creative producer', treating directors as vessels for his vision, because in their view that was what *he* really was: an able technician, brilliant on the set, but not the 'author' he later claimed to be. The ego of the auteur was a tendency he downgraded in others, but treasured in himself.

However, as Leone's more sympathetic witnesses tend to note, he tended to fantasize when he should have had his mind on day-to-day matters. 'He was the least practical person I ever met in my life,' says Luca Morsella. 'He was living in a world of his own in some ways.'[54] His constant embroidery of stories, which he knew perfectly well could be refuted by other witnesses, was part of the same syndrome. But like many unworldly individuals, he was particularly sensitive about being bested in arguments and financial transactions: it was like a muscle. When asked about why he collected antiques, he would sometimes say he wanted to make up for the fact that his father lost everything in the 1930s. Another reason, perhaps, why he had acquired his down-to-earth attitude towards accumulation, and his sharp business sense.

Critic David Thomson has asked of Leone's 'wilderness years' in the 1970s: 'Was he ill? Depressed? Was he lazy and fat from *Dollars* still? . . . Or was he striving to escape his funereal West . . . here is a film-maker whose autobiography might be instructive.'[55] Well, taking all in all, the 1970s were not about 'ruinous things' for Leone. It was in many ways an unsatisfactory decade, but he managed to keep busy – six major productions and ten television commercials – and consolidated the wealth he had made in the 1960s. But problematically, at least where English-speaking critics were concerned, most of his productions (and all of his commercials) did not export successfully; which meant that Leone became invisible to them. Only his mistakes were visible: he was the man who turned down *The Godfather*; he was also the man who originated *Un genio*. But by the decade's end, he was poised to return to the fray. Carla Leone recalls, 'When he made films, he would feel all the emotions a person would normally feel – laughter, tears, fear – only in a heightened way. And he missed them a great deal during that decade. A great deal. And when he eventually did get his great project together, he put into it *everything* he had missed in those years.'[56] As Leone asked himself just before shooting *Once Upon a Time in America*, 'How many years have I spent *not* working on this film?'

# Once Upon a Time in America

When Frank Costello introduced Vito Genovese to Bugsy Siegel and Meyer
Lansky, Genovese said, 'What are you trying to do? Load us with a bunch of
Hebes?' 'Take it easy, Don Vitone,' said Costello. 'You're nothing but a fuckin'
foreigner yourself.'

    Rich Cohen, *Tough Jews* (1998)

Bertolt Brecht was staying close by [in New York, late 1935], in fact his apartment was on the same landing. All I had to do was knock and say, 'Hey, what
about a bit of social studies?' Whereupon we would drive off to 42nd Street
and see the gangster films featuring that splendid man Jack Cagney, *Public
Enemy Number One* and so on. Those were our social studies.

    Hans Bunge, *Conversations with Composer Hans Eisler* (1970)

Harry Grey's 400-page novel *The Hoods* was first published in the USA
in May 1953,[1] and a paperback Italian translation was available in
Rome bookshops in the mid-1960s. It was largely written while its
author (real name: Harry Goldberg) was in Sing-Sing prison. After his
release, he specialized in writing for newspapers, radio and television
about Jewish gangsters in 1920s and 1930s New York. Apart from *The
Hoods*, his best-known work was a biography of the racketeer and
gang leader Arthur Flegenheimer (1902–35), dubbed 'Dutch' Schultz
despite his family's German origins. (The book was adapted as the low-
budget Warner Brothers film *Portrait of a Mobster* in 1961, with Vic
Morrow as Schultz.) In Grey's publicity photographs, he invariably
wore a homburg hat with the brim turned down, and a trenchcoat with
the collar turned up. He would complete the picture by clutching a long
cigar, and scowling at the lens: every inch the movie gangster turned
detective. His unique selling proposition was that his books were semi-
autobiographical – that he was a veteran gangster who had survived the
roaring twenties by walking away at the just right time. Top-drawer
figures such as Schultz, Benjamin 'Bugsy' Siegel, Vincent 'Mad Dog'
Coll and Meyer Lansky had walk-on parts in *The Hoods*, which

focused on a bunch of small-time hoodlums from around Delancey Street in Lower Manhattan, between November 1912 (the month of Woodrow Wilson's election to the presidency) and the early 1930s (when repeal of the 18th Amendment was poised to end the Prohibition era). The only big-time gangster to feature prominently in the story was Frank Costello, who runs 'The Combination', and employs the hoodlums on a contract basis from his luxurious uptown apartment.

The Hoods *begins in the noisy classroom of a tough immigrant soup school where Noodles, Big Maxie, harmonica-playing Cockeye Hymie, Patsy and pudgy little Dominic pore over a pulp Western about the exploits of Jesse James and his gang. Noodles ('You're smart, that's why they call you Noodles, hey?') is the narrator, surrogate for Harry Grey himself: he is also a two-bit punk with a chip on his shoulder and a touch of the street poet about him. Bored at his desk, he indulges in his favourite make-believe: that 'the familiar clamour of New York's Lower East Side through the open window' is 'a discordant operetta', composed of police whistles, horses' hooves, traffic blare and hoarse human cries.*

*The square mile of the Lower East Side – where 344,000 people lived in overcrowded tenements, the most concentrated mass of people in the world – is the setting for the gang's initiation into lives of crime. Big Maxie's adolescent dream is to make a million bucks holding up the Federal Reserve Bank. Noodles is book-smart, but convinced that, in teeming slums ruled by corrupt Tammany district bosses, bent judges and grasping landlords, his only future lies in robbery and violence – protected by Big Maxie's uncle, an undertaker. So he and the gang become apprentice hoodlums, running various cheap scams and hanging around Gelly's candy store on Delancey Street where Gelly's son Fat Moe serves at the counter. At his dingy tenement home, Noodles flirts with Peggy, the janitor's nymphomaniac daughter, argues with his mother and unemployed father, and tries to read Horatio Alger's From Rags to Riches in the hall toilet. At Gelly's, he fantasizes about Fat Moe's pretty brunette sister 'the untouchable Dolores'. Watching her dance in the back room, he feels overwhelming infatuation: 'a clean, uplifting emotion'. But in her haughty company, he is ashamed, of his 'dirty, frayed shirt collar, and the rip in my father's old jacket'.*

*The gang is employed by an Italian ex-convict called 'the Professor' to deliver opium to a shop in Mott Street, Chinatown. One day*

*Noodles and Maxie discover the underage Peggy in flagrante with Whitey, the bent, anti-Semitic local cop. They are delighted to have 'the goods' on him. Meanwhile Noodles' day-job is at a local laundry, where he joins a picket-line and fights against strike-breakers in the pay of the police. This leads to regular work as a 'sort of union organizer' for the local branch of the laundry teamsters. The Professor initiates the gang 'into the soothing, dreamy pleasures of opium'. He also supplies them with 'an assortment of guns and other lethal weapons necessary in the skilled art of committing mayhem'. They rob a small drugstore, only to be chased along Delancey by two cops: Noodles and Maxie get away, but sluggish little Dominic is shot dead by the sergeant. Noodles is later caught and sent to a Jewish Reformatory in upstate New York for eighteen months, while Patsy is sent to a Catholic Protectory.*

*Maxie does a deal with the local Tammany leader and manages to get off scot-free. But he is waiting at the gates of the Reformatory on Noodles' release, smoking a cigar and driving a shiny black Cadillac inherited from his uncle. The gang is now more senior in the trade union, Peggy has become a professional prostitute, Whitey has been promoted to sergeant, Dolores is 'a minor dance sensation in a Broadway musical comedy' and Prohibition has become law. Soon the gang is running a chain of speakeasies from its headquarters at 'Fat Moe's'. Noodles is the head bookkeeper, and their 'front' is Maxie's undertaking business. They join a Combination run by 'the most honourable and boldest hoodlum in the city, Frank or Francisco'.*

*But Noodles has problems adjusting to the big time and to taking orders. And his infatuation with Dolores has turned into a full-time obsession. He idles away hours daydreaming about her in an opium den. When Maxie is asked to do a big diamond heist on 45th Street, Noodles is reluctant to join in, but he is steamrollered by the adamant Max. The heist is based on information from an insurance executive whose wife Betty works in the office of the jewellery wholesaler. While the robbery is taking place she becomes sexually aroused by the violence: so does Noodles, who feels 'a sensual thrill' as he wrenches open the safe. Trying to understand himself at such moments, he takes a notion to write his own book about the gang's exploits: 'Why not be mob historian? . . . The actual facts would land me and everybody else in jail. I'll treat it as escapist stuff, omitting time and slightly camouflaging the place . . . After I write it, I guess I'd better keep it for twenty years or so.' But much of their work is boring and small-time: escorting truckloads of bootleg whisky, giving protection to the Jewish victims of goy loan-sharks.*

*Dolores reluctantly agrees to a date with Noodles at the Arrowhead Inn, before she leaves for Hollywood. Although Noodles hasn't spoken to her more than 'five times in about ten or twelve years', he intends to ask her to marry him. They will leave 'the stink of the city'; and, unlike in 'all the loused-up movie stories of hoodlums breaking away from the mob', he will retire gracefully. But the conversation in the chauffeur-driven limousine does not go according to plan: she remains out of reach, he imagines himself in her eyes as 'a filthy, stinking East Side bum'. Finally, he lunges at her in the back seat of the car and tears off her dress. The chauffeur intervenes, Noodles is shamed, and they return to the city in silence. The next day Noodles watches at Grand Central as Dolores walks out of his life. In his anguish, Noodles discovers that the gang is beginning to lose confidence in him. But a substantial contract from 'Frank' – to lean on a crooked local politician in South Jersey – brings them all together again. And Noodles tries to console himself with the length and depth of his friendship with Max ('We'd been pretty close as far back as I could remember . . . I'd bet he and I could converse without using words, just by a glance . . . Funny how neither of us got married').*

*Next, the gang gets involved – on behalf of the Combination – in helping a strike by elevator workers along Broadway: this involves destroying a rival mob led by a gay gangster called Salvy the Snake, and confronting the real estate agent – Mr Crowning – who runs the Broadway buildings. Noodles particularly enjoys giving this man his come-uppance, because: 'He belonged to every flag-waving, anti-Semitic, reactionary group out to make trouble and frig the little people of this country.' He also enjoys giving the two elected union delegates – Fitzgerald and Jimmy – exactly what they want (a 48-hour week, 40 cents an hour and recognition of the union), provided they are prepared to work in future for the Combination.*

*Noodles meets a chorus-girl, Eve McClain, and begins to think of settling down; Maxie spends time with the masochistic Betty, who has re-entered their lives, together with her insurance executive husband John (who is turned on by hearing about her sexual exploits). Noodles is increasingly disgusted by their behaviour, and by Maxie's short temper, megalomania and excessive brutality. While Max evolves a crazy*

20 Sergio Leone visits Monument Valley with designer Carlo Simi (left), while preparing for *Once Upon a Time in the West*

21 Leone nervously watches as financial arrangements for *Once Upon a Time in the West* are discussed: note the proposed casting of Robert Hossein, Robert Ryan and Enrico Maria Salerno
22 Leone demonstrates how to hold a gun, on the 'Morton railway carriage' set of *Once Upon a Time in the West*

23/24 Inspecting Henry Ford's hat, and miming a gunfight, on the 'Sweetwater' set of *Once Upon a Time in the West* in May 1968

25 Claudia Cardinale (Jill McBain) is photographed by Leone using an antique camera in Almeria

26 Leone lines up an extreme close-up of Henry Fonda (Frank) for the final duel sequence of *Once Upon a Time in the West*, June 1968

27 The director, by now bearded, surveys the 'Sweetwater' set on horseback

28 Rod Steiger (Juan) has an intense conversation with director Sergio
Leone on the set of *Giù la testa* in May 1970
29 Leone rehearses the 'don't talk to me about revolution' speech with
James Coburn (Sean)
30 Demonstrating how to hold a British army rifle on the 'Dublin pub'
set of *Giù la testa*

31 Discussing the final duel sequence of *My Name is Nobody* with director
Tonino Valerii (left foreground), while Terence Hill (Nobody) and Henry Fonda
(Jack Beauregard) wait in a New Orleans street, April 1973

32 Supervising the 'Wild Bunch' climax of *Nobody* in Almeria, with Henry Fonda and Terence Hill,
June 1973

33 Sergio Leone examines some of his art collection at home in the Via Birmania

34 In conference with composer Ennio Morricone,
in the early 1970s
35 Different shapes: Leone with Darlanne Fleugel (Eve) at the Prietralata set while shooting *Once Upon a Time in America*, 1982

36 Robert De Niro (Noodles) discusses a sequence with Leone on the 'Fat Moe's diner and speakeasy' set near Rome
37 Leone demonstrates to the young Noodles how to fight with Bugsy (James Russo)

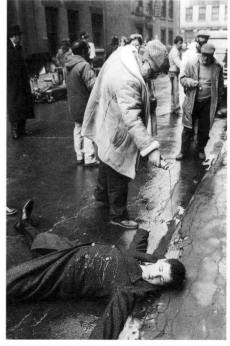

38 Robert De Niro (Noodles) and Elizabeth McGovern (Deborah) rehearsing with Leone and Tonino Delli Colli (left) on the beach near the Excelsior Hotel in Venice, August 1982
39 Leone dispenses the gore, while Tonino Delli Colli watches, on a Montreal location in September 1982

40 At the party after the gala screening of *Once Upon a Time in America* in Cannes, 20 May 1984. From left to right: James Woods, Jennifer Connelly, Sergio Leone, Robert De Niro, Arnon Milchan, Joe Pesci and Danny Aiello

41 With Michelangelo Antonioni, on a visit to the Cannes Film Festival

*plan of his own invention to rob the Federal Reserve Bank, Noodles resolves to inform the Prohibition Agents of an appointment the gang has made to escort a consignment of bootleg whisky up to Westchester: 'I hate to do it, but it's better to do eighteen months on a Prohibition rap than face certain death.'*

*Max persuades Noodles, Cockeye and Patsy to withdraw their considerable savings from the bank and place the cash in four safes hidden inside four large trunks – to evade an income-tax clampdown. Max will let them know after the Westchester operation exactly which warehouse the trunks have been taken to. Noodles puts $50,000 in Eve's bank account, and puts the rest of his money in one of the safes. He then phones the Prohibition Agents and retreats into Joey the Chinaman's opium den – where he reads in a newspaper that his three associates have been killed in a gun battle between the bootleg guards and the agents. After frantically searching (in vain) for the four trunks – which contain over a million dollars – he visits his dying mother and is discovered by three hit-men, the Combination's 'killer squad' sent to execute him for blowing the whistle. He is taken to a warehouse where he expects to be shot and then buried 'in a cement kimono at the bottom of the Hudson River': but he manages to persuade the hit-men that a key kept at Fat Moe's will unlock a million dollars, which he will share with them on a fifty–fifty basis. Fat Moe spikes their drinks, and Noodles returns to Joey the Chinaman's. When he hears that the hit squad has returned, he creeps out of the back door of the opium den, hitches a lift on a Mack truck, throws away his gun and leaves the city. 'But how I got away, where I holed up – that's another story.' He laughs to himself. God bless America.*

Sergio Leone first encountered *The Hoods* when Fulvio Morsella read it to him in Italian. He was 'not particularly enthusiastic about it as a piece of literature'. But the possibility that it could be 'the autobiography of a real-life gangster' was thrilling; even if the gangster in question was no Frank Costello; rather, 'a very humble man who only touched his epoch as if he was a ghost'.[2]

Noodles was at pains to distance himself throughout the book from phoney 'moving picture holdupnicks', 'loused-up stories of hoodlums' and the fast-talking heroics of Hollywood professional criminals. Since *The Hoods* was supposed to end in 1933, he must have had in mind Mervyn LeRoy's *Little Caesar* (1930), William Wellman's *The Public*

*Enemy* (1931) and Howard Hawks's *Scarface* (1932), three very popular films which chronicled the rise and fall of gangsters from lower-class ethnic backgrounds. And yet, as Sergio Leone was quick to notice, the book seemed to have been written by the screenwriter of a low-grade 'B' movie. The first-person narrator even reminded him of a Hollywood voice-over: 'The grotesque realism of this elderly gangster who, at the end of his life, couldn't stop himself using a repertoire of cinematic citations, of gestures and words seen and heard thousands of times on the big screen, stimulated my curiosity and amused me. I was struck by the vanity of this attempt and by the grandeur of its bankruptcy.' When the fable takes over from the actual life of the author, 'that could be a great subject for a film'.[3]

Noodles, the critic of Hollywood gangsterdom, nevertheless talks like Caesar Enrico Badillo, becomes a fall-guy and is sent to a Reformatory like the young Rocky Sullivan in *Angels with Dirty Faces*, describes his headmaster as if he was exactly like Pat O'Brien's Father Connolly in the same movie, hides his hardware in a box under his car like Cody Jarrett in *White Heat*, dresses expensively and tastelessly to show off his newfound wealth like Tony Camonte in *Scarface*, fantasizes about 'the untouchable Dolores' as if he was Jay Gatsby dreaming of the unattainable Daisy in Scott Fitzgerald's novel, expresses his frustration as if he was Eddie Bartlett lusting after Jean Sherman in *The Roaring Twenties*, develops an uneasy relationship with Maxie which mirrors that between Cagney and Bogart in the same movie, gets involved in a detective agency trying to break a strike of elevator workers which reads like a subplot from Dashiell Hammett's *Red Harvest*, and visits his dying mother in a mirror-image of the equivalent sequence at the end of *Public Enemy*. With such beloved sources held in common, small wonder that Sergio Leone 'developed an almighty urge to meet this Harry Grey in person'.

The classic 1930s gangster films had been shot on studio backlots, and their cityscapes had seemed almost unworldly despite the fact that their stories were set in or near the present day. These Hollywood films had created the impression that the underworld of the Prohibition era was largely Italian-American, or in the case of James Cagney, Irish-American. Yet, as Edward Behr, the most recent historian of the Prohibition era, has pointed out, the reality was more complex and much more ethnically diverse.[4] Arnold Rothstein, one of the biggest owners of speakeasies, clip-joints and New York night clubs ( and the man who was thought to have fixed the 1919 Baseball World Series) was Jewish. So were 'Dutch' Schultz, Meyer Lansky, probably the most astute underworld entrepreneur of all, and Benjamin 'Bugsy' Siegel. Rich Cohen's study *Tough Jews* (1998) provides a richly detailed 'family tree' of the most influential Jewish gangsters of New York during this era, and charts their respective ascents. After the pre-history of the gangs in New York, the Wild West period, the Irish were the first on the scene, then the Eastern Europeans, then the Italians. According to Cohen the myth of Italian domination of organized crime in New York was deliberately promulgated by law-enforcement agencies, and by senior Jewish gangsters who were more than happy to keep a low profile. He concludes: 'Most people have never heard of Jewish gangsters. They do not believe they ever existed. The very idea of a Jewish gangster goes against basic stereotypes of Jews, stereotypes that explain the place of Jews in the world . . . Even the few Jewish gangsters who are widely known are viewed through these stereotypes. They are seen as number crunchers, financial geniuses who could have worked their craft as easily on Wall Street as on Hester Street . . . How can people believe in violent Jewish mobsters? Jews don't do that.'[5] Well, adds Cohen, don't let the yarmulke fool ya!

The biographies of movie gangsters, as distinct from their real-life counterparts, had sometimes mirrored those of the first-generation movie moguls who put their money into the stories which depicted them.[6] Carl Laemmle, founder of Universal Pictures, originated from Laupheim, Württemberg, in southwestern Germany and emigrated to the Lower East Side where he worked as an errand boy for an alcoholic chemist. Adolph Zukor, who built up Paramount Pictures, originated from Risce in Hungary, and emigrated to the Lower East Side where he earned a few dollars a week as a boxer and street fighter (he had a cauliflower left ear for the rest of his life); William Fox, who founded the Fox Film Corporation, contributed to the family economy by peddling stove blacking from room to room on the Lower East Side; Louis B. Mayer, who headed MGM, emigrated to Canada from Dymer in Russia with his family and later claimed that he had lost all his papers in the process: he adopted the Fourth of July as his birthday; financier Marcus Loew was born on the Lower East Side and later recalled, 'I was poor, but so was everyone around me . . . It's an advantage to be poor in one sense. That's why so many successes came from the East

Side. The ones with talent for better things have every incentive there to exercise them.'[7]

And yet Edward G. Robinson changed his name from Emmanuel Goldenberg and made his name playing an Italian. John Garfield changed his name from Julius Garfinkle, at Jack Warner's specific request. The early moguls had an intuitive understanding, based on personal experience, of the dreams and aspirations of other immigrants and members of the urban underclass – the backbone of cinema audiences in the 1920s and 1930s. And by 1908, there were 100 movie houses in the Jewish quarter of New York alone. But in disseminating and to some extent creating 'the American Dream', the moguls submerged their own ethnic identity and avoided subjects that could in any way arouse prejudice against them. Their families had experienced enough of that back in Europe. The low esteem in which the movies were held by the WASP cultural establishment made the film industry the perfect route for the complete assimilation of the moguls into the host community. For obvious reasons, Jewish gangsters were *out*.[8]

Only in the historical 'gangster revival' of the late 1950s had Hollywood begun to pay close attention to the activities of gangsters from Eastern European backgrounds, with another trio of films: Budd Boetticher's *The Rise and Fall of Legs Diamond* (1960), Joseph M. Newman's *King of the Roaring 20s: The Story of Arnold Rothstein* (1961) and Joseph Pevney's *Portrait of a Mobster* (1961). By then, the first-generation moguls had made way for a new Hollywood establishment, far less sensitive – fifteen years after the Second World War – to controversial subjects such as gangsters who happened to come from Jewish backgrounds. None of these films turned the ethnic background of their hero-villains into an issue: the emphasis was on shoot-'em-ups and on keeping one step ahead of television. Thematically, their concern was chiefly with the decline of the freelance 'lone wolf' hoodlum, and the rise of corporate crime and nationwide syndicates presided over by men in grey pinstripes.

For Sergio Leone's purposes, the over-lit and well-scrubbed films of the early 1960s had made little or no effort to create a credible sense of period. Obvious anachronisms abounded. And he was interested in 'hoods', not celebrated gangsters. So Sergio Donati was commissioned to fill in some of the historical gaps, from New York newspaper archives, during the post-production phase of *The Good, The Bad and The Ugly*. He would have gleaned from his researches that the Lower East

Side, which had been the centre of New York Jewish life at the turn of the century, by the 1920s and 1930s was the home of a diminishing percentage of the Jewish population. The building of the Williamsburg Bridge in 1903 and the Manhattan Bridge in 1909 had led to an exodus towards the suburbs. Of those who remained, though, many lived in cramped and dilapidated two-room apartments with no bathroom and worked in sweatshops. Donati reported back to Leone with a strong sense of just how complex the project might turn out to be if it went ahead. 'What on earth do we know about the Jewish East Side?' he asked. Why not stick to Westerns?[9]

Robert Warshow wrote, famously, in his 1948 essay on the gangster movie, that 'In ways that we do not easily or willingly define, the gangster speaks for us, experiencing that part of the American psyche which rejects the qualities and the demands of modern life, which rejects "Americanism" itself. The gangster is the man of the city, with the city's language and knowledge . . . carrying his life in his hands like a placard, like a club . . . The gangster is lonely and melancholy, and can give the impression of a profound worldly wisdom. He appeals most to adolescents with their impatience and their feeling of being outsiders, but more generally he appeals to that side of all of us which refuses to believe in the "normal" possibilities of happiness and achievement; the gangster is the "no" to that great American "yes" which is stamped so big over our official culture and yet has so little to do with the way we really feel about our lives.'[10]

Warshow was contrasting the gangster with the more honourable cowboy hero, whereas Leone's cowboys tended to behave like gangsters. Nevertheless, the equation 'gangster' and 'Americanism' would certainly have struck a deep chord with Leone, who knew about the essay.

At this stage, he was thinking about a film which concentrated on the early childhood chapters of *The Hoods*. And he began to talk seriously to American producers about the possibility of backing a film version. In his initial excitement about the book, he may even have included Charles Bronson's harmonica in *Once Upon a Time in the West* because he had recently read about Cockeye's harmonica in *The Hoods*. And there's a scene in *The Good, The Bad and The Ugly* – set in Padré Ramirez's monastery – which closely resembles the section of the novel where Noodles' brother criticizes him for never visiting his sick mother and for choosing the easy way out by becoming a gangster. 'You make me laugh with your show-off devotion,' says the unnamed brother. 'Why don't you come around more often, big shot?' To which Noodles replies, 'Next time I come round, if you start that crap I'll throw you out of the window.' Where *Giù la testa* was concerned, Juan's life-long dream of robbing the bank at Mesa Verde mirrors Maxie's equivalent dream of robbing the Federal Reserve Bank.

Shortly after shooting *Once Upon a Time in the West*, on a visit to New York to discuss the marketing of the film, Sergio Leone phoned Harry Grey's literary agent, a lawyer, who told him that his client had no wish to discuss business affairs in person. The conversation gave Leone the distinct impression that the rights to the novel were available. But, he explained to the lawyer, he wanted to meet the author for other reasons: 'I would like to have a conversation with the man who wrote this book . . . If I buy the film rights of *The Hoods* it will not be to make a straightforward adaptation. So I must have several discussions with the man who wrote it – discussions which have nothing at all to do with your business affairs. We will talk money, you and I. But afterwards! For now, I want to meet the man who calls himself Harry Grey.'[11] His appeal fell on deaf ears: 'Harry Grey's lawyer kept saying "no" on principle. He spoke as if Harry Grey didn't care to speak to anyone.'

Frustrated in this line of attack, Leone decided to enlist the help of Charlie Bluhdorn, his friend and the tough tycoon who was boss of Gulf and Western. This did not help, as Leone recalled: 'Nothing doing. Harry Grey was not available, even to God Almighty. Lee Van Cleef enjoyed killing Western gunmen; this lawyer enjoyed smashing the telephone receiver on the noses of poor Christians. Could I start thinking about this project without even knowing Harry Grey? Yes, easily. Of course I could. This wasn't an issue. I just wanted to get to know the man. Curiosity, at that moment, obsessed me. I'm obsessed about detail, as everyone knows, and I wanted to reconstruct the America of Harry Grey exactly as it was, through his eyes. Speakeasies, synagogues, opium dens and everything. Only Grey, or some New York archivist who had a hot line to the Almighty, could help me. I preferred Grey.

'Two days went by. I was really getting fed up with New York, with films, with the offices of Paramount, with all those secretaries wearing glasses, with air-conditioning units: I simply couldn't find a way of getting the spider from his web. On the third day, just as I was on the point of returning to Italy, I got a telephone call in my hotel. Just like when I tried to contact Lee Van Cleef. Another magic moment. I honestly believe that if the telephone hadn't been invented, I would have remained a "B" movie director – or, worse still, a lawyer. Who was calling? Harry Grey in person.'[12]

A gravelly voice on the other end of the line announced: 'Mr Sergio Leone, I am Harry Grey.' When retelling this story, as he often liked to do, Leone would imitate the line in English. The voice was dry, distant and remote. At first, Leone thought it must be some kind of a joke, since he had let everyone who would listen know about his quest for the author of *The Hoods*. But the call was genuine, and it transpired that Grey had seen all Leone's 'Dollars' Westerns and enjoyed them. He agreed to meet their director later that same evening 'provided there were no witnesses'. Leone remembered how Harry Grey had carefully covered his tracks in *The Hoods*, in case the Combination – or the law – was still on his trail. But 'no witnesses' would be impossible, he said. He did not speak English very well and needed an interpreter – his brother-in-law Fulvio Morsella, who had lived in the USA for several years, knew a bit about American literature and his presence 'wouldn't be anything to worry about'. Grey agreed to this condition with a grunt, and hung up. As Leone later told *Cahiers du Cinéma*, it was only then that he realized, with a rush of excitement, that 'it was Noodles himself who had phoned me'.[13]

Leone continued: 'We left immediately, to go to a certain bar in Manhattan which Harry Grey had mentioned. I don't remember the name of it. It was near the New Calvary Cemetery, just off Greenpoint Avenue ... The bar, it was dark and sordid – of course, just as you'd expect. Furtive creatures were sitting at little tables in the shadows, whispering strange secrets to one another. A couple of prostitutes, with long stiletto boots of red plastic and aquamarine wigs. I couldn't tell if they were white or black. The barman was fat, but seemed benign and of uncertain sexual orientation. He was silently moving back and forth, behind the marble shelf, like a wind-up gnome. He was exactly in the mould of Fat Moe in *Once Upon a Time in America*. And this place – relaxing and secretive at the same time – was maybe the model for the 1968 version of Fat Moe's bar. The sequence where Noodles, after forty years' absence, comes back to New York and calls Fat Moe from a telephone kiosk in front of his bar – that was exactly like how we met Harry Grey. We sat next to a window, under a big neon advertisement for Coca-Cola . . . He arrived after a few minutes, as dead on time as a quartz watch. He waited a few moments, at the entrance, nodded "hello" to the barman and made a beeline in our direction. He was short and thick-set, with a bull neck, a very smooth face and the rosy complexion of a child, and he wore a hat which was already out of fashion when Claudette Colbert was young. Grey looked something like Edward G. Robinson, yet he was over seventy by some distance. We shook hands. He sat down and ordered a whisky, which he never actually drank. He studied it, coolly, for some time. Maybe he had cholesterol problems and ordered the drink only for appearances' sake – as is sometimes the custom in America. Where appearances play such a big part. He was a man of very few words. Yes, no, maybe. He had the vocabulary of a Dashiell Hammett gangster, speaking only about essentials. And acting for an invisible public.'[14]

Leone, through Morsella, started to talk about the book. Silence. Harry Grey looked at these two Italian film people gabbling away excitedly – and then at his whisky. Leone explained that he had really enjoyed *The Hoods* and really, really wanted to make a film out of it. Silence. Grey looked at Leone. The director confessed that he had filmed *The Good, The Bad and The Ugly* with *The Hoods* very much on his mind. He added that he had been trying to convince American studios to back a film version of the book since before *Once Upon a Time in the West*. There was silence. The elderly gangster was still looking at him, expressionless.

Fulvio Morsella was by no means certain that Grey understood what was going on: 'Grey was an old man, very humble-looking and you wouldn't give a cent for his intelligence . . . He was bright, and in fact full of ideas, but he didn't look it at all.'[15]

Leone was to recall, 'My brother-in-law, to help me out, asked if Grey might be willing to act as a consultant on the film. A very slight nod. He didn't seem enthusiastic. He didn't seem enthusiastic about *anything*. We really would be thrilled, added my brother-in-law, to share his memories of old New York – of his childhood in the ghetto, of the rise of the large-scale criminal organizations, of the books he'd read, of Prohibition, of corrupt cops, of platinum blondes, of his escape across America pursued by hitmen from the Mafia Combination, of the Statue of Liberty, of the gangs, of his misfortunes, of speakeasies, of the great bridges across the Hudson. Still silence. Grey studied his little glass of whisky. Okay, he said, finally. We managed to get a couple of answers out of him as if drawing teeth without an anaesthetic. Yes, no, maybe. He answered as if talking tortured his throat muscles. The other people in the bar must have thought that we three, sitting beneath the neon Coca-Cola sign, were exchanging forbidden secrets. I'm surprised no one called the police. It was tough. We were sweating on his every word. But after fifty minutes of this we had certainly entered the dark American night of Harry Grey. Half the film – I'm serious about this – had formed itself in my mind that night. *We* had outlined this idea to *him*, projected it on to him, while he, the old man, guided us with monosyllables, through a labyrinth of monosyllables. Yes, no, maybe.'

Then, just as suddenly as he had arrived, Harry Grey stood up, said goodbye, and began to walk towards the door. Sergio Leone asked if he would like a coffee, perhaps at an all-night high stool. No. Then the two Italians hailed a taxi and returned to their uptown hotel. 'I had wanted to speak to Harry Grey: well, I *had* spoken to him. In a way.' In the course of that fifty minutes, which over the years was to become some-thing of a party-piece for Sergio Leone, he had learned a few new things. He had learned that Noodles was not, decisively not 'Paul Muni in *Scarface* or James Cagney in *The Public Enemy*'. Nor was he Dutch Schultz or Al Capone. Noodles was 'a poor man who had tried his luck, a long time ago, with a machine-gun in his hand and a Borsalino on his head: *his* destiny was to become obscure and miserable . . . There was no Homer to sing the song of Harry Grey who, however, had attempted to write his own poem of crime.'[16]

The meeting reinforced Leone's gut feeling about *The Hoods*. 'After the childhood episodes in the book, which he had evidently lived per-sonally, everything was enmeshed in cliché. My intuition was con-firmed. The only authentic aspects of this story were the childhood episodes. So I said to myself – starting with the moment where the imaginary takes precedence over lived experience, to the point where even the author thought he was doing something new with the com-monest of stereotypes – we have well and truly reached the heart of the myth. And at that moment, I just *knew* I had to make a film about that idea – I had found my starting-point. I would make a homage to the *film noir* and a homage to cinema itself.'[17]

*The Hoods* had been prepared while its author was serving time in Sing-Sing: as for the actual writing, Leone gained the distinct impres-sion that 'he had received a lot of help from his wife, who it transpired had been a primary school teacher'.[18] Clearly, Harry Grey felt that he had lost time. Fancifully or not, Leone felt that growing up in the stultifying atmosphere of Mussolini's Rome had deprived him similarly. Both men had lived a surrogate life through the cinema. Whether or not Leone was simply projecting his preoccupations on to the monosyllabic old man he had waited so long to meet, this sense of 'lost time' seems to have made a deep impression on him: 'Neither of us wanted to depart in oblivion [Leone was approaching forty; Grey was in his seventies]. I wanted to mix my own souvenirs and memories with his, and to make a film about my lost time and his, and perhaps we would both find it again in this film. It could be subtitled "Once Upon a Time Was a Certain Cinema that No Longer Exists".'[19]

Leone left that Manhattan bar convinced that the best approach to filming *The Hoods* would be to have the elderly Noodles revisiting his childhood and youth as a small-time gangster; just as Harry Grey had revisited his early life when writing the book and Leone had visited Grey in 1968. The passage of time would be the central theme. The film would centre on the pivotal moment in 1933 when Noodles betrays his friends in order to save them, then retreats from the implications of his action, into the romance of the opium den: this, at the moment of the repeal of Prohibition, and the split between gangsters who can't move with the times (Noodles) and those who can and will (Max). Like the relationship between Harmonica and Frank (and, indeed, Juan and Sean, in the film Leone was poised to make), the main characters would be men who were mirror-images of each other: 'It seemed to me important, at that precise moment in my life, to film the almost futile existence of a person who left no trace and whose sole strength was the sentiment of friendship ... Something which has always touched me, and which I have treated in all my films, maybe because I was an only child.'[20]

It seems strange that a man of forty should be having such autumnal thoughts ('I must admit', Leone later remarked, 'that I was beginning to read the obituaries – when I never used to'), and identifying himself so strongly with a man nearly twice his age. The small-time American gangster and the wealthy Italian director had risen to very different estates in life. Allowing for hindsight in Leone's reminiscences, some of them sixteen years after the event, it is likely that Leone's insecurities about his place in film history, and the fact that he had never made a film he could truly consider 'personal', were dogging him. At the same time, he had clearly happened on a piece in which he could explore his fascination with time and memory (the chiming watch in *For a Few Dollars More*, the blank clock-face in *Once Upon a Time in the West*, the explanatory flashbacks which gradually come into focus) and with the theme of friendship. His adaptation of *The Hoods* could become a summation of his life's work, and at the same time the autobiography of an adult man who had a love–hate relationship with the Hollywood of his childhood. It would also have something to do with death; about a nobody who is drawn like a sleepwalker towards oblivion.

Fifteen years after it happened, he was to fantasize about 'someone placing a stone with an inscription in that Manhattan bar: the unveiling ceremony will be a party for cinephiles and executioners. But first a Leone buff would have to be elected Mayor of New York.' From the late 1960s onwards, Sergio Leone would meet Harry Grey several more times: 'sometimes in some god-forsaken bar, other times in Central Park or under the neon advertisements of Times Square. And once he invited me to his house where we ate overcooked spaghetti. We even became friends.' As he gained confidence, Harry began to tell some very tall tales. His wife, who dutifully cooked the spaghetti as a tribute to their distinguished guest, was even more inscrutable than her husband. She was, as Leone remembered her, 'tired of everything, and silent. She was an elderly ex-schoolteacher who had lived her whole life waiting for him, shaking with nerves every time the phone or the doorbell rang.' Leone would always bring someone with him – a prospective screenwriter or someone involved in developing the project. He liked showing Harry Grey off as a walking, talking piece of history.[21]

At the end of that first one-way conversation with Harry Grey, Leone had discovered one more thing, which jolted him in his seat. The film rights to *The Hoods* had already been sold, to producer Joseph E. Levine. Grey wasn't certain, but he thought they had since been sold on to someone else. Leone and Morsella cancelled their flight back to Italy and stayed in New York to find out more. A telephone call to Levine confirmed Grey's recollection. Levine had indeed sold *The Hoods* on to Dan Curtis, who at the time was producing NBC television's daytime 'Gothic' soap-opera *Dark Shadows* and who flatly refused to release the rights to Sergio Leone.[22] He intended to produce and direct *The Hoods* himself. Leone was profoundly dejected: 'I returned to Rome and tried hard to turn over another page and find another subject.

Nothing doing . . . Whatever I did, the well-spring of Harry Grey's novel had become a terrible inspiration.'[23]

To compound Leone's woe, his scriptwriting colleagues were far from convinced by his new central idea of having Noodles vanish without trace, only to return to a Manhattan bar and reappraise his past. Sergio Donati considered this 'extremely naïve', as did Luciano Vincenzoni and Ernesto Gastaldi.[24] Donati observed, 'A gangster who disappears from Chicago in 1933, retires into the countryside rubbing out all his traces and then reappears in New York twenty years later. This would have been possible in the Wild West in 1833, but in 1933, with the FBI, it surely wasn't.' Vincenzoni's take: 'Can you imagine in the USA, a man that was a gangster thirty years ago disappears, and becomes a governor of Massachusetts under another name? I mean, come on! . . . If a man wants to be a governor in the USA he has to expose his whole family history for three centuries. It is an idiocy.'

During the hiatus between *Once Upon a Time in the West* and *Giù la testa*, Leone discussed the problem of acquiring the rights to the novel with French producers André Génovès and Gérard Lebovici. Their company had made several films with Claude Chabrol and they were keen to participate in a Leone co-production. They agreed to make *Once Upon a Time, America* or *Once Upon a Time in America* together on condition that Génovès could succeed in acquiring the rights. Maybe Gérard Dépardieu could play the young Max, and Jean Gabin the same man twenty or thirty years later. Dépardieu was certainly interested. He told an interviewer in 1976 that the project reminded him of Bertolucci's *Novecento*: 'the history of a country told through the destinies of two men of the same age'.[25] Leone had 'described the role to me in person . . . it kept on changing every time he told it'. The director claimed, quite apart from the demands of the proposed co-production deal, to be taking the idea seriously: 'Maybe I could direct the French who lived in America. Gérard Dépardieu is a great actor, who was dying to play Max. He was prepared to learn English – with an impeccable accent – if Max was not after all to be French. I was tempted . . . but it eventually became apparent that the "fit" wasn't right.'[26] Gabin, for his part, agreed in principle, provided he would not be expected to fly to America: he preferred to travel by sea, and to 'discuss the role' at leisure during the voyage. Génovès tried hard to buy the book and even offered '$250,000 for a property which wasn't worth more than $20,000'. But Dan Curtis wouldn't budge. Following negotiations lasting eighteen months, during which Leone kept his word and did not discuss the project with anyone else, the idea collapsed. Then, as Luca Morsella (soon to become Leone's assistant) remembers, 'there was another guy, Rossellini's son, who tried to acquire the rights around 1973. He was the head of Gaumont. He tried but didn't manage. I think he spent quite a lot of time with Sergio trying to organize things.' After that, the concept of a French co-production died.[27]

In 1976 Leone turned to Alberto Grimaldi, and made an informal arrangement to the effect that if the producer could manage to acquire the rights to the novel, 'We will then talk.' 'Sergio and I had had a professional separation for a while,' Grimaldi was to recall. 'And I hadn't exactly been involved in this film from the beginning, but . . . I met Dan Curtis in LA, and persuaded him to find a replacement film project which I'd produce and he'd direct. In exchange, he would give me the rights to *The Hoods*.' That same day Grimaldi sent a copy of the novel to Leone's house in the Via Birmania, on a silver platter he'd bought at Bulgari, with a note saying he had the screen rights in the bag.[28] Grimaldi was at that time entering the most ambitious phase of his producing career. The replacement film turned out to be *Burnt Offerings* with Oliver Reed and Bette Davis, funded to the tune of $2 million. At last Sergio Leone could start planning *Once Upon a Time in America* in earnest. He was, as usual, nervous about directing it himself and made a series of trips to New York to discuss the adaptation with some possible candidates. By now Leone had had plenty of time to rehearse his storytelling skills, as Carla Leone remembers: 'He would always start with a single image. And, building on that image, would move outwards to the bigger story. In Rome, he would gather together all his friends after supper, and tell them what he had imagined so far. Slowly, slowly, the story would evolve. And everyone would say, "And then? And then?" And he would conclude by saying, "Wait until it comes out in the cinema, because I've no idea at this moment what happens next." '[29]

Leone didn't have a written script. For about ten years, from 1967 to 1977, according to Sergio Donati, 'he only had an opening scene'. Luca Morsella confirms this: 'I remember, because later on I went to Rafran to look for something and I found the two pages sent to the Authors' Copyright Protection Company, and these two pages about *Once Upon a Time in America* had nothing to do with the film. Not even two pages. Just "Gangster Story – New York in the 1930s". Some of the names were different as well. Probably it was just prepared to protect the name, the title and things like that.'[30]

His opening scene first emerged in a treatment written with Ernesto Gastaldi just after the script of *Un genio* was completed. Gastaldi recalls that Leone gave him *The Hoods*, which he liked, and then introduced him to Grey, 'who looked like Frank Sinatra'. Gastaldi was especially taken with a tale of Grey's, concerning how he had once eluded the Mob by driving his car into the Hudson River and pretending to kill himself: 'My treatment began this way: an old killer is escaping, followed by police cars, and falls into the river. The camera follows him as he plummets underwater, leaving him as he drowns to dwell on the wrecks lining the river bottom: modern sports cars slowly dissolve into antique ones. When the camera emerges from the river, we are back in the New York of the 1930s.' Leone certainly remembered this opening, but claimed 'I wrote it with an American screenwriter [Robert Dillon] who immediately afterwards made a film with John Frankenheimer: he practically stole the whole of this first part by giving it to *99 and 44/100 % Dead* (1974) . . . which had at the beginning the sequence I wanted to make, a cemetery under the water of the Hudson River.'[31]

Whoever was responsible for this idea (maybe Gastaldi's treatment turned into Dillon's draft script, and in any case it was derived from the Model T Ford at the bottom of the river in *The Night of the Hunter*), it was the basis of Sergio Leone's dramatic monologue whenever he wanted to attract attention to his project. It took him a quarter of an hour to describe this one scene. Grimaldi was convinced that 'a project like this needed an excellent American writer', and so Leone performed his party-piece to several.[32] On one such occasion, he met crime writer and journalist Pete Hamill and director Miloš Forman in a suite at the Pierre Hotel, New York. Leone began his presentation as usual, with a single attention-grabbing image. Two men have dragged a heavy corpse to the edge of a wharf, at night. The feet of the corpse are set in concrete – he is the victim of a gangland execution. The camera follows the corpse as it sinks to the bottom of the river. There, we see other corpses: men chained to cars; women still wearing jewels. Then the camera travels through a sewer to another underwater cemetery – this time with more impoverished-looking corpses: one tied to a cart; another in rags. Clearly, the bottom of the river has 'neighbourhoods' just like New York. Finally, the camera rises to the surface again, and reveals

the Statue of Liberty, reflected in the moonlight. Title: ONCE UPON A
TIME IN AMERICA.

After the film's eventual release, Pete Hamill recalled Leone's pitch
to Forman and himself. The Italian had inevitably relied upon a young
woman translator, plus Alberto Grimaldi, as he relayed the thrilling
details: ' "The body comes down, down, down. And then: close-up. Big,
big close-up. A green eye! And . . ." For forty-five minutes, with gestures and words and a voice that shifted from a whisper to a booming
bass, Sergio described scenes, characters, places and camera shots.
Sergio's performance was magnificent, but while I heard his tale of
gangsters, I was also remembering the gangsters of my own youth in
Brooklyn: cheap hoodlums, muscle boys, creeps who peddled heroin
and used knives and guns to fight people they couldn't beat with their
bare hands. I understood the romantic myth of the gangster, and the
enormous appeal of the man with the machine-gun, played by Cagney
or Bogart or Raft, the man whose choice was to make his own rules in a
world where most rules were hypothetical. But those gangsters were the
product of art: real gangsters were slime. Sergio was talking about the
gangsters of legend – the gangsters of the movies. The performance was
remarkable and for a long time, as the coffee grew cold, I could look at
nobody else but Sergio. But then there was a pause, as Sergio called to
Grimaldi for help with a word, and I glanced at Miloš. Miloš Forman
was sound asleep. Sergio slammed the table to emphasize a point and
shouted: "Tragedy! Like Shakespeare!" And Miloš was suddenly
awake. "Well," Sergio said, "what do you think?" Miloš nodded "Interesting," he said. We rose to say our goodbyes. Sergio and Grimaldi said
they would be in touch with us. Neither of us heard from them again!'[33]

At about the same time, Sergio Leone made initial contact with Fred
Caruso, a specialist in the production management of films made in the
New York area. Complicated logistics were his stock-in-trade; he had
recently looked after this side of things for *The Godfather*. Caruso
recalled of his encounter with Leone: 'We met at the Navarro Hotel.
Out of the bedroom of his suite came this huge bulk in a bathrobe,
slippers and a beard. I introduced myself, and he grunted. We shook
hands, and he grunted. Sergio loved to sit around in a bathrobe, but
he's big, and the bathrobe is wide open and he's wearing this brief
bikini jockstrap underwear and looking at me through these octagonal
eyeglasses, and the whole image is very weird to me.'[34] Leone asked
Caruso, as a favour, to estimate a very rough budget, and to do some

preliminary location scouting. Caruso reckoned that, on the evidence presented, the film was likely to cost in the region of $12 million to $15 million; and he agreed to recce a few locations. No fee was mentioned, and Caruso did not hear from Leone again for seven years.

Another 'potential director', in Leone's estimation, was John Milius, whose first feature *Dillinger* had impressed him a great deal. Set in Indiana and Illinois in 1933–4, the film had shown bank-robber John Dillinger (Warren Oates) and G-Man Melvin Purvis (Ben Johnson) as men equally obsessed with the creation and promotion of their own legends. Milius was a confirmed admirer of Leone, and set up a suitably flamboyant meeting in the Los Angeles hills, which Leone was to remember fondly: 'He came to pick us up, to drive us to dinner at his place. We travelled in his open car. As we approached his house, I heard the music from all my films playing in the sky. He had put powerful loudspeakers around his house which overlooked the hill. The sound echoed everywhere. When we reached his house, he opened a locked room. I thought it must contain jewels or something. But it was his gun collection.'[35]

Milius enthused about his years at the University of Southern California film school, where he, and classmates like George Lucas, 'took apart all Leone's films, shot by shot'. Then, the summit of Milius's ambition had been to spend his life writing and directing 'B' Westerns. The generation of film-makers soon to be dubbed 'the movie brats' (Milius, Lucas, Spielberg, Coppola, Carpenter and Scorsese) had all admired Leone's Westerns, and they shared his admiration for the old masters, and his disappointment with the seeming inability of contemporary Hollywood to create magic as it used to. Most of them were 'baby-boomers', born after a war which Leone had lived first-hand. But they identified with his use of film language and his unfashionably firm belief in the possibilities of cinema. Milius then amiably disparaged what had been done to his scripts for *The Life and Times of Judge Roy Bean* and *Jeremiah Johnson*. The former had been made 'too soft and too cute' by John Huston and Paul Newman: 'Roy Bean was harsh and he was cynical – "I know the law. I spend my entire life in its flagrant disregard" – and I was certainly influenced by the cynicism in the Leone movies there.' Similarly, *Jeremiah Johnson*, once mooted for Clint Eastwood and Sam Peckinpah and originally called *Liver Eating Johnson*, had become a more moderate work in the hands of Robert Redford and Sydney Pollack. Both films, Leone recalled Milius telling him, 'had been written thinking of me'. They chatted about Ford and Kurosawa (Milius's favourite directors). And then, finally, they got round to discussing the idea of John Milius directing *Once Upon a Time in America*. But Milius wasn't in a position to commit to the film. According to Leone, this was because 'he was in the process of scripting a story called *Apocalypse Now*'. Unless the conversation happened very early in the project's development, the reason Milius couldn't commit was actually that he was preparing his second feature *The Wind and the Lion*, a child's eye view of Teddy Roosevelt's overseas adventures.[36]

Grimaldi was still convinced that the film had to be written by an American, and preferably a well-known one. He eventually decided on Norman Mailer. A poster touting the combination of Leone and Mailer sounded like a dream ticket. Mickey Knox, a close friend of Mailer, arranged the introductions. Leone, a longstanding fan, was disappointed at their first meeting to hear that Mailer reckoned he was 'completely insane to deal with a subject like this' – one which would go down like a cement kimono in the Hollywood film community. As someone who 'thought of himself as more of a gangster than a Jew', he seemed to know what he was talking about.[37] But Mailer was prepared to give it a whirl. A deal was struck and, as Leone remembered it, Mailer 'really let himself go . . . He barricaded himself in a Rome hotel room with several bottles of whisky, a typewriter and some boxes of Cuban cigars. He "posted" sheets of paper under the door of his room, as he wrote them, to carriers who were standing by. And he remained there, in that room, without ever going out, for three weeks flat. We could hear him singing, cursing and shouting for ice cubes from about ten blocks away!'[38] Then Norman Mailer and Harry Grey met in New York: 'It was a priceless meeting . . . And the elderly Grey said, "Yes, no, maybe," while Norman Mailer acted the part of Norman Mailer. A great drinker, a great talker, a great smoker. The old man just watched him all the time, without any expression on his face. Then he stood up, put his hat on and went out of the bar without saying goodbye to anyone. Nothing else. He'd had enough and he was going back home.' Mailer wrote part of his script in the Philippines, where he was covering a boxing match.[39]

After this interlude, Leone reflected, 'I'm sorry to say [Mailer] only gave birth to a Mickey Mouse version. Mailer, at least to my eyes, the eyes of an old fan, is not a writer for the cinema.' Enrico Medioli took over where Mailer left off, and reckoned that 'there were no new solutions, nothing that one might really have hoped for from Mailer, who is himself a New York Jew of humble origins'. Franco Ferrini recalls that '[Mailer's] script had a hallucinatory and choppy construction in flashbacks with continuous jumps in time which made very little sense and kept the story from ever developing a structure'. Grimaldi adds that 'sadly, the contacts between Sergio and Norman Mailer yielded nothing good. I tried to interrupt the writing when I saw what was happening, but because we had signed an agreement, Mailer quickly wrote a text that . . . was, frankly, very bad.'[40] The net result, according to Leone, was that the production 'lost three months . . . and I decided I could manage to work without him. So I turned to my Italian scriptwriters.' The script Mailer delivered 'made no sense at all', and Grimaldi, it seems, initiated a lawsuit (the first of many on this project) to extricate himself. As Mickey Knox recalls, 'In the end there was warfare. they didn't want to pay Mailer his last payment. Mailer won the case, of course, and they had to pay him.'[41]

This concluded Leone's interest in an American collaborator, and he turned to two of the most respected writers in the Italian film business: Franco Arcalli (known to his friends as Kim) and Enrico Medioli. Since co-scripting and helping to edit *Django Kill*, ex-actor Arcalli had become Bernardo Bertolucci's editor and scriptwriter on *The Conformist* (1970) and *Last Tango in Paris* (1972). At the time he was working on *Novecento*. Arcalli's speciality lay in approaching scenarios from the perspective of an editor's visual language. Bertolucci's cousin Giovanni had introduced the director to Arcalli while *The Conformist* was in preparation, and Arcalli's input galvanized the film. Accustomed to seeing editing as 'a necessary evil', Bertolucci realized that, 'with a magnificent editor such as Kim, it's possible to watch the structure of the movie materialize, piece by piece'.[42] *The Conformist* was shot as a chronological narrative; in the final version, it employed continuous flashback. From 1970 to Arcalli's premature death from cancer in 1978, he and Bertolucci were very close collaborators. For at least three of those years, Arcalli was also contributing to the 'cutting and shaping' of Leone's gangster treatment. Since the story involved several time-shifts, Leone valued Arcalli's uncommon understanding of editing time and visual memory. He would provide the basic structure, not so much as a writer, but more as an improviser who could talk for hours and suggest ideas as they came to him. According to Enrico Medioli, Arcalli produced 'the crux of the film' in precisely this way.[43]

Medioli, on the other hand, had come to specialize in epic, operatic psychodramas of lost time, in collaboration with Luchino Visconti. Their partnership began with *Rocco and his Brothers*, and hit its stride with *The Leopard*, *The Damned* and *Ludwig*. Most tellingly for Leone's purpose, the writer had recently completed a twenty-hour television script for Visconti, based on Proust's *A la recherche du temps perdu*. As Medioli recalled in 1983: 'I think Leone wanted someone to contradict him. I had never been involved in an action film before ... None of us [screenwriters] was American, none of us a Jew, none of us a gangster; but we had encountered all of it, filtered through the cinema rather than through literature. The secret thread that winds through the story is a more European one. The sense of certain mistakes made, of deceit, of treachery, of bitterness, of time that is definitively lost ... The point of departure for our work was, frankly, a great love of old American movies.'[44] Medioli's involvement helped to create a remembrance of crimes past. In the script, when Noodles is asked by Fat Moe 'what have you been doin' all these years?' he replies, 'Been going to bed early,' an unmistakable echo of the celebrated first line of the overture to *Swann's Way*.

After several months' work – which Medioli likened to 'the construction of a cathedral'[45] – Leone, Arcalli and Medioli completed a draft script of some 300 pages. While Arcalli worked on finding practical solutions to the draft's time games, Leone took Medioli to New York to 'inspect locations', and introduce him to Harry Grey. This time the old man was a little more forthcoming, revealing that he had been associated with an Italian called 'Frank' who could only be Mr Costello. Moreover, 'He admitted that the sole liberty he had taken in *The Hoods* was on the question of Max. In reality, Max was not dead at all.' Now seventy, according to Grey, he had survived thanks to Murder Incorporated, the anonymous society of assassins run by Lepke, known as 'the Rabbi', and still accepted one or two contracts a year, to pay the rent. But, as Leone told Grey's tale, 'Max still had big ideas. So, at seventy years old, he proposed to Grey that they do a hold-up together. Harry's wife was seriously opposed to this collaboration. She said to him, "If you dare do that, at seventy, after all these years I've waited for you, I will leave you." And so he turned down the proposal. He didn't have too many regrets, though, because a few weeks later he saw Max being arrested on television. Max had attempted the job all by himself. And as a result found himself back in the slammer.'[46] So the 1968 section of the film, which post-dated the end of the novel, and for which Leone had expected to 'invent everything', now had an autobiographical basis as well: Noodles would encounter the elderly Max, whom he *thought* was dead and about whom he had been suffering pangs of guilt for thirty years, via a television news broadcast seen in a bar in 1968. And the four safes hidden inside four large trunks, which in the book simply disappear, would be part of Max's deliberate plan to exit from the Prohibition era in style.

Whenever Leone visited New York on business he took the opportunity to do some on-the-spot research into the social background to Noodles' escapades, by talking to other veterans from the Lower East Side: 'prostitutes and gangsters always considered cinema people as members of the same criminal fellowship and even as confessors ... And I listened to them so that I could get the flavour of the Jewish ghetto. Very soon, I came to understand that a Jewish gangster, even a very bad one, could become very religious as he got older. He wraps himself up in his religion. This happened to Meyer Lansky, for example ... When he was ill, at seventy, Lansky decided to give it all up to die and be buried in the promised land of Israel. But the authorities refused ... This reality fascinated me, because it made credible the attitude of Max at the end of my film. He is eaten away by guilt. He feels the need to be pardoned by his best friend. This would not be possible with an Italian ... The Mafiosi completely ridiculed religion. They only used it as a pretext.'[47] As usual, cinema was as potent as history in Leone's memories, and his comments on Meyer Lansky owe much to the fictional character of Hyman Roth (Lee Strasberg) in *The Godfather, Part Two* (1974). Roth was closely based on Lansky, who did indeed apply to settle in Tel Aviv in 1970–2, but who was extradited. Golda Meir famously said of him, 'No Mafia in Israel.' Coppola's film, as much as Leone's researches on the streets of New York, probably gave Leone justification for Max's autumnal crisis of conscience at the end of *America*. It may also have boosted his confidence about the dramatic and unexpected time-shifts between the 1920s and the 1960s which by now were a key feature of the script he had commissioned.

Leone had derived a wealth of background material from *Murder, Inc*, a 500-page exposé written by former Assistant District Attorney Burton Turkus, with journalist Sid Feder, and first published in 1951.[48] From this, he gleaned that it was at least possible, if very difficult, to evade both the vengeance of The Combination and the investigations of the FBI. Leone enjoyed telling a particular story: 'There are, in Chicago, two associates. One of them is approached by The Organization, with the order to kill the other. He doesn't question the order; he simply goes and kills the other man. The plan was for him, after the assassination, to abandon his vehicle and get into one of The Organization's cars, which will then take him to a safe place. However, what actually happens is that after the assassination, the man gets out of his car and, instead of entering the car which is following him, he rushes full speed into a wood beside the road and disappears. After thirteen years the gangsters see him again – in the cast of a Hollywood movie!'[49] The two associates were in fact from Brooklyn. The killer was Gangy Cohen, the victim Walter Sage. After stabbing Sage thirty-two times with an icepick, Cohen raced into the Catskill woods and disappeared. A few years later, a couple of hoods happened to be watching the boxing movie *Golden Boy*, with William Holden and Barbara Stanwyck, and they recognized Cohen, now calling himself 'Jack Gordon', as a heckler in the crowd scene at Madison Square Gardens. They didn't stay for the rest of the picture, but immediately spread the word to 'the troop'. The boys made no attempt to contact 'Gordon' direct, but three years later he was arrested in Hollywood and brought back to New York. No wonder Leone remembers this story from *Murder, Inc.* Just like Noodles, a man had outrun the Organization – if only for a while.[50]

There were other historical details from *Murder, Inc* (and from biographies of Rothstein, Schultz and Siegel published in the 1950s and 1960s), which either found their way into the script or reinforced what Harry Grey had said and written. Lepke and Jacob 'Gurrah' Shapiro, in some ways a prototype for the relationship between Max and Noodles, had first met as children while trying to steal from the same pushcart on a street in the Lower East Side. There were, indeed, a cluster of opium dens around the Chinatown intersection of Doyer, Mott and Pell streets. In 1931, as part of a season of strikes, the most influential garment workers' union – the giant Amalgamated Clothing Workers – split into factions, and gangsters with *schlammers* or lengths of lead pipe were called in by both sides. Lepke and his gang were involved, as was union boss Sidney Hillman who, a decade later, in a different incarnation, became Franklin D. Roosevelt's policy adviser on industrial production and 'very close to the White House'. Hillman has his parallel in the script of *Once Upon a Time in America*: Jimmy

O'Donnell. It was possible, after all, for a senior political figure to cover his tracks.

Gangster Pretty Levine made a speciality of driving around in a garbage truck, where he used sometimes to dump dead bodies. One of Lansky's dockland lieutenants was called Cockeye; a Brownsville hood went by the name of Noodles. Benjamin Siegel used to get very angry indeed whenever anyone dared to call him 'Bugsy' – meaning crazy in the head. Just like Max. And amateur-boxer-turned-gangster Irving 'Puggy' Feinstein was stabbed and tied up in a ball by Kid Twist Reles, Bugsy Goldstein and Pittsburgh Phil, before being doused with petrol and torched: by the time they had finished with Puggy only his shoes and socks, a few teeth and his wristwatch were recognizable. That was on Labour Day night in 1939. 'What had once been a man', wrote Turkus, 'was mostly scorched charcoal.' So the unrecognizably charred corpse in *Once Upon a Time in America* – another aspect of the script which Leone would be told was too far-fetched – had an historical precedent as well.[51]

When Leone returned to Rome he was convinced that he 'needed some more scriptwriters' for the section of the story now set in 1922 and so he called in the prolific writing team of Leonardo (or Leo) Benvenuti and Piero De Bernardi to develop the treatment and draft. Since 1955 the pair had collaborated on nineteen separate occasions. The film that particularly attracted Leone to them was one of their most recent efforts *Amici miei/Friends for Life* (1975) written for director Franco Rossi: 'The theme of friendship had been very well handled by them in that film. I thought they had just the right talent to develop to perfection everything connected with the childhood of Noodles, Max and the others . . . I spoke to them about my own childhood, about Trastevere, about many elements which had been in the script I wrote when I was much younger: *Viale Glorioso*.'[52] (They also shared memories of *The Bicycle Thieves*, and Leone happily reminisced about his own contribution to De Sica's film.) In all, Leone now had a team of collaborators to cover all the different historical periods of the story: Benvenuti and De Bernardi for 'childhood' in 1922, Medioli for Prohibition in the 1930s, and Arcalli (until 1978) for the time-shifts; with Leone himself holding it all together. He didn't write much himself. According to Medioli he preferred to 'oversee our work closely: he rejected, accepted, modified. As a screenwriter he was the polar opposite of his approach as a director. In the script he wanted everything to flow – he didn't want pauses, maybe because he knew that when putting the page on film he would certainly drag out the *tempi*.' Leo Benvenuti recalls that 'We left both the book and Norman Mailer's script behind us ... Sergio provided a sense of grandeur which was totally unrealistic but very cinematographic.'[53]

Leone also seconded a young film critic called Franco Ferrini to his team. Ferrini had freelanced on various specialized magazines after studying literature at the University of Pisa, and in 1971 had been commissioned to devote a complete issue of the journal *Bianco e Nero* to 'Leone and the Antiwestern'. Leone was cutting *Giù la testa* at the time: he set the young Ferrini up in a Rome apartment and gave him access to his personal prints, as well as a moviola to view them on. The resultant issue served as an 'apology' on behalf of the critical fraternity for not taking the maestro's work seriously enough. An evidently flattered Leone encouraged Ferrini, as he had encouraged Dario Argento in similar circumstances four years before. He was delighted to be taken so seriously by the Centro Sperimentale di Cinematografia, an experience which in Italy at least was by no means common in the early 1970s. A British author, writing a book entitled *Western Movies* at this time, was informed by the Italian Minister of Tourism that he didn't consider Leone's work to be acceptable public relations for his country's culture.

Ferrini recalls what happened next: 'One evening, probably I was half drunk, when Leone was driving me home in his brown Rolls-Royce, I plucked up the courage to ask him to let me collaborate on the script of *Once Upon a Time in America* and he agreed. That night I didn't sleep a wink, partly because there was an electric blanket in the apartment which I didn't know how to unplug, so I was anxious about it turning into a sort of electric chair.'[54] In the event, progress on the picture was so slow that Ferrini moved permanently to Rome from La Spezia and established himself as a scriptwriter with a 'conventional detective film', *Poliziotti violenti* (1976), and a couple of television scripts, before returning to Leone's work-in-progress.

Ferrini began by reading several histories and novels of the 1910s and the Prohibition era (including Herbert Asbury's 400-page *The Gangs of New York*, 1927) and studies of Jewish history such as Maurice Samuel's *The World of Shalom Alaikem*, about life in a Russian village during the pogroms. He also read the essay on the early New York gangster 'Monk Eastman' (Edward Osterman) by Borges in

*A Universal History of Infamy* (1933). Ferrini remembers that 'the shadow of the two *Godfather*s weighed heavily on Leone', and he was determined to avoid the clichés associated with Italian gangsters in the movies. His advice to Ferrini was 'don't write a history of gangsterism, but look at its mythology seen through European eyes'. He recalls: 'Leone always asked us to link one scene with the next, especially the links from the present to the past and vice versa. He asked us to write editing passages in the script: the links could be associations, traumas, musical themes or false trails. He did not want arbitrary flashbacks; they had to be motivated by the action and visually explained.'[55] Leone himself recalled that Ferrini was brought back to help polish 'the definitive script' at a stage when the main ideas were 'already cooked'. Before that, he was an onlooker like Argento during the *West* discussions. But, according to Luca Morsella, at a late stage, 'Ferrini was the one who thought of the swapping of the children – which became a substitute for some long scenes involving the strike and Police Chief Aiello: that's why I think Sergio decided to put his name on the opening credits.'[56]

Leone was still far from having a workable shooting script, but by now he had enough of a draft to see the way forward. He had already visited Canada late in 1975, to scout locations around Montreal, where there were 'more buildings and details of the 1930s than in New York itself. Besides which, Montreal was the capital of Prohibition – most of the bootleg alcohol passed through that city.' During the trip, he had dinner on 10 October with Pierre Trudeau and formally declared that shooting would start the following May. The cast, he said, would include Gérard Dépardieu as Noodles and Richard Dreyfuss as Max. Dreyfuss had impressed Leone the previous year, with his performance as a nervy Jewish adolescent on the make in *The Apprenticeship of Duddy Kravitz*. He had also been 'remarkable' in *Jaws* earlier in 1975, and Leone even had fond memories of his hysterical 'Baby Face Nelson' in Milius's *Dillinger*. Dreyfuss was, apparently, 'enthusiastic' about the project. Jean Gabin would play the older Max, and maybe James Cagney the older Noodles. And there could be guest appearances by some of the great stars of the golden age, such as George Raft, James Stewart, Henry Fonda and Glenn Ford. Dean Tavoularis, Coppola's art director on both *Godfather* films, would be on hand as consultant to ensure that the film looked authentic. There would also be an important part for French-Canadian singer-actor Robert Charlebois (fresh from *A Genius*). And part of the story would be set in Canada.[57]

At this stage, French actors were still in the frame, unless Leone was merely flattering his distinguished Canadian audience. In the event, Leone recalled, James Cagney proved to be 'flattered by the proposition, but he showed me his trembling hands as if to warn me'. So that idea led nowhere. Richard Dreyfuss did not feel it was the right moment for him to take on Max: to Leone's mind, 'a great pity'. Dépardieu disappeared from the project. So Leone announced that shooting would be delayed for over a year, until March 1977. The script was still 'inferior to the concept' and there were numerous 'material problems'. At the Cannes Film Festival in 1978 he unveiled *Marco Polo*, but spoke frequently of *America*.

By October 1981 he had a 317-page shooting script for a very long film, perhaps a film in two parts like *Novecento*.[58] But, given Leone's general tendency to 'drag out the *tempi*' of the written word on film, those two parts would certainly be very long parts.

*The script begins in a New York shadow puppet theatre in December 1933, where the puppets act out a version of the* Ramayana, *the Asian creation myth. Three hitmen burst in and brutally search the auditorium. The theatre is a front for an elaborate Chinese opium den, where Noodles lies, blissed out, clutching a newspaper with the head-line 'Bootleggers trapped by Feds: Three Slain – an anonymous phone call yesterday tipped off federal agents'. We hear the sound of a tele-phone ringing, which 'continues to echo in Noodles' head'. As he stares at the burning wick of a lamp, we see a snow-lined street where the corpses of Patrick Goldberg, Philip Stein and Maximilian Berkovicz are lying near their crashed Cadillac. 'Max's face looks like badly ground hamburger.' We then see – in the same nightmarish mono-chrome, sapped of contrast by the opium – the corpse of an old man, stretched out on the marble slab of a mortician's parlour. Noodles and his three friends are larking about with the corpse, much to the morti-cian's disgust, and 'turning him into a life-size Groucho Marx doll'. Then we are in Fat Moe's speakeasy, where the black and white decor sets off 'the white satin slink à la Harlow of the dames and the black tuxes à la Cagney of the dudes'. Noodles' friends are dancing and enjoying themselves, but the man himself is nervous as he gets up and goes into the private office. He walks over to a phone and dials: the hand of Sergeant McWillis, in a police station, reaches for a receiver. The ringing of the phone reaches a crescendo and stops.*

*At an abandoned dock, Sal and Carmine douse the unconscious Noodles with petrol while Pasquale lights a match, blows it out and flips it at his victim. 'I thought you was tougher,' says Pasquale in a heavy Italian accent. 'They tell us "Watch out for this one, he got balls, he got brains, he sold his three pals like Judas." But you go get yourself doped up . . . You wanna say the Ave Maria?' Carmine interjects: 'He's a Jew.' 'Say the Ave Jehovah then. Then you gonna burn.' Noodles manages to reply, 'A million dollars is going to burn with me,' and persuades the hitmen to accompany him to find the key which will unlock the loot. They go to Fat Moe's speakeasy, which has an 'In Mourning' sign hanging outside it, where Noodles asks for a drink. 'Make it four. Private stock.' Fat Moe's eyes are rimmed with red as he pours the drinks. Noodles leads the hitmen into the private office, as a grandfather clock ticks away, and watches as they begin to collapse. The drinks have been spiked. After a violent struggle, he shoots each of them, grabs the key to the desk and another key attached to it and leaves. At a subway station, he opens a locker – only to discover that the beat-up suitcase inside it is full of old newspapers and nothing else. At a level crossing on the outskirts of New York, Noodles thumbs a lift from a truck driver (with 'Merry Christmas and Happy 1934' emblazoned on his old truck). 'We hear the roar of its wheels and the wail of a train's whistle, and the view across the tracks is blocked by the engine, the tender, and the cars – car after car laden with Model Ts or whatever Ford was turning out in 1933 . . . The train keeps passing, but the cars are no longer laden with 1933 Fords. They've become 1968 models in pink and turquoise and emerald green, announced by a title that fills the screen:* ONCE UPON A TIME IN AMERICA. *The train disappears, taking its rattle with it, and the barriers rise. But we are no longer staring out over open countryside. We see instead an endless row of high-rises, a cement City of Oz. Heading the row of cars that face us at the crossing is a 1960 Chevy. The driver is in his sixties too . . . Noodles, forty years later.'*

*Outside a synagogue in the City (summer 1968), he sees the Beth Israel cemetery being bulldozed: it is on the street where Noodles grew up 'and not all that changed by time'. Inside the building, he discusses a letter he has received with the Secretary of the Synagogue (in whose office there are 'a bright poster advertising Israel . . . and a colour photo of Golda Meir'), and learns that the three bodies he is looking for have been re-interred out at Riversdale. His name, he says, is Robert*

*Williams. But the letter was not in fact sent by the Synagogue. From a phone booth in front of Fat Moe's, Noodles makes contact with his friend for the first time in thirty-five years – and enters the now-shabby diner with the words 'I brought back the key to your clock'. Noodles examines some old photographs on the wall of himself and his three friends – Max, Cockeye and Patsy – and hears the song they used to sing, 'Amapola', in a corner of his brain. As if drawn by the music, he goes to a little door at the back of Moe's diner, gets up on a seat and looks through a little opening 'which oddly enough seems to be flooded with sunlight'.*

*There, in a cluttered back room, we see a thirteen-year-old girl, 'slim and boyish in her leotard and ballet slippers, dancing to "Amapola" played on an old wind-up Victrolo with a horn'. We are in 1923, and the fourteen-year-old Noodles ('unkempt, uncombed, dressed in ratty hand-me-downs') is secretly peeping at Deborah from on top of a toilet as she goes through her paces. But she is aware of his presence, and 'shows off her little sweet tush as she puts the shoes in a bag'. As Deborah leaves for her elocution lesson, through Gelly's Bar ('men make up most of the crowd in the café, men with the faces and garb of Ashkenazi Jews from Western Europe'), she asks her brother Fat Moe to 'put some bug-killer in the toilet'. Noodles chases her into the street – where he bumps into Patsy, Cockeye and the eight-year-old Dominic – and grabs her by her long black braid. She holds her own in spite of the pain: 'You're filthy, you make me sick, you crawl up the toilet wall just like a roach.'*

*The four boys saunter off to a newsstand, and after leafing through copies of the* Police Gazette, *set fire to it and run like hell. At Monkey's speakeasy, they then select a drunk to roll. The unfortunate man has a massive gold watch on a chain, and just as they are about to roll him, in a dead-end alley, Whitey the neighbourhood cop happens to walk by. A horse-drawn wagon heaped with crummy, beaten-up furniture also happens to be passing, and sitting on it is a boy 'playing his own serious game of King of the Mountain'. It is the young Max, and 'like a guardian angel' he manages somehow to hike the drunk up on to the wagon and drive off. Cockeye pulls out his little flute, his pipes of Pan, and tootles a cheery mini-march on it as the disappointed gang saunters down the street.*

*On the steps outside his tenement block, Noodles catches sight of Max again. He dashes up the stairs to the third floor, and goes into a dingy apartment shouting, 'Mameh, I'm hungry.' 'So eat gefilte fish and bread, boyeleh,' comes the reply. His father is at prayer, and his brother – who seems to have eaten all the food – is asleep on the kitchen floor. There is a scuffle, while the father, in a prayer shawl and phylacteries, intones in Yiddish, 'Hear O Israel, the Lord our God, the Lord is One.' Noodles: 'Yeah, yeah, O Israel, about the man who eats the food out of his own kid's mouth.' Mother: 'David ben Isaac, honour your father! You're a Godless child.' Noodles: 'No I ain't. I got my God. Money, shekels, mazuma.' Noodles storms out and locks himself in the lavatory to read a book. He unlocks the door when he hears Peggy coming, and they flirt with each other: 'I don't like to do it free. Bring me a charlotte Russe with whipped cream, and I'll let you.'*

*At the Grammar School, teacher Miss Mons is calling the roll: 'Aaronson, Aiello, Bernstein, Cochrane, Di Salvo, Fitzpatrick ... Katz, Levine, Matriciano, O'Connor, Ramirez ...' Max Berkovicz enters the classroom ('my uncle just enrolled me'). He is very self-assured: 'Maximilian Berkovicz, you're of Russian-Jewish extraction?' 'Polish. But I was born in America. I lived in the Bronx. My father died, so we moved here to my uncle's. He runs a funeral home, and I hope to help him when I've finished my homework – to learn and to earn, as you might say.' Max pulls out a watch, on a massive gold chain. This infuriates Noodles, who has a fistfight with Max in the corridor outside until the newcomer says, 'What are you trying to do, kill time?' They both have a good laugh. In a pawn shop, the gang (with Max) exchanges the chains and watch fob for an old switchblade. After discussing whether or not to tell Bugsy about it (Dominic: 'He's the boss'/Max: 'I don't need a boss'), they rob a passer-by at knife point, pull off his trousers and shoes, and run for it. Max stays behind to deal the man 'four vicious, senseless blows', and then catches up with them.*

*It is the Sabbath, and Noodles pursues Deborah into Gelly's bar, as the merchants are closing up their shops and heading for the synagogue in their Sabbath best. Inside, she 'prays' with him by quoting from The Song of Songs in the Old Testament. Deborah rounds off this poetic encounter by saying, 'He is altogether lovable ... but he'll always be a two-bit punk. So my beloved isn't my type, which is a crying shame.' Max's voice interrupts them ('Go on home, your mother's calling you'), and in the alleyway outside he tells Noodles that he has offloaded their most recent lot of ill-gotten gains to 'Old*

*Shitzy' Lipschitz. Then, the celebrated Bugsy and his gang appear and savagely beat up the two boys. Noodles turns to Deborah for help: 'Her face is full of sadness, but she doesn't answer and her mouth is sternly sealed'. The two boys stagger into the funeral home belonging to Max's uncle, to recover. They discuss how to get rid of Bugsy, who 'owns' everybody, including Whitey the cop. Then we are in Gelly's bar, where Patsy selects a charlotte Russe with cream: he goes to Noodles' house, and while he is waiting for Peggy to get out of the bath, sits on the stairs and proceeds to eat the delicious treat. Patsy then watches Peggy meet Whitey the cop, on the roof among the water tanks and chimneys. He fetches Noodles who, with Max, photographs Whitey in flagrante 'with your kishka up the tochis of a minor'. The two boys persuade this 'Irish cop' to pay for them to go with Peggy – Noodles in too much of a rush, Max too nervous to perform – and to stop protecting Bugsy from the Feds.*

*Behind Monkey's speakeasy, Bugsy and his gang supervise the unloading of a truckful of bootleg whisky, but two cop cars suddenly arrive and the Feds arrest everyone in sight before smashing the bottles and flooding the alleyway with booze. Max, Noodles and the gang watch with delight from a roof across the way. Cockeye pulls out his flute and joyously leads them, like the Pied Piper, down the fire-escape. In a hidden distillery behind the Capuano Brothers' paper plant, the boys try to make the Italians an offer they can't refuse, 'doing what Bugsy did'. Dominic plays up his Italian accent to show he's one of the family. The Brothers Al, Fred and Johnny aren't interested until they see the boy's latest invention, which will save bootleg booze thrown overboard during Coast Guard raids. In Lower New York Bay, the invention proves its worth, but Noodles is very upset when he thinks Max has drowned.*

*At a subway station, the gang – 'in handsome overcoats, shiny shoes, caps, even gloves yet' – led by Max, solemnly swears always to put 50 per cent of their profits into a straw suitcase. Fat Moe, who will not know what it is for, will be the keeper of the key. The boys march off, only to bump into Bugsy – who shoots Dominic in the back: 'the boy collapses beside Noodles and says, as if amazed and apologetic at the same time, "I tripped." Noodles rushes out, his switchblade at the ready (while Max holds back and watches) and stabs Bugsy over and over again. When two mounted policemen try to intervene, he then stabs one of them in the chest. Max, Patsy and Cockeye wave goodbye to*

*Noodles as he is bundled into prison in a paddy wagon. There is an inscription over the door.*

*1968: The same inscription from Isaiah 3.25, 'Your men will fall by the sword, your heroes in the fight,' is seen over the entrance to an elaborate marble mausoleum in Riversdale cemetery. As Noodles enters, he hears 'music he hasn't heard in years' – Cockeye's flute, piped into the building from two loudspeakers. When he closes the door, it stops. It is the tomb of Maximilian Berkovicz 1908–1933, Patrick Goldberg 1909–1933 and Philip Stein 1909–1933, and the building has apparently been 'erected to their everlasting memory by their friend and brother David Aaronson – Noodles. 1967'. As Noodles reaches for a little key – hanging from the 'd' in Noodles – the woman director of Riversdale enters the tomb and tells him that Mr Aaronson 'left the whole thing up to us', sent a tape of the music, and paid through a foreign bank. She is upset that the gardener let Mr Williams into the mausoleum when he isn't a relative.*

*At the subway station, he unlocks the old straw suitcase and finds 'advance payment for your next job' (there were evidently two keys, and two lockers). As he walks along the street, clutching the suitcase, a frisbee skims the top of his head – and the hand which catches it turns into Max's hand as he grabs a suitcase from Noodles, outside the prison, on 11 June 1933. Noodles has served six years. Max, who is dressed to the nines, is there to pick him up in a majestic black hearse ('my uncle died and left it all to me') complete with a hooker – laid on for Noodles' benefit – in the coffin. They go into Fat Moe's modernized speakeasy, where the gang welcomes him back, and Peggy comes on like Mae West. Noodles has a tentative conversation with Deborah ('Anyway, you came to welcome me back'/'Not really. I still live here . . . I'm at the Royal, every night at eight-thirty . . . You can come and spy on me if you like'), before going to the delicatessen with an impatient Max to meet the elderly Frankie Esposito and Joe from Detroit. Frankie: 'They're all here, the four horsemen of the Apocalypse. Did you happen to see that movie, Joe?' Joe has asked Frankie, as a favour, to arrange a diamond robbery in Detroit – after which the jewels will be taken to Canada for export to Amsterdam. Noodles is unconvinced, but reluctantly goes along with the plan.*

*On the runway of St Louis airport, the gang clambers on to a plane ('Hughes Airlines, St Louis') just as it is about to take off. They are met at Detroit airport, by an insurance-man-turned-informer who guides* them to 112, 44th Street in downtown Detroit and Van Linden's jewellers. During the violent robbery itself, Carol – the insurance man's wife and Van Linden's secretary – is 'turned on by these thugs and their violence'. Noodles obliges her. At a customs checkpoint on the Canadian border, the boys show their passports: on a 'city street, Canada', they hand the jewels over to Joe – who is shot by Patsy while he inspects the loot through a jeweller's eyeglass. One of Joe's gang escapes the ensuing mayhem, and Noodles chases him into a feather-cleaning plant: the man is smothered in 'a Niagara of feathers', and then shot at point-blank range for good measure. The gang of four jump off a pier and 'dive bare-ass into a lake', but Noodles' mood suddenly changes. Noodles: 'Good thing you didn't tell me – 'cos I would have said no. I would have said yes to rubbing out Joe for the diamonds – but no to working for Frankie'/'Frankie's as big as they come. He runs the Combine . . . '/'Aren't you the guy who told me once you didn't need a boss?' Cockeye has climbed back on to the pier and is playing the gang's little march, 'slowly this time, sadly'. At the end of the argument, a motorboat sidles up to the dock – which turns into a similar boat outside a Long Island mansion in summer 1968.

As the elderly Noodles sits behind the wheel of his car, looking on, the boat is blown to smithereens. He picks up a newspaper, with the headline circled in red: 'Pension Fund Scandal: Senator Bailey to appear before Committee'. And written in red beside it: 'To the attention of Mr David Aaronson – Noodles'. As the cops and fire brigade arrive, we realize we are now viewing the scene on a television set over Fat Moe's bar: 'It was only by chance', says the newscaster, 'that Senator Bailey missed his regularly scheduled fishing expedition . . .' The newscaster then interviews Jimmy O'Donnell, General Secretary of the Transport Union, who denies any connection between 'the Bailey scandal' and his union: 'all my life I've fought like a tiger to keep my boys clean'. Noodles: 'He's still saying the same thing.' As another customer, a boy in a kaftan, changes the television channel to an old Bob Hope movie, we are back in 1932, and Jimmy O'Donnell – 'twenty-five or so, with the red hair and greenish eyes we like to think are typically Irish' – is laughing with a large audience of striking steelworkers at a makeshift entertainment. Jimmy warmly thanks the entertainers for showing solidarity with the workers and asks a ventriloquist's dummy if he can see the cops outside the steel mill: 'Yeack!'/'On your way out, ask them what they're doing there.'

413

*Afterwards, Jimmy is summoned by Mr Fitzpatrick (Fitz) to be intro-
duced to Max and the gang: Fitz wants to use the gangsters' influence in
support of the strike against scabs and cops alike; Jimmy doesn't. 'Get
used to it, pal,' warns Max. 'This is a growing country. Certain diseases
you're better off having before you grow up.' Suddenly, two hoods
(Salvy the Snake and Willie the Ape) break into Jimmy's room at the
factory and open fire ineffectively with machine-guns, before leaping
out of the window. A siren signals the arrival of Captain Aiello and his
cops, who claim to be on 'the side of public order – somebody was
shooting in here'. 'Who let them in?' asks Jimmy. At this point, the boss
Mr Crowning, a ruddy-faced hulk on the brink of apoplexy, joins in the
conversation: 'Use your God-given reason. That's what unions are for,
not for dragging honest, hard-working men out on useless strikes.'
Aiello wants to get away ('my wife, she had a baby this afternoon') and
Jimmy, realizing he has lost this round, calls off the strike. Noodles,
who cannot understand Jimmy, is relieved by the ways things have
turned out: 'we got nothing to do with them'.*

*In Peggy's brothel, the boys are collecting their 50 per cent of the weekly
profits. Cockeye is bending over a spy-hole 'in the middle of a wall alive
with nymphs and satyrs'. Noodles announces that from now on the
place will belong to Peggy, so no more pay-offs – but she turns down
the offer on the grounds that 'everything is as smooth as silk around
here on account of everyone knows you boys are my partners'. Cockeye
notices that Carol, the wife of the Detroit insurance man, has appeared
in the Grand Salon; Max summons her in. Carol lines the four men up
for inspection ('let's see you pick the birdie') and selects Max as the one
whom she already knows with 'any degree of intimacy'. He's the one
she now fancies. It transpires that she comes into the salon at weekends, with her husband: she 'takes on twenty–twenty-five johns and
her hubby watches through the peephole'.*

*The party breaks up when Sharkey, a Congressman who is putting
pressure on Peggy's business, is sighted entering the salon. In one of the
bedrooms at the brothel, Sharkey asks if 'we gonna lend a hand to these
boys who are out on strike?' He tells them that scabs, with police
protection, have moved into the factory – the same in Newark – and he
offers to arrange payment if the gang will agree to protect the workers
('Who's gonna pay us?'/'You don't want to know who, you want to
know how much'). Sharkey stresses that 'the future is in the union and
in the happiness of the working man'. Noodles sees things more simply:*

'All you have to do is get rid of that asshole cop.' Sharkey: 'We got the big business interests to think about. We just put through a law to make things easier for the unions nationwide. We don't want to push our luck.' The Chief of Police has been 'bought' by boss Crowning with 500 shares in Anaconda Copper, as a birthday present for his newborn son Vincent Aiello junior. 'All he cares about is his family.'

Cut to the maternity ward of a hospital, where the boys – dressed as doctors – switch babies around, while Patsy tries to keep a tally of exactly who has gone where. In a private room in the hospital, Mr and Mrs Aiello and their six little girls – 'You girls are gonna learn that after me, the boss in the home is the baby' – are desolated to discover that the name-tag for Vincent is now attached to a girl. Noodles phones the Police Chief from Fat Moe's and tells him that to find out which cot the baby is now in, he must lay off the strikers. After Noodles hangs up, Patsy admits that in all the excitement he has lost his tally – but he seems to remember that the even numbers are boys . . .

In the steel factory, the scabs are called out under police cordon, much to the alarm of Crowning (not to mention Salvy the Snake and Willie the Ape). Outside, the strikers, led by Jimmy and Fitz, prepare to move back in. Jimmy tells the workers that 'we can be proud that we've got where we are by our own efforts.' The Four Musketeers have arrived on the scene. Noodles: 'Doesn't he know?' Max: 'Sure he knows. He doesn't want them to know.' As Max and the others join the strikers, Noodles retires for a night out at the theatre. 'The whole cast is on stage for the finale, supporting the star of the show – Deborah.' At the stage door, Noodles – 'spiffy as a head waiter' – shares a few barbed cracks about Jewish gangsters and Mafiosi with the chauffeur, also Jewish, of his hired Rolls-Royce. Deborah comes out of the stage door: 'Been waiting long?' 'All my life.'

The Rolls takes them to a plush seaside restaurant: it has been opened, off-season, especially for Noodles, and the deserted room is full of sumptuous vulgarity. He is seriously out of his depth in this setting, whereas Deborah evidently knows her way around. Noodles reckons she is beginning to sound 'just like Max'. They dance to a quiet little waltz. On the beach outside, lying on a huge Persian carpet, Deborah abruptly announces that she is leaving the next day for Holly-wood. 'I had to see you like this to tell you.' On the way back into New York, the other side of Noodles' nature grips him, and he brutally rapes her, out of a mixture of despair and anguish. The car screeches to a halt.

*The chauffeur shames Noodles, and drives Deborah away, leaving Noodles alone in the night. At a speakeasy on 52nd Street, a drunk and dishevelled Noodles meets the buxom Eve, who tries to comfort him. He gives her a thousand-dollar bill. In Noodles' hotel room, evidently his residence, he goes to bed with 'Deborah' but passes out. At Grand Central station, the real Deborah – 'looking elegant and pale' – finishes her coffee and walks towards a platform. Noodles, still in his evening clothes, looks through the window of her carriage. 'She lowers the window shade and cuts him for ever out of her life.'*

*In the office at Fat Moe's, Noodles sees Max sitting on a huge gilded chair, with the rest of the boys at his feet. Carol is there too. 'It's a throne. Belonged to the king of Romania,' Max explains. It transpires that the union has paid them handsomely for services in a gangland battle, while Noodles was away on holiday. Noodles is upset they didn't contact him. 'We did,' says Max. 'Cockeye found you at the Chink's, so full of the weed you didn't even recognize him.' Cockeye: 'You called me Deborah.' Noodles derides Carol, but learns with disgust that Max and she are now an item. Max counters, defensively, 'I don't give a shit about her and you know it!' The tension mounts, broken by Noodles' sudden uncontrollable laughter. Carol leaves, wordlessly, as the telephone rings. It is Jimmy, phoning from a drugstore downtown: 'I'm going to need you boys tonight.' A black car pulls up beside him, and Salvy and Willie let fly with a machine-gun.*

*At the Plaza Hotel, Crowning reports on events to a nameless tycoon, then leaves flanked by Salvy and Willie. As they cross 59th Street, the two thugs are shot by Noodles and Max. At a hospital suite, the gang – plus Sharkey – is celebrating the workers' victory. They toast the newest head of American unionism – Jimmy O'Donnell. Sharkey talks of the end of Prohibition, and suggests the gang move into the trucking business – hundreds of vehicles run by a national organization and supported by a powerful teamsters' union. Noodles is unimpressed. 'You'll carry that Lower East Side stink with you till you die,' Max sneers. Noodles counters, 'Where the fuck did you grow up? Oyster Bay? I like that stink, Max old buddy.'*

*Sharkey tells Max he is carrying a dead weight; Noodles leaves for a vacation in the sunshine. In the hospital corridor, Noodles gets into one elevator car as Frankie 'the Mafia boss' gets out of another. Eve gets into Noodles' elevator, and they agree to meet that evening at the Fortune Hotel. There, Noodles gives her a box containing a dozen lace* brassieres. *Eve defiantly drops her bra into Noodles' lap 'along with two large rubber falsies'. 'Liar,' he says as they go to bed together. Max kicks the hotel-room door open, wearing a flashy summer suit, clutching a fishing rod. Carol is with him 'in virgin white'. They are, it seems, all going to the beach. On a crowded Miami Beach, a lifeguard drops down on all fours and digs a bottle out of the sand: at last he can drink in public. A newspaper headline reads: 'Volstead Act Repealed; Prohibition Ends in December'. Noodles: 'There it is. We're out of a job.' Max (angrily): 'We got other prohibitions to keep us busy.' While the girls discuss money, Max draws a picture in the sand of the Federal Bank of Manhattan, 18 Fifth Avenue. 'You're nuts'/'Don't say that, Noodles. Don't ever say that.'*

*Cut to the glass porch of a rest home in 1968 where Carol is stretched out on a chaise longue. She thinks Noodles might be visiting her after all these years to talk about Eve: 'Oh, how she waited, but you never showed up ... She shut the windows and locked the door, and nobody bothered to check. She was in there all the time, with her little capsules ... there was nobody at the funeral but me.' Upstairs, Carol asks if Noodles has a 'guilt trip' about having killed Max, and reveals that he was better off dead because 'he had the syph'. If he wasn't already crazy, he soon would have been.*

*Cut to the Federal Bank in 1933, where Max and Noodles – dressed as industrial cleaners – case 'the whole vast warren of the building'. Everywhere there are cops. 'It's suicide,' observes Noodles. Back at Fat Moe's, a monumental row is in progress. Max sits on his throne and accuses Noodles of going soft. Noodles looks at him the way he'd look at a madman. As he and Eve enter his hotel, Carol pulls up outside and asks Noodles to get in the car. She tells him she plans to spill to the cops, and suggests that Noodles puts Max in jail 'just long enough for him to get over the idea'. Max already knows that Noodles has considered informing on him: 'He knows you inside out.'*

*At Fat Moe's speakeasy, Noodles tells Eve that he has to go out on 'our last shipment', just beating the end of Prohibition. She says she'll wait up for him, but he replies, 'I won't be home tonight ... or the day after. But I want you to wait for me.' As the band plays, Max toasts the demise of Fat Moe's speakeasy, and drinks with the boys 'to our last shipment'. Noodles half-heartedly raises his glass, goes into the private office and phones the 22nd Precinct. After he has made the tip-off, Max enters the office and accuses Noodles of 'getting shikker 'cause you ain't got no guts.' 'You really are crazy, Max.' Max raises the butt of his gun and brings it down hard on Noodles' head.*

*Back to 1968, Carol's bedroom in the rest home, where it is getting dark. She is telling Noodles that Max really wanted to die: 'He didn't want to end up in no hut house. He wanted to die on the job, with a gun in his hand. So he deliberately got us to think about turning him in.' What about Patsy and Cockeye? asks Noodles. 'He didn't give a flat fuck about them ... But he didn't want you involved in the suicide.' On the word 'suicide', we cut to Deborah in summer 1968 playing Cleopatra in the death scene from Shakespeare's tragedy. After the show, Noodles visits her in her dressing room; she is still wearing her make-up, which is like a Kabuki mask. 'It's like it was written for you: "Age cannot wither her".' As she peels off her make-up, Noodles asks if he should accept an invitation to a party the following night, at Senator Bailey's place on Long Island. He is convinced she knows Bailey. A young man called David knocks on the door: 'I'm not ready ... wait outside,' says Deborah. She is very reticent about discussing anything to do with Senator Bailey. Noodles: 'Why can't you bring yourself to tell me you're his mistress ... that you've been living with him for fifteen years?' Deborah: 'All we have are a few memories. If you go to that party, you won't even have them any more.' As Noodles leaves the dressing room, he sees, on Cleopatra's throne, the image of Max – 'Max as he was thirty-five years ago – though his blond hair now reaches his shoulders.' 'This is Senator Bailey's son. He's David ... like you.' It is unclear whether the boy is hers.*

*The Senator, Max ('much more changed over the years than Noodles'), surveys his party from an upper window at his elaborate seaside garden. The party-goers circulate 'with the conscious satisfaction of the very, very, very rich', Deborah and David among them. Max turns away, and crosses his oak-panelled study. Jimmy O'Donnell sits in an armchair, a walking-stick by his side. A wall of television monitors gives Max glimpses of how his party is going. Jimmy salutes his bravura gesture, in the midst of the Federal Investigation. Max accuses Jimmy's union of trying to blow him up. 'All we want', he responds, 'is thirty million bucks back in the pension fund.' Max protests tersely that he has been investing union money for twenty-five years; Jimmy upbraids him in turn for an abortive scheme to 'invest in that crazy African emperor and his puppet-show'. Max grabs Jimmy by the lapels:*

'*You wouldn't hit an old cripple, now, would you?*' *asks the union boss.* '*Maybe one of your high-tone guests can save your ass, Max.*'

*After Jimmy leaves, Noodles is ushered into the study by the butler. He sits in a large leather armchair and constantly addresses Max as* '*Mr Bailey*'. *Max talks about the suitcase and the advance payment for the next job.* '*You, Mr Bailey?*' *he says.* '*I haven't had a gun in my hand for I don't know how long. My eyes aren't what they used to be, even with my glasses on . . .*' *Max is impatient:* '*Cut the comedy, Noodles. I'm already dead! You know that. I'll never make it to the investigating committee. I made you come here for this . . . to even the score between us.*'

*He pushes a gun towards Noodles, across the mirrored surface of the table. Noodles stares at it, as* '*out of nothing, or perhaps out of his deep font of nostalgia and regret, joyous images rise like flowers*': *to the music of Cockeye's Pan pipes, we see Max arriving on the wagon, the two of them in the seat of a Ferris wheel at a funfair, Max diving in among the coloured balloons in Lower New York Bay, then a corpse disfigured to the point of unrecognition stretched out on the sidewalk in the snow. Noodles looks up:* '*I don't know what you're talking about, Mr Bailey. You don't owe me anything.*' *Max:* '*I took your whole life away from you; I've been living in your place. I took every-thing – your money, your girl . . . what are you waiting for?*' *Noodles:* '*There's my side to it, my story . . . Many years ago I tried to save a friend of mine by turning him in. He was a very close friend. Things worked out bad for him and for me.*' *He opens a little door set into the woodwork (Noodles has throughout his life always left by the side door).* '*I hope the investigation turns out good for you . . . Goodnight, Mr Bailey,*' *he says.*

*On a side street near the Senator's house, the engine of a giant gar-bage truck starts up. Noodles sees a man on the sidewalk in evening dress, who* '*seems to be Max*'. *When the truck passes Noodles, the man disappears.* '*It is as if he has been wiped out by the night . . . In back [of the truck], the great maw gapes open and the meshed teeth grind in slow steady rhythm with the speed of the truck.*' *Soon all Noodles can see are two red reflectors over the back wheels. The reflectors turn into the headlights of an old Ford, full of party-goers* '*wearing the clothes of the early thirties*'. *Two more cars of the same vintage are driven past:* '*a bunch of drunks, it appears, dolled up in clothes they found in the attic*'. *A woman in the last car tosses a bottle out of the window, as*

*Noodles hears a crescendo of music, horns and voices. We are in New York's Chinatown, on 3 December 1933, the night Prohibition came to an end, and the street is full of frenetic revellers. Noodles is unshaven, and he is carrying the newspaper that announces the death of his friends. He slips into the opium den, walking through the shadow puppet theatre where Rama and Ravana, in silhouette, act out their struggle of good and evil on a white screen. In the den upstairs, he draws smoke from a long-stemmed pipe into his lungs. 'The smoke is harsh and kind and cleansing. It wipes out memories, strife, mistakes . . . and Time.'*

*Once Upon a Time in America* was likely to be very long indeed, giving Leone's imagination plenty of time and space to sprawl. It was also likely to be very expensive, considering its procession of set-pieces. And if the audience expected characters to root for, it was in for a shock: the main character in this story had become Time itself. Guilt was more important than revenge, introspection was no longer a sign of weakness, relationships – for the first time in Leone's cinema – really mattered and the violence was messy. This was to be a 'personal' film at last, the product of fifteen years' emotional investment. But when Alberto Grimaldi read the script he immediately wrote a long letter to Leone listing what he saw as the big problems: 'too long [it would have run for five hours]; the American distributors would forcibly cut it down to two hours; the protagonist Noodles is too negative for the American public – he rapes a woman and kills people without reason, which makes these acts seem unacceptable . . . so either the script will have to be redone, or I will not produce it'.[59]

The script of October 1981 departed from the original novel in several interesting ways. There was more explicit sex; Noodles' sentence in prison was nine years, rather than eighteen months; there was a whole new sequence set in Lower New York Bay; a subway locker replaced the four safes inside four trunks; the time-scale of the early scenes had been telescoped from 1913–33 to 1922–33. The casino subplot was gone, elevator workers had become steelworkers, and Ferrini had provided the farce in the maternity ward. Conspicuously, visual indications of the passage of time, in the form of messages to the art director, were presented in considerable detail – and had in many cases become more significant than the dialogue. There was much more sociological background in the script than the novel, but all references to real-life criminals (notably Frank Costello) had been excised, in line with Leone's firm belief that actors playing famous historical figures tended to appear like waxworks; an unnecessary distraction for the audience, and a barrier to identification with the characters. Noodles' homophobia (strongly present in the novel, in a series of scenes set in Lutke's Turkish Bath and the Eden Garden Club, where the manager is an outrageous music-hall queen) had turned into a recurring phrase of Max's, about 'getting it right up the ass'. The childhood sequences now included various memories from Leone's own experiences in Trastevere, courtesy of *Viale Glorioso*. The most beautiful scene in the film, where Deborah takes Noodles through The Song of Songs was a new addition. But for the sections concerned with 1922 and 1933 the script had derived most of its big ideas from *The Hoods*. The most significant change, apart from the time games and the foregrounding of 'memory' and Noodles' relationship with the whole narrative, was the deletion of all explicit references to American history.

In place of these, Harry Grey's unconscious reworkings of movie clichés became a full-blown homage to Hollywood in the prewar era, 'the kind of cinema', as Leone put it, 'which obsessed *me*'. The scriptwriters had structured the entire modern section of the story as if it was Orson Welles's *Citizen Kane* retold as a gangster epic. While Noodles searches for his Rosebud – the gold watch, symbolizing the revelation that Max is still alive, via other childhood icons such as the key and the battered old suitcase it unlocks – he gathers evidence, like a veteran investigative journalist, from the hard-bitten resident of an old people's rest home (Carol rather than Jed Leland), a loyal and self-effacing assistant (Fat Moe rather than the equally loyal and self-effacing Bernstein), an ex-vaudeville singer turned classical actress (Deborah rather than Susan Alexander) and a multi-millionaire American tycoon whose increasingly ruthless methods have isolated him from the rest of humanity (Secretary Bailey rather than Charles Foster Kane). The mausoleum resembles the Thatcher Memorial Library, there is a picnic in Florida and the key flashback takes place in the snow. Like *Kane*, the script is constructed in the same way as an intricate jigsaw puzzle. In the 1922 and 1933 sections, there were now citations of the Marx Brothers (the flashback to Groucho in the mortuary), Shirley Temple (Deborah's dance), Charlie Chaplin's *The Kid* (the charlotte Russe incident), Busby Berkeley (Deborah's stage performance at the musical theatre), and Valentino (*The Four Horsemen*). Leone used to argue that the character of Noodles in some ways 'resembled a certain son of a veterinary surgeon called Valentino', and at one point there had been 'a scene in a cinema, where the gangsters steal jewellery from Rudolph Valentino fans, completely undisturbed'.[60]

But the key citations came from the genre loosely known as 'gangster movies', from D.W. Griffith's *The Musketeers of Pig Alley* in 1912 right through to Fritz Lang's *The Big Heat* in 1953, from the first-generation lone-wolf hoodlums to the era of big business and the Syndicate. Leone had come not to praise the genre, or even to bury it, but to explore the 'B' movie going on in Noodles' head, which gives shape and meaning to his confused existence in the present day. At the same time, the director was immersing himself in his own cultural memories. Many of the key narrative devices of 'the gangster film' were in evidence; but this was to be 'a gangster story without glory', through which the central character drifts like a sleepwalker. The framing device – where shadow puppets enact the *Ramayana* – would locate these citations within an exploration of myth itself, mediating the contradictions and complexities of everyday life, and of how Noodles yearns for the reassurance it can bring. In some sense, the trappings of the genre were a ruse, as Leone was at pains to point out: 'It is not a film about gangsters. It is a film about nostalgia for a certain period and a certain type of cinema and a certain type of literature.'[61]

Nevertheless, the 'citations' were certainly there: from the Chinese theatre (*The Lady from Shanghai*, 1948) to the contract killing (*The Killers*, 1946) to the gangster revisiting his childhood neighbourhood (*Angels with Dirty Faces*, 1938; *Dead End*, 1937); with one protagonist feeling nostalgic about the anarchic early days (*High Sierra*, 1941), the other becoming increasingly megalomaniac (*White Heat*, 1949) and both having to confront a complicated new world of unions and politics (*Bullets or Ballots*, 1936). The suitcase at the subway station recalled *Cry of the City* (1948) and *The Killing* (1956); Noodles' relationship with Deborah resembled Eddie Bartlett's with Jean Sherman in *The Roaring Twenties* (1939), and the elderly Noodles' arrival at Senator Bailey's Long Island party mirrored Police Sergeant Bannion's arrival at the affluent mansion of Mike Lagarna, head of the crime syndicate, in *The Big Heat* (1953). The switching of the babies ('We're like the Lord God Almighty') chimed with the mid-1930s 'moral' cycle of gangster films, where the roots of gangsterdom – nature or nurture – were explored. The misogyny of the gang, who behave like overgrown little boys obsessed with their cocks, belongs to a long tradition: from Tom Powers pushing a grapefruit into Kitty's face (*The Public Enemy*, 1931) to Vince emptying a coffee percolator over Debbie's face in *The Big Heat*. The inscription 'Your men will fall by the sword' was a variation on the opening of *Little Caesar* (1930): 'For they that take the sword shall perish by the sword' (Matthew 25.52). And so on.

But *Once Upon a Time in America* would not be concerned with rags-to-riches gangsters, or charismatic action men – except at the level of fantasy. The film would be centrally concerned with Noodles' attempt to make some sense of his life by piecing together his memories, jigsaw puzzle-fashion; and with his failure to do so. Like memory itself, the story would be full of the audacious jump-outs and shifts of register which Leone had asked the scriptwriters to emphasize. Like the little girl in the Isaac Bashevis Singer story who says she likes tales in which someone says, '. . . and suddenly'. From 1933 Fords on a train to 1968 models in pink and turquoise and emerald green; from the elderly Noodles looking through a peep-hole behind Fat Moe's diner in 1968 to the young Noodles spying on Deborah in 1923; from the inscription over a prison door in 1924 to the inscription over a mausoleum in Riversdale cemetery in 1968; from Noodles ducking a frisbee under the cement supports for elevated trains in 1968 to Max welcoming him out of prison in June 1933; from a motorboat and steam shovel on a Canadian lake in 1934 to an exploding motorboat and garbage truck outside a Long Island mansion in 1968; from a television set showing an old Bob Hope movie to a union official reacting to an entertainment at a steelworkers' strike in 1932; from Miami Beach in 1933 to the porch of an old people's home in 1968; from the bedroom upstairs to the Federal Reserve Bank in 1933; from the private office beside Fat Moe's speakeasy back to the old people's home in 1968 – whence, on the word 'suicide', the action shifts to a performance of *Antony and Cleopatra*; from Senator Bailey's oak-panelled office to the Lower East Side in 1923 to Coney Island to a Westchester street in 1933 and back to the office in 1968; from a garbage truck – seamlessly – to the costly orgy of an end-of-Prohibition party and back into the opium den where the story began, and where Noodles now knows that his act of betrayal was itself an illusion of memory.

Noodles' betrayal and retreat into the opium den were always at the heart of the story, and in the script of 1981 the possibility is already there that the entire saga may have taken place in Noodles' head at that precise moment. This could explain why so few people in the 1968 section seem to have moved on from where they were in 1933; and why Noodles simply interacts in his future with the people he already knew in his past. It is as if time really did stand still when the grandfather clock stopped, only to be reactivated by the man who brought back the key. Of course, if the 1968 sequences are projections of Noodles' imagination, then how to explain the television set, the cars, the high-tech mausoleum and so on? Still, the ambiguity was there, reminiscent of John Boorman's *Point Blank* (1967), where Walker's (Lee Marvin) tale of revenge may be just wish fulfilment as he is left for dead on a deserted Alcatraz. Leone, a fan of Boorman's film, encouraged the interpretation: 'Opium can create visions of the future . . . As far as I'm concerned, it is possible that Noodles never leaves 1933.' He elaborated: 'Maybe this is the first time a film has actually finished on a flashback. It could all have been a journey of the imagination.' Whatever critics wished to make of the claim, Leone would not be pinned down: 'The film offers a double reading – I say it here and I deny it here . . . certainly, in 1933, Noodles is already morally and materially dead.'[62]

If this reading is correct, the story would be completely circular, and self-contained as a cinematic experience. It would include some images and themes from Leone's earlier works: a cemetery (this time being dug up – another symbol of memory), a coffin, a stop-watch, a reference to Judas, the friendship and betrayal of two male friends, the death of a small child, a character who plays a musical instrument, the drawing of a bank in the sand (like Indio's model of El Paso), the lifetime ambition to rob it (like Juan and Mesa Verde), a characteristic emphasis on how the main characters enter the scene (Noodles always prefers the side door; Max goes through the front door; entrances are usually shown as delayed drops), the repetition of catchphrases and epigrams, the arrival of a train at the beginning. The scene where Noodles looks at his dead companions in the rain is similar to the scene where Sean watches the firing squad in *Giù la testa*. The story would even include echoes of the dialogue of *Once Upon a Time in the West*. 'You wouldn't hit an old cripple now, would you?' asks Jimmy in 1968 (a reference to union boss Jimmy Hoffa, who mysteriously disappeared after a garbage truck had been seen outside his house for several days), which is almost exactly what Mr Morton says to Frank. And, in a new version of Frank's valedictory statement to Harmonica just before the settling of accounts,

Max says to Noodles, 'I took everything – your money, your girl . . . what are you waiting for?' Everything that made him a gangster has been taken away from him. Only this time, there would be no settling of accounts at the point of dying (Noodles usually evades potentially disturbing confrontations by 'going for a swim'), just as there will be no iconic heroes and villains and no resolution of emotional conflicts through violence. When Max offers Noodles his gun, the wronged man refuses it. 'You do not', said Leone, 'kill your own memories.' The entire story is about postponement – the postponement of immediate answers, the postponement of judgement on the characters, the post-ponement of gratification which in the end never comes.

It is not even clear at the fade-out whether Max has thrown himself into the garbage truck; the man standing on the sidewalk in evening dress just 'seems to be Max'. Leone insisted on the ambiguity: 'since it is the whole world that Max has built up that is worthy of being chucked into the dustbin of today's America. It is no longer a question of the individual'; 'maybe Noodles is living everything he *wants* to see after the death of his friends: one reason for the ambiguous ending. It is not, definitely not, Max who disappears. *Someone* disappears. For Noodles, this someone is Max.'[63]

So the story's image of modern America would be one of dreams *not* coming true: the promise of the West is a thing of the past, and it has given way to corruption in high places, despair, and the impossibility of individuals making any difference. Noodles would spend most of the film just looking. Or as Leone put it, 'Someone like Harry Grey seems to have looked at everything through the window of a bar: America flows past him without the possibility of his touching or changing it.'[64]

Even the music played a different role, in keeping with the general atmosphere of melancholy. The shooting script was full of explicit ref-erences to musical themes. But Sergio Leone had strong views about the particular melodies he wanted, which owed nothing to Harry Grey and a great deal to his own biography: 'I asked for a different kind of score from Ennio Morricone this time. We began with a song of the period – "Amapola". And I wanted to add to this some very precise musical themes: "God Bless America" by Irving Berlin, "Night and Day" by Cole Porter, "Summertime" by Gershwin. In addition to the original score by Morricone, and these "mythic" melodies to conjure up an epoch, I added something from today: "Yesterday" by John Lennon and Paul McCartney. I chose these . . . because they were such a lucid form of nostalgia in my head and maybe in reality, because for me they were touching base.'[65]

Irving Berlin's 'God Bless America' had been written in 1918 to celebrate the end of the First World War, but it did not become a public anthem until Armistice Day in 1938, when Kate Smith's live version was recorded. Thus, strictly speaking, associating it with celebrations at the end of Prohibition in December 1933 was a slight anachronism. But the song was another immigrant's fairy-tale, and Leone wanted the irony of its use in this context. 'Yesterday', recorded by the Beatles in 1965, subsequently the most 'covered' song in history, was called upon to provide a bridge to the first 1968 sequence, albeit rearranged as muzak. It was to be reprised as if played at the Long Island party, during Noodles' climactic discussion with Senator Bailey.

Leone had started discussing the music for *Once Upon a Time in America* immediately after completing *Giù la testa*, and the score was more or less complete by 1975–6, seven years before a foot of film was shot, which must be a record. Ever since Leone came to Morricone with the ready-made *deguello* theme for *Fistful of Dollars*, the composer had been very sensitive about starting with a piece of music found by someone else. On this occasion, though, Carla Leone confirms that '"Amapola" was chosen by Sergio'. Originally a Spanish tune by Joseph M. La Calle, it had been given English lyrics by Albert Gamse and become one of the greatest hits of 1924. A 1930s recorded version had been arranged by Jimmy Dorsey. Leone may have been reminded of it in 1971 when he heard the soundtrack of *Carnal Knowledge*, where Jules Feiffer's script called for 'dance music of the forties' in the opening sequences, and director Mike Nichols selected a version of 'Amapola' rearranged by Al Dubin and Harry Warren. In 1989, Morricone reflected, 'I think Leone's choice was on this occasion justified. The film needed historical reference-points, whether this one or other well-known pieces, all corresponding to precise dates or events.'[66] (After the film was released, 'Amapola' re-entered the pop operatic repertory; it reached a sort of apotheosis in the final medley sung by the 'Three Tenors' at the Baths of Caracalla in July 1990.)

'Amapola' was to be heard first, in a 1924-style arrangement, on Deborah's wind-up gramophone; later, in an over-lush string arrangement, played by the seaside restaurant orchestra during Noodles' big night out. The tune was also to be woven into Morricone's 'Deborah's Theme' – transposed from A to E major – as if the two had blended in

Noodles' memory. The 'found music' tended to correspond to real moments in the narrative, with its source shown on screen. As did 'Cockeye's Song', played on the pipes of Pan as the children strut their stuff around Delancey Street, and superimposed by Morricone on Hebraic themes to evoke the ethnic community in which they grew up. This was a development of the 'cross-referencing' of Leone's earlier films. As Morricone recalls: 'The musical construction arose from our conscious mixture of two musics – some from the musical reality of a given epoch, some specially composed. To illustrate the 1920s and 1930s, for example, I carefully kept the orchestration of the period, so that the audience could immediately identify the historical time when the action takes place. Where the original themes were concerned, they had to evoke less palpable things – such as the passage of time, or particular emotions such as nostalgia, love or joy.'[67]

Instead of using the score to beef up big action sequences, or to provide ironic punctuation to the image, for *Once Upon a Time in America* it would have a quasi-religious feel to it – as if calling Noodles back to his distant past. It had a traditionally melodic feel, in more mainstream arrangements usually in the key of E. As Leone was to put it, 'This time the emotions were so sharply defined, so strong and so romantic, that we agreed the music ought to be less emphatic than usual . . . it ought to come from a long way away.' He opted for the pipes of Pan 'because Gheorghe Zamfir, the great Romanian concert performer, had enchanted me, and because the pipes are the most haunting of instruments – like a human voice *and* like a whistle'.[68] A piece which Leone almost turned down in its early stages, fearing a resemblance to the *Once Upon a Time in the West* theme, became 'Deborah's Theme'. Leone was to remember that 'this love theme was, I think, originally composed for a Zeffirelli film but was never used', and its selection continued his time-honoured tradition (going back to *Fistful* days) of re-evaluating Morricone music that other directors had earlier rejected – and then, when the theme proved to be a success, telling all and sundry how clever he had been to spot its potential.

The theme consists of a series of short, hesitant musical phrases, with a few beats of silence between them: each time they return, the phrases are enriched with new embellishments, until the climax when the soprano voice of Edda Dell'Orso is introduced. It is a direct musical expression of Noodles' frustrated desire, compounded by moments from 'Amapola'. But the human voice, scored as another musical

427

instrument, was much less in evidence in *Once Upon a Time in America* than in the previous two Leone films. Morricone explains: 'There is a reason why I used less of Edda dell'Orso's voice in this particular score . . . and it was right not to use it in the childhood scenes. The voice seemed perfect for moments which lament the passing of childhood, to lead the audience to think about times past – the thirty lost years of Noodles.' One such moment was the very last image of the film, when the main title theme was repeated, with soprano harmony, as Noodles inhales the smoke of an opium pipe, lies on his back and, finally, smiles. Such music, said Morricone, 'comes into the film when the camera looks into the eyes of the character. The theme then singles out what he is thinking at that moment, what is going on inside.'[69]

The overture to Rossini's *Thieving Magpie*, another piece of 'found' music, which accompanies the baby-switching sequence, was selected by Carla Leone, as were some of the jazz inserts played in Fat Moe's speakeasy. For the 'Prohibition Dirge', a stately New Orleans funeral march which turns into hot jazz as the party gets into full swing, Morricone followed the script by providing an arrangement in the mid-1930s style of Louis Armstrong.

The main themes were all composed by 1976, ready for refining and recording when at last the schedule was finalized: Leone intended to play the music on the set 'with a few instruments, not necessarily the full orchestra' – to create the right atmosphere, focus concentration and 'to help the chief camera operator find the *softness* necessary to make tracking shots, as if he was playing a violin'.[70] That was the plan, anyway. Final revisions would take just one month, and recording another. But, as Morricone emphasizes, 'Sergio and I always think through our work to the very end, without ever declaring ourselves satisfied'. And Leone would keep having second thoughts: 'Every so often, Sergio, when the music was already written, would phone me and say, "Listen, let's have a quick meeting – because I'm beginning to have doubts about that theme for Deborah." Then he would listen to it, and calm down again. Because he still liked it, after all. This went on about every three months . . . And for the scriptwriters it seemed sometimes as if everything would become a crisis, and they would have to start doing everything all over again. With me, however, he just seemed to want his judgement confirmed every now and again.'[71]

Where visual references were concerned, Leone turned to ready-made images from the 1920s to 1940s in briefing sessions with his

428

regular production designer Carlo Simi and director of photography Tonino Delli Colli. 'It was no longer a question of Max Ernst or Giorgio De Chirico,' Leone said, 'as it had been with *The Good, The Bad and The Ugly.*'[72] The sequence showing the young Deborah's dance would be lit like a Degas painting. But the chief 'stimuli' would be the paintings of Edward Hopper, the illustrations of Norman Rockwell, the drawings and paintings of Reginald Marsh and assorted archive photographs. For the scenes set in the crowded Lower East Side tenements of 1923, Leone made use of the halftones and drawings based on photographs taken by Danish immigrant Jacob Riis and published in his influential exposé *How the Other Half Lives* (1890). Riis had been a crime reporter for the New York *Tribune* in the 1880s, and in his book sought to present 'the misery and vice that I have noted in my ten years of experience', particularly in the Mulberry Street area. He tended to photograph the inhabitants of cheap lodging houses and tiny rooms without their permission, so in the resulting pictures they look surprised, angry and brutalized.

For other perspectives on New York in 1923 and 1933, Leone assembled a reference portfolio of photographs from the 1920s and 1930s; for the massacre of the gang in Westchester, he referred to a night-shot of a group of police cars and fire engines in 1932; for the shooting of Salvy and Willie a crime reporter's photo of a body on a sidewalk, with parked cars (1933); for the shooting of Joe a photo of Benjamin 'Bugsy' Siegel's corpse shortly after he was gunned down by the Syndicate's hitmen in Beverly Hills (1947), plus – for the car window shattered by machine-gun bullets – a still from *Scarface*. The visual link between Long Island in 1968 and New York in 1933 he derived from a flashlit photograph of two cars crammed full of drunken revellers racing each other at the end of Prohibition. These were all subsequently published, next to the scenes they inspired, in the book *C'era una volta in America – Photographic Memories* (1988).[73]

The New York paintings of Edward Hopper which Leone found most useful, for reference purposes, were *Drug Store* (1927) and the artist's signature piece *Nighthawks* (1942), both of which provided the visual inspiration for Fat Moe's speakeasy-turned-diner. Also *New York Movie* (1939) was the template for the scene where Carol meets the elderly Noodles in the hallway of the Bailey Foundation, and *From Williamsburg Bridge* plus *Manhattan Bridge Loop* (both 1928) provided ideas for the set-dressing of the Lower East Side. Hopper, who spent most of his life in New York, specialized, as he put it, in 'painting the loneliness of the big city'. His people, when they appear, tend to be stranded in a night-time limbo – and his best-known paintings have the eerie, artificial quality of studio-bound cities in gangster movies, like stills or snapshots from a *film noir*. They are echoes of the real city, isolated from their context. Such paintings, said Leone, 'worked on my imagination'.[74]

One of Norman Rockwell's cheery, hyper-realist cover illustrations for the *Saturday Evening Post* was to appear on the Delancey Street newsstand which the children torch, next to the latest issues of *Life*, *Liberty* and the *Police Gazette*. The cover shows a rotund old man playing a cello, with a little girl trying to dance, clumsily, just in front of him – a visual memory of Deborah's rather more elegant dance, which we have just seen. The particular issue of the *Post* was published on 3 February 1923, but Rockwell's association with the magazine lasted nearly half a century from 1916 to 1963, and his many images of American childhood throughout this period – kids standing by a fire hydrant, or talking to a neighbourhood cop, or sitting in a pastry shop, or driving a car made out of wooden crates, or struggling to do joined-up writing, or running past a 'no swimming' sign clutching a towel (a famous cover dating from June 1921) – are like a storyboard of the New York life of average Americans as seen through rose-tinted spectacles, and provided many useful details for the sequences set in 1923. Leone referred to Rockwell's work as 'a catalyst'.[75]

When, in the finished film, Noodles leaves New York in 1933 (shuffling off to Buffalo, by train) and returns to exactly the same spot in 1968, he pauses for a long moment, as he departs, by a large mural full of advertisements for Coney Island. 'Visit Coney Island,' it blares across the top in yellow letters, and the mural consists of five gaudy posters in 1930s style; bustling crowds of punters walk by in the foreground of the picture. This is, in fact, a clever collage of two paintings by the New York artist Reginald Marsh, who specialized in images of New York as 'one continuous performance' (his words) in the 1930s: *Smoko, the Human Volcano* (1933), the source for the posters in the film 'Fatalist Supreme' and 'Smoko'; and, carefully sandwiched between them, *Pip and Flip* (1932), the source for 'Pip and Flip Twins', 'World Circus' and 'Major Mite'. Marsh's drawings and paintings (partying crowds on *Fourteenth Street* (1934), shopgirls walking past a *Twenty Cent Movie* (1936), victims of the Depression lying in the doorways of The Bowery or commuters trying to read newspapers on the subway, the boardwalks, beaches and amusement arcades of Coney Island) presented city life in the 1930s as a fantastical, tawdry carnival where 'the best sculpture and decoration done today, though not profound, are shop windows'.[76] Across the top of the Marsh mural Carlo Simi added 'Mrs Legs Diamond Attraction'. By extreme contrast, the over-the-top interior of Peggy's brothel was based on the opulent 'gold style' paintings of Austrian artist Gustav Klimt. Its turn-of-the-century art nouveau decorations – all gilt and glitter and writhing patterns – were a world away from Reginald March's sordid streets, where the employees presumably originated.[77]

Working from these research materials, and visits to New York, Tonino Delli Colli decided to differentiate visually between the 'three eras of the film ... For 1923, we had a brownish hue, which recalled to mind the photographs of the period. For 1933, we tried to make the image more neutral – with a cold, metallic, black-and-white look, in order to get as close as possible to the gangster films of that time. For 1968, no particular effect: we would use a bit of Rn, a special bath [with a little more silver] copyrighted by Italian Technicolor which makes the blacks less velvety – less dirty – which lowers the tone of the colour, makes everything look more luminous and reinforces the contrasts.'[78]

Of his working relationship with designer Carlo Simi, Leone was to recall, when the film was finally released: 'The decors are built with a scrupulous attention to detail and authenticity, some taken from this place, some from that. I use many, many photographs of the period. I do very careful research which even amazes my American friends, such as Spielberg and Scorsese. When they came to Rome, they were astonished by the number of photographs, by this complete visual documentation which starts out from small detail to arrive at the total effect ... all these interiors and scenes represent an incredible amount of work on our part, almost impossible to do again.'[79] Simi recalls customizing the real-life street on the Lower East Side with 'details that gave it character: exterior fire-stairs, decorative features at the tops of buildings, cornices, windows, shop signs, all crafted in Rome out of fibreglass, sculpted wood and metal and then shipped to America to be installed by Italian craftsmen who had flown over.' The other big task was remaking a section of the New York street in Rome. Simi measured the numbered sections himself, to be *certain* the facsimiles would match.[80] But for once the costumes were not designed by Simi. They

were selected by Leone with designer Gabriella Pescucci and her assistant Raffaella Leone, having been researched or found in New York, Los
Angeles and London, 'all as authentic as possible'. Some also came
from Rome, where, as Leone explained: 'Tirelli has many garments of
1920–25, as well as all the costumes used by Visconti . . . When I work
with my visual collaborators – on the decors, the costumes, the objects
– we have to work as a complete team. Nothing is left to chance. For
example, if in an interior a person has a maroon shirt, I ban certain
other colours such as reds and blues. So everything is filtered through
me. When Noodles drinks a cup of coffee he does not use a round cup
but a hexagonal one with little floral motifs of the 1930s.'[81]

If everything intended for the eye of the lens was looking just right,
Leone's relationship with producer Alberto Grimaldi was going seriously wrong. When Grimaldi had first acquired the rights to *The
Hoods*, he had been riding high on the international success of *Last
Tango in Paris* (1972). Since then, two of his multinational productions
– Bertolucci's 325-minute *Novecento* (1976), distributed in two parts,
and Fellini's 150-minute *Casanova* (1977) – had fared very badly at the
box office and, according to Leone, 'Grimaldi was panicking, because
he had lost the support of the major companies'. On the one hand, 'he
hoped that our film would get him out of trouble': on the other, he had
learned the hard way that a two-part film (which *Once Upon a Time in
America* was turning out to be) was no longer a viable investment.
Hence the various go–stop–go announcements of a start-date. This led
to yet another lawsuit since, according to Leone, 'Grimaldi had made
me lose three or four years when he effectively immobilized me'.[82]
Leone later said he was hoping, through the courts, to 'break our
agreement and regain the rights to the novel – but Grimaldi refused
to let go'. If he could regain control of the project, Leone had hopes
of finding a new producer – or even of producing the film himself –
to realize the fully fledged version of *Once Upon a Time*. Alberto
Grimaldi denies nearly all of this, insisting he was not 'nearly bankrupt', nor was he obstructing the production. 'I withdrew solely for
professional reasons. I did not believe in the script or in the success of
the film. I have the letter I wrote about this in my archives. Sergio asked
if I would agree to release the rights in exchange for reimbursing my
expenditure. We agreed on a sum of $500,000.'[83]

Then, through a French contact, Yves Gasser, Leone met Israeli mil-
lionaire Arnon Milchan in 1980. Milchan had produced some plays in

Paris, Jack Gold's *The Medusa Touch* (1978) and an epic mini-series for American television about Romans versus Israelites (recut for theatrical distribution in Europe) called *Masada*. He had clinched a deal to produce Martin Scorsese's $20 million *The King of Comedy*, his first Hollywood venture, with Robert De Niro as kidnapper-turned-celebrity Rupert Pupkin. And he had been trying in 1980 to negotiate tax-shelter money to save David Lean's two-part version of *Mutiny on the Bounty* which Dino De Laurentiis had been bankrolling for several years. Milchan had taken *The Bounty* to United Artists, but they were reeling from the *Heaven's Gate* fiasco and, like all the majors, were extremely wary of productions shot by big-name directors outside the immediate environs of Hollywood. Milchan remained very keen to break into the big time.[84]

When first he met Sergio Leone, the *Once Upon a Time in America* project must have seemed hopelessly bogged down in legal complications. And in confusion Leone now talked of Paul Newman as the older Noodles and Tom Berenger as his youthful counterpart; or maybe Dustin Hoffman as Max; or maybe Jon Voight or Harvey Keitel or John Malkovich, with Liza Minnelli as Deborah. As Sergio Donati observed, 'There was no actor who wasn't promised a role in that movie.'[85] Detailed negotiations with Milchan began in late summer 1980. Milchan clinched the deal over the rights to *The Hoods* from Grimaldi and set about arranging a distribution deal with the Ladd Company and Warner Brothers. He could raise $18 million for the film, ten of it up front from Ladd and much of the rest his own money, if Leone would agree to make certain changes. As Leone recalled three years later, 'He didn't want to know anything about two films, *Novecento*-style ... And he led me to understand that if we didn't start immediately, it would not prove possible to make the film at all. So, during the time we had to work on it, I cut what I could, although I knew that the film was already likely to be long enough for two films when it finally came out.'[86] Yet, to *Cahiers du Cinéma* in the same year, Leone claimed he had been given 'carte blanche to make a film of four and a half hours ... with the aim of turning it into a film in two parts': only 'four months before we began shooting' was he then told that 'some distributors cannot cope with a double distribution', and he would have to wield the knife to make a three-hour film.[87] Either way, for a film-maker who was already famous for overrunning, this was an ominous start. Warner Brothers were under the impression that Leone was contracted to deliver a film of 160 minutes. Leone was expecting to make a film at least 100 minutes longer than that. Luciano Vincenzoni's wry comment on the affair? 'You give a block of stone to poor Michelangelo, and tell him to create a *Pietà*; if what he ends up with is a couple of Siamese Madonnas, he's got everything wrong; whereas in the cinema you could always cut them apart and sell them separately.'[88]

Luca Morsella reckons that Milchan did in fact ask Leone to cut the script down to the length of a single, manageable film *and* that Leone realized in a vague way that the film he was about to make was far too long. Leone embarked on the film, hoping against hope that the length question would somehow sort itself out: 'You know he wasn't very practical . . . He was living in his own world in a way, so I don't think he was being dishonest, thinking, "I'll make a longer film and then they'll accept it." I think he was just thinking, "It's going to be all right." And I don't think he could really tell how long it would be before shooting.'[89] Whatever the facts of the matter, *Once Upon a Time in America* was 'on' again, with Milchan as producer, at the beginning of 1981. It would, said the press release, commence shooting in January 1982. In the event, the start date would be postponed for six months to June. Meanwhile, Leone divided his time between interviewing more than 3,000 actors for over eighty speaking parts (500 auditions were videotaped); scouting locations, this time for real; and supervising the pruning and reshaping of the script.

The project had been in gestation since 1967. Now everything seemed to be happening in a rush. One priority was to turn the dialogue into more convincing American-English. It still read in places like a translation. Luca Morsella's solution was to suggest that Leone contact Stuart Kaminsky. Morsella recalls: 'He was teaching cinema in Chicago. So I said to Sergio, "If you're looking for someone – he's Jewish, he writes mysteries set in 1940s Hollywood, I know you're after the 1920s but still, he is fascinated by cinema, he admires your work. I don't think you can do better than that." '[90] Kaminsky had written about Leone's films in the film journals *Take One* (1973) and *The Velvet Light Trap* (1974), in which he had concluded that Leone's Westerns were 'comic nightmares about existence' and celebrations of 'male style in the face of horror'. He had also written a series of crime novels, featuring private investigator Toby Peters, set in and around Hollywood studios: such as *Never Cross a Vampire* (1980), which begins with Bela Lugosi receiving poison-pen letters written in animal blood and involves a murder for which suspicion falls on William Faulkner.

Stuart Kaminsky was approached in summer 1981. He recalled, a couple of years later, that 'Medioli was the only Italian writer who spoke English. Leone spoke very little English. The working procedure . . . was for the Italian script to be translated into English and given to me. I would rewrite dialogue and make other suggestions for cutting, change, and defining character; and the script would be retranslated into Italian. This process was followed through five versions with supervision by Leone.'[91] Since then Stuart Kaminsky has been more specific about the division of labour: Benvenuti devised the physical and visual action, Medioli ensured 'that we remembered the epic nature of the film to be shot', while he 'turned the characters [Noodles and Max] into distinct individuals representing opposite ends of the spectrum' and crafted the English-language version of all the dialogue.[92] Luca Morsella reckons that Kaminsky could perhaps have offered more – beyond retranslation and helping to shape the long script: 'He was trying, but he didn't manage because maybe there was a lot of jealousy among the Italian writers.'[93] Kaminsky was to be credited on the finished film for his 'additional dialogue'. Leone's recollection of exactly what this meant was not quite the same as Kaminsky's: 'For the film, I needed a Jew, Polish or of Polish extraction, who knew a little Yiddish and who could also write. Kaminsky fitted the bill to perfection . . . His intervention was limited; of a technical nature. He added nothing; he simply adapted faithfully and freely certain things which seemed too "translated".'[94] Leo Benvenuti remembers that 'writing the definitive script at the same time as its translation led to us working closely with the translator. We started on page one, the interpreter did a literal translation, then Kaminsky did his version. And so it went on, give or take a few rows because Kaminsky was a strict Jew and didn't like it when De Niro said to McGovern that in prison he used to masturbate while reading *The Song of Songs*! "No! Never!" yelled Kaminsky and it was changed.'[95]

While Kaminsky retranslated the dialogue, Leone attributed the 'miraculous conclusion of the screenplay' to Leo Benvenuti. Luca Morsella explains what actually happened: 'From autumn 1981 to the beginning of 1982, the writers were cutting the long script. Sergio was away. Benvenuti and De Bernardi are great writers, but the only serious, meticulous person of the three was Medioli. They were doing their job well, but not caring really about the length of the film so the only control could have come from Medioli. But the strong relationship was between Sergio and Benvenuti and De Bernardi. So although they cut a lot, they didn't cut as much as they could. Then during the shooting, Sergio was working on these things and sometimes pages were coming in like new versions of scenes and things like that. On one or two occasions, they came a couple of days before shooting.'[96]

By the time Sergio Leone approved the final script, in New York in May 1982, various important changes had been made. The story now opened with Eve being shot by The Combination's hired killers; thereafter, three of the killers brutally beat up Fat Moe, forcing him to reveal Noodles' whereabouts. Much of the sociological background (Noodles' parents, the schoolroom scene, Nathan's funeral parlour) was deleted; a garbage truck now appeared as a link between 1933 and 1968 (foreshadowing the bizarre sight Noodles witnesses outside Senator Bailey's party); the steelworkers' strike was radically compressed – rushed, even; and some very costly set-ups (the airport, the Coney Island funfair) vanished. The resulting script was more focused, the verbal cross-references between historical periods were more memorable, and the dialogue now had some terrific one-liners. 'Noodles, I slipped'; 'So he'll never be my sweetheart. What a shame'; 'It's 9.32 and I've got nothing left to lose.' But it was still a very long story.

When Leone started filming, on 14 June 1982, the title *Once Upon a Time in America* was still to appear against an elaborate sequence of a 1933 trainload of cars turning into a 1968 trainload. According to Luca Morsella, Leone was determined 'to do that scene, right to the very end – but he wanted to do the scene without cutting! With Noodles being young and old at the same time. Impossible!'[97] Instead, Leone had finally to settle for credit titles, in 'period' Letraset, against a black background, before the opening sequence: the dullest titles of any Sergio Leone film, more akin to a Woody Allen movie. Thus, instead of hitching a lift at the level crossing, Noodles goes to a railway station in 1933, asks for a ticket on the next train out (to Buffalo) and looks at 'a girl primping herself by a mirror'. As the music changes to 'Yesterday', the elderly Noodles – thirty years later – looks in a mirror, and we see part of a wall painting behind him, which has changed to the Big Apple ad for New York.

During shooting Leone reluctantly had to sacrifice the dialogue scene between Noodles and the chauffeur prior to his dreadful 'date' with

436

Deborah: 'where you can feel intuitively their mutual scorn and where the difference between the Italian Mafia and the Jewish equivalent is explained. The Jewish people did not admire their gangsters, unlike the Italo-Americans. For the record, the chauffeur was played by the film's producer. The moment where he refuses a tip made all his friends smile.'[98] The scene was in fact shot, but Leone's reasons for cutting it were not entirely to do with running time, as Luca Morsella remembers: 'Sergio had promised the part of the chauffeur to Arnon Milchan, but at the end of the Canadian location – just before the crew moved to New Jersey – he lost his nerve about this. He was worried that having taken so much trouble over casting everyone else, this might not work. So he said no. Milchan was offended and asked Robert De Niro to intercede. There was a row with Sergio, who finally agreed to shoot it. He shot it then cut it, and then told interviewers Milchan had made him cut it!'[99]

One side-effect of the changes made between autumn 1981 and May 1982, and during the shoot, was that the Italian references in the film had become increasingly obvious, despite the 'shadow of the two Godfathers' which Leone claimed he was determined to shake off. Dominic saying to the Capuano Brothers 'we da best escort-a you ever gonna get'. The Thieving Magpie in the maternity ward sequence. The Romanian throne which symbolizes Max's megalomania, which had become 'a gift to a Pope. Cost me 800 bucks . . . it's from the seventeenth century.' This may well have been a sly reference to Sergio Leone's own taste in antique furniture, but it also created the impression that despite the fragments of Yiddish in the dialogue, the jokes about deli food and the spectacular scenes of crowded ghetto life on Pesach, there was very little that was Jewish about these particular hoods. When John Landis heard that Sergio Leone was making a film about Jewish gangsters from the Lower East Side, knowing his lack of sensitivity on racial issues, his initial reaction, he says, was 'Oh no!' But Landis was reassured to discover 'it was about Italians after all'.[100] At one stage, the characters were to have spoken Yiddish with English subtitles. And actors such as Richard Dreyfuss, Harvey Keitel and Dustin Hoffman had been approached. Now Leone was casting Italians.

The reason Arnon Milchan had managed to get the film off the ground where others had failed was entirely because of Robert De Niro. The actor recalled the sequence of events, for the RAI documentary C'era una volta il cinema: 'I had met Sergio and talked to him about the movie. In fact I'd met him nine years ago.' He was thinking of Gérard Dépardieu for the film at that time.' He was also thinking about three actors to play each of the protagonists.[101] De Niro was making *The Godfather Part II* and they met in New York. His only film which had been noticed by the critics was Martin Scorsese's *Mean Streets* (1973). De Niro recalled the conversation in an interview for *American Film*: 'He was a big guy and I liked him: but I wasn't sure about him as a director. I knew he'd done what they call spaghetti Westerns, but they weren't taken seriously, in a way, I guess – I hadn't seen any of them. But I liked him. He was very Italian, very sympathetic, *simpatico*.'[102]

By the time Arnon Milchan reintroduced De Niro to Leone, the actor had *Taxi Driver*, *New York New York*, *Raging Bull* and *The Deer Hunter* to his credit. He was about to start work on *The King of Comedy*, which was expected to be a huge hit. At the first of their 1981 meetings, in New York, Leone was impressed that De Niro recalled their earlier conversation: 'He remembered *Once Upon a Time*; the story seemed to have touched him.' It still touched him after Leone 'over about seven hours, in two sittings, had described the whole story to me'.[103] 'For the three ages of Noodles,' Leone remembered, 'I had resigned myself to using three different actors, when the producer told me he had managed to get hold of De Niro – whom I'd thought about in the first place. It was as if they had said to Carlo Collodi "make Pinocchio with a real boy". This had to be a very mythical, fairy-tale-like film, and yet the extreme *truthfulness* of De Niro would introduce a much more realistic tone to it. If De Niro did commit, the film would become a little different to the films I'd made until then – where the game of the puppet-master, the *burattinaio*, was to squeeze one more orgasm out of the story.'[104]

Given Leone's by now much-publicized comments on working with Actors' Studio graduates such as Rod Steiger, and his use of iconic actors as walking pieces of mythology, the casting of Robert De Niro would be more than 'a little different'. It would represent a radical rethinking of the whole project. De Niro was already famous for his total immersion – mind and body – in whatever part he played and for researching every nuance of character in fanatical detail. As Jerry Lewis, his co-star in *King of Comedy*, drily put it, 'De Niro has obviously never heard Noel Coward's advice to actors about remembering their lines and trying not to bump into the furniture'. He was a perfectionist, discussing with his director why take after take had not quite hit the spot, and depending to an unusual extent on co-operation with other actors. The results were often very impressive, but they were not 'acting' in the traditional sense at all: more a case of getting right inside someone else's skin. This was a far cry from Leone's concentration on surfaces. Moreover, Leone was the sort of personality who liked to establish who was boss, from the word go. A collision of opposites could be envisaged.

Leone told De Niro the story 'practically shot by shot' and left him the 1981 script, plus the choice of either Noodles or Max. There was then a delay of two months, as De Niro began his researches. He screened 'three or four of Leone's films', including Martin Scorsese's prized print of Once Upon a Time in the West. It had been Scorsese who helped to give Milchan confidence in Sergio Leone's abilities in the first place. 'The films were interesting,' De Niro remembered. 'Leone didn't take himself too seriously, even the way he did the credits. Anyway, there was something about him I liked. We met again. We talked. I went to Italy: he showed me the locations – they were gonna do it, with or without me [which was not strictly true]. But I knew it was a big commitment. Maybe two years. And that's what it was. Two years.'[105]

Leone, for his part, began to discover that De Niro's obsessive temperament and perfectionism were 'something like my own'. This would have to be a much closer working relationship than he was accustomed to; he had collaborated before, but never like this: 'He identifies himself totally with his character, and lives it one thousand per cent. When he had to play an old man, he *was* an old man . . . Bob lives with his script: he repeats it to himself 100,000 times at home, and when he comes on the set he gives off a sense of improvisation and spontaneity . . . I would go on the set and play his part to him – and then he would say to me, smiling, "You're very good," before doing it much better than I ever could.'[106] As De Niro recalled it, he was often keen to receive a Leone line reading, if only for research purposes: 'I'd sometimes say to him, "Show me how you would do it." If you hit the moment right then you get the language in a very organic way from the director. When he did that I'd say, "Okay, I've got it. You're not giving me the performance but I see the way you did it." After that, I had a way to do it.' At an early stage, Leone recalled, De Niro 'made it clear that he has needs to be fulfilled . . . so for the first time, in this film, I would have to follow an actor's ideas without destroying my own. Yes, Bobby will have his *interpretazione artistica*.'[107]

After two months, and after satisfying himself that Sergio Leone really was *simpatico*, De Niro signed to play Noodles, for a fee which was reported to be the first ever to top $3 million. It was essential that he played the same character in 1933 and 1968 – which would, of course, have implications for all the other actors appearing in both periods. One of the first things he did, was to study the behaviour of elderly people, to arrange a series of make-up tests and to practise ageing his voice: a mirror-image of his research for *The Godfather Part II*, where he had watched videotapes of Marlon Brando's performance as Don Vito Corleone repeatedly, to 'get the *beginning* of the rasp in his voice'. For *Raging Bull* of three years before, he had turned *himself* into an obese has-been: this time he would have to entrust his appearance to someone else. He told Pete Hamill, 'It took so long to put the make-up on – four to six hours – that I was so tired I *had* to look old. You get up at three, start at four, and go to work at eight or nine.' Leo Benvenuti found all this 'a bit over-serious' and decided to play a joke on De Niro: 'The best way to handle the role', he told him, 'is to shoot the first part with you as you are now, stop, wait thirty years, then film the end when you are really old.' He didn't laugh, apparently. Instead, De Niro decided to shoot all the 'young' sequences in continuity, followed by the 'old' sequences – an idea, Benvenuti recalled ruefully, 'which cost the production an extra million and a half dollars'.[108]

De Niro's first choice of make-up artist was Christopher Tucker, who had transformed John Hurt into *The Elephant Man* the previous year. But Leone was not convinced. Noodles was not Quasimodo or 'some such monster'. As Luca Morsella put it, 'he was not supposed to look like a Muppet'. He was a quiet old man who had gone to bed early for thirty-five years. After ten weeks of tests, Leone proved his point: 'And I took on a young Italian who did fantastic things [one of the great make-up jobs in movie history, in fact, credited to Nilo Jacoponi, Manlio Rocchetti and Gino Zamprioli]. De Niro put on that make-up . . . for two and a half months. And he had to shave his head and his cheeks . . . He entered into the spirit of things with a mad love, a professionalism and a total obedience – even though I'd been told that he was difficult to work with. He loves his craft so much.'[109] Meanwhile, De Niro began to read books about New York in the 1920s and 1930s, to wander around the period buildings of the Lower East Side and to look at archive photographs. The pre-publicity for the film said he 'spent a great deal of time with a Jewish family of the neighbourhood, comprising three generations, so that he might study their cadences and gestures'. 'I talked to certain people', De Niro added, 'to get a feeling for the things I didn't know. I didn't know about Jewish gangsters. There were quite a few of them in the old days. One of the people De Niro talked to was a disc jockey friend from Philadelphia, who knew a gangster called Little Nicky Scarfo, who in turn knew the aged Meyer Lansky himself. De Niro apparently tried to get Scarfo to arrange a meeting with Lansky to find out first hand about Jewish gangsters – but Scarfo declined. It would have been as fascinating and bizarre an encounter as Leone's with Harry Grey.[110]

De Niro's casting as Noodles made Leone begin to 'rethink the whole idea of the film – with even more reality within the dream'. It also provided a starting point for the casting of all the other characters, for, 'having chosen Bob, we then had to have common accents – which all had to be from New York'. Leone spent several weeks in Hollywood scouting talent, but found only 'people from Texas or San Francisco'. So he resolved to set up a long series of auditions in New York itself, with Robert De Niro, Brian Freilino and an American assistant on the interviewing committee with him. This was a procedure which De Niro had successfully used with Martin Scorsese, even though it was very time-consuming. Two hundred actors were auditioned for the part of Max alone. It was, said Leone rather ambiguously, fortunate that other actors wanted so much to work with Robert De Niro: 'Bob wanted me to cast one of his friends in the part. And we did numerous tests with his cronies. Happily, he is an honest man. When he saw these tests, he had to agree with me that none of his friends could really play Max.[111]

'The case of Joe Pesci was different. Milchan had promised him the part of Max. I thought he was terrific in Raging Bull [as Jake La Motta's manager brother Joey] but I had warned him that he would not be right for this particular part. I would take him on for another role – which he could choose [in the end, Frankie, The Combination's man]. But De Niro did lead me towards another of this friends: Tuesday Weld. I remembered her from her very first films: in those, she was just as beautiful as Brigitte Bardot. From the very first tests, it was self-evident that she was indeed able to play the character [of Carol, the gangster's moll].'[112] Leone associated Weld with her earliest teen movies, rather than her cult performances in Lord Love a Duck (1966), Pretty Poison (1968) and

*Looking for Mr Goodbar* (1977). Her screen image as sex-kitten-turned-nasty seemed tailor-made for the detached, nymphomaniac Carol who has seen better days. Tuesday Weld was pleased to be involved again with a large-scale movie 'that sweeps you away like a book or a person can do'. Claudia Cardinale, who had hoped to be cast as Carol, was disappointed, but Leone explained that since the film was now to feature characters 'in a New York style' she would no longer be suitable.[113]

Leone wanted 'a new face' for Max. He was first taken to see the thirty-five-year-old James Woods on the New York stage in the early 1970s. He later noticed him in the television mini-series *Holocaust* (1978), in which he had played a young concentration camp artist. 'After *Holocaust*', Woods told a French reporter, 'I was offered so many parts as young, tormented Jews, that if I had accepted them, I would have become an honorary member of the Knesset.'[114] Since being 'noticed' as Barbra Streisand's college boyfriend in *The Way We Were* (1972), Woods had chiefly distinguished himself as a psychopathic cop killer in *The Onion Field* (1979). Since then, he had become typecast in character roles as twitchy, intense villains. 'I liked his theatre performance,' Leone recalled. 'His screen test was not conclusive, but I sensed an on-the-edge neurosis – a driven energy – behind his offbeat looks . . . And I convinced De Niro that he ought to be hired for the part.'[115]

So, as Woods remembered, 'Leone calls me and tells me I have the role of a lifetime and I say, "Wonderful." This will be the role that turns it all around.' Woods was fascinated to watch Leone 'learning something new' as the piece came to life in the hands of his actors. 'Leone was used to iconographic film-making, operatic, using actors as marionettes – stand there, look into the distance, do this . . . We would work up scenes and do them completely differently than he anticipated, and he'd try to cover it rather than create it. He said, "I always had my shots set up and I'd just plug the actors in. Now you guys come in and completely redefine the scene, and I have to cover it as if I'm a documentarian – I've never worked this way but I find it invigorating." '[116]

Where Woods himself was concerned, he used the experience of acting with De Niro to fuel the onscreen relationship between Max and Noodles: 'I was a known, respected, still-to-be-proven character actor on the cusp of some kind of success, playing opposite the widely acknowledged and acclaimed greatest actor in the world. I thought, "Well, my challenge is to go toe to toe with him in every scene and prove that I'm of the same mettle as him." So I used that challenge of being in an actors' ego competition, in a subtle way, to infuse the relationship between Max and Noodles with the same sense of affection and yet dire competition. And Bobby was aware of it and it was good for the film.'[117]

It helped that De Niro's interpretation of the character of Noodles chimed with that of Woods: 'two of the main things that interested me in the movie', he said to Diego Gabutti in the RAI documentary, 'were this friendship and this betrayal, and also tied in with the betrayal was the romantic part with Deborah ... he's the ultimate betrayer, and that's the thing – I can only say what I say in the last scene'.[118] The two actors managed to persuade Leone to use direct sound as a way of capturing the electricity between them, and this was used for the more intimate scenes. After much discussion, though, they settled for sometimes 'filming with music', to the point where – as Leone observed – 'Bob preferred to post-synch and give up direct takes ... dubbing was also necessary at times because he speaks in a very quiet voice, probably because deep down he is ashamed of acting. Which makes him even greater.' Music was always played during rehearsals, and just before the take; for the bigger scenes, dialogue was recorded on a guide-track. Leone estimated that in the end 65 per cent of the film was recorded direct, the rest post-synchronized.[119]

James Woods came to enjoy soaking up the atmosphere through prerecorded music: 'We go on the set, and we sit for a few hours, and we have cappuccino, and we listen to the score for the movie ... You always imagine, as an actor, walking down a dirt road with a shotgun next to Bill Holden at the end of *The Wild Bunch* and having that music playing. Of course, it never happens when you're an actor; you're walking down, and there's people gawking, and the guys are tripping over the cables. But when you're there with Leone, it's just like in the movies. You're sitting looking at the other guy, and there's a hundred guys on violins playing. You go, "This is exactly like I thought it was gonna be. This is why I became an actor. This is the magic, the absolute magic, of being a movie star in a great movie." '[120]

There were, of course, some tensions on the set. On one occasion (which Leone later enjoyed recalling) Robert De Niro questioned a set-up and Leone invited him to look through the viewfinder himself. De Niro conceded that the director was right after all and Leone could not resist saying, 'I'm glad you think so, Bob, since I am the director.' On another – when they were shooting the scene were Noodles returns to the gang, to find Max sitting in his throne – De Niro decided during rehearsal that he would like to add 'a homage to Sergio Leone, in the movies I've seen of his'. He would pick up a cup of coffee, and stir it over and over and over again while his childhood friends looked on. 'It seemed right for the scene – and the kind of thing you'd imagine in one of his films.' Leone conceded that the actor was right.[121]

Raffaella Leone (who was assistant costume designer) remembers that, during the first sequence to be filmed in mid-June 1982 (the opium den, shot in Rome), De Niro wanted unusual sounds to be played on set, to help him wake up suddenly and convincingly: 'We tried all sorts of sounds, and many, many takes. After this had been going on for some time, one of the grips was heard to ask, "Is there a scene in this film where he has to cry? If so, I'll volunteer to be the one who kicks him in the balls."' She also recalls the long discussions with Sergio about Noodles' hat and exactly where its crease should be: 'It had to be ironed over and over again.'[122] During pre-production, in early March 1982, De Niro had discussed with John Belushi a possible part in Leone's film. This is one reason why he was with the actor at the Chateau Marmont Hotel the night before he died of a drug overdose. Maybe he had Belushi in mind for Fat Moe. While *America* was being filmed, four months later, De Niro gave evidence about the circumstances of his friend's death by telephone from Rome. The police were by then treating the case as a homicide inquiry, and had tried in vain to get the actor to appear in person. This made him particularly tense.

At about the same time, Danny Aiello, the New York actor who had had a walk-on in *The Godfather Part Two* and more recently played a cop who murders a Puerto Rican kid in *Fort Apache, The Bronx* (1981), let it be known he wanted to act with De Niro in *America*. Leone responded formally and asked him to give a reading. Aiello remembered a couple of years later, 'That whacked me out, cut into my confidence. Then I figured, hell, maybe Sergio never saw me before, so I went. He said to me, "You got a *bella* face, a *bella* face. I seen your *bella* face somewhere." So I say to him: "*Fort Apache, The Bronx*?" "No, no. I didn't see that," he says. "*Hide in Plain Sight*?" I say. "No, no. I don't know where," he says. He can't remember, and then it's over. I figure I must have been terrible. I'm going to the door, and Sergio says, "You are, of course, going to be in my picture" … A picture with Sergio Leone and Bobby De Niro. Great! Then I go around the various hangouts in New York, where actors go, and I bump into, I swear to

God, a hundred actors who say the same thing. And I begin to think I'm not gonna be in it.' But he had at least been given a script by Leone, and of the three parts on offer, he chose his namesake, a corrupt police commissioner called Aiello.[123] After another meeting, two more readings (one videotaped), and a brief but nerve-racking wait, Aiello was in: and all for two short sequences, the residue of a much more substantial part in the original 1981 shooting script.

For the casting of the children, in the 1923 sequences, Leone relied upon Cis Corman, the casting director who had often worked with Martin Scorsese. He did not want child stars, he said, but 'spontaneous urchins I could direct'. According to Leone, the successful candidates 'came from the Jewish quarter and had never acted before'. In fact, Corman selected children with experience in theatre or television commercials; only Scott Schutzman (Young Noodles) was a complete newcomer. Of the actors playing the same characters as grown-ups, Larry Rapp (Fat Moe) was also a newcomer to film – he was a garment salesman who sent his photograph to a casting agent friend on the off-chance – while Amy Ryder (Peggy) was a cabaret performer at the Duplex in New York who also modelled for the 'Big Beauties Modelling Agency'. Darlanne Fleugel (Eve) had shown up briefly in *Eyes of Laura Mars* (1978) and *Battle Beyond the Stars* (1980) but had established herself as a fashion model. 'When I was directing them', said Leone, 'I played all the parts as usual and then said, "I want this – now see if you can do better than I did" – a process which allowed me to avoid interpreters. For the scene of Young Patsy [Brian Bloom] eating a charlotte Russe, we did this four times using three cameras. The little actor was delighted to eat four charlotte Russes.'[124]

Elizabeth McGovern had appeared, fresh out of the Julliard School of Dramatic Art, as Timothy Hutton's girlfriend in *Ordinary People* (1980). Leone had loved her performance as turn-of-the-century Broadway star Evelyn Nesbitt in *Ragtime* (1981). So, he was prepared to squeeze into a narrow wooden seat at a tiny off-Broadway theatre to study her at closer range. McGovern remembers: 'The whole group of them came to this rinky-dink little theatre that was on top of this hotel and it was the very first play this theatre company (the Second Stage) had ever staged . . . I was quite basking in the glory of this Hollywood success, but I wanted to do a play because I wanted to figure out how to do that. The play was written by a girl called Wendy Kestlemann and it was loosely based on the same historical incident as

Genet's *The Maids* – these two sisters who commit this atrocious murder. After the theatre, you had to get into this rickety elevator, and the highlight of my entire life was when all these hulking Italians, I think with De Niro, all came up this rickety little elevator to see this tiny play. Unbelievable!'[125] Leone then asked McGovern to sit comfortably and listen to his story. She recalls: 'He sat me down, and I remember literally the sun moving across the sky as hour after hour I had this story told to me.' Clearly, she acknowledged, this director was a performer at heart.

But Robert De Niro needed a lot of persuading that McGovern was right for the part of Deborah. One reason: 'She wasn't from New York [born in Evanston, Illinois]', Leone recalled, 'and he would have liked all the actors to have come from New York – with the original Brooklyn accent.' At some of the subsequent readings and tests, De Niro was present and McGovern recalls: 'I certainly had the sense he had mixed feelings about my casting. Because we were at odds, actually, the whole time: De Niro was so fixated on realistic detail and Sergio couldn't care less about realistic detail, and in my heart of hearts I couldn't care less about realistic detail either ... On the other hand, it was inspiring to see somebody work as hard as De Niro does. Unbelievable powers of concentration.' After the readings came the screen test, about which McGovern (unlike Danny Aiello) had no qualms: 'I was deeply insecure about doing the part, because actually on the page it was a very difficult part to bring to life ... though obviously she has an ambition and certain characteristics, the point of the part is that she is an imaginary woman. I was aware of that at the time and I *wanted* to have a screen test because I wasn't sure I could feel very comfortable in it.'

Of the shooting, McGovern admits, 'I did struggle with his way of directing quite a lot ... Sergio would say, "Turn your eyes up there and your cheek down there" and this kind of thing. And I passionately wanted to fulfil his vision, and at times I unfortunately didn't know how to marry that with the few tools I had as an actress: my work was more based on a spontaneous response to actors in the scene ... If you look at the acting in a lot of his movies, there's a kind of falseness to it, a frozen-ness. But he had a lot of patience for actors – even if it was a struggle. I know that the scenes with no dialogue felt the most fluid to do. The dialogue was certainly the thing to overcome in that movie – rather than the other way around.'

Leone was to tell *Cahiers du Cinéma* in May 1984 that 'McGovern was remarkable: to play as she did, at twenty-one years old, the make-up scene where she was supposed to be fifty! My model for that scene was an Italian woman such as the actress Valentina Cortese, who is always young.' He particularly liked the idea that, like Cleopatra, in Noodles' imagination, 'age cannot wither her'.[126] Elizabeth McGovern was much less sure about whether the scene would come off: 'He said I looked fifty? Well it was more like, "When are you gonna get out of high school?" In all the 1968 scenes, I can't ever really get past the old-age make-up. In my case, it was hopeless. But what can you do? Sergio shot the scene from *Antony and Cleopatra* [which explains why Deborah is wearing mask-like Kabuki make-up] but thankfully cut it out because it stopped all the action at a point where you couldn't afford to take the time suddenly to get used to the Shakespearean language . . . It was very strange to have a death scene Kabuki-style at that point in the movie. And I had this Shakespearean coach hanging around for months on end . . . and he brought along Robert Stephens who'd go on and on and knew all the Shakespearean monologues. It was all like a dream. In Rome. And of course I'd never done a Shakespeare play in my life. You don't just instinctively do it well.'

*America* is also about a romantic relationship between Noodles and Deborah, however dark and unfulfilled, which is contrasted with the decadence of Max's relationship with Carol. When the film was first released, it was this aspect – particularly the two rape scenes – which proved to be by far the most controversial: they went well beyond the usual conventions of 'molls and mothers' within the gangster genre. During the robbery, Carol (Tuesday Weld) – who has already been described as a slut – is turned on by the orgy of violence, bent face-down over a desk and shafted from behind by Noodles. Later, she is humiliated by Max when she dares to interrupt him while he is trying to impress Noodles. What is worse, she seems to thrive on such treatment and always comes back for more: in the case of the robbery, the scene is played for laughs ('We're goin'', 'You comin'?'). Where Deborah is concerned, after giving Noodles a condescending kiss on the cheek (not mentioned in the script) she is brutally raped, twice, in the back seat of the chauffeur-driven limousine. The sequence goes on for a very long time – too long for comfortable viewing. It is relentlessly nasty and the actors are neither favoured nor spared by Leone. There is no music. Both scenes unsettled audiences and critics alike, and at the Cannes Film Festival in May 1984 a member of the audience screamed at

Robert De Niro: 'As a woman, I feel deeply embarrassed to have witnessed it. I feel totally demoralized.' Another publicly accused Leone of
'blatant misogyny and anti-feminist sadism'. Leone did not exactly help
his case when he argued publicly that Noodles' rape of Deborah was an
'act of love by a man who has lost the only thing he ever wanted'. A
month later, on 6 June 1984, the headline in the *Los Angeles Times*
read 'Rape Scenes are "Love" in Sergio Leone's eyes'.[127]

Admittedly, all the members of Max's gang are meant to be emotionally retarded, like small boys obsessed with their equipment who have
no idea how to relate to flesh-and-blood women: they are not so much
misogynists as pre-sexual children who only feel at home among their
own kind in the playground playing with their new toys. But Leone did
not always seem to be aware of just how contemptible his main
characters were, and as usual he enjoyed celebrating the carnival. It was
as if, said some critics, he was making a 1960s movie in the 1980s – and
attitudes had changed a lot in the meantime. In *The Hoods*, although
the narrator is certainly cocksure and adolescent, neither the Carol
character nor the Deborah character is raped: the two scenes were
added during the drafting of the 1981 shooting script.

Elizabeth McGovern's take on this is that the limousine scene 'didn't
glamorize violent sex: it is extremely uncomfortable to watch and it is
meant to be ... He is making a gangster film, and to a certain extent
you can't make that kind of film unless you profile an extremely violent
lifestyle and an extremely brutish and limited kind of person. And if
you say, "this violence is wrong", you'd have to enlarge that to say, "all
violence in movies is wrong" and then you'd have to say, "you can only
make movies about good people who obey the law and do right things"
which a) excludes a lot of what life is and b) makes for some very
boring movies. Where do you draw the line? I don't think he would
make a gangster movie without including some violence in it and I
include that rape scene: I don't differentiate that from taking out a gun
and shooting somebody ... The question of misogyny is a different
thing altogether and there's some truth in it: it's very Italianesque
which is one reason why I struggled with the part ... the female
characters are the Madonna and the whore, and it is part of Italian
culture, of Italian-American culture.'

Questioned about the scene, Leone would argue that it was 'central
to the film' in two ways: first, the failure of Noodles to have an adult
relationship with the only person 'from whom he can hide *nothing* of

himself' tells us a lot about his state of mind, his tendency to romanti-
cize. Second, Deborah's impact on both Noodles and Max makes her
as strong a character as Jill in *Once Upon a Time in the West*. But what
of Deborah as a person, apart from her ambitious 'agenda'? Leone
always replied by changing the subject to Noodles: 'The accusations of
misogyny are too absurd. The rape scene is a cry of love! Noodles has
just spent many years in prison. He has thought about nothing but this
woman, who lives on the outside. He has always been madly in love
with her . . . She is going away to become an image in Hollywood. And
become an image again for Noodles. He wants her to leave with a
memory she will never shed. And he destroys her with the maximum
violence he can muster.'[128]

At the time of the film's release *American Film* asked Leone the more
general question 'Do you have anything against women?' He replied,
somewhat archly: 'I have nothing against women and, as a matter of
fact, my best friends are women. What could you be thinking? . . . I
even, imagine this, *married* a woman and, besides having a wretch of a
son, I also have two women as daughters. So if women have been
neglected in my films, at least up until now, it's not because I'm misogynist or chauvinist. That's not it. The fact is, I've always made epic
films and the epic, by definition, is a masculine universe.'[129]

Looking back, Elizabeth McGovern reckons that the segments of the
film that work best are not the ones which attempt to understand
Noodles and Deborah as adults, but the flashback childhood segments:
'You feel there's something so magical there, that's never quite achieved
in the adult sections.' One problem with the 1930s and 1960s episodes
is the bond between Max and Noodles, which in her view doesn't seem
to have enough to do with either friendship or compulsion. It isn't *sexy*
enough: 'A thing I know that Sergio had in his mind, when he described
his vision of the film to me, was the idea of the relationship between
Max and Noodles being a love affair that had gone wrong. And I don't
think the final film played that way because there isn't that onscreen
chemistry between Jimmy Woods and De Niro. It's hard to have that
chemistry. But it's not something that happens with De Niro. He has
his genius, his vision, his myopia, but it's not ever about a connection
between people.'

Nevertheless, McGovern was touched by the streak of wistfulness
that the film revealed in its creator: 'Sergio certainly had a melancholy
streak in him – with this story about this exile who never quite gets

back, while the ones that just play the game, like Max, rise to the top. The ones who don't have much heart. Noodles coming back was like Sergio coming back to his favourite stories, and seeing this man who played the game walk away with all the rewards. That's the chord he strikes, but he never hits the hammer right on the nail.'

This melancholy film would avoid the visual expansiveness of Leone's Westerns. As he himself put it: 'the camera moves, this time, only while following the characters . . . and *America* is noticeably less spectacular, since I put technique in the service of emotions rather than as a way of discovering a world, a history or a universe, as I did with *Once Upon a Time in the West*. I'm aware that *America* appears to be more static . . . but this stasis is the stasis of time: everything grinds to a halt in the opium den.'[130] Originally, it was to have been filmed in Cinemascope, but after the first tests with Tonino Delli Colli, Leone changed his mind. One reason, he said, was that a lot of 1980s cinemas were no longer adequately equipped to screen films in 'scope, and the results could be fuzzy at the edges and ill-defined. Another was that Leone had the misfortune to watch *Once Upon a Time in the West* on television, in an American hotel room, with Delli Colli. It was a pan and scan print, which made it look like a lot of big faces with no background: 'a total mess', Delli Colli recalls. Since the days of *Once Upon a Time in the West*, the video revolution had occurred as well – not to mention the spread of television ownership, and the proliferation of channels across Italy. All in all, Leone felt it was best that *America* be shot in the standard 1.85:1 aspect ratio instead of his trademark letterbox.[131]

When the schedule was all set to begin on 14 June 1982, Sergio Leone contacted Harry Grey again. A clause in the contract selling the film rights of his novel stipulated that Grey would be a 'consultant to the production'. A few weeks before shooting began, Leone called him in New York to let him know the good news that at last – 'after all the problems' – the adventure was to begin. Re-establishing contact was a big symbolic moment for Leone: '*Once Upon a Time in America* was a monument to Harry Grey's life in the shadow of the big statue which welcomed immigrant ships into the harbour. So I called him with the news. His wife replied. Dry, distant, tired. Can I speak to Harry Grey? Harry Grey, she told me, died a few weeks ago.'[132] It would have been fascinating to hear the old man's reaction to his considerably larger-than-life monument.

As ever, the 'visual details' were important to Leone, 'to give realism to this dream'. So the Grand Central station of the 1930s, which no longer existed, was filmed at the Gare du Nord in Paris (in one shot, the sign 'Voie 13' can clearly be seen). As he pointed out, 'Grand Central was only a replica of the Gare du Nord, in any case . . . made of the same materials'. Its buffet, where Deborah waits for her train, was filmed in the Brasserie Julien on the Rue St Denis. The lockers where the children hide their battered suitcase were at Hoboken station. The entrance to Senator Bailey's Long Island home was at Lake Como, and the garbage truck at Pratica di Mare on the outskirts of Rome. The Florida beach sequence was filmed at the Don Caesar Palace at St Petersburg, Tampa, near Miami. The art deco hotel where Noodles tries to impress Deborah, but doesn't even know which wine to order, was the Excelsior in Venice. This was because, as Leone pointed out, 'there were no longer hotels of that kind on Long Island, but they were copies of Venetian palaces: so I filmed the sequence in Venice. It's logical.'[133] In Venice, too, was the scene where the boys wait for kegs of bootleg booze to come to the surface of Lower New York Bay: this was filmed in Porto Marghera.

The drive to and from the hotel was through northern New Jersey (near Deal). The Lower East Side street scenes were shot a few blocks below the Williamsburg Bridge in Brooklyn, on 8th Street South near the corner of Bedford Avenue and 'all the streets around there' – except the 'most rundown bits which were in Rome'. The feather factory was 'a real, working feather factory near 8th Street'. Leone had been offered the streets used in *The Godfather Part Two*, but he wanted more depth of field – four blocks all the way down to the river – plus one of those 'great bridges'. Two hundred metres of 8th Street South and surroundings were duplicated by Carlo Simi and his team back home near Prietralata on the Via delle Messid'oro. 'This location', recalls Luca Morsella, 'belonged to De Paulis Studios. A section of 8th Street, Brooklyn, was reconstructed there as well as Fat Moe's speakeasy and diner and the gang's private office. The outside of the speakeasy was both New York and Rome, the inside only Rome. The alley where Bugsy beats up Max and Noodles was Rome, because the alleyway in Brooklyn was far too small. And also where Deborah dances in the warehouse was Prietralata.'[134]

The setting for Jimmy O'Donnell's beating by strikebreakers was an old abattoir in the centre of Rome, Mattadoyo di Roma. There, someone mentioned to Leone that he had seen 'a rat so large that the cats are having heart failure'. By lunchtime Leone was claiming with relish that he was the one who'd seen the rat, and that they were everywhere. But, where 'authenticity' was concerned, the director's most helpful discovery was the surprising number of unspoiled 1920s and 1930s buildings in and around Montreal: 'Even there, between the recce and the filming, many of the places I found had already been destroyed.'[135]

The sequences filmed in Montreal included the newsstand which the boys torch; the prison where Noodles is locked up; the fire and the deaths of Noodles' associates; the club outside which Crowning's hit-men are mown down with a machine-gun; and the Federal Reserve Bank. Montreal was also the source of 'a fabulous collection of vintage cars'. The scene where Joe (Burt Young) is shot in the eye was filmed at Trois Rivières near Quebec, as was the car driving off the pier: for Carlo Simi, 'the place where the St Lawrence seems like the ocean, and where the road is lined with the carcasses of rotting boats' was his favourite location.[136] The jewel robbery that precedes this sequence was shot on a sound stage at Cinecittà. There, the opium den, the Reginald Marsh/Big Apple screen, Peggy's brothel, the hospital interior and the study in Senator Bailey's house were also filmed. The shadow puppets performed in a 'then derelict Roman theatre' called Teatro la Cometa, operated by Indonesian and Dutch puppeteers found by the Italian embassy in the Hague and watched by members of the Chinese community in Rome (with some of the older faces from Paris). When asked why they had an Indonesian puppet theatre in a Chinese opium den, Luca Morsella replied, 'None of us ever thought of that.'[137]

Filming took place in Rome from 14 June to July 1982, moved on to the Gare du Nord and the Brasserie Julien in Paris (four days), then to Venice, then back to Rome, then to Canada (late August), New Jersey, Florida (four or five days) and New York (mid-October to December), then back to Rome and Venice (for the scene in New York Harbour) and finally to Belaggio at Lake Como and Rome again. The exact length of the schedule, says Luca Morsella, is complicated to work out: 'After we came back to Rome from New York we suspended the film for a little while. It was not continuous. We came back to Rome and shot non-stop to February 1983. Then we went to Venice. Then there was a gap. Then we went to Como. And then the last scenes were in Rome, in Pratica di Mare, where we shot part of the exterior of Bailey's villa. And also we shot the scene where the car, the Cadillac, explodes ... At one point, they had done a close-up. When the car explodes . . . the camera saw the number plate clearly and it was different from the close-up we had done before. We'd done the close-up in the cemetery in Queens, with shots of a sinister black car following Noodles around. So we abandoned that idea. From the start in June 1982 to the finish around March/April 1983 I'd say was a total of nine months' filming, with a gap of fifteen days in the schedule.'

Fred Caruso, who had at last been signed as 'executive in charge of production' in February 1982, was responsible for planning the complicated logistics: 'We had [the Lower East Side street] in Rome, a set', he told *American Film* in June 1984, 'and we had an actual street in Brooklyn but we had to do it in Montreal too. And they all had to match exactly, so we could shoot reverses. We went to Montreal because we couldn't find enough old buildings in New York, buildings that weren't all junked up with modern signs, modern streetlights, modern telephone poles . . . and it was only an hour from New York, so it was also accessible. [Leone himself opted for the 8th Street South location, out of a range of possibles.] He loved it because it had the Williamsburg Bridge in the background. He said, "That's America. That type of bridge can't be found in Europe. It tells everybody 'this is New York, this is America, this is the Lower East Side'." It had some other advantages too. On one side of the street, a lot of houses were owned by the city or abandoned or boarded up. On the other side, a knish factory took up two-thirds of the block, so we only had to deal with one landlord on that side. Still, there were problems.'[138]

False store-fronts had been built (Mario's grocery store became S. Cohen's Hebrew Bookstore, for example); shop windows had been decorated with English and Yiddish lettering; a little synagogue and graveyard had been moulded out of fibreglass by Simi's Italian craftsmen; 500 actors had to dress up as Hasidim and the real inhabitants (mostly Puerto Ricans) had to be persuaded to live with their front windows boarded up for a total of four months. A hundred thousand dollars was spent on lumber alone to customize 8th Street. When Leone and his crew arrived, in a bitterly cold October 1982, they had already shot most of the matching details and interiors in Rome. During the filming of the two big crowd scenes – an approximation, on a much grander scale, of the equivalent shots in *Angels with Dirty Faces* – a couple of real-life Hasids, onlookers, were heard by a *New York* reporter to mutter 'the men and women are going to *shul* together. They're *touching*

one another! This is very bad . . . This is supposed to be a movie in the
1920s, and the street is filled with people dressed like us, but there were
very few Hasids in America then. We did not come until after the Holocaust.' On being informed that the film being shot was 'about crime',
another onlooker became thoroughly confused: 'Crime – and *Hasids*?'
Hasids disapprove of films on principle. And yet, to confuse matters
further, ex-members of the sect were to be found among the extras.[139]

Luca Morsella, who assisted at the New York location, recalls the
director's perfectionism – obsessive, even by his standards: 'We were
shooting in Brooklyn and working with some eight hundred extras.
And there were fifteen period cars and pickup trucks and animals of all
sorts because this was a market scene and Sergio was watching it all
from a Chapman crane . . . We had to shoot this scene thirty-five times,
because either there was a hole in between the extras, or one car didn't
start at the right time or this or that. There was always something that
Sergio didn't like and so we had to repeat it. Eventually when we were
on the twenty-sixth or twenty-seventh take, everybody was holding his
breath because this is the good one, *this is the good one*, everything will
be all right. And instead all of a sudden about two or three seconds
from the end of the shot Sergio was screaming like crazy and saying
"kill that one" and he meant it, and everybody was really surprised
because they thought everything was just perfect that time. Instead,
when he came down from the Chapman crane he said that there was a
girl twenty metres or so away from the camera who had actually *looked
into the camera* while he was shooting . . . He was checking every single
thing, and the framing and the movements and the lot until the very
end.' Tonino Delli Colli adds, 'When he had something on his mind,
*nothing* could be done about it . . . He would see things which would
never have shown up on film. I tried to tell him they were insignificant,
but for him everything had to be perfect. I was sometimes beside
myself, but that's how he saw things.'[140]

When he wasn't on the crane, Leone – in a bulky blue sweater and a
long red scarf, his bespectacled eyes taking it all in – was rushing from
Hasid to Hasid, adjusting their dress, or else making sure that the
young Noodles was wearing his hat exactly as the older Noodles would
later do – not to mention double-checking that the De Niro mole on the
boy's right cheek was firmly in place. Or negotiating with Puerto Rican
teenagers who had been hired by the producer as 'minders'. Or giving
quotable soundbites to reporters such as 'detail is important, but it is

not everything: the vision is everything'. With forty-five Italians, plus American counterparts, trying to film hundreds of American actors in a rundown part of New York, under the watchful eye of understandably suspicious Hispanic and Hasidic locals, Caruso also had his work cut out: 'There was always the language problem, too, but that wasn't as bad as you might think. We had a lot of Italians that Sergio brought with him. In Montreal, some of the Italians spoke French and some of the Canadians spoke Italian. Some of the Americans – like me – spoke Italian, and some of the Italians spoke English. But I remember at one point the chief Italian gaffer was trying to explain something to the chief American gaffer, and they had to settle on using Spanish. But the international language is pointing. If anybody didn't understand, they pointed.'[141]

To complement his Italian crew of about forty-five people, Leone had to hire a shadow American crew 'who, to tell the truth, were not terribly useful to me . . . I negotiated in the USA with the lesser of the two big trade unions they have in this area, and we paid a certain number of American technicians less than my technicians – paid them to stay at home while I worked with my own crew which created a conflict between the two unions, but still helped us to save a lot of money. If you're filming in New York, it is madness. Say you have a hundred parked cars, you must pay a hundred drivers at $1,300 a week each.

'By using a minority union, I was able to engage fewer people. The majority union then became angry and made itself heard through important voices – those of Reagan and Ted Kennedy, who were called to the rescue. The union mounted a campaign, with typical slogans: "While America has economic problems, why should an Italian crew be allowed to invade our country?" In fact, we had to leave before the agreed date.'[142] The Reagan reference was not a Leone exaggeration: on 30 March 1983, *Variety* reported – under the headline 'IATSE Opposes Import of Foreign Crew' – that the President had asked the Department of Labor to investigate the importation of 'foreign crew members' during the Brooklyn shoot of Sergio Leone's film. By then, though, Leone was safely back on his home turf shooting 8th Street South on duplicate sets.[143]

When he filmed at the real 8th Street South, he had particularly wanted to show the Williamsburg Bridge in the distance. This involved irritating not just the trade union, but the traffic police – as Luca Morsella remembers only too well: 'It was a 1923 period scene, and we could clearly see the bridge. The New York authorities gave us permission to shoot from, say, eleven o'clock to twelve o'clock. And this was special treatment. Obviously, and everybody knew it would happen, Sergio wasn't happy by twelve o'clock and wanted to do "just one more", as ever. He managed to convince them to ask for one more shot. Caruso and the Italian production supervisor Mario Cotone went with walkie-talkies, with their cars on the bridge, in front of everyone, when the bridge was still closed. And as soon as the police said, "Buster, we have to open it," the cars started coming and they let the first cars pass and then they blocked the bridge with their own cars, pretending that they had broken down. Just for the time to get the shot. And Sergio, obviously, took quite a time to do it. So the police became furious and on the day after in a New York paper it said, "This has to be the last time we give permission for a foreign film to come and shoot here." '[144]

Ted Kurdyla, billed as New York 'production liaison', had to contend with further logistical complications while the crews were still in America. He recalled: 'There's a scene in which Robert De Niro picks up Elizabeth McGovern at a New York theatre, and takes her for a ride out to Long Island, to this unbelievable art deco restaurant on the beach. At the restaurant there are violins and champagne, then a dance on the shore, then the ride back. This all takes place in the 1930s. On the screen, it will probably take five minutes. But we shot the interior of the theatre in Montreal; the exterior of the theatre was actually an old hotel here in New York; the drive was through northern New Jersey . . . and the shore of the Atlantic was actually the Adriatic. It wasn't that we couldn't have found locations that came *close* to what Sergio wanted. We had to get *exactly* what he imagined. For example, he saw a garbage truck in some book. And he wanted it for the picture; he had to have it. The scene he had imagined was based on the teeth of the mechanism that crushed the garbage. Well, we looked everywhere. We must have looked at every garbage truck in the nation, and we couldn't find that one. He wouldn't settle for something like it. And we had to build it. That's the thing that makes him so special. I mean, every director is like that to some extent, but Sergio is kind of a combination director and art director.'[145] And the truck had to have the number 35 painted on it, the number of years Noodles had been away.

Back in Italy, the press was already commenting on the scale and ambition of the project – as Luciano Vincenzoni noted: 'People are already talking about the atmosphere of *Once Upon a Time in*

*America*. [Leone] managed to create an opium cloud which was as big as the Stazione di Termini, with clouds of smoke and bunk beds . . . this is, of course, an exaggeration because the only clouds of opium you will actually see in the Chinese Quarter are rather squalid, but the little man sitting in the middle of the cinema, who watches this gigantic screen where in close-up he sees a head six metres by three metres, is almost assaulted by these images and when he leaves the cinema he carries with him the strong impression that he has been affected. Leone always has to *make an effect* – every time.'[146] Leo Benvenuti had pointed this out to Sergio: 'If one of the smokers who is on a high-up bunk falls, he will kill himself! It's an impossible structure. But common sense was not his thing, and so Simi made an opium den like a cathedral.'[147]

His way of working was expensive. Arnon Milchan's original estimate for the film had been $18 million and a twenty-week schedule. This had been officially raised, as the production grew, to a revised total budget of $23 million and a thirty-week schedule. The thirty-week schedule had grown to thirty-six weeks or even more than that. Leone's own estimate of what was actually spent was $15 million 'on the line – that is to say, without including my salary, De Niro's, principal actors' and post-production: I can be certain of that because I would have been penalized on my salary if I had overshot it.' Luca Morsella estimates the cost as 'slightly above $20 million'. *Variety* reported, when the film was finally released, that its total cost was more than $30 million. Fred Caruso was quoted in *American Film* as stating, 'it is unfair to say we went over budget', but he did accept that the gap between what was written on the page and what was actually filmed was unusually wide. Which made life difficult. 'In the script you could read something and it seems like a nice little scene. But in Sergio's imagination, every scene is a huge, monumental visual epic . . . it was always double, triple, ten times the scope of what you read in the script. I say this in a good sense. Sergio visualizes what other people don't.'[148]

The last sequence to be shot was outside the gates of Bailey's mansion, where *someone* is seemingly chewed up by that garbage truck: a suitably disgusting end to a corrupt empire. James Woods had overrun his contract and returned to America; and Sergio Leone needed a figure in a dinner jacket. Even before Woods left, Leone had told the actor, 'I want it to be sort of you, but not you.' As he explained, Bailey was based on Jimmy Hoffa, the disappeared head of the truckers' union, who gambled the members' pension funds by loaning them to the

Mafia, among others. 'We know in our hearts', Leone confided, 'he's in that garbage truck. But we never actually have any proof of it: I want to leave it that way.' There was a week's break before filming, and executive producer Claudio Mancini suggested they use it to find a double. Leone was far from convinced; this was stretching the ambiguity. But Luca Morsella managed to track down a man who had once doubled for Gregory Peck, and whose physique was fortuitously similar to that of Woods. They dressed him up as Senator Bailey, put a plastic make-up shell over his face, and Morsella asked Leone to 'come out a second' from his editing suite at Rafran, in the Via Birmania. The double walked towards him, from the bottom of the road, 'like James Woods would have done, a bit limping when he was old'. Leone was impressed, though he wasn't about to show it publicly: 'Come here; I'll show you how to do it,' he said. But at last the director had his man.[149]

After the garbage truck has passed by, Noodles sees a car full of drunken party-goers, and, according to the script, the scene somehow changes to New York's Chinatown, on 3 December 1933, the night Prohibition ended. Leone had hoped to film this street party in style, as Luca Morsella remembers: 'The Chinatown scene was in the script, but cut out. Before going into the opium den, Noodles walks around Chinatown. Among the revellers. Instead of this, we shot the scene of the cars approaching him with the bright lights. At the same place as the gates to the mansion, Pratica di Mare. You can see a pagoda structure in the background. And then we see De Niro inside the opium den. The scene in which he wandered around the streets of Chinatown – Sergio was determined to shoot it in Hong Kong! With something like two thousand extras. Sailors, drunken revellers, people celebrating . . .'[150] Carlo Simi's drawing of 'Chinatown' makes it look like one of the most elaborate sequences in the film.

By February 1983, Sergio Leone had ten hours of usable footage in the can. With help from editor Nino Baragli, who had joined the director for the Italian-shot sequences, this was pruned to six hours. Then, finally accepting that there was unlikely to be a two-part version, Leone delivered a fine cut of three hours and forty-nine minutes. His ideal running time, he said, would have been 'between four hours ten minutes and four hours twenty-five minutes'; but he very reluctantly excised between forty-five and fifty minutes' worth of 'significant material'. No longer would Noodles return home to his tenement, in 1922, to discover his parents at prayer and no food on the table; certain visual *leitmotifs* – a black limo tailing Noodles, an ominous garbage truck – had to make way. Senator Bailey's dispute with the elderly Jimmy O'Donnell over the pensions scam was lost, as was Noodles' opium-rich flashback to himself, Max and the gang as children. Leone's biggest regret over the lost material was that 'most of it concerned relationships with women'. To the cutting-room floor were consigned all of Louise Fletcher's performance as the director of Riversdale cemetery, most of Darlanne Fleugel's as Eve (including her meeting with Noodles, and his revelation that she sports 'falsies'), some of Elizabeth McGovern's work (including her Busby Berkeley and Shakespeare routines), and Tuesday Weld as Carol, telling Noodles about Max's syphilis from her rest home.

By mid-April 1983, as Leone was interviewed at length by *Cahiers du Cinéma*, there were already rumblings from the Ladd Company in Hollywood, the American distributor, that the film would require further cuts, to bring it closer to the 165 minutes Leone had been contracted to deliver. There was a note of panic in his replies. Four months later, there was talk of agreeing to a film of 180, perhaps 210, minutes. But 229 was out of the question. By 27 December 1983, according to the *New York Daily News*, Ladd Company executives were becoming apprehensive about the resistance of exhibitors to screening such a long film. Maybe it wasn't a question of cutting half an hour out: maybe the solution was to dismantle the entire story, possibly shedding the flashback structure and reassembling it into chronological order. The company's position was that, because Leone had failed to meet his target length, he had forfeited the right of final cut. Leone's position was that his original agreement with the producer had been misinterpreted. He thought they *wanted* a two-part version. And he was understandably agitated. While busily putting the finishing touches to the 229-minute version, he was being threatened with a rival version, over an hour shorter, edited by someone else on the other side of the Atlantic, and without his authorization or supervision.[151]

A particular problem was the deliberately confusing and very brutal opening, culminating in the inexorable ringing of the telephone, which took the full length of the film to explain. Mary Corliss of *American Film* imagined the scene: 'The rings are very long and loud, and there are twenty-two of them, screaming through scenes that no member of the audience could yet comprehend. It's easy to imagine that after about five rings, Alan Ladd Jr was trying to determine what Leone was up to; that after ten rings, he decided it was to inflict pain on the audience; that after fifteen rings he envisioned members of that audience shouting out, "Answer the bloody phone!"; that after twenty rings, he wished he was in some other business; and that on the twenty-second ring, he resolved to cut the damn movie down to a running time that exhibitors would find acceptable.'[152]

At three hours forty-nine minutes, *Once Upon a Time in America* would be longer than any film released by Hollywood since Bertolucci's *Novecento*, and the Ladd Company was still reeling from the recent disaster on the American domestic market of *The Right Stuff*, which ran for a mere three hours and fourteen. The point was now raised that Robert De Niro had not appeared in a profit-making project since *The Deer Hunter* five years earlier. On 17 February 1984, a sneak preview in Boston of a 227-minute version, shorn of two minutes' violence, confirmed the distributors' worst fears. Most of the audience's reply cards bore the words 'Confused', 'Angry', and 'Too long'. A second sneak, scheduled for the following day in Washington, DC, was immediately cancelled.

Leone poured out his anxieties to *Cahiers*: 'Now they want to cut another hour, notably at the beginning. The only way to do this would be to suppress my flashback construction – and I am not prepared to ... I have retained a very good French lawyer, Léo Matarasso (Orson Welles's lawyer), since the contract was in fact signed in France under the Napoleonic Code. I've also retained a lawyer in the USA to try to hold up the distribution of any truncated version. But my first line of attack is to instigate an action against the producer, who is based in France ... The truth is that at the American end the project has no champion, no patron. The Ladd Company depends on Warner Brothers, and at Warner Brothers there is no single executive, but many, who all think the same way and play things by the rule book ... They don't want to do battle with the distributors and take responsibility for the outcome ... What I've made is a film about time, memory and cinema ... My film isn't *The Godfather I* and *II* [which had, in 1978, been re-edited to make a continuous four-part television mini-series]: you can't see it in chronological order ... The truth is, these gentlemen are scared for their jobs which change all the time in the major companies ... It is difficult to fight an enemy who doesn't exist.'

At Cannes on 20 May 1984, where *America* was shown in its three-hour forty-nine-minute version *hors de competition*, many critics rushed for their superlatives; the 'full version' attracted the best reviews worldwide of any Leone film. But some female members of the audience attacked both De Niro and Leone for the 'blatant, gratuitous violence' of the rape scenes. De Niro, who was wearing a woolly hat because his hair was still growing back, pulled the hat over his eyes and sat in silence. Immediately afterwards he drove straight back to his hotel at Cap d'Antibes. It was his last public attempt to promote the film. On the way out of the screening, Leone met Dino De Laurentiis who said that *America* was terrific, but that it would surely benefit from 'having at least half an hour cut out of it': Leone snapped back that Dino was the last person to offer an opinion on the subject, since 'he made two-hour films which felt like four hours, whereas I make four-hour films which feel like two'.[153]

Despite Leone's various attempts to save his film through litigation, *Once Upon a Time in America* was indeed re-edited for the American market, by Zach Staenburg, under instructions from the Ladd Company. It emerged at 144 minutes: that is, over twenty minutes *less* than the contracted length and almost exactly the same running time as the cut version of *Once Upon a Time in the West*. This version jettisoned the flashbacks, began with Deborah's dance in 1923, removed some of the childhood escapades of the gang, as well as all of Deborah's 1968 scenes, had characters cropping up without explanation, dubbed in a few explanatory lines, and ended with a gunshot on the soundtrack as Senator Bailey unambiguously committed suicide. The telephone rang only once. It played like a disjointed attempt to put a yarmulke on Don Vito Corleone. When Leone first heard about a Burbank screening of this truncated version – which, an executive claimed, had played 'infinitely better' than the February preview – his reaction made the front page of the *Hollywood Reporter*. He was considering withdrawing his name from the picture: 'I didn't remake *The Godfather*. The stories and the anecdotes I tell aren't horses' heads bleeding on satin sheets! They are something much more complex and profound.' He conceded that he had been contracted to deliver a feature of 165 minutes. But that could not possibly justify the company's decision to mutilate the work 'to which I devoted all my mature years'.[154] The publicity department at Ladd expressed surprise at this eruption, saying, 'We have a very close and cordial relationship with Sergio.'

When the Ladd Company's version opened in America on 1 June, the critics tended on the whole to agree with Leone. Vincent Canby described it in the *New York Times* as 'an inscrutable trailer' which had been 'edited on a roulette wheel'. The headline in the *Wall Street Journal* was 'A Jewish Godfather: Oh no, Sergio'. For Sergio Leone, this was the unkindest cut of all. He had always been sensitive about comparison with *The Godfather*, and now his film had been 'barbarously massacred' to make it resemble Coppola's. He never saw the American release print, lamenting that, 'You know Fellini's *8½*? Well, if they'd taken out the flashbacks in that, all you'd have had left is Fellini wandering round the studios. It was never my intention to make a gangster film, but the American version looks like one now because they have left only the squalid episodes, one after the other.' He maintained that the luxurious pacing of a densely textured work deserved and demanded respect: 'When you cut a film that was designed to be long, the film always seems longer because it is more boring – mainly because it is more incomprehensible.'[155]

Catastrophe duly descended, as *America*, in its truncated version, made only $2.5 million in US rentals. The film was released in Europe in a 227-minute version, approved by Leone, and it reopened in this form at the New York Film Festival on 12 October 1984, followed by a 'showcase' presentation at the Gemini 2 Theater in Manhattan. *Once Upon*'s American re-release was, it was said, thanks to pressure from the critics, and Leone publicly thanked them.[156] But the film still made no money. It is often rumoured that Leone's 270-minute cut, reinstating the sequences removed in February 1983, has been shown on German or Italian television. It hasn't. The cans of film certainly exist, but they have not been dubbed. Leone hoped to get the actors together again, but it never happened.

Elizabeth McGovern's first view of *America* was at a Ladd Company screening in Los Angeles: 'My heart just sank. I was hardly in it. But by then I was relatively out of touch with what Sergio must have been going through. Then I took a trip to Paris to publicize another film I'd done, and went and paid to see the film in a theatre with my sister. I had the strong sense that it would never ever play in that version in America. It was clear why it hadn't. The pace of it was European.'[157] James Woods was much more outspoken: 'Three weeks before the film is released, they have the assistant editor of *Police Academy* chop it to fucking ribbons. I mean, do you think maybe I was suicidal? The film got fucking slaughtered by the critics, as well it should have. What chance did the studio think the picture was going to have in hell of pleasing the critics when they've already created the political scandal of interfering with a great artist's film? Such a stupid move. They were fucking dead in the water.'[158] He refused even to see 'the aborted version' of the film, saying only, 'I hope they burn the fucking negative'. Leo Benvenuti is less charitable to Leone: 'Any director could have shot that script to last two and a half hours. *America* is two and a half hours for the film, then another half hour for "Leone-ness"!'[159]

Andrea Leone, Sergio's son, looks back on his father's campaign of March–June 1984 more in sorrow than in anger: '*America* could have appealed to the mass audience and the intellectual one as well. It was a big success in the whole world except in America ... My father did not lose his love for America, but he did feel cheated by some institutions which dominate there.'[160] Andrea had reason to look back in sadness. When he was six months into the shooting of *Once Upon a Time in America*, in the cold winter of 1982, Sergio Leone complained that he was not feeling well. He was diagnosed as having a heart disease called 'dilating myocardiopathy', which meant that his heart muscle was not functioning properly. Whether this was because of a virus or for congenital reasons was not clear. Filming was shut down for a few days. By the time of the post-production battle, he had undergone a series of check-ups in Rome, and was aware of the seriousness of his condition. Leone was advised by his doctors to avoid stressful situations – at precisely the same time as he entered into litigation against his producer and against Hollywood. In April 1983, he made an extraordinary statement: 'It isn't coincidental that Visconti made *Death in Venice* at the end of his days; it's a reflection of a certain position we have in time vis à vis life and death. This film *Once Upon a Time in America* seemed very important to me at this precise moment in time.' When he said this, he had recently celebrated his fifty-fifth birthday.

# I2

## A Certain Cinema

In the City Museum of History in Leningrad there are a few torn pages of a
child's notebook, ABC pages in the Russian alphabet: A, B, V, G, D and so on.
On them there are scrawled under the appropriate letters simple entries in a
child's hand:

Z – Zhenya died 28 December, 12:30 in the morning, 1941.
B – Babushka died 25 January, 3 o'clock, 1942.
L – Leka died 17 March, 5 o'clock in the morning, 1942.
D – Dedya Vasya died 13 April, 2 o'clock at night, 1942.
D – Dedya Lesha, 10 May, 4 o'clock in the afternoon, 1942.
M – Mama, 13 May, 7: 30 a.m., 1942.
S – Savichevs died. All died. Only Tanya remains. I am left all alone.

The entries were made by Tanya Savicheva, an eleven-year-old schoolgirl. They
tell the story of her family during the Leningrad blockade.
   Harrison E. Salisbury, *The 900 Days* (1969)


We begin – Sergio Leone would say, taking a puff on his double corona,
looking like a tribal storyteller – with a big close-up of the hands of
Dmitri Shostakovich, playing his piano.[1] He is searching for the notes
of his Seventh Symphony, a symphony dedicated to a city: the *Leningrad Symphony*. Leone would open his hands and thump them on a
table. The music is slow and soft, to begin with. And as the composer
finds the notes, the piano is joined by an insistent side-drum, then by
three instruments, then ten, then twenty, then a hundred in a huge and
violent crescendo. From drum to violins to woodwind to brass to the
full power of the orchestra. A military theme, repeated over and over
again like Ravel's *Bolero*, becomes a massive requiem for the dead. The
close-up of the hands is filmed through an open window, and the entire
opening sequence will be built around this music: the first movement,
which Shostakovich called 'invasion'. It will be a single shot, like
you've never ever seen before.
   We pull back from the window and begin our journey through the

'gaping wound' of the city of Leningrad at dawn. Two civilians, carrying rifles, walk down the street and get on an early morning tram. The camera follows them on their journey through hell. Long queues waiting for the shops to open, brutal couplings under the stairs, piles of frozen corpses, abandoned funerals in public gardens, floggings of captured German soldiers, drunks crying, orators shouting on street corners, peasants wearing the infected rags of Breughel. The tram stops several times, and more civilians get on – all carrying guns. The camera hovers over this city, like an angel in flight, looking at the bottomless pit of Dante's inferno – so deep that the buried have no idea of the light any more. The texture of the music continues to thicken. The tram reaches a suburb, and stops at a square where other tramways crisscross. Next to them, some beaten-up lorries are waiting to pick up the armed men. The camera now follows these lorries on their bumpy ride. No cuts, no inserts, still the same single shot.

Now we arrive at the trenches that have been dug to protect the city, and the music, played by more and more instruments, becomes explosive, catastrophic. The Russian men settle into their trenches, and we move across the river towards the wide-open steppe beyond the city. The camera crosses the steppe, taking it all in, to discover a black legion of 1,000 German Panzers waiting for the order to fire. A *thousand*. As the first tank fires a shell, exploding with the death march of the music, we cut! For the first time! Then a curtain opens on a concert where Shostakovich is playing his Seventh Symphony, accompanied by 150 musicians, before an audience of 4,500. It is the first performance in Leningrad. MAIN TITLE. A hellish version of the *Iliad* is to be retold from within the walls of Troy.

Leone would pause for breath at this point, enjoying the effect he was having on his listeners, and add as a footnote: 'When the siege was over, at the victory celebration there was a performance of the same symphony in the very same concert hall in Leningrad. Everything had been left as it was. The ordered rows of seats. And the same people were invited as had attended the première. But this time there were only nine musicians and forty-six spectators. All the others had been killed.'[2]

Sergio Leone's party-piece, which he perfected in the 1980s, acquired new details in every telling. It was a description of the most expensive single shot in movie history. Sergei Eisenstein had once managed to persuade the inhabitants of Odessa to rush down those steps pursued by mounted Cossacks, but Leone would go even further. He would completely redecorate the streets of Leningrad, with façades authentic to the two and a half years of the siege (1941–44), and he would somehow persuade the locals to 'vacate the city'.[3] Sometimes, he would refer to two archive photographs he had seen. One showed Shostakovich in fireman's helmet and thick glasses, standing on the roof of the Leningrad Music Conservatory, on fire-fighting duty during the incessant Nazi bombardment. (He had enthusiastically volunteered for active service, but was rejected because of bad eyesight; he was, however, permitted to work in the Leningrad fire brigade.) The other showed the bespectacled composer sitting by himself among chairs arranged for a concert, listening hard to a piece of music being performed off-camera in 1942, during the period when he wrote the Seventh. The opening sequence would in some ways 'bridge' these two photographs. Leone would also refer to a piece of newsreel footage showing Shostakovich at his piano working on the symphony, in a Leningrad apartment with blackout blinds.

Carla Leone remembers her husband rehearsing the story, after supper, to various groups of friends, 'as usual starting from a single image. The Russians were very happy that the film was going to be made there . . . But they were afraid that there might be things in the film which the regime would not approve of. The bureaucracy moved along at a snail's pace. Every time Sergio brought up the subject he had to ingratiate himself with a new person, a new party functionary, a new politician.'[4]

Often as not, the punchline would be Leone's paraphrase of what some twitchy apparatchiks in the Brezhnev era had said to him, after listening to the big presentation: You want to make film about the 900 days of the siege? But the Khrushchev era has been over for a while. We have entered a great new phase in our society and politics, and the powers-that-be don't want to be reminded of the misdeeds of Comrade Stalin, who mined Leningrad and would have blown the city up as soon as the Nazis invaded in order to protect Moscow. No, is not right, *tovarich* Leone. So why not reduce the 900 days to the ten days that shook the world, by John Reed? Okay? Is agreed then. But, on second thoughts, it would perhaps be better to have no days at all, and to start with Reed's reporting of Mexican Revolution. Eisenstein did the same thing, so is fine. And we can do it again, no? Mexican Revolution is better for you. Russian Revolution we are not so sure about, so is better to leave on one side. Some old party members could be upset about it. You know how these apparatchiks are, don't you, *tovarich* Leone? Like little children, not like *us* at all.[5]

Leone had bought a book about the siege, at Fiumicino airport, when flying to New York in the hope of luring investment for *Once Upon a Time in America*. The book was *The 900 Days – The Siege of Leningrad* by Harrison E. Salisbury, a *New York Times* journalist who had been foreign correspondent in that city during the lifting of the siege. It was published in 1969, following serialization in *Reader's Digest*. When Leone returned home, Fulvio Morsella read Salisbury's book to him, in Italian, from cover to cover. Its effect was striking. Sergio Donati remembers hearing Leone expound the idea around this time: 'One day we were working on a moviola and there came to Rome Mikhail Kalatozov, the veteran Soviet director, with the cinematographer who shot *La tenda rossa/The Red Tent* [1969, an Italian–Soviet co-production directed by Kalatozov], about the North Pole expedition. And they wanted to meet Leone. Sergio said to me, "Who is this guy Kalatozov?" I replied, "Didn't you ever see the film *The Cranes Are Flying*, about ten years ago, which had an international reputation?" He said, "Okay, okay." And they arrived, and this Kalatozov was a very important man because he was President of the Soviet Association of Film-makers. Influential. And Sergio, who spoke good French, started talking about Chekhov, and then he said, "O, j'ai vu votre film," which wasn't true. "Ou êtes-vous trouvé tous ces paysages?" If you remember the movie, it was actually shot in two streets of Moscow! Kalatozov said, "But it's just Moscow. No landscapes." And Sergio just said, "Yes, well, you know." And then he started explaining his *Leningrad* to the Russians. He said, "One morning, a German sentinel hears the throbbing engines of tanks – ten tanks, twenty tanks, thirty tanks . . . two hundred tanks. This great division of tanks moves towards the river. And the German says, 'Crazy!' And then all two hundred tanks *cross the river*. Because in the night, someone has put just under the water a kind of pontoon bridge." And Kalatozov's cinematographer said, "It's true, it's true, Mr Leone, but there were only two tanks. I was there." Sergio just shrugged.'[6]

Leone first went public about the idea in a 1969 interview with a French cinéaste while promoting *Once Upon a Time in the West*: 'I really would like to change genre and I believe a director should be like a *chef d'orchestre*: capable of performing anything, Verdi as well as Mozart, Wagner as well as Stravinsky.'[7] He had been inspired by hearing the first movement of the *Leningrad Symphony*, and in particular the 'invasion' theme, which starts five minutes into the movement and builds for some nine relentless minutes. It was composed during September 1941, just three months after the Nazi invasion of the Soviet Union was launched, and had its Leningrad première on 9 August 1942, the same day the German High Command announced, 'We will enter Leningrad.'

Describing the invasion theme, which evokes the mechanical, armoured advance of the Nazi war machine, Shostakovich said, 'The simple, peaceful life of the people of Leningrad is shattered by war; not a naturalistic depiction of war – clanking guns, exploding shells, etc. – but I am trying to convey the idea of war emotionally.' The result is not subtle. Its repetitiveness and musical clichés were parodied by Bartók a year after its first performance, in the fourth movement of *Concerto for Orchestra* (1943), and one modernist critic of the time referred to its 'longitude and platitude'. Shostakovich himself later dropped the titles he gave to each of the movements, because they made the piece seem too literal and specific.[8] But the theme undeniably packed a considerable punch, and its historical significance was great. To complete the symphony, Shostakovich had to be airlifted further east to the wartime Soviet capital Kuibyshev: its performances, in Allied concert halls, turned the composer into a very special kind of war hero, especially a famous broadcast by Toscanini with the NBC Symphony Orchestra. As Leone remembered, 'On listening to Shostakovich's Seventh, a film immediately came into my head.'

Stimulated by Salisbury's book, the music and the two photographs, a story began to take shape in his mind: a love story, involving a cynical American newsreel cameraman and a young Soviet girl, against the epic background of the siege. The heroic self-sacrifice of 3 million people in defence of their city would 'open the American's eyes' (*à la For Whom the Bell Tolls*, in Leone's mind[9]). The cameraman would be commissioned to 'spend twenty days in Leningrad covering the battle', but would stay for the rest of the siege, even though 'he doesn't give a damn about the cause'. But love would change his mind.

'A lost love, lost in hell. A love story with a party member who is not permitted to live this passion. If she is discovered with a Westerner, she could be condemned to spend twelve years in prison. But she's prepared to take the risk. Their doomed affair is very, very intense. A child is born and, just as the city is about to be liberated, he is killed, camera in hand, as he records the final images of the siege. A worker's death. This may be even more pessimistic than my other films. And I will touch on things I've never attempted before . . . But I will not show how he dies.

We will learn about it with the girl he loves. She is watching some newsreels in the cinema. She recognizes the battle footage on the screen, and knows that he filmed it. She recognizes his way of showing combat, with a hand-held camera [Germans fleeing, the Russians pursuing, grenades coming from all sides and then an explosion just in front of the camera]. While she sits there, she sees the lens jump. And she realizes that he must be dead. [She has their little girl in her arms, a few months old.]'[10] On other occasions, Leone was more upbeat about the ending: 'This will be a film about life, not death. The heart is always the finest part of a hero, and my hero, believed dead, will live at the end. Is Cinema, or is it not, a grand illusion?''[11]

The story clearly awaited its cinematic interpreter. Stalin himself, Leone added, had vetoed any fictionalized film about the siege at the time; although one short film called *Solo*, directed by Konstantin Lapusansky, had told the story of a violinist who somehow keeps performing through the ghastly 900 days. A stirring compilation of newsreel footage had been issued to Soviet schools in 1959, with Shostakovich's Seventh on the soundtrack. And in 1972, a documentary film commemorated the thirtieth anniversary of the Leningrad première of Shostakovich's Seventh Symphony. But Leone believed that this piece of history was obscure in the public memory: 'Speaking with various intellectuals, Italian and French included, I realized that they were always confusing the battle of Leningrad with that of Stalingrad. So did the public. This made me want to read Harrison Salisbury's book in detail. I was struck by the Leningrad people's readiness to sacrifice their lives. In three years about forty per cent of the population of the city died – a total of 1,300,000 people. In a newsreel of the time, you can see the faces of the workers when the siege was announced. The camera pans across their faces and you just know that the Germans will never be able to enter this city. And Hitler was banking on a successful air attack. He even had tickets printed for a concert of Wagner's music that was to take place at the Leningrad Philharmonic ten days after the siege began. There were some cruel facts, too, episodes of cannibalism and scenes of women who were unable to move their dead because their corpses were frozen. I was particularly moved by a little girl, a kind of Anne Frank, who made entries in her diary about the deaths of her relatives – her grandmother, her sister, her mother . . . and at the very end ". . . and today, I have been left all alone". Only her diary was ever found [and it was on public display at the Museum of the History of

Leningrad on the Neva embankment]. In the midst of this apocalypse, an American and a Russian, the two world powers that today hold the destiny of the world in their hands. But with many smaller, intertwining stories. This will be no *Zhivago*, though.'[12]

Leone had been surprised to discover, in the early 1970s, that his 'Dollars' films had developed something of a cult following in the Soviet Union. *The Good, The Bad and The Ugly* had been screened, he said, in a huge stadium with an audience of thousands: 'the sequence in the cemetery, when everything rotates around Eli Wallach, was given a standing ovation, which was strange because there was not much love lost between the USSR and the Western'. Following the success of *The Magnificent Seven* there, Western movies had in fact been officially categorized 'crude American propaganda', to Leone's bafflement: '*The Magnificent Seven* can be read as a classic communist parable. There are the defenceless farmers, the feudal bandits who let the people die of hunger, and the Bolshevik Party of hired guns who fly to their salvation.'[13]

As Leone understood it, his films were at first shown only to a select few: party functionaries, members of the cinema trade unions, carriers of the correct cards, or people who knew which officials to bribe. But somehow the cult of Leone spread, and when he was visiting Moscow a representative of the Supreme Soviet of Film Production asked if he would be interested in 'preparing a film to be made in the USSR'. Leone immediately suggested *The 900 Days*. If the project got off the ground, it would be the first time the Soviet authorities had officially allowed a foreign, non-communist, director to film an important chapter of post-revolutionary history. The discussions which ensued became part of Leone's after-dinner repertoire. In 1980, he turned down the offer to direct *Reds* – another story of an American reporter working in Russia, this time during the October Revolution. He preferred 900 days to ten, Leningrad to Moscow, and a Soviet co-production to an American one.[14]

French critic Gilles Gressard would observe, 'Rarely has a film-maker spoken so much and so often about a film he has not yet made.'[15] Whenever Sergio Leone appeared as president of a jury or as a guest at a film festival from the mid-1980s onwards (Cannes, Venice, Annecy), he was asked about how *The Siege* was progressing. At Italian Film Week in Nice, as covered by *Screen International* on 22 December 1984, he announced that his next project would be filmed 'either in the Soviet Union or in China': the Chinese project was, apparently, a version of Malraux's *Human Condition* and its development would depend on enlisting the help of French minister of culture Jack Lang to persuade Chinese investors to co-produce; the Soviet project was *The 900 Days*, 'the most likely of the two to take off'. Mosfilm had given their blessing, but they were 'waiting to see the final script before signing the deal'. Leone, the report went on, 'has promised the Soviets to keep politics out of the story, and Salisbury himself will not collaborate on the script [which the director himself is writing, with an Italian screenwriter]. Leone says, "I have promised the Russians it will be an epic film that highlights the heroism and human qualities of the Soviet Resistance when the Nazis invaded their country."' Maybe Robert De Niro would play the American cameraman. Unlike *Once Upon a Time in America*, though, Leone had 'promised producer Nello Santi that I will not go over three hours this time'.[16]

In February 1987, he announced in Rome that 'the Russians have said they'll decide within the week. I expect a reply any day now.' The liberal director Elem Klimov, a supporter of the project, had in summer 1986 become head of the Union of Film-makers, and 'with perestroika at last the wind has started to blow in the right direction'. Moreover, the Italian minister for foreign affairs had kindly intervened on Leone's behalf. The following March, the film was announced in *Pravda*. Amid much speculation about the yes–no attitude of Russian officials, Leone held a press conference in Moscow on 7 February 1989, at which he revealed that after four years of negotiation, a co-production deal had at last been agreed with a consortium of three partners: Sovifilm, Sovexportfilm and Lenfilm studios, with 'his Sergio Leone corporation and RAI in Italy', and with 'the state cinema committee of the USSR standing as guarantors'. Leone was in town, with Carla, to collect a Soviet award. He enthused, 'This is a dream I've had for a long time . . . The actors are still to be found. Only one is for certain – the "young" Robert De Niro, unless he becomes old by the time the film is actually started.'[17] The joke went down well.

*Screen International* reported four days later that 'Robert De Niro has been consistently mentioned in interviews by Leone as the probable American star'. But when queried, De Niro said he had never been formally contacted by Leone about the project, and he certainly had not agreed to it. He vaguely remembered Sergio talking about *Leningrad* on the set of *Once Upon a Time in America*, but his own participation had not been brought up as far as he could remember.

They did agree, though, that they would enjoy working together again some day.

'There will be two or three other Americans,' Leone continued at the Moscow press conference. 'A team of Germans, because the German people will have to be played by real Germans. And, naturally, Russians. I will take a lot of screen tests and then decide. The protagonist, a woman, will be Russian but she has not been chosen yet . . . The music will be by Ennio Morricone, but the *Leningrad Symphony* will feature prominently as well.'

Someone from the floor asked for more details of the story: 'Think of *Gone with the Wind*. A love story, against the background of a war. This will be a huge cinematic fresco, at least three hours' screen time . . . There will not be an emphasis on the war, although I have to say that I asked for 400 tanks when in fact I will be requiring at least 2,000.'

He first fell in love with the idea, he said, after reading *The 900 Days* but then he had visited Moscow in 1987 and discovered the 'even more splendid' historical account by Danijl Granin and Alex Adamovic, *Blokadnaja kniga/The Book of the Siege*. (This book, he later informed *L'Europeo*, 'told of the siege day by day, and it was recommended by the Moscow correspondent of *L'Unità*'. He added that 'I can't mention Salisbury over there, because the Russians don't have very good memories of him'.)[18] 'At present, the idea is entirely in my own head, but I will be using an international team of screenwriters to turn it into a script: Arnold Yanovich Vitol, who wrote a local television film about the siege; plus I will try to convince the American writer Alvin Sargent, who won an Oscar for Fred Zinnemann's film *Julia*; and two old Italian friends I've worked with in the past, Leonardo Benvenuti and Piero De Bernardi.' Leone had referred to Vitol, in the French film journal *Studio* the previous year, as the 'official' Soviet writer on the team: 'He is a man who lived in Leningrad and who has 150 medals pinned to his chest – which at least creates the impression that he has the confidence of the Party.'[19]

The researching and writing of the script, he estimated, would take a year (five months of it in Leningrad), the filming another year, and the post-production six months: so it would be a two-and-a-half-year project, at least. Leone concluded the conference by saying that the film would have to be a co-production 'because I'm not sure the Soviets are able to raise the full amount', that he hoped his technicians and their Soviet counterparts could work happily together (he could only make films 'one way', and this time he would be his own producer), and that most of the filming would take place in Leningrad itself: 'but I hope I don't have to destroy the city a second time'. A representative of Sovifilm then wrapped up by saying this would be the most ambitious multinational project ever made in any studio, anywhere, and that 'we hope we can count on the support of the Soviet army'.

Just before he left for Moscow, Leone had talked to the French film magazine *Première*, in one of his last published interviews as it turned out. He had recently presided at the Venice and Annecy film festivals, and the interview was happening just after he had finished a picnic while trying to perch on the bonnet of a car. Not exactly a gourmet experience. He was in a truculent mood, and his replies were unusually brisk: 'The Russians have said yes. From the strictly administrative point of view, everything seems to be going fine. But this response means nothing without a signature on a piece of paper. The contracts are ready, the lawyers are studying the small print . . . Now is the time to test their will to let me direct the film I want to make, and on which I will not compromise this time. And to find out if they'll put at my disposal everything I need . . . The project is so immense that I don't just need a production house, I need a state!'[20]

The image of the Soviets on one side, the Americans on the other and Sergio in the middle might have impressed even the Man with No Name. Leone had negotiated with the Russians on his own behalf, and spent a considerable amount of his own money in the process, to secure half of the investment he needed. The industry gossip about his meanness with money and reluctance to invest in his own projects had no grounds at all in the late 1980s, as Andrea Leone confirms: 'This was quite a difficult project, insofar as it was to be a co-production between Italy and Russia [an RAI/Soviet consortium]. Also difficult because he had only written three or four pages and he had the whole thing in his head . . . He made his contract with a country where until now there were only film service facilities for foreign companies, never co-productions with foreign films. From this point of view, he signed an important page in the history of cinema when he went to Moscow.'[21]

Without a definite title, a star, or a script, Leone had still managed to raise over $15 million of investment and services in Russia on his track-record and the sheer force of his personality. More than four years before, he had stated publicly that the Russian co-producers were 'waiting to see the final script before signing the deal'. They still hadn't seen a script, and yet they had signed the deal. Where casting was concerned, he had made some vague comments about Robert De Niro or maybe a young Robert De Niro. And, in response to a rumour that Meryl Streep plus Russian accent might play the lead, he had said: 'Meryl Streep? Not on your life. She is not the kind of actress who is made for me. No, I intend to audition a lot of Soviet actresses. It is even possible that I'll use an unknown.'[22] So casting was still on the drawing board. Leone's rough estimate of the total cost of the picture was around $30 million, assuming that it would be filmed almost entirely in the Soviet Union, with the co-operation of the Soviet army and an endless supply of tanks. (Some press reports inflated this figure to $100 million, which would have made it the most expensive film of all time. *Variety*'s estimate was 'in the $70 million range'.) According to Luca Morsella, Leone did not even have the three- or four-page treatment Andrea speaks of. 'A very short page was copyrighted in order to protect the title [*Leningrad*] and the idea, but since Sergio was well aware he couldn't protect either, the page apparently was written by some lawyer's secretary just in case.'[23] Sergio Donati recalls that after Sergio's death, 'some producers came to Benvenuti and De Bernardi and asked, "Where is the script, the treatment?" And there was nothing. Only the opening scene, as told by Sergio himself.'[24]

Of his colleagues, Alberto Grimaldi (who might have helped produce the film) says, 'There was no script, just the Salisbury book and a Russian account.' Tonino Delli Colli (who would have photographed it) recalls, 'Sergio just loved telling "beginnings". He would embroider the story around them. For the *Leningrad* opening sequence, which was all he had, I said , "Careful, camera magazines only hold 300 metres of film: with everything you've told me, the reel will be finished mid-shot."' Leo Benvenuti has in his archive a long letter he wrote, with De Bernardi and Enrico Medioli, beginning, 'Dear Union of Soviet Socialist Republics', and outlining the project to an un-named official. After stating, 'We have no concrete proposals yet,' the letter describes the opening sequence and the ending, praises Leone as 'a magic link between two cultures' and between art and the people, and concludes that 'We do not want to make a political film . . . a love story will avoid excessive historicism and propaganda.' The presence of an American newsreel cameraman in Leningrad is laboriously justified: 'Maybe the accredited American journalist (a marginal figure, we assure you) has invited him over from London, where he has settled after the French Front, or maybe he has fled by the last helicopter from Finland, after the battle with the Germans.' Benvenuti's defensiveness about Harrison Salisbury (the 'accredited journalist') arose because Leone had discovered just how controversial a figure he was in the USSR. *The 900 Days* had never been published there, a *Pravda* review had judged that Salisbury demeaned the role of the Communist Party in the city's defence and over-emphasized 'the heroism of the people', and his chapter about Stalin's hostility to Leningrad as 'the crucible of the revolution of 1917 which might turn against him' had been received particularly badly by official-dom. According to Benvenuti, the changing fortunes of the project mirrored global politics: 'Meeting of Gorbachev–Reagan in Switzerland, excellent results – the project advances; summit meeting in Iceland, bad atmosphere – the project retreats. After that, we received a telegram saying there was a solution to "the problem of the love story between an American journalist and a young Russian woman". The solution was to change round the gender of the protagonists, so the journalist is kissed by a young Russian man. That, apparently, will be okay.'[25]

Would Leone ever have made the film? Did he even believe it could be made, or was he playing out an elaborate game? Was the whole project absurdly overambitious? Or was it in direct line of ascent from his previous work: from a stick of dynamite to an exploding bridge to 1,000 Panzers. Sergio Donati is not sure, but says it is as well to remember that 'also for *Once Upon a Time in America*, for ten years he had only the opening scene. We thought he would never make that film either. But in the end he did.'[26]

When asked in 1986 whether he regretted the years spent in inertia, waiting for the Soviets to agree, Leone had replied somewhat testily: 'I don't underestimate the difficulties of the project, but I'm drawn towards difficult challenges. It is not worth the bother of dealing with a "routine" film in the meantime . . . Kurosawa and I – and a few other surviving directors, so long as such a race of people exists – we are not the type to have withdrawal symptoms. You can't shoot film as if you were putting salami into its skin. From a project like *Ran* or *Once Upon a Time in America*, you come away dry in the mouth, with your head in flames and your soul in shreds. I do not work much at the moment through philosophical choice, because I do not want to die with my eyes glued to the viewfinder. When I do shoot film, I do it because I chose to a long time ago – not because I was condemned to do it by a tribunal.'[27]

After the blissed-out smile of Robert De Niro, he told another interviewer, 'What can possibly follow that dream of America lost? . . . Death. And this new film will certainly be about death.'

At least, in these waiting years, Sergio Leone remained *highly* visible within the film community in Italy. The annual Festival Unità, organized by the communist newspaper, was in 1984 centred on *Once Upon a Time in America*. Leone delivered the opening address: 'I don't want to be remembered as a philosopher, unlike so many of my celluloid brothers. I want to be remembered as an entertainer, or you may as well forget me completely. My interest in America, indeed the universal interest in America, is because of the tale. America, to my eyes, appears like a long and cruel Arabian Night, which is why my cinema is populated with thieves of Baghdad, kidnapped princesses, nasty magicians, birds which sing rock 'n' roll . . . I must try to tell the story of Scheherezade, and capture the attention of the public – or the death sentence will be carried out at dawn.'[28]

The following year, Leone wrote an article for *L'Unità* commemorating the ninetieth birthday of cinema, in which he speculated about the future of cinema-going in the age of video and deregulated television channels. 'Cinema', he said at the time, 'is invading our homes more and more. Some television screens are now almost big enough to create the impression of watching a feature film in a cinema. I have seen some measuring four metres by two metres in certain homes, taking up all of one wall. I have been told that in Japan they even build houses and villas with built-in projection systems. Obviously, cinema is going to end up in the home. But, like all great popular forms of entertainment, it *cannot* be a purely home-based pastime. Clearly, the exact opposite of what is happening now will begin to occur. The great, old cinemas in the big cities of France have become seven small cinemas. This is the problem: to try to pay expenses and avoid half-empty houses. In the future, though, I see gigantic stadiums. Each city will only have three cinemas but they will be huge stadiums. They will seat ten or twenty thousand people, the screens will measure fifty metres and certain kinds of film will be appropriate to be shown on them . . . Obviously the sensation you get from a huge screen with stereophonic sound, 20,000 people surrounding you, 25,000 people buzzing with conversation, living and breathing with the show they are watching – that can never be replaced by a television screen, however big it may be.'[29]

Leone had seen *Once Upon a Time in the West* projected on to a thirty-metre screen, with 5,000 spectators, at the Maxence Basilica in Rome: 'I was moved, very moved, and I was the person who made the film; imagine what the others must have been feeling.' Did these opposing tendencies – home entertainment versus public spectacle – amount to a 'crisis' in the Italian film industry? Leone preferred to see the collision as part of a 'period of transition'. The industry statistics for the 1980s were certainly alarming. By 1989, of the 117 films produced in Italy that year, only eighty-nine were given theatrical distribution: of these, just under half were screened in fewer than five cities. Seventy per cent of Italians never went to the cinema at all: a figure roughly in line with neighbouring countries, but still the most dramatic fall in attendances (60 per cent since 1980) in the whole of Europe. In the 1960s and the heyday of the Cinecittà assembly-line, Italians went to the cinema more often – per week, per adult – than any other audiences in the world. And, more often than not, they went to see co-productions with a strong Italian presence, or Italian films. But by the late 1980s, American films accounted for somewhere between 70 and 80 per cent of box-office takings in Italy; and in the post-*Star Wars* era, these films, to Leone's eye, increasingly resembled 'videotapes of Michael Jackson rather than Gershwin symphonies'.[30]

Some 80 per cent of Italian feature films were now backed by RAI and Finivest, the two biggest television channels. Meanwhile, Italy had spawned by far the highest number of local TV stations in Europe, and the country purchased the most imported programmes. Leone himself had, perhaps as a result, developed a new habit: 'I have become a night-time televiewer. I channel-hop to find the old films in black and white. The films of the 1930 and 1940s. The television image has colonized the cinematic image. We have been visually brain-washed. Oscars are now awarded to television films such as *Terms of Endearment*.'[31] This, at a time when Giuseppe Tornatore's *Cinema Paradiso* (1988), a deeply nostalgic flashback film about the experience of cinema-going in the 1950s, won an Oscar and a prize at Cannes; while Maurizio Nichetti's *The Icicle Thief* (*Ladri di saponette*, 1989), a satire on the cut-throat world of the Italian media industries, won the Grand Prix at Moscow Film Festival. But *Cinema Paradiso* was not a success in Italy until it attracted international legitimacy by distribution in America; while *The Icicle Thief* did no business at all on the domestic market.

One worry, for Leone, was that a lot of the up-and-coming film-makers were 'joining the profession to become famous, for the status of the director', rather than 'for the love of cinema'. They didn't seem to have cinema in their guts. Internationally, directors such as John Boorman, Peter Weir and Martin Scorsese had cinema in their guts, but the young Italians were careerists in comparison. Federico Fellini, always alert to developments in the industry he loved, made *Intervista* in 1987 – a tour of the landmarks of his career in the form of a Japanese television crew videotaping him at work on his latest project, a bizarre version of Kafka's *Amerika*, while the rest of Cinecittà is being used for tacky television commercials. At one point, the Cinecittà archivist shows the television crew 'the pool of *Ben-Hur*, *Quo Vadis*? and the naval battle in *Cleopatra*', which has now become a small decorative pond in front of an apartment block: the value of the real estate has become higher than its value as a studio backlot. The film climaxes with Fellini's crew, trapped in a polythene tent on the open-air set of an American main street during a thunderstorm, being attacked by Red Indians waving television aerials. 'We'll never surrender. Stop!' they shout.

Maybe the business would indeed polarize into home entertainment and gigantic screens watched by 20,000 people. But if so, apart from Leone, Bernardo Bertolucci (in his multinational phase) and maybe Dario Argento (if he went mainstream), which Italian film-makers would be capable of making 'the kinds of film appropriate to be shown on them'? Films that would attract and excite a mass cine-literate audience? And where would the investment come from, if not from the dreaded US majors? Leone's article finished on the comforting thought that problems such as these would just have to be resolved 'through agreement between the film and television industries'. Maybe . . .

Sergio Leone wrote several other newspaper pieces at this time: a homage to John Ford in *Corriere della Sera*, and a defence of Charlie Chaplin (particularly of *Modern Times* and *Monsieur Verdoux*) in *L'Unità*. For the *Gazzette dello Sport* of 10 May 1987, he created in inimitable style a 'hypothetical movie' of the build-up to the football League Cup in Naples: 'The promotion of this movie is already happening. I know that Naples is full of flags and blue umbrellas, wigs and effigies of Maradona, big scarves, fetishes and countless other useless ornaments – all of them blue . . . The movie will not follow a pre-ordained script, but will consist of small episodes, one by one, and will not be interrupted by any big dramatic set-pieces. The pleasure of the director will be that the point of view of his hundred cameras will not be planned or fixed, but will amount to the very free and natural story of a mass movement and a shared affection. I don't see well-known characters as actors, because the neo-realist method should predominate, and as in *The Bicycle Thieves* this collective fiesta should have the people as its actors in a story which has already been constructed . . . I also imagine Naples as the main character, Naples forced into an off-limits zone as happened after the war, a solid traffic jam without sound which is animated by the movement of the flags, like an immense blue sheet covering the whole city with the team's colours, a city under siege by its own passion, full of motionless people watching the skies and waiting for a "messianic" revelation: summoned up by all these arcane prayers, the figure of destiny will appear, dressed in the robes of San Gennaro with the hair of Maradona, appearing between fireworks over the Bay of Naples.'[32]

Shortly before writing this article, in spring 1987, Leone spoke at the International Festival of Youth Cinema at Giffoni Valle Piane where he was guest of honour, and where the jury consisted entirely of children under fourteen. He told them that he felt especially drawn to the imaginative world and openness of children. He also contributed to the journal *Bianco e Nero* an impassioned defence of Ermanno Olmi's *The Legend of the Holy Drinker* (1988) which, as President of the Jury at Venice, he had worked hard to persuade his fellow jurors to support for that year's Golden Lion.[33]

Meanwhile, where his public face was concerned, his reputation for having a considerably larger-than-life style continued. He sailed to the Cannes Film Festival every year in his private yacht ('my little boat') which he had purchased in the mid-1980s. He continued to maintain his house in Paris. He entertained lavishly at his Roman villa in the Via Birmania, with plentiful supplies of expensive wine (Brunello di Montalcino being a favourite) and the best of heavy Roman and Neapolitan cuisine. When greeting visiting journalists he liked to wear a voluminous white kaftan and velvet slippers, and enjoyed talking at them about cinema as if he was some bearded Old Testament patriarch. He did not mind the fact that he could now be compared with Orson Welles in terms of his girth as well as his taste for expensive Havana cigars. In 1988, Leone wrote a short article on the aesthetics of double coronas in which he confessed that 'physically and sensually, they suit me perfectly'. The man who insisted that Clint Eastwood continue to smoke a very thin, very dark and very strong toscano (as a symbol of control and invincibility) in sequels to *Fistful of Dollars* was himself billed in *The Illustrated History of Cigars* (1989) as 'one of the few great Italian cigar connoisseurs'.[34]

In 1988, the Leone family moved from Via Birmania to a large villa in Via Nepal about half a mile away. The villa had been built for Alberto Grimaldi, who lived there for a couple of years before basing himself in America; Sergio Leone purchased it from an Arab emir. It was designed by Carlo Simi, his longstanding production designer, who had also designed Grimaldi's PEA offices near by. On the imposing high-security gate of the villa was the brass head of a lion, and outside the front door a pair of seated stone lions: a pride of Leones. Indoors, his elaborate seventeenth- and eighteenth-century Roman furniture and fine silverware in cabinets shared space with huge sofas, metaphysical and surrealist paintings, and a gallery of family photos of Carla and the three children. Over the desk in his study (or 'batcave' as he sometimes called it) were a still from *Raging Bull* (signed 'To Sergio from Bobby – you're the best'), and a picture of the elderly John Ford dressed in clothes too big for him (signed 'To Sergio Leoni. With admiration'). There were small dogs everywhere.

By 1988, Leone was becoming lethargic, and his stamina – as legendary in the business as his workaholism – was visibly diminishing. It could not escape attention that when Leone presided at the Venice Film Festival that summer, his physical condition had deteriorated. His beard was grey, his cheeks sunken, and he seemed to have shrunk. He was always photographed sitting down. Since his heart problems of 1984, he had attempted to diet. But by now he couldn't walk up the stairs without feeling seriously out of breath. In an RAI television documentary made in 1985, *C'era una volta il cinema. Sergio Leone e i suoi film*, he had walked up a few of the steps of the public staircase on the Via Glorioso, while describing his childhood; but the effort had evidently been considerable, and he had had to recover his balance by resting against the railings. There was talk of a heart transplant, but Leone did everything he could to avoid even thinking about it. Morricone remembers: '*Leningrad* was the first of our projects about which he didn't want to talk with me. He knew he was going to die. He'd been advised to have a transplant, his sole chance maybe, but he'd refused.'[35]

His interviews, which had been possessed of an autumnal quality ever since the completion of *Once Upon a Time in America*, now seemed to contemplate a leave-taking. His valedictions to cinema were becoming more abstract, meandering and melancholic than ever: 'The old golden vein, in California's movieland, where these riches once glistened so close to the surface, unfortunately seems almost completely dried up now. A few courageous miners insist on digging still, whimpering and cursing television, fate, and the era of spectaculars which has impoverished the world's studios. But they are dinosaurs, delivered to extinction.'

Clint Eastwood, one such miner, visited him in autumn 1988. Eastwood was in Rome for the opening of *Bird*, and Leone invited him to lunch. The two men met again that same evening for dinner and Leone arrived with his friend, the film director Lina Wertmüller. According to Eastwood, Sergio was in a mellow and nostalgic mood. Although he knew he was very ill, he did not once mention it. The acerbic quality of Leone's comments about 'his actor' seemed a thing of the past: 'we got along better than in all the times we had worked together'. Eastwood is convinced that Leone 'had called up to say goodbye'.[36]

Their careers had gone in very different directions. As Clint Eastwood recalled: 'It's not that we drifted apart, but I think we just became philosophically different . . . He got into larger, epic pictures and I got into smaller, more personal pictures.'[37] In press interviews, they had engaged in a twenty-year running battle (Eastwood gently, Leone fiercely) about who was responsible for what in the 'Dollars' films. At a press conference in Cannes to discuss *Pale Rider* three years before, a genial exchange had taken place wherein an intense French critic put it to the fifty-five-year-old Eastwood that his films constituted an 'Oedipal destruction' of his 'cinematic father', fifty-six-year-old Papa Leone. Eastwood fielded that one with ease: 'If he is my father, Sergio must have conceived me at a very early age.'[38]

Whatever waters had passed under the bridge, after saying farewell to Clint Eastwood in Rome, Sergio Leone turned to Luca Morsella and joked, 'We'll have to create a part for him, too.' The part would have been in a television mini-series he was then developing, entitled *Colt, an American Legend*. Its plan was to tell the story of a single weapon, from its manufacture at the factory in Hartford, Connecticut, to its various uses and abuses in the Wild West. As Morsella put it, 'The revolver, passing from hand to hand, would have told the history of the West . . . Sergio's idea, after meeting Clint Eastwood, was to have a magnificent stranger [Eastwood] travelling by train from Arizona to Hartford,

Connecticut, to watch a gun being made for him, and customized in exactly the way he wanted. Eastwood would stand over the gun-maker until he got it right. Then, back to Arizona, where he meets a badman – scruffy, from the bottom of the social ladder. There is a duel, with the usual close-ups. And this badman shoots Clint Eastwood right in the middle of his forehead, or maybe in the back. The badman picks up the revolver, and the adventure begins. This was Sergio's idea for the beginning of *Colt*.'[39]

The idea for the mini-series went back to the previous year, when Sergio Leone contacted Sergio Donati for the first time since their blazing row over Carlo Verdone's first film. As Donati recounts, with a hint of déjà vu: 'In 1987, Fulvio Morsella called me and said, "Oh, come on Sergio, there was a misunderstanding."' Donati called upon Leone and found him, after his recent heart troubles, 'much more human, more calm'. Leone explained that he had an offer to produce a Western mini-series, and was toying with the idea of basing it on a saloon in Santa Fe, New Mexico, telling the stories of the kinds of folk who drifted into the old place. Donati thought this was a touch hackneyed; and besides, he had something better. 'I had written a small story called *Gun*, which is the oldest story of the movies, with *La ronde*, *Carnet de bal* and so on; the same gun which passes from hand to hand. "But," I said, "*but*, it's a chance to have different stories – dramatic, ironic, historical, every kind of story." And we started to talk *à la* Leone, that is to say in his house while eating rigatoni.'[40]

Donati had already explored his fascination with the effects of handguns upon their users in his script for *The Toy/Il giocattolo* (1979). Leone's enthusiasm for the topic was written all over the screen. As they set to serious discussion, the two Sergios were sometimes joined by visitors, as Donati recalls: 'There was Mickey Rourke, who was shooting *San Francesco* with Liliana Cavani. Next Sunday came Richard Gere, who was shooting some biblical thing [*King David*]. And they liked the idea of *Colt*, but to do cameo parts in it. And so Sergio started to say, "But why don't you do a story about two sonofabitches?" Every Leone Western started this way, no? "Two sonofabitches who . . ." I said, "Sergio, it is twenty years after. We do a Western, we have to do something different." We discussed something quite similar to the Clint Eastwood movie [*Unforgiven*]. I said, "Why don't we tell the Western story like it really was? With guns which couldn't hit a cow at ten metres; with a Pinkerton man who was shooting people through the doors while they were sleeping." That was the real West – no? . . . Then the thing took biblical time, Leone time.'[41]

Meanwhile, Luca Morsella was contacted by Leone early in 1988 to discuss a proposed feature Western, to be constructed around the director's esteemed visitors: 'In 1987, Sergio had been contacted by Mickey Rourke and some weeks later by Richard Gere. Both actors, independently of one another, wanted to make a Western with Leone. Sergio had conceived a television series, and thought it could have been possible to produce a feature as the pilot of this series . . . He would not have directed it, but as producer and artistic supervisor he could have guaranteed the quality of the film. He offered me the post of director, as long as we came up with a good story. As you can imagine, I could not believe it, and I started reading and researching ideas for the script. But the more we talked about it, the more we came to the conclusion that the structure of *Colt* was not suitable for two actors such as Rourke and Gere. We decided we needed something different and closer to the classic Leone Western. After six months of research we started writing with the aid of a young writer, Fabio Toncelli, and we came up after a few months with *A Place Only Mary Knows* . . . It was the last thing Sergio wrote for cinema.'[42]

So while Donati thought about a revisionist Western, Morsella and Leone went ahead with planning a more Leone-style production. This time the director would be the son of Fulvio Morsella, the man who had produced Leone's Rafran films from the late 1960s to the mid-1970s, and who had spent a lot of time reading to him. Some critics claimed that Leone liked picking eager young directors so that he could stage-manage them without taking responsibility for the finished product. Others preferred to say that Leone had a flair for finding young film-makers (and actors) and for giving them their first chance in the industry. Whatever his motives, he felt ready to announce the project in *Il Messaggero*, early August 1988: 'The Western is back in fashion. Official. Official that is, according to Sergio Leone, the director who in the sixties created an unparalleled genre which is still widely imitated, especially in America: the "Spaghetti Western". The Italian maestro intends to produce a new "pistolero", to be directed by a young first-timer (don't forget that the director of *Giù la testa* gave Carlo Verdone his début). With two outstanding actors, two superstars: Mickey Rourke and Richard Gere, both delighted to be working with the father of the Spaghetti Western.'[43]

*A Place Only Mary Knows*, according to the treatment, is 'a homage to the inspired work of several American authors': Edgar Lee Masters (*Spoon River Anthology*), Ambrose Bierce (*An Occurrence at Owl Creek Bridge*), Mark Twain (*A Military Campaign that Failed*), Stephen Crane (*The Red Badge of Courage*) and 'naturally, Margaret Mitchell: *Gone with the Wind*'. It tells the story of 'two sonofabitches' whose paths keep criss-crossing during the American Civil War. One is Mike Kutcher from Georgia, whose job it is to enrol men into the Union army. The other is Richard Burns, a shady businessman 'who flaunts his elegance, is jauntily self-possessed, and who likes to give the impression of being tough'. A third leading character, Francesco, a young cook from Rome, arrives at the port of Boston on an immigrant ship during the opening sequence. Their adventures take them from Boston in 1863, to a mining camp in Colorado, to Atlanta, Georgia (just as General Sherman arrives there in 1864), where the gold is buried inside an unmarked grave, dug in a place 'only Mary knows'.[44]

Mary, it is explained, was at one time Mike's girlfriend, and the gold is the proceeds of a robbery. Richard is conned into enlisting, becomes an agent for 'Major Allen' (alias Alan Pinkerton), is captured with Mike and taken to a Confederate prison camp, joins a Gold Rush through Indian territory, meets a war photographer called Matthew Douglas and a wagon train of strolling players, finds himself sleeping rough with Mike in the no man's land that divides two armies, and eventually reaches Atlanta – where Mike is about to be hanged as a spy. In a sequence that owes much to Ambrose Bierce's famous short story, Mike seems to escape and run towards his beloved Mary when in fact he is seeing his whole life flash before him at the moment of death. Richard buries him in the unmarked grave they have been looking for throughout the film (Mary has of course taken the money and run), and bumps into Francesco on the day Atlanta falls. Francesco simply looks at Richard and asks him if he wants something to eat. 'Here is the Victory Menu: on the card there is written the date of the conquest of Atlanta and the name of only one dish, Potato Stew Sherman. On the back is written the next day's date and nothing else. "What about tomorrow?" asks Richard. "Tomorrow . . ." answers Francesco, shrugging, "I'll think about it tomorrow . . . After all, tomorrow is another day." Our view rises to include Atlanta finally conquered and destroyed. And that sparse group of men, clinging to a wisp of smoke.[45]

At last Leone was having a go, albeit none too piously, at *Gone with the Wind. Mary*'s characteristic cynicism is tempered by an exploration of loyalty and motivation, and packs in much more history than the 1960s Westerns ever managed. The characters of Mike and Richard were clearly intended for Rourke and Gere, while Francesco would have provided an Italian name above the title. While Luca Morsella worked on this project, Sergio Leone was delighted to see his daughter Raffaella's name beginning to appear as 'assistant costume designer' on the credits of some Italian–American co-productions. She had helped with the costumes on *Once Upon a Time in America*, and subsequently worked on *Aurora* (1984), a Sophia Loren/Alex Ponti television movie, *Detective School Drop-Outs* (1985), a *Police Academy* spinoff, and Carlo Verdone's *Troppo Forte* (1986). It was a start.

Then, in late January/early February 1989, against everyone's advice, Sergio Leone travelled with Luca Morsella to Zimbabwe, to shoot a commercial for the Renault 19: the one with the rope bridge and the elephants. According to Morsella, 'he was behaving as though he was in perfect condition – oblivious to stress and fatigue, and even of danger'. Twenty-five years of experience had not diminished Leone's fear of air travel. But 'during that month in Zimbabwe he was travelling back and forth on either choppers or small aircraft much more than he needed to ... He no longer seemed to care about his personal safety. One day we were about to hit some wires with the chopper because he wanted to go down. "Down, down, down," he kept on saying.'[46]

Morsella also remembers that Leone's concern for the safety of others took an alarming slump. On one occasion he signalled from the ground for the helicopter pilot to land, even though the blades of the chopper would pass perilously close to the raised camera crane, on which the operator sat, exposed. Neither the operator nor the grips could see the approaching blades for dust, though Morsella and his wife Alexi, watching from a distance, spotted the potential danger and were able to intervene in time. This was, Morsella noted, a very rare lapse on Leone's part: 'everyone who knew him was amazed'. But Leone was approaching even this commercial work with his customary diligence: 'He would wake up at three o'clock in the morning in order to be on the set at three-thirty, to be ready to shoot at four when it was still dark ... He wanted the very first light. He was really being almost hyperactive.'[47]

When Leone departed for his Moscow press conference on 7 February 1989, Morsella took over the direction of the commercial. Upon his return, Leone immediately started editing his and Morsella's footage in Rome. 'It was one of the last times I saw him,' says Luca Morsella. 'I was worried that the stuff I'd sent over was not that good, but he said, "No, no, you did a great job." In front of everybody in the mixing studio, which was nice . . . Sergio was about to go to America. The last period he looked obviously older, shall we say? But he was quite well spirited. Once he accepted the fact that he was sick, and that he had to do something serious in order to save himself, and that maybe nothing would save him, he decided to live less worried. He was about to have a check-up with a heart specialist in LA who would have made a transplant . . . But I think he decided it wasn't worth it. He wanted to live well to the very last minute.'[48]

Following the reunion dinner of his elementary school 'class of 1937' at the restaurant Checco er Carettiere in Trastevere, Leone had had the idea of adding a prologue to *Viale Glorioso*, a script which still lay in his desk drawer. A middle-aged film director arrives early at just such a reunion, examines the fading photographs on the wall of class 5A and the empty chairs around the dinner-table, and flashes back to his childhood in Rome during the late 1930s. In the original photograph there were forty-nine well-scrubbed children: in the press picture of the reunion, there are fourteen middle-aged men, standing behind a table covered in empty bottles and glasses with their backs to a mural of fruit trees, the restaurateur to the right. The grey-bearded Sergio seems the oldest: much older than his sixty years. And he is standing in the shadows, behind the rest of the group, Morricone on his right. He does not look well; and he does not look as though he has been on a diet.

The man whose first experience of cinema was on the streets of postwar Rome with Vittorio De Sica had never once pointed his camera in the direction of Rome in the here and now. When asked why he had dwelled upon America, specifically the West, and had never made a film in Italy about Italy, he replied: 'The Western is a consumer item in Japan, Nigeria, Colombia, England, Italy, Germany and France – all over the place. It belongs to the world now . . . When you write a story about Italy, unfortunately you can write only about Italy. In America, though, even in the smallest town, you can write about the world. Why? Because it is a conglomeration of all these communities. You can find the world in America. I mean the world, with all its customs, defects and strengths. As a European, the more I get to know of America, the more it fascinates me *and* the more distant I feel – light years away.'[49]

Leone was drawn, throughout his film-making career, to artificial, faraway worlds where realistic surface details were carefully researched, so as to chime with the audience's suspension of disbelief. But the stories belonged to the realm of myth, where the characters were not *bourgeois* Romans but giants and where theatre mattered more than the mundane. These were his fairy-tales for grown-ups. In this sense, it took him much of his life to see like a child, and to make the uninhibited Hollywood movies he, as an Italian, wanted to see. The words that critics were beginning to use to describe his work included 'mannerist', 'carnivalesque', 'exhibitionist', 'excessive' (meaning bad) and 'excessive' (meaning good). What he was trying to do was to re-enchant the cinema, while expressing his own disenchantment with the contemporary world and conveying the exhilaration he personally felt when watching and making movies. He was the first modern cineaste to make really popular films, a bridge between 'art films' and popular cinema, and a source of deep confusion to the critics. Fulvio Morsella, who favoured the word 'spectacularist', reckons that 'fifty years earlier, Sergio would have been a great master of lyrical operas. Because he had that sense of the sound, the visual, the spectacular, the overall effect.'[50]

Early in the morning of Sunday, 30 April 1989, Sergio and Carla Leone were watching television together in bed, at their villa on the Via Nepal. They were watching *I Want to Live!*, Robert Wise's harrowing film of 1958, which shows the execution in a California gas chamber of Barbara Graham (Susan Hayward), for a crime she probably did not commit. Suddenly Sergio leaned his head against Carla's shoulder and said, 'I'm sorry, I don't feel very well.' Within a few seconds, he was gone. Carla called an ambulance shortly after 1.30 a.m., but it was already too late. Although all the obituaries were to give the cause of death as a heart attack, he in fact died because his heart simply stopped beating. He was resting at home, before a planned flight to Los Angeles on 2 May in the company of Andrea Leone and Attilo D'Onofrio, a specialist in co-production deals. The plan was to discuss American investment in *Leningrad* with the Movie Group; and to keep that appointment with the heart specialist. Maybe Sergio had inherited his weak heart from his father Vincenzo, who was excused active service in the Italian army in 1915 because of a heart condition. But Vincenzo lived to the age of eighty, having retired from the industry ten years previously. Several reports gave Sergio's age as sixty-seven. He was only sixty. Most referred to him as the 'Spaghetti Western inventor', an epitaph he would certainly have disliked. One obituary erroneously said Francesca Bertini was his mother; another that Andrea was his daughter rather than his son.[51]

Before the funeral service on Wednesday, 3 May, at 11.30 a.m. in the basilica of San Paolo Fuori Le Mura, Sergio Leone's body was laid out in his wood-panelled private screening room, facing the wide screen on the wall, in front of the five rows of green padded benches with lattice backs where friends used to be invited to watch his movies. Francesco Cossiga, the President of Italy, sent a telegram of condolence, and Franco Carraro, Minister of Tourism and Entertainment, came to pay respects to his friend and golfing companion. Others who went into the screening room for this final performance, and who were not away from Rome for the May Day holiday, included Federico Fellini, Bernardo Bertolucci, Michelangelo Antonioni, Tonino Delli Colli and Ennio Morricone. In the projection booth was a print of *Once Upon a Time in America* – 'Cinecittà reels. Vers. Lunga'. As the hearse left the villa, it passed a blue French street sign – '16e Avenue Sergio Leone' – which had been superimposed on 'Via Nepal'. Carla Leone remembers that 'a French cinéaste gave him that sign, and he liked it a lot'. At the basilica, someone had draped a banner around one of the columns which read, 'Thank you Sergio! You are the greatest, greater than John Ford'.

As the coffin arrived, Ennio Morricone played a slow version of the main theme from *Once Upon a Time in the West* on the organ, and the capacity congregation burst into a round of applause. Fellini stood up and said, 'I have the impression of a colleague who worked joyfully at something that made him happy: a presence and a voice, full of love for the cinema.' Morricone said, 'We fought for many years about the sound and the silence of his films: now there is only the silence.' Claudia Cardinale removed her dark glasses to wipe away the tears. Flash cameras punctuated the gloom. Francis Ford Coppola sat near Bertolucci, Damiani, Argento and Ettore Scola. Clint Eastwood sent a telegram from California: 'Sergio Leone had a great influence on my career. I learned a lot from him as an actor and as a director. And he was an extraordinary human being. His loss is one of the saddest of my life.' Three years later, Eastwood was to dedicate his *Unforgiven* 'For Sergio and Don', in memory of Leone and Don Siegel. Robert De Niro sent another telegram: 'To work with Leone was almost child's play. We were both perfectionists.' At the end of the service, the coffin left to another round of applause and there was a reprise of *Once Upon a Time in the West*. It was chaotic, but it was just right.[52]

Italian Western actor Tony Anthony had recently met Sergio Leone in a restaurant in Rome, with director Ferdinando Baldi. Leone enthused about *Leningrad*, and his projected star, Mickey Rourke ('I believe in this guy, Mickey Rourke'). Not long after, Anthony found himself in Brazil, acting in a Mickey Rourke picture entitled *Wild Orchid*. Early one morning, he was informed of Leone's death, and decided to seek out Rourke, who had just arrived on the production: 'Mickey was working out, jumping rope. I went over to him and said, "This is a terrible way to say hello . . . I'm Tony Anthony. I just wanted you to know I heard from Italy that Sergio Leone has died." His mouth dropped open, he was destroyed. He ran inside to call his wife and everyone else. He came back out and said, "God! I just spent two months with him, and this was going to be his big, big film – the story of Leningrad." '[53] *Screen International*, on 6 May 1989, reported that Leone's sudden death had 'put in jeopardy one of the most ambitious co-productions ever contemplated . . . After the funeral, one of Leone's close associates said, "It will be up to the Soviets to decide whether the film now goes ahead." ' It hasn't; nor has *A Place Only Mary Knows*. *Colt*, according to various articles in the French press, may still be made one day (six ninety-minute films 'which will remain faithful to the spirit of Sergio Leone') under the aegis of Canal Plus, RAI and Andrea Leone films, plus an American independent.

There were no tributes to Leone from the writers of his Westerns. They were still angry at him for taking so much of their credit, and claiming a retrospective knowingness about his movies which was not in evidence during their making. When I asked Sergio Donati about his verdict on Leone today, he replied: 'It's terribly difficult, because I had at the beginning a complete faith in Sergio, and he was so cynical about this aspect of his work. At bottom yes, he was a wonderful man to talk with, in some perspectives a great film-maker. But . . .' Luciano Vincenzoni's verdict is that Leone was 'very intelligent, and had a great sense of humour . . . an incredible businessman . . . very good for action movies . . . a great director on the set'. But, 'he took himself too seriously', and 'he started to put himself on top of all the people that worked and made his future, including me. And so in the end I told myself, "That's a son of a bitch!" ' Vincenzoni, though, did regret, that he never made his peace with the man: in characteristically patrician style, he said 'We both behaved like idiots, especially me. Because I'm a little more cultured than he was, I should have had the intelligence to make peace.'[54]

In October 1989, the Annecy Film Festival instituted a 'Sergio Leone Prize', to be awarded to 'a French or Italian director who does most to keep alive the memory of a film-maker who died so prematurely'. If the prize had been extended to Hollywood, the list of contenders would have been a very long one. It would include some of the American 'movie brats' who took Hollywood by storm as the old studio system crumbled around them and who, as Leone put it, 'watched *Once Upon a Time in the West* on a moviola in college, to discover its secrets'. John Carpenter, for example, gave the 'something to do with death' line to one of his characters in *Assault on Precinct 13* (1976); he reckoned that *West* was 'one of the classics of all time, a movie that states the essence of the Western, and the essence of mythology, and maybe finished off the genre'. Carpenter had its music played at his wedding.

Leone could discern other debts of love paid to his work amongst the leading lights of Carpenter's generation: 'When I saw the opening sequence of Spielberg's *Close Encounters*, I thought, "That was made by Sergio Leone." You know, the dust, the wind, the desert, the planes, the sudden chord on the soundtrack . . . George Lucas has told me how he kept referring to the music and the images of *Once Upon a Time in the West* when he cut *Star Wars*, which was really a Western – series B – set in space. All these younger Hollywood directors – George Lucas, Steven Spielberg, Martin Scorsese, John Carpenter – they've all said how much they owe to my work . . . But none of them has ever been tempted to make a Western which is actually a *Western*.'[55]

The list of potential Leone Prize-winners would also include the 'video brats' of twenty years later: Quentin Tarantino and Robert Rodriguez. In 1983, Tarantino got his job at Video Archives on Sepulveda Boulevard by talking incessantly to the owner about Sergio Leone. *Reservoir Dogs* and *Pulp Fiction* both end with a 'Mexican stand-off', and the advice Tarantino gave to actor Samuel L. Jackson before shooting the latter was, 'We're gonna start with the opening shot of *Casablanca*, then go into something Sergio Leone did in *The Good, The Bad and The Ugly* and finish up with a kind of Wile E. Coyote thing.' The triangular shootout in *The Good* was, for Tarantino, 'one of the best action sequences of all time'. Of the black suits, black ties and shades in

*Reservoir Dogs*, he has said, 'My genre characters are in uniform . . . like Sergio Leone's dusters he'd have his characters wearing.' And what about the incessant ringing of the telephone in *Jackie Brown*? Meanwhile, Robert Rodriguez's *El Mariachi* (1992) and its remake *Desperado* (1995) transposed *Fistful of Dollars* to modern-day Mexico, and armed its Man with No Name with automatic weapons hidden inside his guitar case.

If the list was extended from directors to actors, then it would have to include the post-1960s blockbuster action heroes, from Eastwood to Bronson to Stallone to Schwarzenegger to Willis to Van Damme and beyond, who substitute one-liners, skill and anti-heroics for the honour and glory of their pre-*Fistful* antecedents. In terms of genre, Leone clearly transformed the Western. Sam Peckinpah acknowledged a debt to Leone – or rather, *Leone* said he did. Peckinpah's authorized biographer does not mention Italian Westerns once, an omission which is shared by most American critics and film historians, who have consistently refused to acknowledge their significance. At the 1981 Santa Fe Festival of the Western, there was a heated debate about whether the Italians had killed off the Western, or saved it. Katy Jurado, the dark lady from *High Noon*, announced that a great tradition had fallen victim to the Spaghetti Western's 'lack of respect'. James Coburn was not sure: 'Well, Serge! Serge has his own ideas.' A few delegates supported the motion, 'Let's hear it for irreverence.'[56]

Casting the net wider than Hollywood, we can sense the shade of Leone in films as diverse as: Nils Gaup's *Pathfinder* (1987, Norway), described by its director as a 'reindeer Western', the opening sequence of which was inspired by the McBain family massacre; Richard Stanley's *Dust Devil* (1993, GB/South Africa), which features a supernatural Eastwood-lookalike hitchhiker in a long duster; Perry Henzell's *The Harder They Come* (1972, Jamaica), a celebration of the impact of Leone's and Corbucci's Westerns on a Rasta rude boy; Ales Verbic's *Once Upon a Time* (1989, Yugoslavia), which treats life as a train journey and is 'dedicated to Sergio Leone who once travelled on this train'; the complete thrillers of John Woo, from *The Killer* (1989) to *Broken Arrow* (1996), which has John Travolta's badman being heralded on the soundtrack by a baritone guitar played by Duane Eddy; and George Miller's *Mad Max* (1979, Australia). When Miller's sequel was poised for release in the USA, the director was seeking a new title, as the first film had not done great business there. Since the plot posited petrol as a form of currency in a post-nuclear desert, the present writer suggested (on BBC Radio's *Kaleidoscope*) *For a Few Gallons More*. They chose *The Road Warrior* instead. Many Chinese historical epics made since 1984 (especially Tsui Hark's *Once Upon a Time in China*) seem to be refracted through the structure and atmosphere of Leone's final film. Guy Richie's *Lock, Stock and Two Smoking Barrels* (1998, GB) has two Leone-style shootouts involving smalltime London gangsters.

And if the prize list went beyond world cinema to popular music, it would have to give prizes to everything from Jamaican ska to gangsta rap, at the sharp end; through numerous rock videos and 'found' pieces of Morricone's Leone soundtracks on digital collages; to, at the blunt end, Mike Oldfield and Jean-Michel Jarre, and advertising jingles worldwide. As I write, a London advertising hoarding for a trucking company screams 'Lee VAN Cleef' and features a giant drawing of the actor's snarling face from *The Good, The Bad and The Ugly*. Another, for chili hamburgers, claims in Western-style lettering that these may be had 'For a fistful of small change'. One of Lee Van Cleef's last roles (before he died in December 1989 at the age of sixty-four) was as a gunfighter striding into a sepia saloon, dressed in a long leather duster, accompanied by wailing harmonica soundtrack – to shoot some beer bottles and enjoy a well-earned Bavarian bier. This was for a Dutch television commercial.

Thirty-five years after they first appeared, Leone's images of show-downs and duels are still in the pantheon of visual clichés. Like Janet Leigh in the shower, Judy Garland on the Yellow Brick Road, Humphrey Bogart at the airport, Marcello Mastroianni and Anita Ekberg in the Fontana de Trevi, they are instantly recognizable, and can register in seconds. The French philosopher Jean Baudrillard called Sergio Leone 'the first post-modernist director' – the first to understand the hall of mirrors within the contemporary 'culture of quotations'. Thus, it is appropriate – necessary, even – that his work should have since been reflected by so many others. Clint Eastwood rode into San Miguel on a mule, and wound up traversing the globe – to the strains of Morricone.

But the Sergio Leone Prize is intended for a French or Italian director, and there Leone's adherents are harder to spot. A French director such as Luc Moullet, perhaps, whose *Une Aventure de Billy le Kid* (1970, France) has Jean-Pierre Léaud discussing the meaning of life with his girlfriend as they wander around the rocks of High Provence, on the run from the law. Moullet wrote in 1983: 'within genre moviemaking Sergio Leone beats all records for provocation ... [his] genre films often turn out to be more personal and artistic than the films of auteur cinema which nowadays are much too often reduced to a kind of left-wing reminiscence or fanciful flight of the aesthete'.[57] Or an Italian director such as Dario Argento, whose stylish horror films of the 1970s and 1980s (powered by thunderous music, opulent sets and elaborate technical effects) attempted to raise the 'splatter movie' to the level of mannerist painting. Argento, who has been called 'the Sergio Leone of the Gothics', said of his mentor after his funeral, 'He gave me a sense of rhythm, a taste for fantasy and a rigour in my framing. He was a friend, a unique director with a loyalty to and a love of his work.'[58] But there are no French or Italian directors who have managed to bridge 'popular cinema' and 'art cinema' Leone-style, while at the same time achieving international success.

One problem is that the Italian film industry which sustained Sergio Leone has gone: the victim of television, satellite, video and the economics of distribution. And it was because Leone was an Italian (specifically, a Roman with Neapolitan ancestry) that he made the kinds of film he did. They are as much about Italian culture and society in the postwar period as they are about American history and Hollywood dreams. Nevertheless, when asked, 'How do you think you fit among Italian directors?' while editing *Once Upon a Time in America*, Leone characteristically side-stepped the question: 'Without a doubt, I, too, occupy a place in cinema history. I come right after the letter "L" in the director's repertory, in fact a few entries before my friend Mario Monicelli, and right after Alexander Korda, Stanley Kubrick and Akira Kurosawa ... That's my place in cinema history. Down there between the Ks and Ms, generally to be found somewhere between pages 250 and 320 of any good film-makers' directory. If I'd been named "Antelope" instead of "Leone", I would have been number one. But I prefer Leone: I'm a hunter by nature, not a prey.'[59]

At the end of May 1993, there was a sixteen-day auction of all the furniture and props from Cinecittà studios. Among the 5,000 lots on offer, stored in eight separate warehouses, were the ballroom furnishings from *The Leopard*, the throne from *Cleopatra*, the scriptorium from *The Name of the Rose*, some white telephones used in 1930s

SERGIO LEONE

comedies, and an assortment of beds, as used in seduction scenes by Marcello Mastroianni. Thrown in were some wagon wheels, and the fixtures and fittings of a Mexican cantina. It closed an amazing chapter in Italy's cultural history. As the auction took place, only one production was being filmed at Cinecittà: a television programme. A representative of the Rome-based auctioneers explained why the sale had to take place: 'The movie industry is a big industry and has to be managed as such nowadays. Only if you have great organizational skills like the Americans can you have a proper movie industry today. Italians have imagination and creativity, but lack the organizational skills.'[60]

Once upon a time, as Sergio Leone liked to say, there was a certain cinema . . .

CUT!

# Notes

## Chapter 1: *Once Upon a Time in Rome*

1 See Noel Simsolo: *Conversations avec Sergio Leone* (Stock, Paris, 1987) pp. 21–22. Leone also reminisced about this in *C'era una volta il cinema*, a documentary directed by Gianni Minà and broadcast on RAI in 1985.

2 Simsolo, pp. 22–23. For historical context James Hay: *Fascist Italy – the Passing of the Rex* (Indiana University Press, 1987) pp. 64–98.

3 Italo Calvino: *The Road to San Giovanni* (Vintage International, New York, 1994) pp. 37–73, 'A Cinema-Goer's Autobiography'.

4 Federico Fellini (with Tonino Guerra): *Amarcord – Portrait of a Town* (Abelard-Schuman, London, 1974). Also James Hay, loc. cit.

5 James Hay, loc. cit. Also Marcia Landy: *Fascism in Film* (Princeton University Press, New Jersey, 1986) pp. 3–29, 33–71, and Mira Liehm: *Passion and Defiance Film in Italy from 1942 to the Present* (University of California Press, Berkeley, 1984) pp. 21–40.

6 Simsolo, pp. 22–23 (Leone on Charlie Chan) and pp. 23–24 (Leone on comics). See also Diego Gabutti: *C'era una volta in America* (Rizzoli, Milan, 1984) pp. 90–93. One of Sergio Leone's first cinema experiences, which he was to remember for the rest of his life, was going to see *Charlie Chan's Secret* (1936, directed by designer Gordon Wiles) with its climactic sequence where a clock in the living room of an expressionist house triggers a high-powered rifle when the clock strikes the hour. On comics of the period, see (ed.) Aghina and Saccabusi: *Annitrenta* (Comune di Milano, 1982) pp. 449–65.

7 Simsolo, and Gabutti, loc. cit.

8 Gilles Lambert: *Les bons, les sales, les méchants et les propres de Sergio Leone* (Solar, Paris, 1976) p. 40; interview with Sergio Leone for Channel 4/Large Door *Visions* (broadcast May 1984), November 1983; Simsolo, p. 97. On the *Burattini* and the *pupi Siciliani*, see Antonio Pasqualino: *L'opera dei pupi* (Sellerio, Palermo, 1989), Bill Baird: *The Art of the Puppet* (Ridge Press, Macmillan, New York, 1965) pp. 119–129, Michael Byrom: *Punch in the Italian Puppet Theatre* (Centaur, London, 1983) appendix A, and Henry Festing Jones: *Diversions in Sicily* (Alston Rivers, London, 1909) pp. 82–93. Gilles Cèbe: *Sergio Leone* (Henri Veyrier, Paris, 1984) pp. 87–133 is good on Leone and the carnivalesque.

9 Lambert, pp. 93–94; also Simsolo, pp. 20–21.

10 *Visions* interview; also (ed.) Luca Verdone: *Per un pugno di dollari* (Cappelli, Bologna, 1979) interview with Leone pp. 11–20; and author's interview with Leone February 1982.

11 Simsolo, pp. 17–20. For historical context, Charles F. Delzell: *Mediterranean Fascism 1919–45* (Harper & Row, New York, 1970) pp. 133–155. For Fellini's version, *Amacord* pp. 17–24.

12 Derek Elley: *The Epic Film* (Routledge & Kegan Paul, London, 1984) pp. 84–85; Maria

495

Wyke: *Projecting the Past – Ancient Rome, Cinema and History* (Routledge, London, 1997) pp. 20–22; *Bianco e Nero special*, August 1939; James Hay, pp. 150–180.

13 Author's interview with Sergio Leone, February 1982.

14 Lambert, pp. 30–32; Simsolo, pp. 21–23.

15 Calvino, pp. 37–73.

16 Author's interview with Sergio Leone, February 1982, confirming remarks in Lambert and in Guy Braucourt's interview for *Cinéma 69*, November 1989, pp. 81–90.

17 Luciano Vincenzoni, in Oreste de Fornari: *Tutti i film di Sergio Leone* (Ubulibri, Milan, 1984) pp. 171–173.

18 Bernardo Bertolucci, interview in *Positif*, March 1973, p. 37.

19 Tonino Valerii, interview for BBC television documentary *Viva Leone!*, directed by Nick Jones and David Thompson and broadcast December 1989. Interview in Rome, November 1989.

20 Clint Eastwood, cited in Christopher Frayling: *Spaghetti Westerns* (Routledge & Kegan Paul, London, 1981) pp. 126–127, 145–146.

21 Franco Ferrini, interview with Sergio Leone in *Bianco e Nero*, September/October 1971, pp. 37–42.

22 Verdone, interview pp. 11–20.

23 Verdone, also Gianni Di Claudio *Il cinema western* (Libreria Universitaria, Chieti, 1986) interview pp. 13–21.

24 Simsolo, pp. 190–191, 195–196.

25 Simsolo, pp. 25–26

26 Gilles Cèbe: *Sergio Leone* (Henri Veyrier, Paris, 1984) pp. 34–35, quoting Leone.

27 Simsolo, pp. 28–30.

28 Simsolo, p. 30.

29 See, for example, Luca Beatrice: *Al cuore, Ramon, al cuore* (Tarab, Florence, 1996) pp. 156–160, 162–166.

30 Interview with Leone in *Take One*, May 1973, pp. 27–32.

31 Diego Gabutti, pp. 90–92; also Leone's essay in (ed.) Marcello Garofalo: *C'era una volta in America – Photographic Memories* (Editalia, Rome, 1988) pp. 9–15.

32 Gabutti, Garofalo, loc. cit.

33 Christopher Frayling: *Spaghetti Westerns*, p. 65.

34 Author's interview with Carla Leone, Rome, 1 July 1994.

35 Gabutti, Garofalo, loc. cit.

## Chapter 2: *Bob, Son of Robert*

1 Aldo Bernardini and Vittorio Martinelli: *Roberto Roberti – direttore artistico* (Le giornate del cinema muto edizioni, Pordenone, 1985) pp. 8–15. This publication accompanied the 1985 silent film festival at Pordenone, which included a discussion with Sergio Leone about his father, 3 October 1985.

2 Noel Simsolo: *Conversations avec Sergio Leone*, pp. 9–12.

3 Simsolo, loc. cit.

4 Bernardini and Martinelli, p. 31.

5 Bernardini and Martinelli, pp. 10–15.

6 Emilio Ghione, cited in Pierre Leprohon: *The Italian Cinema* (Secker and Warburg, London, 1972) pp. 43–44, 55–58. On Ghione, also see Maria Wyke: *Projecting the Past*, p. 171.

7 Bernardo and Martinelli, pp. 41–42.

8 Simsolo, p. 12.

9 See Monica Dall'Asta: *Un Cinema musclé 1913–26* (Editions Yellow Now, Crisnée, Belgium, 1992) pp. 25–167; also Vittorio Martinelli and Mario Quargnolo: *Maciste & Co* (Edizioni Cinepopolare, Udine, 1981).

10 For Leone on Pagano, see – among many other references – Guy Braucourt's interview for *Cinéma 69*, November 1969, pp. 81–83 and Simsolo pp. 9–12.

11 See Dall'Asta, loc. cit.

12 For Campogalliani's letter, see Dall'Asta p. 137.

13 Bernardini and Martinelli, pp. 61–62

14 Mira Liehm, pp. 19–20 and *passim*. On Francesca Bertini, see her memoirs *Il resto non conta* (Giardini, Pisa, 1969) pp. 100–165.

15 Simsolo, pp. 12–13

16 Simsolo, pp. 13–14; Bernardini and Martinelli pp. 23–24.

17 See, for example, Simsolo, p. 13.

18 Simsolo, loc. cit., and Braucourt, loc. cit. In most interviews about his early life, Sergio Leone included one version or another of this story.

19 Denis Mack Smith: *Mussolini* (Weidenfeld and Nicolson, London, 1981) pp. 15–17.

20 Gian Piero Brunetta: *Storia del cinema Italiano 1895–1945* (Riuniti, Rome, 1979) p. 236 and Bernardini and Martinelli pp. 24–27.

21 See Francesco Savio: *Ma l'amore no* (Sonzogno, Milan, 1975) p. 332 and Bernardini and Martinelli pp. 99–101.

22 See (ed.) Franco Marietti: *Cinecittà tra cronica e storia 1937–1989* (vol. 1, Presidenza del Consiglio dei Ministri, Rome, 1990) pp. 227–230; also, Gianni Di Claudio: *Directed by Sergio Leone* (Libreria Universitaria, Chieti, 1990) pp. 12–13.

23 Carla Del Poggio, in Francesco Savio: *Cinecittà anni trenta 1930–43* (vol. 2, Bulzoni, Rome, 1979) pp. 440–443.

24 Francesco Savio, p. 48; Bernardini and Martinelli pp. 101–102.

25 Author's interview with Carla Leone, 1 July 1994.

26 Author's interview with Tonino Valerii, Udine, 26 April 1997.

27 Carla Leone interview.

28 Tonino Valerii interview.

29 Author's interview with Sergio Donati, Fregene, 23 May 1998.

30 Simsolo, pp. 31–34.

31 Simsolo, pp. 30–31. See, for historical context, Gian Piero Brunetta: *Storia del cinema Italiano, 1945–1980s* (Riuniti, Rome, 1982) pp. 24–25.

32 Carla Leone interview. A striking sequence from *Le serpe* (1920) is included in Gianni Minà's RAI television documentary *C'era una volta il cinema*.

33 Interview with Andrea Leone for *Viva Leone!*, Rome, November 1989.

34 Simsolo, pp. 33, 37–38.

## Chapter 3: *Hollywood on the Tiber*

1 Diego Gabutti: *C'era una volta in America* (Rizzoli, Milan, 1984) pp. 64–69.

2 Loc. cit.; and Noel Simsolo: *Conversations avec Sergio Leone* pp. 35–36.

3 Simsolo, loc. cit.

4 Gabutti, loc. cit.

5 Simsolo, pp. 33–34. See also Federico Fellini: *Cinecittà* (Studio Vista, London, 1989) pp. 23–25.

6 *Italian Cinema 1945–51* (Unitalia Film, for the diffusion of film abroad, 1951) pp. 57–58. For historical context, see Paul Ginsborg: *A History of Contemporary Italy* (Penguin, Middlesex, 1990) pp. 72–120, 210–253.

7  Gian Piero Brunetta: *Storia del cinema Italiano 1945 to the 1980s* pp. 476–480; see also (ed.) Jeremy Tambling: *A Night in at the Opera* (John Libbey, London, 1991) pp. 279–284.

8  See Raymond Durgnat: *Eternal Triangle – Opera, Film, Realism* (*Monthly Film Bulletin*, October 1990, pp. 282–284); Jean-Paul Bourre: *Opéra et Cinéma* (Editions Artefact, Veyrier, Paris, 1987); and Tito Gobbi: *My Life* (Macdonald and Jane, London, 1979), Chapter 8.

9  Gabutti, pp. 64–69.

10  Among Leone's many comments about his dislike for opera, see interviews in *Cahiers du Cinéma*, May 1984 (pp. 7–11, 56–60), *Take One*, May 1973, pp. 31–32 and Simolo, pp. 174–175.

11  *Italian Cinema, 1945–51*, pp. 55–56. See also, on *Fabiola*, Simsolo, p. 36 and, for background, Maria Wyke: *Projecting the Past*, pp. 49, 55–56.

12  Simsolo, pp. 34–38.

13  Gabutti, pp. 64–69.

14  Gabutti, loc. cit.

15  Francesco Savio: *Cinecittà Anni Trenta* (vol. 2) p. 521. Leone's recollection is that he did 'film certain scenes' in Fabrizi films, Simsolo pp. 51–52. Writer Luciano Vincenzoni agrees.

16  Gabutti, pp. 82–83; Simsolo, pp. 28, 39–41.

17  Simsolo, pp. 40–41.

18  Simsolo, p. 53.

19  See Orson Welles and Peter Bogdanovich: *This is Orson Welles* (HarperCollins, London, 1993) pp. 267–268.

20  Lambert, pp. 12–13; Simsolo, pp. 45–46.

21  Oreste de Fornari, pp. 157–158 and author's interview with Tonino Delli Colli, Rome, 18 December 1981.

22  Oreste de Fornare, pp. 171–173; also Luciano Vincenzoni, interview with Cenk Kiral, 25 April 1998.

23  Oreste de Fornari, pp. 158–60.

24  Author's interview with Sergio Donati, Fregene, 23 May 1998.

25  Oreste de Fornari, pp. 166–170 (Valerii).

26  Luciano Vincenzoni, interviews with Cenk Kiral 2 and 13 May 1998.

27  Simsolo, pp. 53–54.

28  Wyke, pp. 138–148.

29  Fabio Melelli: *Eroi a Cinecittà – stuntmen e maesti d'armi* (Mercurio Editrice, Perugia, 1998) pp. 138–150. On background to this era, see Fellini, p. 25.

30  Simsolo, pp. 43–44; Lambert, pp. 14–15; author's interview with Leone February 1982; Braucourt, loc. cit.

31  Lambert, loc. cit.

32  Simsolo, pp. 43–44.

33  Simsolo, pp. 54–56; also Fred Zinnemann: *An Autobiography* (Bloomsbury, London, 1992) pp. 154–171; Alexander Trauner and Jean-Pierre Berthomé: *Décors du cinéma* (Jade-Flammarion, Paris, 1988) pp. 138–142, and National Film Theatre booklet October–November 1984, *Alexander Trauner – designs for living*.

34  Simsolo, pp. 54–56.

35  Author's interview with Fred Zinnemann, 2 November 1990.

36  Ibid.

37  Author's interview with Luca Morsella, 20 December 1991.

38  Charlton Heston: *The Actor's Life – Journals 1956–76* (Penguin, Middlesex, 1980) pp. 39–61 and Charlton Heston: *In the Arena* (HarperCollins, London, 1995) pp. 180–206.

39 Frayling: *Spaghetti Westerns*, p. 97.

40 For some of Leone's many versions of working on *Ben-Hur*, see *Cinéma 69*, November 1969, pp. 81–82; *Ciné-Magazine* January 1977; Lambert, pp. 13–14 and Simsolo, pp. 53–54, 56–57. In the author's interview of February 1982, he admitted with a smile that some journalists may have exaggerated his role a little.

41 Joanne D'Antonio: *Andrew Marton Interviewed* (Directors' Guild of America and Scarecrow Press, New York, 1991).

42 See note 40.

43 D'Antonio, op cit.

44 Simsolo, pp. 53–54, 56–57.

45 Ibid.

46 Author's interview with Charlton Heston, 19 November 1995; see also Heston: *In the Arena* pp. 189–90.

47 Leone on working as an assistant director: *Take One*, May 1973, pp. 29–30; *Cinéma 69*, November 1969, pp. 81–83; *Ciné-Magazine*, January 1977; Lambert, p. 23; Simsolo, p. 51–52, Gilles Cèbe, op. cit., pp. 36–37; Frayling: *Spaghetti Westerns*, pp. 96–101.

48 Gabutti, pp. 64–69.

49 Interview with Sergio Leone by Jean A. Gili in *Positif*, June 1984, pp. 6–15.

50 *Take One*, May 1973, pp. 29–30.

51 Frayling: *Spaghetti Westerns* pp. 58–60; on Leone's politics, see *Take One*, May 1973, pp. 28–29; Simsolo, pp. 100–101, 163–4; Gabutti, pp. 116–117

## Chapter 4: Economic Miracles

1 Frayling: *Spaghetti Westerns*, pp. 54–57.

2 Patrick Lucanio: *With Fire and Sword* (Scarecrow, NJ, 1994) pp. 12–13; on the culture of bodybuilding pp. 22–25. See also Geoffrey O'Brien: *The Phantom Empire* (W. W. Norton, New York, 1993) pp. 129–172.

3 Domenica Paolella: *La psychanalyse du pauvre* (Midi-Minuit Fantastique, 12, May 1965) pp. 1–10; Frayling pp. 53–55.

4 Paolella, pp. 9–10.

5 See Pierre Leprohon, *The Italian Cinema* (Secker and Warburg, London, 1972) pp. 174–179.

6 Christopher Wagstaff: *A Forkful of Westerns – Industry, Audiences and the Italian Western* (in *Popular European Cinema*, (ed.) Dyer and Vincendeau, Routledge, London, 1992) pp. 245–261.

7 Franco Ferrini: *Interview with Sergio Leone* (*Bianco e Nero*, September/October 1971, pp. 37–42).

8 Simsolo, pp. 66–67.

9 Ibid.

10 Author's interview with Carla Leone, 1 July 1994.

11 Simsolo, pp. 59–61. See also Richard Whitehall: *Days of Strife and Nights of Orgy* (*Films & Filming*, vol. 9 no. 6, 1963, pp. 8–14); Raymond Durgnat: *Epic* (*Films & Filming*, vol. 10 no. 3, 1963, pp. 9–12); Patrick Lucanio: *With Fire and Sword* pp. 289–291.

12 See Maria Wyke, pp. 147–182; also Wyke: *Cinema and the City of the Dead* ((ed.) MacCabe and Petrie, *New Scholarship from BFI Research*, BFI, London, 1996, pp. 140–56); also Derek Elley: *The Epic Film*, pp. 121–122; Lucanio, pp. 200–202.

13 Simsolo, pp. 62–63.

14 Simsolo, pp. 65–66; also author's interview with Sergio Leone, February 1982.

15 (ed.) Franca Faldini and Goffredo Fofi: *L'avventurosa storia del cinema Italiano 1960–9* (Feltrinelli, Milan, 1981) pp. 286–288.

16 Faldini and Fofi, p. 286; Gabutti, pp. 82–85

17 Author's interview with Sergio Leone, February 1982.

18 Simsolo, pp. 66–67; Lambert, pp. 14–15; Gabutti, pp. 83–85.

19 Gabutti, loc. cit.; see also Derek Elley, p. 74; (ed.) Lutz Becker and Martin Caiger-Smith: *Art and Power* (Hayward Gallery, London, 1995) pp. 14–17, 30–31.

20 Simsolo, p. 66.

21 Simsolo, pp. 68–70; Lambert, p. 15; Gabutti, p. 84.

22 Simsolo, p. 70.

23 Author's interview with Sergio Leone, February 1982; also Simsolo, pp. 72–73.

24 Oreste de Fornari, pp. 15–16.

25 Elley, p. 77.

26 Author's interview with Sergio Donati, 23 May 1998; Vincenzoni interview by Hubert Corbin in *Cinéma Méditerranéen Montpellier* catalogue, 23 October–1 November 1998, pp. 65–66.

27 Simsolo, pp. 49–50.

28 Author's interview with Carla Leone, 1 July 1994.

29 Carla Leone interview.

30 Carla Leone interview.

31 Author's interview with Fulvio Morsella, Rome, 24 May 1998.

32 For Aldrich and *Sodom and Gomorrah*, see Richard Combs: *Robert Aldrich* (BFI, London, 1978) p. 44; Edwin T. Arnold and Eugene L. Miller: *The Films & Career of Robert Aldrich* (University of Tennessee Press, Knoxville, 1986) pp. 95–97; Mike Munn: *Stories behind the Scenes of the Great Epic Films* (Illustrated Publications Co, Argus Books, 1982) pp. 33–35; Lucanio, pp. 293–296.

33 Faldini and Fofi, pp. 178–80.

34 Simsolo, pp. 75–76.

35 Lucanio, and Combs, loc. cit.

36 Ken Adam's storyboards for the sequence were exhibited at the Palais de Tokyo, Paris, April–June 1992, and published in the catalogue *Storyboard – le cinéma dessiné*, (ed.) Peter, Faton and de Pierpont (Yellow Now, Paris, 1992) p.146.

37 Faldini and Fofi, loc. cit.

38 Arnold and Miller, loc. cit.; also interview with Aldrich in *Positif*, 182, June 1976.

39 Simsolo, loc. cit.

40 Goffredo Lombardo, quoted in Faldini and Fofi, pp. 179–180.

41 Simsolo, loc. cit.; Oreste de Fornari, pp. 15–16.

42 Faldini and Fofi, p. 180.

43 Simsolo, pp. 74–75.

44 *Annuario del Cinema Italiano* – Sezione 1, p. 99 (1961).

## Chapter 5: *Fistful of Dollars*

1 On the *Yojimbo* visit, see Oreste de Fornari pp. 166–168, and *Cinéma Méditerannéen Montpellier* pp. 61–63; confirmed by my interview with Carla Leone. On *The Eagles of Rome*, see *Cinéma Méditerannéen Montpellier*, interview with Tonino Dolli Colli, pp. 71–72. The project was still being discussed as late as 1975, as a possible vehicle for Elliot Gould and Donald Sutherland.

2 Carla Leone interview.

3 Carla Leone interview; see also De Fornari and Faldini and Fofi, pp. 287–288

4 Author's interview with Sergio Leone, February 1982.

5 Oreste de Fornari, p. 39.

6 Frayling: *Spaghetti Westerns*, p. 39.

7 Ibid. pp. 147–150.

8 See Frayling, p. 101. Also Carlos Aguilar: *Sergio Leone* (Catedra, Madrid, 1990) pp. 76–86; Peter Besas: *Behind the Spanish Lens* (Arden Press, Denver, 1985); Masegosa, Mañas and Vizcaíno: *La produccion cinematografica en Almerià* 1957–75 (Institute of Almerian Studies, Almerià, 1997) pp. 13–18, 32–40; Vicente Vergara: *10,000 dolares para una masacre* (Cine español, cine de subgéneros, (ed.) Fernando Torres, Valencia, 1974). Plus author's interview with Joaquin Luis Romero Marchent, Udine, 26 April 1997.

9 Aguilar, p. 82.

10 Author's interview with Marchent, 26 April 1997.

11 See Frayling, pp. 121–137. Also author's interview with Sergio Donati, 23 May 1998.

12 Simsolo, pp. 89–90.

13 Carla Leone interview, also *Patrick McGilligan: Clint: the Life and the Legend* (HarperCollins, London, 1999) pp. 130–131.

14 Faldini and Fofi, pp. 288–290; Simsolo, pp. 87–88.

15 See Franco Ferrini's interview in *Bianco e Nero* (September/October 1971), Leone's interview introduction to *Per un pugno di dollari* (Cappelli, Bologna, 1979) pp. 11–20, and interview with Leone for *Visions* (Large Door/Channel 4) November 1983.

16 Simsolo, pp. 112–114.

17 Author's interview with Sergio Leone, February 1982.

18 Ibid.

19 Vincenzoni interview with Hubert Corbin, in *Cinéma Méditerranéen Montpellier*, p. 65–66.

20 *Visions* interview, November 1983. See also Frayling: *Spaghetti Westerns*, pp. 160–175.

21 Frayling, pp. 60–63, 180–191.

22 Ibid., pp. 147–150.

23 Tonino Delli Colli interview with Hubert Corbin, in *Cinéma Méditerranéen Montpellier*, pp. 71–72.

24 De Fornari, pp. 166–168.

25 Ibid.; also *Montpellier*, pp. 61–62.

26 De Fornari and *Montepellier*, loc. cit.

27 Author's interview with Carlo Simi, Montpellier, 24 October 1998; also see *Carlo Simi – l'Amérique de Sergio Leone* (*Cinéma Méditerranéen Montpellier*, 1998, (ed.) Corbin) pp. 4–6.

28 Author's interview with Tonino Valerii, Udine, 26 April 1997; also De Fornari, pp. 166–168.

29 Author's interview with Carlo Simi.

30 Lambert, pp. 23–24.

31 Author's interview with Valerii; see also *Montpellier* pp. 61–63.

32 *Montpellier*, p. 60.

33 Fabio Melelli, interview with Benito Stefanelli, pp. 138–150.

34 See Steven Whitney: *Charles Bronson* (Dell, New York, 1975); Richard Harrison's foreword to Gary A. Smith: *Epic Films* (McFarland, North Carolina, 1991) pp. xiii–xiv and (ed.) Danny Peary, *Close-Ups* (Galahad Books, New York, 1978) pp. 535–536.

35 Author's interview with Sergio Donati.
36 Author's interview with Tonino Valerii.
37 Ibid.
38 Author's interview with Sergio Leone.
39 Guy Braucourt: *Interview with Sergio Leone* (*Cinéma 69*, November 1969) pp. 81–90; also Frayling: *Spaghetti Westerns*, pp. 145–146.
40 Pete Hamill interview with Leone (*American Film*, June 1984) pp. 23–25; Elaine Lomenzo interview (*Film Comment*, August 1984) pp. 21–23; and Christopher Frayling: *Clint Eastwood* (Virgin, London, 1992) pp. 53–67.
41 Richard Schickel: *Clint Eastwood* (Cape, London, 1996) pp. 131–133, 134–150. I am indebted to this biography as well as to Daniel O'Brien: *Clint Eastwood* (Batsford, London, 1996) pp. 42–70, Minty Clinch: *Clint Eastwood* (Coronet, Hodder & Stoughton, London, 1995) pp. 49–72, 'Directed by Clint Eastwood' in *Projections* 4½, (ed.) Boorman and Donohue (Faber, London) pp. 60–62, Douglas Thompson: *Clint Eastwood, Sexual Cowboy* (Smith Gryphon, London, 1992) pp. 32–36, Michael Munn: *Clint Eastwood, Hollywood's Loner* (Robson, London, 1992) pp. 44–66, De Witt Bodeen: *A Fistful of Fame* (*Focus on Film*, 9, spring 1972 pp. 12–24), Paul Smith: *Clint Eastwood, a Cultural Production* (University of Minnesota Press, 1993) pp. 1–28 and Iain Johnstone: *The Man with No Name* (Plexus, London, 1981) pp. 35–51.
42 Schickel, loc. cit.; Frayling, *Clint Eastwood*, loc. cit.
43 Schickel, loc. cit.
44 Frayling, *Clint Eastwood*, loc. cit.
45 Author's interview with Tonino Valerii.
46 Schickel, pp. 134–135.
47 Johnstone, *Clint Eastwood*, pp. 36–37.
48 Frayling, loc. cit.
49 Simsolo, pp. 92–93.
50 *Projections* 4½, pp. 60–62; Frayling, *Clint Eastwood*, loc. cit.
51 *Projections*, Christopher Frayling, David Downing and Gary Herman: *Clint Eastwood, All-American Anti-Hero* (Omnibus Press, London, 1977) pp. 28–52.
52 *Montpellier*, interview with Franco Giraldi, p. 60.
53 Schickel, p. 141.
54 Clint Eastwood interview, in the television documentary *Sergio Leone . . . Les Westerns* (Blue Dahlia Productions and Canal Plus, directed by Philip Priestley, 1997).
55 Frayling: *Spaghetti Westerns*, pp. 146–147, and *Westerns all'Italiana* (Anaheim, California, nd.) *Gian Maria Volonté memorial issue*.
56 Frayling, *Spaghetti Westerns*, loc. cit.; Simsolo, p. 96.
57 *Montpellier*, p. 60.
58 Simsolo, pp. 89–92.
59 Frayling: *Clint Eastwood*, p. 56.
60 Simsolo, pp. 92–93.
61 Frayling, *Spaghetti Westerns*, pp. 59–60.
62 Frayling, *Spaghetti Westerns*, pp. 63–64; Schickel, pp. 145–146.
63 Guy Braucourt, pp. 86–90.
64 Schickel, p. 147.
65 Schickel, p. 150.
66 Author's interview with Tonino Valerii.
67 Schickel, p. 144.
68 Author's interview with Tonino Valerii

69 Thompson, pp. 32–36; Munn, pp. 44–66.
70 Lambert, pp. 29–30.
71 De Fornari, pp. 166–168; *Montpellier*, pp. 61–63; author's interview with Tonino Valerii.
72 Author's interview with Fulvio Morsella, 24 May 1998.
73 Author's interview with Tonino Valerii.
74 Ibid.
75 Ibid. See also De Fornari, pp. 166–168.
76 Simsolo, p. 88.
77 Author's interview with Carla Leone; *Montpellier*, pp. 71–72; Simsolo, pp. 104–105; Gianni Di Claudio: *Directed by Sergio Leone* (Libreria Universitare, Chieti, 1990) pp. 43, 67.
78 Frayling: *Clint Eastwood*, pp. 61–62; author's interview with Sergio Donati, 23 May 1998.
79 Simsolo, pp. 93–95; Anne and Jean Lhassa: *Ennio Morricone* (Favre, Lausanne, 1989) pp. 51–56; *Ennio Morricone* BBC television documentary (directed by David Thompson, spring 1995).
80 *Ennio Morricone* television documentary; on Morricone's music for Leone's films, see Robert C. Cumbrow: *Once Upon a Time – The Films of Sergio Leone* (Scarecrow, New Jersey, 1987) pp. 199–216.
81 Lhassa, pp. 23–33, 45–50; H.J. de Boer and M. van Wouw: *The Ennio Morricone Musicography* (Amsterdam, 1990) pp. 1–33.
82 Interview with Ennio Morricone for *Viva Leone!*, Rome, November 1989; Lhassa, pp. 201–214; De Fornari, p. 165.
83 Lhassa pp. 57–72; *Viva Leone!* interview; Christopher Palmer: *Dimitri Tiomkin* (TE Books, London, 1984) pp. 64–65, 87–91.
84 Author's interview with Sergio Leone, February 1982.
85 Lhassa, loc. cit.
86 *Viva Leone!* interview with Ennio Morricone; see also Lhassa, and De Fornari, loc. cit.
87 Author's interview with Alessandro Alessandroni, Rome, 22 May 1998; see also Lhassa, pp. 80–83.
88 Lhassa, pp. 57–72, 201–214; *Ennio Morricone* television documentary; see also musicologist Sergio Miceli's explanatory booklet in Morricone's boxed set *The Italian Western* (RCA ML/MK 3 1543). Miceli's book *Morricone, La Musica, Il Cinema* (Ricardi Mucchi, series Lesfere No. 23, 1994) is good on the composer's early life, pp. 26–39, 65–105, and on Nuova Consonanza, pp. 195–205.
89 Author's interview with Sergio Leone, February 1982.
90 Simsolo, p. 97.
91 Author's interview with Sergio Leone.
92 Lambert, p. 32; Ferrini's interview (*Bianco e Nero*, September/October 1971) pp. 37–40.
93 Interview with Stefanelli in Fabio Melelli: *Eroi a Cinecittà*, pp. 138–150.
94 Frayling: *Spaghetti Westerns*, pp. 129–130.
95 Lambert, pp. 32–33.
96 Simsolo, pp. 103–104.
97 Author's interview with Tonino Valerii; see also De Fornari pp. 166–168.
98 Author's interview with Sergio Donati, 23 May 1998.
99 Interview with Dario Argento for *Viva Leone!*
100 Sergio Leone, interview introduction to *Per un pugno di dollari* (Capelli, Bologna, 1979) pp. 12–20; Simsolo, pp. 63–64.
101 Schickel, pp. 152–154.

Chapter 6: *For a Few Dollars More*

1 On Leone's 'creative paralysis', see Lambert, p.37 and Simsolo, pp. 105–106.
2 Author's interview with Sergio Donati, 23 May 1998; see also De Fornari pp. 158–159.
3 Simsolo, p. 106; Gianni Di Claudio, p. 67.
4 *Montpellier*, pp. 72–73; Simsolo, pp. 105–106.
5 Author's interview with Carla Leone, 1 July 1994.
6 Author's interview with Sergio Donati.
7 See, for an extensive if not always accurate filmography, Thomas Weisser: *Spaghetti Westerns – The Good, the Bad and the Violent* (McFarland, N. Carolina, 1994) and for a more accurate one Luca Beatrice: *Al cuore, Ramon, al cuore* (Tarab, Florence, 1996) pp. 184–248.
8 Author's interview with Sergio Leone, February 1982.
9 As recounted by Luca Morsella, 21 December 1991.
10 Burt Reynolds: *My Life* (Hodder & Stoughton, London, 1994) pp. 111–119.
11 Author's interview with Tonino Valerii, 26 April 1997. See also De Fornari, pp. 166–168 and *Montpellier*, pp. 61–63.
12 Interviews with Luciano Vincenzoni by Cenk Kiral, 25 April, 2 May and 13 May 1998. See also De Fornari, pp. 171–2. For Vincenzoni's career, see (ed.) Everardo Artico and Silvano Mezzavilla: *Luciano Vincenzoni – Sceneggiatore* (Comune di Treviso, 1986).
13 *Montpellier*, pp. 65–66.
14 Ibid.
15 De Fornari, pp. 171–172.
16 Author's interview with Fulvio Morsella, 24 May 1998.
17 Schickel, pp. 154–155; Gianni Di Claudio, pp. 67–68.
18 Author's interview with Tonino Valerii, 20 April 1997. See also De Fornari, pp. 166–168.
19 Schickel, p. 156; author's interview with Carla Leone, 1 July 1994.
20 Simsolo, pp. 107, 109–110.
21 Author's interview with Tonino Valerii; see also De Fornari, pp. 167–168.
22 Interviews with Cenk Kiral, April–May 1998.
23 Simsolo, pp. 107–108.
24 See Mark Twain: *Roughing It* (University of California Press, Berkeley, 1972) pp. 86–104 (Twain's account) and pp. 542–5 (Orion Clemens's account); Prof. Thomas J. Dimsdale: *The Vigilantes of Montana* (reprinted Time–Life Books, Virginia, 1981) pp. 166–177.
25 Some variations on the Slade story are summarized in Jay Robert Nash: *Encyclopedia of Western Lawmen and Outlaws* (Paragon House, New York, 1992) pp. 284–285.
26 Frayling: *Spaghetti Westerns*, pp. 125–126; Lambert, p. 9; Simsolo, p. 108.
27 Guy Braucourt interview, *Cinéma 69*, November 1969, pp. 81–90; Lambert, pp. 8–9; Frayling, *Spaghetti Westerns*, p. 120.
28 Cenk Kiral interviews, April–May 1998.
29 See Peter Bogdanovich: *John Ford* (University of California Press, Berkeley, 1978), for Ford's comments on printing the legend. On bounty-hunters, a useful source is Kim Newman: *Wild West Movies* (Bloomsbury, London, 1990) pp. 127–138. The Mann quote is cited in Christopher Wagstaff, p. 245.
30 See Frayling: *Clint Eastwood*, pp. 1–20, based on author's interviews with Budd Boetticher.
31 Interview with Sergio Leone for *Visions* documentary (Large Door/Channel 4), November 1983; author's interview with Leone, February 1982; Simsolo, pp. 110–112; author's interview with Carla Leone, 1 July 1994. On Van Cleef's life, see Mike Malloy:

# NOTES

*Lee Van Cleef* (McFarland, N. Carolina, 1998) pp. 3–31 and *Westerns all'Italiana*, 'Lee Van Cleef Memorial Issue', 1990.

32 As note 31, plus Cenk Kiral interview with Vincenzoni, April–May 1998. Also William R. Horner: *Bad at the Bijou* (McFarland, N. Carolina, 1982), pp. 43–60.

33 Horner, loc. cit.; Romany Bain interview with Van Cleef (*TV Times*, 14 February 1980, pp. 4–7) and Frank Garvan interview (*Weekend*, London, 21–27 November 1979, pp. 24–25).

34 De Fornari, p. 17.

35 Horner, loc. cit.; and Munn, pp. 53–57.

36 Author's interview with Fulvio Morsella, 24 May 1998.

37 Author's interview with Carla Leone.

38 Cenk Kiral interviews, April–May 1998.

39 Clint Eastwood interview in *Sergio Leone . . . Les Westerns* (Blue Dahlia/ Canal Plus Production, 1997). On dubbing, see Anthony Burgess's essay in (ed.) Michaels and Ricks: *The State of the Language* (University of California Press, Berkeley, 1980) pp. 297–303.

40 De Fornari, p. 52.

41 Author's interview with Sergio Donati, 23 May 1998.

42 Ibid. See also De Fornari, pp. 158–159 and Schickel, pp. 159–161.

43 De Fornari, pp. 171–173.

44 Simsolo, pp. 108–109.

45 Frayling: *Spaghetti Westerns*, pp. 168–169.

46 Author's interview with Carlo Simi, 24 October 1998; see also interview in the television documentary *Sergio Leone . . . Les Westerns*.

47 Author's interview with Simi; see also Hubert Corbin's catalogue *Carlo Simi – L'Amérique de Sergio Leone*, pp. 8–12.

48 Author's interview with Luis Beltran, at Leone ranch, Almeria, 18 September 1998.

49 Author's interview with Tonino Valerii; see also De Fornari, pp. 166–168. Also interview for *Viva Leone!*, November 1989.

50 Interview with Carla Leone. This *may* in fact be an anecdote about *Once Upon a Time in the West*, where there are small children in the Flagstone station sequence, and the Leone girls were photographed on set.

51 Luis Beltran interview, 18 September 1998.

52 Carla Leone interview.

53 Lhassa, pp. 201–214; Hubert Niogret: *Ennio Morricone sur trois notes* (*Positif*, 266, April 1983, pp. 2–11); interview with Ennio Morricone for *Viva Leone!*, November 1989; Simsolo, pp. 118–119; De Fornari, p. 165.

54 *Ennio Morricone*, BBC television documentary, directed by David Thompson (spring 1995).

55 Sergio Miceli, loc. cit; and Miceli: *Morricone, La Musica, Il Cinema* (Ricordi Mucchi, 1994; Le Sfere No. 23).

56 Author's interview with Sergio Donati, 23 May 1998.

57 Sergio Miceli, loc. cit. And Miceli: *Morricone, La Musica, Il Cinema*, pp. 103–122.

58 Leone on the flashback: interview in *Take One*, May 1973, pp. 30–31; Simsolo, pp. 112–113.

59 Author's interview with Carlo Simi.

60 *Ennio Morricone*, BBC television documentary.

61 Author's interview with Gillo Pontecorvo, 7 October 1995.

62 Author's interview with Sergio Donati; and Sondra Locke: *The Good, The Bad and The Very Ugly* (William Morrow, New York, 1997) pp. 230–231.

63 Schickel, pp. 165–168.

64 Wagstaff, loc. cit.
65 Interview with Dario Argento for *Viva Leone!*, November 1989.


Chapter 7: *The Good, The Bad and The Ugly*

1 De Fornari: pp. 171–173; Cenk Kiral interviews, April–May 1998.
2 Author's interview with Sergio Donati, 23 May 1998.
3 Cenk Kiral interviews, April–May 1998; De Fornari, pp. 171–173; *Montpellier*, pp. 65–66.
4 Lambert, pp. 56–58; Simsolo, pp. 125–126.
5 Lambert, loc. cit; Simsolo, pp. 123–124; interview in *Cinéma 69*, November 1969, pp. 81–90.
6 Simsolo, pp. 123–124; Frayling: *Spaghetti Westerns*, pp. 121–137.
7 On Hollywood and the American Civil War, see Kim Newman: *Wild West Stories*, pp. 21–33, Jack Spears: *The Civil War on the Screen* (Barnes, New Jersey, 1977), pp. 11–16 and *The BFI Companion to the Western* (Deutsch, London, 1988), pp. 88–90.
8 Author's interview with Sergio Leone, February 1982.
9 Simsolo, p. 125.
10 Ambrose Bierce: *An Occurrence at Owl Creek Bridge and Other Stories* (Penguin, Middlesex, 1995) pp. 59–76.
11 Franco Ferrini's interview with Sergio Leone (*Bianco e Nero*, September–October 1971), pp. 37–42; author's interview with Carlo Simi; Hubert Corbin: *Carlo Simi – l'Amérique de Sergio Leone*, pp. 14–18.
12 Munn and Horner.
13 *Westerns all'Italiana* (Anaheim, California) No. 49, 'Eli Wallach issue', 1997; interview in *Sergio Leone . . . Les Westerns* (Blue Dahlia/ Canal Plus, 1997); interview in Eli Wallach video (Bill Shaffer, 1991); interview by Alvin H. Marill (*Films in Review*, August–September 1983, pp. 400–408).
14 Johnstone, p. 46; *Sergio Leone . . . Les Westerns*, interview with Clint Eastwood; Richard Schickel, pp. 174–175; see also chapter 5, note 41.
15 Bound transcript of seminar, in the AFI library, Los Angeles.
16 Frayling: *Spaghetti Westerns*, pp. 139, 157; Simsolo, pp. 121–122; *Cinéma 69*, November 1969. This was a favourite Leone reference, post-1968.
17 Cenk Kiral interviews, April–May 1998.
18 Author's interview with Sergio Donati, 23 May 1998. See Louis–Ferdinand Céline (tr. John Marks): *Journey to the End of the Night* (Chatto & Windus, London, 1934). Sergio Leone often referred to the novel: see, among many examples, Simsolo, pp. 83, 173–4; interview in *Cinéma 69*.
19 Author's interview with Fulvio Morsella, 24 May 1998.
20 Francesco Mininni: *Leone* (Il castoro cinema, Florence, 139, January–February 1989) p. 6; also Simsolo, p. 122.
21 Author's interview with Sergio Donati; Cenk Kiral interviews with Luciano Vincenzoni, April–May 1998.
22 Simsolo, pp. 124–125.
23 Author's interview with Sergio Donati.
24 De Fornari, pp. 171–173.
25 Lorenzo Codelli: interview with Age and Scarpelli (*Positif*, 193, May 1977, pp. 2–9).
26 Simsolo, pp. 131–132.
27 Author's interview with Carla Leone.
28 Schickel, pp. 169–170.

29 Patrick McGilligan and Paul Buhle: *Tender Comrades – a backstory of the Hollywood blacklist* (St Martin's Press, New York, 1997), interview with Mickey Knox, pp. 385–387; Cenk Kiral's interviews with Mickey Knox, 18 January and 1 February 1988.

30 McGilligan and Buhle, op cit; Kiral interviews.

31 Author's interview with Sergio Donati; see also De Fornari, pp. 158–160.

32 Simsolo, p. 128.

33 Simsolo, pp. 126–127; author's interview with Sergio Leone, February 1982.

34 See note 13.

35 Eli Wallach: *In All Directions* (*Films and Filming*, May 1964, pp. 7–8).

36 *Westerns all'Italiana* No. 49, 'Eli Wallach issue'; interview by Marill in *Films in Review*, August–September 1983, pp. 400–408.

37 Simsolo, pp. 126–128.

38 Eli Wallach video (Bill Shaffer, 1991).

39 Schickel, pp. 174–175.

40 See, among many other versions, the reference in Clinch, pp. 60–72.

41 *Westerns all'Italiana*, No. 49.

42 Ibid.; and Eli Wallach video (Bill Shaffer, 1991).

43 Eli Wallach video (Bill Shaffer, 1991).

44 Simsolo, pp. 126–128. The sequence is a distant echo of James Cagney/Pat O'Brien gangster films too.

45 See Hubert Corbin: *Carlo Simi – l'Amérique de Sergio Leone*, pp. 14, 18.

46 Interview with Luca Morsella for *Viva Leone!* (November 1989).

47 De Fornari, pp. 172–173.

48 De Fornari, pp. 157–158.

49 Author's interview with Tonino Delli Colli, 24 October 1998; see also *Montpellier*, pp. 71–72.

50 *Sergio Leone . . . Les Westerns*, interview with Clint Eastwood.

51 Eli Wallach video (Bill Shaffer, 1991).

52 Simsolo, pp. 131–132.

53 Author's interview with Sergio Leone, February 1982; see also Simsolo, pp. 77–81, where Leone goes into some detail about his taste in paintings.

54 Author's interview with Tonino Valerii, 26 April 1997.

55 Author's interview with Carla Leone.

56 Author's interview with Sergio Donati.

57 Simsolo, pp. 77–81.

58 Ibid.

59 *Montpellier*, pp. 157–158; in conversation Delli Colli observed that Leone may have overdone the *explicit* references to paintings in order to impress arty interviewers.

60 *Simsolo*, pp. 128–129.

61 Author's interview with Allessandro Alessandroni, 22 May 1998.

62 Lhassa, pp. 57–72, 201–214.

63 Ibid, p. 237; also interview with Morricone for *Viva Leone!*, November 1989.

64 Interview in *Cinéma 69*, November 1969, pp. 81–90.

65 Simsolo, pp. 130–131. Delli Colli recalls that two cameras were used for Eli Wallach's run around the tombs, and that 'the rhythm was achieved in the editing room, with the music'.

66 Eli Wallach video (Bill Shaffer, 1991); Munn, pp. 53–57; Horner, pp. 43–60.

67 Interview with Dario Argento for *Viva Leone!*, November 1989; De Fornari, pp. 149–150.

68 De Fornari, pp. 150–151.

69 Author's interview with Sergio Donati; De Fornari, pp. 171–173; Cenk Kiral interviews, April–May 1998.
70 Author's interview with Sergio Donati.
71 Ibid.
72 Ibid.
73 Author's interview with Fulvio Morsella, 24 May 1998; see also De Fornari, p. 23 for Leone's version; also Simsolo, pp. 177–178.
74 *The Hoods* was first published in America in May 1953 (Crown Publishers Inc. for New American Library of World Literature, pp. 1–371). The first British edition was in September 1965 (New English Library, Four Square Books, pp. 1–416). It was dedicated 'to my true and loyal mob M,B,H & S'.
75 Lambert, pp. 79–82; *Take One*, May 1973, p. 27; Gilles Cèbe: *Sergio Leone*, pp. 46–47; Simsolo, pp. 135–136.
76 Author's interview with Sergio Donati; also De Fornari, pp. 159–160.
77 Interview in *Cinéma 69*, November 1969, pp. 81–90.
78 Author's interview with Carla Leone; Simsolo, pp. 135–136; Lambert, pp. 79–82.
79 Author's interview with Fulvio Morsella.
80 Author's interview with Sergio Leone, February 1982.

## Chapter 8: *Once Upon a Time in The West*

1 Enzo Ungari and Don Ranvaud: *Bertolucci by Bertolucci* (Plexus, London, 1988) p. 51; Bernardo Bertolucci: *Once Upon a Time in Italy* (*Film Comment*, July–August 1989), pp. 77–78; author's interview with Bertolucci, ICA, London, 25 February 1988; interview with Bertolucci in *Positif*, March 1973, p. 37.
2 De Fornari, pp. 149–151; interview with Dario Argento for *Viva Leone!*, November 1989; Luca Palmerini and Gaetano Mistretta: *Spaghetti Nightmares* (Fantasma Books, Florida, 1996) pp. 16–21.
3 Ungari and Ranvaud, childhood section.
4 Ungari and Ranvaud, op cit; author's interview, 25 February 1988.
5 De Fornari, pp. 151–153; author's interview.
6 Author's interview with Carla Leone, 1 July 1994.
7 Simsolo, pp. 135–137.
8 De Fornari, pp. 149–151.
9 *Positif*, March 1973, p. 37.
10 Author's interview with Sergio Leone, February 1982.
11 *Positif*, March 1973, p. 37; De Fornari, pp. 151–153.
12 De Fornari, pp. 149–151; interview with Dario Argento for *Viva Leone!*, November 1989; *Positif*, March 1973, p. 37.
13 Author's interview with Tonino Delli Colli, Montpellier, 24 October 1998.
14 Interview with Dario Argento for *Viva Leone!*, November 1989.
15 Author's interview with Bernardo Bertolucci, 25 February 1988; Frayling: *Spaghetti Westerns*, p. 195.
16 Author's interview with Bertolucci; interview with Argento for *Viva Leone!*
17 Author's interview with Sergio Leone, February 1982.
18 Author's interview with Bertolucci.
19 Ibid.
20 See James K. Lyon: *Bertolt Brecht in America* (Methuen, London, 1982) pp. 3–39 and John Willett: *Brecht in Context* (Methuen, London 1984).
21 Author's interview with Sergio Leone, February 1982.

22 De Fornari, pp. 149–151.

23 Author's interview with Sergio Leone; Simsolo, pp. 100–101, 143–144.

24 Author's interview with Sergio Leone, February 1982.

25 See, among many other sources, Dan Ford: *The Unquiet Man* (William Kimber, London, 1979).

26 Frayling: *Spaghetti Westerns*, p. 129.

27 Author's interviews with Raffaella and Carla Leone, 1 July 1994.

28 De Fornari, pp. 151–153.

29 Ibid.

30 Author's interview with Sergio Leone.

31 De Fornari, pp. 149–151.

32 Author's interview with Sergio Donati, 23 May 1998.

33 Ibid.

34 Ibid.

35 Among many examples, interview with Dario Argento for *Viva Leone!*, December 1989.

36 The details of 'who did what', of the length of the treatment, and of the extent of Argento's contribution, were the subject of a heated internet exchange, 22 July 1988.

37 Author's interview with Sergio Donati.

38 De Fornari, pp. 158–160.

39 Ibid., pp. 151–153; also *Film Comment*, July–August 1989, pp. 77–78.

40 Braucourt, pp. 81–90; also Simsolo, pp. 139–141.

41 Author's interview with Carla Leone, 1 July 1994; see also Gianni Di Claudio: *Directed by Sergio Leone*, pp. 94–95. Some Internet buffs have claimed that the heavily disguised Leone never in fact appeared in this film. But his participation is confirmed by everyone I have spoken to about it.

42 Simsolo, pp. 137–139; also *Sergio Leone . . . Les Westerns* (Blue Dahlia/ Canal Plus, 1997) for the press conference of spring 1967 and (ed.) Danny Peary: *Close-ups* (Galahad Books, New York, 1978) pp. 535–536 'Sergio Leone remembers Henry Fonda'.

43 Henry Fonda (and Howard Teichmann): *My Life* (New American Library, New York, 1981) pp. 305–307; also Fonda: *Dialogue on Film* (American Film Institute, November, 1973).

44 Simsolo, pp. 137–139.

45 Cenk Kiral interviews with Mickey Knox, 18 January and 1 February 1998.

46 Simsolo, loc. cit.

47 Frayling: *Spaghetti Westerns*, pp. 141–145.

48 Simsolo, loc. cit.

49 Henry Fonda (and Howard Teichmann): *My Life*, pp. 305–307; see also AFI: *Dialogue on Film*.

50 De Fornari, p. 19.

51 Simsolo, loc. cit.

52 (ed.) Peary, pp. 535–536.

53 Cenk Kiral interviews with Mickey Knox.

54 Ibid; see also Patrick McGilligan and Paul Buhle: *Tender Comrades* (St Martin's Press, New York, 1997) pp. 351–388.

55 (ed.) Peary, loc. cit.; Simsolo, pp. 137–139.

56 Author's conversation with John Landis, London, 21 January 1998.

57 Schickel, p. 184.

58 Simsolo, pp. 139–140.

59 Jerry Vermilye: *The Films of Charles Bronson* (Citadel Press, New York, 1980) pp. 153–158; Steven Whitney: *Charles Bronson, Superstar* (Dell, New York, 1978) pp. 148–150.
60 Simsolo, pp. 139–141; *Cinéma 69*, November 1969, pp. 81–90.
61 Simsolo, loc. cit.
62 Vermilye, and Whitney, loc. cit.
63 Interview with Franco De Gemini, *Westerns all'Italiana* (Anaheim, California) vol. 1, no. 2.
64 De Fornari, pp. 155–156.
65 Simsolo, pp. 141–142.
66 Ibid.
67 De Fornari, pp. 158–160.
68 Simsolo, pp. 141–142.
69 Author's interview with Fulvio Morsella, 24 May 1998.
70 Simsolo, p. 143.
71 De Fornari, pp. 155–156.
72 Claudia Cardinale (with Anna Maria Mori): *Lo, Claudia – Tu, Claudia* (Edizione Frassinelli, 1995), pp. 150–152.
73 De Fornari, pp. 155–156; Cardinale, pp. 150–152; interview in *Photoplay*, November 1968, pp. 13–15, 55.
74 *Photoplay*, November 1968, pp. 13–15, 55.
75 Ibid.
76 Ibid.
77 De Fornari, pp. 155–156.
78 Ibid., p. 19.
79 Author's interview with Tonino Valerii, Udine, 26 April 1997.
80 De Fornari, pp. 155–156.
81 Simsolo, pp. 141–142.
82 *Cinéma 69*, November 1969, pp. 81–90.
83 Author's interview with Sergio Donati, 23 May 1998.
84 De Fornari, p. 165; interview with Ennio Morricone for *Viva Leone!*, November 1989.
85 Lhassa, pp. 57–72, 201–214. On the music for *Once Upon a Time in the West*, see Robert C. Cumbrow: *Once Upon a Time: The Films of Sergio Leone* (Scarecrow, New Jersey, 1987) pp. 199–216; also H.J. de Boer and M. van Wouw: *Ennio Morricone Musicography* (ISV, Amsterdam, 1990) pp. 60–76.
86 Simsolo, pp. 146–147; Lhassa, loc. cit.
87 Author's interview with Alessandro Allessandroni, 22 May 1998.
88 Woody Strode (and Sam Young): *Goal Dust* (Madison Books, New York, 1990) pp. 233–237.
89 Interview with Ennio Morricone for *Viva Leone!*, November 1989.
90 Author's interview with Carlo Simi, Montpellier, 24 October 1984; also Corbin: *Carlo Simi – l'Amérique de Sergio Leone*, p. 20.
91 Lhassa, loc. cit.
92 Ennio Morricone interview with Hubert Niogret, *Positif.* 266, April 1983.
93 *Photoplay*, November 1968, pp. 13–15, 55.
94 Ibid. Corbin: *Carlo Simi*, pp. 20–24.
95 Ibid.; also author's interview with Carlo Simi, 24 October 1998.
96 Ibid.
97 Author's interview with Sergio Leone, February 1982; also De Fornari, pp. 20–21.
98 Corbin, loc. cit.

# NOTES

99 See Carlo Gaberscek: *Il West di John Ford* (Arti Grafiche Friuliane, 1994) pp. 81–3; also Carlo Gaberscek: *Dove Hollywood ha creato il West* (Udine, 1988) pp. 28–29.

100 De Fornari, pp. 171–173.

101 Author's interview with Tonino Delli Colli, Rome, 18 December 1981.

102 De Fornari, p. 20.

103 Author's interview with Sergio Leone, February 1982; Cenk Kiral interviews with Mickey Knox, January–February 1998.

104 Author's interview with Carla Leone, 1 July 1994.

105 Author's interview with Sergio Leone.

106 Simsolo, pp. 144–145.

107 Author's interview with Sergio Donati.

108 The original scenes have been published in Franco Ferrini: *L'Antiwestern e il caso Leone* (*Bianco e Nero*, September/October 1971) pp. 43–60; see also Frayling: *Spaghetti Westerns*, pp. 269–279.

109 Author's interview with Tonino Valerii, Udine, 26 April 1997.

110 Author's interview with Sergio Leone.

111 Cenk Kiral interviews with Mickey Knox, January–February 1998.

112 Kiral, loc. cit.; McGilligan and Buhle, pp. 358, 385–7.

113 Kiral, loc. cit.; author's interview with Sergio Donati.

114 McGilligan and Buhle, pp. 385–387.

115 McGilligan and Buhle, pp. 363–364.

116 Author's interview with Sergio Leone; Luca Morsella confirms that this was a favourite Leone story.

117 Author's interview with Luca Morsella, Rome, 21 December 1991.

118 Author's interview with Sergio Leone.

119 Simsolo, p. 147, *Cinéma 69*, pp. 81–90.

120 Author's interview with Sergio Leone. In Britain, Paramount could not decide whether to market the film as an 'epic' (with a poster showing the main characters standing on the front of a train) or as an 'action film' (with the three *pistoleri* biting the dust). Female interviewees preferred the former; male the latter. See *Once Upon a Time in the West – advertisement test* (London, 1968).

121 John Boorman: *Money into Light – A Diary* (Faber and Faber, London, 1985) pp. 22–23.

122 Author's interview with Sergio Leone, 1982; also Simsolo, pp. 207–208.

123 Wenders' review in (ed.) Sheila Johnson: *Wim Wenders BFI Dossier*, No.10 (1981), pp. 45–46; also Wenders: *Emotion Pictures* (Faber and Faber, London, 1989) pp. 24–25. Author's interview with Wim Wenders, on the road to Cambridge, May 1984.

124 Bertolucci in *Positif*, March 1973, p. 37; author's interview with Umberto Eco, Milan, May 1984.

125 Cenk Kiral interviews with Luciano Vincenzoni, April–May 1998.

126 Author's interview with Sergio Donati, 23 May 1998.

127 Bertolucci, in *Film Comment*, July–August 1989, pp. 77–78.

## Chapter 9: *Keep Your Head Down*

1 Simsolo, pp. 149–151.

2 Ibid. pp. 81–83.

3 See Gilles Gressard: *Sergio Leone* (J'ai lu, Paris, 1989) pp. 100 ff.

4 Author's interview with Fulvio Morsella, 24 May 1998.

5 Author's interview with Tonino Valerii, Udine, 26 April 1997.

6 Author's interview with Sergio Leone, February 1982.

7 Simsolo, p. 149.
8 See Paul Ginsborg: *A History of Contemporary Italy* (Penguin, Middlesex, 1990) pp. 254–297, 298–347; also (ed.) Gaston Haustrate: *Le cinéma Italien des années soixante* (74, Sept–Oct 1974), pp. 34–265.
9 Interview with Leone in *Take One*, May 1973, pp. 28–9; Simsolo, pp. 149, 159–160; (ed.) Franca Faldini and Goffredo Fofi: *L'avventurosa storia del cinema Italiano 1960–69* (Feltrinelli, Milan, 1981) pp. 300–303.
10 *Take One*, pp. 28–29.
11 Simsolo, pp. 100–101, 164; author's interview with Sergio Leone, February 1982.
12 De Fornari, pp. 22–23.
13 Faldini and Fofi, pp. 302–305
14 See James Roy Macbean: *Film and Revolution* (Indiana University Press, 1975) and Frayling: *Spaghetti Westerns*, pp. 217–244.
15 Faldini and Fofi, p. 301; Luca Beatrice: *Al cuore, Ramon, al cuore* (Tarab, Florence, 1996) pp. 130–134; Christopher Frayling: *The Wretched of the Earth* (*Sight & Sound*, June 1993, pp. 26–29).
16 Faldini and Fofi, p. 306; Beatrice, pp. 156–160.
17 Piernico Solinas: *Gillo Pontecorvo's The Battle of Algiers* (Scribners, New York, 1973) pp. 192–201; Faldini and Fofi, pp. 302, 305; author's interview with Gillo Pontecorvo, Rome, 7 October 1995.
18 Author's interview with Marchent, Udine, 26 April 1997.
19 Author's interview with Franco Nero, Udine, 27 April 1997.
20 Author's interview with Sergio Donati, 23 May 1998.
21 Frayling, *Spaghetti Westerns*, pp. 225–226.
22 Simsolo, pp. 151–154.
23 Author's interview with Sergio Donati.
24 Author's interview with Sergio Donati; Eli Wallach in Bill Shaffer video, 1991.
25 Simsolo, pp. 151–153.
26 Peter Bogdanovich: *Two Beeg Green Eyes* (*New York*, 26 November 1973).
27 Ibid. Cenk Kiral interviews with Luciano Vincenzoni, April–May 1998.
28 Bogdanovich, loc. cit; Ian Hamilton: *Writers in Hollywood 1915–51* (Heinemann, London, 1990) pp. 166–180; Peter Bogdanovich: *John Ford* (University of California Press, Berkeley, 1978).
29 Diego Gabutti: *C'era una volta in America* (Rizzoli, Milan, 1984) pp. 115–118; *Take One*, May 1973 p. 28.
30 Ibid.
31 Author's interview with Peter Bogdanovich, London, 26 November 1982.
32 Ibid.
33 Cenk Kiral interview with Vincenzoni, April–May 1998; author's interview with Peter Bogdanovich.
34 Author's interview with Sergio Donati, 23 May 1998.
35 Simsolo, p. 153. No biographies of Sam Peckinpah even mention this intriguing possibility, or indeed the undoubted influence of Leone on Peckinpah – very different in attitudes though they were.
36 Cenk Kiral interviews with Vincenzoni, April–May 1998.
37 *Montpellier*, p. 66.
38 Author's interview with Sergio Donati; Leone's version is in *Bianco e Nero*, September/October 1971, pp. 37–42.
39 Author's interview with Carla Leone, 1 July 1994; Simsolo, pp. 153–154
40 Simsolo, pp. 158–159, Cèbe, pp. 34–5, Lambert, pp. 85–88.

41  *Take One*, May 1973, pp. 27–28.

42  Simsolo, pp. 161–163.

43  Ibid. pp. 148–149.

44  Ibid., pp. 161–163; *Bianco e Nero* September/October 1971, pp. 37–42.

45  Simsolo, pp. 159–161; *Bianco e Nero* September/October 1971, pp. 37–42; Cèbe pp. 49–50.

46  Sergio Leone: *A John Ford* (*Corriere della Sera*, 20 August 1983); Lambert, p. 92; *Take One*, May 1973, pp. 27–28. Simsolo translates the Ford essay into French, pp. 203–207.

47  De Fornari, pp. 171–173.

48  Author's interview with Sergio Donati.

49  Cenk Kiral interviews with De Fornari, pp. 158–60 for background.

50  Lhassa, pp. 95–97, 201–214; Simsolo, p. 119; on the music for *Giu la Testa*, see *Ennio Morricone Musicography*, pp. 118–120, and Cumbrow, pp. 205, 208–209.

51  Hubert Niogret: *Ennio Morricone* (*Positif* 266, April 1983); De Fornari, p. 165; interview with Ennio Morricone for *Viva Leone!*, November 1989.

52  Sergio Miceli's brochure in Ennio Morricone: *The Italian Western*, RCA boxed set ML/MK 31543; Lhassa, pp. 201–214.

53  Gabutti, pp. 116–117; *Take One*, May 1973 p. 28; Simsolo, pp. 158–160. The complete release script of *Giù la testa* is published in *Bianco e Nero*, September/October 1971, pp. 61–107.

54  Gabutti, loc. cit.

55  Cumbrow, pp. 85–98.

56  Simsolo, pp. 161–163.

57  *Take One*, May 1973, p. 31.

58  Claire Bloom: *Limelight and After* (Weidenfeld and Nicolson, London, 1982) pp. 152–155; see also Claire Bloom: *Leaving a Doll's House* (Virago, London, 1996) pp. 117–136.

59  *Take One*, May 1973, pp. 27–28.

60  Simsolo, pp. 155–157; also De Fornari, p. 22.

61  Author's interview with Carla Leone, 1 July 1994.

62  Ibid.

63  Cenk Kiral, interviews with Luciano Vincenzoni, April–May 1998; De Fornari, pp. 158–160 for background; author's interview with Sergio Donati.

64  *Photoplay*, September 1972; Barbra Paskin: interview with Rod Steiger on the set of *Giu la testa* in Almeria (typescript).

65  Barbra Paskin interview with Rod Steiger, California, June 1997.

66  Author's interview with Sergio Donati.

67  Barbra Paskin interview with Rod Steiger, June 1997.

68  Michael Munn, interview with James Coburn (*Film Review*, December 1981, p. 11).

69  Simsolo, pp. 155, 158.

70  Barbra Paskin interview with James Coburn on the set of *Giù la testa* in Almeria (typescript).

71  Simsolo, p. 155.

72  Author's interview with Carlo Simi, 24 October 1998; also Corbin, p. 29. Filming in Guadix was extensively covered by photographer Yvan Dalain and the results published in Dalain: *Western Spaghetti* (Photoarchives, editions Ides et Calendes, Neuchatel, 1995).

73  John Martin interview with David Warbeck (*Giallo Pages*, 1, pp. 18–19); see also Palmerini and Mistretta: *Spaghetti Nightmares*, pp. 152–157

74  De Fornari, pp. 21–23.

75  Gianni Di Claudio: *Directed by Sergio Leone*, p. 138; Bertolucci in *Positif*, March 1973, p. 37; Gilles Gressard: *Sergio Leone* (J'ai lu, Paris, 1989) pp. 98–100. Pasolini defended *Giù la testa* against left-wing dismissal, saying that 'Leone is incapable of making an uninteresting film'.

76  Frayling: *Spaghetti Westerns*, pp. 184–185, 232–233, citing De Fornari: *Sergio Leone* (Milan, 1977).

77  Simsolo, pp. 165–166.

78  On Pinelli and the Piazza Fontana massacre, see Ginsborg, pp. 333–334; also Enzo De Paoli: *Il Cinema e la Prima Republica* (Marna, Como, 1995) pp. 88–99 and Di Claudio, p. 192.

79  Author's interview with Luca Morsella, 24 May 1998.

## Chapter 10: *Entr'acte*

1  Author's interview with Tonino Valerii, Udine, 26 April 1997; see also *Montpellier*, pp. 61–64 and De Fornari, pp. 168–170.

2  Bogdanovich: *Two Beeg Green Eyes*.

3  Author's interview with Tonino Valerii; also interview for *Viva Leone!*, November 1989.

4  Ibid.

5  Interview with Ennio Morricone for *Viva Leone!*, November 1989.

6  Simsolo, pp. 173, 183–184; Lambert, p. 89.

7  Author's interview with Fulvio Morsella, Rome, 24 May 1998.

8  Diego Gabutti, pp. 21–31, 135–137.

9  Interview with Sergio Leone for *Visions* (Large Door/Channel 4), November 1983; Simsolo, pp. 150, 167–168.

10  Ibid.

11  Diego Gabutti, pp. 136–137.

12  Author's interview with Sergio Donati, 23 May 1998.

13  Interview by Tim Lucas with Ernesto Gastaldi in *Video Watchdog*, 39, 1997, pp. 48–51.

14  See Ron Chernow: *John Ford – The Last Frontiersman* (*Ramparts*, April 1974) pp. 45–48 for an account of his death.

15  Lambert, p. 89; Frayling: *Spaghetti Westerns*, pp. 247–255.

16  Interview with Ennio Morricone, *Positif*, April 1983; also interview with the composer for *Viva Leone!*, November 1989.

17  Author's interview with Tonino Valerii; interview for *Viva Leone!*, November 1989; De Fornari, pp. 166–170; *Montpellier*, pp. 61–64.

18  Author's interview with Sergio Leone, February 1982; see also Simsolo, pp. 169–170.

19  For background on Hill and Spencer, see (ed.) R. Jacquet: *Terence Hill and Bud Spencer* (Star System 2, Paris, 1980). Jacquet wrongly states, though, that Mario Girotti is the son of Massimo Girotti of *Ossessione* fame – a mistake often made.

20  Author's interview with Gillo Pontecorvo, Rome, 7 October 1995.

21  Interview with Tonino Valerii for *Viva Leone!*, November 1989.

22  Author's interview with Tonino Valerii; also De Fornari, pp. 168–170.

23  Author's interview with Fulvio Morsella, 24 May 1998.

24  Author's interview with Tonino Valerii; also De Fornari, pp. 168–170.

25  Ibid.; also *Montpellier*, pp. 61–64.

26  Neil Summers: *Terence Hill and My Name is Nobody* (*Westerns all'Italiana*, 26, Summer 1990).

27  Francesco Minnini: *Leone* (Il castoro cinema, 139, Rome, January–February 1989)

p. 11. This statement, which Leone concluded by stating 'without false modesty I directed all the scenes the public remembered the most', particularly infuriates Valerii. 'Of course it is a lie . . . and does wrong to the name of Sergio who gained no advantage whatsoever from uttering it.'

28 Interview with Ernesto Gastaldi, *Video Watchdog*, 1997, pp. 48–51.

29 De Fornari, pp. 168–170; interview with Valerii for *Viva Leone!*, November 1989.

30 Simsolo, p. 168; Henry Fonda: *My Life*, p. 312; Beatrice, pp. 150–154.

31 Stephen Mackey: *An Analysis of Les Valseuses by Bertrand Blier* (RCA MA dissertation, unpublished, 1993); Simsolo, p. 171; Beatrice, pp. 132–134.

32 Ibid.

33 Author's interview with Fulvio Morsella, 24 May 1998.

34 Ibid.

35 De Fornari, p. 96; Simsolo, pp. 171–172.

36 Diego Gabutti, pp. 136ff; Simsolo, p. 172.

37 Author's interview with Fulvio Morsella, 24 May 1998.

38 Ibid.

39 Author's interview with Sergio Donati, 23 May 1998.

40 Ibid.; Georgette Ranucci and Stefanella Ughi: *Carlo Verdone* (Dino Andino, Rome, 1997), pp. 3–12, 17.

41 Enrico Giaconelli: *La commedia all'Italiana* (Gremese, Rome, 1990) pp. 122–125.

42 Interview with Sergio Leone for *Visions* (Large Door/Channel 4), November 1983; compare Verdone's account in Ranucci and Ughi, pp. 3–12, 16–21

43 Author's interview with Luca Morsella, 24 May 1998; Ranucci and Ughi, pp. 21–23.

44 Author's interview with Raffaelle Leone, 24 May 1998; Ranucci and Ughi, pp. 32–34.

45 Simsolo, pp. 175–176; *Catalogue de la Production Cinématographique Française t.II* (Centre National de la Cinématographie, Paris, 1975). Many of Sergio Leone's television commercials were screened on videotape as part of the exhibition *Omaggio a Sergio Leone*, Galleria D'Arte 'La Scaletta', Rome, December 1991.

46 De Fornari, p. 177; Simsolo, pp. 175–176; *Montpellier*, p. 87; Corbin, p. 41.

47 On Barthes and car advertising, see Bent Fausing: *The Genius of Design* (in (ed.) Susann Vihma: *Objects and Images*, UIAH, Helsinki, 1992), pp. 180–192.

48 Author's interview with Luca Morsella, 20 December 1991.

49 Author's interview with Luca Morsella, 24 May 1998.

50 Simsolo, pp. 175–176.

51 On Leone's various projects, see Cèbe, pp. 51–53; Di Claudio, p. 192; Lambert, pp. 93–95; De Fornari, p. 178; *Cinéma 69* interview, pp. 89–90.

52 Author's interview with Fulvio Morsella, 24 May 1998.

53 Cenk Kiral interviews with Luciano Vincenzoni, April–May 1998.

54 Author's interview with Luca Morsella, 24 May 1998.

55 David Thomson: *Leonesque* (*American Film*, 10 September 1989, pp. 26–30, 56).

56 Author's interview with Carla Leone, 1 July 1994.

## Chapter 11: *Once Upon a Time in America*

1 Harry Grey: *The Hoods* (Crown Publishers Inc for New American Library of World Literature, May 1953). The paperback edition was issued in England and Italy in autumn 1965.

2 Author's interview with Fulvio Morsella, 24 May 1998; Gabutti, pp. 21–34; Di Claudio, pp. 94–5.

3 Interviews with Sergio Leone in *Positif*, June 1984, pp. 6–15; *American Film*, June 1984,

pp. 23–25; *La Revue du Cinéma*, June 1984, pp. 50–60; *Film Comment*, August 1984, pp. 21–23; *Cahiers du Cinéma*, May 1984, pp. 7–11, 56–90.
4  Edward Behr: *Prohibition* (BBC Books, London, 1997) p. 175.
5  Rick Cohen: *Tough Jews* (Cape, London, 1998) pp. 23–67; 130–132. See also, among many other sources, Robert Lacey: *Little Man – Meyer Lansky and the Gangster Life* (Little, Brown & Co, Boston, 1991).
6  See Neal Gabler: *An Empire of Their Own* (W.H. Allen, London, 1989) pp. 187–236; Philip French: *Kings of the Underworld* (*The Movie*, 4, Orbis, London, pp. 68–72).
7  Gabler, pp. 18–20.
8  On this aspect of the history of the gangster film, see John McCarty: *Hollywood Gangland* (St Martin's Press, New York, 1993) pp. 55–59; Raymond Durgnat: *The Gangster File* (*Monthly Film Bulletin*, April 1991) pp. 93–96; Carlos Clarens: *Crime Movies* (Da Capo, New York, 1997) pp. 100–170; (ed.) Phil Hardy: *BFI Companion to Crime* (Cassell, London, 1997); Ian Cameron: *A Pictorial History of Crime Films* (Hamlyn, London, 1975); Colin McArthur: *Underworld USA* (Secker & Warburg/BFI London, 1972) pp. 11–70.
9  Author's interview with Sergio Donati, 23 May 1998; De Fornari, pp. 158–160. On the Lower East Side in the 1920s and 1930s, see Beth S. Wenger: *New York Jews and the Great Depression* (Yale University Press, 1996) pp. 83–84.
10  Robert Warshaw: *The Gangster as Tragic Hero* (in *The Immediate Experience*, Atheneum, New York, 1975, pp. 127–134).
11  Simsolo, pp. 177–179.
12  Gabutti, pp. 21–31.
13  Ibid.; *Cahiers du Cinéma*, May 1984, pp. 7–11, 56–90.
14  Gabutti, loc. cit.
15  Author's interview with Fulvio Morsella, 24 May 1998.
16  Gabutti, loc. cit.
17  For various versions of this statement, see interviews listed in note 3.
18  De Fornari, pp. 23–26.
19  Brian Case: *Once Upon a Time* interview (*Sunday Times Magazine*, London, 30 September 1984).
20  On the 'friendship' theme in these three films, see Trevor Willsmer: *Leone's Fairytales* (*Movie Collector*, vol. 2, issue 2, 14 March 1995, pp. 62–67).
21  Gabutti, loc. cit.
22  Ibid.; De Fornari, pp. 23–26.
23  Simsolo, pp. 177–181.
24  Author's interview with Sergio Donati; Cenk Kiral interviews with Luciano Vincenzoni, April–May 1998; interview with Ernesto Gastaldi in *Video Watchdog*, 1997, pp. 48–51.
25  Guy Braucourt: interview with Gérard Départieu in *Ecran 76*, 15 February 1976; Cèbe, pp. 51–54.
26  Simsolo, pp. 179, 184–185.
27  Author's interview with Luca Morsella, 24 May 1998.
28  *Montpellier*, pp. 72–73.
29  Author's interview with Carla Leone, 1 July 1994.
30  Author's interview with Luca Morsella, 24 May 1998.
31  Interview with Ernesto Gastaldi in *Video Watchdog*, 1997, pp. 48–51; Jean A. Gili interview with Sergio Leone, *Positif*, June 1984, pp. 6–15.
32  *Montpellier*, pp. 72–73; Simsolo, pp. 185–187.
33  Pete Hamill: *Once Upon a Time in America* (*American Film*, June 1984, pp. 20–29, 54).
34  Ibid.

35 Simsolo, pp. 186–187.
36 Interview by Louise Swan with John Milius, California, October 1995 for the author's BBC radio series *Print the Legend*; also author's interview with John Milius, London, 1981.
37 Simsolo, p. 186; Gabutti, p. 32.
38 Gabutti, loc. cit.; Cèbe, p. 51.
39 Carl Rollyson: *The Lives of Norman Mailer* (Paragon House, New York, 1991) p. 275. Rollyson dates the Manila trip to the 'fall of 1975'. *The Los Angeles Times* of 10 June 1984, on the other hand, dates Mailer's involvement to 1970 (sec c:23), which is impossible since Leone did not yet own the screen rights to the novel. Norman Mailer has not responded to my faxed requests for further information.
40 *Montpellier*, pp. 72–73; De Fornari, pp. 161–163 (Ferrini), 163–164 (Medioli).
41 Cenk Kiral's interviews with Mickey Knox, January–February 1998.
42 See Enzo Ungari and Don Ranvaud: *Bertolucci by Bertolucci* (Plexus, London, 1982).
43 De Fornari, pp. 163–164.
44 Ibid.
45 Cuel and Villiers: *interview with Medioli* (*Cinématographe*, 72, November 1981, pp. 21–23); Cèbe, pp. 52–53.
46 De Fornari, pp. 23–26; Gabutti, pp. 21–31; Simsolo, pp. 181–182.
47 Simsolo, pp. 182–184.
48 Burton Turkus and Sid Feder: *Murder Inc* (Da Capo, New York, 1992) especially pp. 46–47, 80–85, 94–95, 331–362.
49 Jean A. Gili: *Interview with Sergio Leone* (*Positif*, June 1984, pp. 6–15).
50 Turkus and Feder, pp. 46–47.
51 Turkus and Feder, pp. 80–85, 331–362. The gangster biographies in print at the time Leone and his team were researching included Ted Addy: *The Dutch Schultz Story* (Monarch, Connecticut, 1962), Leo Katcher: *The Big Bankroll – The Life and Times of Arnold Rothstein* (Da Capo, New York, 1958), Paul Sann: *Kill the Dutchman* (Da Capo, New York, 1971) and Dean Jennings: *We Only Kill Each Other* (Fawcett World, 1968). But Turkus and Feder seems to have been the main historical source.
52 Simsolo, pp. 180–181.
53 De Fornari, pp. 163–164; *Montpellier*, pp. 76–77.
54 The *Western Movies* book was by Walter C. Clapham (Galley Press, London, 1976) p. 146; the Ferrini interview is in De Fornari, pp. 161–163.
55 De Fornari, pp. 161–163; Jorge Luis Borges: *A Universal History of Infamy* (Penguin, Middlesex, 1975) pp. 51–60 on 'Monk Eastman, purveyor of iniquities'.
56 Author's interview with Luca Morsella, 24 May 1998.
57 Cèbe, pp. 51–52; interviews with Sergio Leone in *Cahiers du Cinéma*, May 1984, *La Revue du Cinéma* , June 1984 and *Positif*, June 1984.
58 Script of *Once Upon a Time in America* dated October 1981 (Embassy International Pictures).
59 *Montpellier*, p. 73.
60 De Fornari, pp. 23–26.
61 On some of the genre elements in *Once Upon a Time*, and Leone's treatment of them, see Adrian Martin: *Once Upon a Time in America* (BFI, London, 1998).
62 On the 'opium' interpretation, see Nick Redman: *To Dream or Not to Dream* (*Movie Collector*, 14 March 1995, pp. 68–69), Chris Peachment: *Once Upon a Time in America* (Film Yearbook, 1986, pp. 96–97), and Adrian Martin, op cit. Leone's teasing statements about it include Simsolo, pp. 191–92.
63 For variations on this quote, see interviews in note 3.
64 Jean A. Gili: *Interview with Sergio Leone* (*Positif*, June 1984, pp. 6–15).

65 Simsolo, pp. 193–194.

66 Interview with Ennio Morricone for *Viva Leone!*, November 1989; also Lhassa, pp. 209–212, 243–244. On the music for *Once Upon a Time*, see Cumbrow, pp. 209–211 and *Ennio Morricone Musicography*, pp. 222–223.

67 Lhassa, loc. cit.

68 Leone may well have been introduced to Zamfir's work by the soundtrack of Peter Weir's *Picnic at Hanging Rock* (1975), a film he greatly admired.

69 Ennio Morricone interview for *Viva Leone!*; Lhassa, loc. cit.

70 Interviews with Leone in *Positif*, June 1984; *La Revue du Cinéma*, June 1984; *Cahiers du Cinéma*, May 1984.

71 Interview with Ennio Morricone for *Viva Leone!*, November 1989.

72 Simsolo p. 193; (ed.) Garofalo, pp. 9–15, Sergio Leone's 'presentation'.

73 Alexander Alland, Sr; *Jacob A. Riis, Photographer and Citizen* (Gordon Fraser, London, 1975); and Otto Steinert: *Jacob A. Riis* (Museum Folkwang Essen, November 1971). Riis's photograph of a market in Mulberry Street, 1900, is very similar to Leone's/Simi's street scenes in *Once Upon a Time*, while his 'What the Boys Learn on Their Street Playground' resembles the antics of Noodles and Max as children, and his 'Mullen's Alley, Cherry Street' is very like the alleyway near Gelly's Bar in the 1920s sequences. Also, Garofalo, op cit; *Once Upon a Time in America* production information (The Ladd Company, 1984).

74 Simsolo, loc. cit.; see also Gail Levin: *Edward Hopper – The Art and the Artist* (W.W. Norton, New York, 1980) especially pp. 45–61, 185–197, 264–279.

75 Simsolo, loc. cit.; see also Christopher Finch: *Norman Rockwell's America* (Harry Abrams, New York, 1975) especially pp. 48–78 ('Growing Up') and 268–305 ('*Evening Post* Covers'); and Thomas S. Buechner: *Norman Rockwell — A Sixty-year Retrospective* (Harry Abrams, New York, 1975) especially pp. 13–52 (on the 1910–1929 period).

76 Marilyn Cohen: *Reginald Marsh's New York* (Dover and the Whitney Museum, New York, 1983).

77 Garofolo, pp. 19–38.

78 De Fornari, pp. 157–158, *Montpellier*, p. 71, author's interview with Tonino Delli Colli, 24 October 1998 ('when discussing composition, we did talk about Norman Rockwell and Edward Hopper, but not while we were actually shooting. Just to set the scene').

79 Leone interview in *Positif*, June 1984, pp. 6–15.

80 Corbin, pp. 30–38.

81 Leone interview in *Positif*, June 1984, pp. 6–15.

82 Simsolo, pp. 187–188.

83 *Montpellier*, pp. 72–73.

84 De Fornari, pp. 23–26. Kevin Brownlow, *David Lean* (Richard Cohen Books, London, 1996), pp. 639–40.

85 Author's interview with Sergio Donati, 23 May 1998.

86 De Fornari, loc. cit.

87 *Cahiers du Cinéma*, May 1984, pp. 7–11.

88 De Fornari, pp. 171–173.

89 Author's interview with Luca Morsella, 24 May 1998.

90 Ibid.

91 Stuart M. Kaminsky: *American Film Genres* (second edition, Nelson–Hall, Chicago, 1985) pp. 47–48.

92 See Martin, pp. 25–27.

93 Author's interview with Luca Morsella.

94 Interview with Sergio Leone, *Positif*, June 1984, pp. 6–15.
95 *Montpellier*, p. 76.
96 Author's interview with Luca Morsella.
97 Ibid. This section is based on a close comparison between the script dated October 1981 and the shooting script in the BFI Library which was received on 27 March 1984.
98 De Fornari, pp. 23–26.
99 Author's interview with Luca Morsella, 22 May 1998.
100 Author's conversation with John Landis, 21 January 1998; see also review by Michael Sragow (reprinted in (ed.) Richard T. Jameson: *They Went Thataway*, National Society of Film Critics, San Francisco, 1994, pp. 12–16).
101 *C'era una volta il cinema*, directed by Gianni Minà, RAI, 1985.
102 Pete Hamill in *American Film*, June 1984, pp. 20–29
103 Gianni Minà documentary; *American Film*, June 1984. Also see John Parker: *De Niro* (Vista, London, 1995) pp. 190–203; Patrick Agan: *Robert De Niro* (Robert Hale, London, 1996) pp. 114–118; Andy Dougan: *Untouchable – Robert De Niro* (Virgin, London, 1997) pp. 199–214.
104 Variations on this story appear in many interviews of May–June 1984; see note 3.
105 Pete Hamill, loc. cit.
106 De Fornari, pp. 23–26; *American Film*, June 1984, pp. 23–25; *Film Comment*, August 1984, pp. 21–23.
107 *American Film*, June 1984, pp. 23–25.
108 *Montpellier*, pp. 76–77.
109 *La Revue du Cinéma*, June 1984, pp. 50–60; *Cahiers*, May 1984, pp. 56–90.
110 Dougan, pp. 199–214.
111 Simsolo, pp. 188–189.
112 Ibid.
113 De Fornari, pp. 155–156.
114 *Ciné Revue*, 11 August 1983, pp. 24–25.
115 Simsolo, pp. 188–189; De Fornari, pp. 25–26.
116 Interviews with James Woods in *American Film*, May 1990, pp. 51–53 and *Film Comment*, January–February 1997, pp. 58–59.
117 Ibid.
118 Robert De Niro in Gianna Minà's RAI documentary.
119 De Fornari, pp. 23–26.
120 Interview in *American Film*, May 1990, pp. 51–53.
121 Case: *Once Upon a Time*; the De Niro biographies listed in note 103; Minà's RAI documentary.
122 Author's interview with Raffaella Leone, 24 May 1998.
123 Hamill, pp. 20–29.
124 De Fornari, p. 25.
125 Author's interview with Elizabeth McGovern, London, 7 November 1997; also for subsequent quotes.
126 *Cahiers* interview, May 1984, pp. 7–11, 56–90.
127 For the critical reaction, see references in Adam Knee: *Notions of Authorship and the Reception of Once Upon a Time in America* (*Film Criticism*, Meadville, PA, vol. x, no. 1, Fall 1985, pp. 3–17).
128 Simsolo, pp. 195–197.
129 Interview in *American Film*, June 1984, pp. 23–25.
130 *La Revue du Cinéma*, June 1984, pp. 50–60; *Cahiers*, May 1984; *Positif*, June 1984, pp. 6–15; Simsolo, p. 194 for various versions of this idea.

131 De Fornari, pp. 157–158; author's interview with Tonino Delli Colli, 24 October 1998.
132 Gabutti, p. 34.
133 Simsolo, pp. 193–194.
134 Author's interview with Luca Morsella, 24 May 1998.
135 Interview in *Positif*, June 1984, pp. 6–15.
136 Corbin, p. 38.
137 Author's interview with Luca Morsella, 24 May 1998; also for subsequent quotations.
138 Pete Hamill, *American Film*, June 1984, pp. 20–29, 54.
139 Joe Klein: A Film Grows in Brooklyn (*New York*, 24 January 1983, pp. 16–17).
140 Interview with Luca Morsella for *Viva Leone!*, November 1989; *Montpellier*, p. 71; author's interview with Tonino Delli Colli, 24 October 1998.
141 Hamill, loc. cit.
142 De Fornari, pp. 23–26; and interviews listed in note 3.
143 *Variety*, 30 March 1983, p. 7.
144 Author's interview with Luca Morsella, 24 May 1998.
145 Hamill, loc. cit.
146 De Fornari, pp. 171–173.
147 *Montpellier*, p. 76.
148 Hamill, loc. cit.
149 Author's interview with Luca Morsella, 1 July 1994.
150 Author's interview with Luca Morsella, 24 May 1998; Corbin, p. 37.
151 For press reaction to these different versions, see Knee, op cit. *Variety* reported on 24 August 1983 (p. 13) that the film would 'unspool as one epic, not two'; on 21 March 1984 (p. 3) *Variety* headlined 'Sergio Leone reacts to threat to trim *Once Upon a Time*; on 13 June 1984 (p. 2) *Variety* covered 'Leone speaks out on recut America'.
152 Mary Corliss: *Once Upon a Time* (*Film Comment*, July–August 1984, pp. 18–21). She was the only major critic to *prefer* the cut version.
153 Simsolo, pp. 196–198.
154 *Hollywood Reporter*, 21 March 1984, p. 26 'Sergio Leone considers withdrawing his name'.
155 Leone on long films: interview for *Visions* documentary (Large Door/ Channel 4), November 1983.
156 *Variety*, 17 October 1984 (p. 5) 'Leone thanks critics at Fest conference'.
157 Author's interview with Elizabeth McGovern, 7 November 1997.
158 Interview with James Woods in *Empire*, June 1991.
159 *Montpellier*, p. 76.
160 Interview with Andrea Leone for *Viva Leone!*, November 1989.

## Chapter 12: *A Certain Cinema*

1 The *Leningrad* opening sequence is compiled from Gabutti, pp. 138–140; Simsolo, pp. 211–212; Di Claudio, pp. 18, 192; and reminiscences of various interviewees. Leone's primary source was Harrison E. Salisbury: *The 900 Days – The Siege of Leningrad* (reprint Da Capo, New York, 1985).
2 Di Claudio, loc. cit.
3 Gabutti, loc. cit.; Gianni Di Claudio, loc. cit.; Francesco Minnini, pp. 98–100. The *Potemkin* comparison was made by Leone himself: see Giles Gressard: *Sergio Leone* (Editions J'ai lu, Paris, 1989) p. 136.
4 Author's interview with Carla Leone, 1 July 1994.
5 Gabutti, loc. cit.

6  Author's interview with Sergio Donati, 23 May 1998.

7  Braucourt, pp. 89–90.

8  Liner notes by Philip Taylor for recording of Shostakovich's Seventh Symphony conducted by Gennadi Rozhdestvensky (Collets, CML 2036, 1991) and by Eric Roseberry for the Seventh Symphony conducted by Valeri Polyansky (Chandos, 9621, 1998).

9  Gressard, pp. 130–139; De Fornari, op cit. pp. 178–179; Di Claudio, loc. cit.; Simsolo, pp. 209–210.

10  Gabutti, loc. cit.; De Fornari, loc. cit.; Di Claudio, loc. cit.

11  Laurent Bachet: *Interview with Sergio Leone* (*Première* (French version), December 1988, p. 45). A very late interview.

12  See note 10. Leone tended to exaggerate his 'historical sources' as he retold the story. The anecdote about the performance of the Seventh during the 'victory celebration' is a garbled version of what happened at the Leningrad première in August 1942 when the surviving fourteen players of the Radio Orchestra, plus elderly and emaciated musicians, performed the piece. The story of Hitler printing tickets for a Wagner concert is based on his real-life plans to stage 'an elaborate military parade' in Palace Square. And, although Leone could not have known the fact, the famous photo of Shostakovich fighting fires has been proved a composite – issued for propaganda purposes.

13  Gabutti, p. 137–138.

14  Di Claudio, p. 192.

15  Gressard, p. 134.

16  *Screen International*, 22 December 1984, p. 6 ('Next project Soviet Union').

17  Giuletto Chiesa: *Leone a Mosca*, *L'Unità*, 12 January 1989 and 10 February 1989; *Screen International*, 11 February 1989.

18  De Fornari, pp. 178–179.

19  Gressard, pp. 136–137.

20  Bachet interview, *Première*, December 1988, p. 45.

21  Interview with Andrea Leone for *Viva Leone!*, November 1989.

22  Bachet interview, loc. cit.

23  Author's interviews with Luca Morsella, 2 July 1994 and 24 May 1998.

24  Author's interview with Sergio Donati, 23 May 1989.

25  *Montpellier*, p. 73 (Grimaldi), p. 71 (Delli Colli, plus author's interview 24 October 1998), pp. 76–79 (Leo Benvenuti). Benvenuti adds that Leone 'was unbeatable on the subject of Tom Mix, but his knowledge of Russian geography was more shaky', and that the screen writers' correspondence with Soviet officialdom began 'in the Brezhnev era, before the invention of faxes'. For background on the fortunes of *The 900 Days* see Salisbury's introduction to the Da Capo edition, pp. vii–x.

26  Author's interview with Sergio Donati.

27  Di Claudio, p. 18.

28  Brian Case: *Once Upon a Time* (*Sunday Times Magazine*, London, 30 September 1984).

29  See, among many references, Sergio Leone: *Per il novantenario del cinema* (*L'Unità*, 28 December 1985); Jean A. Gili: *Interview with Sergio Leone* (*Positif*, June 1984, pp. 14–15); interview for television documentary *Visions* (Large Door/ Channel 4), November 1983.

30  Morando Morandini: *Paradiso Lost* (*Sight and Sound*, June 1991, pp. 18–21); Simsolo, pp. 208–209; Di Claudio, p. 190.

31  Simsolo, loc. cit.

32  'Sergio Leone "films" his own football league cup', article in the Neapolitan newspaper *Gazette Dello Sport*, 10 May 1987.

33 Di Claudio, p. 192; Sergio Leone: *Venivamo da ogni parte della terra* (*Bianco e Nero*, Venezia 88 issue, December 1988 pp. 7–8).

34 Bernard Le Roy and Maurice Szafran: *The Illustrated History of Cigars* (Harold Starke publications, London, 1993; first published France, 1989) pp. 128–129.

35 *Montpellier*, p. 75.

36 Schickel: *Clint Eastwood*, pp. 438, 464.

37 Frayling: *Clint Eastwood*, pp. 64–65.

38 Ibid., pp. 25–26.

39 Author's interview with Luca Morsella, 24 May 1998; letter from Luca Morsella, 28 September 1994, pp. 1–3.

40 Author's interview with Sergio Donati, 23 May 1998.

41 Ibid.

42 Letter from Luca Morsella to author, 28 September 1994.

43 Cited in Di Claudio, p. 174.

44 Sergio Leone, Luca Morsella and Fabio Toncelli: *A Place Only Mary Knows* (treatment, written in Rome, dated 1988), pp. 1–27.

45 Ibid., pp. 26–27.

46 Author's interview with Luca Morsella, 24 May 1998.

47 Ibid.

48 Ibid.

49 Interview with Sergio Leone for *Visions* (Large Door/Channel 4), November 1983.

50 Author's interview with Fulvio Morsella, 24 May 1998. On Leone's reputation among critics, see Adrian Martin: *Once Upon a Time in America* (BFI, London 1998), especially the introduction.

51 Minnini, pp. 98–101; *Westerns all'Italiana*, 'In Memoriam Sergio Leone', Fall 1989; Di Claudio, p. 189. Schickel, p. 135, reports that Leone claimed to have been born in 1929 but 'in fact [he] was born 23 January 1921, nine years earlier than Clint'. This is wrong, as the school photo on the wall of Checco er Carettiere and interviews with relations confirm. He did, however, look much older than his age from the mid-1980s onwards.

52 Based on a home video, shot at Leone's funeral; and articles collected in *Westerns all'Italiana*, Winter 1989–1990.

53 Interview with Tony Anthony in *Westerns all'Italiana*, Spring 1991.

54 Author's interview with Sergio Donati, 23 May 1998; Cenk Kiral interviews with Luciano Vincenzoni, April–May 1998; *Montpellier*, p. 66.

55 Author's interview with Sergio Leone, February 1982.

56 Scott Simmons: review of Christopher Frayling's *Spaghetti Westerns* in *The Journal of Popular Film and Television*, Fall 1981, p. 149.

57 Luc Moullet, in De Fornari, p. 9.

58 Kim Newman: *Nightmare Movies* (Bloomsbury, London, 1988) pp. 105–109; Di Claudio, p. 189; Minnini, pp. 98–101.

59 Interview with Sergio Leone in *American Film*, June 1984, pp. 23–25.

60 On the Cinecittà auction see David Willey in the *Observer*, London, 23 May 1993, pp. 22–23; Carla Pilolli in *Il Messagero*, Rome, 27 May 1993, p. 12 and 28 May 1993, p. 14; also the auction catalogue, dated May 1993.

# Bibliography

In addition to specific references, the following studies – devoted in full or part to Leone's films rather than his life – provided useful background.

Carlos Aguilar: *Sergio Leone* (Ediciones Cátedra, Madrid, 1990)
Luca Beatrice: *Al cuore, Ramon, al cuore* (Tarab, Florence, 1996)
Gilles Cèbe: *Sergio Leone* (Veyrier, Paris, 1984)
Lorenzo Codelli: *Nickelodeon Gazette* (Udine, April 1997, on 'Eurowestern')
Hubert Corbin: *Sergio Leone, une retrospective* (20 Montpellier Festival, October 1998)
Robert Cumbrow: *Once Upon a Time* (Scarecrow, New Jersey, 1987)
Oreste De Fornari: *Sergio Leone* (Moizzi, Milan, 1977)
Oreste De Fornari: *Sergio Leone* (Tutti i film, ubulibri, Milan, 1984; 1997)
Lorenzo De Luca: *C'era una volta il Western Italiano* (Instituto Bibliografico Napoleone, Rome, 1987)
Gianni Di Claudio: *Directed by Sergio Leone* (Libreria Universitaria, Chieti, 1990)
Franco Ferrini: *L'antiwestern e il caso Leone* (*Bianco e Nero*, September/October 1971)
Christopher Frayling: *Spaghetti Westerns* (Routledge and Kegan Paul, London, 1981; new edition Taurus, London, 1998).
Diego Gabutti: *C'era una volta in America* (Rizzoli, Milan, 1984)
(ed.) Marcello Garofalo: *C'era una volta in America – Photographic Memories* (Editalia, Rome, 1988)
Gilles Gressard: *Sergio Leone* (Editions J'ai Lu, Paris, 1989)
Gilles Lambert: *Les bons, les sales, les méchants et les propres de Sergio Leone* (Solar, Paris, 1976)
Roberto Lasagna: *Sergio Leone* (Edizione Ripostes, Salerno, 1996)
Gian Lhassa: *Seul au monde dans le Western Italien* (3 vols, Grand Angle, Mariembourg, 1983)
Francesco Mininni: *Leone* (Il castoro cinema, Rome, January–February 1989; second edition April 1994)
Massimo Moscati: *Western all'Italiana* (Pan Editrice, Milan, 1981)
Philippe Ortoli: *Sergio Leone – une Amérique de légendes* (Editions L'Harmattan, Paris, 1994)
Noel Simsolo: *Conversations avec Sergio Leone* (Stock, Paris, 1987; reprint 1998)
Thomas Weisser: *Spaghetti Westerns – the Good, the Bad and the Violent* (McFarland, N. Carolina, 1992)

## Writings of Sergio Leone

A John Ford (*Corriere della Sera*, 20 August 1983)
Preface to Harry Grey's *Mano Armata* (Longanesi, Milan, 1983)
Preface to Diego Gabutti's *C'era una volta in America* (Rizzoli, Milan, 1984)

# BIBLIOGRAPHY

Essay in *Es war einmal in Amerika* (Bastei-Lübbe-Paperback, Bergisch Gladbach, 1984)

Per il novantenaro del cinema (*L'Unità*, 28 December 1985)

Tout est entre les mains d'Allah in (ed.) Laura Delli Colli: *Les métiers du cinéma* (Liana Levi, Paris, 1986)

Introduction to Gianni Di Claudio: *Il cinema western* (Libreria Universitaria, Chieti, 1986)

Sergio Leone 'films' his own football league cup (*Gazzette Dello Sport*, 10 May 1987)

Per il decimo anniversario della morte di Chaplin (*L'Unità*, 26 December 1987)

'Presentation' to (ed.) Marcello Garofalo: *C'era una volta in America – Photographic Memories* (Editalia, Rome, 1988)

*Venivamo da ogni parte delle terra* (*Bianco e Nero*, Venezia 88, December 1988)


Also sources of inspiration: the magazine *Westerns all'Italiana* ((ed.) Tom Betts and Tim Ferrante, Anaheim, California, 1983– ); the exhibition 'Omaggio a Sergio Leone' at Gallerie D'Arte 'La Scaletta', Rome, December 1991; Mikhail Bakhtin: *Rabelais and his World* (Indiana University Press, Bloomington, 1984) and Sergio Leone's collection of paintings.

# Complete Filmography

## As Assistant Director

Leone was seldom credited on his earliest work; his roles ranged from third to second to first assistant, also second-unit assistant and production secretary. These credits emphasize the people with whom he later worked.

### 1944
*Il folle di Marechiaro* (originally *I fuochi di San Martino*) directed and written by Roberto Roberti, completed 1949; with Aldo Silvani (the madman), Polidor (the old fisherman) and Tatiana Farnese (the vamp); songs by Beniamino Gigli

### 1946
*Rigoletto* directed by Carmine Gallone; with Tito Gobbi (Rigoletto), Marcella Govoni (Gilda – voice by Lina Pagliughi)

### 1947
*Ladri di biciclette* directed by Vittorio De Sica, from a script by Cesare Zavattini, Oreste Biancoli, Susso Cecchi D'Amico, Adolfo Franci, Gherardo Gherardi, Vittorio De Sica and Sergio Amidei (uncredited); with Lamberto Maggiorani (Antonio Ricci) and Enzo Stajola (Bruno, his son)

*Fabiola* directed by Alessandro Blasetti, adapted from the novel by Cardinal Nicholas Wiseman by fourteen scriptwriters – not all credited; with Michèle Morgan (Fabiola), Michel Simon (Fabius) Massimo Girotti (Sebastian) and Gabriele Ferzetti (Claudio); American version (1951) adapted by Marc Connelly and Fred Pressburger

### 1948
*La leggenda di Faust* directed by Carmine Callone, from Goethe, Gounod's opera and Berlioz; with Gino Mattera (Faust), Italo Tajo (Mephistopheles), Nelly Corradi (Marguerite – voice by Onelia Fineschi)

### 1949
*La forza del destino* directed by Carmine Gallone; with Tito Gobbi (Don Carlos), Nelly Corradi (Leonora – voice by Caterina Mancini)

*Il trovatore* directed by Carmine Gallone; with Gianna Pederzini (Azucena), Vittorina Colonnello (Leonora – voice by Franca Sacchi)

### 1950

*Il brigante Musolino* directed and co-written by Mario Camerini; produced by Carlo Ponti and Dino De Laurentiis; story by Antonio Leonviola, Mario Monicelli and Steno; with Amedeo Nazzari (Beppe Musolino) and Silvana Mangano (Mara)

*Il voto* directed by Mario Bonnard; screenplay by Mario Bonnard, from the comedy *O voto* by Salvatore Di Giacomo and Alfredo Cognetti; photographed Tonino Delli Colli; with Doris Duranti (Carmela), Giorgio De Lullo (Vito) and Maria Grazia Francia (Cristina)

*Taxi di notte* directed by Carmine Gallone; music from the operas of Ruggero Leoncavallo and Gaetano Donizetti; with Beniamino Gigli (the taxi-driver), Danièle Godet (Laura Morani), William Tubbs (William Simon, American industrialist)

### 1951

*Quo Vadis?* directed by Mervyn Le Roy; screenplay by John Lee Mahin, S.N. Behrman and Sonya Levien, based on the novel by Henryk Sienkiewicz; with Robert Taylor (Marcus Vinicius), Deborah Kerr (Lygia), Peter Ustinov (Nero) and Leo Genn (Petronius)

### 1952

*Jolanda (or Iolanda) la figlia del corsaro nero* directed by Mario Soldati; produced by Carlo Ponti and Dino De Laurentiis; from a novel by Emilio Salgari; screenplay by Ennio De Concini, Ivo Perilli, Franco Brusati (not credited) and Mario Soldati; photographed by Tonino Delli Colli; edited by Roberto Cinquini; music by Nino Rota; with May Britt (Jolanda), Marc Lawrence (Van Gould), Renato Salvatori (Ralf, son of Morgan)

*I tre corsari* directed Mario Soldati; produced by Carlo Ponti and Dino De Laurentiis; from the novel *Il corsaro verde* by Emilio Salgari; written by Ennio De Concini, Age and Scarpelli, Franco Brusati; photographed by Tonino Delli Colli; music by Nino Rota with Ettore Manni (Enrico, the black pirate), Renato Salvatori (Rolando, the red pirate), Cesare Danova (Carlo, the green pirate)

*L'uomo, la bestia, la virtù* directed by Steno [Stefano Vanzina]; based on Pirandello's comedy; music by Angelo Francesco Lavagnino; assistant director Lucio Fulci; with Orson Welles (Captain Perella), Totò (Prof. Paolino), Viviane Romance (Assunta Perella)

*La tratta delle bianche* directed and co-written by Luigi Canencini; produced by Carlo Ponti and Dino De Laurentiis; edited by Nino Baragli; production secretary: Sergio Leone; with Eleonora Rossi Drago (Alda), Ettore Manni (Carlo), Silvana Pampanini (Lucia), Marc Lawrence (Marquedi), Vittorio Gassman (Michele)

### 1953

*Friné, cortigiana d'Oriente* directed and co-written by Mario Bonnard; based on the Greek legend; music by Giulio Bonnard; with Elena Kleus (Friné, alias Afra), Pierre Cressory (Iperide) and Giulio Donnini (Lamarco)

### 1954

*Elena di Troia/Helen of Troy* directed by Robert Wise; 'based on the *Iliad* of Homer'; second-unit director Raoul Walsh (not credited); art director Edward Carrère assisted by Ken Adam; with Rossana Podestà (Helen), Jacques Sernas (Paris), Cedric Hardwicke (Priam), Stanley Baker (Achilles), Brigitte Bardot (Andraste)

*Tradita/La notte delle nozze* directed by Mario Bonnard; screenplay by Mario Bonnard and Vittorio Nino Novarese; photographed by Tonino Delli Colli; music by Giulio Bonnard; with Lucia Bosè (Elisabetta), Pierre Cressoy (Franco Alberti), Brigitte Bardot (Anna)

*Questa è la vita* (fourth episode of four called *Marsina stretta*) directed and written by Aldo Fabrizi; based on a short story by Pirandello; with Aldo Fabrizi (Prof. Fabio Gori), Walter Chiari (Andrea), Lucia Bosè (Angela Reis)

*Hanno rubato un tram* directed by Aldo Fabrizi (begun by Mario Bonnard); story by Luciano Vincenzoni; screenplay by Mario Bonnard, Ruggero Maccari, Aldo Fabrizi; photographed by Mario Bava; music by Carlo Rustichelli; with Aldo Fabrizi (Cesare Mancini), Carlo Campanini (Bernasconi), Lucia Banti (Marcella, daughter of Mancini)

## 1955
*La ladra* directed and co-written by Mario Bonnard; with Fausto Tozzi (Nino), Carlo D'Angelo (parroco don Pietro), Henri Vilbert (lawyer)

## 1956
*Quai des illusons/La legge mi incolpa* directed, produced, edited and co-written by Emile Couzinet; music by Joseph Kosma; Dyaliscope; consultant to the Italian version Sergio Leone; released three years after it was shot; with Lise Bourdin (Lise Vincent), Fausto Tozzi (Fausto) and Gaby Morlay (Mme Vincent)

*Mi permette, Babbo!* directed by Mario Bonnard; music by Giulio Bonnard; with Alberto Sordi (Rodolfo), Aldo Fabrizi (Allessandro Biagi)

## 1957
*Il maestro* directed and co-written by Aldo Fabrizi; with Aldo Fabrizi (maestro Giovanni Merino), Edoardo Nevola (Antonio, his son), Mary Lamar (the schoolteacher)

## 1958
*Afrodite, dea dell'amore* directed by Mario Bonnard; screenplay by Ugo Moretti, Sergio Leone, Mario Bonnard, Mario Di Nardo; with Isabelle Corey (Lerna), Antonio De Teffè (Demetrio), Irene Tunc (Diala) and John Kitzmiller (Tomoro)

*Il figlio del corsaro rosso* directed and co-written by Primo Zeglio; 'freely adapted from the novel by Emilio Salgari'; edited by Roberto Cinquini; with Lex Barker (Enrico di Ventimiglia), Silvia Lopez (Carmen di Montelimar) and Vira Silenti (Néala)

*The Nun's Story/La storia di una monaca* directed by Fred Zinnemann; art director Alexander Trauner; second-unit photographer Enzo Barboni; with Audrey Hepburn (Sister Luke, Gabrielle Van Der Mal), Edith Evans (Mother Superior) and Peter Finch (Dr Fortunati)

## 1959
*Ben-Hur* directed by William Wyler; music by Miklos Rozsa; art directors William A. Horning and Edward Carfagno; second-unit directors Andrew Marton, Yakima Canutt and Mario Soldati; credited assistant directors Gus Agosti, Alberto Cardone; with Charlton

Heston (Judah Ben-Hur), Jack Hawins (Quintus Arrius), Haya Harareet (Esther), Stephen
Boyd (Messala) and Hugh Griffith (Sheik Ilderim)

## As Actor

### 1941
*La bocca sulla strada* (as a small boy)

### 1944
*Il folle di Marechiaro* (as a GI)

### 1947
*Ladri di biciclette* (as a young priest)

### 1968
*Cimitero senza croci/Une corde, un colt* (directed by Robert Hossein; co-written by Dario
Argento; as a hotel clerk)

### 1979
*An Almost Perfect Affair* (directed by Michael Ritchie; as himself – at the Cannes Film Festival)

## As Credited Writer

### 1958
*Afrodite, dea dell'amore* (co-screenplay, with three others)

*Nel segno di Roma/Sign of the Gladiator* directed by Guido Brignone (completed by
Michelangelo Antonioni); second unit Riccardo Freda; story and screenplay by Francesco
Thellung, Francesco De Feo, Sergio Leone, Giuseppe Mangione, Guido Brignone; music by
Angelo Francesco Lavagnino; edited by Nino Baragli; assistant director Michele Lupo; with
Anita Ekberg (Zenobia, Queen of Palmyra), Georges Marchal (Marcus Valerius), Folco Lulli
(Semanzius), Jacques Sernas (decurion Julian) and Chelo Alonso (Erika)

### 1959
*Gli ultimi giorni di Pompei/The Last Days of Pompeii* (co-screenplay, with four others)

### 1960
*La sette sfide/Seven Challenges* directed by Primo Zeglio; screenplay by Sabatino Ciuffini,
Sergio Leone, Ambrogio Molteni, Roberto Natale, Ernimmo Salvi (also producer), Giuseppe
Taffarel and Primo Zeglio; music by Carlo Innocenti; with Ed Fury (Ivan), Elaine Stewart
(Tamara), Roldano Lupi (The Great Khan) and Furio Meniconi (Amok)

### 1961
*Romolo e Remo/Romulus and Remus/Duel of the Titans* directed by Sergio Corbucci; second
unit Franco Giraldi; story by Luciano Martino, Sergio Leone, Sergio Corbucci; screenplay
Ennio De Concini, Franco Rossetti, Duccio Tessari, Luciano Martino, Sergio Leone;
photographed by Enzo Barboni; music by Piero Piccioni; designed by Giancarlo Simi; director
of production Franco Palaggi; stunt director Benito Stefanelli; with Steve Reeves (Romulus),
Gordon Scott (Remus) and Virna Lisi (Julia)

1962
*Le verdi bandiere di Allah* directed by Guido Zurli, supervised by Giacomo Gentilomo; story by Umberto Lenzi; screenplay by Umberto Lenzi, Sergio Leone, Arnaldo Marrosu, Adriano Bolzoni, Guido Zurli; with José Suarez, Linda Cristal, Mimmo Palmara and Walter Barnes

1973
*Il mio nome è Nessuno* ('from an idea by Sergio Leone')

## As Director

1957
*Taxi . . . signore?*
A short, filmed on location in Rome (listed by some sources)

1959
*The Last Days of Pompeii/Gli ultimo giorni di Pompei* (It/Sp/Ger)
Directed by Mario Bonnard (Sergio Leone took over, after pre-production)

*Cast*: Steve Reeves (*Glaucus*), Christine Kauffman (*Ione*), Fernando Rey (*High Priest*), Barbara Carroll (*Nydia*), Annemarie Baumann (*Julia*), Mimmo Palmara (*Gallinus*), Guillermo Marin (*Ascanius*), Angel Aranda (*Antonius*), Mino Doro (*Second Consul*), Carlo Tamberlani (*Leader of the Christians*), Mario Berriatúa (*Praetorian guard*), Mario Morales (*Praetorian guard*), Angel Ortiz (*Praetorian guard*), Ignazio Dolce, Antonio Casas, Tony Richards, Lola Torres, Vicky Lagos, Ignaz Cole.

*Script*: Ennio De Concini, Luigi Emmanele, Sergio Corbucci, Roberti Sergio Leone, Duccio Tessari
*Story*: adapted from the novel *The Last Days of Pompeii* by Lord Edward George Bulwer-Lytton
*Art director*: Aldo Tomassìni, Ramiro Gómez
*Construction*: Francisco R. Asenzio
*Costumes*: Vittorio Rossi
*Costume assistant*: Giuliana Bagni
*Make-up*: Angelo Malantrucco
*Volcano special effects*: Erasmo Baciucchi
*Director of photography*: Antonio López Ballesteros
*Process and colour*: SuperTotalScope and Eastmancolor
*Colour photography consultant*: Jorge Grau
*Sound*: Mario Amari, Giovanni Percelli
*Second unit director of photography*: Enzo Barboni
*Second unit director*: Sergio Corbucci
*Assistant directors*: Duccio Tessari, Sergio Leone, Antonio Fenollar
*Editors*: Eraldo Da Roma, Julio Peña
*Music*: Angelo Francesco Lavagnino
*Sound mixer*: Fausto Ancillai
*Production managers*: Cesare Seccia, Eduardo De La Fuente
*Production secretary*: Alfonso Fabrizio
*Production companies*: Cineproduzioni Associate (Rome), Procusa (Madrid), Transocean (Munich)

*Distributed in USA by United Artists*
*Running times*: It: 100 mins, GB: 97 mins, US: 103 mins.

1960
*The Colossus of Rhodes/Il Colosso di Rodi* (It/Sp/Fr)
Directed by Sergio Leone

*Cast*: Rory Calhoun (*Dario*), Lea Massari (*Diala*), Georges Marchal (*Peliocles*)
Conrado Sanmartin (*Thar*), Angel Aranda (*Koros*), Mabel Karr (*Mirte*) Mimmo Palmara
(*Chares*), Roberto Camardiel (*Serse*), Alf Randall [Alfio Caltabiano]
(*Creonte*), Jorge Rigaud (*Lisippo*), Yann Larvor (*Mahor*), Carlo Tamberlani (*Senone*), Félix
Fernandez (*Carete*), Antonio Casas (*Phoenician ambassador*), Fernando Calzado (*Sidione*),
Ignazio Dolce.
*Uncredited*: José Suarez, José Vilches (*Etéocle*), Arturo Cabre, Angel Menendez, Carlo
Gualtieri, Giovanni (*Nello*) Pazzafini (*striker of the gong*).

*Script and story*: Ennio De Concini, Sergio Leone, Cesare Seccia, Luciano Martino, Aggeo
Savioli, Luciano Chitarrini, Carlo Gualtieri
*Interiors*: Cinecittà (Rome), Istituto Nazionale Luce (Rome), CEA (Madrid)
*Exteriors*: the port of Laredo, between Santander and Bilbao (Spain)
*Art director*: Ramiro Gómez
*Assistant art director*: Giuseppe Ranieri
*Set decorator*: Jesus Mateos
*Sculptor of the Colossus*: Socrate Valzanis
*Construction*: Francisco R. Asenzio
*Key grip*: Aldo Colanzi
*Costumes*: Vittorio Rossi
*Costume assistant*: Antonio Cortes
*Costume suppliers*: Casa D'Arte di Firenze
*Wardrobe*: Irma Tonnini
*Wardrobe assistant*: Maria Pia Mancini
*Footwear*: Pompei
*Make-up*: Angelo Malantrucco, Carlos Nin
*Wigs*: Palombi
*Choreography*: Carla Ranalli
*Stunts*: Alfio Caltabiano
*Weapons and props suppliers*: R. Sormani of Rancati
*Special effects*: Erasmo Baciucchi, Vittorio Galliano
*Director of photography*: Antonio López Ballesteros
*Second unit director of photography*: Emilio Foriscot
*Process and colour*: Totalscope and Eastmancolor
*Lens and technical equipment*: ATC (Rome)
*Camera operator*: Eduardo Noé
*Camera assistants*: Franco Frazzi, Gianni Maddaleni
*Sound*: Giuseppe Turcio, Mario Amari
*Continuity*: Jose Castañer, Maria Isabel Ruiz-Capillas
*Special assistant to the director*: Michele Lupo
*Assistant director*: Jorge Grau
*Director's assistants*: Mahnahen (May) Velasco, Luis Lasala
*Production managers*: Cesare Seccia, Eduardo De La Fuente
*Laboratory*: Tecnostampa (Rome), Riera (Madrid)

*Optical effects*: Tecnostampa (Rome)
*Sound effects*: Tonino Cacciottolo
*Editor*: Eraldo Da Roma
*Assistant editor*: Marisa Mengoli
*Music*: Angelo Francesco Lavagnino
*Music publishers*: Nazional Music (Milan)
*Dubbing studio*: CDC
*Executive producer*: Michele Scaglione
*Production companies*: Cineproduzioni Associate (Rome), Procusa Film (Madrid), Comptoir Français de Productions Cinématographiques (Paris), Cinéma Télévision International (Paris)
*Distributed in USA*: MGM
*Running times*: It: 142 mins, GB: 127 mins, US: 128 mins.

[Some sources list Sergio Leone as director of *Vacanze in Argentina* (1960), an Italian–Argentinian co-production: it was in fact directed and co-written by Guido Leoni]

## 1961

*Sodom and Gomorrah/Sodoma e Gomorra* (It/Fr/US)
Directed by Robert Aldrich. Second unit director Sergio Leone, billed on Italian posters as co-director.

*Cast*: Stewart Granger (Lot), Anna Maria Pierangeli/Pier Angeli (Ildith, wife of Lot), Anouk Aimée (Queen Berah of Sodom), Stanley Baker (Astaroth, brother of Queen Berah and prince of Sodom), Rossana Podestà (Shuah, daughter of Lot), Scilla Gabel (Tamar), Rik Battaglia (Melchior), Claudia Mori (Maleb, daughter of Lot), Giacomo Ross Stuart (Ishmael), Aldo Silvani (Nakur), Antonio De Teffè (Captain), Giovanna Galletti (Malik), Gabriele Tinti (Lieutenant), Feodor Chaliapin (Alabias), Mimmo Palmara (Arlok), Daniele Vargas (Segur, leader of the nomads), Enzo Fiermonte (Eber), Mitzuko Takara (Orfea), Alice and Ellen Kessler (Dancers), Massimo Pietrobon (IIssaak), Liana Del Balzo (old Hebrew woman), Mimmo Poli (bodyguard), Nazzareno Natale (soldier), Vittorio Artesi, Primo Moroni, Calogero Chiarenza, Andrea Tagliabue, Tom Felleghi, Renato Terra Caizzi, Valenino Macchi, Renato Giuia

*Script*: Hugo Butler, Giorgio Prosperi
*Art directors*: Ken Adam, Giorgio Giovannini
*Set decorators*: Gino Brosio, Emilio D'Andria
*Costumes*: Giancarlo Bartolini Salimbeni
*Costumes assistant*: Giuliana Ghidini
*Choreography*: Archie Savage
*Special effects*: Lee Zavitz, Serse Urbisaglia, Wally Veevers
*Dialogue director*: Michael Audley
*Directors of photography*: Silvano Ippoliti, Mario Montuori, Alfio Contini
*Colour*: Technicolor
*Sound*: Kurt Dubrowsky
*Second unit director*: Sergio Leone (listed as co-director in most sources)
*Assistant directors*: Gus Agosti Giorgio Gentili, Franco Cirino
*Production managers*: Giorgio Zambon, Mario Del Papa
*Production assistant*: Giorgio Adriani
*Special photographic effects*: Cyril Knowles
*Titles*: Maurice Binder
*Editors*: Mario Serandrei, Peter Tanner
*Music*: Miklós Rozsa, conducted by Carlo Savina

*Executive producer*: Maurizio Lodi-Fé
*Producer*: Goffredo Lombardo
*Production companies*: Titanus (Rome), SN Pathé (Paris), SGC (Paris)
*Distributed in USA*: 20th Century–Fox
*Running times*: It: 150 mins, GB: 153 mins, US: 154 mins. Original cut: 171 mins.

1962
*Il cambio della guardia/En avant la musique/The Changing of the Guard* (It/Fr)
Directed by Giorgio Bianchi (sometimes attributed to Maurizio Lucidi); completed by Sergio Leone.

*Cast*: Gino Cervi (Mario Vinicio), Fernandel (Attilio Cappellaro), Franco Parenti (Virgili), Andrea Aureli (Luciano Crippa), Frank Fernadel (Gianni Cappellaro), Milla Sannoner (Aurora Vinicio), Dada Gallotti (Silvana Crippa), Gerhard Herter (German official), Amelia Perrella (Bianca Vinicio), Giuseppe Giannetto (don Fausto), Giuseppe Fortis (Mezzanotte) Pietro Vivaldi (Vernazza), Jimmy il Fenomeno [Origene Soffrano] (the street cleaner)

*Script*: Albert Valentia, Jean Manse, from the novel *Avanti la musica* by Charles Exbrayant
*Exteriors*: Ardea (Latina)
*Art director*: Sergio Canevari
*Costumes*: Fiammetta Petrucci
*Director of photography*: Giuseppe Aquari
*Assistant directors*: Aldo Florio, Milo Panaro
*Editor*: Nella Nannuzzi
*Music*: Mario Nascimbene, conducted by Alessandro Derevitsky
*Executive producer*: Franco Dodi
*Producer*: Aldo Pomilia
*Production companies*: APO Film (Rome), Paris Elysées Productions (France)
*Running time*: 92 mins.

1964
*Fistful of Dollars/Per un pugno di dollari* (It/Sp/Ger)
Directed by Bob Robertson [= Sergio Leone]

*Cast*: Clint Eastwood [dubbed by Enrico Maria Salerno ] (The Stranger), Marianne Koch (Marisol), Johnny Wels [= Gian Maria Volonté] [dubbed by Nando Gazzolo] (Ramón Rojo), Wolfgang Lukschy (John Baxter, the sheriff), Sieghardt Rupp (Esteban Rojo), Joe Edger [= Josef Egger] (Piripero, the undertaker), Antonio Prieto (Miguel Rojo, called 'Benito' in Italian print), José 'Pepe' Calvo (Silvanito, the cantina owner), Margherita Lozano (Consuelo Baxter), Daniel Martin (Julián), Benny Reeves [= Benito Stefanelli] (Rubio), Richard Stuyvesant [= Mario Brega] (Chico), Carol Brown [= Bruno Carotenuto] (Antonio Baxter), Aldo Sambrell (member of Rojo gang). Uncredited: Fredy Arco (Jesus), Antonio Vica, Raf Baldassarre, Umberto Spadaro, Johannes Siedel, José Orjas, Antonio Molino Rojo, Lorenzo Robledo (blond Baxter gunman)

*Script*: no credit given (Duccio Tessari, Victor A. Catena, G. Schock, Sergio Leone, from the screenplay *Yojimbo* by Ryuzo Kikushima and Akira Kurosawa)
*Story*: no credit given (Sergio Leone, after Kurosawa)
*Dialogue*: Mark Lowell
*Exteriors*: La Pedrizia di Colmenar el Viejo, near Madrid; Almeria
*Art director, set decorator and costumes*: Charles Simons [= Carlo Simi]
*Make-up*: Sam Watkins [= ?]
*Special effects*: John Speed [= Giovanni Corridori]

*Stunts*: W.R. Thompkins [= Bill Tompkins] and Benito Stefanelli
*Photography*: Jack Dalmas [= Massimo Dallamano], assisted by Federico Larraya
*Process and colour*: Techniscope and Technicolor
*Camera operator*: Steve Rock [= Stelvio Massi]
*Sound*: Edy Simson
*Continuity*: Tilde Watson
*Unit manager*: Fred Ross [= ?]
*Production managers*: Frank Palance [= Franco Palaggi], Günter Raguse
*Second unit director*: Frank Prestland [= Franco Giraldi]
*Negative*: Eastmancolor
*Editor*: Bob Quintle [= Roberto Cinquini]
*Music*: Dan Savio/Leo Nichols [= Ennio Morricone]
*Trumpet player*: Michele Lacerenza
*Guitar, whistle, and choral arrangement*: Alessandro Alessandroni
*Choir*: I Cantori Moderni di Alessandroni, soprano Edda dell'Orso
*Dubbing facilities*: Titanus and CDC
*Music publishers*: RCA Italiana
*Titles*: Luigi Lardani
*Producers*: Harry Columbo [= Arrigo Colombo], George Papi [= Giorgio Papi]
*Production companies*: Jolly Film (Rome), Ocean Film (Madrid) and Constantin Film
(Munich/Monaco)
*Distributed in USA*: United Artists (1967)
*Running times*: It: 100 mins, Fr: 96 mins, US: 96 mins, GB: 95 mins.

1965
*For a Few Dollars More/Per qualche dollaro in più/La muerte tenia un precio* (It/Sp/Ger)
Directed by Sergio Leone

*Cast*: Clint Eastwood ('Monco', the bounty-hunter), Lee Van Cleef (Colonel Douglas
Mortimer), Gian Maria Volonté (El Indio), Mara Krup (Hotelier's wife), Luigi Pistilli
(Groggy), Klaus Kinski (Wild, the hunchback), Josef Egger (The Old Prophet), Panos
Papadopoulos, Benito Stefanelli (Luke, a member of Indio's gang), Aldo Sambrell (Cuchillo),
Roberto Camardiel (station clerk), Luis Rodriguez, Tomás Blanco, Lorenzo Robledo
(Tomaso, the betrayer), Sergio Mendizabal, Dante Maggio (El Paso bank guard), Diana
Rabito (girl in tub), Giovanni Tarallo, Mario Meniconi and Mario Brega (Niño). Uncredited:
Carlo Simi (bank manager), Rosemary Dexter (Mortimer's sister), Peter Lee Lawrence [= Karl
Hirenbach] (Mortimer's brother-in-law), Diana Faenza (Tomaso's wife), Aldo Ricci, Ricardo
Palacios (saloonkeeper), Antonio Ruiz (child in El Paso), Francesca Leone (baby).

*Script*: Luciano Vincenzoni, Sergio Leone
*Story*: Sergio Leone, Fulvio Morsella
*Dialogue*: Luciano Vincenzoni
*Interiors*: Cinecittà (Rome)
*Exteriors*: Almeria; Guadix (Spain)
*Art director, set decorator and costumes*: Carlo Simi
*Assistant art directors*: Carlo Leva, Raphael Ferri [Jorda]
*Head make-up artist*: Rino Carboni
*Make-up*: Amedeo Alessi
*Special effects*: Giovanni Corridori
*Stunts*: Benito Stefanelli
*Director of photography*: Massimo Dallamano

*Process and colour*: Techniscope and Technicolor
*Camera operators*: Eduardo Noé, Aldo Ricci
*Assistant camera operator*: Mario Lommi
*Sound*: Oscar De Arcangelis, Guido Ortenzi
*Continuity*: Maria Luisa Rosen
*Assistant director*: Tonino Valerii
*Director's assistants*: Fernando Di Leo, Julio Samperez
*Production manager*: Ottavio Oppo
*Production supervisors*: Norberto Soliño, Manuel Castedo
*Production secretary*: Antonio Palombi
*Supervising editor*: Adriana Novelli
*Editors*: Eugenio Alabiso, Giorgio Serralonga
*Music*: Ennio Morricone, conducted by Bruno Nicolai
*Music publishers*: Eureka Edizioni Musicali
*Whistle and choral arrangement*: Alessandro Alessandroni
*Choir*: I Cantori Moderni di Alessandroni
*Guitar*: Bruno D'Amario Battisti
*Recorded at*: RCA Italiana Studios
*Synchronization*: International Recording
*Dubbing studios*: CDS
*Mixing*: Renato Cadueri
*Titles*: Luigi Lardoni
*Producer*: Alberto Grimaldi
*Production companies*: PEA [Produzioni Europee Associate] (Rome), Arturo Gonzales
(Madrid), Constantin Film (Munich/Monaco)
*Distributed in USA*: United Artists (1967)
*Running times*: It: 130 mins, GB: 128 mins, US: 128 mins.

1966
*The Good, The Bad and The Ugly/Il buono, Il brutto, Il cattivo* (It/USA)
Directed by Sergio Leone

*Cast*: Clint Eastwood ('Blondie'), Eli Wallach (Tuco [Benedicto Pacifico Juan Maria] Ramirez),
Lee Van Cleef ('Angel Eyes'; 'Sentenza' in Italian print), Aldo Giuffrè (Union officer), Luigi
Pistilli (Padré Pablo Ramirez), Rada Rassimov (Maria, the prostitute), Enzo Petito
(storekeeper robbed by Tuco), John Bartha (Sheriff), Livio Lorenzon (Baker), Antonio Casale
(Jackson, alias 'Bill Carson'), Claudio and Sandro Scarchilli, Benito Stefanelli (member of
Angel Eyes' gang), Angelo Novi (Monk), Antonio Casas (Stevens), Aldo Sambrell (member of
Angel Eyes' gang), Al Muloch (one-armed bounty-hunter), Sergio Mendizabal, Antonio
Molino Rojo, Lorenzo Robledo (Clem, a member of Angel Eyes' gang), and with Mario Brega
(Corporal Wallace). Uncredited: Chelo Alonso (Stevens's wife), Antonio Ruiz (Stevens's
youngest son), Silvana Bacci, Frank Brana

*Script*: Age [= Agenore Incrocci], [Furio] Scarpelli, Luciano Vincenzoni, Sergio Leone (and
Sergio Donati uncredited)
*Story*: Luciano Vincenzoni, Sergio Leone
*English dialogue*: Mickey Knox
*Interiors*: Elios Film (Rome)
*Exteriors*: Almeria; Colmenari Burgos
*Art director, set decorator and costumes*: Carlo Simi
*Assistant art director*: Carlo Leva

*Make-up*: Rino Carboni
*Hairdresser*: Rino Todero
*Equipment suppliers*: Tani
*Costume suppliers*: Western Costume Co., Antonelli
*Special effects*: Eros Bacciucchi
*Stunts*: Benito Stefanelli
*Director of photography*: Tonino Delli Colli
*Process and colour*: Techniscope and Technicolor
*Camera operator*: Franco Di Giacomo
*Assistant camera operator*: Sergio Salvati
*Sound*: Elio Pacella, Vittorio De Sisti
*Continuity*: Serena Canevari
*Assistant director*: Giancarlo Santi
*Director's assistant*: Fabrizio Gianni
*Production supervisor*: Aldo Pomilia
*Production manager*: Fernando Cinquini
*Production assistants*: Carlo Bartolini, Federico Tofi
*Production secretaries*: Antonio Palombi, Luigi Corbo
*Editors*: Nino Baragli, Eugenio Alabiso
*Titles*: Luigi Lardani
*Music*: Ennio Morricone, conducted by Bruno Nicolai (Lyrics of the song 'The Soldier's Story' by Tommie Connor)
*Orchestra*: Orchestra Cinefonico Italiana
*Solo performers*: Bruno D'Amario Battisti (guitar), E. Wolf Ferrari, I. Cammarota, F. Catania, Michele Lacerenza (trumpet), N. Samale, Franco De Gemini (harmonica), F. Traverso
*Choir*: I Cantori Moderni di Alessandroni
*Whistle*: Alessandro Alessandroni
*Vocals*: Alessandro Alessandroni, E. Gioieni, F. Cosacchi, G. Spagnolo, Edda Dell'Orso
*Recorded at*: International Recording (by Giuseppe Mastroianni)
*Music publishers*: Eureka Edizioni Musicali
*Sound mixing*: Fausto Ancillai
*Sound dubbing*: Goffredo Potier
*Dubbing studio*: CDS
*Synchronization*: NIS Film
*Producer*: Alberto Grimaldi
*Production company*: PEA [Produzioni Europee Associate] (Rome)
*Distributed in USA*: United Artists (1968)
*Running times*: It: 180 mins, Fr: 166 mins, US: 161 mins, GB: 148 mins.

## 1968
*Once Upon a Time in the West/C'era una volta il West/Hasta que llego su Hora* (It/USA)
Directed by Sergio Leone

*Cast*: Claudia Cardinale (Jill McBain), Henry Fonda (Frank), Jason Robards (Manuel 'Cheyenne' Gutierrez), Charles Bronson (Harmonica), Gabriele Ferzetti (Mr Morton), Paolo Stoppa (Sam), Woody Strode (Stony), Jack Elam (Snaky), Marco Zuanelli (Wobbles), Benito Stefanelli (member of Frank's gang), Keenan Wynn (Sheriff of Flagstone), Frank Wolff (Brett McBain), Lionel Stander (trading-post owner and barman), Levio Andronico, Salvo Basile, Aldo Berti, Marilù Carteny, Luigi Ciavarro, Spartaco Conversi (member of Frank's gang shot through Cheyenne's boot), Bruno Corazzari, Paolo Figlia, Stefano Imparato, Frank Leslie, Luigi Magnani, Claudio Mancini (elder brother of 'Harmonica'), Umberto Marsella, Enrico

Morsella, Tullio Palmieri, Renato Pinciroli, Corrado Sammartin, Enzo Santaniello (Timmy McBean), Simonetta Santaniello (Maureen McBain), Sandra Salvatori, Claudio Scarchilli, Ivan Scratuglia, Fabio Testi (member of Frank's gang), Dino Zamboni. Uncredited: Al Muloch (Knuckles), John Frederick (member of Frank's gang), Dino Mele (Young Harmonica), Aldo Sambrell (member of Cheyenne's gang), Michael Harvey (Frank's aide), Raffaella and Francesca Leone (girls at Flagstone station), Luana Strode (Indian woman)

*Script*: Sergio Donati, Sergio Leone
*Story*: Dario Argento, Bernardo Bertolucci, Sergio Leone
*English dialogue*: Mickey Knox
*Interiors*: Cinecittà and Luce (Rome)
*Exteriors*: Guadix, Almeria, Arizona, Utah
*Art director, sets and costumes*: Carlo Simi
*Assistant set builder*: Enrico Simi
*Furniture suppliers*: Cimino, Ellis Mercantile, Matheos
*Set dressers*: Carlo Leva, Raphael Ferri
*Assistant set dresser*: Tonino Palombi
*Key grip*: Franco Tocci
*Gaffer*: Alberto Ridolfi
*Wardrobe*: Marilù Carteny
*Head dressmaker*: Valeria Sponsali
*Costume and footwear suppliers*: Safas, Western Costume, Antonelli, Pompei
*Make-up supervisor*: Alberto De Rossi
*Make-up*: Giannetto De Rossi
*Make-up assistant*: Feliziani Ciriaci
*Hairdresser*: Grazia De Rossi
*Assistant hairdresser*: Antonietta Caputo
*Wigs*: Rocchetti
*Special effects*: Eros Bacciucchi and Giovanni Corridor
*Stunts*: Benito Stefanelli
*Director of photography*: Tonino Delli Colli
*Process and colour*: Techniscope and Technicolor
*Camera operator*: Franco Di Giacomo
*Assistant camera operator*: Giuseppe Lanci
*Sound*: Claudio Maielli, Elio Pacella, Fausto Ancillai
*Continuity*: Serena Canevari
*Stills*: Angelo Novi
*First assistant director*: Giancarlo Santi
*Director's assistant*: Salvo Basile
*Production manager*: Claudio Mancini
*Production supervisor*: Ugo Tucci
*Production assistants*: Camillo Teti, Manolo Amigo
*Production secretary*: Glauco Teti
*Production accountant*: Raffaello Forti
*Negative* : Eastmancolor
*Editor*: Nino Baragli
*Assistant editors*: Andreina Casini, Carlo Reali
*Sound effects*: Luciano Anzilotti
*Sound effects editors*: Italo Cameracanna, Roberto Arcangeli
*Editing, mixing and synchronization*: NIS, with the participation of CDC
*Music*: Ennio Morricone, conducted by Ennio Morricone

*Music edited and recorded at*: RCA Italiana S.p.A.
*Harmonica*: Franco De Gemini
*Vocals*: Edda Dell'Orso
*Whistling*: Alessandro Alessandrini
*Executive producer*: Fulvio Morsella
*Producer*: Bino Cicogna
*Production companies*: Rafran, San Marco
*Distributed in USA*: Paramount (1968)
*Running times*: It: 168 mins, Fr: 164 mins, US: 144 mins, GB: 145 mins.

1971
*A Fistful of Dynamite/Duck you Sucker/Giù la testa/Il etait une fois la Revolution/*
*Todesmelodie/Agachate, maldito* (It/USA)
Directed by Sergio Leone

*Cast*: Rod Steiger (Juan Miranda), James Coburn (Sean Mallory), Romolo Valli (Dr Villega), Domingo Antoine [billed as Jean Michel Antoine on English-language print] (Col. Gunther Reza/Gutierrez), David Warbeck (Sean's friend in flashback), Maria Monti (Adelita, the woman on the coach), Rick Battaglia (Santerna), Franco Graziosi (Don Jaime, the governor), Giulio Battiferri, Poldo Bendandi (executed revolutionary), Omar Bonaro, Roy Bosier (landowner), Vivienne Chandler, John Frederick (the American), Amato Garbini, Michael Harvey (a Yankee), Biagio La Rocca ('Benito'), Furio Meniconi (executed revolutionary), Nazzareno Natale, Vincenzo Novese (Pancho), Stefano Oppedisano, Amelio [Meme] Perlini (a peón), Goffredo Pistoni (Niño), Renato Pontecchi (Pepe), Jean Rougeul (monsignor on coach), Corrado Solari (Sebastian), Benito Stefanelli, Franco Tocci, Rosita Torosh, Anthony Vernon (coach passenger). Uncredited: Antonio Casale (the notary), Franco Collace (Napoleone)

*Script*: Luciano Vincenzoni, Sergio Donati, Sergio Leone
*Additional dialogue*: Roberto De Leonardis, Carlo Tritto
*Story*: Sergio Leone, Sergio Donati
*Interiors*: De Laurentiis Studios
*Exteriors*: Dublin, Co. Wicklow, Almeria, Guadix, Burgos
*Art director*: Andrea Crisanti
*Set decorator*: Dario Micheli
*Assistant set decorators*: Franco Velchi, Ezio Di Monte
*Furniture suppliers*: Cimino, Rancati
*Key grip*: Franco Tocci
*Gaffer*: Massimo Massimi
*Costumes*: Franco Carretti
*Costume and footwear suppliers*: Tirelli, Pompei, Nathan, Western Costume
*Wardrobe supervisor*: Luisa Buratti
*Jewels*: Nino Lembo
*Make-up supervisor*: Amato Garbini
*Hairdresser*: Paolo Borzelli
*Wigs*: Rochetti
*Arms and explosions*: Eros Baciucchi
*Armourers*: Giovanni Corridori, Tonino Palombi
*Special effects*: Antonio Margheriti
*Stunts*: Benito Stefanelli
*Director of photography*: Giuseppe Ruzzolini

*Camera operator*: Idelmo Simonelli
*Assistant camera operators*: Alessandro Ruzzolini, Roberto Forges Davanzati
*Process and colour*: Techniscope and Technicolor
*Second-unit directors*: Giancarlo Santi and Martin Herbert [= Alberto De Martino]
*Second-unit director of photography*: Franco Delli Colli
*Continuity*: Serena Canevari
*Stills*: Angelo Novi
*Assistant director*: Tony Brandt
*Production manager*: Camillo Teti
*Production supervisor*: Claudio Mancini
*Production secretary*: Vasco Mafera
*Production accountant*: Raffaello Forti
*Negative*: Eastmancolor
*Editor*: Nino Baragli
*First assistant editor*: Rossana Maiuri
*Assistant editors*: Gino Bartolini, Olga Sarra
*Synchronization*: NIS Films, and CD
*Music*: Ennio Morricone, conducted by Ennio Morricone
*Music recorded by* : Federico Savino at International Recording Studios
*Orchestra*: Unione Musicisti di Roma Symphony Orchestra
*Music publishers*: Bixio – Sam (Milan)
*Mixer*: Fausto Ancillai
*Dubbing director*: Giuseppe Rinaldi
*Sound editor*: Michael Billingsley
*Associate producers*: Claudio Mancini, Ugo Tucci
*Producer*: Fulvio Morsella
*Production companies*: Rafran Cinematografica, San Marco Films, Miura, plus Euro
International Films
*Distributed in USA*: United Artists (1971)
*Running times*: It: 154 mins, US: 138 mins, GB: 138 mins, Fr: 150 mins; restored to 160 mins.

## 1984
*Once Upon a Time in America/C'era una volta in America* (USA)
Directed by Sergio Leone

*Cast*: Robert De Niro [dubbed by Ferruccio Amendola] (David 'Noodles' Aaronson), James
Woods [dubbed by Sergio Fantoni] (Max Bercovicz), Elizabeth McGovern [dubbed by Rita
Savagnone], (Deborah Gelly), Joe Pesci (Frankie Menaldi), Burt Young (Joe), Tuesday Weld
[dubbed by Maria Pia Di Meo] (Carol), Treat Williams (Jimmy Conway O'Donnell), Danny
Aiello (Police Chief Vincent Aiello), Richard Bright (Chicken Joe), James Hayden (Patrick
'Patsy' Goldberg), William Forsythe (Philip 'Cockeye' Stein), Mario Brega ('Mandy', the
heaviest leader of Eve's killers), Darlanne Fleugel (Eve), Larry Rapp (Fat Moe Gelly), Richard
Foronji ('Whitey' the patrolman), Robert Harper (Sharkey, the labour fixer), 'Dutch' Miller
(Van Linden, the diamond merchant), Gerard Murphy (Crowning, the businessman), Amy
Ryder (Peggy), Olga Karlatos (woman in Chinese shadow theatre), Ray Dittrich ('Trigger',
Eve's killer), Frank Gio ('Beefy', third of Eve's killers), Karen Shallo (Mrs Lucy Aiello),
Angelo Florio (Willie the Ape), Scott Tiler (Young Noodles), Rusy Jacobs (Young Max, and
David Bailey), Jennifer Connelly (Young Deborah), Brian Bloom (Young Patsy), Adrian
Curran (Young Cockeye), Mike Monetti (Young Fat Moe), Noah Moazezi (Dominic), James
Russo (Bugsy), Frankie Caserta (member of Bugsy's gang), Joey Marzella (member of Bugsy's
gang), Clem Caserta (Al Capuano), Frank Sisto (Fred Capuano), Jerry Strivelli (Johnny

Capuano), Julie Cohen (Young Peggy), Marvin Scott (Marvin Brentley, the TV reporter), Mike Gendel (Irving Gold, Bailey's lawyer), Paul Herman ('Monkey', the barman), Ann Neville (girl in a coffin), Joey Faye (old man beside the hearse), Linda Ipanema (Nurse Thompson), Tandy Cronin (first reporter), Richard Zobel (second reporter), Baxter Harris (third reporter), Arnon Milchan (limousine chauffeur), Bruno Iannone (thug), Marty Licata (cemetery caretaker), Marcia Jean Kurtz (Mrs Bercovicz, Max's mother), Estelle Harris (Peggy's mother), Gerritt Debeer (drunk 'rolled' by Max), Margherita Pace (body double for Jennifer Connelly), Alexander Godfrey (newsstand proprietor), Cliff Cudney (first mounted policeman) Paul Farentino (2nd mounted policeman), Bruce Bahrenburg (Sergeant P. Halloran), Mort Freeman (street singer), Sandra Solberg (friend of young Deborah), Jay Zeely (warder), Massimo Liti (Macrò, in Chinese shadow theatre). Uncredited: Louise Fletcher (cemetery proprietor, deleted) T. Scott Coffey, Claudio Mancini (Jimmy O'Donnell's assistant in newsreel)

*Script*: Leonardo Benvenuti, Piero De Bernardi, Enrico Medioli, Franco Arcalli, Franco Ferrini, Sergio Leone
*Additional dialogue*: Stuart Kaminsky
*Story*: based on the 1953 novel *The Hoods/Mano Armata* by Harry Grey
*Interiors*: Cinecittà, Rome
*Exteriors*: New York City, New Jersey, St Petersburg Beach (Florida), Montreal, Paris, Venice Lido, Bellagio, Pietralata
*Art director*: Carlo Simi
*Assistant art director*: Giovanni Natalucci
*Art director* (New York): James Singelis
*Set builders* (New York): Otto Jacoby, George Messaris
*Set dressers*: Bruno Cesari, Osvaldo Desideri, Gretchen Rau (New York)
*Assistant set dresser*: Nello Giorgetti
*Scenic painter* (Montreal): Alain Giguere
*Key grips*: Augusto Diamanti, Steve Baker (New York), Normand Guy (Montreal)
*Construction co-ordinators*: Tullio Lullo, Joey Litto (New York)
*Chief carpenter* (Montreal): Claude Simard
*Furniture suppliers*: GRP, Rancati
*Rattan furniture suppliers*: Italo Gasparucci – Sant'Ippolito (P.S.), Italy
*Props*: Gianni Fiumi, Steve Kerschoff (New York), Ronald Fauteux (Montreal)
*Casting*: Cis Corman, Joy Todd
*Extras casting* (Montreal): Flo Galant, Sylvie Bourque
*Costumes*: Gabriella Pescucci
*Costume associate* (New York): Richard Bruno
*Costume assistants*: Raffaella Leone, Marina Frassine, Elouise Meyer (Rome), Helen Butler (New York)
*Costume suppliers*: Modelli Tirelli (Rome)
*Wardrobe costumes*: Umberto Tirelli
*Furs suppliers*: Fendi
*Hat suppliers*: Borsalino
*Footwear suppliers*: LCP
*Jewellery suppliers*: Bulgari, Hedy Martinelli
*Make-up*: Nilo Jacoponi, Manlio Rocchetti, Gino Zamprioli, Randy Coronato (New York)
*Dental make-up*: Henry R. Dwork, DDS
*Hairdressers*: Maria Teresa Corridoni, Renata Magnanti, Enzo Cardella
*Wig suppliers*: Rocchetti-Carboni
*Location managers*: Attilio Viti, Robert Rothbard (New York), Pierre Laberge (Montreal)

*Location controller* (New York): Herb Hetzer
*Transportation*: Romana Transporti Cinematografici
*Transportation captain* (New York): James Giblin
*Stunts*: Benito Stefanelli
*Car stunts*: Julien Remy (or Remy Julien)
*Period car adviser* (New York): Sonny Abagnale
*Director of photography*: Tonino Delli Colli
*Process and colour*: Technicolor
*Camera operator*: Carlo Tafani
*Camera assistants*: Antonio Scaramuzza, Sandro Battaglia, Crescenzo Notarile (New York)
*Camera suppliers*: Arco 2 (Rome)
*Gaffers*: Romano Mancini, John Newby (New York), Walter Kymkiw (Montreal)
*Sound*: Jean Pierre Ruhu
*Boom operator*: Bruno Charrier
*Dialogue director*: Brian Freilino
*Continuity* (New York): Jennifer Wyckoff, Francesca Alatri
*Stills*: Angelo Novi
*First assistant director*: Fabrizio Sergenti Castellani
*Second assistant director*: Luca Morsella
*Negative*: Eastmancolor Kodak S.p.A.
*Titles and optical effects*: Studio 4
*Special effects technician* (Montreal): Gabe Vidella
*Special effects assistant* (Montreal): Louis Craig
*Editor*: Nino Baragli
*First assistant editor*: Vivi Tonini
*Assistant editors*: Ornella Chistolini, Patrizia Cerasani, Alessandro Baragli, Giorgio Venturoli
*Editing co-ordinator*: Maurizio Mancini
*Synchronization studio*: Cinecittà
*Synchronization technicians*: Fabio Palmisano, Massimo Rinchiusi
*Sound mixer*: Fausto Ancillai
*Sound dubbing*: Adriano Torbidone
*Sound effects*: Cooperativa di Produzione e Lavoro Studio Sound s.r.l., Cine Audio Effects s.r.l.
*Dubbing studio*: CDC
*Dubbing director*: Riccardo Cucciolla
*Dubbing assistant*: Adriana Iannuccelli
*Dubbing editor* (English version): Robert Rietti
*Dubbing technician* (New York): Paul Zydel
*Postsynch editors* (English version): Nicholas Stevenson, Gabrio Astori
*Music*: Ennio Morricone, conducted by Ennio Morricone
*Orchestra*: Orchestra Sinfonica dell'Unione Musicisti di Roma
*Pipes of Pan*: Gheorghe Zamfir
*Solo vocalist*: Edda Dell'Orso
*Music recording studio*: Studio Forum
*Music recording mixer*: Sergio Marcotulli
*Songs*: 'God Bless America' (Irving Berlin/singer: Kate Smith), 'Summertime' (George Gershwin/Dubose Heyward/Ira Gershwin), 'Night and Day' (Cole Porter), 'Yesterday' (John Lennon/Paul McCartney), 'Amapola' (Joseph M. La Calle/Albert Gamse), 'La Gazza Ladra' Overture (Rossini, conducted by Francesco Molinari Pradelli)
*Music publisher*: Hapax Music – Warner Music Group

Unit manager: Walter Massi
Production accountants: Gianna Di Michele, Dominique Bruballa (New York), Lucy Drolet
(Montreal)
*Assistant accountants*: Fausto Capozzi, Sergio Rosa, Diana Di Michele
*Production supervisor*: Mario Cotone
*Production manager* (Montreal): Ginette Hardy
*Production assistants*: Piero Sassaroli, Tonino Palombi
*Production liaison* (New York): Ted Kurdyla
*Unit publicist* (New York): Bruce Bahrenberg
*Director's assistants* (New York): Dennis Benatar, Amy Wells
*Production co-ordinator* (New York): Gail Kearns
*Consultant to the producer*: Robert Benmussa
*Executive in charge of production in USA*: Fred Caruso
*Executive producer*: Claudio Mancini
*Producer*: Arnon Milchan
*Production company*: The Ladd Company (a PSO International Release)
*Distributed in USA*: Warner Brothers (1984)
*Running times*: It: 218 mins, GB: 228 mins, US: 139 mins; US restored print: 227 mins.

## As Producer

### 1971
Sergio Leone's name, together with that of several other Italian directors, was on the credits of
12 *Decembre/Document on Giuseppe Pinelli* – 'a film of counterinformation'.

### 1973
*My Name is Nobody/Il mio nome e Nessuno* (It/Fr/Ger)
Directed by Tonino Valerii. Some sequences directed by Sergio Leone.
*Cast:* Henry Fonda (Jack Beauregard), Terence Hill (Nobody), Jean Martin (Sullivan), Leo
[V.] Gordon (Red), Neil Summers (Squirrel), R.G. Armstrong (Honest John), Steve Kanaly
(false barber), Geoffrey Lewis (Wild Bunch leader), Piero Lulli (Sheriff), Mario Brega (Pedro),
Mark Mazza (Don John), Benito Stefanelli (Porteley). Uncredited: Alexander Allerson (Rex),
Franco Angrisano (train driver), Emile Feist, Antonio Luigi Guerra (official), Carla Mancini
(mother), Humbert Mittendorf, Ulrich Muller, Angelo Novi (barman), Antonio Palombi,
Remus Peets (Big Gun), Tommy Polgar (Juan), Antoine Saint Jean/Domingo Antoine (Scape),
Claus Schmidt

*Script*: Ernesto Gastaldi
*Story*: Fulvio Morsella, Ernesto Gastaldi, from an idea by Sergio Leone
*Interiors*: De Paolis
*Exteriors*: Almeria, New Orleans, New Mexico
*Art director*: Gianni Polidori
*Assistant art director*: Dino Leonetti
*Set dresser*: Massimo Tavazzi
*Key grip*: Gilberto Carbonaro
*Costumes*: Vera Marzot
*Costume suppliers*: Tirelli, Western Costume
*Footwear suppliers*: Pompei
*Equipment*: Gianni Fiumi
*Make-up*: Nilo Jacoponi
*Hairdresser*: Grazia De Rossi

*Wigs*: Rochetti-Carboni
*Special effects and firearms*: Eros Baciucchi, Giovanni Corridori
*Stunts*: Benito Stefanelli
*Director of photography*: Giuseppe Ruzzolini (Italy and Spain), Armando Nannuzzi (USA)
*Colour and process*: Technicolor and Panavision
*Camera operator*: Elio Polacchi, Giuseppe Berardini, Federico Del Zoppo
*Continuity*: Rita Agostini
*Stills*: Angelo Novi
*Sound*: Fernando Pescetelli
*Assistant director*: Stefano Rolla
*Production supervisor*: Piero Lazzari
*Unit managers*: Franco Coduti, Paolo Gargano
*Editor*: Nino Baragli
*Assistant editor*: Rosanna Maiuri
*Sound effects*: Roberto Arcangeli
*Sound mixing*: Fausto Ancillai
*Music*: Ennio Morricone, conducted by Ennio Morricone
*Guitar solos*: Bruno D'Amario Battisti
*Music editing*: General Music (Rome)
*Music publisher*: Nazionalmusic
*Executive producer*: Fulvio Morsella
*Producer*: Claudio Mancini
*Production companies*: Rafran Cinematografica S.p.A. (Rome), Les Films Jacques Leitienne s.r.l. (Paris), La Societé Imp. Ex. Ci. (Nice), La Societé Alcinter s.r.l. (Paris), Rialto Film Preben Philipsen GMB and Co. KG. (Berlin)
*Distributed in USA*: Universal (1973)
*Running times*: It: 118 mins, US: 115 mins, GB: 116 mins.


1975
*Nobody's the Greatest/Un genio, due compari, un pollo* (It/Fr/Ger)
Directed by Damiano Damiani (with Giuliano Montaldo and for one scene Sergio Leone); line producers Fulvio Morsella and Claudio Mancini for Rafran Cinematografica; story by Ernesto Gastaldi and Fulvio Morsella; screenplay by Ernesto Gastaldi, Fulvio Morsella and Damiano Damiani; photographed by Giuseppe Ruzzolini; sets by Carlo Simi and Francesco Bronzi; music by Ennio Morricone; with Terence Hill (Joe Thanks), Robert Charlebois (Steamengine Bill), Miou-Miou (Lucy), Patrick McGoohan (Major Cabot), Klaus Kinski (Doc), Jean Martin (Colonel Pembroke) and Mario Brega


1977
*Il gatto/Qui a tué le chat?*
Directed by Luigi Comencini, with Massimo Patrizi; produced by Sergio Leone and Romano Cardarelli for Rafran; story by Rodolfo Sonego; screenplay by Rodolfo Sonego, Augusto Caminito with Fulvio Marcolin; photographed by Ennio Guarneri; edited by Nino Baragli; sets by Dante Ferreti; music by Ennio Morricone; with Ugo Tognazzi, Mariangela Melato, Jean Martin, Philippe Leroy and Mario Brega


1978
*Il giocattolo*
Directed by Giuliano Montaldo; line producers Claudio Mancini and Fulvio Morsella for Rafran; story by Sergio Donati; screenplay by Sergio Donati, Nino Manfredi, Giuliano

Montaldo; photographed by Ennio Guarnieri; sets by Luigi Scaccianoce; edited by Nino Baragli; music by Ennio Morricone; with Nino Manfredi, Marlène Jobert, Arnolda Foà and Mario Brega

## 1979
*Un sacco bello*
Directed by Carlo Verdone; line producer Romano Cardarelli for Medusa Cinematografica; story and screenplay by Leo Benvenuti, Piero De Bernardi, Carlo Verdone; photographed by Ennio Guarnieri; sets and costumes by Carlo Simi; edited by Eugenio Alabiso; music by Ennio Morricone; with Carlo Verdone (Leo, Ruggero, father Alfio, the Professor, Anselmo, Enzo), Veronica Miriel (Marisol) and Mario Brega (father of Ruggero)

## 1981
*Bianco, rosso and verdone*
Directed by Carlo Verdone; produced by Romano Cardarelli for Medusa; story and screenlay by Carlo Verdone, Leo Benvenuti, Piero De Bernardi; photographed by Luciano Tovoli; sets and costumes by Carlo Simi; edited by Nino Baragli; music by Ennio Morricone; with Carlo Verdone (Pasquale, Furio, Mimmo), Irina Sanpiter (Magda), Lella Fabrizi (the grandmother) and Mario Brega (the truck driver)

## 1985
*Troppo forte*
Directed by Carlo Verdone (one sequence directed by Sergio Leone); produced by Augusto Caminito; story by Carlo Verdone and Rodolfo Sonego; screenplay by Carlo Verdone, Rodolfo Sonego, Alberto Sordi; photographed by Danilo Desideri; sets by Franco Velchi; costumes Raffaella Leone; edited by Nino Baragli; music by Fabio Liberatori; with Carlo Verdone (Oscar Pettinari), Alberto Sordi (lawyer Pignacorelli), Stella Hall (Nancy) and Mario Brega

Television Commercials

## 1974–89
Glaces Gervais, Renault 18 (ruins of Petra), Renault 18 (diesel unchained), Riz Lustucru, Pain Bonne Fournée, Whisky J & B, Europ Assistance, Palmolive, Talbot Solara, Dany Danone and Renault 19.

# Index

544

INDEX

*Yellow Sky* (film), 229
*Yojimbo* (film), 118, 119, 122, 124–5, 126, 128, 129, 147, 148, 149
Young, Burt, 452
Young, Lyman: *Cino and Franco*, 7
*Young Mr Lincoln* (film), 126
Yugoslavia, 88, 105, 191

Z (film), 364
Zagreb, Yugoslavia, 105
Zamfir, Gheorghe, 427
Zampi, Luigi, 241
Zamprioli, Gino, 440
Zapata, Emiliano, 160, 312, 337

Zapata, Emiliano, 160, 312, 337
Zavattini, Cesare, 50–51, 309, 347
Zeffirelli, Franco, 76, 427
Zeglio, Primo, 105
Zimbabwe, 374, 375, 485
Zimbalist, Sam, 73
Zingarelli, Italo, 26
Zinnemann, Fred, 70–71, 76, 94, 205, 337, 472
*Zorro the Avenger* (film), 123, 124, 132, 191
Zukor, Adolph, 385
Zurli, Guido, 119